A MOST DETERMINED WOMAN

Emma Blair

SPHERE BOOKS LIMITED

A SPHERE BOOK

First published in Great Britain by Michael Joseph Ltd 1988
Published by Sphere Books Ltd 1989

Printed and bound in Great Britain by
Richard Clay Ltd, Bungay, Suffolk

Sphere Books Ltd
A Division of
Macdonald & Co. (Publishers) Ltd
Orbit House, 1 New Fetter Lane, London EC4A 1AR
A member of Maxwell Pergamon Publishing Corporation plc

'I'm told she was brought up as a collier's daughter in some horrid little mining village, or whatever,' Carrick said, and laughed nastily.

'It's true,' Henrietta sniggered. 'I could hardly believe it when I found out.'

'But true it is,' Carrick steamrollered on. 'Henrietta has it on the best of authority. Miss Sarah Hawke may be dressed in silk and satin when she sits down at table tonight, but underneath she's common as muck.'

'I say, steady on!' Charles Knox exclaimed.

Ian, trembling with fury and humiliation for Sarah, started to rise from the settee, but Sarah restrained him.

'God knows what the mother's like, the one who married this miner. Some trollop no doubt,' Carrick said, and laughed nastily again.

Sarah saw red at that. Leaping to her feet she marched from the 'snug room' into the drawing-room. Her eyes were blazing, her expression glacial . . .

To the memory of The Emira Sammia Jazaery
—we all miss you Sammy!

PART 1
Noise and Smoky Breath

A sacredness of love and death
Dwells in thy noise and smoky breath.

ALEXANDER SMITH
(from a poem about Glasgow)

Chapter 1

A lark sang high in the heavens above, a right bonny sound that caused Sarah to pause in her white claying of the front step to listen in appreciation. It was a June day, the year 1890, with a boiling sun belting down out of a cornflower-blue sky. Sarah closed her eyes, sighing with pleasure as the heat and sun beat against her face.

She gave a little smile when the lark sang again. They were joyous uplifting moments – those last few moments before her life would change forever.

Opening her eyes again, she blinked several times to readjust them to the strong light, and saw the flat cart appear round the corner, simultaneously being pushed and pulled by a handful of colliers from the pit. On top of the cart was a man lying stretched out.

It was too far for her to make out who the prostrate figure was, but somehow, instinctively, she knew it was Bob, her step-da. She continued kneeling there, quite motionless, as the cart trundled towards her, along the unpaved street with the open drain that ran down its middle, as open drains did in all the streets of Netherton.

Her mind was numb, frozen with shock. Vaguely she could hear her ma moving about inside the house. Oh Ma! she thought. Oh Ma! The nightmare all miners' women dread had come true for them – the cart was coming to their house.

She could see now there were five colliers pushing and pulling the cart, Jack Bonner, wee Mo Ford, Davey Hardy, Davey's brother Mal, and Tom Crayk. All of them Bob's close pals.

Somehow she rose to her feet, the white claying forgotten, the step only half done. 'Ma, you'd better come away out!' a voice called. A voice she suddenly realised was her own.

'What is it?' Myrtle shouted back.

'Come away out, Ma.'

There was something in Sarah's tone that made Myrtle frown. Something that told her this was no ordinary request, that this was different.

Myrtle appeared in the doorway, wiping wet hands on her pinny. 'Aye lass?'

'It's Bob, Ma.'

Myrtle's gaze flicked up the street to fasten on to the cart moving in their direction. Uttering a strangled cry, her hand flew to her mouth, for the cart was now so close there could be no mistaking who it was bearing.

Neighbours had appeared at their windows and doors, each of them secretly relieved – though hiding it well – that it was Bob Sunter being carted and not their own husband or son.

Myrtle joined Sarah outside, her hand still at her mouth. She was gnawing it, without realising she was doing so.

The cart halted beside Myrtle and Sarah. 'He's not dead,' Jack Bonner said quickly, doffing his cap. The other four did likewise.

Instantly Myrtle was by Bob's side. His eyes were shut, his breathing extremely shallow.

'There was no accident, no fall of stone or anything like that. He was chaffing to wee Mo here when he just fell over. We think it must have been a heart attack,' Jack Bonner explained.

Myrtle could see that underneath the coal-dust covering his face, Bob was white as milk. 'The doctor, we must get the doctor,' she said.

There wasn't a doctor at the pit where all the men of Netherton grafted, or even in Netherton itself. The nearest, Doctor Elson, was nearly a mile away on the Bearsden Road.

'I'll go,' offered Mal Hardy.

'The manager said we should bring him home first. He said that was the right thing to do,' Tom Crayk said.

Aye, Sarah thought cynically. The pit manager would say that. He would be saving the pit the five-shillings fee that the doctor charged. 'No, I'll go,' she told Mal Hardy, knowing she'd be far faster.

'Hurry, then,' Myrtle pleaded, anguish and despair contorting her features.

Sarah kicked off the clogs she was wearing, and took to her heels. As she flew down the street, her long auburny hair streamed out behind her.

'We'll get him inside and on to his bed,' Jack Bonner said to Myrtle, and gave a nod to the others who replaced their caps and organised themselves to lift the stricken Bob.

As Bob was carried up over the step that Sarah had been white claying he gave a terrible groan which caused Myrtle to burst into tears when she heard it.

*

Sarah and Myrtle sat in the darkened house – they'd closed the curtains back and front, watching while Doctor Elson examined Bob. Jack Bonner and the others had left on Elson's arrival, returning 'down by' – as the pit was often called – to finish their shift.

'Can you hear me, Mr Sunter?' Elson asked in a soft yet commanding voice. When he got no reply, even though Bob's eyes were open and staring, he tried again. 'Can you hear me, man?' Again he received no reply.

Myrtle was holding a large linen hanky. She was continually wrapping it round her left hand, then unwrapping it again. Every ten seconds or so she took a particularly deep breath which she exhaled in a sort of gasping choke. She couldn't believe this was happening.

Sarah was thinking of Gordy McCallum, the chap she'd been walking out with for the past year. Seventeen years old, the same age as herself, he too worked down the pit, and had done since he was twelve. What if one day he too was taken home on the cart, and it was her he was brought to? She shuddered at the thought. She was supposed to have been seeing Gordy later, but he wouldn't be expecting her to turn up now, for he would have heard about Bob. The news would have gone round the pit – and then Netherton – like wildfire.

'Could you give me a bit of help?' Elson appealed, slipping Bob's braces down. Between the three of them, they got Bob out of his working trousers – his boots had already been removed – then out of his collarless shirt. Bob's skin gleamed palely in contrast to his clarty face and neck.

'Is it a heart attack? Is that's what happened, Doctor?' Myrtle queried, the question she'd been bursting with since Elson's arrival.

'I'll speak to you when I'm done,' Elson evaded, wanting to be certain of his facts before he made his pronouncement. He glanced at Sarah. 'I could use a cup of tea, lassie, if that's possible.'

'Aye, right,' Sarah replied, and hurried over to the range – a vision of shining black, matt white, silver grey and burnished brass – where the kettle was steaming on the hob, as it nearly always was. She made a good cup of tea, thick and strong enough to stand a spoon up in, as the saying went. Bob had once confided to her, with one of those fly winks of his, that she made a better cup of tea than her ma, but not to let on mind or he'd be wearing the next potful

5

Myrtle brewed rather than drinking it. Dear Bob, a real smasher, one of the best. He'd been like a real father to her, always treating her as if she was his own flesh and blood instead of someone he'd inherited through Myrtle.

It was a long examination, nearly an hour before Elson was completely satisfied. With a sigh he began packing away his instruments and the other bits and pieces he'd used. There was no doubt whatever in his mind about what was wrong with Bob. If only it had been a heart attack. But Bob hadn't been that lucky.

Grim-faced, Elson went over to the sink, pumped some water into the enamel bowl, and slowly washed his hands. He was only too well aware of Myrtle and Sarah's eyes boring into his back.

He dried his hands, then rolled down his shirtsleeves. Buttoning the cuffs, he rucked the sleeve material up round the silver armbands he wore. 'It's bad news, I'm afraid. Bad indeed.'

Myrtle wet her dry and bloodless lips, and waited. Sarah had gone all cold inside, cold as a burnie in winter. The same icy water might have been coursing through her veins. She'd never known herself this way before.

'He's had a massive stroke that's left him paralysed down the entire right side of his body,' Elson stated.

Myrtle jerked from head to toe like a fish that had just been gaffed. Her eyes widened while her mouth pursed into a silent *o*.

'He's also lost the power of speech,' Elson added.

Myrtle tried to ask a question but couldn't get the words out. 'What does all this mean?' Sarah asked for her.

Elson's expression became stony. 'It means he'll be like he is now for the rest of his life,' he replied.

'He'll never work again?' Myrtle queried in a croaky whisper.

Elson shook his head. 'He'll never walk again, or talk. I can't be specific about the extent of damage that's been done to his brain, but it would appear to be substantial.'

'He'll live though!' Myrtle burst out.

'Oh aye.' If you want to call it that, Elson thought to himself. 'For no saying how long. Of course a lot of that depends on how well he's looked after.'

'My God!' Myrtle whispered, her gaze returning to where Bob lay sleeping peacefully, thanks to the injection Elson had given him.

'I eh . . . I really am most dreadfully sorry,' Elson said.

Sarah went to her ma and put her hands on Myrtle's shoulders in

6

a gesture of solace. 'You're certain, absolutely certain, that nothing can be done for him?' she asked.

Elson shook his head. 'I may only be a local doctor so to speak, but I have seen a fair amount of strokes in my time to know what I'm talking about. However, if you wish a specialist's opinion, that's up to you. It will cost you several guineas and I assure you that he'll only tell you the same thing.'

'Will there be any improvement?' Sarah queried.

'Fractionally perhaps, no more.'

Elson put on his jacket. 'I'll come back tomorrow if you want. My advice though is to save your money.' He looked thoughtful. 'Is there a son at home you can fall back on now?'

'No,' Myrtle replied softly.

'Does that mean the two of you are on your own then?'

'I have a lad, but there's nothing official between us yet,' replied Sarah.

'I see.'

'We have relatives mind, though no one here in Netherton. I'm sure they'll help,' added Myrtle.

'I'm sure they will.' Elson coughed discreetly. 'I'll be getting on my way then.'

'Thank you for coming so quickly, Doctor,' Myrtle said, rising.

Elson glanced at the mantelpiece clock, and hoped he wasn't going to have to ask for his money. He hated doing that.

It was Sarah who twigged. 'The doctor's fee, Ma. Will I take it from what's in the barrel?'

Myrtle realised she'd forgotten all about the doctor's money, unforgivable considering how kind he'd been. 'Aye, do that.' The old biscuit barrel was where Bob's wages were kept, replenished every Friday night when Bob handed over his pay packet to her. From now on there weren't going to be any more pay packets from 'down by'.

Sarah counted out the cash from the barrel, and handed over a halfcrown, florin and two silver thrupennies to Elson, who immediately pocketed the assorted coins. 'So would you like me to come again tomorrow or not?' he queried gently.

'Yes, I would.' Myrtle told him. 'Even if there's nothing you can do I would find it reassuring.'

Elson nodded, he could understand that. 'Fine. I'll call sometime during the morning.'

7

Sarah saw Elson out, shut the door behind him, and leant against it. She and her mother stared at one another, volumes passing between them in that silent stare. Then Myrtle turned and crossed to where Bob lay sleeping.

She thought of that morning when she'd seen him off, as she did every working morning, up the road to the pit. There had been the usual hug and kiss for her, before he stepped out of the door, and then he'd been away, whistling quietly to himself, to meet up with Jack Bonner and his other pals. Who would have thought then, who would have dreamt it! that before the day was out her lovely beautiful man would be reduced to what he now was.

A sob racked her, and then another bigger one. Crystal tears bubbled from her eyes to roll down her cheeks. Never walk or talk again, and awful damage done to his brain!

An animal sound escaped her lips as she sank to her knees. 'Oh Bob, Bob, Bob,' she whispered.

Sarah went to her mother, and dropped down beside her. The pair of them fell into one another's embrace, clutching each other tightly like a couple of lost babes. Babes beside themselves with grief.

Sarah woke with the first blush of dawn, knowing as she did that there would be no more sleep for her that night. A terrible fear had taken hold of her, fear for Bob, fear for her ma, fear for herself. Now that Bob was unable to work, how were they going to make ends meet? And if the rent wasn't paid, as it had to be every Saturday morning, then that would be it, they'd be out on the street, lock stock and barrel.

What were they going to do? *What?* The fear turned to panic, blind panic that threatened to engulf her.

Desperately she fought the panic, telling herself that Gordy was the answer. Gordy whom she loved, and who loved her. Gordy whose kisses were sweet as sugar toffee, in whose arms there had been times when she'd almost swooned with happiness.

Yes, Gordy was the answer.

When Sarah saw her ma in the morning she thought Myrtle had aged a dozen years overnight. There were black patches under her eyes, and lines deeply etched where none had been before. She looked haggard as hell.

8

'It's just beginning to actually sink in,' were Myrtle's opening words.

'Did he sleep all night?'

'Aye. That injection the doctor gave him really knocked him out. But he's beginning to stir now.'

'In a way it's . . .' Sarah trailed off.

'What?'

Sarah shook her head. She'd been going to say that in a way what had happened was actually worse than Bob being dead, but had decided her ma wouldn't appreciate such sentiments. At least not yet. 'I'll rouse the fire up and put the kettle on,' she said instead.

Myrtle pulled her dressing-gown—her 'goonie' as she called it—more tightly around her, then went over to the old biscuit barrel and counted what little cash was left.

'How much?' Sarah asked.

'Seven and ten.'

Sarah bit her lip. After Elson had paid them a return visit that would leave them only two shillings and ten. How far could they go on that? Not very. 'There is of course what Bob's due for this week, three full days. The pit manager will have to give you that,' she said.

Myrtle ran a hand through her hair. It had gone limp and straggly, and felt to her like a right bunch of rats' tails. 'Things aren't quite as bad as they seem.'

'How do you mean?'

'I have a plank. A wee something put by against a rainy day.' She gave a hollow laugh. 'And if this isn't a rainy day I don't know what is.'

A plank, a secret hoard. It seemed quite uncharacteristic of Myrtle. Sarah was amazed. Maybe she didn't know her ma as well as she thought. 'How much is this plank?' she queried.

'Wait here.' Myrtle left her daughter, disappearing out back to where the toilet and bins were. When she returned she was carrying a flat cocoa tin.

'Where did you have that then?' Sarah asked.

'Behind a loose brick at the rear of the toilet.' She explained further when she saw Sarah's puzzled expression. 'The loose brick is only half a brick, this tin fitted behind it.'

Myrtle opened the tin and emptied its contents out on to the table. It was all change with the exception of a solitary ten shilling note. Most of the change was comprised of tanners and single shillings.

'How much is there?' Sarah queried.

'No idea. Haven't counted it in goodness knows how long.'

Sarah placed the filled kettle on the hob, then joined Myrtle who was now sitting at the table totting up her plank. Sarah began helping her.

'Eight pounds one and thrupence,' Myrtle announced.

'Not exactly a fortune, but an awful lot better than seven and ten.'

'Aye,' Myrtle agreed. 'But what happens when this runs out?'

Sarah thought about Gordy again; the sooner she saw him the better. If he didn't come round after tea she'd go to his house and suggest a walk and chaff in Bluebell Wood. That was their favourite place. But then again, it was the favourite place of all courting couples in Netherton.

Bob made a noise, and right away Myrtle was on her feet and hurrying to him.

She took him by the hand, and gave him a smile. 'What is it, Bob? Do you want something?'

The eyes that looked into hers were vacuous, reminding Myrtle of that idiot boy Charlie Forbes who the children in Netherton referred to as Big Daftie, or 'him that's only elevenpence three farthings in the shilling'. She shuddered, unable to stop herself.

Bob opened his mouth, but only a gurgle emerged. That and the spittle which ran down the side of his chin. Using the hem of her dressing-gown, Myrtle wiped the spittle away.

'Perhaps he's trying to tell you he's hungry?' Sarah suggested.

'Aye, that could well be it. For he won't have had anything since yesterday's dinnertime piece.'

'I'll cut the bread,' Sarah said. Bread, butter and jam was their usual breakfast. Except in late autumn and winter when they also had porage.

'I've just thought,' Myrtle said, tears welling inside her again. 'I'm going to have to hand-feed him from here on in. He's incapable of doing it for himself.'

Sarah cut thick slices, the doorstops Bob had always been partial to. The jam was apple and ginger which she had made the previous year, and which they were now rapidly running out of. Apple and ginger was far and away Bob's favourite.

'Only tea for me, I couldn't eat a thing,' Myrtle said, coming over to Sarah and lifting the plate Sarah had placed Bob's doorstops on.

Sarah saw the glint of tears in her mother's eyes. 'Me neither. I feel like I'll never be hungry again,' she replied.

Myrtle nodded. It was exactly the same with her.

Suddenly a foul stench filled the room, a smell that was unmistakeable. The two women swung their attention to Bob, the source of the stench.

She wasn't only going to have to hand-feed him, there were other, more unpleasant duties she was going to have to cope with, Myrtle realised. She put the plate back on the table. 'It wasn't that he was hungry. That must have been what he was trying to tell me,' she said. 'I'll clean him and the bed up and he can have his breakfast after.'

'I'll help,' Sarah offered.

'No, leave this to me.'

As her mother began attending to Bob, Sarah opened the windows to let some fresh air in.

Gordy came directly after his tea, as Sarah had hoped he would. His face was creased with concern and he'd combed his hair using water, which was something he normally only did on the sabbath when he went to the kirk.

'Come in,' said Sarah, ushering him into the kitchen.

His gaze flicked to Bob lying in the wall-bed, then back to Sarah. 'I nearly came last night, but then decided you'd prefer to be left alone.'

'Probably for the best. Ma and I were a bit emotional last night as I'm sure you can understand.'

'Aye.'

Myrtle, who'd been out back, came into the room.

'I'm awful sorry for what's happened to Mr Sunter,' Gordy said to Myrtle in a rush of words, with obvious sincerity.

'You never know the minute till the minute after, do you?' Myrtle replied, attempting a brave smile that came out so twisted it was more of a grimace than a smile.

'No, I suppose you don't.' His eyes flicked again to where Bob lay. 'A stroke, I heard?'

'And a right bad one too,' Sarah said softly.

There was a knock on the door which turned out to be another neighbour come to sympathise. Friends and neighbours had been in and out all day. 'If you two are going out, away you go,' Myrtle told them.

11

'You'll be all right, Ma?'

'Aye, of course I will.'

The neighbour who'd chapped the door was Mrs Geddes, she and her hubby and three weans lived further down the street. She went into the house as Sarah and Gordy left it.

'I thought we might go to Bluebell Wood,' Sarah suggested.

'That's fine by me.'

'We'll get some privacy there.'

'How are you yourself? It must have been a terrible shock.'

'That's putting it mildly.'

'It's being said that . . .' Gordy cleared his throat. 'That Mr Sunter will never go "down by" again?'

'He'll never walk or talk again either, according to Doctor Elson. The stroke caused considerable damage to his brain.'

'Jesus!' Gordy swore softly, and kicked a small stone out of their path.

He took her hand and they walked in silence till they reached Bluebell Wood and the secluded spot – a little haven surrounded by bushes – where they did their courting.

Normally the first thing Gordy would have done, would have been to take Sarah into his arms and give her a long, lingering kiss. That didn't seem appropriate on this occasion however, so he flopped to the ground and Sarah sat beside him.

'So how are you and your ma going to manage?' he asked.

'That's the question, isn't it? I wish I knew the answer.'

He gave her a sideways glance. She was beautiful right enough, the prettiest lass in Netherton by a long chalk. Aye, and not only Netherton but as far as Temple itself. He'd counted it his lucky day when he'd got off with her.

'Gordy?'

'Aye?'

She slipped her feet out of her clogs and ran them up and down through the cool grass. A large butterfly flitted by, followed by another. The wood was renowned for its butterflies. 'I do love you, you know.'

'I know, Sarah. And I love you too. As God is my judge I do.'

She came close, and pressed herself to him, her full breasts flattening against his chest. With a sigh he laid a hand on her right thigh.

She looked down at the hand which was blue – streaked along

12

its back with ingrained coal-dust. All the men of Netherton had similar blue streaks on the backs of their hands, along their arms, and on their bodies. Ingrained coal dust that would never come out, no matter how hard you scrubbed or how much soap you used. After a few years down the pit you were marked forever.

'At seventeen we're old enough to get married,' she said.

The scent of her in his nostrils was driving him wild with desire. But then it always did. He pulled away from her, though most reluctantly. 'I do intend to marry you some time, Sarah, but I can't right now. It's impossible.'

'I know there are problems. But where there's a will there's a way,' she argued.

'Not in this instance.' He fumbled for his makings, and proceeded to roll a cigarette with trembling hands. 'Don't you think I thought about this after I heard about Mr Sunter? But it's just not on. Heaven knows I wish it could be, but it can't.'

When he'd finished rolling his cigarette Sarah took his makings from him and proceeded to do one for herself. She tried not to let her acute disappointment show.

'I have responsibilities, Sarah. My ma and the twins.' He was the sole breadwinner in his house ever since his father had perished in a gas explosion 'down by' eighteen months previously.

He struck a match, lighting first her cigarette, then his. 'It'll be two years till the twins are old enough to graft. Till then I have to look after them.' The twins were his younger brothers, now aged ten. There had been a big gap between him and them.

'Surely we could work something out!' she pleaded.

'Tell me what and I'll do it! For a start, if we got married where would we sleep? Our house is the same as yours, a bedroom and a kitchen. The twins and I are in the bedroom, Ma in the kitchen. I couldn't ask her to share with the boys, they're too big for that.'

'What about our house?'

Gordy broke off a dock leaf and threw it from him. 'That would mean me supporting two households which is quite out of the question on my wage.'

She could see now that she hadn't thought this through at all; that she'd been grasping at straws.

'I'm between the devil and the deep blue sea,' he said wretchedly. 'I can't even get a bigger house to accommodate us all because I can't bloody well afford that either.'

He was right, she had to acknowledge. If there was a way out of this then it didn't involve him, or their marriage.

Gordy pulled deeply on his cigarette. 'Everything will change once the twins start down the pit, then we will be able to afford that bigger house. But till then . . .' He broke off, and shrugged.

Tears misted Sarah's eyes. She and Myrtle seemed to have been greeting non-stop since Bob was brought home on the flat cart. Was it really only yesterday? It felt longer, a lot longer.

Anger erupted in Gordy. 'It's just so unfair, so it is. For you, your ma, for Mr Sunter, and for me.'

'Bob used to say that life was unfair. That was something you had to learn about it, and accept.' She pictured Bob lying at home in the wall-bed. 'That poor man. That poor poor man,' she whispered.

'Aye,' Gordy agreed.

Sarah shook her head. 'I don't know what we're going to do. What will become of us?'

'You must have relatives, someone who'll take you in?'

'We have relatives all right, good folk too. But take us in? I don't see how any of them can do that when they're living hand to mouth just as everyone else is in Netherton.'

'The pit owner might help?' Gordy suggested.

She gave a bitter laugh. 'Sure, and pigs might fly.'

It was a daft proposal, Gordy told himself. Dundonald help? Sarah was right, pigs would fly first, and to the moon and back at that.

'Will you cuddle me, Gordy? I want to be cuddled,' Sarah pleaded in a cracked whisper. She couldn't restrain her tears any longer; they streamed down her face.

Gordy gathered her into his arms, torn apart to see her like this. But what could he do? Nothing, his hands were tied.

Oh but it was a rotten world at times. A rotten, rotten one.

The next evening when the day shift was over and the colliers were making their weary way home there was a knock on the front door. Sarah answered the knock to find Jack Bonner and Tom Crayk standing there.

'Can we speak to your ma, hen?' Jack Bonner asked.

'Of course, come away in,' Sarah replied, beckoning them into the kitchen.

The two men looked over at the wall-bed. 'How is he today?' Tom Crayk inquired.

'The same.'

'Aye, well then,' Tom mumbled.

'Go on over.'

The two men glanced at one another, then hesitantly crossed to where Bob lay.

'How are you doing, you old bugger?' Jack Bonner said, trying to inject a cheery note into his voice.

'The lengths some folk will go to to get to stay in their bed,' Tom cracked.

The vacuous expression that Sarah and Myrtle were getting to know so well was turned first of all on Jack, then Tom. Bob gave no sign of recognition whatever.

'It's us, Jack and Tom,' Tom said.

Bob's mouth fell open, and spittle ran from both corners down to his chin. Jack turned away, his face contorted in anguish.

'Your ma?' Jack Bonner husked.

'She's out in the toilet, shouldn't be a minute,' Sarah replied.

'Do you think . . . Do you think he hears anything?' Tom asked.

'We don't honestly know. But I doubt it.'

'He was such a . . . such a man,' Jack Bonner said.

'Aye,' Sarah agreed. She knew exactly what Jack meant by that.

Myrtle entered the room. 'It's yourself, Jack, and you, Tom,' she said, having recognised their voices before coming into the kitchen.

'How are you bearing up, lass?' Jack Bonner asked softly.

'As well as can be expected, I suppose,' Myrtle answered.

Jack glanced again at Bob. The pair of them had been pals an awful long time, they'd been in the same class at school together. It broke Jack's heart to see Bob in his present state. Like Sarah he felt it would have been better if Bob had died rather than be reduced to what he now was, a travesty of his former self.

'We took a collection, passed the hat round,' Jack said to Myrtle.

'Not one man, not one, didn't give or wasn't pleased to do so,' Tom Crayk added.

'He was well liked, you understand.' Then realising what he'd said, Jack hastily rephrased his statement. '*Is* well liked, Myrtle.'

'Well liked *and* respected,' Tom Crayk added.

Jack Bonner delved into a jacket pocket to produce fistful after fistful of coins which he piled on to the table. The end result was a formidable mound of cash.

'I hope that will make things easier until you can get yourselves sorted out,' Jack said.

'It's a big help. Sarah and I thank you both, and all who contributed. God bless you all.'

'It's little enough. If only . . .' He shrugged.

'I understand, Jack. You've all got wives and bairns of your own, at least most of you have, and what you bring home at the end of the week hardly stretches from one Friday to the next.'

'We're always there if you need us, you appreciate that, don't you?' Jack said in a voice that was just a fraction above a whisper, and tight with emotion.

'I do indeed,' Myrtle replied. Then, impulsively, she went to Jack and hugged him tight. Doing the same to Tom Crayk after that.

'We'd best get on,' Jack Bonner said, not trusting himself to stay any longer in case he broke down.

'Aye,' Tom Crayk agreed.

Myrtle saw Jack and Tom to the door and shook them by the hand. 'I'll drop by in a couple of nights' time to see how you're doing,' Jack promised.

'I'll look forward to that.'

Myrtle waved the two men away, then returned to Sarah who'd already started to count the money the two men had brought. The pair of them were in the middle of this when there was another knock at the door. It was the Reverend Havergal.

'I'm sorry I haven't been before but I've been laid up with my chest again,' he apologised.

Myrtle nodded; it was well known that the minister was a martyr to his chest.

'An awful business,' Havergal commiserated. 'And how is Mr Sunter?'

Myrtle repeated everything that Doctor Elson had told them while Havergal listened gravely. When Myrtle had finally finished he gave a deep sigh. 'God certainly moves in mysterious ways, and it certainly can be most difficult for us poor benighted mortals to see any sense in some of the things he does. But sense there is, Myrtle, we have to believe that.'

He crossed over to where Bob lay to stare down at him, his eyes filled with compassion.

'I think a wee prayer, don't you?'

Myrtle sank on to her knees, and behind her Sarah did the same.

Both women bowed their heads, and clasped their hands in front of them, as did the minister.

When the prayer was over – and a fine prayer it had been too – Myrtle and Sarah rose again to their feet, and Sarah said she'd make a pot of tea.

Havergal indicated the money on the table, roughly half of which was now stacked in piles. 'Have you been to the bank to raid the safe?' he joked.

Myrtle explained to him about the collection taken at the pit and Havergal reached into his pocket, extracted a half-crown, and placed that on the pile that remained to be counted. 'The best I can do,' he apologised.

'Thank you, Minister. That's right kind of you.'

'I only wish I could provide something from the church, but I'm afraid there are no funds available for such a thing. We're an impecunious parish and no mistake, though rich in many other ways.'

'Please sit while you have your tea,' Sarah instructed.

Havergal sat in one of the comfy chairs by the range. 'So what now?' he queried.

'I wish we knew,' Myrtle answered.

There were some Abernethys which Sarah placed on a plate, pleased they had a biscuit to offer the minister. Though goodness knows he must get heartily tired of biscuits and teabread which were forever being thrust at him whenever he visited a member of his large congregation.

'What about relatives?'

'There's my sister, Jessica, and her husband Dandy – he's a miner in Shotts. They're good people, but with a clutch of young bairns of their own to support I can't really ask of them, can I? A miner's wage only stretches so far, as we all know only too well.' Myrtle's expression was grim, her big worry – in fact it terrified her – was that when their money ran out they would end up in the poorhouse. The very thought brought her out in a cold sweat.

'Anyone else?'

'Bob's parents have passed away and he's an only child. He does have cousins but they're all more or less in the same position as Jessica and Dandy.'

'It's a problem then,' Havergal mused, looking thoughtful.

Having filled the teapot, Sarah now put it aside to mask. 'Do you take sugar, Minister? I can't mind.'

'Three spoonfuls if you can manage that. It's a wicked sin to take so much, I know, but it's one weakness I just can't seem to overcome.'

'We've no milk in I'm afraid. Everything's a bit—' She was about to say 'arse for elbow', then remembered it was a man of the cloth she was addressing. 'Well let's just say we're not quite as organised as we normally are.'

'Completely understandable in the circumstances. And I like black tea, anyway.' The latter was a lie, he hated black tea, but you would never have guessed that from either his tone or expression.

'And your own parents, Myrtle, have they also passed on?'

'My da's alive, and lives on his own not far from Jessica. He bides in a single-room house and hasn't got two farthings to rub together, so he's no use to us either.'

Sarah poured the tea, gave Havergal his, while handing him a sideplate.

'Have you considered getting yourself a job?' Havergal asked.

Sarah laughed. 'In Netherton? What work is there for women here?' Women working was a novel concept as far as she was concerned, it just wasn't the done thing.

'It wasn't Netherton I was thinking of. What about going into service?'

'Here, that is an idea!' Myrtle exclaimed.

'You mean being a maid in a posh house?' Sarah queried, frowning.

'What you would earn would more than pay the rent here. And at the same time you would be being kept, fed and watered at your employer's expense.'

'It is a thought,' Sarah mused. To be truthful, she wasn't at all keen on the notion of being somebody's servant, there was a large streak of stubborn pride that ran all the way through her, but beggars couldn't be choosers. And, God knew, they desperately needed some sort of regular income if they were to keep their heads above water.

'How would she go about getting such a job?' Myrtle inquired, seeing this as a definite way out of their predicament, a sudden light at the end of a pitch-black tunnel.

Havergal accepted an Abernethy from the plate Sarah offered him. 'I do have many connections outside Netherton. I could make inquiries if you wanted me to.'

'That would be awful good of you, Minister,' Myrtle enthused.

'I've no experience, mind,' Sarah said.

'I'll make sure whoever I approach appreciates that – and your need for the job as well,' Havergal answered.

It was going to mean leaving Netherton, Sarah thought with mixed emotions. Up until then Netherton and its environs had been her entire world. Leaving Netherton *and* Gordy!

As though reading her mind, Havergal said with a smile, 'You will get days off, and be able to come back here and see everybody then.'

Sarah forced herself to match the minister's smile, though inside she was filled with a nauseous, sinking feeling.

'I've no option, have I?'

Havergal focused his attention on Myrtle. 'And what about you, Myrtle, maybe we could arrange something for you?'

'Oh I couldn't be parted from Bob, he's totally dependent on me, you understand,' she replied quickly.

'I'm not speaking of you being parted from him. But tell me, do you have a decent mangle?'

A mangle! What was the man driving at? 'I do, Mr Havergal, a new one bought only last year when the old one gave up the ghost.'

Sarah was ahead of Myrtle; she'd twigged what the minister was about to propose. 'You're thinking of Ma taking in washing?' she queried. 'But there's no one round here with the wherewithal to pay for that kind of luxury.'

'Maybe not here, but they do in Bearsden which isn't all that far away.' He turned again to Myrtle. 'If I could get something organised for you in the washing line, would you be interested?'

'Too right and I would, Minister. I'd be interested in anything that brings in a shilling or two. Why if Sarah did get a job in service, and I had washing to take in, we'd be well home and dry. Our worries would be over.'

'Then I'll see what I can do for the pair of you.'

Myrtle's eyes shone with gratitude and relief. 'You're a proper Christian right enough, Mr Havergal.'

'Aye well,' he replied drily, 'there's more to being a minister than just praying and sermonising, you know.'

The stench of defecation wafted through the room causing Myrtle's face to drop in embarrassment. 'I'm terribly sorry, Mr Havergal, it's Bob he—' She broke off.

19

Havergal laid his cup and plate on the floor, and rose to his feet. 'Don't fash yourself, woman, I understand. Bob doesn't communicate at all then?'

'No,' Myrtle whispered.

He nodded.

'I'll be on my way so you can attend to him. You'll both be hearing from me just as soon as I have any news.'

The two women accompanied him to the front door where he paused, then said to Myrtle, 'It's a hard boat you've been landed with to row, there's no denying that. But do try to pray, I promise you you'll find strength and comfort in it.'

'I will, Minister.'

'God bless you all.'

As soon as Havergal was gone, Myrtle hurried over to the wall-bed while Sarah set about opening the windows.

It looked as if from now on in she was going to have to do a wash every day, Myrtle thought as she started stripping the bedclothes off Bob.

The Craufurds lived in Park Circus, one of the swankiest streets in all Glasgow. The folk who stayed there – and the roads round about – were all swells, real toffee-noses who spoke as if they suffered permanently from constipation.

Sarah, hands clasped in her lap, was sitting in the kitchen waiting to be interviewed by Mrs Craufurd. Her feet were murdering her for, instead of her usual clogs, she had on a pair of lace-up shoes that had been borrowed from a neighbour. Myrtle owned a lovely pair of shoes, right smashers, but unfortunately her ma's feet were far smaller than hers.

Her dress was her 'Sunday go to kirk' one, while her straw hat with made-up flowers was a present from Mrs Havergal, who had insisted she not only wear it for the interview, but keep it afterwards.

The cook, a Miss O'Donoghue, was preparing vegetables. Glancing over, she regarded Sarah with what could only be described as a glower. 'What's your name again?' she demanded in a growl.

'Sarah, Cook.'

'*Miss O'Donoghue* to you, girl.'

'Miss O'Donoghue,' Sarah repeated, thinking she didn't like the look of the cook at all. There was something brutish about the woman, the sort of person who probably enjoyed hurting others, and making their life a misery.

A female a few years older than Sarah bustled into the kitchen, gave Sarah the briefest of smiles, then said to Miss O'Donoghue, 'The mistress has asked for tea and sandwiches to be served in an hour's time, after she's dealt with this lassie here. Apparently she's expecting two of her friends to drop by then, Miss O'Donoghue.'

The cook swore, which shocked Sarah. It wasn't that she wasn't used to swearing – you couldn't be brought up in a mining village and not be – but to hear a *woman* use the c-word and so venomously too. *That* was completely new to her.

'It's not my fault, I'm only delivering the message,' the girl said.

The cook stuck her face into the girl's. 'Mind your lip you. I won't take cheek from anyone.'

'I wasn't being cheeky, Miss O'Donoghue.'

'If I say you were being cheeky, you were.'

The girl was suddenly very much on edge, giving Sarah the impression that she was scared. 'I'm sorry, Miss O'Donoghue, if that's how it came across, I certainly didn't mean it to,' she apologised.

The cook grunted. 'Tea and sandwiches for three in an hour's time, you say?'

'Yes, Miss O'Donoghue.'

'Did she say what sort of sandwiches?'

The girl shook her head. 'No, just sandwiches.'

'Right then, hoof it.'

What a thoroughly unpleasant piece of work, Sarah thought. A real bully.

The girl turned to Sarah. 'The mistress will see you now. Please follow me.'

Sarah was instantly on her feet, smoothing down her dress and making sure everything was just so. She followed the girl out of the huge kitchen into a dingy hallway.

'What's Mrs Craufurd like?' Sarah asked in a whisper.

'She smiles a lot,' the girl replied ambiguously.

'What does that mean?'

'It means just that. Now come on.'

The girl bustled off again, Sarah hurrying after her. On the ground floor – the kitchen was in the basement – they encountered the butler, a tall thin man with a face like a prune. He watched them go by, but didn't speak.

The inside of the house was very elegant, Sarah thought, as they mounted a sweep of stairs, but somehow there was something missing. Something that should have been there. And then it dawned on her – there was no love. No feeling of love whatever.

They came to a cream-painted door at which the girl knocked. A voice answered from within, the words too low for Sarah to make out what they were.

The girl opened the door, and indicated for Sarah to enter. She herself didn't go in, but closed the door behind Sarah.

Mrs Craufurd, the room's only occupant, was lying on a *chaise-longue*, and was younger than Sarah had expected. For some reason she'd expected Mrs Craufurd to be in her late forties or early fifties. Sarah doubted she was much over thirty.

Underneath a crown of corn-coloured hair, Mrs Craufurd was smiling, but it wasn't a smile that Sarah liked at all. The smile was an out-and-out lie.

Mrs Craufurd had a pale complexion, and light blue eyes. When Sarah got closer, she also noted that Mrs Craufurd had a scar traversing her nose, a scar her heavy make-up failed to hide.

She had hardly any breasts at all, and even at that distance and angle, Sarah couldn't fail to appreciate that she had a very large bottom, one that was quite out of proportion to the rest of her.

'Good afternoon, ma'am,' Sarah said.

'Good afternoon. Sarah, isn't it?'

'Yes, ma'am.'

Mrs Craufurd crooked a finger. 'Come and stand here where I can see you properly.' She pointed to a spot about three feet in front of her.

Sarah walked slowly forward, feeling as if she might be *en route* to the gallows, and stopped at the indicated spot. Mrs Craufurd's smile never wavered.

'I have a letter here about you,' Mrs Craufurd said, picking up a sheet of paper which lay beside her, and waving it at Sarah.

Sarah didn't know if she was supposed to reply or not, and decided to say nothing. A spider, she thought suddenly, that's what Mrs Craufurd made her think of, a smiling blonde spider.

'Your poor father's had a stroke, I believe?'

'My step-father, ma'am. And yes, he has.'

Mrs Craufurd leant forward a little, her eyes glittering. 'Paralysed down his entire right side?'

Sarah nodded.

'Unable to speak?'

'Yes.'

'And eh . . . damage to the brain?'

The spider was enjoying this conversation, Sarah thought. 'Yes, that's true.'

'How awful!'

Sarah stared down at the floor.

'Look at me when I talk to you, Sarah.'

She glanced up again to find the damned woman still smiling. 'Sorry, ma'am.'

'And now you need a job?' When Sarah didn't reply she went on. '*Very badly* need a job.'

Sarah couldn't help squirming where she stood. She felt humiliated, though there was no real reason why she should have done. It was the spider's tone that did it, and what lay behind the smile.

'Very badly, ma'am,' she confirmed.

'And you've no previous experience of being in service?'

'None, ma'am. Of course I am well used to working round our house. Cleaning, cooking, baking, sewing, stitching, knitting – I can do all those.'

Mrs Craufurd waved the letter again at Sarah. 'I must say your Mr Havergal certainly sings your praises. It would appear he thinks very highly of you.'

Sarah blushed.

'He tells me you know how to apply yourself, and that you're thoroughly honest. Is that true?'

'Yes, ma'am, on both counts.'

'One thing I won't stand for is thieving. Try it in this establishment and your feet won't touch the ground till they land in a police cell.'

'I am not a thief, ma'am,' Sarah replied stiffly. 'You have my word before God on that.'

'Hmm!' Mrs Craufurd mused, and tapped her teeth with the edge of the letter.

Sarah wondered what Mr Craufurd was like. He was a banker, she'd been told, and extremely wealthy.

'I think I'll start you as an assistant to Miss O'Donoghue, our cook . . .' Sarah's heart sank to hear that. 'Do well with her and there will be promotion for you. But as you haven't been in service

23

before, I believe it will be for the best if you begin at the foot of the ladder.'

Sarah swallowed hard. Working with Miss O'Donoghue! Her life in the kitchen was going to be sheer unadulterated hell, she'd bet a pound to a penny on that.

'Can you start on the first of the month?'

'Yes, ma'am.'

'Good.' Mrs Craufurd nodded approvingly. 'Good.'

'And er . . . Not wishing to be forward, ma'am, but how much will I be paid?'

Mrs Craufurd named a sum that was most generous, considerably more than what Sarah had been expecting.

'Is that suitable?'

'Yes, ma'am.'

'I thought it might be,' Mrs Craufurd said drily. Then, 'There's a bell pull by that Landseer on the wall, could you give it a tug please.'

Mrs Craufurd was still smiling when Sarah finally left the room.

'Oh Gordy, what's to be my bedroom is absolutely tiny, and worse than that it's the most cheerless room I've ever been in. It looks directly on to a high wall and must never get any decent light at all,' Sarah said miserably. She and Gordy were in Bluebell Wood; it was late evening of the same day she'd been to Park Circus.

He was distraught to hear her tale. 'But if this Mrs Craufurd is as awful as you claim, why not just apply for another post in some other house?'

'I can't. Mr Havergal really put himself out for me with her, and I don't feel I can land the job and then let him down by not taking it – don't forget we've got to keep in his good books as he's going to arrange taking in washing for Ma. And possibly even more important, the Craufurds pay more than other people – I suspect because they've had trouble keeping staff in the past – and I need that extra money. Every ha'penny is going to count in our house from here on in.' She paused, then added, 'I know it always did in the past, but even more so now.'

Gordy took a deep breath. 'When do you start?'

'The first of the month.'

'And you say she smiles all the time?'

'She made me think of a smiling blonde spider.' Sarah shuddered.

'She fair gave me the creeps. As for the cook Miss O'Donoghue whose assistant I'm to be, God help me there.'

Gordy angrily stubbed his cigarette out underfoot. 'It's a bleak prospect for you right enough. Bleak enough to make a cat weep.'

'Aye, it is that,' she agreed.

'From what you say it's going to be purgatory.'

'I doubt there'll be many laughs.'

'If only the twins were older. If only . . .' He trailed off, grinding his right fist into his left palm.

At least she had to the end of the month, Sarah told herself. She did a quick mental calculation, that was eight days of freedom left to her.

'You haven't said yet, what time off do you get?'

She brightened at that. 'The time off is excellent, like the money. One full day off every week, two full days on the last day of the month. Not a week will pass but I won't be able to get back to Netherton.'

Gordy cheered up. 'Well, that is good news,' he enthused.

'Aye, it is that.'

He stared deep into her eyes, thinking to himself how gorgeous she was. She was the stuff that male dreams are made of.

'Kiss me,' she whispered urgently.

Their lips met, and his tongue sank into her mouth. She squirmed in his embrace, not with humiliation as she had in front of the awful Mrs Craufurd, but with pleasure, the most wonderful feelings coursing around inside her.

Together, entwined, they sank into the lush grass.

It was the worst summer storm that Sarah had ever experienced, thunder crashing and booming in the night sky, a sky that every few seconds was being lit by streaks of lightning.

Myrtle jumped when a particularly loud peal of thunder cracked the heavens – it might have been some monstrous cannon being fired directly above them.

'That's set my ears ringing,' she said to Sarah.

Rain rattled against the window-panes. In the quieter moments between thunder crashes the wind could be heard sighing and moaning as it swept through Netherton.

'Not a night to be out in,' commented Sarah to her ma, crossing to Bob to see how he was.

'Aye, you can say that again,' Myrtle agreed. Lightning didn't bother her too much, but thunder did. She'd hated thunder, and been scared of it, since wee.

Sarah needn't have worried about Bob; his vacuous gaze was directed at the ceiling. Was anything going on inside his head?, she wondered. Was he away in his own little dreamland? Was that what had happened to him? Or were there only vague passing shadows that meant nothing whatever to him?

'Listen,' said Myrtle, pausing in what she was doing.

There was the unmistakable sound of hooves which came to a halt outside their front door. A horse snorted loudly, then snorted again.

'Must be Mr Havergal's sulky,' Myrtle said, hastily drying her hands.

'I'll let him in,' Sarah declared, and hurried to the door. Now why had Mr Havergal, who owned the only gig in all Netherton, and a battered old item it was at that, come calling in the middle of such a storm? Whatever the reason, it had to be important.

She threw open the door, staggering a little as the rain lashed against her, to discover a man standing there. He was about six feet tall, wearing a dark cloak and top 'lum' hat. It wasn't Mr Havergal, but a total stranger. Behind the man was a carriage and pair, the driver hunched against the wild elements.

The man stared at her, his eyes boring into her. They were hard eyes, fiercely intent, but not unkind.

'We thought you were the minister,' Sarah found herself saying. The man didn't answer.

'Who is it?' Myrtle queried. She came to the door herself, and pulled the door further open. When she caught sight of the man's face, her mouth fell wide open.

The biggest sheet of lightning so far lit up the sky. 'Hello Myrtle,' the stranger said.

Sarah suddenly realised that the man's face was strangely familiar, though she was absolutely certain she'd never seen him before. She glanced at Myrtle. Why was her ma standing transfixed? It was as though Myrtle was seeing a ghost. 'Ma?'

'Aren't you going to ask me in, Myrtle? It's hardly the night to converse on the doorstep.'

He knew her ma's name. So presumably they were acquainted with one another.

'Well?' the man prompted.

26

'Have you come to cause trouble?' Myrtle demanded in a dry, croaky voice.

'That's the last thing I have in mind, I assure you.'

'You'd better come in then.'

The two women moved backwards to allow the man entrance. What was this all about, Sarah wondered. It was a right mystery.

The man removed his hat as he stepped into the kitchen, and as he did, his stern features relaxed into an easy smile.

Why did his face seem so familiar? If she had heard of the expression, Sarah would have called it *déjà vu*.

Inside the kitchen, the man looked round the room, missing nothing. The only time his gaze stopped moving was when it lit on the wall-bed, and Bob inside it. And that was only for the briefest of seconds.

'I never ever thought to see you again,' Myrtle said.

'No?'

Myrtle shook her head.

'Aren't you going to introduce me to Sarah? She must be wondering who I am.' He turned to Sarah, and said very softly, 'You are Sarah, aren't you?'

'That's correct.' From his clothes he was a gentleman, no doubt about it. And a monied one at that. And how did he know *her* name?

Myrtle opened her mouth to speak, found she couldn't, and swallowed instead. The stranger waited patiently.

'Sarah, this is Jock Hawke, your father.'

Sarah felt she'd been poleaxed. Her senses swam, confusion filled her. 'But he can't be—my father's dead!' she blurted out.

'So you told her I was dead,' Jock said to Myrtle, steel in his voice.

'It seemed the best thing.'

'Did it indeed?'

Suddenly Myrtle was indignant. 'You said you hadn't come to cause trouble!'

He held up a pacifying hand. 'And neither have I.'

'You . . . you really are my father? My real father?' Sarah asked incredulously. No wonder Myrtle had looked as if it was a ghost she was seeing!

'Yes, Sarah.'

And then it dawned on her why his face seemed so strangely familiar. It was an older, male version of her own. She was his spit.

'Can I take off my cloak?' Jock inquired. Myrtle nodded and he whipped it from his shoulders, draping it over a wooden chair.

'Have you any whisky in? I could take a dram.'

'I'm sorry, we don't.'

'Then you won't be offended if I supply my own.' He produced a leather-bound flask from an inside pocket. 'You do have glasses though, I presume?'

'I'll get you one,' Sarah told him. Her father wasn't dead after all, but standing right here in front of her. For as long as she remembered she'd believed her father to be dead, dying young of consumption.

'Will you have a gill?' Jock asked Myrtle.

'I don't normally have a taste for strong liquor, but considering the shock of you appearing out of the blue like this, yes I will.'

There were a thousand questions Sarah wanted to ask, all of them dancing on the end of her tongue. So he knew her age – that meant he'd thought about her, remembered her. She was intrigued by him, how could she not be? Her father, alive, well and gey prosperous by the looks of things. She still couldn't believe it.

'And you, Sarah? At seventeen you're old enough.'

'A small one, thank you, with lots of water,' she replied shyly.

As she reached for the glasses in the press she pinched her wrist to convince herself she wasn't dreaming, or away with the fairies.

'How eh . . . how did you know where to find me?' Myrtle queried.

'I've known for a dozen years where you were. I made it my business to know,' he answered, the steel back in his voice.

Myrtle nodded.

Sarah placed three glasses on the table, and Jock poured. He gave himself a very large one, a middling one for Myrtle, and a slightly wee-er one for Sarah. She pumped fresh water at the sink into a stone jar which she put beside the glasses. Jock said he'd have his neat, Myrtle added a little water to hers, Sarah lots.

Jock lifted his glass in a toast. 'To fresh beginnings!'

Now what did that mean, Sarah wondered as she sipped her drink.

'I suppose I have to ask the obvious. What brings you out on a night the Devil himself wouldn't venture abroad in?' Myrtle queried.

Jock chuckled, a deep rumbling sound at the back of his throat. 'The Devil wouldn't but Jock Hawke would?'

Myrtle glanced down into her drink.

'Or maybe you think of the Devil and Jock Hawke as one and the same?'

Myrtle threw what remained of her drink down her throat, and didn't reply.

'I came tonight because I only learned about Sunter late this afternoon. I've been abroad on business, to Canada – the ship that brought me back docked at half-past three,' Jock said softly.

Myrtle was puzzled. 'So who told you about Bob?'

'Charlie Dundonald. There was a letter from him waiting for me in my office.'

Puzzlement gave way to amazement. 'Dundonald the pit owner?'

'He's a good friend of mine. We belong to the same club.'

'And does he know that I was your wife?'

'That you *are* my wife, Myrtle,' Jock corrected her. 'We were never divorced.'

This was another shock for Sarah. Myrtle and Bob not married! Another long-held belief had just gone down the plughole.

Myrtle, her thoughts in turmoil, brushed a stray wisp of hair from her forehead. 'What you say is true of course, though it's a long time since I've thought of you as my husband. We may not be wed in the eyes of the church, but as far as I'm concerned Bob Sunter is my man and husband, and that's that.'

'Fair enough. But as you admit, there's nothing legal between the pair of you. No piece of paper.'

Myrtle went over to one of the comfy chairs by the range and sank into it. Her heart was hammering nineteen to the dozen.

'There was a full account of what's happened to Sunter from Charlie who got the details from a Doctor Elson. For what it's worth, and I hope you'll believe this, I'm truly sorry. I wouldn't wish that on anyone, not even my worst enemy.'

'So why are you here now then if not to gloat?'

Jock turned to Sarah. 'You've grown up into a fine-looking lass, girl.'

'Thank you.'

'You were only two when . . . when Myrtle left me for Sunter over there. You don't remember me at all, I take it?'

Sarah shook her head.

'You used to be a chubby wee thing with a mass of curls. That's how I've reminded you down all this long while.' He took a gulp of his whisky, and coughed. Whether the latter was from the drink or emotion wasn't clear.

'So what's to become of you all now that Sunter is unable to provide for you any more?'

'That's all taken care of already, thank you very much,' Myrtle answered quickly.

Jock raised an eyebrow. 'Oh?'

'Yes, Sarah has landed herself a job.'

'Indeed! And what sort of job is that?'

'I'm going into domestic service in a real posh house. I'm to be assistant to the cook there,' Sarah informed him.

Jock's geniality vanished, and a thundercloud settled on his brow. 'Domestic service, eh?'

'It was the best we could think of. And it's honest work,' Sarah said simply.

'And bloody hard work. Morning, noon and night with hardly any let-up.'

'There's good time off, and the Craufurds pay more than most families.'

Jock grunted, and looked thoughtful. 'But that's not going to be enough. You're going to need more than an assistant cook's wages to replace what Sunter was earning as a miner.'

'The minister is being right helpful. It was him that got Sarah the job, and he's going to arrange for me to take in washing. From that and what Sarah earns we should just get by,' Myrtle said.

'Take in washing?' Jock whispered. Myrtle dropped her eyes, unable to hold his gaze. She could feel the back of her neck burning.

'Taking in washing beats starving to death, or the poorhouse, any day,' Sarah said hotly, defending her mother.

'Skivvying,' Jock stated.

'Aye, skivvying, her and me,' Sarah retorted fiercely.

Jock looked from one to the other, then went over to the wall-bed. Sarah joined him there.

He stared at Bob who vacuously stared back. Then suddenly mists seemed to clear from Bob's eyes, and for a second or so there was recognition in them.

'Ah . . . ah . . .' Bob muttered, causing spittle to spill from his mouth and run down his chin. His body jerked several times as he appeared to be trying to haul himself on to an elbow.

'Ma, come quickly!' Sarah cried out.

Myrtle was instantly out of her chair and over to Bob, her face lined with worry. But it was already over, Bob lying flat on his back, his expression completely vacuous again.

'Oh, my bonny, my bonny,' Myrtle whispered, wiping the spittle from his chin with the rag that had been set by the bedside for that purpose.

'That's the first time he's reacted to anyone,' Sarah said to Jock.

Jock didn't reply, instead he returned to the flask on the table and poured himself another hefty dram. Although he didn't show it, the incident at the bed had shaken him.

After a short while, Myrtle went back to her chair, and Sarah came to stand by her side. 'It's obvious you've done well for yourself, but then I always knew you would,' Myrtle said to Jock.

Slowly, with emphasis, each word equally weighted, Jock replied. 'You asked why I've come here tonight. I've come to make you a proposition.'

He's still in love with me, Myrtle thought, believing she'd guessed what the proposition was going to be. 'A proposition?'

Jock ran a hand through his swept-back hair, the same auburny colour as Sarah's. Then he extracted a pocketbook, laid down his glass, opened the pocketbook and took from it a thick sheaf of fivers. Myrtle gasped to see so many. It was a king's ransom she was staring at.

'A hundred pounds precisely,' Jock stated, throwing the fivers on to the table.

'That's a . . . an awful lot of money,' Sarah said, wide-eyed.

'To me it's nothing at all, a mere bagatelle as the saying goes.'

'You've made it that big then?' Myrtle queried.

His eyes slitted with the pleasure of telling her. 'Bigger, far bigger than you've any idea.'

Myrtle rose, went over to the table, and lifted up the sheaf of fivers. What she could do with a hundred pounds! 'And what's this for?'

'You.' He paused, then added softly, 'If you want it.'

'You're giving me this for old time's sake, is that it?'

'Not quite.'

Myrtle gave a low laugh. 'No, I didn't think so. Not after what I did to you. So what do I have to do for it?'

'How much was Sunter earning?'

Myrtle stated an average sum of what had been in Bob's pay packet on a Friday night.

'I'll give you the hundred pounds, plus double per week of what Sunter was bringing in. Your money troubles will be over, and there will be no need for skivvying.'

Sarah was silently watching this by-play between her mother and father. She was fascinated. She'd already noted that Jock had tremendous charisma; he seemed to exude it.

Myrtle regarded Jock with a sideways look. 'Again I ask, what do I have to do for all this?'

'You? Nothing. But Sarah, yes.'

That threw Myrtle, she'd been certain it was herself he was after.

'Me!' Sarah exclaimed, as thrown as Myrtle.

Jock produced a cigar, clipped it, then crossed to the mantelpiece on which stood a brass container filled with spills. Choosing a green spill he lit it at the range, then lit his Havana.

'You,' he said finally to Sarah through a cloud of smoke.

Sarah shook her head. 'I don't understand.'

But Myrtle was beginning to. 'You want to take her away with you, is that it?'

Jock stared at his daughter, the daughter who'd haunted him these past fifteen years. 'I'm a very rich man, Sarah, you'd want for nothing. Instead of being the servant, you'd be the one who had the servants. Instead of being ordered about, you'd be the one doing the ordering.'

Sarah was flabbergasted, not knowing what to think.

To Myrtle, Jock said. 'That's my proposition then. A hundred pounds in cash, plus double Sunter's wages every week which will arrive here every Friday without fail – you have my word on that. In return I want Sarah to come and live with me as my daughter.'

'Where?' Sarah asked.

'Where what?'

'Where do you live?'

'I have a big house, it's called Stiellsmuir, in Newton Mearns, which is on the southern outskirts of Glasgow,' Jock answered.

'No,' said Myrtle, the words tumbling out of her mouth, 'no you can't have her. I won't let you.'

'You'd prefer to take in washing, and for her to be forever at someone's beck and call?'

Myrtle was clearly agitated. 'If that's how it's going to be then that's how it's going to be. But you're not going to get your claws into her.'

Jock regarded Myrtle coldly. 'Isn't that somewhat selfish of you? Denying Sarah the good things in life, the very best that life has to offer?'

Myrtle stuck a thumb into her mouth, and began worrying its nail. Everything had been so simple until Bob had fallen down with his stroke. She'd literally have given her right arm to have him back as he'd been.

'How do you feel about coming to live with me?' Jock asked Sarah.

'I don't know. I don't know you.'

'You'll have anything you want. Gowns, jewellery, a carriage of your own. And you'll make new friends of course, friends of your new social standing. There will be teas and soirées and grand balls. It'll be a fairy tale come true.'

Sarah had to admit, it was certainly a dazzling prospect. Too much really, coming as it did on top of the reappearance of her father, for her to take in all at once. A carriage of her own! Her mind boggled at that thought. And jewels! In her mind's eye she pictured a cascade of falling, glittering gems. Stones, the colours of the rainbow.

'I think you should go now, Jock,' Myrtle said, rising.

'Could it be that you're jealous?'

'I beg your pardon?'

'I was watching your face when I said it was Sarah I wanted. Did you think I'd come for you?'

Myrtle blushed. 'No, I didn't.'

Jock laughed, a cutting laugh that told Myrtle he rightly thought her a liar.

'Mind you, you're still a fine-looking woman, Myrtle, there's no denying it. Though how long you'll retain those looks with Sunter having to be danced attendance on, goodness only knows. The money I'm offering would make it all so much easier for you. Why, you could even afford to hire a lassie to help you out, take some of the burden off your shoulders.'

'I already have Sarah.'

He blew a stream of blue smoke in her direction. 'No you don't. You're forgetting, she's going into service.'

Myrtle bit her lip, she *had* momentarily forgotten that.

Jock swung on Sarah. 'It's a decision you'll have to make yourself. But not tonight, I don't want to rush you. I want you to think this over.'

33

'Goodnight, Jock and goodbye,' Myrtle said emphatically.

Jock took another puff on his cigar, a long slow puff. 'There is one more thing, a condition to Sarah coming to Stiellsmuir.' He paused for effect, then said. 'And that is, if she agrees to live with me she never returns here ever again.'

Sarah sucked in her breath, feeling like a fish who's been contemplating a fat juicy worm and suddenly been made aware of the hook underneath.

'To get back at me of course,' Myrtle hissed at Jock.

'You've had her all to yourself these past fifteen years. Now I want her all to myself. It's as simple as that.'

'Never see Ma again?' Sarah murmured, dazed.

'That's the condition.' Jock drained what remained of his whisky, placed the empty glass on the table, and the flask back in his pocket, then picked up the sheaf of fivers.

'The day after tomorrow, at 9 am, my carriage will be outside your door. The driver will have this hundred pounds which he will hand over to you if Sarah is ready to go with him. If she chooses to remain here then he'll hang on to the money.' Having said that, Jock replaced the wad of fivers in his pocketbook, and that too disappeared into a pocket.

'I do hope you'll come, Sarah, with all my heart I do,' he said. Then, throwing his cloak round his shoulders and replacing his hat on his head, he strode to the door. A fierce gust of wind swept round the room, causing the candles to flicker.

'The day after tomorrow, 9 am,' he said. He looked Sarah straight in the face, his eyes boring into hers the way they had when he'd first arrived, and then he was gone, the door clicking shut behind him.

A command rang out, a whip cracked, followed by the sound of the carriage and pair moving off into the night.

Myrtle sagged, and had to grab hold of a chair to steady herself.

'Are you all right, Ma?' Sarah asked anxiously.

'A bit shaken—it'll pass in a minute. I could use a cup of tea though.'

'I'll get that for you.' Sarah's thoughts were whirling as she set about making the tea. What had just taken place, the reappearance of her father from the dead, his offer, was just—well, was just fantastic!

Myrtle sat down again, and remained there in brooding silence

34

while Sarah made the tea. 'Thank you,' she said quietly when Sarah handed her the cup. She sipped the contents, closing her eyes in appreciation. There was nothing in the world to beat a good cup of tea.

'Ma?'

Myrtle looked up at her daughter.

'Why did you lie to me all these years by telling me my father was dead?'

Myrtle sighed, and sipped more tea.

'And that you and Bob were married?'

Myrtle's gaze strayed to the wall-bed where Bob lay, then she brought her gaze back to Sarah.

'I never dreamt in a million years . . .' She broke off, licking her lips, then sipped again. 'It's a smashing cup this, you make grand tea, Sarah.'

'Ma, I think I should have some answers. I'm entitled to.'

Myrtle took a deep breath. 'You musn't go to Jock, I won't let you.'

'Do you have a reason? I mean a particular reason? Or is it just because of you and him and whatever happened between you in the past?'

'Sarah, your father is . . .' Myrtle paused, wrestling with herself as how best to put this. 'He can be rather odd.'

'Odd? What does that mean?'

'It's why I left him. He can be odd, strange.'

Sarah shook her head. 'I don't understand what you're trying to tell me, Ma.'

Myrtle's thoughts were back in time, to that first day she'd clapped eyes on the new clerk at Poulson's Pit, that fine upstanding young man with the sort of handsome face and slim build that was guaranteed to melt a lassie's heart.

'He was aye ambitious your da, determined to get ahead. He was an orphan you see, his own mother and father both dying of the consumption.'

Sarah was fascinated. Myrtle had never spoken of Jock before. Whenever she'd brought up the subject of her da in the past – and she had on innumerable occasions – Myrtle had always put her off with some vague excuse or other. She'd come to believe that Myrtle refused to talk about the supposedly dead Jock because of grief. That was clearly wrong.

35

'Consumption was what you told me he died of.'

'He might well have done too when he was small if he hadn't been physically strong, with the constitution of a horse.'

'So how old was he when his parents died?'

Myrtle had to think about that. 'Nine, I seem to remember. The two of them went within weeks of each other.'

'And what happened to him then?'

'He went to bide with an aunt. But she was a bitch of hell according to him, her husband a brute who used to knock the living daylights out of Jock. Jock stayed with them only a few months and then struck out on his own.'

'At nine!' Sarah exclaimed, amazed.

'He not only got by on his own, but continued his education. For the most part Jock Hawke is a self-taught man.'

'And where did you meet him?'

'Shotts, of course, where I was born and brought up, and where your aunt Jessica and granda still live. I was just your age when Jock came to work at Poulson's Pit as a new clerk.'

'He was never a miner then?' For some reason she'd always thought he had been. Myrtle had never actually said, but that had been the inference.

'Not your da. He wasn't one to toil with his hands; he had a brain and knew how to use it. Poulson himself, not a man to be generous with compliments, said more than once that Jock was the smartest clerk who'd ever worked at the pit.'

It was all spilling out now, Sarah thought, the story she'd been dying to hear for as long as she could remember. And it wasn't at all as she'd expected it to be. 'So how did the pair of you meet?'

'At that year's gala. There was dancing, as there always was, and I was standing chaffing to Peggy McIlhone – who later got married to a chap who went to work in the Kent pits – when up he comes, bows to me . . .' Myrtle broke off to smile at the memory of that, 'and asks me on to the floor.'

'And that was the beginning of it? You started courting after that?' Sarah queried eagerly.

'He didn't ask me out at the gala, but about a week afterwards. From there it sort of snowballed until finally we got engaged, then wed.'

Myrtle drank more of her tea. Those days seemed so long ago, an eternity away. And yet, in other ways, they might just have been the previous week.

36

'Did you love him when you married him?'

'Why do you ask that?'

'You couldn't have been married that long before you left him, and surely you don't leave someone you love?'

'He was a fair old catch was Jock Hawke,' Myrtle replied slowly. 'A lot of the lassies in Shotts would have given their eye teeth to get off with him, but it was me he favoured. He had prospects you see, he was going places in life.'

'So you didn't love him?' Sarah prompted.

Myrtle's lips curved into a wry smile. 'At the time I thought I loved him, and you were certainly conceived in what I would call love. But whatever it was I felt for him drained away after we moved to Maryhill, and he started to turn funny.'

'Why did you go to Maryhill?'

'Jock got a better job with an import/export firm. There was nothing to hold him in Shotts, which as you know is a quarter of the way to Edinburgh, after that. And so we moved to Glasgow, which was convenient for his new office.'

Sarah was puzzled. 'And that was when he started being funny? Odd and strange, you called it.'

'Aye, I think it had something to do with his parents dying when he was so young and him having to bring himself up. But it was in Maryhill, just after we'd arrived there, that he had for the first time – or at least the first time I'd seen it – one of his "moods".'

'What kind of moods, Ma?'

'He'd become withdrawn, and talk to himself. He'd get a peculiar look in his eyes which used to send ice-cold shivers racing up and down my spine.'

'Are you saying he hit you?'

'No, he was never violent. But you thought that at any moment he might be. That he might suddenly lash out and knock you right across the room.'

'Having his parents dying on him when he was so young and then having to bring himself up must have left its mark on him. It couldn't have done otherwise,' Sarah agreed.

'I only know he changed after we went to Maryhill, and the more he changed the more we grew apart.'

'Do you mean the pair of you grew apart, or just you from him?' Sarah asked shrewdly.

Myrtle finished her tea, and laid the cup on the floor. 'Me from him. Jock was always besotted by me. Yes, I believe that's the correct word and not too strong. Besotted, he worshipped the very ground I walked on.'

'And you left him?'

Myrtle's gaze went back to the wall-bed where Bob was snoring. He snored a great deal now, something he'd rarely done before his stroke. She couldn't imagine how the two things were connected. 'I re-met Bob whom I'd more or less grown up with.'

'How did that come about?' Sarah prompted.

'Before she died your grandma used to get bad spells of being ill. During one of them, when Jessica was also laid up, I returned to Shotts from Maryhill to look after your grandma – granda was still grafting at the time – and it was then that I re-met Bob.'

Myrtle's face lit up in a soft, warm, smile. 'I was coming out of Curley's grocery shop when I bumped into him. "It's yourself then, Myrtle," he said. "And it's yourself, Bob Sunter," I replied, thinking he'd changed somehow. Later I discovered he'd thought exactly the same about me, that I'd changed.

'Anyway, we had a bit of a natter, and then off I went and in he went to Curley's. Well next night, out for a breather, don't I bump into him again and him off to the pub for a pint. There and then he asked me if I'd like to go with him, said it was better than just wandering the streets aimlessly, and I quite surprised myself by agreeing.'

'And you a married woman? Wasn't that scandalous? Didn't folk talk?' Sarah queried, knowing full well what village life was like – an eye behind every curtain, and you couldn't do anything – well hardly ever unless it was terribly well planned and organised – without everyone finding out about it, and commenting on it.

'It wasn't seen as scandalous to begin with. As I say Bob and I had known each other all our lives. Everyone knew that and thought he was being kind the way a brother might. And that's how it began, like brother and sister.'

'And how did it become more than that?'

'To be truthful Sarah, I don't really know. He started taking me out regularly for a drink and a chat, all above board like, but then something began developing between us, and like Topsy that something just grew and grew till before long we were head over heels in love with one another.'

'I presume by then it had clicked with the others in Shotts? They'd realised what was going on?'

'Oh aye, by then it was obvious. When we were together we seemed to spark off each other. There was almost a physical bond between us. Then Grandma recovered, and I had a choice to make.'

'And you chose Bob?'

Myrtle remembered only too well the astonishment, and profound hurt, on Jock's face when she told him she was leaving him for another. There had been anger, ranting and raving, then he'd cried when she'd walked out the door. Wept like some big wean.

Myrtle went on. 'Bob and I decided to leave Shotts and make a fresh start elsewhere, somewhere we weren't known. He cast about and came up with the job here in Netherton. When we arrived we said we were Mr and Mrs Sunter, and who was to know any different? I considered passing you off as our child, but Bob wouldn't have it. He said that wouldn't be right for you, or Jock, and so we told folk that you were the child of a previous marriage on my part, and that your da had died young of consumption.'

Silence fell, the only sounds in the kitchen being Bob's snoring and the steady tick-tock of the wag at the wa' clock.

After a while Sarah asked, 'Was Jock against you taking me with you? Did he want to keep me himself?'

'He did indeed want to keep you, desperately so. But I argued with him, and he saw the sense in my argument. How could he look after a two-year-old? Impossible unless he employed someone, and he wasn't yet earning enough to do that. At least I don't think he was. But what really got through to him was how cruel it would be to take a bairn away from its ma, a ma who knew how to care for that bairn the way a bairn should be cared for. A ma who loved the bairn with all her heart and soul.'

'So you took me and Jock was left with nothing,' Sarah stated.

An expression of guilt crept over Myrtle's face. 'That's how he saw it. But it was common sense for you to come with me, far better in both the short and long terms. And you can't deny Bob did the right thing by you, that he always treated you as his own.'

'That's very true, I can't deny it,' Sarah agreed.

Myrtle let out a long sigh. 'I was so relieved the day I left Jock, relieved that my life with him was over, and that I was going to Bob.'

'And yet, as you admit, Jock worshipped the ground you walked on.'

'But he scared me, Sarah.'

'Nonetheless you were his wife, still *are* his wife as he pointed out. And agreed to be so in sickness and in health.'

Myrtle stared levelly at Sarah. 'Are you criticising what I did?'

'No, Ma, only trying to understand.'

Myrtle locked her fingers together and twisted them against each other. 'I don't regret what I did, nor one moment with Bob. He and I were meant for one another, I'm sure of it.' Again she looked across at the wall-bed. 'Even now I don't regret it. Not one jot.'

Sarah was trying to sort out her thoughts; so much of this new information would have to be digested.

'You're not to go to him, Sarah, I forbid it. Even if the money would solve all our problems. Well, at least financially anyway.'

Being forbidden outright like this rankled with Sarah, put her back up a bit. She was seventeen after all, and a fairly mature seventeen at that. 'Don't you think I'm old enough, or capable of making up my own mind, Ma?'

'I don't trust him. As I told you, he can be odd, very odd indeed.'

'Odd he may have been, but he never hurt you, did he?' Sarah probed.

'He never laid a finger on me. Except once when—' Myrtle broke off, blushing furiously. 'That's something I can't tell you about. It was eh . . .' She groped for a suitable way of putting it. 'Fun, shall we call it.'

Sarah was intrigued. 'Fun?'

Myrtle's redness turned almost to scarlet. 'Aye, well, you know. Things husbands and wives do to one another.'

The penny dropped. It was something they'd got up to in bed. 'And he hurt you then?'

'But only in fun, as an accident. He didn't mean to. He wasn't in one of his "moods".'

All sorts of pictures were flashing through Sarah's mind as she conjectured what her mother and father had been doing. One of those pictures made her want to burst out giggling, but she forced herself not to, knowing full well Myrtle would be mortified if she did.

Myrtle changed the subject.

Sarah awoke with a start to find herself covered in a cold sweat, this even though the night was extremely hot. The heat wave was continuing.

She reached up to touch her hair. It was soaking and her scalp itself was awash.

She remembered then, she'd been dreaming. She'd been working for Miss O'Donoghue who'd been giving her a right lambasting, and while Miss O'Donoghue had shrieked at her the awful Mrs Craufurd had been standing nearby, smiling as she watched what was happening.

Sarah shivered, and drew the bedclothes up to her chin. In another part of the dream she'd seen her mother mangling a veritable mountain of laundry, bent almost double at the task, her arm going round and round and round while piece after piece of laundry shot through the mangle to go flying out the other side. Behind her mother was a huge copper that hissed and spat as it boiled even more laundry that was to go on the mountain.

One hundred pounds, cash in hand, and double Bob's wages every week, Sarah thought. How very much easier that would make what lay ahead for Myrtle. As for herself, if she agreed to go and live with Jock there would be no Miss O'Donoghue and Mrs Craufurd. She'd be completely spared the cook and blonde spider.

Instead it would be the life of Riley for her. A grand house to bide in, servants to do her bidding, gowns, jewels . . . Oh, but it was tempting right enough.

But if she did accept, there were penalties to be paid: she would never see her ma again, or Bob, or Netherton, or Gordy. At least if she went to Park Circus she'd get home every week and Gordy's arms would be waiting for her. Gordy's arms and Bluebell Wood.

Then again there was something else to consider, Jock's 'moods' as Ma called them. The moods that had scared her into leaving him. But did he still get these moods? He could well have grown out of them by now, it being fifteen years since Ma had packed her bags. He'd certainly seemed pleasant enough when he'd come to the house.

Hours later Sarah was still tossing and turning, agonising over the decision she was going to have to make.

Gordy was appalled. 'Never see you again!' he breathed, his face white and tight with shock.

They were in Bluebell Wood where Sarah had arranged to meet him, having left a note with Mrs McCallum earlier on that day. A note she'd written shortly after she'd made her decision.

41

'I have my mother to think about, and Bob, my step-da. This way they'll both be taken care of.'

'But us, you and I!' Gordy cried out in despair.

She took him by the hand. 'This is an opportunity which I'd be downright stupid to let go by. I'll have everything I want—everything.' She shuddered. 'The alternative is Park Circus and those two women there.'

'But at least if you were at Park Circus I'd see you at weekends. Now . . .' He trailed off in anguish.

'Do you think this isn't hurting me as much as it is you? I do love you, you know.'

'And yet you've chosen not to see me ever again. I find that a funny sort of love.'

'You're not thinking straight, Gordy. You're thinking with your heart and not your head.'

'And you are, I suppose!'

Tears bubbled into her eyes. She'd promised herself she wouldn't cry, and now she was. 'I'm doing the right thing, I just know I am.'

'But what about us?' he protested bitterly.

'Gordy, when I suggested we get married you explained to me you had your responsibilities towards your ma and the twins. Well I also have responsibilities towards my ma, Bob, my step-da, and not least myself.' Her voice was suddenly shrill and accusing. 'Do you want me to have to go out skivvying, as my father put it, for those two dreadful females I've told you about? Well, do you? And if you do, what sort of love is *that*?'

He hung his head. 'It's just that . . . that . . .' He groaned. 'Never to see you again.'

Luckily, she'd had a hanky on her which she'd used to mop away her tears, and now blow her nose. She was as distraught as he, but doing her best not to show it. 'I'll never forget you, I want you to know that.'

He looked up to stare at her, drinking her in, searing her face as it was at that precise moment into his memory. 'It's like having a knife stuck in you, stuck in and waggled about,' he husked.

'Yes, isn't it?'

'We just weren't to be, I suppose.'

She didn't reply.

'And I'll never forget you, Sarah, never as long as I live.'

They continued staring at one another. Then abruptly, without

42

uttering anything further, Gordy turned round and walked away out of their secluded spot, out of her life forever.

'Oh Gordy!' she whispered when he was gone. 'Oh Gordy!'

She gave him a full five minutes' start, then followed him back to Netherton.

The carriage and pair came to a halt outside their house at 9 am precisely. Sarah was waiting inside with the small bundle of personal things she intended taking with her.

Myrtle was beside herself at the prospect of losing her daughter. Her face clearly showed her distress.

'It's time then,' Sarah said as there was a knock on the front door.

Myrtle put a clenched fist to her mouth, and began chewing one of her fingers. She just couldn't believe this was actually taking place. In such a short while her entire world had come crashing in ruins round about her. First Bob, now Sarah.

Sarah opened the front door to discover the carriage driver standing there holding a large brown envelope.

The driver touched his hat. 'Miss Hawke?'

'Yes.'

'I've to inquire whether you're staying or coming with me, Miss Hawke?'

'I'm coming with you.'

He again touched his hat in salute. 'Very good, Miss Hawke, in which case this is for you.' And with that he handed her the large brown envelope.

'I'll just be a moment,' Sarah said, and half shut the door. Going to Myrtle, she gave her mother the envelope.

Myrtle tried to speak, but was too choked to do so. She threw her arms round Sarah and hugged her daughter as tightly as she could.

'I'll just say farewell to Bob,' Sarah whispered, disentangling herself. Myrtle's head bowed, and she was racked with sobs, her entire body shaking with them.

There was spittle on Bob's chin which Sarah wiped away. He stared at her vacuously, his mouth slightly agape. 'There's no need to worry, Ma will be well looked after from here on in,' she told him as if he could actually hear and comprehend what she was saying.

She pecked her step-da on the cheek, then forehead. 'I'll be praying for you,' she said softly.

It was time to go, time to leave home, and Netherton. Taking a deep breath she turned away from Bob to give her ma a weak smile.

'My baby, my wee baby,' Myrtle wept.

Sarah picked up her bundle, knowing if she didn't get out of there quickly she wouldn't go at all.

'Goodbye Ma, take care,' she said, so filled with emotion she felt she must surely burst from it.

She rushed at Myrtle, kissed her on the lips, and then flew out of the front door. The door crashed shut behind her.

'Can I take that for you, Miss Hawke?' the driver inquired, indicating her bundle.

'Please.' She thrust it at him, then allowed him to help her into the carriage which smelt beautifully of polish and leather.

The driver climbed up on to his seat, and cracked his whip over the horses' backs. With a jolt the carriage moved off.

They passed Curley's grocery shop, and McHarg's the newsagent. At that point Sarah had a perfect view of Dundonald's Pit which dominated Netherton, and which was Netherton's lifeblood. The big wheel, an integral part of her memories for as far back as she could remember, was slowly spinning in the direction which denoted that someone – the shift had gone down hours previously – was descending to the coalface.

She listened vaguely to the steady clip-clop of hooves as the houses and streets of Netherton slipped by.

And then they were out of Netherton, and that was that.

Chapter 2

A flap which allowed the driver to speak to whoever was inside the carriage flipped open. 'That's Stiellsmuir over on the right, Miss Hawke. I thought you might like to know,' he said.

Sarah thanked the driver, wondering what he made of Jock's daughter being dressed as she was, and wearing clogs, then looked in the direction he had mentioned. What she saw caused her to gasp in awe.

The architecture was very Scottish in the grand house tradition. Baronial, slightly Gothic in appearance, Stiellsmuir was constructed of red sandstone that was topped by a copper-green roof adorned with ornamental turrets, a turret at each corner.

Bonnie Prince Charlie, Sarah suddenly thought. It was the sort of grand house she would have expected Bonnie Prince Charlie to come striding out of. And from here on it was going to be her home.

She smiled wryly as she compared the house she was now looking at to the one she'd left behind in Netherton. There couldn't have been a greater difference. It was the proverbial chalk and cheese.

The carriage clattered over a stone bridge below which a burn slowly meandered, and then through open wrought-iron gates which brought them to the approach, and then the driveway to the house.

As they got closer, Sarah saw a face pressed to a window, and recognised it as Jock's. As if by magic the face abruptly vanished.

When the carriage reached the front of Stiellsmuir Jock was there to greet her. He threw open the door nearest him the moment the carriage had come to a stop. 'You came then,' he said simply, his broad beam broadening even further. He was clearly overjoyed to see her.

She accepted his hand, and stepped down on to the gravel that scrunched underfoot. She was nervous, yet at the same time calm inside. It was a strange combination of sensations.

'Welcome to Stiellsmuir, Sarah,' he said. Drawing her to him he kissed her first on one cheek, then the other. His eyes were sparking like diamonds, green diamonds shooting off shafts of fire.

'Here I am,' she replied. It was all she could think of to say.

'Yes, here you are. At long last,' he agreed, and shook his head in disbelief. 'Anyway, let's away inside. There's no point in standing here.'

They ascended a short flight of stone steps that brought them to the twin main doors, oak decorated in iron, then went through those into a marbled hall. Instantly the temperature dropped from the heat that had been outside, and for Sarah in the coach.

'When did you buy the house?' Sarah asked as they headed for a sweeping staircase, her clogs rat-a-tatting as they went.

'I didn't buy it, I had it built.' His expression became one of intense pride. 'I can't wait to show it to you.'

Some of the walls they passed were wood-panelled, others painted a clotted-cream colour. There was thick pile maroon carpeting on the staircase, the banisters' oak the same as that of the main doors. What furniture Sarah saw was undoubtedly antique. Indeed a few pieces were Jacobean, which married perfectly with her idea about Bonnie Prince Charlie.

'I intend to take the rest of the week off work in order to spend it with you,' Jock informed her as they reached a landing.

'Don't feel you have to.'

He touched her lightly on the arm. 'Believe me, it's something I very much want to do. To get to know my daughter a little.'

'And I'm looking forward to getting to know my father. My real father.' She glanced back down the stairs to see a manservant carrying her bundle.

The bedroom Jock took her into was huge. It contained a double fourposter bed, white marble fireplace, with Chinese rugs scattered over the highly polished wood floor. Sun streamed in the three windows whose curtains were a buttercup yellow colour.

Sarah gazed about her in wonder. 'It's . . . wonderful.'

'This is my principal guestroom which will be yours on a temporary basis. The bedroom that will eventually be your own is on the floor above this. I shall have it completely redecorated before you move in.'

Completely redecorated for her! That was a luxury indeed. Most thoughtful of him.

'Obviously I didn't know whether you'd come today or not, but hoping you would I had Mrs McGuffie – that's my housekeeper – buy in a few clothes to keep you going until such times as your dressmaker can deliver the wardrobe we'll be ordering for you.'

He went to a built-in press and threw it open to reveal a variety of

46

skirts, blouses and other garments. 'I hope these fit, I had to guess at your size,' Jock told her.

Sarah crossed to the press, and took one of the blouses. She'd never touched silk before, but there was no question that was what she was now feeling.

'There are some shoes of varying sizes, and hopefully at least one pair will fit. We'll order a couple of dozen pairs after we've been to the dressmaker,' Jock said.

Sarah nearly burst out laughing. A couple of dozen pairs of shoes! The thought was just incredible.

She indicated what she had on, her 'Sunday go to kirk' dress. 'I hope I haven't let you down in front of the servants by coming in this, but it's the best I had.'

'You haven't let me down at all, Sarah. And as for the servants, it's not their place to judge, but to serve. However, as I'm sure their curiosity has been well roused I'll have Mrs McGuffie have a word with them to explain something of the situation.' He paused, then went on. 'Which reminds me, I haven't got a proper lady's maid here as I haven't had need for one. However, now that you're in residence we clearly do. I'll instruct Mrs McGuffie to take one on as soon as a suitable female can be found.'

A maid all to herself! And to think if Jock hadn't turned up out of the blue as he had she would shortly have been starting as an assistant cook for the awful Mrs Craufurd. How the pendulum had swung in her favour.

'Would it be possible for me to interview the maid myself? Or would that be stepping on Mrs McGuffie's toes?'

'You'd like to interview the candidate yourself? Then by all means. I'm sure Mrs McGuffie won't mind.' His forehead creased in a frown and he added, 'But maybe it would be just as well if Mrs McGuffie also agreed to your choice. I feel that would be diplomatic, don't you?'

'If you say so. I don't want to disrupt anything, or make enemies.'

Jock laughed. 'You won't make an enemy of Mrs McGuffie, she's the original treasure. But why possibly offend when it's unnecessary to do so?'

There was a great deal of warmth in Jock's voice when he spoke about his housekeeper, Sarah noted. 'Do you have a butler?'

'No, Mrs McGuffie is in charge. She's been with me since I moved into Stiellsmuir, and I rely on her entirely.'

'When do I meet her?'

Jock gestured at the clothes hanging in the press. 'Get yourself changed and then come downstairs. You can meet her then, after which I will give you a personally conducted tour of the house and gardens.'

'Right,' she smiled.

He went to the door, paused, then turned back to her. 'I can't tell you how happy you've made me by coming today. Thank you.' And with that he left the room, closing the door behind him.

Sarah gazed again round the bedroom thinking how absolutely splendid it was. Kicking off her clogs, she ran to the bed and threw herself across it.

My God but it was soft. The bed she'd had at Netherton was like a board compared to this. She had a peep under the counterpane to discover that the sheets were crisp white linen of the highest quality.

She was still sprawled across the bed when there was a knock on the door. Instantly she was on her feet and with a single sweeping motion of her arm smoothed the bed where she'd rumpled it.

'Yes?'

The lassie was about her own age and wore a black poplin dress with fitted bodice and long plain sleeves. A white lawn apron, with embroidered edging, was tied round her waist, its bib pinned in place on her bosom. On her head she was wearing a small mob-cap of white muslin.

'Please Miss, I'm Hettie, one of the parlourmaids. Mrs McGuffie has sent me up to ask if you'd care for a bath before joining the master?'

A bath sounded just the ticket. 'That would be lovely, thank you, Hettie.'

'I'll run the bath for you now then, Miss.' Hettie bobbed, then left the bedroom.

Hettie was back in under ten minutes to say that the bath was ready. Sarah, changed into a dressing-gown that had been in the press, accompanied the parlourmaid who showed her where the bathroom was.

After Hettie had left Sarah locked the bathroom door, then stared about her. She'd never been in a proper bathroom before; in Netherton you bathed in the zinc tub in front of the range.

The bath itself was white procelain encased in wood, and enormous.

She could have got two if not three of her in it, no bother at all. Fragrant-smelling steam rose from the pink-tinged water that it held.

Towels had been laid out, fluffy ones that were gorgeously soft, and these were carefully draped over the side of the bath.

There was a thick carpet on the floor, midnight blue in colour, which went with the walls which were a delicate pale blue. The ceiling was the same colour as the carpet.

Sarah tossed her dressing-gown over a towel-rack, on which there were other towels, then went to the bath to test the temperature of the water. It was perfect, not too hot, not too cold, just right. Stepping into the bath she sank on to her bottom.

This was bliss, sheer unadulterated bliss she thought, closing her eyes and slipping further down till the water was lapping her neck. Something had been put in the water to tint it and make it smell so nice, but she didn't know what. Whatever, it was lovely. The tension and nervousness she'd felt about coming to Stiellsmuir started to seep out of her, replaced by a soporific, contented feeling.

'Aaahh!' she sighed. Then 'Aaahh!' again.

Jock rose as she entered the library. He'd been sitting talking to an earnest looking woman whom Sarah presumed, correctly, to be Mrs McGuffie the housekeeper.

'So how was your bath?' he demanded.

'Marvellous. Simply marvellous.'

'Excellent.'

Mrs McGuffie had also risen by now to stand staring at Sarah. There was no smile or any other sign of welcome on her face.

'You're good at guessing women's sizes, the clothes fit perfectly,' Sarah told her father.

'And the shoes?'

She pointed her right foot to reveal it encased in soft satin. 'Three pairs I can wear.'

Jock took hold of her hands, and squeezed them. Then he swung round to the housekeeper. 'Mrs McGuffie, this is my daughter Sarah – Sarah Hawke.'

Mrs McGuffie gave a small bow. 'I'm pleased to meet you, Miss Hawke.'

She didn't look pleased at all, quite the contrary, Sarah thought with a sinking heart.

'And I'm pleased to meet you.' Should she shake hands or not? She decided she would.

Mrs McGuffie hesitated for a fraction of a second, then came forward to accept the proffered hand. 'I hope you'll enjoy living at Stiellsmuir, Miss Hawke,' she said, her tone formal, precise.

'I'm sure I will.' About forty, Sarah judged. Her figure was slim, her features the type that are often described as handsome rather than pretty. Her hair was pepper and salt, worn swept upwards and held in place at the crown of the head by a brace of black combs.

'This calls for a celebration,' Jock said to Sarah, and crossed to where an ice-bucket stood atop an occasional table.

'Champagne, nothing less, will do for the return of my daughter,' he declared, pulling the bottle from the bucket.

'There's a towel there,' Mrs McGuffie said quietly, nodding.

Jock picked up the towel and wrapped it round the bottle. 'Now to make it pop,' he smiled at Sarah.

Mrs McGuffie went over to an ornately designed cabinet and opened it to display an assortment of glasses. From these she produced two crystal flutes.

'Have you had champagne before?' Jock asked Sarah, knowing full well what the answer would be.

She shook her head.

'I thought as much.' The wire was off and his fingers were working on the cork. It went suddenly, going off with a most satisfactory bang and sailing clean across the far side of the library. Mrs McGuffie was there with the glasses as the wine frothed from the bottle.

'Only two glasses, Mrs McGuffie, where's yours?' he queried.

'I thought this was a private celebration, between you and your daughter,' came the cool reply.

'Don't be daft woman, get another glass.'

When the three glasses were filled, Jock raised his in a toast. 'To Sarah, come home to me at long last.'

'To Sarah,' Mrs McGuffie echoed.

As they drank Sarah was aware that Mrs McGuffie's eyes were watching her over the rim of her glass. Eyes that were ever so slightly narrowed, and glinting.

*

'Well, did you enjoy that?' Jock asked Sarah as their carriage clattered along Sauchiehall Street. They had just left Madame Baptiste's, a Frenchwoman – with some Negro blood in her as her darkish skin betrayed – who was the best, and most exclusive, dressmaker in all Glasgow. She was patronised by everybody who was anybody.

'Enjoy it, I positively revelled in it!' Sarah exclaimed, her delight and enthusiasm making Jock laugh. 'The money it's going to cost, it must all add up to a small fortune!'

'Don't you worry your head about that. I can well afford it, I assure you.'

Sarah's mind was still reeling at the number of dresses she'd been measured for, dresses for all occasions from simple day-wear to those to be worn to a high-falutin ball. *Her at a ball!* She just loved the idea.

Jock took out his fob watch, and glanced at it. 'I know I said I'd take the rest of the week off work, but would you mind if I make a couple of calls before taking you to lunch?'

'Not at all.'

'You might find them interesting.' He rapped the front carriage partition with his cane and a few seconds later the flap there was opened.

'Yes sir?' the driver asked.

'Take us to the *Good Intent*. It's berthed at Queen's Dock, North Basin,' he instructed.

'Yes sir.' The flap was shut again.

'We're going to the docks?' Sarah queried, thinking that sounded exciting.

'One of my ships came in this morning and I want a word with the captain.'

'You own ships?' she exclaimed.

'Four of them, and I'm hoping to add to that number.'

'So your money comes from ships then?'

'Partially so. Basically I import and export, and owning my own ships increases the profit margin.' He smiled at her. 'Why pay for transport when I can transport myself and save expense?'

She thought about that. 'I don't know anything about business, but it sounds good Scots sense to me.'

He laughed. 'Spoken like Jock Hawke's daughter.'

As their carriage turned down towards the Clyde she said. 'Can I ask a personal question?'

'Certainly. Though I don't promise to answer.'

'Why did you never divorce Ma and remarry? Even if you did continue to . . . to care for her, you must have known she was never going back to you?'

He took out a cigar, clipped, then lit it.

'You could have had other children,' she persisted. 'And a good home life.'

He blew a long stream of smoke that was slowly sucked out of the carriage.

'I'm sorry, I shouldn't have asked you. Obviously you don't want to talk about it,' she apologised.

His eyes met hers, fastened on to hers. And suddenly it was as if she'd been pinioned against her seat. Once more she was acutely aware of his personal charisma.

'I never wanted to be married to anyone other than your mother. I'm a person who doesn't settle for second best, and that's what marrying another woman would have meant for me.'

'I see.'

He raised an eyebrow. 'Do you?' He was thinking she was young after all, inexperienced in the world.

As though reading his thoughts she replied. 'I think I do. If for no other reason than she is my mother, whom I love, and you're my father.'

He looked away from her, and as he did her shoulders slumped a little. She felt she'd been physically released. If Jock was feared by some, she thought, she was beginning to understand why. The man was not of the common herd.

'You must hate Bob, my step-da,' she said quietly.

Seconds ticked by, seconds that became a full minute. Finally Jock replied in a voice that was a stabbing stiletto. 'I did consider having him taken care of – killed. But what good would that have done me? None. It wouldn't have destroyed what Myrtle felt for him, or made things again as they'd once been between Myrtle and me. But I can tell you this though, lass, I was tempted, sorely sorely tempted.' He drew deeply on his cigar, and his voice softened. 'What I would never have done is wish on Sunter what's happened to the bugger. As I said in Netherton, I wouldn't wish that on my worst enemy.'

'And is he your worst enemy?'

Jock gave a dry chuckle. 'I might have thought that once, but not for many a long year now. No, that position is held by McIvor. Ranald Cyril McIvor.'

'And who's he when he's at home?'

'My chief competitor and business rival. You'll meet him, we bump into each other quite a lot socially.'

A few minutes later Jock pointed out of the open carriage window. 'That three-masted wooden barque tied up over yonder is the *Good Intent*. Her master is Captain Wilson, and he's as fine a master as ever sailed out the Clyde. Though for goodness' sake don't let on to him I told you that or he'll be asking for more money out of me.'

The ships tied up in Queen's Dock fascinated Sarah. There was something sleek and terribly romantic about them. She could just imagine them sailing to strange and exotic ports all over the globe.

The carriage stopped beside the *Good Intent*'s for'ard gangplank, and Sarah and Jock got out. A sailor came running down, saluting as he did, and asked them aboard. Captain Wilson was in his cabin and would receive them there.

Even though the ship was tied up, it still moved beneath Sarah's feet as she followed her father and the sailor across the deck. It was the queerest sensation, she thought. And decided she rather liked it.

Captain Wilson was pouring out drams when they entered his cabin. She'd been expecting some grizzled old sea-salt, crusty and barnacled—the reality couldn't have been more different.

Captain Wilson had a cleanshaven, open face, and a slim, lithe build. His grey eyes were keen with intelligence and good humour. What surprised her most was his age, he could only have been about twenty-five, certainly somewhere in his mid twenties. Terribly young for a ship's captain.

'Good day sir,' Wilson said, giving Jock a small nod of the head that had absolutely nothing subservient about it.

'Good day to you Mathew. I'd like you to meet my daughter, Sarah.'

Wilson's eyebrows shot up. 'I had no idea you had a daughter, Mr Hawke.'

'Well I do, and now she's come to live with me at Stiellsmuir.'

'You know the house do you, Captain?'

'Oh aye indeed, Miss, I've been out there often.'

That pleased her, she liked this Captain Wilson.

'I poured drams for your father and myself. Would you care for a sherry?' Wilson asked her.

'I'll have a dram same as you two. If that's acceptable, that is.'
She glanced quickly at Jock to see if she'd made a gaffe in saying
she'd take whisky. But she hadn't.

'Drams all round then,' Wilson said, and poured out another
generous gill which Sarah requested to be topped up with water.

'So how was the trip?' Jock asked.

'I don't think you'll find cause for complaint. I have the
documentation all here for your study,' Wilson replied, indicating
several ledgers and other sheets of paper that stood in a pile on what
he used as a desk.

'There's another cargo ready and waiting for you. Can you catch
tomorrow evening's tide?'

'What's the cargo?'

'Heavy machinery bound for Boston.'

Wilson made rapid mental calculations. 'And where from
Boston?'

'The Canaries via Bermuda, then back here.'

'In which case I'll need to replenish my food and water. Or I
could do it in Boston if that was preferable?'

'No, leave it to me. I'll see you're fully replenished before you
sail. Now can you give me half an hour with these books? Perhaps
you'd like to show Sarah round your ship?'

'That would be my pleasure, sir. Would you care to step this way,
Miss Hawke?'

He finished his whisky, she had another sip and laid her glass
aside. Then he assisted her through the cabin door which was not
only low but narrow. A tremor ran through her when his hand
accidentally brushed against hers.

Up top a wind had sprung up, a wind in off the sea that brought
the tang and taste of salt with it. Sarah breathed in deeply and
appreciatively, you never got a wind like this in Netherton.

'First time on a ship?' Wilson smiled.

She nodded. There had been a lot of firsts for her since leaving
Netherton the previous day. Was it really only twenty-four hours
ago? It seemed far longer than that.

'She's a Scots vessel, built in Montrose in '69,' Wilson explained.

'She's very handsome,' Sarah replied. Thinking, just like her
master.

'She's a trim craft right enough. As sweet as any I've sailed on.'

'And how long have you worked for my father, Captain Wilson?' she asked.

'A few years now. I've also commanded the *Edward Wake* for him. That's another of his ships, a barque the same as this, only smaller, about a third less tonnage.'

He led her aft to an open hatch, explaining that it dropped away to a hold. 'We were carrying casks of sherry in there which have already been unloaded.'

'The same sherry you offered me in your cabin?'

A soft smile curled the corners of his mouth. 'The same sherry Miss Hawke, but that particular kilderkin was a personal gift to myself from the Spanish agent I dealt with. Everything is above board, I can assure you. Any breakages or losses on my ship are genuine.'

She was blushing furiously. 'I'm sorry, I didn't mean that to sound the way it did.'

He took off his cap and ran a hand through fine blondish-brown hair. 'Many captains benefit from what they see as perks at the owner's expense, but not I. I just don't believe in that sort of thing. It's downright dishonest, and I would find it difficult to live with myself if I was that.'

She smoothed and straightened her skirt, not because it needed smoothing and straightening but because it gave her something to do. She was highly embarrassed. 'I seem to have got off on the wrong foot altogether with you, Captain Wilson. Again, I can only say I'm sorry. The inference was unintended.'

'That's all right then.'

She looked up to find his eyes were twinkling. 'You can inspect the hold if you like, but I think you might consider it rather too dirty.'

'I'll stay up here, thank you.'

He took her by the arm. 'Let's go astern and I'll show you the wheel.'

They got on like a house on fire, and Sarah's time aboard the *Good Intent* seemed to simply fly by.

Carlton Place was a splendid row of buildings on the south bank of the Clyde, overlooking the river. 'The firm,' Jock said with undisguised pride, pointing at a brass plate which bore the legend in plain script,

The plate shone like a new pin. 'Do you have it polished every day?' Sarah asked, tongue in cheek.

'I do. Wullie the caretaker does it early every morning, before we open for business.'

'Sundays too?'

He twigged she was teasing him. 'You wouldn't have me make someone break the sabbath, would you? No, when I said every day I meant every working day.'

Sarah glanced across the water at the customs houses facing. 'It's a prime position.'

'And you should see the view from the roof. I'll take you up there before we leave.'

They went inside the building, and then up a flight of stairs. The ambience was of success, Sarah thought. Success and hard work.

A clerk emerged from an open doorway. 'Good morning, Mr Hawke sir,' he said quickly.

'Good morning, Smith. Would you be so kind as to inform Mr Moffat that I'm here. And send young Tennant to me.'

'Certainly sir. Right away sir.' And with that Smith scurried off.

'He looked terrified of you,' Sarah said quietly.

'He was. I rule with a rod of iron.'

'Are you saying you're a tyrant?'

'Genghis Khan had nothing on me. You'd better believe that.'

She did.

They went along a corridor, at the end of which he threw open a door and bade her enter. 'The holy of holies, the inner sanctum, *my* office,' he informed her.

She gazed about her. There was a roll-top desk strewn with papers with a leather-covered captain's chair in front of it, highly polished wax linoleum on the floor, and a most unusual type of blind on the windows. 'What sort of blinds are these?' she queried, going over and peering at one.

'Venetian. Look, this is how they operate.' And with that Jock demonstrated how they opened and closed.

'Ingenious,' she commented, shaking her head in amazement. 'Whatever will they think of next!'

She brought her attention back to the office as a whole. Besides what she'd already taken in, there was also a small fireplace with a fancy tiled surround, several pictures of landscapes and, dominating one wall, an extremely large wooden piece – she couldn't imagine what to call it – made up for the main part of what appeared to be hundreds of pigeon-holes. Many of these holes had papers stuffed in them.

Jock noted what had caught her attention. 'My personal filing system,' he explained. 'Had it built especially. I find it a far easier way to lay my hands on something than rifling through innumerable cabinets.'

There was a discreet tap on the office door. 'Come in!' Jock called out.

The leading man was old with white hair, the man behind him young, only a few years older than herself, Sarah judged. White hair looked a right sourpuss.

'Mr Moffat, I'd like you to meet my daughter, Sarah Hawke,' Jock said.

Moffat was the sourpuss. He had sallow skin and beady eyes. 'Pleased to meet you, Miss Hawke,' Moffat said unctuously, and bowed from the waist.

'Mr Moffat is my Chief Clerk,' Jock explained.

Sarah did her best to seem impressed. 'And I'm pleased to meet you, Mr Moffat.'

'And this is Adam Tennant. Adam is under Mr Moffat.'

A mental picture flashed into Sarah's mind of Adam lying on the floor with Mr Moffat sitting on top of him. *Under* Mr Moffat! Laughter bubbled up inside her, laughter she managed to control and convert into a broad smile.

'How do you do, Adam?'

'Very well, Miss, thank you,' Adam replied in what was a very pleasant-sounding voice.

'Adam, could you organise a cup of coffee for Sarah, and entertain her until I'm finished with Mr Moffat,' Jock instructed.

'How do you take your coffee, Miss Hawke?' Adam queried. When he had that information he excused himself and hurried from the room.

What a nice young man, Sarah thought.

'Will you be all right on your own until Tennant gets back?' Jock asked her.

'I'll be fine. You go ahead and do what you have to. Don't worry about me.'

Jock nodded his approval, and turned to Moffat. 'I've just come from the *Good Intent* and want to speak to you about that, and then there are several matters.' Moffat, brow furrowed, was listening intently as the two men left the office.

Sarah moved towards the pigeon-holed filing system, and in doing so realised for the first time that there was a return to one wall. In this return, and quite hidden from where she'd been standing previously, was a display cabinet containing the models of four ships. She immediately recognised one of them as being the *Good Intent*.

She was still staring thoughtfully at the model of the *Good Intent* when Adam returned with her coffee.

'Here you are,' he said, handing her a steaming cup.

'Thank you. Aren't you joining me?'

He gave her a sheepish look. 'I was told to get you coffee – if Mr Hawke had wanted me to have one as well he would have said.'

She had a sip of the coffee, which was delicious. 'I was aboard the *Good Intent* before coming here,' she said, indicating the model.

'They've brought in sherry, wine and timber from the Baltic.'

'Yes, Captain Wilson told me that. He showed me round the vessel.' She paused, then asked as casually as she could. 'Is he married? He never said.'

'Oh, he's married all right.' Sarah's heart sank to hear that. To immediately rise again when Adam added, 'To the sea, that is. He's a real sailor is Captain Wilson.'

She probed further. 'Not married eh? Engaged surely?'

'Not that I know of. I'm sure I would have heard if he was.'

So, Mathew Wilson was unmarried, and not engaged. Now that was interesting. Yes, very interesting indeed. With a sudden flush of guilt Sarah thought of Gordy whom she loved, and who loved her. Gordy in whose arms she'd been only several days since. But Adam was speaking again. She forced herself to forget Gordy and Mathew Wilson and concentrate. 'I beg your pardon? I was daydreaming.'

'I said, you could have knocked us all over, the entire staff, with the proverbial feather when we heard that your father was taking the rest of the week off.'

'Oh?'

'Mr Hawke *never* takes time off. It's unheard of.'

Sarah's curiosity was roused. 'He must stay at home when he's ill?'

Adam shook his head.

'Well, what about holidays?'

'Mr Hawke doesn't have holidays. Even on New Year's Day when everyone – and I mean everyone – has time off, he comes in and works at his desk.'

Taking time off work was a monumental gesture on her father's part she realised, something she hadn't appreciated up until now. It showed the depth of his feeling about her going to live with him at Stiellsmuir.

'I suppose it was just as big a shock for you all to learn that he had a daughter?' Sarah said.

'No one knew that, not even Mr Moffat.'

She had another taste of her coffee, and decided to change the subject. 'So tell me what you do here, Adam?' she inquired.

She was still quizzing Adam about his job and the firm in general when Jock and sourpuss arrived back.

Jock raised an arm and made a broad sweeping gesture. 'Glasgow in all its glory!' he declared.

Sarah and Jock were standing on a flat area by the lower part of the roof, access to which was gained from french windows which opened out on to it.

Sarah had to agree. Jock had promised her a tremendous view on the way up there and that's precisely what it was. Straight in front of her was the great main sprawl that was Glasgow, sandstone stretching as far as the eye could see.

'It's a braw sight right enough,' she said.

'I come up here a lot you know, it inspires me. I find this big ugly city of ours quite exhilarating. Living in it, working in it, makes me feel so alive. You can keep your Edinburgh and London and all the other cities – Glasgow is the city for me. There's something about its hustle and bustle, its noise and smoky breath that's very very special for me.'

'I must confess I've never thought of it like that, but then I've been in Netherton all my life. I can count on the fingers of one hand the number of times I've been further than the Bearsden Road – until yesterday when your carriage arrived to take me away forever.'

He swung on her, his eyes glowing. 'You'll never regret coming to me, Sarah, I promise you that. I swear it.'

'I'm beginning to understand how much it means to you.'

'Oh yes,' he breathed softly, 'it most certainly does. It means the world.'

On impulse she kissed him on the cheek. He touched the spot she'd kissed with the tips of his fingers, his mind filled with memories of another pair of lips, and a mouth that one moment was soft as silk, the next fiery as blazing coal. Lips and a mouth that at one time he would have died for.

'So you approve of my business?' he asked, a husk in his voice.

'Very much so. I know the firm is now J. Hawke, but did you start it up yourself or was it under another name, the one you joined when you went to live in Maryhill?'

The glow went out of his eyes. 'What has your mother told you about Maryhill?'

'She said that was where you lived when you first came to Glasgow from Shotts.' Sarah paused, then added, 'I didn't know anything at all about you until after you came to Netherton. Ma had always refused to discuss you. Whenever I brought the subject up she shied away.'

'Except to lie to you that I was dead,' he said bitterly.

'Yes.'

'And what do you know now?'

'That you were orphaned at nine, went to live with an aunt and uncle whom you didn't get on with, and that you ran away from them to bring yourself up. The only other thing I know is that when you left Poulson's Pit you came to Glasgow to work for an import/export firm.'

Jock's expression blackened, and became one of sheer hate. 'My aunt was called Lena Crerar, and a bigger bitch of hell never lived. I can't even begin to describe how ghastly it was in her house. As for her husband John, he was nothing more than a dim-witted pig. He used to knock me around, the bastard, slap and punch the living daylights out of me. Until that last day when I took the breadknife to him.'

'You didn't!' Sarah exclaimed, shocked.

'I did. I'd finally had enough, a right bellyful. I picked up the breadknife and told him I was going to stick him with it. And he believed me, he could see I meant what I said.'

'What happened then?' Sarah couldn't wait to hear.

Jock's expression lightened a little. 'The funny side was that he had nothing on at the time – he was stark naked, which no doubt made him feel far more vulnerable than he would have done otherwise. He was always going round the house with nothing on when the weather was good, a disgusting thing to do when there was a child of my age in the house, a child not even his own.'

'So what happened?' Sarah prompted.

'I went for him, chased him round the kitchen and then he ran outside into the street.'

'Stark naked!'

Jock was grinning now. 'Stark naked into the street. And down the street with me in full pursuit and the neighbours hanging out of their windows having a good old laugh at his expense. I must have chased him half a mile before I gave up and went home again to find my aunt Lena having hysterics, thinking I'd murdered her husband. I packed what few clothes I had and left the house – and never saw either of them again.'

Jock threw back his head and laughed. 'I'll never ever forget the sight of that man running in his bare scuddy with me after him. I can just see that hairy backside of his flashing away in front of me.'

'Would you really have killed him? I mean not merely stuck him with the knife, but killed him?'

Jock stopped laughing, and his face became sober again. 'Oh yes, I most certainly would have done. No doubt about it.'

Sarah shuddered. It was a funny story, but at the same time an awful one.

'But you were asking me about the firm. I started J. Hawke myself after leaving McIvor, McIvor and Devereaux.'

'McIvor? Didn't you tell me he was your worst enemy?' she queried.

'Ranald Cyril, yes. Old man McIvor is still alive, though retired, and Ranald is his son, and head of the company. The other McIvor of the name is long dead, as is Devereaux.'

'And you were employed by them?'

'I learned a great deal from McIvor, McIvor and Devereaux, and also made a lot of contacts through them. They never forgave me when I struck out on my own.'

'But why?' Sarah questioned, frowning.

'Because all my initial business was stolen from them, as indeed much of my subsequent business was.'

'Gamekeeper turned poacher, eh?'

'You could put it that way.'

'But how did you get the capital to start up on your own? You couldn't have saved enough from your earnings as a clerk to start your own firm?'

Jock took a deep breath, and stared downriver where the White Star liner *Adriatic*, a combined sail and steam vessel, was heading out to sea. 'I don't wish to talk about that if you don't mind,' he replied emphatically.

'I see.'

'Whatever you're thinking I came by the money honestly and legally. There was no jiggery pokery, I promise you.'

That had crossed her mind, though she wouldn't have dreamt of saying.

Jock rubbed his hands together briskly. 'I don't know about you but my stomach's beginning to think my throat's been cut. How about lunch?'

'Marvellous.'

'Let's away then. I'm going to take you to a restaurant that serves food fit for the gods.'

And with that he began telling her about the restaurant which was situated in the old part of the city near the Tolbooth.

She was in Bluebell Wood, lying on the grass in Gordy's arms. 'Oh Gordy, my darling Gordy!' she whispered.

And there was Bob Sunter her step-da as he'd been before his stroke, laughing and waving as he floated on by.

'Bob!' she cried out, delighted to see him well and whole again.

'Sarah!' he cried back, waving even harder.

'I thought you were . . .' But he was gone, vanished into thin air.

Gordy's face melted to re-form as the face of another, Captain Wilson of the *Good Intent*.

'You're not Gordy,' she said, which seemed a stupid and senseless thing to say.

'Who's Gordy?' Wilson asked, fondling her breast.

'Netherton for me, Netherton for me, if you're not in Netherton you're no use to me!' Myrtle sang.

Sarah looked in the direction the singing had come from, and there was her mother doing the washing, up to the elbows in suds.

'He keeps me busy, you know!' Myrtle shouted.

'But he doesn't do it in the bed any more, he's all right now,' Sarah shouted back.

From nowhere Myrtle produced a soiled sheet. 'That's what you think!'

Sarah returned her attention to Captain Wilson to discover he'd become Gordy again, but Gordy in the captain's uniform.

'I have my responsibilities to the twins, you see,' Gordy said, gently rotating her breast.

'And I have mine to my mother and step-da.'

Gordy kissed her neck, the kiss changing to a suck as he attempted to give her a love bite. 'No, no!' she protested, pushing him away.

'Don't you like that?' Captain Wilson smiled.

'No I do not. I'd be mortified if people saw that sort of thing on my neck. It's not considered nice.'

'They're just jealous, that's all,' Captain Wilson replied, and stuck a hand up her skirt.

'Nor that either. I don't know you!'

'What do you mean you don't know me?'

Bob was suddenly there again, his face black as if he'd just come off shift. 'I feel strange,' Bob said.

The flat cart appeared in the distance, trundling in her direction. When it arrived it was Jock it was carrying. 'But that can't be right, he isn't a miner,' Sarah protested to Jack Bonner who, along with wee Mo Ford, Davey Hardy, Davey's brother Mal, and Tom Crayk, was in attendance.

'Netherton for me, Netherton for me, if you're not in Netherton you're no use to me,' Myrtle sang, arms going like the clappers as she pounded away at her washing.

'Let me show you the hold where the sherry was,' Captain Wilson suggested with a leer.

Over his shoulder she spotted Gordy lying on the grass with another girl, the pair of them kissing deeply and passionately. It was Betty Redhead who had always fancied Gordy.

'You leave Gordy alone, he's mine!'

'Not any more, sweetie,' Betty yelled back.

Sarah woke with a gasp, and sat bolt upright. What a dream, what a nightmare! She'd been dreaming a lot since Bob had his stroke, the beginning of the dramatic alteration to her life.

Realising she badly needed to wee she slipped from underneath the covers to grope below the bed for the chanty pot that was kept there, but couldn't find it. 'Damn!' she swore softly.

She lit a candle, and had a look under the bed. There was no sign of the chanty, it definitely wasn't there. That was a black mark against Hettie, the person responsible for the room.

Sarah got off her knees, and stood up. There was nothing else for it, she'd have to make the journey to the nearest toilet which adjoined the bathroom.

The candle cast weird flickering shapes on the walls and ceiling as she padded down the corridor leading to the toilet. She wondered what time it was—certainly after midnight. The stillness permeating the house suggested to her it was probably some time in the early hours of the morning, somewhere between one and three o'clock, she guessed.

When she'd finished in the toilet she went into the bathroom where she washed her hands and rinsed her face. When she'd dried herself she picked up her candle again and stepped back out into the corridor. 'Aaahh!' she exclaimed, coming up short, her entire body going rigid with fright.

There was a figure in the shadows, a tall figure, appearing to be staring directly at her.

'Who is it?' she queried, voice quavering.

There was no reply, nor did the figure move. A ghost? Or was she really still in bed dreaming? A tiny droplet of candle grease sputtered on to her hand, the pinprick of pain it caused answering her question. She was wide awake.

The figure moved suddenly, taking several silent steps towards her. She shrank against the wall behind her.

'Who is it? Who are you?' she demanded, trying not to sound as frightened as she felt, and failing totally.

It was a man, she could make that out now. And the shape of him was familiar. 'Jock? Is that you, Father?'

The man came closer still, and into the penumbra of the light cast by her candle. It was indeed Jock, his features twisted into an expression of profound anguish.

'Father?'

He blinked his eyes, as if trying to bring himself back from some place deep within his mind.

'It's me, Sarah. You gave me an awful fright. For a moment there I thought you were the bogeyman.'

'Sarah?' He sounded as if he'd only just recognised her.

She went to him. 'Yes, Jock, it's me. But what are you doing up so late, and still fully dressed?'

He shrugged himself out of her grasp. 'Don't touch me,' he breathed angrily.

Her fear returned. 'I'm sorry, I . . .'

'What are *you* doing up?' he demanded harshly, grabbing hold of her arm.

She grimaced. 'That's sore!'

'I said, what are you doing up? You weren't spying, were you?'

'Spy on what?' she answered in alarm. 'I had to go to the toilet, that's all.' She was remembering what Myrtle had told her about Jock's 'moods'. She'd been in Stiellsmuir for three weeks now and this was the first time she'd encountered one, for that's what it had to be.

'The toilet, eh?'

'The maid forgot to leave my chanty and I woke up having to go.'

With a grunt he released her. 'I heard a noise, wondered what it was. I thought . . .' He shook his head. 'I don't know what I thought.'

'Are you all right, Jock? Is there anything I can get for you?'

'I'm fine. Just not tired though. I've always been something of an insomniac, which is a curse as I loathe the night.'

'Even if you aren't feeling tired I think you should go to bed, it's terrible late,' she urged.

He looked past her, his eyes focusing as though he was seeing something in the far distance. 'Some nights I don't go to sleep at all. When that happens I never suffer any ill effects afterwards. You'd never know I hadn't had a full eight hours.'

'Mr Hawke, sir, can I help?'

Sarah gave a startled exclamation. She'd heard nothing whatever of Mrs McGuffie's approach; the housekeeper might have materialised straight out of the woodwork.

Jock turned to gaze hard at Mrs McGuffie, then nodded. 'Perhaps a warm glass of milk. Yes, I think I'd enjoy a warm glass of milk.'

'Then if you'd care to come downstairs I'll get it for you.'

'Thank you, Maud.'

Mrs McGuffie looked inquiringly at Sarah.

'I'll eh . . . I'll get back to my bed. Unless there's any way I can assist?'

65

'I'll manage on my own, thank you very much,' Mrs McGuffie replied firmly.

The woman didn't like her, Sarah thought to herself. And not only didn't like her but resented her as well.

'Sorry if I gave you a fright, lass, didn't mean to,' Jock apologised to Sarah.

'It's just that I wasn't expecting to find anyone else up at this time of the morning.'

To Mrs McGuffie, Jock said, 'She thought I was the bogeyman.' He laughed at that, and so did Mrs McGuffie. And with their laughter the atmosphere returned to normal.

'Do you want my candle?' Sarah asked, offering it to them.

'You keep it. Neither Mr Hawke nor I need a light to find our way round Stiellsmuir. Do we, sir?'

'No, we do not,' Jock agreed.

'Goodnight then, Miss Hawke.'

'Goodnight, Mrs McGuffie.' Going to her father she kissed him on the cheek. 'Goodnight, Jock.'

'Goodnight, Sarah.'

Sarah proceeded along the corridor, but hadn't gone far when she stopped to glance behind her at the retreating figures of Jock and the dressing-gowned Mrs McGuffie. The housekeeper and her father were suddenly thrown into sharp relief by moonlight streaming in through a window. Then they were gone, disappeared round a corner.

Sarah shuddered. That little episode had scared the living daylights out of her. It was a long time before she was able to drop off to sleep again.

'Let's have a gander at you then,' Jock said, rising from the chair where he'd been sitting sipping a whisky and soda as was his nightly custom before dinner.

Sarah slowly turned about, showing off the first of Madame Baptiste's dresses that she'd picked up from the Frenchwoman earlier that afternoon.

'You don't think it's too old for me?' she asked anxiously.

'It certainly makes you look older, but I wouldn't say it's too old for you,' Jock replied, shaking his head. He thought her a vision, and could hardly credit this was the same lassie who'd come to him in clogs from Netherton.

'You're simply stunning,' he stated.

Sarah adored the evening dress which was of cream-coloured satin with a crossover bodice and puffed sleeves. It had a big stiffened collar, also of cream satin, edged with lace, which stood up with a winged effect over the shoulders, dipping at the back, and following the crossover line of the bodice in front. Her sash was of black satin, tied at the back. In length the skirt just kissed the ground, forming a train at the back.

Her hair, done by her new personal maid Elinor, was fashioned in a thick, curled fringe brought forward on to her forehead with short locks over the temples. The remainder of her hair was drawn up into a high chignon at the back of her head, leaving her ears exposed.

'And my hair, what do you think of that?'

'Absolutely gorgeous.'

Sarah clapped her hands in glee. 'I hardly recognised myself in the looking-glass. I felt I was staring at a totally different person.'

He gave her a warm smile. 'No, it's still you, Sarah. Let's just say you're embellished somewhat.'

'You make me sound like an iced cake,' she laughed.

There was a tap at the door. 'Come in!' Jock called out.

It was Roderick, one of the footmen. 'Dinner is served, sir,' he announced.

Jock finished off his whisky, then went to Sarah and crooked an arm. 'Shall we?'

'Delighted,' she replied, placing a hand on the crook of his arm. From there they strolled to the dining-room.

'So how is Elinor turning out?' he inquired as they entered the dining-room. Elinor, the promised lady's maid, had just started two days previously.

'She's excellent, seems to know everything about everything. I'm very happy with her.'

'Good.'

Sarah shot her father a sideways glance, remembering how difficult the interviews for her lady's maid had been. Mrs McGuffie hadn't been at all pleased that she'd wanted to be in on the interviewing. In fact she'd been downright disapproving.

There had been four candidates for the position, and after all four had been seen, there had been no doubt whatever in her mind whom she wanted, the one called Elinor. The trouble was that Mrs

McGuffie favoured a horsy-faced woman by the name of Belle who came with very high references indeed.

She hadn't taken to Belle at all and had said so straight out, which hadn't pleased the housekeeper one little bit. But she hadn't declared Elinor to be her choice, suspecting if she had done so that it would have been the end of Elinor's chances. Unless of course she had insisted, against Mrs McGuffie's wishes, that Elinor be hired, which she hadn't wanted to do. For that would have meant direct conflict between herself and Mrs McGuffie, which she most definitely wanted to avoid.

What she'd done was appear to be keen on a young girl called Thirzie and then in the end had agreed – appearing slightly reluctant about it – on Elinor as a compromise choice. In other words, by some fancy footwork and by sending out the wrong signals she'd finally managed to get her own way, and Elinor as her maid.

'No regrets there then,' Jock said.

'None at all.'

'And when do you go to Madame Baptiste's again?' Jock inquired after they'd sat down.

'Day after tomorrow. She'll have another two dresses ready for me then, and a walking suit.'

As she ate Sarah thought back to the previous night, and her encounter with Jock in the corridor. 'Tell me more about your childhood?' she asked. Then, with a winning smile, 'I want to know all about you.'

Jock signalled for his wine glass to be topped up. It was a Spanish rioja, not a fashionable wine but one he enjoyed very much. And if he enjoyed it he'd drink it – and to hell with fashion.

'You mean after I ran away from the Crerars?'

She nodded.

He pushed a piece of meat round his plate as his mind flooded with memories. Some of them pleasant, some of them anything but.

'If you don't wish to tell me, or prefer to do so another time I'll understand,' she said softly, thinking of the profound anguish she'd seen on his face the night before.

He laid down his knife and fork, and sipped some wine. Then he asked the servants to leave them. He'd ring the small brass handbell in front of him when he wanted that course cleared, and the next served.

Jock waited patiently till the dining-room door had clicked shut, and he and Sarah were alone.

Taking his time about it, he said, 'For some months after the Crerars I lived rough. I found a cave which I used as a place to live, and from there I went out scrounging and stealing what I could.'

'You cooked for yourself?'

He gave a hollow laugh. 'Oh yes, I did that. And a dab hand at that sort of cooking I became too. Speciality of the house was garbage soup.'

'What!' Sarah exclaimed.

'Garbage soup. You put into it all kinds of things that other people throw away. Potato peelings for instance.'

Sarah screwed up her nose. 'It must taste awful. Quite revolting.'

He treated her to a thin, sardonic smile. 'Hunger is excellent sauce. Garbage soup can taste like a dish fit for a king.' He paused, then added, 'When you're hungry enough, that is.'

'What else did you cook?' She was intrigued, fascinated.

'Literally whatever I could get hold of. I roasted four sparrows once, and another time I cooked a hedgehog. The hedgehog was delicious.'

She didn't think she would have found it delicious at all. How could you eat something that spent most of its life covered in fleas? Then again, as Jock said, hunger was excellent sauce. Starvation even better. 'So how long did you stay in this cave for?'

'Till the winter of that year, and then I had the good fortune to meet Rence. His real name was Clarence but he hated that as a jessie name and insisted he be called Rence.'

Jock leaned back in his chair, and swirled the wine round his glass. 'Rence became a true friend, a true friend. Without him it's almost certain I wouldn't have lasted the winter, which was a vicious one.'

'You went to live with this Rence then?'

'Yes, in his caravan.'

'A caravan!' That sounded exciting.

'Gaudily painted in all colours of the rainbow, just like a gypsy one.'

'Was Rence a gypsy?' she queried eagerly.

Jock shook his head, then sipped more wine. He could see Rence as clearly as if it was only yesterday.

'He was Scots and a retired sailor. Having been at sea man and boy he'd dreamt of retiring to the country, which was precisely what he did when he got too old to work the ships. The caravan he bought from a tink, and then did it out and painted it himself. He used to call it his wee palace, and that's precisely what it was.'

'You were fond of him, that's obvious,' Sarah stated.

'I was that. While I was with him he was like a father to me, and I was like the son he'd never had.' Jock cleared his throat of the emotion that had started to creep up it. 'When he found out I had no one in the world he took me in, because as he said, he had no one either. Except Mr Murphy that is.'

'And who was Mr Murphy?'

'Mr Murphy, Sarah, was a cockatoo, or a galah to be more precise. He had a rose-coloured breast and a grey back, and came from Australia. He and Rence were as close as a man and animal can be. He was also the cause of Rence's death.'

Jock sighed, and finished off his wine. Getting up, he went over to where the bottle was on a side-table, and poured himself some more. When he returned to the dinner-table he was shrouded in gloom.

'How did your friend Rence die?' Sarah asked softly.

'I was thirteen at the time, having lived with him in the caravan for four years. One night, very late, there was a bad thunder-and-lightning storm.'

'Like that night you came to Netherton?'

He nodded. 'Very similar. Thunder crashing and banging, lightning zig-zagging all over the sky. We were both lying awake, having been woken up by the storm, chaffing about this and that, when suddenly there was the most almighty explosion which sounded as if it had come from just outside the caravan. So of course we had to get up and investigate.'

Jock took a deep breath, reliving that terrible night in his mind. 'When we got outside we discovered that a nearby chestnut tree had been struck by lightning, and was blazing like billyo. It was all too close for comfort, so we decided to shift the caravan, which we had to do ourselves as there was no horse, the caravan being permanently sited on common ground.

'We'd just started to budge the thing when a finger of fire curled round the top of it, setting it instantly alight. Within a couple of seconds the roof—which had just recently been retarred—was on fire from end to end.'

This time Jock didn't sip his wine, but swallowed a mouthful savagely. Sarah wasn't certain, but she thought she could see a hint of moisture in his eyes.

He went on. 'We tried to fight it, but it was a losing battle. I've never seen fire spread so quickly. And then Rence and I—simultaneously—realised that Mr Murphy was still inside.'

There was now no question—there was moisture in his eyes.

'Rence got to the double doors first and threw them open, calling to Mr Murphy who was quite used to flying in and out when he wanted to. Only Mr Murphy had fallen off his perch on to the floor, overcome by the smoke I presume. He was lying there feebly fluttering in the midst of what can only be described as an absolute inferno. I shouted to Rence not to go in after the bird; that it would be madness, but nothing would stop him. In he plunged to rescue his pal.'

Jock took out a cigar and clipped it. 'I saw Rence get to Mr Murphy, then I was beaten back by the heat which, as you can imagine, was extremely fierce. All of a sudden the caravan . . .' Jock trailed off, took another deep breath, then lit his cigar with trembling hands.

In a voice that Sarah had to strain to hear he added, 'There was one solitary moment when Rence screamed, a bloodcurdling sound that made me clap my hands over my ears. And then that was it for him. In the morning I buried what was left of the pair of them—precious little—and took to the road.'

'What a horrifying story,' Sarah breathed.

Jock fished out a hanky, and blew his nose. 'If it hadn't been for Rence I wouldn't be where I am today.'

'How so, Jock?' she prompted.

'Rence had a great many books in that caravan of his, books he treasured albeit he couldn't read himself. When he found out I could read he made me read them, and when I'd finished that lot he arranged with a local laird, whom he'd built some model ships for, that I have access to the laird's private library. Thanks to that library I was able to educate myself properly, including learning accountancy.' He puffed on his cigar, and blew out a smoke-ring.

'Next course now?' he queried.

'I'd rather hear what happened when you went on the road.'

He puffed again on his cigar, then studied its tip as if seeing something in the ash. 'Ever hear of a "farmed-out house"?'

She shook her head. 'No.'

'If anything in this life is truly degrading they are. I went to Edinburgh where I did a succession of odd jobs, this and that, anything that would turn a ha'penny. And during that period, until I landed a full-time position with Mr Love, the undertaker, I stayed in a succession of "farmed-out houses".'

He paused to flick the ash he'd been studying on to his plate, there not being an ashtray on the table. '"Farmed-out houses" are houses whose owners pack their rooms with derelict humanity. One such owner was Big Margie Colquhoun. Many's the time I slept at Big Margie's – never in a bed of course, they took up far too much space. No, you slept stretched out on the bare floor, or if you'd arrived too late to get stretched out, then it was your back propped up against a wall. In the morning, and included in the price of your night's lodging, you got a slice of bread and a soused herring.'

'How many to a room then?'

'As many as could be squeezed in. It was nothing for there to be two dozen men all squashed together tight as sardines in a can.'

'My God,' Sarah breathed. Forget how uncomfortable it must be, she could just imagine the sheer stink of such a situation.

Jock returned to the winebottle and refilled his glass. 'A far cry from that to this, eh?' he said suddenly, and laughed.

'I should say.'

'There were many nights I used to wake up and listen to the coughing; there was always someone coughing, usually with the consumption which my own parents died of. That was something I never got used to, the coughing always bothered me. Particularly if there were a number of them going hard at it.'

He waved his glass at her. 'Then my luck changed. I went to work for Mr Love, the undertaker, doing his books which neither he or his wife could ever manage themselves.'

'Were they nice?'

'What they were was completely misnamed, a more unloving couple you'd travel far and wide to meet. They weren't cruel, nothing like that, just unloving and uncaring, cold and emotionless through and through.'

'So where did you stay when you were with them?'

'Above the undertaking parlour, as they did themselves. Nor was that the only undertaking parlour they had – they owned eight in all, which was why they needed a bookkeeper. I also doubled as wages clerk.'

Jock wrinkled his forehead in memory. 'They were as different to Rence as the proverbial chalk to cheese. Rence used to be warm and outgoing, a great one for a laugh. I don't think I ever heard the Loves laugh. They were the original dreich couple, a right wet Monday morning the pair of them.'

'Did they pay you well?'

'A thirteen-year-old lad? Not likely. I got bed and board, and occasionally a few coins. Though that did change a bit as I grew older; they had to pay me more then. But it was still nothing like a proper wage for the job.'

'And then you left them?'

He nodded. 'Aye, for Poulson's Pit and Shotts where I met your mother.'

She stared at him. What a tragic childhood he'd had, so unlike her own which had been happy and carefree. Her heart went out to him.

'Did you tell her all this?'

His mouth twisted into a cynical downward curve. 'Bits and pieces. To be truthful, Sarah, she never really seemed all that interested.'

That shocked Sarah. It was so unlike the Myrtle she knew. But she believed Jock; there was the ring of truth about what he'd said.

They spoke a little more, then Jock rang the handbell and instructed the next course to be brought.

'You know, Mrs Forrest is an excellent cook,' he said, having sampled the contents of the bowl in front of him, 'but she can't make a clootie dumpling anywhere near as good as Myrtle could. I used to adore Myrtle's clootie dumpling.'

Sarah had to agree with him. Mrs Forrest's clootie dumpling did leave something to be desired. 'If you like I'll make you one for tomorrow night. Ma has always said that I make an even better clootie dumpling than hers.'

Jock's eyes lit up. 'Done! I'm looking forward to it already.'

Sarah laughed. She'd make him one of her best, one that would just melt in his mouth. If he was already looking forward to eating it, she was already looking forward to making it.

She was going to enjoy that.

Sarah hummed to herself as she worked in the currants and sultanas. Coming down to the kitchen after breakfast she'd discovered it was Mrs Forrest's day off, so instead of asking her where everything was she'd had to ask Katy who assisted Mrs

Forrest—the same job she herself would have occupied had she gone to work for Mrs Craufurd, the smiling spider.

A little more milk now, she thought. Taking a ladleful from the churn she slowly began dripping it in. It was the consistency of the dumpling that was the key; it had to be just right.

What a smashing smell, she thought, inhaling deeply. Cinnamon, ginger, brown sugar and syrup were amongst the various ingredients, all combining to give off a rich mouthwatering aroma. And if it smelt good now it smelt ten times better when it was cooking. That was the sort of smell that might come straight from Heaven.

She glanced over at the stove to check if the water in the large pan was boiling, which it was. The next step was to put the mixture into the cloth, or cloot.

'What do you think you're doing!'

The voice was shrill, outraged, and belonged to Mrs Forrest who Sarah hadn't heard enter the kitchen. The cook was dressed in a coat and hat and had either just come in, or was on her way out. A huge pin that must have been all of nine inches long skewered her hat to her hair.

'I'm making a clootie dumpling,' Sarah replied.

Mrs Forrest sucked in a breath that puffed her chest out like a pigeon's. 'I'm the cook here. I do all the cooking and baking. This is my kitchen, Miss Hawke, you have no right to be using it, none at all.'

Sarah was taken aback by this attack. 'I'm sorry, I did intend asking your permission but you weren't here.'

'And if I had been you certainly wouldn't be doing what you are now. It's unheard of for someone from upstairs to come down and try to cook.'

Sarah was beginning to get angry. 'I'm not trying to, I *am* cooking,' she snapped in reply.

'Not in my kitchen you're not!' Mrs Forrest hissed, glaring at Sarah.

Katy was in the kitchen now, attracted by the sound of the argument. So too was Elinor, and Pansy, another of the parlourmaids. They were all looking fearfully at Mrs Forrest who was known as something of a martinet.

'Pansy, run and find Mrs McGuffie. Tell her she's needed here,' Mrs Forrest not so much said as commanded. Pansy scampered out of the kitchen.

Sarah crossed to the sink and pumped water over her hands and arms to wash the flour off them – as part of the process the cloot had to be well dredged with flour prior to the mixture being put into it. Then she dried herself on the rough towel that hung from a peg to one side of the sink.

She was angry, confused, and very upset by all this. But she was damned if she was going to give in to the cook. Sod that! as Bob her step-da used to say.

'Impertinence,' Mrs Forrest mumbled, just loud enough for Sarah to hear.

A few minutes later Mrs McGuffie appeared. 'Miss Hawke, Cook,' she acknowledged, her expression wary.

Mrs Forrest pointed an accusing finger at Sarah. 'She's been using my kitchen, and without so much as a by-your-leave,' she said in the same shrill tone she'd employed previously.

'I couldn't ask Mrs Forrest's permission to use her kitchen as it was her day off,' Sarah explained quietly.

'Someone from upstairs coming down to cook, whoever heard the like! She's certainly no lady,' Mrs Forrest said.

Sarah flushed; the woman couldn't have been more right. The last thing she was was a lady, of that sort anyway.

'Would you please ask her to leave, Mrs McGuffie, and never to come messing up my kitchen again.'

'If I wish to use the kitchen then I'll use it,' Sarah stated levelly.

'Hmmm!' Mrs Forrest ejaculated, and folded her arms over her bosoms.

'It's most irregular,' Mrs McGuffie said, eyes narrowed and glinting precisely the same way as when Sarah had first met her.

'Unless I'm assured that my kitchen is mine and mine alone I'll hand in my resignation,' Mrs Forrest said. Then, the penny dropping, 'And why was she making a clootie dumpling, which I served up last night? Is she inferring that mine wasn't good enough?' Mrs Forrest's voice rose even higher. 'Is that it?'

Sarah bit her tongue to stop herself from making the obvious reply.

Mrs McGuffie turned to Sarah and arched an eyebrow.

Sarah decided the best thing to do was evade the accusation. 'So what do you intend to do?' she asked the housekeeper.

'I think . . .' Mrs McGuffie paused, then said. 'I think this is a matter for Mr Hawke himself.'

'It's nothing but an insult so it is,' Mrs Forrest huffed.

Sarah removed her apron and draped it over a chair. She then walked from the kitchen, all those she'd left behind watching her go.

Jock's face was stony as he listened to Mrs McGuffie's account of what had taken place that morning. When she had finished he glanced at Sarah.

'Is that correct in every respect?'

'Yes,' she replied. Mrs McGuffie's account of the proceedings had not only been correct, it had also been completely unbiased, which had surprised Sarah.

Jock's gaze swung round to the cook. 'Have you anything to say, Mrs Forrest?'

'Only that I'll resign if the kitchen isn't to be my sole preserve.'

'You're presumptious, woman,' Jock said.

Mrs Forrest blinked.

'Not only presumptious, but insolent. If my daughter wants to cook in *my* kitchen then she's damned well entitled to do so. You seem to have forgotten that you're an employee in this house, Mrs Forrest, nothing more.'

Mrs Forrest had paled – as cook she ranked only below housekeeper in domestic importance. Hers was a position of authority and responsibility.

'So-called ladies don't come into the kitchen to cook. It's just not done!' she protested.

Jock leant forward a fraction in his chair. 'I don't know whether you're aware of it or not, but I wasn't born into the moneyed classes – I dragged myself up by my bootstraps to become what I have become. And one of the things I learned *en route* was not to obey other folks' rules, but to make my own. Mrs Forrest, should either my daughter or myself decide to come down to the kitchen to cook then that is precisely what we'll do, whether it's the done thing or not.' He added, his voice a whiplash, 'Do you understand?'

Mrs Forrest recoiled from his verbal onslaught. 'In that case I offer my resignation,' she retaliated.

'You can't, for you were fired five minutes ago. I just hadn't got round to telling you yet,' he replied.

She swallowed hard. 'I'll work my notice and . . .'

'You'll do no such thing,' he interjected. 'You'll leave this room, go straight to your own and pack your belongings. I expect you to be out of this house within the hour.'

She'd been pale before, now she was white as a freshly-laundered sheet. 'But you'll need longer than that to make up my notice money and write my reference.'

Jock stared levelly at her. 'No notice money. You get paid until today, and that's it.'

'But it's my right. If I resign, or am . . .'—she swallowed hard again—'am sacked, then I work a month's notice to give you time to replace me, and myself time to find another position. That's accepted practice.'

Jock smiled thinly. 'You didn't listen, woman. I said I make my own rules and don't abide by the rules of others.'

'But . . . but I've nowhere to go!' she wailed.

Jock didn't reply to that, just continued to stare at her.

The cook's hands started to flap in front of her. 'You can't throw me out in the street, Mr Hawke. Please?'

'Who says I can't?'

'Father, I . . .' Sarah's voice trailed off when Jock held up a hand to her that bade her be quiet.

'My reference, I'll have to have—'

'No reference,' Jock stated.

Mrs Forrest slumped in on herself. The proud, arrogant female of a few minutes previously had been reduced to a shaking wreck. 'I must have a reference, Mr Hawke sir, that's essential for me.'

'No,' Jock said emphatically, with finality.

Mrs Forrest burst into tears, looking to Mrs McGuffie for help. But there was nothing the housekeeper could do.

Ruthless, Sarah thought of her father. Totally ruthless.

'You may leave us now,' Jock said to the cook. Then, to Mrs McGuffie, 'Make up her wages as to and including today. Pay her as she leaves the house.'

A thoroughly beaten and destroyed Mrs Forrest trailed from the room, Mrs McGuffie behind her.

'Would you care for a dram?' Sarah asked Jock as soon as the two women were out of the room.

He nodded. 'Aye.'

She poured him a large one and a small one for herself. They were in the library where an ample supply of alcohol was always kept.

'Give her the reference,' Sarah said as she handed him his whisky and soda.

He sipped his drink, took a larger swallow, then looked up at her. 'The woman asked for what she got.'

'I'm not arguing with that. But I do think you were unduly harsh. You could well be denying her future employment.' To Sarah that was a terrible sin, her working-class background and values made it so.

'I made the decision and I won't go back on it. Occasionally you have to crack the whip – it makes the others sit up and pay heed.'

'You mean every so often set an example?'

He grinned. 'Precisely.' His grin faded. 'I'll have no disrespect towards you in this house and now they all know that.'

She was curious. 'Do you ever change your mind once you've made a decision?'

'Rarely.'

'And if you're wrong?'

'I said I do, though rarely. The trick is not to make a decision unless you've properly thought it through.'

'And you'd done that with Mrs Forrest?'

'There wasn't much to think through. If I'd let her get away with that the other servants would have got the idea that they could take liberties with you.'

'She did have a point about it being unusual for someone from upstairs going downstairs to use the kitchen.'

He gave her a sideways look, and suddenly there was a twinkle in his eyes. 'As I said, I've learned to make my own rules in life. Perhaps that's something you should resolve to do as well.'

She replied with a smile, and excused herself for the moment, saying she'd be right back.

'Mrs McGuffie!'

The housekeeper was on her way to the small study where she did all her paperwork. She was going to work out what was due to Mrs Forrest, and extract whatever that sum was from petty cash. She stopped and turned round to see Sarah hurrying after her.

'Yes, Miss Hawke?'

Sarah was clutching two five pound notes which she held out to Mrs McGuffie. Mrs McGuffie's brow furrowed in puzzlement as she stared down at the money.

'I feel I was partially at fault for what happened. Would you please give this to Mrs Forrest, but not let on it came from me.'

Mrs McGuffie looked at Sarah, a warmth in her expression that had never been there before. 'Is this your pin-money?' She knew that Jock had given Sarah an allowance which he had told her he would replenish when it ran out.

'Yes.'

'Then it's a most kind and generous offer.'

Sarah shrugged. 'I can't bear the thought of anyone being thrown out on the street. And without a reference . . .' She trailed off.

Mrs McGuffie took one of the five pound notes, leaving the other with Sarah. 'I'll think up some story to explain this. Ten pounds would be over generous. As you say, you might have been partially at fault, but the silly woman brought what happened on her own head.'

'I tried to get him to change his mind about the reference, but he wouldn't.'

Mrs McGuffie nodded. 'No he wouldn't. I could have told you that.'

Sarah and the housekeeper stared at one another. 'I'll get back to him then,' Sarah said eventually.

The housekeeper, eyes narrowed but this time not glinting, gazed after Sarah until she had vanished from sight.

Looking down at the five pound note she folded it once, then folded it again. This would make a big difference to Mrs Forrest's immediate circumstances.

She was already inventing a suitable story to explain the money when she entered her study.

A great wave of homesickness rose up within Sarah to swamp and engulf her. She staggered where she stood, one hand clutching her stomach, the other raised to her face.

How she missed Netherton, and Myrtle, and the wee house the two of them had shared with Bob. Tears ballooned in her eyes as she remembered the faces and places she'd never see again.

She lurched across the garden to the nearest tree, and leaned against it. There was a dull soreness in her heart, and she felt as if she might be sick.

Gordy whom she loved, and who loved her. What was he doing now? Right then he'd be 'down by', she knew that. But, was there a new lassie in his life yet? Surely not, it was too soon for that. And yet ... there again ...

And how was her ma coping all on her own with Bob? And how was her ma? Was Myrtle well?

She could almost smell Netherton. The combined smells of soot, and dug coal, and the people who bided there.

She could see again Bluebell Wood, and that secluded spot, special to her and Gordy, where the pair of them had done their courting.

Bile rose in her throat, she was going to be physically sick after all. Bending over, she let it come. A hot, scalding, evil-tasting liquid that gushed from her mouth.

'Oh Ma!' she whispered to herself when it was all over. 'Oh Ma! Oh Gordy!'

Sarah was in the library, which she now visited every afternoon for several hours, deeply engrossed in *Pride and Prejudice*. She was finding the story fascinating, totally gripping.

She had decided to do what her father had done as a lad, which was read extensively and comprehensively.

She glanced up when there was a tap at the door, a hint of annoyance on her face at being interrupted. 'Come in!'

It was Mrs McGuffie. 'I'm interviewing candidates for the position of cook tomorrow morning, starting at ten. I presume you'll wish to interview with me?'

Sarah frowned. 'Why should I?'

'You were most insistent about that where your maid was concerned.'

It suddenly dawned on Sarah what the problem was between Mrs McGuffie and herself, or at least part of the problem. How slow of her, she berated herself. She should have twigged long before now!

'Mrs McGuffie, would you please take a seat.'

The housekeeper appeared uncertain, seemed to be about to refuse, but then sat as requested.

'I think there may be a misunderstanding between you and me,' Sarah said slowly. 'I have no wish to intrude on any of your duties, or take over any part of them.' She paused to let that sink in. 'I was only anxious where Elinor was concerned because the person chosen was to be my personal maid. I wouldn't dream of sticking my oar in where the choice of other staff was concerned.'

Mrs McGuffie, who'd been sitting ramrod straight up until then, now relaxed a little. Her features also softened.

Sarah went on. 'My living in this house will make no difference where your job is concerned. If I am now the house's mistress, it's in name only. I have no intention of even trying to run it my own way, if for no other reason than the simple one that I have absolutely no experience whatever in running a big house like Stiellsmuir. You're the expert at that, and it would be downright stupid of me to meddle where an expert is already doing the task extremely well indeed.'

'Thank you, Miss Hawke,' Mrs McGuffie said, relief in her voice.

'Do we understand one another now?'

Mrs McGuffie nodded. 'Yes, the situation is now clear.'

'Good.'

Mrs McGuffie began to rise, but stopped when Sarah said, 'I haven't finished yet, there's more.'

Mrs McGuffie sank back on to her chair.

'It's become quite obvious to me since arriving at Stiellsmuir that my father thinks of you not merely as an employee, but as a personal friend. It would give me great pleasure if we, you and I, could also be friends. I should like that very much indeed.'

Sarah studied Mrs McGuffie's face while the housekeeper considered that. She was wearing an expression that Sarah couldn't quite interpret. Was it one of wariness? Then the expression disappeared, to be replaced by a smile.

'That would give me great pleasure also, Miss Hawke,' Mrs McGuffie said, rising and extending her hand.

'From now on it's Sarah in private,' Sarah said as they shook hands.

'And I'm Maud.'

Sarah felt a lot better now that the air was cleared between them.

Sarah and Jock were returning from church having been to morning service, and were almost home.

'By the by, I have a surprise for you,' Jock said.

'A surprise? Honestly, Father, you're spoiling me, you're forever giving me things.' It was November 1890 and Sarah had been living at Stiellsmuir for five months.

'What's a father for if not to spoil his daughter? Anyway, I'm only making up for all those lost years when you were with Myrtle and Sunter.'

She placed a hand on his. 'You're awful good to me.'

'I promised you I would be, and whatever else Jock Hawke is, he's not one for breaking his word.'

That was true enough, she thought. He was known for it. 'So what is this surprise?'

'You'll see shortly. Just bide your time.'

She laughed, thoroughly enjoying this. 'It's back at the house, then?'

'I said bide your time, woman,' he repeated, pretending to glower at her.

'I can't think what it is, and to be given on the sabbath too.' The latter was unusual.

They clattered to a halt outside Stiellsmuir. 'We've got company,' Sarah said, pointing to a magnificent carriage and pair of black geldings that stood a little way over on the driveway.

Ferguson the driver, the same man who'd come to Netherton to fetch her, leapt down and helped Sarah out. He was grinning hugely for he was in on the surprise.

Jock came round to join Sarah, having let himself out. 'Fancy a drive then? I've got another surprise for you.'

'What do you mean *another* surprise? I haven't had the first one yet.'

'You're staring at it.'

She was mystified. Staring at what? The only thing she could see was . . . 'This carriage!' she gasped. 'Is that it?'

'I told you in Netherton that you'd get a carriage of your own if you came to stay here. Well, that's it.'

She went to the carriage, and gently placed a palm against its side. The colour was deep maroon picked out in black, the interior upholstery black leather. 'It's fabulous,' she breathed.

The horse nearest her snorted, and pawed the gravel. 'That's Royal, and the other – his brother – is Regal,' Jock explained with a smile.

'They're absolutely gorgeous. And they're mine as well?'

Jock nodded.

'I don't know what to say. I'm bowled over.'

A young man in livery whom Sarah had never clapped eyes on

before appeared from round the side of the house, from the direction of the mews. The colours of his livery matched those of the carriage perfectly.

'This is Sheach, he's to be your driver,' Jock further explained.

When Sheach reached them he doffed his hat, and gave Sarah a small bow. 'Delighted to meet you, Miss Hawke,' he said.

'And I'm delighted to meet you, Sheach.'

She turned to Jock, her face glowing. 'Thank you Father, this is a wonderful wonderful surprise.' And with that she kissed him on the cheek, a big sloppy smacker.

'I thought you'd like it.'

'Who wouldn't!'

Laughing, she climbed aboard the carriage, Jock assisting her up and in, then he also got in to sit facing her. 'Now for the second surprise which I hope you like as much as this one.' Reaching up he rapped the roof which was the signal for Sheach to move off. Smoothly without the hint of a jolt, the carriage got under way.

'Where are we going?' Sarah queried.

Jock tapped the side of his nose. 'Wait and you'll find out.'

'Jock!'

'I told you before, bide your time woman. The surprise wouldn't be the same if I told you what it was. Now would it?'

She had to admit he was right. 'I suppose not,' she agreed reluctantly.

Down through the south side they drove, heading in the direction of the Clyde. On reaching the river they swung into Carlton Place where Jock's firm was located, drawing up outside the building.

For the life of her Sarah couldn't imagine why they'd come there on a Sunday. What on earth was Jock up to now?

'I want to show you something,' Jock said, opening the carriage door. Sheach helped her out, Jock following.

'There we are, what do you think of that?' Jock said, pointing at the brass plate by the side of the door.

It was a brand new brass plate, and it bore a new legend. This one read, again in plain script,

J. HAWKE & DAUGHTER
GENERAL IMPORTERS & EXPORTERS

'Wullie the caretaker fixed it there yesterday,' Jock said.

'It's, eh . . .' She was lost for words.

'It means that you're now my beneficiary.' His brow gathered darkly. 'Providing you don't go back to Netherton, that is. The day you do, you're disinherited.'

'Beneficiary,' she spoke to herself, quite shaken by this.

'To put it bluntly, when I die you get the lot. Lock, stock and barrel. I've made that official.'

'Everything?' she queried, still unable to believe this. Inheriting was something she'd never actually thought of.

'Everything,' he confirmed.

She took a deep breath, then another. She needed both. 'I take it you're pleased with me then. That you approve of your daughter.'

'Pleased! Approve! Of course I do lassie. I think the sun shines out of your . . .' He gave her a wicked grin. 'Out of your lovely green eyes.'

She looked again at the plate. *& DAUGHTER.* 'If I'm on the plate I'd like to learn something of the business. Perhaps work for it in some capacity?'

'Nay, girl, nay,' he said, chucking her under the chin. 'A woman's place is in the home, not out working. But I appreciate the thought, all the same.'

'You employ women, Mrs McGuffie for instance,' she protested.

'That's different, that's domestic. I don't have any females in the firm, and that's the way it's going to stay. Now I'll hear no more on the matter.'

The subject was firmly closed, that was clear. Which was a pity; she might have actually enjoyed working for her father.

'I'll tell you what, we should celebrate this, and what better way to celebrate than by having a party? It'll give you the perfect opportunity to meet all my friends, and they you.'

She clapped her hands in glee. 'A party sounds tremendous!'

'Then we'll organise it.'

Sarah wondered if Captain Wilson would be in port when the party took place. Perhaps she could arrange one to coincide with the other?

She hadn't seen the captain since that day aboard the *Good Intent*, the day after she'd come to Stiellsmuir. Ever since then she'd been looking forward to seeing him again.

Chapter 3

'Sarah, I'd like you to meet the Honourable Ian Monteith,' Jock said, introducing her to a good-looking young man in his early twenties. He was exceptionally broad shouldered with straw blond hair and, strangely for that colouring, liquid brown eyes.

'How do you do,' Ian Monteith said, and taking Sarah's hand he brought it to his lips and kissed the back of it.

'Watch this one, he can charm the birds down out of the trees,' Jock warned with a laugh.

'It's absolutely true. It's a gift I have; I was born with it,' Ian confirmed with a disarming smile.

'I can see humility isn't one of your virtues,' Sarah smiled back.

'Why be humble? I have nothing whatever to be humble about.'

In anyone else it would have been bumptious and off-putting, but not with the Honourable Ian Monteith. He got away with it. 'You think a great deal of yourself, then,' she countered.

'Oh yes, a great deal.'

She laughed, he was fun.

'Excuse me,' Jock said, and left them. He'd spotted someone he wanted a word with.

'It was a good party before, but it's ten times better having met you,' Ian said.

'Why thank you.'

'It's true,' he added.

He had a beautiful speaking voice, she thought. Cultured and soft, with the hint of a caress in it. 'How do you come to know my father?' she asked.

'Through *my* father, Viscount Ascog. The pair of them are members of the same club, and both are on the wine committee.'

'I see. Is your father here?'

'Was invited, couldn't make it. His liver is playing up so he's taken to his bed for a few days.'

'Oh dear, I hope he gets well soon.'

Ian gave her a small bow. 'I shall convey that message to him, which I'm sure he'll be delighted to receive. Particularly when I tell him about the stunning creature that sent it.'

'I'll bet you say that to all the girls,' she teased.

'You're quite right, I do. Only in this case I mean it.'

Jock was correct, she thought. He probably could talk the damned birds down out of the trees. He was silver-tongued and no mistake.

Sarah glanced round the room, spotting Adam Tennant from the firm chatting to another man called Rose who also worked for Jock in Carlton Place, and whom she'd been introduced to earlier. Everyone from the firm had been invited to the party, Adam and Mr Moffat the Chief Clerk—old sourpuss—the only two who'd turned up without partners. In Mr Moffat's case because his wife was home in bed with a heavy cold.

Adam saw her staring in his direction, and waved. She didn't know it but he was in the process of steeling himself to ask her up to dance. He thought she looked smashing, quite the belle of the ball.

Sarah was wondering about Captain Wilson who, as far as she was aware, hadn't arrived yet. Though he might have done and could be in another room, the entire ground floor of Stiellsmuir being used for the party.

'What do you do?' she asked Ian, bringing her attention back to him.

'Do? I shoot a bit, and hunt a bit—'

'No, I mean, what do you work at?'

'I don't work, Miss Hawke, I'm a *gentleman*.' He said that last word in a very haughty and disdainful manner, but with his tongue firmly in his cheek.

He might be laughing at her, but he was also laughing at himself. Yes, she thought, there were some very admirable qualities about Ian Monteith.

'I do a fair amount of riding over and above the hunting, just adore riding.'

'You have your own horse then, I presume?'

'Three actually, all damned fine beasts.'

'You still live at home I take it? Or do you have your own house?'

Ian treated her to a thin smile. 'I still live at home, can't afford a house of my own. Wish I could.'

This puzzled Sarah; the information he was giving her appeared to be conflicting. 'Are you saying your family aren't well-to-do?' How could they not be when he had three horses and his father was a viscount?

'We have an estate which manages to pay for itself and upkeep the

86

bricks and mortar. But as for actual cash in the bank, our cup doesn't exactly overflow with that. And what money there is belongs to Pa.'

'Well, at least one day the estate will be yours, including the bricks and mortar.'

His thin smile thinned even more. ''Fraid not, I'm the second son. James my elder brother succeeds to the title and everything else. I shan't get a bean.'

'You can't mean that, surely? The estate and house should be sold and the money realised split fairly betwen you.'

Ian laughed. 'I'm afraid you don't know much about the upper classes, Sarah – may I call you that?'

She nodded.

'The last thing one ever does is sell or divide the land and all on it, one has to be in absolutely dire straits to do that. It's logical if you take time to think about it. For example, if I got half of what Pa owns now, and James the other half, and then say we each married and had two sons of our own, what would happen when we died? My half would be split into another two halves as would James's, which would divide the original into four. And so on and so on till before you knew where you were there would be a large group of descendants sitting on about six feet square each. No, the way we do it may seem grossly unfair to everybody other than the firstborn son, but it does mean the continuation of the land as a whole.'

'So James gets everything, and you nothing?'

'That's it.'

She was curious. 'And your three horses?'

'Well, technically they belong to the estate. Should I leave I'd have to ask James if I could take them with me. And knowing him he'd say yes, he's a good egg, James.'

'And lucky to be the firstborn.'

'Yes indeed Sarah, very lucky indeed.'

Somebody was smoking close by, she could smell it. She would have loved to have a cigarette herself, but it just wasn't done for a woman to smoke in polite society. Jock heartily disapproved of her even doing so in private, but hadn't put his foot down and forbidden her from doing so.

'Tell me then, and may I call you Ian?'

'I'll be most upset if you don't,' he replied, and gave her a small bow.

'Tell me, Ian, what will you do when your brother does succeed?'

'Depends whether or not he's married at the time. If not I'd no doubt stay on; if he was I'd be obliged to leave.'

'And do what?'

'Traditionally it's the army or navy, or India – that sort of thing. Or I might try my hand in the diplomatic corps; I see that as being fairly attractive. Then again I might just marry someone who has money in her own right, and that would be me off the hook, so to speak.'

'You mean you would marry just for money?'

He laughed at her outraged expression. If she found him fun, he found her highly amusing – the latter without condescension. 'Amongst the upper classes and landed gentry there's nothing unusual about that. They've been doing it time out of mind.'

'But it's . . . it's . . . well, it's just not right!'

'I do believe you're a romantic, Sarah,' he teased.

There was something in his tone which got to her, making her quite embarrassed. She blushed bright red. 'There's nothing wrong with that,' she protested.

She glanced over at the door, and there was Captain Wilson. Nor was he alone; a gorgeous woman clung to his arm.

Sarah felt her insides sink. Her embarrassment gave way to bitter disappointment. It had never entered her head that he would bring a partner, and such a beautiful one too. She hated the female instantly.

Ian's gaze followed the direction of her eyes. 'Someone you know?'

'No . . . well yes, actually. I mean I've only ever met him once before. He works for my father.' She struggled to concentrate again on Ian, but was still terribly aware of Captain Wilson and the woman he was with.

'I think you would do well in the diplomatic corps,' she said.

'I take it that's a compliment,' he jibed.

'Of course, what else?'

They both laughed. Hamish the footman appeared by their side carrying a tray of wine. Sarah immediately stopped him and took a glass, saying to Ian she was parched. In fact she just wanted the alcohol, something to take the edge off her disappointment.

She'd been a fool, she told herself. She might have thought often of Captain Wilson, but now it was clear he hadn't of her. He would hardly have brought a partner to her party if he had.

'You're a bit of a mystery, aren't you?' Ian said to her.

She immediately knew what he was referring to. 'Am I?'

'Popping up out of thin air as you did. People have been frightfully curious.'

'Have they indeed?'

'Yes they have.' He smiled at her, clearly waiting for an explanation.

She and Jock hadn't discussed what she would say if asked about her background. She certainly wasn't ashamed of it. On the contrary, she was proud of it. Nor would Jock be embarrassed in the slightest if she told the truth – up to a point, that is. He wouldn't wish her to speak other than on a surface level about him and Myrtle.

'I was abducted by a Chinese gang when I was two years old, and it's taken me all this while to escape their evil clutches,' Sarah replied, absolutely straight-faced.

'You don't say!'

'I do. They took me to Shanghai where I stayed in a prince's castle. When I was old enough I was to be his wife.' Captain Wilson was moving in her direction. Was he coming over to speak?

She was pulling his leg of course, Ian thought, but it was awfully amusing. And convincing – she was a born actress. 'Fascinating,' he murmured.

'Not only his wife, but his fifteenth!'

He decided to play her little game, to go along with it. Why not! 'And were the wives all European?'

'Oh no, only me. The others were Chinese. I was destined to be his first non-Chinese spouse.'

'And so you escaped before . . .' said Ian dramatically, '. . . a fate worse than death?'

'Exactly.' Wilson was definitely coming to speak. Out the corner of her eye she could see him looking at her as he and his companion crossed the room.

'You have led quite a life, Sarah,' Ian mocked gently.

'You wouldn't believe the half of it.' What would he know about the likes of Netherton and 'down by'? His world must be as different to the one she'd previously inhabited as champagne is to cider.

'Your father must have been overjoyed to get you back?'

'Oh he was! Quite overjoyed. He'll tell you himself, he thought he'd lost me forever.'

Ian was about to get Sarah to expand on her escape from the Chinese prince and gang when a new voice spoke.

'Miss Hawke, how nice to see you again.'

She turned to Wilson with a smile. 'And how nice of you to come to the party, Captain Bilson.'

His face fell fractionally. 'Wilson,' he corrected. 'Captain Wilson.'

'Oh please forgive me, I am dreadful with names,' she pretended innocently. Gesturing at Ian she said, 'This is the Honourable Ian Monteith.'

The two men shook hands. 'And I'd like you to meet Miss Bessie Wallace from Boston, Massachusetts.'

'Delighted,' Ian replied.

The bloody woman was even more gorgeous up close, Sarah thought in despair. She made her feel positively plain by comparison.

'And what brings you to Glasgow?' Sarah sweetly asked the American.

'My grandfather hailed from Scotland, and ever since a child I have promised myself a trip to the old country to visit all the places I've heard so much about. My family are direct descendants of Sir William Wallace, the great Scottish patriot.'

'How interesting,' Ian muttered politely.

What was it the English did to Wallace? Hung, drew and quartered him? Sarah would gladly have visited the same on his gushing descendant.

'How did you two meet?' Sarah asked.

'In Boston last year, through some mutual acquaintances,' Bessie explained.

'I see,' Sarah smiled.

'So when I found myself in Glasgow I just had to look Mathew up, hoping desperately he would be here and not at sea. And wasn't I lucky to find he was!' And with that Bessie snuggled up against Wilson.

Still smiling, Sarah swallowed hard.

'Speaking of being lucky, I consider myself that to be in port at the same time you were having your party,' Wilson said to Sarah.

Of course he'd been in port, she'd damn well arranged the date of the party for when he would be. Suddenly she felt foolish and reluctant to talk to Wilson and this Bessie Wallace any more.

'I think you promised me a dance, Ian,' she prompted.

He was too much the well-bred gentleman to show any surprise, but took up his cue immediately. 'Then shall we?'

She placed a hand on the arm he extended to her. 'I hope you enjoy yourselves,' she said to Wilson and Bessie, and with that she and Ian headed for the dining-room where the dancing was taking place.

Stupid, foolish and fuming, she thought as Ian swept her into his embrace. Fuming at herself more than anything.

When the dance was over they stayed up for the next, after which they came off the floor.

'I could use another drink, how about you?' Ian asked.

'Not for me thank you, but you go ahead.' It was very warm in the dining-room, to the point of being stuffy.

Ian glanced about, but there were no drinks in sight. 'Will you excuse me for a few moments,' he apologised, and left her to go hunt for a tray-carrying servant.

Jock entered the room with a man she recognised right away. Jock looked round, spotted her, said something to his friend, and then they both headed in her direction.

'Here's someone I don't have to introduce you to, you know Charlie of old,' Jock said. The Charlie he was referring to was Charlie Dundonald, owner of the pit at Netherton.

Nervousness had replaced her other emotions. In Netherton Dundonald was almost a godlike figure. No, not almost, *was*. He was the owner, without him there was no work, and without work there was no roof over your head, clothes on your back or food on the table.

'How do you do, Sarah,' he said softly.

'How do you do, sir.' If she'd been Gordy or Jack Bonner or Tom Crayk or any of the other colliers in Netherton she'd have touched her forelock. As it was she only just stopped herself in time from bobbing to him.

'I must say you look a proper treat.'

'Thank you, sir.'

Charlie glanced at Jock, then back at Sarah. 'I think in these new circumstances it might be more proper for you to call me Mr Dundonald. We're on an equal footing now you know.'

'Yes, Mr Dundonald.'

'And from here on in I want you to consider me a friend, as your father and I have been friends this long while.'

Consider the Netherton pit owner a friend! *That* was going to get some getting used to. By God and it was. 'Thank you, sir . . . I mean Mr Dundonald.'

'Would you do me the honour of dancing with me then, Sarah?'

She hadn't expected that. 'I'm the one who'd be honoured, Mr Dundonald.'

'Nay lass, it's me who'll be honoured,' he said gently. 'I can assure you.'

What a different image he projected to the one he had in Netherton. Why he was quite pleasant really, not at all the ogre Netherton folk thought him. But then, as he had rightly said, he was amongst his own here. They were all on an equal footing as he'd termed it. At least certainly he, Jock and that like were. The Honourable Ian and his ilk were something else again.

The music struck up again; there were four musicians playing, and Sarah and Charlie Dundonald moved off.

'Your father tells me you've settled in well in Stiellsmuir. I'm glad,' Dundonald said.

'It's quite a change for me, as you can imagine.'

He chuckled. 'Yes, I can.'

She saw Wilson and Bessie Wallace come into the room, the pair of them deep in conversation. Without further ado they took to the floor.

'Young Monteith's father Jock and myself all belong to the same club you know.' The club he was referring to was the Albion in Royal Exchange Square.

'Yes, Ian mentioned that.' Jock went to The Albion at least once a week, often twice.

'We have a ladies' night the last Saturday in every March. I hope Jock will bring you to the next one.'

'I'd enjoy that.'

'Good,' Dundonald said, nodding approvingly.

There was a question she was dying to ask, but dare she? 'Mr Dundonald, Jock would be angry if he knew I'd asked you this, but it's important to me. How are my mother and stepfather? Do you know?'

Dundonald's eyes flicked round the room, but there was no sign of Jock. 'I don't know all the ins and outs of Jock and his wife, but I'm able to guess at quite a bit of it. This is strictly between you and me? I don't wish to lose a good friend.'

'Strictly, Mr Dundonald.'

'Sunter is, I believe, just the same as when you left Netherton. No better, but then no worse. And from what I'm told your mother is managing just fine.'

Relief surged through Sarah. Oh, but it was marvellous to hear that. 'Thank you,' she whispered.

'You won't let on mind?'

'I won't let on, Mr Dundonald. Cross my heart and hope to die if I do.'

When that dance was concluded they came off the floor to where Jock had reappeared. As the three of them started chatting, Sarah glanced towards Wilson, he and Bessie having remained up. For the briefest of seconds their eyes met. Then, casually, she brought her attention back to her father and Mr Dundonald. Not visually snubbing Wilson, but not giving him any particular visual acknowledgement either.

She was wondering where Ian had got to when Adam Tennant came up to them with the silliest of grins plastered all over his face.

'I was wondering if I may be so bold as to ask your daughter up to dance?' Adam requested of Jock.

'If it's my permission you're after then granted. But whether she'll dance with you or not is up to her,' Jock replied.

'Of course I'll dance with you,' Sarah told Adam, at the same moment spying Ian re-entering the dining-room carrying the drink he'd gone in search of.

'Thank you, Miss Hawke,' Adam answered, and, still grinning, bowed low in a formal manner.

They took to the floor, blending smoothly into the dance now in progress.

'What are you grinning like that for?'

His eyebrows shot up in surprise. 'Am I?'

'It makes you look demented.'

The silly grin vanished. 'Sorry, I wasn't aware of it. I . . .' He trailed off, then added, 'I've been screwing up my courage to ask you to dance. The grin must have been nerves.'

'Well there's no need to be nervous with me, Adam. I don't bite.'

He sucked in a deep breath, which seemed to calm him. His shoulders dropped into a more natural, relaxed position.

'That's better,' she smiled, and he smiled back.

'I think you look absolutely smashing, the belle of the ball,' he told her.

'Why thank you, Adam!'

'No I mean it, I really do,' he persisted. 'I wasn't just being polite or trying to ingratiate myself. You are quite the belle of the ball.'

She glanced over to where Bessie Wallace was. If only that were true, but the American woman knocked spots off her. The bitch.

'There are lots of people here tonight.'

'Yes,' she agreed.

'Have you met many of them before?'

He was a surprisingly good dancer, she thought. He had a natural grace and fluidity. 'Some, not all that many.'

He was thinking how intoxicating she smelt; it was going straight to his head. Why was it neither Olivia or Primrose ever smelt like that? Or if they did, he'd certainly never noticed. Then again, maybe you didn't with your sisters.

'Have you made some chums since coming to live in Stiellsmuir?'

'What do you mean by chums?' she queried.

'You know, girl friends, that sort of thing.'

She thought of her lonely days round the house, loneliness she was still having to come to terms with. Still, it wouldn't be so bad now she had a carriage of her own. She could go to the park whenever she wanted, or drive into and round town. The carriage was going to make a big difference to her.

'I'm afraid not. But I'm sure that'll come in time.'

He glimpsed something of her current loneliness in her face, which disturbed him. Was there any way he could help? And then he had it, a suggestion.

'I eh . . . I wonder . . .' He was suddenly all tongue-tied, damn it! Come on, spit it out, he told himself.

'Yes?'

'This is difficult, you being the boss's daughter and that. I don't want to be seen to be trying to . . .' He groped for the correct word.

'Be ingratiating yourself?' she prompted, using the word he'd used earlier.

He laughed. 'Exactly.' He laughed again, and she with him.

'I have two sisters, Olivia and Primrose, you might find interesting. Olivia is nineteen, Primrose seventeen. If you'd care to meet them perhaps you might come to tea this Sunday? Or if that wasn't convenient how about the Sunday following?' Having got it out he was amazed at his own audacity. He'd gone through torture to bring himself to ask her to dance, and now, not only that, he'd asked her to his house for tea. With the intention of meeting Olivia and Primrose of course!

She'd have to tread warily here, Sarah thought. Adam worked for Jock who might not wish her to socialise with his staff and the staff's families. The party was one thing, but going to a member of staff's home might be quite another.

'I'll have to speak to my father first,' she smiled in reply.

'Naturally! I perfectly understand.' And he did.

The Tennants' parlour was identical to a million other middle-class parlours to be found the length and breadth of Britain. Heavy flock wallpaper, antimacassars on the backs of chairs and settee, the obligatory aspidistra standing in the window, a fire burning in the grate because it was winter and they had a visitor.

'Another cup of Lapsang Souchong, Miss Hawke?' Mrs Tennant asked. She was a cheerful body, plump, with enormous bosoms.

Sarah was already awash. If she had any more tea she felt sure it would start leaking from her ears. 'No thank you, I've had sufficient,' she replied. This was proving to be excruciatingly boring, and she had long since wished she hadn't come.

Mr Tennant was sitting stiff as a poker. He'd hardly uttered a word, but when he had it had been in monosyllables. Sarah was convinced he was terrified of her because she was Adam's boss's daughter. Douglas Tennant was a clerk with the Glasgow & South Western Railway.

'Or perhaps another potato scone?' Primrose, the younger of the two daughters inquired. Primrose was plumpish, and took after her mother. Olivia was similar in looks and temperament to Adam, neither of which seemed to take after either the mother or father.

Sarah held up a hand that said no, and wondered how much longer she would have to decently wait before she could escape.

Adam was fidgety, knowing full well that Sarah's visit was going badly. He'd been so looking forward to it, and now it had turned out to be a disaster. The conversation had been like trying to wade through thick glutinous mud.

'Terrible summer don't you think?' Mr Tennant said suddenly.

Sarah blinked at him. What was the man havering about? The summer had been brilliant, one of the best she could remember. Her reply was a sound that neither agreed or disagreed with him.

'We did have some nice days though,' Mrs Tennant smiled.

God, Sarah thought with a mental groan, this was going from bad to diabolical.

Olivia, only too painfully aware of the situation, had a brainwave. 'Adam, why don't you show Miss Hawke some of your pictures? I'm certain she'd like to see them.'

A tinge of pink crept into Adam's cheeks. 'Och, I'm sure not.'

'Pictures? What pictures are these?' Sarah queried.

'Adam draws and paints,' Olivia informed her.

'Just a hobby you understand,' Adam said quickly.

'He's very good,' Primrose said. Adam shot her a murderous look.

'I would like to see them. Yes, indeed,' Sarah enthused. Anything was better than this present stifling dreariness.

'Go and get some then,' Olivia urged her brother.

He was genuinely reluctant. 'I don't know . . .'

'Our guest has indicated that she would like to see them,' Mr Tennant said with emphasis.

He was coming on, Sarah thought to herself. Two full sentences out of the man. Positively loquacious compared to what he'd been up until a minute ago.

'Aye, well, if you insist,' Adam said, shooting daggers at Olivia.

'Adam has been drawing ever since he was a wee lad. It used to keep him busy and out of my hair for hours on end,' Mrs Tennant informed Sarah.

Adam left the parlour, returning shortly with an armful of drawings. 'You can see these first, and if you're still interested I'll show you a couple of paintings,' he said to Sarah.

'Here I'll help,' Olivia volunteered, springing to her feet.

The drawings were all higgledy-piggledy, but with Olivia to assist him Adam soon sorted them out. 'The Botanic Gardens,' he said, handing Sarah a sheet of paper that was roughly eighteen inches square.

It was a palm tree, with bananas on it, surrounded by shrubs. 'Hmmm!' she mused, nodding.

The next was of a bench in the same gardens with a young couple seated on it. A young couple very much in love – Sarah could tell that immediately from the expressions they wore. The couple were so lifelike they seemed to leap out of the paper at her.

The next was of a swan on a stretch of water, the one after that of people in a street. When she came to the last it was of a young working-class girl sitting on the edge of a pavement with her bare filthy feet in the gutter. The sort of girl to be found in every street in Netherton, indeed the sort of girl Sarah herself had been at that age.

Adam shuffled in embarrassment when she was finished. 'It occupies some of my spare time, you understand,' he said defensively.

She looked up at him, a new respect in her eyes. 'Those are rare, Adam. Can I see your paintings?'

He brightened visibly. 'You mean that? You're not just being polite?'

'I mean it. I'd like to very much indeed.'

This time he walked briskly from the parlour.

While he was gone Sarah went through the drawings again. Their realism, depth and sheer excellence fascinated her. She was staring avidly at the couple on the bench when Adam returned carrying three middling-sized paintings. Olivia immediately went to help him.

'This is the Broomielaw,' Adam said, holding the first one in front of Sarah while Olivia minded the other two.

It was as if the bustling Broomielaw had been suspended in a split moment of time. Ships were tied up, cargo was being loaded and unloaded, folk were toing and froing, seagulls dipping and weaving, the whole thing exactly as you'd see it any working day. Adam had even caught the Glasgow light and its effect on colours precisely as they were in real life.

Adam gave the picture back to his sister and took the second one which he now gave Sarah a viewing of. The subject was an older man, so pompous and stuffy and full of his own importance Sarah couldn't help but burst out laughing.

'That's my uncle Robert the bank manager,' Adam explained, glancing at his father—whose brother Robert was—who was looking most unamused.

'I thought it a very good likeness,' Douglas Tennant said stiffly, which made Sarah laugh again, and him frown because he couldn't understand what was funny. Olivia and Primrose were both grinning broadly, they understood all right. As for Mrs Tennant, if she did she wasn't letting on.

'And this is our coalman with his horse and cart,' Adam said, exchanging the second painting for the third.

The horse was a Clydesdale, a huge beast now bowed and bent with age and years of back-breaking graft. The coalman was old too, and sucking on a battered briar. There was a spiritual light in the man's face. Here was a reflection of all that was good and honest in the working class, a face that had the spark of God in it.

'They're magnificent, all three,' Sarah pronounced simply.

'That's what I think,' Olivia said.

'I know nothing about art as such, but I don't have to to appreciate you have talent, real talent,' Sarah smiled at Adam who, on hearing that, blushed and immediately looked down at the carpet.

'Have you ever thought about taking it up professionally?'

'I eh . . .' Adam trailed off, and shrugged.

'Couldn't do that!' Douglas Tennant said coldly.

Sarah turned to Adam's father who was no longer poker-stiff. 'Why not?'

'It's a ridiculous notion. People such as us don't become artists,' he said derisively.

'Why shouldn't someone like Adam become a professional artist?'

Douglas Tennant laughed, a nasty mocking laugh that made Sarah dislike him intensely. It was a laugh direct from a small, constrained mind. A mind with about as much vision as the inside of a matchbox. 'He's got a fine job right now, with prospects. If he watches his p's and q's he can go far. He doesn't want to go mucking about with any arty-crafty nonsense.' Douglas Tennant took a deep breath and stuck out his thin chest. 'It may be all right as a hobby, nothing against that, but not as a way of life. No money in it, lass, no money in it. Besides which, it's not respectable.'

That was the key, Sarah thought, respectability. Folk such as Douglas Tennant was revealing himself to be worshipped respectability almost above all else. It went with the antimacassars and aspidistras in the window.

'And what do you say, Adam?' she queried.

Adam kept staring at the carpet. 'I don't really know if I'm *that* good.'

'I think you are,' Olivia stated defiantly.

One up for you! Sarah thought, smiling at Olivia. She was rapidly taking a shine to the elder Tennant daughter.

Douglas Tennant snorted dismissively. 'Being an artist is for Frenchmen and Spaniards, those sort of breeds. Scotsmen don't become professional artists, the idea is absurd.'

'And what's your opinion, Mrs Tennant?' Sarah asked.

Mrs Tennant glanced at her husband, got the message he was glaring at her, then brought her gaze on to Sarah. 'I wholeheartedly agree with Douglas. Ideal as a hobby, a Sunday afternoon relaxation, but that's as far as it goes.'

Sarah looked again at the painting of the coalman and his horse and cart. If she said much more she would be being rude, and that she didn't want. She was a guest in their house for the first time after all, and it really had nothing to do with her.

'I believe I will have another cup of tea,' she announced, and proceeded to completely change the subject.

Mrs Tennant poured her a fresh cup while Adam put away his paintings and drawings.

Douglas Tennant went back to being monosyllabic.

Tap tap tap!

Sarah drifted upwards into that state which is neither asleep nor awake, but somewhere in between. Was she really hearing tapping noises, or was she dreaming them?

Tap tap tap!

There they were again. Urgent, insistent, and far far away. She was dreaming them, she decided, and turned over in her bed. Cosy, warm, lovely and warm, she thought as she felt herself falling back into sleep proper.

Tap tap tap!

She opened her eyes. She wasn't imagining or dreaming the tapping noises, they were real enough. But what were they?

Tap tap tap!

This time they seemed to come from right outside her bedroom door. Her own bedroom that she'd moved into in August after Jock had had it done up for her.

Tap tap tap!

What on earth was going on? It sounded as if somebody, or something, was tapping the corridor walls. Gooseflesh sprang up on her shoulders, and despite the fact she'd been beautifully warm only seconds previously she was now cold all over. It was the something that worried her.

You're being daft! she chided herself. It wasn't something, but somebody. Should she investigate?

Tap tap tap!

She slid out of bed, and into her heavy woollen dressing-gown that was just the dab for this time of year when there was snow on the ground, and the winds that whistled round Stiellsmuir could cut you to the bone if you weren't properly wrapped up against them. She stuck her feet into her lambswool slippers, another necessity, before padding to the bedroom door. On reaching the door she placed an ear against it, and listened.

Tap tap tap!

After the last tap a few moments' silence, followed by a long-drawn-out sigh.

She opened the door a fraction to peer out, to see Jock on his hands and knees.

Tap tap tap! Jock tapped the wall just above the skirting board with the forefinger knuckle of his right hand.

'Jock, what are you doing?' she whispered.

He glanced up to stare at her standing framed in the doorway. He frowned, as if trying to place who she was.

'What are you doing?' she repeated, again in a whisper.

'Looking for her.'

Now it was Sarah's turn to frown. 'Who?'

'*Her.*'

Sarah came out of the doorway to go and squat beside him. 'Who do you mean?'

'Don't you know?'

Sarah shook her head.

'She always comes in the middle of the night. And when she does I never fail to know she's about.' He suddenly grabbed hold of Sarah by the arm. 'Never!' His eyes bulged as he said that.

Sarah wasn't sure whether she was scared or frightened or what. One thing was certain however, Jock was having another of his 'moods'.

'But who is she?'

He peered to the left, and then to the right. 'The blue lady,' he whispered.

'The blue lady?'

'That's what I call her. I've no idea what her real name was.'

Sarah's gooseflesh was back. '*Was?*'

'Yes, she's a ghost now, you see. She died long ago.'

The hair at the nape of Sarah's neck shot right out to become spikes. 'A ghost?'

'She tells me things.'

'What sort of things?'

Jock smiled, and tapped his nose. 'Just things,' he replied mysteriously.

Still holding her by the arm, he pulled her closer. 'Is that you,

100

Myrtle?' he queried in a cracked, hoarse voice.

That really made Sarah go all peculiar inside. 'No Father, it's Sarah.'

His eyes went moist. 'Not Myrtle?'

'No Father, her daughter. Your daughter.'

'Not Myrtle,' he repeated, and released Sarah. Putting his head in his hands he began rocking back and forth.

She wanted to ask him why he'd been tapping the wall, what that had to do with this blue lady, but he seemed beyond further questioning. She grasped him gently by the shoulders. 'Come on, Jock, I'll get you back to bed, that's the best place for you.'

He offered no resistance as Sarah raised him to his feet. He still had his head in his hands as she led him away. Behind the hands he was quietly sobbing.

She took him along the corridor, then down a flight of stairs to the level below, where his bedroom was located. She was almost at his bedroom door when it flew open to reveal Mrs McGuffie frantically tying the cord of her dressing-gown. The housekeeper's feet were bare.

Mrs McGuffie froze when she saw Sarah. Her complexion paled, and turned a muddy colour. Her hair, normally up and held in place by a brace of black combs, was free, tumbling over her shoulders and down her back.

Sarah's mind was whirling. Why was Mrs McGuffie in her father's bedroom, and why had her dressing-gown been undone? On reaching the bedroom door she automatically glanced inside.

'Where was he?' Mrs McGuffie asked quietly, and anxiously.

'Upstairs, outside my room. He was tapping the wall and it was that which woke me.'

Her father's bed had been slept in on both sides. Both pillows were dented, both sides of the bedclothes thrown back. *Her father's bed had been slept in on both sides!* Mrs McGuffie had been in bed with her father. She felt shocked, sick, repulsed all at the same time.

The two women stared at one another, Mrs McGuffie's expression grim as could be. You could have cut the atmosphere between them with a knife.

'I'll look after him now, see he's all right,' Mrs McGuffie said softly. Adding, 'Don't worry, I'm used to this. It'll soon pass, it always does.'

Jock took his hands away from his face to reveal it streaked with

101

tears. He appeared distraught in the extreme. He sighed again, a lost lonely sound that came from the very depths of his being.

'This way, Jock,' Mrs McGuffie said to him, and taking him by the hand as though he was a child, led him back into the bedroom, closing the door behind them.

Sarah glanced at the door, wincing a little – though she couldn't think why – when she heard the snib being shot home.

Mrs McGuffie and Jock. Jock and Mrs McGuffie. *Her father* and Mrs McGuffie! She'd had no inkling, no idea. This was a bombshell, a lightning bolt right out of the blue.

Sleeping together! Lovers!

She made her way back to her own bed where it was hours before she finally dropped off again to sleep. But when she eventually did so much that had worried and puzzled her in the past now made sense.

She always had breakfast with Jock before he left for work, seeing that as a duty on her part. A duty she enjoyed. Sometimes they spoke more than just the usual morning pleasantries, that morning they hadn't.

She'd searched his face for signs of guilt or embarrassment; there had been neither. Jock had been himself, exactly as he normally was. There hadn't even been a hint in his behaviour that anything untoward had happened the previous night.

After he'd kissed her goodbye and left for Carlton Place, she rang for more coffee. It was Mrs McGuffie who answered.

Mrs McGuffie bit her lower lip. 'We have to talk, Sarah,' she said.

Sarah nodded. 'In half an hour's time in the library?'

'Yes, that would be fine.'

'I was ringing for more coffee, but perhaps we could have it then?'

The fact that Sarah had said 'we' wasn't lost on Mrs McGuffie; she was grateful for that. 'I'll bring it myself.' And with that she left the breakfast room, and Sarah alone again.

The housekeeper had looked awful, Sarah thought. Haggard was the right word to describe her. Haggard and, something she'd never have applied to Mrs McGuffie before, very unsure of herself.

*

'Come in!' Sarah called out when there was a rap on the library door.

Mrs McGuffie entered, carrying a silver tray on which were two cups and saucers, a silver coffee pot with matching sugar bowl and milk jug.

Sarah had already pulled two chairs together, and set a small table between them. 'Put the tray down here,' she said, indicating the table. As Mrs McGuffie did that she lit a cigarette, for she too was nervous.

'Shall I pour?' Mrs McGuffie asked, sitting.

'Please.'

Sarah took a deep draw and studied the housekeeper through the smoke she exhaled. Despite her revulsion and other feelings of the night before she was determined to keep an open mind about this. She wanted to learn the housekeeper's side of things. That was only fair.

'Can I have one of those?' Mrs McGuffie asked suddenly.

Sarah didn't understand. 'I beg your pardon?'

'Your cigarettes. I very occasionally indulge, and I'd like to now. If it's all right with you, that is.'

Sarah offered her packet, and Mrs McGuffie picked one out of it. Sarah handed her the box of matches.

Mrs McGuffie passed Sarah her coffee, then lit up. She inhaled as if she was a drowning person who'd just made it back to the surface.

'Do you hate me?' she asked abruptly.

It threw Sarah slightly that Mrs McGuffie had taken the initiative – she'd intended doing that. 'Hate? No, I don't think so.'

'I thought you might. I was fully prepared for that.'

'How long have you . . .?' This was difficult with a woman so much older than herself. 'How long have you and Jock . . .?'

'Eighteen months after I came to Stiellsmuir.'

'And that was why you were so cold towards me when I arrived here. It wasn't merely that you thought I'd usurp your duties as housekeeper, and domestic mistress of the house, but you thought I threatened, or came in the way of, your relationship with my father.'

'I want you to understand something, Sarah. I love him,' Mrs McGuffie replied simply.

Sarah digested that. 'And does he love you?'

103

Mrs McGuffie shook her head. 'I'm under no illusions. He's very fond of me, but the only person he loves in that way is your mother.'

'And knowing that you continue to love him?'

'With all my heart and soul.' Suddenly, vehemently, full of passion, she said, 'Jock is a great man, a *great* man.'

Sarah had another puff of her cigarette, a dozen and more questions crowding her mind.

'Can I make something clear between us? The something that has made me fear you ever since you put in an appearance here,' Mrs McGuffie said.

Sarah nodded.

'If what you've discovered upsets you so much that you force him to choose between us, he'll choose you. I'll be the one to go.'

Sarah's heart softened towards the housekeeper. No wonder the woman had been the way she had to her. Everything had been going along hunky-dory for the housekeeper until she'd appeared on the scene, a potential terminal threat to the housekeeper's situation if ever there was one.

'I won't force him to choose. You have my word on that,' Sarah replied.

Mrs McGuffie sagged where she sat. 'Thank you, and thank God,' she whispered.

Sarah had a sudden thought. 'Is there a Mr McGuffie somewhere?'

'No, I've never been married. I only assumed the title of Mrs because it gave me more authority over the staff, and it also makes things easier, more acceptable shall we say, with me looking after a single gentleman.' She corrected herself. 'As I was until you came.'

'I see.'

Mrs McGuffie's face cracked into a smile, and she barked out a laugh. 'At the risk of sounding impertinent, you should have seen your face last night. It was a picture and no mistake – as I'm sure mine was. I've been terrified of you finding out.'

Sarah was intrigued. 'Do you go to him every night?'

Mrs McGuffie picked up her cup, and gazed into its contents. 'Twice a week on average. Occasionally more, but that tends to be unusual.'

'And you *are* physical lovers?' She wanted to be quite certain about that, to have the confirmation from the housekeeper's own lips.

Mrs McGuffie glanced at Sarah, then back down into her cup. 'We are.'

Sarah sipped some coffee. Her nervousness had vanished.

'That must be difficult for you to come to terms with?' Mrs McGuffie ventured after a few silent seconds had ticked by.

'Last night I was shocked, I won't deny it. In fact I was more than shocked, I was totally stunned by the revelation of . . . of you and him.'

'And now?'

'I suppose I'm getting used to the idea.'

Mrs McGuffie drew on her cigarette, thinking that she couldn't conceive of life now without Jock. Without him there was no life for her – he was her life. 'Do you approve or disapprove?'

Sarah stared the housekeeper straight in the eyes. 'It's not my place to do either. What Jock does is his own business.'

'You disapprove then?'

'I didn't say that. What I did say was that the idea takes some getting used to.'

'I know he'll never marry me, Sarah, he's made that plain. He'll never marry me, just as he'll never divorce your mother. I've long since accepted both these things. I . . .' She swallowed. 'I bring him what happiness and support I can, and am content with that.'

Sarah believed the housekeeper, her words rang with sincerity. 'Does he remember anything about last night, Maud?'

Mrs McGuffie shook her head. 'Sometimes he does, other times not. Last night was one of the latter.' She paused, then asked bluntly, 'What do you know about Jock and last night, and that other night when . . .?'

'He was in one of his "moods" as my mother calls them,' Sarah interjected.

'Yes.'

'Very little, Maud. My mother warned me just before I left Netherton that Jock had these "moods". And because of them – and how they'd scared her in the past – she was totally against me coming here.'

'They can be scary,' Mrs McGuffie agreed. 'Until you get used to them, that is, and then they stop being that. At least they did for me.'

'Ma says he never hurt her while he's been like that. What about you?'

'Never. Well, he has bruised my arm once or twice, but that was inadvertently on his part. He's never hit me or threatened me with violence.'

At least that hadn't changed since he'd been with Myrtle, Sarah thought with relief. 'And how often does he have these "moods" of his?'

'He goes through phases. It's been very good since you took up residence at Stiellsmuir—it's only happened a handful of times. Your presence seems to have had a settling effect on him.'

'I'm glad about that. But tell me, do they only happen at night?'

Mrs McGuffie nodded. 'During the day he manages to immerse himself in his work, and keep his mind occupied with that. It's at night when he starts to brood and hark back to the past that what you and your mother term "moods"—I call them "funny turns"—come on him.'

'But what exactly are they?' Sarah queried.

'To be truthful, I have no idea.'

'Has he been to see a doctor?'

Mrs McGuffie gave Sarah a cynical smile. 'He won't hear of that. Refuses point blank to go to the doctor.'

'But why?' Sarah burst out.

'Perhaps,' Mrs McGuffie replied slowly, 'he doesn't want to hear what the doctor might tell him.'

Sarah sipped more coffee, which had now gone cold. She topped up the housekeeper's cup, and then her own. 'This ghost he was searching for, the blue lady, is that common?'

'Oh yes, he often claims to have spoken to her. Though he's never actually confided in me what about. He always shrugs that off.'

Sarah was fascinated. 'Are there any other ghosts?'

'He says there are. Though the blue lady is the one he sees most, and the only one he calls by name. Or title if you will.'

Sarah shivered. This was so unlike the Jock she knew of the daytime. But there was no arguing that the other night-time Jock did exist, she'd met him twice now.

'He thought I was my mother,' Sarah said.

A sheen of tears came into Mrs McGuffie's eyes. 'I'm not surprised. He's often called me Myrtle when he was having a "funny turn".'

'How awful for you,' Sarah sympathised.

'Yes, if there's a hardest bit about the whole affair it's when he thinks I'm Myrtle. Particularly when . . .' Mrs McGuffie broke off, thinking she couldn't continue with that, not with his daughter.

'The pair of you are in bed together?' Sarah prompted, guessing what it was.

The housekeeper dropped her head, not wanting Sarah to see her expression. 'Yes,' she replied, in a cracked voice.

'What about when he's abroad? When he came to visit us in Netherton he said he'd just returned from Canada.'

Mrs McGuffie, without looking up, replied in the same cracked voice. 'Thankfully it's rare for him to have to go away from Glasgow, overseas or otherwise. When he does all I can do is pray everything will be all right which, thank the Lord, up until now it has been.'

Sarah stubbed out her cigarette, forcing herself to ask the next question. 'Maud, is he insane?'

'No!' Mrs McGuffie exclaimed in anguish, her face suddenly dead-white. She stared at Sarah. 'He's no such thing. He's just . . . eccentric, that's all.'

A lot more than eccentric, Sarah thought, at least as she understood the word.

'He's not insane,' Mrs McGuffie repeated adamantly. 'He just has these "funny turns" – wandering in his mind, that's all.'

Silence fell between them again, each immersed in her own thoughts. The only sound to disturb the silence being the tick-tock of the mantelpiece clock, and its sonorous chiming when it struck the hour.

'I'd better get back to work,' Mrs McGuffie said when the chiming was over.

'There will be no choosing between us, I promise you,' Sarah repeated.

Mrs McGuffie flashed Sarah a grateful smile, a smile of intimacy, a shared secret.

'If you make my father happy, then I'm happy,' Sarah declared softly.

Mrs McGuffie gathered the coffee cups and saucers back on to the silver tray. 'Thank you,' she choked.

There was more than just a sheen of tears in her eyes when she left the library.

Sarah sat knitting, Jock smoking a cigar and frowning at the sheet of figures he was studying. Beside him was a large whisky and soda.

107

It was evening, five nights after the one Sarah had found Jock outside on her landing. Looking at him now she could hardly believe that the event had taken place, and yet it had.

Picking up a pencil he made a mark on the paper, then angrily another. 'Damn and blast!' he muttered, and took a deep swig of his drink.

Sarah was thinking about Adam Tennant and his sisters, and about asking them to Stiellsmuir. A return visit for the one she'd paid to their house. She was keen to have them come, having quite taken to Olivia. The thing was, with Christmas and Hogmanay looming on the horizon should she ask them before, or after? She wanted to discuss that with Jock.

'Jock?'

'Yes?' he snapped back irritably.

Now wasn't the time, she thought looking at his thunderclouded face. 'Is something wrong?'

'How do you mean?'

'Well you're not exactly in the best of humours, are you? You nearly bit my head off there.'

'Did I?' He looked genuinely surprised. 'Sorry, I didn't mean to.' He had another pull at his drink, which finished it, and got up to pour himself another.

'What about you?' he queried, waving the bottle at her.

'No, thank you.'

'This is Macallan – whisky doesn't come any better.'

'Maybe later.'

He grunted, and poured himself another large one, adding soda to it. He was well aware it was considered a sacrilege to add soda to malt, and the very best of malt at that, but that was how he liked it, so to hell with the traditionalists.

'Something's troubling you,' Sarah said softly, giving him a small smile.

He shrugged. 'Business.'

She'd realised that, he hadn't had to tell her. She nearly said as much but decided not to. 'Anything I can do to help?'

'No, as I say it's business. A few sticky problems, that's all.' He returned to his chair and threw himself down. Picking up the paper again he glared at it.

Sarah knitted on, her needles going clickety-clack. It was a sound she found soothing. 'Anything to do with McIvor?' she asked.

'Aye, he's involved. I'm telling you that man has all the cunning of a polecat.'

'Wouldn't weasel be better?'

He looked at her. 'Weasel? You mean weasel rather than polecat?' She nodded.

Jock laughed, a deep rumbling sound that reverberated round and round the library. 'By God you're right. Weasel is exactly the right word. It fits McIvor to a T.'

Well she'd made him laugh, that was something. She continued knitting—socks she was making for Jock.

He returned to studying the sheet of figures. 'Hmmm!' he murmured, his forehead creasing. Then, 'Hmmm!' again.

Finally he laid the paper in his lap, had another gulp of whisky and soda, and stared up at the ceiling. His eyes were far away, lost in troubled contemplation.

'Would you like to talk about it?' Sarah asked quietly.

'Eh?'

'I said, would you like to talk about it?'

'It's business, Sarah, I told you.'

Her needles clickety-clacked. 'Sometimes it's useful to talk about problems rather than just thinking about them.' She stopped to glance over at Jock who was now staring thoughtfully at her.

'Go on,' he said.

'Use me as a sounding-board if you want. Talk to me, and I'll listen, and maybe ask you the odd question to clarify something if I don't understand it. And by talking and explaining, perhaps you'll come up with the answers to your problems more easily and quickly than if you were just thinking about them, keeping it all inside your head so to speak.'

He blew a long stream of smoke at her. What she was suggesting was something he had attempted to do years ago with Myrtle, but had soon given up when he'd realised she was neither paying attention nor interested in his work.

'A sounding-board?' he smiled.

Clickety-clack, clickety-clack, her fingers and the needles flew.

He spoke slowly at first, but within minutes the words were flowing out of him like a river in torrent.

Sarah listened intently as Jock spoke about McIvor, Nigeria and the palm oil he bought from there, the Manxman Sir George Goldie whom he bought the palm oil from in Nigeria, and so on and so forth.

When it was finally time to go to bed Jock had decided on a plan of action against his adversary, and Sarah knew quite a bit about his dealings with the Royal Niger Company, which Sir George Goldie headed, and the considerable profit Jock made from the palm oil he bought from that company when he resold it in Britain.

Out of the corner of her eye Sarah looked yet again at the brown paper parcel Adam Tennant had brought with him when he and his sisters had come to tea, the return visit for when Sarah had gone to their house the previous month. The date was now January 1891.

The parcel was rectangular in shape, about two feet by three in size, and tied with coarse string. Adam had laid it to one side when he and his sisters had entered the drawing-room, and so far not referred to it once. Sarah was eaten up with curiosity.

'And did you all have a pleasant Christmas and New Year?' Sarah asked the Tennants, addressing herself mainly to Olivia who was seated facing her.

'Excellent, thank you. I think I can speak for all of us when I say we thoroughly enjoyed ourselves,' Olivia smiled in reply.

'Did you stay up to see the New Year in?'

'I did, and so did Adam. But sleepyhead over there went to bed.'

'Well I got tired! I couldn't help it,' Primrose protested, causing Adam to grin and Olivia to give a small laugh. Although Primrose was the same age as Sarah she was nowhere near as mature. There was still far more of the girl in her than there was of the young lady.

'I love Hogmanay, it's my favourite night of the entire year,' Olivia said.

'Well I wouldn't say it was my favourite night of the whole year, but I do enjoy it,' Sarah replied. She preferred Burns' Night with its haggis, bagpipes and recitations of the bard's works. Burns' Night had always been a big 'do' in Netherton, the working class celebrating the working man's poet, as they saw Rabbie.

Sarah glanced directly at Adam. 'You're not saying much.'

He blushed. 'Sorry, am I being boring?'

'Not boring – quiet. They're hardly the same.'

'He never stops talking at home,' Primrose said, which earned her a glower from her brother. 'Well it's true!' she added defensively, thinking to herself that recently that talk had all been about Miss Sarah Hawke here, and how marvellous and wonderful Miss Hawke was, etc., etc.

110

Sarah looked again at the parcel. What was it? Perhaps it was something they were taking on elsewhere, in which case that was a disappointment.

'We had some jolly nice presents at Christmas,' Olivia said.

'Oh yes?'

'And stockings, we each had one of those.' She laughed. 'Stuffed full of apples, oranges, sweeties and all the things you adored as children. It was lovely.'

Sarah produced an enamel and metal cigarette case, and took a cigarette from it. 'Anyone else?' she asked.

'What a beautiful case!' Primrose exclaimed.

The front of the case was sky-blue with clouds and tiny red birds worked into it. The rear was plain sky-blue.

'A Christmas minding from my father. He asked me what I wanted and I said a cigarette case, which didn't please him at all as he's very much against me smoking, even though he himself smokes like a lum. He gave it to me however, and a prettier one I think you'd go a long way to find.'

'Can I see it?' Olivia asked, coming to her feet, and crossing to Sarah. 'It's beautiful, no doubt about that,' she said, caressing the case.

'It's nothing to what he gave me for New Year,' Sarah said, not at all sure she wasn't acting in bad taste by boasting like this, but absolutely bursting with it.

Olivia's eyes opened wide. 'What?'

Sarah held back, teasing it out.

'Come on!' Primrose urged.

'A sable coat.'

'Ahhh!' Primrose breathed, and sank back into her chair. 'A sable coat! How divine!'

Adam was about to comment that must have cost a fortune, but bit back his words. Of course it would have done, but then Jock Hawke could well afford it. The man was stinking.

Adam's heart sank within him. It was best he stop dreaming now, he told himself. Sarah Hawke was about as far beyond him as the moon was. He was only a humble clerk after all, the wage he earned would hardly keep her in buttons. He'd been mad to think of her in any light other than that of his boss's daughter.

'Lucky old you!' Olivia enthused.

Lucky wasn't the word for it, Sarah thought. Why only seven

months ago she'd been living in Netherton, wearing clogs and taking a bath once a week in front of the range. Now she wore the finest dresses, shoes and other attire, and could have a bath every single day of the week if she chose to. Twice a day if she wanted!

Of course the Tennants knew nothing of Netherton. To them she'd always been well-to-do.

Sarah thought of showing off the sable coat to Olivia and Primrose, and reluctantly decided against doing so. That would be lording it over them, and *definitely* in bad taste.

'Yes, lucky old me,' Sarah agreed with Olivia.

'I say, I think I would like to try a cigarette,' Olivia replied.

'Ollie!' Adam exclaimed.

'Why not?'

He wanted to say it was fast for a female to smoke, but could hardly do that when Sarah did.

'Well I'm going to,' Olivia declared defiantly, and accepted a cigarette from Sarah's open case.

'Primrose?' Sarah asked with a twinkle in her eyes, knowing that this would further outrage Adam.

Primrose pretended to consider it, though she had no intention whatever of putting one of those smelly things in her mouth. 'No thank you. I don't believe I will,' she smiled back at Sarah after a few seconds.

Sarah assisted Olivia to light up. 'Turkish tobacco, it'll make your toes curl,' she said.

Olivia puffed without inhaling. 'Very pleasant too,' she declared, and blew smoke in Adam's direction, which made him look cross, as she'd known it would.

'Do you play cards?' Olivia asked Sarah. 'That's my indulgence. I just adore playing rummy.'

'I can play, though I haven't for a while, I must admit,' Sarah replied. She, Myrtle, her step-da Bob and others had often played on Saturday nights in Netherton, all of them drinking beer and shandies, with whisky on the table when that could be afforded.

'Good. I've brought a pack with me. Gives us something to do while we natter to one another.' Olivia opened her Dorothy bag and extracted the referred-to pack of cards. Then she had a thought which made her pause.

'Hadn't you better give Miss Hawke what you brought for her before we get involved in rummy?' she said to Adam.

If Adam had blushed previously, now he went positively scarlet.

'For me!' Sarah exclaimed. That explained the brown paper parcel. It *was* for her after all.

Adam shuffled his feet in embarrassment. He'd been so looking forward to giving the gift to Sarah, now he didn't want to. In fact it was the last thing he wanted to do. He just wished the floor would open up and swallow him.

'It's eh . . .' He cleared his throat, his voice having gone all tight and husky. 'It's nothing much.'

She smiled at him, waiting. This was exciting.

'Get on with it!' Olivia urged, amused to see her brother so windy.

Adam lifted the parcel, jiggled it in his hands before going swiftly over to Sarah and handing it to her. 'As I said, it's nothing really. But I thought you might like it. Consider it a season's token from me, from the three of us.'

'From *you*,' Primrose corrected. 'Ollie and I had absolutely nothing to do with it.'

Adam shot his younger sister a look that would have sunk a battleship.

Sarah laid the parcel across her lap, and began untying the string.

'I've a penknife here,' Adam said, fumbling in his trouser pockets.

'I'll undo it if you don't mind,' Sarah told him. In Netherton she'd been brought up never to destroy a piece of string which might be used again. Waste not, want not, Myrtle had always said.

Finally the string fell away, and she started folding back the brown paper.

'I think it's terrific,' Olivia said, taking another puff of her cigarette, thinking how sophisticated the cigarette must make her seem.

Inside the brown paper was thick cardboard. When Sarah opened that she found an unframed oil painting inside, *of herself*.

'As I said, it's nothing much,' Adam muttered.

Sarah was spellbound. Not by the fact it was a picture of her, but because it was her to the life. It was like staring into a mirror, and yet not staring into one, for there was far more of her in the picture than she'd see in any mirror. Somehow, as if by magic, Adam had translated her very essence into her face, her face now representing her total being, inside as well as out, mental as well as physical.

'You can throw it away if you don't care for it, I won't be offended,' Adam said.

'Don't be daft! It's . . .' She groped for the right word. 'It's superb. Positively superb.'

His face brightened. 'You really mean that?'

'I most certainly do. I'm honoured to accept this, and will treasure it always.'

'He's been going at it hammer and tongs ever since you visited us,' Primrose said, for which she got another sinker.

Sarah gazed at the picture again. It had so much depth, and feeling, and sensitivity. The picture seemed so alive that if it had opened its mouth – her mouth – and spoken to her she wouldn't have been at all surprised.

'Thank you, thank you very, very much,' she said to Adam, who went scarlet for a second time.

'Now what about that rummy,' Olivia smiled.

'So how did it go?' Jock asked. He'd been elsewhere in the house while the Tennants had been there, but had come down to say goodbye, and see them off.

'Fine. They're excellent company, particularly Olivia; I like her a lot.'

'A potential friend eh?'

'I think so.'

'Good, you need a friend of your own age. See that you encourage the relationship. Feel free to invite her and the others over any time you wish.'

She grasped him by the arm. 'Come on into the library, I want to show you something.'

He followed her without protest into the library where Adam's picture of her was standing on a chair.

'What do you think of that?' she asked proudly.

'Why it's . . . it's you.' He went closer to the picture, and stared at it.

'Adam did it. I think it's superb.'

'It's certainly a good likeness. Can't deny that. I recognised you right off.'

'Dad!' she exclaimed, peeved. 'It's a lot more than just a good likeness. It's art, and high quality art in my opinion.'

Jock raised his eyebrows, and had another long look at the

picture. It was on the tip of his tongue to tease her by asking how she would know about high quality art, being brought up in Netherton, a mining village, as she had. But he refrained from doing so, thinking that might be a bit below the belt.

'To be truthful, girl,' he replied instead, 'I wouldn't know art, high quality or otherwise, if I fell across it in the street. It's something I've never interested myself in, possibly because I have no feel for it.'

He gave her an impish grin. 'Now show me a well-kept and balanced ledger and I'll wax lyrical right enough.'

She laughed at that, ledger indeed! But she knew what he meant. 'I'd like it framed, and framed well. It deserves that.'

'Then take it into Glasgow and have it done, the best frame in the shop. That's the least I can do for high quality art,' he said, putting special emphasis on the last three words.

'Are you making fun of me?' she demanded, pretending anger.

'Who, me?'

They both dissolved into laughter. It was moments like these he cherished, and he thanked God for her coming to live with him after all those lost, lonely years for him while she'd been in Netherton with Myrtle.

'You get the very best frame there is,' he repeated, a slight choke in his voice.

Sarah studied the picture yet again. Adam really was so talented, she thought, and fell to brooding about that.

The Honourable Ian Monteith had set her a poser. He'd written inviting her to go bicycling with him, and what did you wear for that! Even the seemingly all-knowing Elinor had been at a loss. Finally, after much consultation between the pair of them they had decided that a sensible jacket and skirt would be the answer.

The tailored jacket they'd chosen was of black cloth, with long lapels and sleeves puffed and gathered at the top; her waistcoat of pale grey satin, with a pattern of dark red dots. Her man's wing collar and dark red knotted tie was worn with a stiff shirt front.

Her flared skirt was of grey tweed with two narrow bands of black braid near the hem. The whole ensemble was in the style known as the 'New Woman'.

Elinor was pinning Sarah's hat into place, a grey felt hat with a black band that imitated a man's Homburg, and which had a combination of black and grey feathers stitched to its front, when there was a knock on the bedroom door.

'Come in!' Sarah called out.

It was Mrs McGuffie, for once looking slightly flustered.

'What do you think, will I do?' Sarah asked, still anxious that she'd chosen the right outfit to wear.

Mrs McGuffie, despite being flustered, stopped inside the door to give Sarah the once-over. 'Turn round,' she said after Sarah's hat was fixed in place.

Sarah complied. 'Well?'

'You'll do.'

'Sure about that?'

'Quite. I certainly can't think of anything else in your wardrobe that would be more suitable.'

That pleased Sarah, and settled her anxiety somewhat. She wasn't particularly bothered at having a rendezvous with the Honourable Ian, but she would have been upset to think she'd let Jock – and herself – down in any way by presenting herself unsuitably dressed.

Mrs McGuffie waved a sheaf of papers at Sarah. 'Mr Hawke left these behind and I just know he's going to need them before the morning is over. As you're already going to the Monteiths could you make a slight detour and drop them off to him at Carlton Place?'

'Of course,' Sarah replied instantly, and accepted the papers from Mrs McGuffie. 'I'm leaving in a few minutes' time, so he should have them within the hour.'

'I wouldn't bother you, but I know they're important.'

Sarah knew they were important as well; she and Jock had discussed their contents the previous night in the library during one of their after-dinner sessions when he used her as a 'sounding-board'.

'You can stop worrying, Mrs McGuffie, leave them to me.'

'Right then.'

Mrs McGuffie crossed to the window and looked up at the leaden sky. 'I hope it isn't going to rain, that might spoil your day.'

'To be truthful, I wouldn't be too upset if it did. I'm not at all certain I fancy the idea of bicycling.'

'Rather you than me, Miss,' Elinor muttered.

'And it's lunch first with the Viscount present?'

'So Ian said in his letter.'

Mrs McGuffie wagged a cautionary finger at her. 'He's a terrible old roué, so make sure you keep well out of range of those wandering hands of his.'

Sarah didn't know what a roué was, but the gist was clear. 'Thanks for the warning. As they say, to be forewarned is to be forearmed.'

'He's an old sweetie really,' Mrs McGuffie said, 'it's just that he does have an awful weakness where women are concerned.'

Sarah would have loved to ask more about Lord Ascog and his awful weakness for women; it sounded intriguing. But there wasn't time for that. Perhaps later if she could get the housekeeper alone.

Elinor went down with Sarah to her carriage while Mrs McGuffie went about her housekeeping duties.

As the carriage clattered away from Stiellsmuir, and across the stone bridge below which a burn normally slowly meandered, but which was now frozen solid, Sarah laid the papers Mrs McGuffie had given her on her lap, and began reading the top sheet.

She and Jock might have discussed what the papers contained the night before, but that wasn't quite the same as actually reading and studying the papers themselves and the problems they contained to which Jock was desperately trying to find solutions.

She was still deeply engrossed when the carriage rattled into Carlton Place.

She recognised the voice while still outside Jock's office: it was that of Captain Wilson. She hadn't realised he was in port. This would be the first time she'd seen him since the party at Stiellsmuir when he'd turned up with the gorgeous Miss Bessie Wallace from Boston, Massachusetts. Or that bloody woman, as she still thought of Miss Bessie Wallace, descendant of William.

Smith, the clerk who was escorting her, didn't so much as knock the door as scratch on it. Sarah didn't wait for a reply, but marched straight in.

'Sarah!' Jock exclaimed, surprised.

There was another man present, an older man than Wilson, but dressed in the same uniform.

'I've brought these, you left them behind,' Sarah explained, and handed Jock the sheaf of papers.

'I . . .' Jock shrugged. 'I hadn't realised. Thank goodness you brought them, I need them this morning.'

'Which is why I made a detour on my way to the Monteiths.'

'Thank you.' And having said that he kissed her on the cheek.

She turned to the watching Wilson and gave him a dazzling smile. 'Why hello Captain, how pleasant to see you again.' She somehow contrived to make it sound as if that wasn't really so.

Wilson frowned a little. 'And it's pleasant to see you again, Miss Hawke.'

'You haven't met Captain MacQuarrie yet, Sarah. He's the captain of my brigantine *Snowdrop*.'

Captain MacQuarrie extended a hand. 'Delighted to meet you, Miss Hawke.'

She shook the captain's hand. 'And you Captain.'

'Captain MacQuarrie has just returned from Nigeria with a cargo of palm oil,' Jock explained.

Sarah already knew that; details of MacQuarrie's voyage were contained in the papers she'd just given Jock. 'How interesting!' she exclaimed, pretending this was news to her, while at the same time contriving to present her back to Wilson.

'Was it an easy trip?' she asked MacQuarrie.

'Fair ma'am, fair.'

Not much of a talker, Sarah thought. Pity that. 'And how long are you ashore for this trip, Captain?'

He glanced at Jock. 'Three days ma'am, then we're off again.'

'Back to Nigeria?' She was already aware that was the *Snowdrop*'s destination.

'Yes ma'am. More palm oil, the good Lord and the Royal Niger Company willing.'

'Have you got time to take coffee with us, Sarah?' Jock queried.

She pulled a face. 'Not really. I'm due at the Monteiths for lunch and it wouldn't do to be late and keep the Viscount waiting, now would it?'

'Most certainly not,' Jock agreed.

She'd totally alienated Wilson now. He was hovering on the periphery, quite out of the conversation. In her mind's eye she stuck out her tongue at him. Bessie Wallace from Boston, Massachusetts, indeed!

'Well I suppose I'd better be on my way,' she announced.

'I'll come downstairs with you,' Jock volunteered.

'No, you stay here and get on with your business. I can find my own way, I assure you.'

She turned again to MacQuarrie. 'Well goodbye, Captain, and I hope we meet again, and for longer. If we do you can tell me all about Nigeria.'

'That I most certainly will do, ma'am, given the opportunity.'

She indulged in a further piece of play-acting.She made as if she was going for the door, then suddenly 'remembered' that Wilson was also present.

'And goodbye to you, Captain Wilson.'

'Goodbye, Miss Hawke.' She was a puzzle right enough, he was thinking. They'd got on so well together that day aboard the *Good Intent*, and now here she was treating him as though he didn't really exist. Or worse still, was some sort of bad smell under her nose. Who would ever understand women? Certainly not him.

'And don't forget, my regards to Lord Ascog,' Jock said, repeating what he'd told her over breakfast, as he walked her the remainder of the distance to the door.

'I won't forget.' At the door she glanced over her shoulder. 'Goodbye again, Captain MacQuarrie.'

Smiling, she swept from Jock's office. Put that in your pipe and smoke it, she thought, referring to Wilson.

But she did have to admit he had looked lovely, lovely enough to eat. That was a saying she'd once heard in Netherton.

The office door was no sooner shut behind her than the smile dropped from her face.

Lord Ascog was a small man with a bald head and huge protruding belly. He also had the same liquid brown eyes that Ian had—come-to-bed eyes she now thought of them as.

'More claret, dear?' he smiled.

She placed a hand over her glass. 'No thank you, I've had enough sir.'

'*Bertie*,' he stressed. 'I insist you call me Bertie.'

She found it difficult calling a viscount, and peer of the realm, by his Christian name; it seemed so presumptious and impertinent on her part. 'Sorry, *Bertie*,' she replied.

'Well I'm going to have some, what.' He signalled to the servant who strode over to refill his glass. Ian declared that he too would have a top-up.

'That really was delicious,' Sarah said, having just finished the main course which had been game pie and winter vegetables, the starter a warming cock-a-leekie soup.

Bertie stared at Sarah over the rim of his glass. 'You're certainly a looker, gel. Can't argue with that,' he said.

Sarah flushed. 'Thank you.'

'Oh she's a cracker all right. An angel descended,' Ian agreed.

Sarah shot him a reproving sideways look. That was going a bit far.

'I was hoping you'd show me round before we start bicycling,' she suggested to Ian.

'Fully intended to.'

Bertie took a deep swallow of his claret. 'So tell me something about yourself, Sarah. Don't know a thing. Jock's kept me perfect stumm about it. Could have knocked me over with the proverbial feather when I heard he was the sire of a young filly that he'd kept tucked away all these years. Damned devious of the chap, what?'

She hesitated. To tell her story, or not?

'Actually she was kidnapped when two years old by a Chinese gang,' Ian said mischievously.

'What!' Bertie's eyes popped. 'You never said, lad!'

Ian ignored that. 'They took her to Shanghai where she stayed in a prince's castle. When she was old enough it was intended she be his fifteenth wife, and the only non-Chinese one. But before the evil sod could have his wicked way with her she escaped. Isn't that so, Sarah?'

'Well I'll be!' Bertie exclaimed, flabbergasted.

She made a decision. 'It's a load of tommy-rot really. I made that tale up the night of the party to amuse myself – and you too of course, Ian.'

'Of course,' Ian agreed, the corners of his mouth twitching in a half-smile.

'Not true, eh?' a disappointed Bertie demanded.

'Not a word of it.'

Bertie threw back his head and laughed. 'Chinese gang, Shanghai, very good!' Then, more soberly, 'That's quite an imagination you've got there, lass.'

'I've always had it. As a little girl I used to make up stories, it helped pass the time.'

Bertie had another gulp of his claret. He was enjoying this conversation – the girl had spirit. Not like some of those more-dead-than-alive creatures that had been brought to meet him in the past.

'Before Stiellsmuir I stayed with my mother,' Sarah explained.

'Jock's ex-wife?' Bertie queried.

Sarah sidestepped that by just not answering the question.

Bertie shook his head in amazement. 'Until Ian mentioned you I had no idea that Jock had even been married. He's kept very closemouthed about the fact.'

They fell silent while their plates were cleared away, and fresh ones laid. Sarah wondered what was for pudding; she adored puddings.

'And where did you live with your mother?' Bertie asked after slices of tart and cream had been placed in front of them.

'Netherton,' Sarah replied.

Bertie looked blank, while Ian was frowning. 'Netherton?' Bertie repeated.

'It's a mining community on the north side of Glasgow. Mr Dundonald owns the pit there, the pit where my step-da worked until he had a stroke.'

'Your step-father was a collier?' Bertie queried.

Sarah nodded.

The corners of Ian's mouth were twitching again; he thought this to be another story.

'It's true. Honestly,' she said to Ian, and got stuck into her tart and cream.

When she glanced up again both men were staring at her as if she'd suddenly sprouted horns. 'Do you wish me to leave?' she asked quietly.

'Certainly not!' Bertie exclaimed.

'That really *is* true?' Ian demanded.

'Yes. I went to Netherton when I was two, and lived there until going to Stiellsmuir. Jock Hawke may have been my father, but I was brought up as a miner's daughter. And . . .' She paused for emphasis. 'I'm proud of it too. I want you to understand that.'

'Well, well, well,' Ian breathed, and saw off what remained in his glass. He instantly signed that he wanted a refill.

'And you say your step-father had a stroke?' Bertie probed.

'Yes.' That was as far as she intended going, there would be no elaboration. Or if there was it would have to come at another time, and from Jock himself.

Bertie and Ian tried to pry further, but Sarah would have none of it. She had told them all she was going to.

After a short while, the message having got home, Bertie changed the conversation to start talking about horses. He was a devotee of horses as were both his sons.

When lunch was over, Ian asked Sarah if she'd care to freshen up before he showed her round, to which she replied she would. As she mounted the stairs, following a servant leading the way, to the nearest toilet and bathroom on the floor above, she could hear Ian and Bertie conversing in low voices below.

About her revelation, no doubt, she thought grimly to herself.

Sarah and Ian were in the stables where he'd brought her directly after taking her round the house, which was far larger than Stiellsmuir. And not only larger but the authentic article, dating back in parts to the early sixteenth century.

'We've got a dozen riding horses in all, and these three beauties are mine,' Ian said, indicating three stalls and the horses in them with a forefinger.

'And the others?'

'Pa has two, James the remainder.'

Sarah was sorry she hadn't met brother James, the one who would inherit, but he was in Perth on estate business.

'You like horses?' Ian inquired, coming closer to her.

'Yes, although I don't ride myself.'

'Didn't get a chance to in Netherton?'

It was the first time he'd referred to Netherton since the lunch table.

'That's right.'

'Who would have thought you were a little peasant, eh?'

It was done before she knew it. Her open hand flashed to crack against his cheek, sending him staggering backwards.

'If I am a little peasant, as you put it, it's extremely rude of you to say so,' she told him, voice as cold as ice.

She was right of course, it had been extremly rude of him. He couldn't think why he had behaved in such an ungentlemanly manner, except there was a quality about her that got under his skin. She was quite unlike all the other girls he knew, or had known. But then none of them had been brought up as a miner's daughter.

He pounced on her, pulling her tightly to him. She struggled, but to no avail; thanks to his exceptionally broad shoulders and

122

surprisingly well-developed arms he was very strong indeed. Far more than a match for her.

Next moment his mouth was pressed against hers, his tongue trying to penetrate the barrier of her clenched teeth.

'Hmmm!' she protested, continuing to try and break free. 'Hmmm!'

He removed his mouth from hers, to kiss her neck. He yelped, then cursed when she bit his.

'Let me go!' she said forcefully.

'You're fabulous when you're angry.'

'Tell me something Honourable Ian, do you always behave like an animal when you're alone with a girl, or do I merit special treatment?'

'I repeat, you're fabulous when you're angry.'

'I think I would like to go home now. Could you please have Sheach summoned for me.' Sheach was with the Viscount's servants, probably in the kitchen.

Ian was right about one thing, she thought. She was angry. In fact she was furious. How dare he assault her like this. Arrogant pig!

Ian released her, and ran both hands through his hair which had become dishevelled in their tussle.

'I eh . . . I am sorry,' he said contritely. He moved away to the closest stall which he leaned up against. His heart was thundering like mad, and there was a dull throbbing in his temples. He was also incredibly sexually aroused.

Sarah waited, wanting him to go and have Sheach summoned. If he didn't do it soon she'd do it herself. She wished to be away from here. Little peasant indeed!

'I don't normally behave like this. I just don't know what came over me.'

'Perhaps it was the thought of "slumming it" that got you all worked up.'

He winced. 'I deserved that.'

'Did you suddenly think I was easy because you'd learned something of my background? Or if not easy, perhaps someone to be abused, ridden roughshod over?' She positively spat the next bit. 'Is that how you treat the maids in the house, the little peasants? Is it a forced kiss and maybe more in the dark corners and broom cupboards? Is that how you treat them, knowing they won't complain because they need the work?'

123

Ian had gone quite pale. 'No I don't. As I said to you, and as God is my judge it's the holy truth, I've never behaved like this until now.'

Despite not wanting to believe him, she did. There was that in his eyes and tone told her so.

'Why me?' she asked softly.

'I find you . . . I just find you . . .' He trailed off, reluctant to verbalise how he did find her.

'I understand.'

'You do?'

She allowed a soft smile to creep on to her face. 'Yes, I think so.'

He bent down, picked up a piece of straw, and whisked the stall door with it. 'I've said I'm sorry, and I meant it. Can we start again? Afresh?' Then, when she didn't reply, 'Please, Sarah?'

She couldn't resist the jibe. 'Even though I'm a little peasant?'

'But a lovely one,' he countered, which made her laugh. Who wouldn't have when his reply was delivered with such charm and sincerity?

'Will you accept my apology, Sarah?'

Her fury had disappeared, completely melted away. 'What surprises me more than anything is for you to be so uncouth. That seems totally out of character.'

'Yes, it is,' he agreed.

Return to Stiellsmuir, or stay on? She was still undecided. She should go home after what had happened, and yet . . . 'Where are these bicycles?' she asked.

He took a deep breath. 'Come on, they're round at the back of here waiting for us.'

As they left the stables she found herself wondering what he'd be like to go to bed with. Imagine being made love to by an Honourable. She almost giggled at the thought.

The air stung her cheeks as they bicycled along, and her eyes had begun to water. Within the last half hour the temperature had dropped considerably.

All her worrying about the actual bicycling itself had been for nothing. The machines, which belonged to friends of James's apparently, were three-wheelers and not two, which meant they were an absolute dawdle to use. A sense of balance, or previous experience, wasn't needed in the least.

She put a little more effort into it, and caught up with Ian who'd been slightly ahead.

'Tremendous fun, isn't it!' he said.

'Fun, but freezing with it. Can we turn back before I solidify altogether?'

They'd cycled roughly four miles, a fair old distance, Ian thought. He'd thoroughly enjoyed it so far, and it seemed Sarah had too. But he had to agree, the cold was becoming penetrating.

'Listen, there's a public house just ahead. Why don't we stop there and warm ourselves with hot toddies?' he suggested.

Hot toddies sounded marvellous, the very dab to give the troops. 'Right!' she agreed, and put a spurt on. 'I'll race you! Last one there is a rotten egg!'

'You're on!' he shouted in reply.

He allowed her to win, feeling he had to. After all, if either of them was a rotten egg that day it had to be him after what he'd said and done in the stables.

The pub was called the Saracen's Head and, much to their delight, had a huge log fire blazing in the lounge. Sarah headed straight for the fire while Ian went up to the bar to place their orders.

God but it was bitter out, Sarah thought as she briskly rubbed her hands together. She smiled with pleasure as the heat washed over her.

While Ian waited for the hot toddies he glanced around. There were a number of others present in the lounge, including the back of a head that looked vaguely familiar.

He was idly wondering who the head belonged to, thinking it must be someone from the estate or environs, when the man turned to present his profile to him.

'Aubrey!' Ian exclaimed in a voice that carried right across the room.

Next moment he was striding over to grasp the hand of an old pal. 'Aubrey, how are you! And what on earth are you doing in Scotland?'

Sarah watched this from in front of the fire.

Aubrey, on his feet now, pumped Ian's hand, while thumping him on the shoulder. 'Dear boy, it's marvellous to see Absolutely marvellous.'

When the toddies were placed on the bar, Aubrey come and meet Sarah and have a dr was drinking a gin and tonic, and Ian immediately ordered him a double.

'Sarah, I'd like you to say hello to an old school chum of mine, and very dear friend. C. Aubrey Smith, this is Sarah Hawke.'

'Delighted,' smiled Aubrey, and taking hold of Sarah's hand kissed her fingers.

'And I'm pleased to meet you,' Sarah replied, thinking to herself that the man was an Englishman, the first she'd ever encountered. English or not he was a handsome devil. Everything about him positively screamed of the aristocracy.

The three of them sat. 'So what brings you to Scotland?' Ian asked again.

Aubrey gestured at the group he'd left. 'A play. We open in Glasgow tomorrow evening.'

'Aubrey's something of an actor,' Ian explained to Sarah. 'He acts when he's not playing cricket.'

Aubrey laughed. 'The two great passions of my life, I have to confess.'

Sarah knew nothing whatever of cricket, it just wasn't a Scottish sport. When played north of the border it was only amongst a rarefied circle.

Aubrey went on. 'The principals of the cast – which are those ladies and gentlemen over there and myself – decided to have a day out in the country while the set-up takes place. Dress tomorrow afternoon, first perf at 8 pm sharp.'

This was double Dutch to Sarah. 'I hardly understood a word of that,' she told Aubrey.

He grinned sheepishly. 'Sorry, I've just been talking shop and forgot you weren't one of the initiated. The set-up is when they assemble the scenery, or set, which usually takes an entire day as it can be fairly involved. The dress is the dress rehearsal, and the first perf is the first performance.'

'I see, I understand now,' she nodded.

'And how long do you play Glasgow for?' Ian inquired.

'Two weeks, then it's through to Edinburgh, with Dundee and Aberdeen after that.'

'And from Aberdeen?' Sarah asked.

He shrugged. 'That's the finish. We're only a touring production, and Aberdeen is the end of the tour.'

'No West End then?' Ian smiled.

126

'Not this time, old boy.'

'Well I for one will be there tomorrow night to cheer you on,' Ian declared. 'Will you come with me, Sarah?'

'Buckets of champagne afterwards if you do,' Aubrey told her, and winked.

'Of course I'll go. Now that I've met you, a member of the cast, how could I possibly not?'

'Jolly good!' Aubrey enthused, and saw off some of his g & t.

'When did you arrive in Glasgow?' Sarah enquired.

'Last night, after a foul journey from Newcastle-upon-Tyne. We were there for a week, Manchester before that.'

The hot toddie had done the trick. Sarah was completely thawed out now. Between the toddie and the fire she felt quite toasty inside and out.

Sarah decided she liked this C. Aubrey Smith, Englishman or not. He was extremely easy to be with and, as was rapidly being shown, tremendous company. She could well understand why Ian was so keen on him.

'But tell me about your cricket – what have you been up to in that direction?' Ian asked, explaining to Sarah, 'Aubrey plays for Sussex as an amateur.' Then to Aubrey again, 'You still do, don't you?'

'Yes. But don't you follow the game any more?' Aubrey replied, looking amazed.

Ian shook his head. 'Lost touch and interest I'm afraid Just one of those things.'

'Well if you hadn't lost touch you would have read that I captained the first English team to visit South Africa. We were there two years ago at the beginning of eighty-nine.'

'I say, that must have been a tremendous experience. And you the captain too!' Ian enthused.

'Fabulous trip, thoroughly enjoyed myself. One of the most spectacular countries I've ever seen.'

'And the grounds you played in, what were they like?'

Aubrey pulled a face. 'Most a bit . . . provincial, shall we say. Though the Wanderers Club in Johannesburg was excellent, couldn't fault that at all.'

Sarah frowned. 'Isn't Johannesburg where they found gold?'

'Indeed they have. Vast diggings everywhere, with fortunes being made overnight. Gold in the Witwatersrand, which is Afrikaans for Ridge of White Waters, and diamonds in Kimberley.'

Ian's eyes gleamed. 'Gold and diamonds, now those are two words to conjure with.'

'It's quite a place, I can tell you, though in many areas very primitive. Johannesburg is still little more than a shanty town, but it does have a great future ahead of it. Unless the gold runs out that is, and so far there's no sign of that.'

'I'm surprised you weren't tempted to stay on,' Ian said.

'To be truthful I was. But there's no theatre as such there. And the cricket, to date, is just not in the same class as that we play here.' He nodded. 'Nonetheless, I was tempted.'

The three of them spoke for a little while longer about cricket and various other topics, then Aubrey took them over to meet the other principals of his play.

When it was time for Sarah and Ian to leave, Aubrey saw them to the pub door, he and his party having decided to stay put a bit longer.

At the door Ian repeated that he and Sarah would be in the audience the following night, and Aubrey said they were to be certain and come backstage afterwards. Then, with Aubrey waving them on their way, they began their return journey.

They hadn't gone far when the germ of an idea was born in Sarah's mind, an idea that had sprung directly from their meeting and conversation with Mr C. Aubrey Smith.

The final curtain rang down to still thunderous applause, no one applauding more enthusiastically than Sarah. Although she hadn't confided it to Ian, this was her first visit to a proper theatre, and the first play she'd ever seen. Throughout the entire performance she'd sat entranced. The play was *The Government Inspector*, written by the Russian dramatist Nikolai Gogol, and Aubrey had taken the title role, the part of Ivan Alexandrovitch Hlestakov.

According to the programme notes – Sarah had devoured the programme from cover to cover before the curtain had gone up – *The Government Inspector*, sometimes called 'The Inspector General', was a landmark in Russian literature, and had initially been performed on 19 March 1836, at the Imperial Theatre in the presence of the Tsar himself, Nicholas I.

'Wonderful, wasn't it,' Ian whispered to her as the applause started to fade.

'Absolutely.'

'Haven't seen Aubrey act in years. He was good then, but even better now.'

'He's excellent,' Sarah agreed.

Finally the applause died away altogether, replaced by excited and appreciative chatter as the audience began filing up the passageways that would take them to the foyer, and the cold crisp night beyond.

At the stage door the doorkeeper said that Aubrey had left instructions and they should go straight to his dressing-room which was number one, to be found on the left just along the corridor.

Aubrey, clad in a satin dressing-gown, greeted them with open arms, and a kiss on the cheek for Sarah.

'You were terrific, old chap,' Ian said, his voice loaded with sincerity.

'Great play and part, difficult to go wrong in either,' Aubrey replied modestly.

'I can't say about that, but you certainly shone out there tonight. Congratulations,' Sarah told him.

Aubrey's reply to that was to give her a second kiss, this time on the other cheek.

As Aubrey opened a bottle of Tattinger that had been cooling in a nest of ice he said, 'I usually go out with some of the others for dinner after the show – would you two care to join me as my guests?'

'That sounds top-hole!' Ian beamed. 'Sarah?'

'Yes, I'd like that very much indeed,' she replied, thinking this suited her own plans perfectly.

As Ian and Sarah sipped glasses of Tattinger, Aubrey slipped behind an exotically decorated screen and changed, while members of the cast and other theatre employees came and went, all having a drink – a second bottle was opened by Ian at Aubrey's request – and generally contributing to the conversation.

It was a jolly atmosphere backstage, Sarah thought as she chatted to a woman called Diana who'd played the mayor's wife, and who looked nothing at all in real life to how she had on stage.

When they reached the restaurant, Sarah grasped Aubrey by the arm. 'Do you think I could sit beside you? There are a few things I'd like to discuss with you if you don't mind.'

Aubrey's eyes were raised in surprise. 'Of course, my dear. The pleasure will be mine.'

Throughout the meal she quizzed him about South Africa, asking him a great many questions, some of which he had the answers to, some of which he didn't.

Jock was sunk in gloom, his eyes unfocused as he gazed down at the large whisky and soda he was holding.

Sarah, sitting opposite, felt this was now the right moment.

'Jock?'

She had to repeat herself, and speak more loudly, to rouse him. 'Jock?'

He cleared his throat. 'Hmmm?'

'Can I have your attention?'

He pulled himself upright in his chair, and swallowed about half of what was in his glass. 'Yes, of course. What is it?'

'I'd like to make a suggestion.' She was tense inside, though confident of what she was about to propose. Her sole worry was that Jock might not take her seriously because she was a woman.

'About what?'

She lit a cigarette. 'Your problems with palm oil.'

He stared at her, his eyes suddenly diamond hard. 'Go on,' he said slowly.

'Your friend Ranald Cyril McIvor has allied himself with Miller Bros. of Liverpool, correct?' She had his total attention now, the diamonds seemed to be boring into her own eyes.

Jock nodded.

'Together they're undercutting the price of Nigerian palm oil in Britain to such an extent that they're rapidly making it prohibitive for other traders to deal in that commodity.'

'Miller Bros. are a huge concern which can afford to undercut for months, if not years, if needs be. And Miller Bros. are the financial backing behind McIvor,' Jock replied.

'Their combined intention would appear to be quite clear. They are out to secure a monopoly of Nigerian palm oil, and once that monopoly is achieved, and they have cornered the home market, they will inflate the price to double or treble what it was originally, perhaps even more, and thereby put themselves in the position to sustain a long-term killing.'

Jock produced a cigar, and clipped it. 'That would appear to be the case. The Royal Niger Company could stop this monopoly happening of course, but as long as they have an outlet for their product I doubt they care one way or the other. Unless, that is, Miller Bros. and McIvor tried to impose terms on them, which would then be a different story, but Miller Bros. and McIvor are far too intelligent for that.'

'You thought you had an answer to all this, but that failed.'

Jock nodded again, the diamonds glittering, shooting off sparks of cold green fire. 'That was before the overall pattern became clear. Now I can't see a way round losing this trade.'

'Which you don't want to lose because it's so profitable?'

'That's right. A difficult cargo to get hold of mind you, due to there being so many traders there vying with you, and entitled to their share. That's why I only have the *Snowdrop* on the Nigerian run. Timewise it just wouldn't be worthwhile putting others on to it.'

'Which is what Miller Bros. and McIvor must have thought as well, until they came up with this little scheme to rid themselves of the competition. Squeezing out the other traders by undercutting, then inflating the price to goodness knows what when they have a monopoly – and, should anyone try to break that monopoly, simply undercutting once more till that trader gives up again.'

'It'll be like a goose laying continual golden eggs for them,' Jock said quietly.

Sarah paused while the mantelpiece clock chimed the quarter hour. Then she went on. 'The other thing I wish to establish with you is that the Royal Niger Company, being founded under a Royal Charter – which it was five years ago – only deals with British firms. There are no foreign firms, or even other members of the Empire, involved here?'

'Correct,' Jock agreed.

'So if I read this correctly, the agreement between Miller Bros. and McIvor is that the Millers get the English, Welsh and Irish markets, McIvor the Scottish one?'

'That has to be it,' Jock concurred. 'I have no idea why Miller Bros. felt they needed a Scottish partner, but no doubt they have their reasons.'

'Perhaps because the original conception of the monopoly was McIvor's? That might explain it.'

That was possible, Jock thought. Now why hadn't he seen it that way round? It was astute of Sarah to have done so.

Sarah continued. 'Now let's talk about palm oil itself. We need it

131

because it's the most important constituent in soap manufacture. And Nigerian palm oil not only comes in abundance, but is of exceptionally high quality. Is that not so?'

'It is.'

'There are other producers of palm oil on the African continent, but the quality of the oil is low, and it isn't in the hands of the British but rather the French, Germans, Portuguese and others.'

'Correct again,' Jock acknowledged. He was impressed, very much so. She really had done her homework. Her grasp of the subject was impeccable so far, her articulacy such that she might have been dealing in business for years.

As though reading his mind, Sarah explained. 'I read and studied those papers I brought to you at the office the other day. I've also been doing quite a bit of research on my own.'

Jock blew out a long thin stream of smoke. 'I'm still waiting for this suggestion you mentioned.'

'I'll come to that in due course – I want to establish the facts first.' She paused, wishing she'd had the foresight to have had a cup of tea to hand which she could have murdered at that point, then plunged on.

'Nigerian palm oil comes to this country where it's made into soap, and only this country. Why?'

Jock looked blank. 'Why only *this* country?'

'Yes, why?'

'It's part of our domestic cycle. We import the palm oil, manufacturers turn it into soap which we then export again. The country as a whole benefits from both actions.'

'But there's nothing dictates you have to import it to Britain, is there?'

Jock chewed the end of his cigar. He was damned if he could see what Sarah was driving at. 'No, there's nothing dictates *that*, there are no binding agreements, or legislation, if that's what you mean.'

'So, and it's blindingly obvious if you think about it, if Miller Bros. and McIvor are hell-bent on securing a monopoly in Britain, why not just take your palm oil elsewhere?'

He stared at her, quite dumbstruck. It *was* blindingly obvious. As obvious as the nose on his face.

'And if you do so, Jock, you won't be subject to undercutting by Miller Bros. and McIvor. In fact I should imagine you'll make even more profit than you have been up until now. Miller Bros.

132

and McIvor will still achieve their monopoly of course, but what's that to you?'

He finished what remained in his glass. It had just never occurred to him to go elsewhere. He imported into Britain, and exported out of it, that was the established practice, tradition if you like. But Sarah was right, why should it remain that way?

'Did you have anywhere in mind?' he queried.

'South Africa,' she shot back instantly.

'Why there?'

'It's the nearest sizeable white market to Nigeria, and a market that's expanding daily. People have been pouring in there since diamonds and gold were discovered.'

She was certainly right about the influx of people into South Africa, Jock thought. He'd read a newspaper article on the subject only the previous week.

Sarah went on. 'At the moment soap is shipped there from Britain, where it must be an expensive item to buy. Now I have no idea if there are any local soap manufacturers, and if there are, the soap they're turning out must be pretty poor stuff. But with our Nigerian palm oil they could transform the quality of their produce to match that which is being imported.'

'And if there aren't any local soap manufacturers, what then?'

'You promise a regular supply of Nigerian palm oil and there soon will be. The venture would be a certain winner with a guaranteed high profit margin,' Sarah argued.

'If it did work,' Jock mused, 'then the other traders that Miller Bros. and McIvor are squeezing out would soon be down in Cape Town with me selling their palm oil.'

'But the important point to remember is that you would have been there first, with all the benefits that entails. You would be in an unassailable position.'

'All right then, let's say I've sold my palm oil. What do I buy to bring back to this country?'

'Cotton, sugar cane, wheat, groundnuts, fruit and vegetables if the *Snowdrop* is fast enough to get them here before they spoil, and sunflower seeds,' she replied.

Jock came slowly to his feet, and went over to where the whisky decanter was. He poured himself another whisky, then one for Sarah.

'What do you think?' she asked, the merest hint of a tremble in her voice.

'I'll have to make a number of inquiries, speak to various folk, but I have to admit your plan makes sense. Off the top of my head I see no reason why it can't be viable.'

A warm glow of satisfaction filled her.

'It just means doing things differently to how I have been, and there's certainly no harm in that,' Jock said.

'And once you establish a toehold in that market there's no saying what it might lead to either.'

That was true, Jock thought. 'But what about the political situation? Didn't they have a war down there not so long ago?'

'There were the ones against the Kaffirs, but you must mean the one against the Afrikaners. That was from 1880–81, and is called by the Boers, who won it, the War of Independence.' She paused, then added, 'If there was another war with them, a possibility apparently, according to some sources, it wouldn't matter to us which side won, they'd still need soap.'

Jock laughed, he couldn't fault her logic. Boer or Britisher, they would still need soap. Though the one perhaps more than the other.

'I might go down there personally,' he thought to himself, but speaking out loud.

That was the single fly in the ointment as far as Sarah was concerned; she didn't want him to do that because of his 'moods'. 'Surely that's unnecessary? And possibly even counterproductive in a way. Wouldn't it be best to leave all the on-the-spot organising, negotiating, working out of details, etc. to a local agent, and local face?'

Again she could well be right, Jock thought. This was something else he was going to have to think through should he decide to go ahead with her plan.

He handed Sarah the drink he'd poured for her. 'You're Jock Hawke's daughter right enough,' he said, and raised his glass to toast her.

It was only when she went to sip hers that she realised he'd poured her an identical measure to his own, a large one. The first time he'd ever done that.

Her warm glow of satisfaction deepened in intensity.

She was smiling as she drank.

PART 2

Between Two Shores

Between two shores of Death we drift.
   Behind are things forgot:
Before the tide is driving swift
   To lands beholden not.
Above, the sky is far and cold;
   Below, the moaning sea
Sweeps o'er the loves that were of old,
   But, oh Love! kiss thou me.

H. RIDER HAGGARD
(From Cleopatra)

Chapter 4

Sarah was engrossed in *The Life of Nelson* by Robert Southey which she'd picked up again after dinner – she was still continuing with her daily bouts of afternoon reading – as she was totally gripped by the story of the great man and dying to know what happened next. She was at the part of the narrative where Nelson had hoisted his flag in the *Vanguard* and been ordered to rejoin Earl St Vincent when Jock spoke. They were in the library where he'd been reading his business letters and documents.

'I beg your pardon?' she said, looking up.

'I said the South African undertaking is going absolutely splendidly. I couldn't be more pleased.'

She had to admit to herself that it was a big relief. In fact it was a huge one. Her plan had been viable in theory, but often theory and practice could prove to be two different things entirely. 'Good.'

'And I'd like to show that pleasure in a more substantial way than merely saying thank you.' With that Jock rose, crossed to a small writing desk and there wrote out a bank cheque. He handed it to Sarah.

She gasped when she saw the amount that had been written. 'But I couldn't possibly accept this, you've already given me so much . . .'

He waved her quiet. 'You've earned every penny piece of that, so no protestations please,' he smiled.

She was flabbergasted, quite stunned by his generosity. She swallowed, then swallowed again. 'What shall I do with it?'

'Buy whatever you will. Or put it in the bank in an account of your own should you care to.'

She stared at the cheque, thinking how long her step-da and Gordy would each have to work to earn that amount. With a start she realised this was the first time she'd thought of Gordy in ages. Gordy and Netherton, they both seemed so long, long ago now. It was October 1891, sixteen months since she'd come to Stiellsmuir.

'Thank you,' she said quietly.

'No Sarah, thank *you*. The idea of selling my palm oil in South Africa and then importing to here from there was a brilliant one.'

She laid the cheque on top of a table beside her chair. Spend the money or save it? She didn't know which. Perhaps she'd do both. Spend some, save some.

Jock cleared his throat, and clasped his hands behind his back. His expression became serious. 'There's something I'd like to ask your opinion of, Sarah.'

She memorised the page she was at, closed her book and placed it beside the cheque. When Jock asked her opinion regarding business matters, as he was doing more and more since her palm oil suggestion, she gave him her full and undivided attention.

'As you know, I've made all my money importing and exporting, starting the firm and building it up. Now I'm considering adding a second string to my bow.'

'Which is?'

'Capital investment overseas. I have a considerable amount of cash lying idle in the bank, so why not put it to good use? The eventual return would be far greater than what I get from where it is now.'

'And this wouldn't affect the firm as it now stands?' she queried.

'No, no, nothing like that. The firm would continue exactly as it is.'

She certainly would have been against anything that would have done that. 'What sort of capital investment overseas?' she asked, frowning.

'I don't know yet. I would do that through a broker who deals in such matters.' He paused, then said, 'Such investment is all the rage now in Scotland. We Scots are investing far more capital overseas than any of the other home countries, and that includes mighty England.'

Her frown deepened. 'But why overseas? Why not invest your capital here?'

'Quite simply the return from overseas investment is far, far higher than I could make from any domestic one. But there's also another point – overseas investment generates orders for ships, coal, steel and railway equipment, all sectors of heavy industry that Scotland is heavily committed to. In other words, not only does the Scottish investor expand his personal capital, he is also boosting Scottish industry.'

'I see,' she replied. She smoothed down the front of her dress while she thought. Providing his facts were correct – and she was sure they were – then his argument made sense. There was no denying that. And yet . . .

Jock went on. 'I rather fancy Canada myself. It's a country I've

138

had many dealings with in the past, and have actually been to. I must say I was much impressed by the people and situation there. Much impressed.'

'Why not just buy yourself another ship, and enlarge the business?' she countered.

'That of course has occurred to me, and is definitely what I shall eventually be doing. But in the meantime I rather thought I'd give the overseas investment a fling, same as a large percentage of the chaps at the club are doing.'

'Is Mr Dundonald going to invest?'

'Charlie already has. He sank a considerable sum into the United States earlier on this year.'

'And Lord Ascog?'

Jock shook his head. 'Bertie's wealth is nearly all tied up in equity, the house and estate. He doesn't have any spare capital to invest.'

Seconds ticked by. 'Well?' Jock prompted.

'My own instinct — and it's nothing more than that — is to stay with what you know, and personally control. Overseas investment may be all very well, but you're putting yourself into someone else's hands, and I don't like that.'

'That's precisely what I did in Cape Town when I took on Burnet as my agent,' Jock argued.

'It's not the same thing at all, and well you know it! What Burnet does is an extension of what you already do, an arm of the firm so to speak. Overseas investment managed by a broker is a different thing entirely.'

'You're against it then?'

'No, I'm not,' she replied slowly. 'I'm sure it's an excellent way of making money. It's just that I have reservations for the reasons I've already given you.'

'Hmmm!' Jock mused, rubbing a hand over his chin. Going to the fire, he picked up the brass tongs and put some more coal on.

Sarah wondered whether or not he was finished with her and if she could go back to her book. She was itching to do so. She was deriving tremendous benefits from all the reading she'd been doing since coming to Stiellsmuir. For one thing, her vocabulary was greatly expanded from what it had been, her understanding and knowledge considerably increased. As Jock had done as a lad, she too was learning accountancy, which delighted Jock who was only too eager to explain anything to her that she had trouble understanding. Like her father she'd discovered she not only enjoyed dealing with figures, but that she had a natural flair for them.

Having finished putting more coal on the fire, Jock, with his back to Sarah, now proceeded to jab at it with a poker, opening up airholes at the bottom of the grate.

'To change the subject completely, Mrs McGuffie tells me that you and she are getting on very well together. Is that so?'

The question took Sarah by surprise. What a strange thing to ask her after all this while. 'Yes we are.'

Jock paused in his jabbing, and when he next spoke there was a tightness in his voice. 'Because if there was any conflict between you she could always be replaced. All you would have to do is say.'

A tightness in his voice, and something else? Fear, Sarah decided. A trace of fear, but why should that be so?

Then the penny dropped. He knew she knew about his relationship with the housekeeper, and that was what he was actually referring to. The first time he'd ever done so. He wasn't really asking how she got on with Mrs McGuffie, he was asking for her approval of the liaison.

'I think Mrs McGuffie is a fine woman, and quite irreplaceable.' Sarah knew precisely what she was saying when she added, 'As far as I'm concerned Mrs McGuffie is part and parcel of the household, almost family you might say.'

Jock returned to poking the fire although it didn't need that any more.

Sarah picked up her book and resumed reading.

Sarah's carriage swung into Rose Street, then a few seconds later came to a halt. Sarah looked at Olivia Tennant sitting opposite her and hoped the pair of them were doing the right thing.

Sheach opened the door on to the pavement. 'The Art School, Miss Hawke,' he announced.

Sarah got out first, then Olivia. 'Bring the pictures and drawings please, Sheach,' Sarah instructed the driver. The pictures and drawings she was referring to were all neatly piled next to where she'd been sitting.

Inside the building there were two young men standing talking. One of these, with dark hair, thick moustache, and intense, intelligent eyes, very animatedly so. Sarah glanced around, but there was no one else about. Nor were there any signs of direction or information of any kind.

'Excuse me,' she said.

The men stopped talking to turn and stare at her. Both smiled in a friendly manner.

'I wonder if you could help me – I mean us. We're looking for the person in charge.'

'Are you now?' said thick moustache's companion.

Moustache took in the load that Sheach was carrying. 'Are you a painter then, lassie?' he inquired of Sarah in a mocking voice.

'Are you?' she retorted sharply.

Moustache made an elaborate, theatrical bow. 'Some people would say I am.'

Cheeky, Sarah thought. Cheeky but nice. 'I'm sure people say a lot of other things about you as well,' she replied in an insinuating tone which made both men laugh.

'Oh aye, they do indeed,' Moustache admitted, and laughed again.

'The person in charge?' Olivia chipped in, wanting to be part of the conversation. She considered both men most attractive.

'It's Fra Newbery you want then,' the companion said.

Sarah raised her eyebrows. 'Fra? What sort of name is that?'

'Short for Francis, but he always gets Fra. I believe you'll find him upstairs.'

Sarah looked all round, but there were no stairs in evidence. 'And how do we get up there?'

'By following us. My friend and I will take you,' Moustache said.

'That's most kind of you.'

Moustache's eyes flicked to the pictures and drawings that Sheach was carrying. 'Not in the least. I'm curious.'

The stairs were hidden round a corner, and very dark. 'Watch your feet,' the companion warned unnecessarily as they climbed upwards.

On the level again they passed a room from inside which came the sound of a man singing. Somewhere close by someone swore, a barked out expletive that caused Olivia to suck her breath in horror. The expletive didn't bother Sarah one whit, she'd heard far worse in Netherton where such words were an integral part of the fabric of daily life.

Sarah suddenly wondered if they'd see any naked models, which she'd heard artists used. If they did Olivia would absolutely die from embarrassment. As it transpired she needn't have worried; they didn't.

Moustache threw open a door. 'Fra, a couple of lassies here to see you!' he proclaimed.

Fra, apparently lost in puzzled thought, was standing in front of an easel staring at a half-completed painting. 'Come and give me your judgement of this, Toshie,' he replied without looking round.

An Englishman, Sarah noted. Which was indeed correct. Newbery had come to the School of Art from the Royal College of Art in South Kensington, London.

Moustache went to stand beside Fra, his companion beside him. Moustache was the one referred to as Toshie, Sarah surmised.

'Old-fashioned and boring, though not without some technical merit,' Toshie eventually pronounced.

'And you, Herbert?'

It was the companion who now replied. 'I agree with Toshie.'

Fra Newbery smiled. 'Everyone can't be "modern" like you two. That's an unreasonable expectation.'

Toshie played with the large bow he was wearing at his neck. 'I don't see why.'

Fra's smile widened, while his face filled with affection. He was clearly very fond of these two young men. 'No you wouldn't, Toshie. You wouldn't.'

His gaze left Toshie to fasten on to Sarah, Olivia and Sheach.

'And who have we here?'

'We're told you're in charge of the Art School?' Sarah said.

'I'm the Director, yes.'

'Then you're who we've come to speak to. We'd like your advice, Mr Newbery.'

He waved a hand at them. 'Call me Fra, everyone else does. We don't stand on ceremony round here.'

Sarah introduced herself, then Olivia.

'I take it you've already met these reprobates?' Fra queried, indicating Toshie and the companion.

'Not properly,' Sarah replied.

'Then allow me to do the honours. This is Toshie, or Charles Rennie Mackintosh to give him his full title.'

Toshie gave them another exaggerated bow similar to the one he'd given them downstairs.

'And his friend is Herbert MacNair.'

'Ladies,' Herbert acknowledged with a nod of his head.

'Toshie has just come back from Italy and the Continent, haven't you, Toshie?'

'That is so.'

'Must have been a marvellous experience,' Sarah enthused.

'Indeed it was. Marvellous, and highly instructive. Have you travelled much yourself?'

'I'm afraid not, though someday I should love to do so.'

'And you?' Herbert inquired, turning towards Olivia.

'I haven't either. A trip "doon ra watter" to Millport is the furthest I've been from Glasgow.' 'Doon ra watter' meant down the Clyde.

They all smiled at that; for the vast majority of Glaswegians the Clyde coast was as far, and that was if they were lucky, they would ever get from home.

'Toshie won the Alexander Thomson Travelling Scholarship it was that financed his trip,' Fra explained proudly.

Toshie was proud of his achievement too, Sarah could read it in his face. Proud, but not overly so. It was pride mixed with humility, both overlaying a great deal of sensitivity. 'You must be an excellent painter then,' Sarah acknowledged.

'Many would say a better architect,' Toshie replied quietly.

'But now let's get back to the object of your visit here,' Fra interjected, addressing Sarah and Olivia. 'How can I be of help to you?'

Olivia looked at Sarah, and nodded that she should do the explaining. 'Miss Tennant's brother draws and paints, and we both think he has considerable talent. We'd appreciate your advice on the matter, Fra, as obviously you're the expert.'

A bemused expression came over Fra's face. 'And why doesn't Miss Tennant's brother come and see me himself?'

'His father has quite undermined his confidence in the matter of his one day being a professional.' She paused for a brief second, then decided she'd quote Douglas Tennant. 'Mr Tennant says that only Frenchmen and Spaniards, those sort of breeds, become professional artists, that Scotsmen don't.'

'Well,' Fra said, rocking slightly back on his heels.

Toshie looked outraged, while Herbert was scowling darkly.

'And you don't agree with that?' Fra probed.

'I think it's nonsense, an excuse for Mr Tennant to hide behind because he doesn't want Adam to become a professional. He prefers

Adam to be in a safe, secure and respectable job, one with prospects.'

Fra nodded. 'One musn't be too hard on the Mr Tennants of this world. They only want the best for their children, as they perceive it, after all, and a life in art, for most engaged in it, can hardly be called that.'

'Adam is happier drawing and painting than doing anything else,' Sarah stated simply.

Fra, Toshie and Herbert all knew exactly what she meant by that.

'And this is Adam's work?' Fra asked, indicating that which Sheach was carrying.

'Yes.'

'Then let's have a gander at it.'

They were the original drawings and paintings that Adam had shown Sarah, with the addition of the picture he had done of her, together with various other drawings and paintings executed since then. All of which, with the exception of Sarah's portrait, Olivia had smuggled out of the Tennant household earlier.

Fra went through the drawings first, studying each in turn before handing it to Toshie, who in turn handed it on to Herbert.

'Hmmm!' Fra muttered to himself. Then, 'Hmmm!' again. Toshie didn't utter a word, nor did Herbert.

Sarah was nervous, her stomach a-flutter with butterflies. And judging from Olivia's expression, Olivia was the same.

Finishing with the drawings, Fra took a picture from Sheach and placed it on the easel, standing the half-completed painting that had been there when Sarah and company entered the room against a wall.

'The Broomielaw,' Olivia said softly, and started to chew a thumbnail.

'Our Uncle Robert, the bank manager ' Olivia went on when that replaced the one of the Broomielaw.

Sarah became mesmerised by Toshie's eyes. They'd become like burning coals set in his face. Although they were quite different they reminded her of Jock's eyes; each had a similar power and sense of purpose behind them. The eyes of men who had enormous personal charisma, and who perceived more than ordinary mortals.

'You of course,' Fra said to Sarah when her portrait replaced Uncle Robert.

'It was a present to me.'

Toshie glanced sideways at her when she said that, then brought his attention back to the picture.

The final painting they came to was the last Adam had done, a young mother, no more than fifteen by the looks of her, with her baby wrapped to her in a shawl. The girl's face was thin and undernourished, her legs bent from rickets, that terrible scourge of the Glasgow working class.

Fra let out a sigh. 'Well Toshie, what do you say?'

'The chap has a great deal of potential – I'm sure you could make something of him. He appears to have a particular feel for people which I think could be developed.'

That was a huge relief to Sarah who flashed Olivia a triumphant smile.

'And you, Herbert?'

'Toshie's right, this lad is good with people. I certainly consider him material for the school.'

'And so do I,' Fra said. To Olivia he added, 'Your brother's work is still raw and young, but he's a born artist if ever there was one.'

'You're saying you will accept him into the school then?' Sarah asked Fra, wanting to be quite clear about that point.

'If he wants to come, we'll have him.'

Part of Olivia was ecstatic to hear that, another part wasn't. 'The trouble is Father,' she said. 'He's dead set against Adam doing this other than as a hobby. I just can't see him allowing Adam to give up his job.'

Sarah was thinking furiously when Toshie said quietly, 'There is a way round that. He could do as I did myself.'

Sarah and Olivia listened intently to Toshie's suggestion.

'They actually agreed to take me!' Adam exclaimed, his face aflame with excitement.

'They certainly did,' Olivia replied.

'And it was the Director, the head man himself you saw? The big cheese?'

'It was,' Sarah answered.

Adam was amazed at what Sarah and Olivia had done, at their boldness and audacity at just walking in off the street like that. If they hadn't been where they were, which was in a Cranston tearoom, he'd have given Olivia a smacker on the cheek, and another to Sarah. Lovely, smashing, beautiful Sarah whom he idolised. A kiss on the cheek? He'd much have preferred to give her one on the mouth. If only he had the nerve.

'I'm most grateful to the pair of you, and very flattered, but of course it's useless.'

'You mean because of Father?'

Adam nodded to his sister.

'Your father approves of your drawing and painting as a hobby, he told me that himself,' Sarah said.

'Yes?'

'So he won't object to you taking *evening classes* connected with that hobby, will he?'

Adam frowned, she'd lost him. 'What are you talking about?'

It was Olivia who explained further. 'You don't need to attend the day course, you can take evening classes which are every bit as good according to the Director Fra Newbery and this Toshie we met. Toshie took the evening classes and now he's with the firm of Honeyman and Keppie as an articled architect.'

Hope dawned in Adam's eyes. 'Evening classes?' he mused.

'Every bit as good as the day course,' Sarah reiterated. 'You get exactly the same teachers, facilities and lessons.'

'And in the meantime you can keep on working, and keep the peace at home with father,' Olivia added.

Adam picked up his cup and gulped down some tea. His hand was shaking to such an extent the cup rattled on the saucer when he replaced it. This was a dream come true.

Sarah said, 'Of course there will eventually come a time when you'll leave the School of Art, and then a decision will have to be made about whether you do take it up professionally, or what, and if you do there will be your father to contend with. But that's all in the future, a bridge that can be-crossed when you come to it.'

'Art School!' Adam breathed. The very thought made him itch in anticipation.

'There is one snag, however,' Olivia said. This was what she'd been dreading getting round to.

'What's that?'

'Day course or evening classes, there are fees to be paid.'

'How much?'

Olivia named a sum that made him blanch.

'It is a lot. And with three terms in the year it certainly adds up.'

'And beyond me, well beyond me,' Adam said miserably, despair settling on his face.

'I hope you don't think me too forward for asking this, but do you hand over your pay packet to your mother at the end of the week, and are then given an allowance in return?' Sarah probed. That was the usual arrangement, she'd come to understand, with young professional unmarried men who were still living at home.

'Yes,' Adam acknowledged.

'Well, couldn't you leave home altogether and set up in some rooms of your own?' she queried, certain she already knew the answer, but wanting it verified.

Adam shook his head. 'That's impossible on what I earn at the moment. In a few years' time perhaps, but not now.'

His reply was exactly the one Sarah had been expecting. Well, she hadn't gone this far to be thwarted; she had a proposal. 'May I suggest a solution?'

Adam, who'd been staring disconsolately into his cup, now looked up at her. 'What solution?'

'Jock gave me a present of money which he told me I was to spend on whatever I wanted. What I want is for you Adam to go to Art School, and so I'd like to pay the fees.'

Adam's reaction was instantaneous as fierce Scottish pride took hold of him. 'I couldn't possibly accept anything like that from you, Sarah, it's quite out of the question.'

'Why is it?'

'Because . . . because it just is.'

Sarah sipped some of her tea, and let a few cooling seconds tick by. 'There's nothing I'd enjoy spending the money on more,' she cajoled. 'And it wouldn't be all the money either, only a fraction of it.'

'It's very kind of you, Sarah, and God knows I appreciate the offer, but my answer has to be no,' he replied stubbornly.

'Olivia?' Sarah appealed to his sister.

'It is extremely kind of you, Sarah, but I can understand Adam saying no. If you were family or a long-standing friend it might be different. But as it is I'm sorry, for his sake, but I believe he's right.'

Damn! Sarah thought. She'd expected support from Olivia. She cudgelled her brains. She could offer him the money as a long-term loan, but doubted he would agree to that either. However, there was no harm in trying. She was just about to put that to him when she had another idea, a far better one.

'If you won't let me give you the money how about earning it?' she said.

His forehead creased in a frown. 'Earn it? How?'

'Jock loved the picture you did of me, and I know would love one of Stiellsmuir to hang in the house. Why don't I commission you to paint one for him which I can give him for Christmas?'

'But . . . but nothing I painted could be worth that amount of money,' Adam protested.

'It would be to me, and Jock.' A mischievous smile lit up her face. 'Regard it as an investment on my part. For who's to say that when you leave Art School you don't go on to become a world-famous, internationally acclaimed painter? Which would make my commission very valuable indeed, worth far more in cash terms than what I originally paid for it.'

'Or valueless if I prove a flop,' he countered.

'Isn't that all investment is, a gamble? In this case I'm willing to gamble on you.'

Sweep her into his arms, hold her tight, then kiss her deeply on the mouth. How he longed to do that.

'Well?' she prompted.

'Art School it is then,' he conceded.

That made Sarah very happy, happy that he was going to go after all, happy that she'd been instrumental in bringing that about. She lifted her teacup. 'To your *hobby*, and the new evening classes connected with it!' she toasted.

Adam and Olivia lifted their teacups, and repeated the toast. Then together, as one, the three of them burst out laughing.

Sarah's carriage came to a halt outside the School of Art. Adam was sitting beside Sarah, Olivia facing them. It was the night Adam started his evening classes and Sarah had insisted that she and Olivia personally accompany him to Rose Street and drop him off on what was for him a momentous occasion.

'You look like you're about to lay an egg,' Olivia said to her brother, and giggled.

Adam gave her a weak grin. He *felt* like he was about to lay an egg. And an ostrich-sized one at that.

Sarah put a hand on his. 'You're bound to be nervous, but that'll soon pass. By the time the class is over you'll be wondering what on earth you were worried about.'

'I can't thank you enough for what you've done, Sarah, and you too, Ollie.'

'Havers man, what do you think friends and sisters are for? Now away in with you,' Sarah replied fondly.

148

I wonder if she knows that Adam's in love with her? Olivia thought to herself. She didn't think Sarah did. It must just be that Sarah couldn't see what was so obvious to her. Adam was head over heels with Sarah Hawke.

Sheach opened the door, and Adam got out. Olivia was about to, then let Sarah hand him the various bits and pieces that he needed for his class.

'Good luck then!' Sarah smiled.

'Good luck!' Olivia echoed.

'And watch out for the nude models!' Sarah teased as Sheach shut the door again.

Adam went rigid with fright. My God, he'd never thought of that! Nude models, why he'd never seen a woman with her clothes off, not one. The prospect was absolutely petrifying.

He was still standing rooted to the spot as the carriage started up once more.

In the carriage Sarah was scolding herself for saying that, but she hadn't been able to resist it. And the look on his face had been priceless!

Sarah was whacked out, looking forward to dinner and bed after that. It had been an exhilarating but tiring day tramping the Monteith estate in the company of Ian, Ian's brother James, Bertie and the other 'guns' that made up the shooting party for that weekend.

The bag had been an excellent one with masses of grouse, pheasant, partridge, ducks, rabbits and a solitary woodcock being taken. The highest individual bag going to James Monteith who it had transpired was a wizard shot.

'It's lovely here,' she whispered to Ian. They were on a settee in front of a roaring fire, the room a small one off the main drawing-room, the 'snug room' Ian had referred to it as, a name that fitted it perfectly.

Ian saw her pottery goblet was empty and refilled it from the earthenware jug of mulled wine he'd brought into the room with him. He was slightly drowsy thanks to the combination of the day's exertions, the fire and wine.

'I'm glad you came for the weekend – thank you,' he whispered back. In that cosy and intimate atmosphere to have spoken any louder would have been quite out of place.

149

It was the first shooting party Sarah had been part of, and she hadn't been at all sure she'd enjoy the experience. As it turned out the slaughter hadn't sickened her as she'd feared. Once she'd got the idea into her mind that the animals were all being killed for food, she'd been able to accept what was taking place.

The other side of the coin was that the walking and fresh air, and the March air had certainly been that, was doing her a power of good. When the weekend was over she knew she'd be feeling the better for it.

'And I'm glad I did come,' she whispered in reply.

She closed her eyes, revelling in the heat from the fire battering into her.

'It appears we're the first ones down,' a voice said in the drawing-room. Sarah recognised it as belonging to Sandy Usher, one of the 'guns', and a great chum of James's. The voice that answered Sandy was that of his wife Gillean.

'Shall we join them?' Ian asked, still whispering.

Keeping her eyes shut, Sarah shook her head. 'I don't want to move from here just yet. Let's wait.'

That pleased Ian; the longer he had alone with Sarah, the better.

'Are you for a game of billiards after dinner, Sandy?' another male voice inquired about a minute later. That was Carrick Holme, a friend of Ian's. His wife was called Henrietta, a snooty bitch, in Sarah's opinion.

'You're on,' Sandy replied. Sandy was an avid billiards player whom Carrick had been trying to beat unsuccessfully for years.

Ian grinned to himself. Carrick would be in a foul mood after he lost, which he undoubtedly would.

Henrietta said something, then there was the noisy sound of another couple arriving in the drawing-room. They turned out to be Charles and May Knox who were regular members of the Monteiths' shooting parties. Charles was somewhat stolid and bluff, but a good egg nonetheless. May was having a torrid affair with Sir Walter Dixon, a neighbour of the Knoxes. Everyone knew about it except Charles.

Sarah sipped more mulled wine which slipped down her throat like warm cream. The sensation reminded her of something from the past, which brought a smile to her face.

Carrick was talking again. He's been drinking in his room, Ian thought. You always knew when Carrick had been imbibing; for

150

some reason he always spoke more quickly than he did otherwise. When he was drunk he positively gabbled.

'So what do you make of Ian's bit of stuff, Sandy?' Carrick demanded.

Something turned over inside Sarah when she heard that. The 'bit of stuff' reference and his tone were both offensive. Slowly she opened her eyes.

'Haven't spoken much to her,' Sandy prevaricated.

'I'm told she was brought up as a collier's daughter in some horrid little mining village, or whatever,' Carrick said, and laughed nastily.

'It's true,' Henrietta sniggered. 'I could hardly believe it when I found out.'

'But true it is,' Carrick steamrollered on. 'Henrietta has it on the best of authority. Miss Sarah Hawke may be dressed in silk and satin when she sits down at table tonight, but underneath she's common as muck.'

'I say, steady on!' Charles Knox exclaimed.

Ian, trembling with fury and humiliation for Sarah, started to rise from the settee, but Sarah restrained him.

'God knows what the mother's like, the one who married this miner. Some trollop no doubt,' Carrick said, and laughed nastily again.

Sarah saw red at that. Leaping to her feet she marched from the 'snug room' into the drawing-room. Her eyes were blazing, her expression glacial.

Carrick's laugh died in his mouth when he saw her. He hadn't dreamed that he'd be heard by anyone outside his present company, all safe 'ears' as far as he was concerned, least of all by the female in question.

Sarah stalked towards Carrick until she was standing in front of him, where she stared directly into his suddenly white face.

'My step-father may have been a miner, but he's ten times the gentleman you are, Mr Holme,' she said, her voice matching her expression.

Carrick swallowed hard.

'As for my mother being a trollop, all I will say is this. She's one of the kindest, sweetest, most lovable women I know, who's only been to bed with two men in her life, my father and my step-father.'

The atmosphere in the drawing-room was like a tautened wire

stretched to the verge of breaking. The only sound to be heard was Carrick's heavy breathing as his chest heaved in and out.

Finally Ian broke the lengthening hiatus. 'You'll apologise to the lady,' he said from behind Sarah.

'Carrick!' Henrietta mumbled when her husband didn't make the demanded apology.

When there was still no apology from the defiant Carrick, Ian said. 'You have ten more seconds. If an apology isn't forthcoming by then I shall take you outside and give you the thrashing of your life.'

Fear crept into Carrick's face. He knew only too well that Ian was strong as a young bull. He would stand no chance whatever against those exceptionally broad shoulders, and the power they contained.

Ian counted silently to ten. 'Right then, outside,' he said.

'I, eh . . .' Carrick cleared his throat. 'I'm sorry, Miss Hawke.' He spoke the words so grudgingly and reluctantly they might have been rare jewels he was giving away. But he *did* speak them.

Another couple, the Forts, were at the drawing-room door staring in. They'd halted there, realising a 'scene' was taking place.

'Now you and Henrietta can go upstairs and get packed,' Ian said. 'I want you out of this house just as soon as you are able. Is that clear?'

Henrietta hung her head as Carrick nodded.

'You are my friend no longer. As from this moment you cease to exist as far as I'm concerned.'

'Come, Henrietta,' a shaken Carrick said to his wife. Taking her by the arm he led her, head still bowed, from the room.

'Unforgivable,' Charles Knox said. 'The man's a prig.'

Now that it was all over, all Sarah wanted was for the floor to open up and swallow her. She felt the size of a ha'penny.

Ian opened his mouth to speak to her, but before he could utter she was heading for the door. She wanted out of there before the tears came, tears that were already crowding her eyes.

In the corridor she went the opposite way to the Holmes, and once round a corner broke into a run. The tears were flooding down her face, and she was sobbing, when Ian, who'd come after her, finally caught up with her and forced her to stop.

He gazed quickly about to register his bearings. 'In here,' he said, and pulled her into Bertie's den. He closed the door behind them.

'I really am most terribly sorry about that. And I want you to know that whoever Henrietta got that from it wasn't me.'

Sarah spotted a decanter of spirit. 'I could use a drink,' she said. God how awful that had been. How absolutely mortifying!

Ian poured large brandies into balloons and handed Sarah one. She took a swig, and immediately felt the fiery liquid steady her a bit.

'Can I borrow your handkerchief please?' she asked.

'Of course.'

She wiped her face dry, having now stopped crying. Smudges of make-up stained the hanky. I must look a right mess, she thought.

'If there was any way I could undo what happened I would,' Ian told her, feeling extremely guilty. For the incident had touched a raw nerve, reminding him as it did of his own behaviour on the occasion he'd taken Sarah bicycling. The memory of calling her a little peasant still made him wince. At least he hadn't done it in company as that bloody insensitive fool Carrick had.

Sarah attempted a smile. 'Yes, I believe you.' She had another swallow of her brandy. 'When I've finished this I'll have Elinor pack, and instruct Sheach to drive us back to Stiellsmuir.'

'No!' Ian exclaimed. 'You musn't do that. I won't allow it.'

'But I can't stay after what's happened.'

'You have to. It's the only thing you *can* do.'

She stared at him, puzzled. 'Why? I don't understand.'

'You can't run away every time your past is brought up, even when it is brought up as horribly as tonight. You've told me yourself you're not ashamed of your background – running away would be tantamount to admitting you are ashamed of it.'

He was right, she could see that now. Except . . . 'How can I face those people though, Ian? I'm so embarrassed.'

'You'll face them because, to put it crudely, you've got guts, because you're strong. And how do I know that? I know it because I've seen it in you. You're entirely capable of not only facing them, but outfacing them.'

She finished her brandy, thinking that staying would be an ordeal, but that she'd go through with it. If she ran now she'd never stop.

'All right,' she smiled.

'Will you marry me, Sarah?'

She was taken aback, convinced she'd heard incorrectly. 'I beg your pardon?'

'Will you marry me? Will you consent to be my wife, Mrs Ian Monteith?'

She hadn't heard incorrectly, he had proposed. Nor was that really a surprise; she had been half expecting him to do so for some while now. It was just his timing that had so thrown her.

'For my money of course. Or the money and other assets, including the firm of J. Hawke & Daughter, which will be mine one day when Jock dies,' she replied in a cool tone of voice.

Ian returned to the decanter and poured himself another. 'I recall telling you that the first time we met, didn't I? That eventually I would be forced to go into the army, navy, diplomatic corps, or to marry for money?'

'Yes you did.'

'Well I won't lie to you, I did start off thinking about you in that latter respect. But then . . . things changed.'

That hint of caress was in his voice which in other circumstances could make her go prickly all over. 'How?'

'You're different, Sarah. I enjoy your company tremendously, you're a delight to be with.' He paused, then said, 'I don't know exactly when it was I fell in love with you, but I have. It wouldn't matter to me now whether you have, or will have, money or not, I'd still want you to be my wife.'

So convincing, she thought. He really could charm the birds down off the trees. It was such a marvellous performance he almost had her believing him. Almost, but not quite.

Ian laid down his glass, strode across to her, put both hands behind her neck, and kissed her.

They'd kissed a number of times during the fifteen months they'd known each other, and the many occasions they'd been out together in each other's company, but there was an urgency in this kiss that had never been there before.

'Oh, Sarah!' he breathed, placing a cheek against hers. 'Say that you accept. Please?'

She was tempted, for he was a fine catch. She could certainly do an awful lot worse for herself than the Honourable Ian Monteith.

Placing a palm against his chest she gently pushed him away. She gazed into those liquid brown eyes, thinking for the umpteenth time what an odd combination they were with his straw-coloured hair.

'I could never marry anyone who was marrying me for my money,' she replied.

'But I've just told you, I wouldn't be doing it for that. But because I love you. Because I've fallen in love with you.'

'And how do I know that you really do love me? That you're saying so isn't just a fib to get me to the altar?' she teased.

'Because it isn't a fib!' he protested, and tried to draw her to him again, but she resisted and broke free.

'My answer's no, Ian,' she stated firmly.

'You haven't had time to think about this, to consider . . .'

'I could think about it till kingdom come and wouldn't change my mind,' she interjected. 'I like you Ian, very, very much. But I won't marry you. I won't be your or any other man's mealticket. I have far too much pride for that.'

Desperation was rising in him, he hadn't foreseen such an adamant refusal. He'd been certain he'd be able to convince her of the truth of his feelings.

'Sarah, I love you with all my heart. Please, please, believe me,' he pleaded.

'It's no use, Ian, you'll have to find someone else to keep you in the manner to which you were born, or else work for a living,' she replied gently and with affection.

'But . . .'

She shook her head.

In that instant he knew that she was lost to him, that, misguidedly, she meant what she said and would never agree to their marriage. If only he had never told her what he had that night at the Hawke party. But he had, and now couldn't convince her that he wanted her for himself and not for her damned money.

'What's the expression, hoist by my own petard?' he said weakly, suddenly feeling totally drained. At the same time filled with a biting frustration.

'We can still be friends though, can't we, Ian?'

He turned away so she couldn't see the pain in his face. 'Yes, of course.'

She took a deep breath. 'I'll have to attend to my make-up before I go in to dinner.'

'I'll walk you up to your bedroom and wait outside. We'll go in to dinner together.' When he turned round again he was perfectly composed. He smiled at her, and she smiled back.

'No more charades, Ian?'

For a moment or two he didn't realise what she meant by that, then the penny dropped. 'No more charades,' he agreed.

*

He was drunk, Ian thought. But what the hell, it was a night for getting drunk. For getting absolutely stinko.

He looked deep into the fire and saw her face there, darling Sarah.

'Ah here you are! Been looking everywhere for you,' Bertie said, coming into the 'snug room' where Ian was sitting slumped on the settee, the same settee Ian and Sarah had been on earlier when they'd overheard Carrick Holme.

'I've got a bottle here, but you'll have to find your own glass,' Ian slurred in reply.

'Sounds to me like you've had more than enough.'

'No, not yet,' Ian replied, and took a swallow of the neat whisky he was drinking.

Bertie sat on a fourteenth-century wooden chair that stood to one side of the fireplace from where he gazed at his younger son who was showing visible signs of the alcohol he'd consumed. Ian's hair was awry, his eyes glazed, and there was a flush on his cheeks and neck that had nothing to do with the heat from the fire.

'Bad business about the gel before dinner. You did the right thing to tell Holme and his wife to leave. Dashed bad manners,' Bertie said.

'I proposed to her tonight, directly afterwards,' Ian mumbled, screwing up his eyes in memory.

'Proposed to her?' Bertie said slowly. 'And?'

'You like her, don't you, Pa?'

'I think very highly of the gel. In fact, though I've never said this to you before, there's something about her reminds me of your mother.'

Lydia had died five years previously. She'd fallen in the garden and broken a hip, and had never really recovered. Her hip had eventually healed, but despite this her general health had deteriorated more and more till one morning she'd collapsed while getting dressed, and died minutes later. Bertie's name had been on her lips at the moment of her passing.

Bertie Monteith had known a legion of women in his life, before and after marriage to Lydia, but although he'd cheated on her consistently, Lydia was the only one he'd ever loved. All the others had been affairs of the flesh, his relationship with Lydia had transcended that.

'Sarah is somewhat reminiscent of mother, isn't she? I hadn't thought of that before,' Ian mused.

'Spirit – your mother had that and so does Sarah,' Bertie continued. 'Spirit and . . .' He thought carefully, then added, 'Substance, yes, that's the very word. Spirit and substance, qualities your mother had which Sarah has also.' He beamed. 'So, when's the wedding?'

Ian saw off what remained in his glass. He was long past the stage of tasting what he drank, or feeling its effect. You can only get so numb after all.

'There isn't going to be one. She turned me down, flat.'

Bertie's eyebrows shot up. 'Did she indeed? Did she say why?'

Ian explained about the Hawke party, and what he'd said to her about marrying for money. 'Now nothing I can say will convince her that's not what I'm trying to do.'

'You actually love her then?'

Ian didn't so much pour as throw more whisky into his glass, slopping some on to the settee in the process. 'Yes.'

'I see,' Bertie replied, rubbing his chin. 'That makes it all rather awkward doesn't it?'

Ian nodded agreement, and immediately wished he hadn't done so as the inside of his head began to spin.

'Then all you can do is keep after her hoping that one day you will be able to convince her to the contrary,' Bertie counselled.

'I don't think that's the solution, Pa. I don't wish to sound negative, but I've lost her, I know it.'

'If you know it then you have,' Bertie said, thinking that if the lad had given up mentally then there *was* no chance of his succeeding in the future. And Ian could well be right, for his son was no fool, even when deeply emotionally and subjectively involved as he was in this instance.

The inside of Ian's head might be spinning, but his thought process was still lucid enough, if a lot slower than usual. He'd said he and Sarah would remain friends, and so they would, but he was going to stop seeing her as often as he had been. In fact, he might just stop seeing her altogether. Why tantalise himself after all? Yes, why tantalise himself?

Bertie watched Ian's head droop. It was a great shame that the gel had turned him down for she was perfect for him. But sometimes certain things were just not to be, weren't on the cards.

Ian would hurt for a while, but he was young, he'd get over it. There were always plenty other fish in the sea. Though, and Bertie smiled sadly, perhaps not another fish that Ian might fall in love with.

Going to Ian he took the glass from his hand, and pushed him backwards till he was sprawled out on the settee. Laying the glass on the floor he lifted Ian's feet up on to the settee, then covered him with a patchwork quilt that had been neatly folded on a stand by the window. The quilt was there because Bertie often had an afternoon nap in that room during the winter months when the fire was lit.

Ian was already fast asleep. 'Sarah!' he whispered. Then again, 'Sarah!'

Heart heavy for his younger son, Bertie kissed him on the forehead.

Ian started to snore.

It certainly was a colourful and Bohemian spectacle, Sarah thought to herself, but then what else would you expect of an art school summer ball? She felt quite drab by comparison to some of the women present, and the men. There were a few of the latter so outrageous she wondered how they'd dared walk the streets to get there, which Adam had told her they'd done.

There was a female with a neckline so plunging and a cleavage so deep it was a miracle her breasts hadn't yet sprung free. Why, the neckline was so plunging as to be positively obscene.

And there again was her favourite so far, a man in black tights (she still couldn't believe her eyes every time she spotted him, a *man* in *tights*!) with a padded-out crotch. Now that *was* obscene, no two ways about it. Obscene and, she had to admit it, very, very funny.

Thank goodness, Adam, who'd invited then brought her to the ball, was dressed more or less conventionally, if somewhat flamboyantly. One thing was certain, she'd have refused point blank to have come with him if he'd turned up wearing tights and a padded crotch! Picturing Adam like that brought a smile to her face.

'Enjoying yourself?' Adam asked.

'Thoroughly, and you?'

'Thoroughly.' At least he had her attention again, he thought as they waltzed on. Half the time her attention was elsewhere, watching the passing scene, taking in this, taking in that. Anywhere, everywhere, but on him.

He didn't really know why he'd asked her to be his partner at the ball, the way she treated him he might just as well have asked one of his sisters.

The answer was of course that he was mad for her and grabbed at every opportunity to be in her company even though he knew it was hopeless, that nothing would ever come of his feelings for her. She just didn't think of him in the same way that he thought of her.

'You really are an excellent dancer. Did you take lessons?' Sarah asked.

'No. I just picked it up as I went along.'

She remembered the local Netherton dances she'd been to with Gordy. What a clumf he'd been, two left feet.

'They'll be opening the buffet fairly soon,' Adam said, for food and a limited amount of wine went with the tickets.

Adam could be difficult to talk to at times, Sarah thought. Like getting blood out of a stone. There were occasions when it was no bother and he and she just rattled along, other times, like tonight, it was the complete opposite. It was something about him she found irritating.

'Who's that chap in the blue and white spotted cravat? He's dancing with a girl in a red gown,' Sarah inquired.

Adam glanced round, saw who she meant, and scowled. 'Oh him!' he muttered darkly. 'Why do you ask?'

'He keeps staring at me.'

'Does he now!' Adam exclaimed, and his scowl got even darker. 'Well, who is he?'

'Jardine, comes here during the day. And a would-be Romeo. Thinks he only has to look at a woman and she'll fall at his feet.' The trouble was, Adam thought, there was a great deal of truth in that, for Jardine with his saturnine sardonic appearance was a handsome bugger. Handsome, and arrogant with it.

Jardine winked at Sarah. She was tempted to wink back, for he seemed interesting, but decided not to. Raffish, was her impression of him.

'What's his painting like?' she asked.

'Who? Romeo?'

'Yes. Does he have talent?'

'He wouldn't be here if he didn't. He's all right, better than some, but not so good as others.'

'And you don't care for him?'

'I can take him or leave him.'

159

'But preferably leave him?'

Adam was getting annoyed now. Damn Jardine for giving his Sarah 'the eye', and damn her for wanting to know about Jardine. But she wasn't *his* Sarah, he reminded himself, that was the trouble. For two peas he'd have gone marching over there and given Jardine a punch on the nose.

'Who's the girl he's with?'

Adam couldn't resist it. 'His wife.'

Sarah glanced at Adam in surprise. 'I thought you said he was a Romeo?'

'I did. Romeos can have wives can't they? And they're the worst sort.'

'Oh!' she said, believing Adam, which both pleased and brightened him up a bit. When he saw that Jardine was now smiling at Sarah he twisted her round so that her back was to Jardine.

'Two children as well,' he added, just hoping he wasn't going too far, overgilding the lily.

Despite being a storyteller herself, one who therefore should have recognised another a mile off, Sarah was completely taken in. 'Well well,' she muttered.

'Let's sit down, shall we?' Adam suggested when that dance was over. Sarah replied that it was a good idea for her feet had swollen a little and were beginning to hurt. Adam steered her in the opposite direction to where Jardine and the girl in the red dress were standing, waiting to resume dancing.

'There's Toshie and Herbert McNair whom you've already met. Shall we join them?' Adam proposed, pointing to the table where the two men in question were in the company of a couple of young women.

'Yes, let's.'

Toshie and Herbert rose when Adam and Sarah stopped at their table, and yes of course they both remembered Sarah. Herbert very gallantly kissed Sarah on the back of the hand while Toshie declared they would be delighted if Adam and Sarah joined them.

Toshie made the introductions, the two young women were called Hannah and Barbara, and Herbert acquired chairs from an adjoining table for the newcomers.

'We're discussing art,' Toshie explained as he sat down again.

'What else!' quipped Herbert, which caused Barbara to giggle.

It was Toshie who'd been holding forth, and he now resumed where he'd left off.

'There are three main constituents in recent artistic ideology which, apart entirely from superficial stylistic influences, prepare the ground for what I, Herbert and others of like mind are trying to do. The first of these, owing its importance entirely to our mutual admiration of, indeed obsession with, John Ruskin, is the idealisation of Nature. Nature is to the rational, the true 'reality'; to the humanist a substitute for the divine; to the artist the inspiration for his beginning and the measure of his achievement.

'The designer, in whatever medium, should go straight to nature to learn the principles of structure, of line and form and mass, of texture, of colour, and of fitness to function.'

Heady stuff, Sarah thought, and noted that Adam was drinking it all in, which of course she would have expected. She knew from previous conversations with Adam that he was a great admirer of Toshie who sometimes taught him at evening class.

Toshie went on. 'The second constituent is the emphasis on material and technique which springs directly from our Victorian emphasis on labour. It is the doctrine of Carlyle, disseminated by Ruskin, and applied by Morris . . .'

Some sixth sense penetrated Adam's concentration, drawing his gaze to another part of the hall where it locked on to Jardine who was staring fixedly at Sarah. There was no doubt about that, it was Sarah that Romeo Jardine was riveted to.

When Jardine rose and began walking towards them he knew that Jardine was going to ask Sarah to dance.

Feeling sick inside, be brought what remained of his attention back to Toshie.

Vera Bryce, barmaid at Milne's Vaults, glanced up from the glass she was polishing to notice what was rapidly becoming a familiar sight of late, that nice young man from the School of Art sitting alone crystal-balling into his beer. Usually he sat in a booth, but tonight he was perched on a stool at the end of the bar. And didn't he look miserable! He always looked that way mind you, but tonight he appeared even more so. He had a face on him the length of Sauchiehall Street.

Seeing he was only a couple of swallows away from finishing his drink she replaced the glass she'd been polishing and went over to him.

'Another bottle of Revolver is it?' she asked, knowing that Younger's Revolver Brand export was his regular tipple.

Adam roused himself from his reverie, and shook his head. 'Can't afford another,' he replied dourly.

'A fine gentleman like you? Surely that's not true?' she teased.

'Sad to say it is. That last one cost me my tram fare so I'll have to walk home.'

'As bad as that, is it?'

He shrugged. 'Walking's good for you. I don't mind it in the least. Gives me time to think.'

He seemed to do an awful lot of thinking, she thought. Which, now she'd come to realise it, impressed her. She liked a man with a head on his shoulders rather than just a turnip. Her George, the biggest mistake of her life, had been one of the turnips.

What she did next was on impulse. She quickly looked round the bar and pub in general, saw what was what and who was where, then said in a low voice, 'Just hang on a wee.'

She whipped open a bottle of Revolver, placed it before him, gave him the slightest of nods, and moved off down the bar.

For free? Adam wondered. It had to be; he'd told her he didn't have money for another. Well, wasn't that kind!

He poured the contents of the bottle into his glass, and when she next glanced over at him he gave her a warm smile.

She was quite a dish too, he thought, sipping his Revolver and studying Vera for the first time. She certainly had a figure, particularly up top. She was well endowed there all right.

When he left a little later he called out goodnight to her, and waved.

A smiling Vera waved back.

It was Friday night of the following week, and Adam had been into Milne's Vaults every week night since that first free beer, and on every occasion there had been more from Vera whom he now called by her Christian name, and she him by his. Tonight he hadn't paid for one single Revolver, all of them appearing magically before him when his glass was nearing empty.

They'd talked a bit, scraps of conversation here and there when there was a chance. Over and above her name he'd learned that she was twenty-five, two years older than himself, was married but had been deserted by her husband who'd run off with another woman, childless, and lived near by. He also knew – for she'd made it plain enough by a multitude of glances, smiles and other signs—that she found him attractive. As he found her.

What are you waiting for! he thought to himself as she served a pint of light at the far end of the bar. He couldn't expect to sit here night after night supping her free beer and not do something about it.

Then he thought of Sarah, and writhed inside. She'd considered it funny that he'd lied to her about Jardine at the ball, and had laughed at him for doing so. How that had hurt, and how foolish he'd felt. Jardine had laughed at him too, and in a way that had been even worse.

Was Jardine seeing Sarah? He didn't know, and was damned if he'd ask either Ollie or Sarah herself. But in his heart he believed Jardine was.

Bastard! he thought, shouting it out in his mind. Bastard! For not only was Jardine a handsome bugger; he also came from an extremely well-to-do family. A family in the same financial bracket as Jock Hawke, which meant Jardine could afford Sarah.

'Come on, cheer up. You're not going to get all down again are you?'

It was Vera speaking; he hadn't noticed her making her way along the bar.

'When you've finished here tonight could I walk you home?' The words were out before he knew it.

Triumph flared in her—this was what she'd been angling after. She took her time in answering, however, not wishing to appear over eager.

'Yes, that would be all right.' She paused for a moment, then added, 'When we close wait on the pavement opposite. I'll be as quick as I can.'

'Right then.'

She moved off again, having been shouted for by 'Tiny' Mitchell, one of the regulars. 'Tiny' was six feet two and a half inches, a giant by Glasgow working-class standards where working men, thanks to a poor diet and living conditions, were traditionally on the short side.

Suddenly Adam had his doubts about what he'd done. Should he have asked to walk her home? Perhaps . . . A picture of Sarah appeared in his mind, making him angry, with himself more than anything else.

Don't be so bloody soft! he told himself.

A fresh bottle of Revolver appeared in front of him.

*

163

He was as nervous as hell as he stood on the pavement opposite Milne's Vaults waiting for Vera as per her instructions. She was a barmaid after all, and working class. Not at all the sort of lassie he should be taking an interest in.

He was only walking her home! he reminded himself. There was no harm in that. And he was an artist, or going to be one anyway, and artists operated outside the normal conventions.

Why, look at the French Impressionists and some of the things he'd heard they got up to, and the women they associated with! Street women, cancan dancers, thieves, all sorts. What was a barmaid compared to those!

He burped – he'd had quite a few Revolvers and although bottled beer it was strong stuff. He was drinking a lot more than he had been but, and he couldn't help smiling, what Glaswegian wouldn't when it was free!

And then there Vera was, slipping out from behind the sliding iron gate which fronted the doors that had been three-quarters pulled shut, waiting to be locked from the inside when the last of the non-living-in staff had gone.

When he made to go to her she gestured that he stay where he was, and crossed over to him.

'Hello,' she said.

'Hello,' he replied awkwardly. She was wearing a shawl round her shoulders, the badge of a female 'workie'.

She started off to their right, and he fell into step beside her.

'It isn't far,' she said.

He already knew that.

'A tenement, three storeys up.'

'The wife in the middle door hit me with a cup,' he shot back, that the second line of a Glasgow street song, the first line of which was similar to what she'd just said.

Vera laughed. 'You're daft!'

The nervousness and tension drained out of him, leaving him relaxed.

'What kind of pictures do you paint?' she asked.

He began talking about his art work, his love and enthusiasm for it fairly bursting out of him. He was still talking when they reached her close, and continued to do so.

Finally, at last, she said. 'I'd better away up before I take root here.'

'You'll be on tomorrow night I presume?'

'Oh aye.'

'I'll see you then.'

'Thanks for walking me home, Adam.'

Suddenly he was awkward again. 'The pleasure was all mine.'

She could see he was just going to walk away, so she took him by the hand and pulled him into the front close. She smiled up at him, parting her lips slightly.

Her mouth was gorgeously soft and sweet, Adam thought as they kissed. Sugar sweet.

'Tomorrow night then,' Vera husked when the kiss was finally over. Turning, she fled up the stairs.

Adam sucked in a deep breath. That had been absolutely marvellous, he felt all bubbles and coloured lights inside.

He felt just wonderful.

'And what time is this to come in!' Douglas Tennant demanded, tapping his brass fob watch.

'I'm sorry, I didn't realise it was so late. I stopped off for a drink after class,' Adam replied. My God but his father had a right dander up.

'Aye, you've been doing more and more of that recently. It's getting so that you're drinking like a fish!'

'Hardly as bad as that,' Adam smiled, trying to placate Douglas.

Douglas stuck his face close to Adam's. 'A fish I say and a fish I mean.'

Adam didn't reply. He certainly wasn't going to agree with his father, even if the old man was right.

Douglas Tennant grunted, and moved away. 'I'm beginning to have serious doubts about this hobby of yours. You're spending so much time at it nowadays, and the drinking that seems to go with it, that it must be affecting your job.'

Alarm blossomed in Adam.

'I think it is for the best you give up these night classes. I can't imagine how I allowed myself to be talked into letting you do them in the first place.'

The alarm was rapidly turning to panic. He couldn't stop his classes now, he wouldn't! Nor could he afford to leave home. 'My classes aren't affecting my job, Dad, I swear!' he gabbled.

'You're trying to burn the candle at both ends and that . . .'

Out of Adam's rapidly mounting panic inspiration was born. 'Rather than affecting my job,' he interjected, 'it's actually helping it.'

Douglas Tennant gave his son a disbelieving stare. 'How do you make that out?'

'Mr Hawke is very keen on art, and has tried his hand at it himself in the past, only to discover that he has no talent whatever in that direction,' Adam lied smoothly.

Douglas Tennant's anger faded from his face, replaced by the ingratiating expression he employed when talking to his own boss, and others in authority. Unknown to him his colleagues referred to it as his 'creeping Jesus' expression. 'You don't say?'

'Mr Hawke was most impressed by the portrait I did of his daughter, Sarah. You remember that, don't you Father?'

Douglas Tennant nodded vigorously.

'*Most* impressed,' Adam reiterated. 'And when he learned from Sarah that I was taking classes he called me into his office to talk about them.'

'Ah!' Douglas Tennant breathed, eyes glinting.

'We've talked about art in general and my classes on several occasions now. And last week, last Thursday in fact . . .' He paused for effect. 'Mr Hawke asked me to paint a picture of his house, Stiellsmuir.' The picture he was referring to of course was the one Sarah had commissioned and which he'd finished in time for her to give Jock as a Christmas present half a year previously. His father knew nothing of that picture because it had been done at the art school, and never brought home. According to Sarah, Jock had been delighted with it.

'A picture of his house, my, my, my,' Douglas Tennant said, 'washing' his hands.

'So you see, Father, rather than hindering my job, my art and classes are actually helping it, because through them Mr Hawke has taken a special interest in me . . .'

'Special interest,' Douglas Tennant repeated softly to himself.

'An interest that I shouldn't be at all surprised led to my rapid advancement within the firm.'

Douglas Tennant waited, making quite sure that Adam had finished.

'Well naturally this puts a whole new complexion on matters. Yes indeed. You must continue your classes, there's no question of you stopping them. No question at all.'

Adam's back was awash with sweat he could feel it coursing down to and over his buttocks.

'And when do you start this painting for Mr Hawke? Or have you done so already?' Douglas Tennant inquired.

'I thought I'd make some preliminary sketches during the summer recess, then start it proper next term,' Adam answered. It was almost the end of that term, next term starting in the September.

'That way your tutors will be able to keep an eye on what you're doing as you go along?'

Which was precisely what he wanted his father to think, to extend the time necessary for this painting as far into the future as possible. 'I wish to give Mr Hawke the very best that I'm capable of.'

'Aye indeed, that's the right way to think son. The right way.'

He'd successfully won the old man round, Adam thought. But it had been a near thing, too damn near.

'I'd better be off to my bed then, don't want to be tired in the morning,' he said.

He dreamt he was back in the close front kissing Vera.

'I want a word with you before I leave for work,' Adam said to Olivia who was sitting beside him at breakfast the next morning. Their father had just excused himself, and risen from the table. Douglas always left the house shortly before Adam, and Mrs Tennant didn't take breakfast. Primrose, a picker at the best of times, made do with a cup of tea in her room.

'About what? Sarah, I suppose?' Olivia teased flippantly.

Adam ignored that, replying in a very serious, level tone. 'I told Dad a story last night and I want you to corroborate it for me should he ask you about it. Which he might well do, as it concerns Sarah and Mr Hawke, and Dad knows you and Sarah are friendly.'

Olivia frowned. 'What sort of story?'

Adam began explaining, but didn't mention anything about Vera. He also reminded his sister that it was because of her and Sarah that he was attending evening classes in the first place.

Adam and Vera were in her back close kissing and cuddling which was where they now ended up every night after he'd walked her home. They hurriedly broke apart when there was the sound of approaching feet.

A man appeared out the darkness of the back court to go striding past them; nor did he attempt to look and see who they were as he went by. Back closes were a favourite spot for courting couples and it was considered bad manners to intrude other than was absolutely necessary. It was only fair that such courting couples had a wee bit privacy after all.

'Mr Cameron, lives on the landing below me,' Vera whispered to Adam as Mr Cameron clattered up the stairs in the tackety boots he was wearing.

'It's high time I wasn't here, though I don't want to go,' Adam whispered in reply. Drawing her to him again, he nibbled her neck.

Vera closed her eyes. 'It's my day off tomorrow so I won't be at the pub tomorrow night,' she whispered.

'I hate it when it's your day off and I don't see you,' he complained.

She opened her eyes to gaze into his. 'You can tomorrow if you want. Why don't you come straight from work and I'll make you some tea? And there will be no need for you to hurry off afterwards as the Art School is closed down for the summer.'

Excitement gripped him. In her house with her, the two of them there alone. What a prospect that was!

'I'd love to come.'

'Good,' she breathed in reply.

This time it was she who nibbled his neck.

Bryce.

Adam stared at the name inscribed on the brass plate, and swallowed hard. His stomach felt as though he'd swallowed a pound of lead, while his legs had gone all weak and trembly. He tugged at the bell pull and heard it clang within.

She opened the door almost immediately, as if she'd been standing directly behind it awaiting his arrival. 'Come in,' she smiled.

He crossed the step, and handed her the half bottle he'd brought. She saw it was the same brand as the half bottle she'd bought in, which seemed an auspicious omen.

She led him down the small hall and into the kitchen. 'It's a room and kitchen, I expect your house is bigger,' she said, placing his bottle by the side of the sink alongside the one already there.

The kitchen was well kept, very neat and tidy, he noted. But

168

then he hadn't expected otherwise. Vera hadn't struck him as the sluttish type.

The walls of the kitchen, as were those of the hall, were distempered a deep yellow colour. The linoleum underfoot was old and highly polished. In front of the sink there was a patch where it had worn right through to the floorboards.

He shifted from one leg to the other, nervous and awkward again as he'd been that first time he'd waited for her on the pavement opposite the pub.

'A dram then?' she asked.

'Lovely.'

'Why don't you sit,' she suggested as she poured.

He sat on one of the two comfy chairs, one of which was on either side of the range as was the usual arrangement. The chairs were as decrepit as the linoleum; he could feel a spring jabbing into his bottom, but not uncomfortably so.

Vera was wearing a dress that Adam had never seen before, a 'good' dress. He wondered if she'd bought it especially for his visit, and was flattered to think she might have done.

She handed him his drink in a tiny glass fashioned in the shape of a thistle, a size and design he'd encountered many times before, that particular glass being extremely popular.

'Slainthe!' she toasted.

'Slainthe!' he responded.

'It's the first time we've had a drink together,' he said by way of making conversation, for bar staff were forbidden either hard or soft drinks while on duty at Milne's Vaults, this common pub practice.

'I've laid in some bottles of Revolvers, just say when you want one,' she replied.

'I wouldn't mind one now.'

'I'll get it then.'

The bottles were behind the curtain that dangled from the sink. He watched her as she squatted and thrust the curtain aside. She moved beautifully, he thought.

'I hope you like liver, bacon and onions? That's what I've got for tea,' she said as she poured out his beer.

'One of my favourite meals,' he answered.

She handed him a tumblerful of Revolver. 'I'll get on with it then.'

'Right.'

Silence fell between them as she busied herself preparing the meal, she being just as nervous of the situation as he was, something she'd never been during any of their previous rendezvous.

'Would you object to me drawing you?' Adam asked after a while. He had a sketchpad and pencil with him, rarely going anywhere without them since joining the art school. He kept them in a capacious inside jacket pocket that Olivia had sewn in for him.

'Draw me!' Vera exclaimed, turning to look at him in surprise. 'No, I don't have any objections. Go ahead if that's what you want to do.' She felt chuffed that he had asked to draw her, very chuffed indeed.

Adam produced his sketch pad, and chose a pencil, a 4B. 'I've often thought of drawing you while in the pub, but that would look awfully pretentious on my part, don't you think?'

She laughed. 'It would at that.' Glasgow pubs just weren't the kind of places where you did that sort of thing at all.

His pencil started to fly, his eyes flicking from the pad to Vera, and back to the pad again.

'Can I continue on as I was?' she queried. 'I mean you don't wish me to stand still, do you? I'll never get the tea ready if you do.'

'You just continue as you were, and forget what I'm up to.'

The lead in his stomach began to melt away, while his legs stopped being weak and trembly. He began to hum, he was finding her easy to capture, which he'd guessed he would, her likeness seeming to appear on the paper with little effort on his part.

Vera was tying on a pinny to protect her new dress — she *had* bought it especially for his visit — prior to flouring the liver, when Adam tore the top sheet of paper from his pad.

'No use, eh?' she smiled in sympathy.

'On the contrary. This one is finished. Come and have a gander.'

It was just like looking into the mirror, she thought, gazing at the portrait he'd handed her. 'It's terribly good. You're very clever,' she told him.

'Thank you. You can keep that.'

Her face lit up. 'Can I!'

'Of course. I'm going to do three or four and you can keep them all.'

She crossed to the mantelpiece and put the portrait on display there, propping it up with a knick-knack. 'I'll treasure this, so I will, Adam. Till my dying day.'

'Let's just hope that's some time off,' he joked, and she laughed again.

He was completely at ease now, as was she. She got on with the meal while he started on the next piece of paper.

'That was delicious,' Adam said, placing his knife and fork together, and slightly pushing the plate away from him.

'Was it enough for you?'

'More than enough.'

'Another dram and Revolver?'

He was already quite tipsy, but what the hell! He was enjoying himself, thoroughly so. In fact he couldn't remember the last time he'd enjoyed himself as much.

While Vera rose to pour fresh drinks for the pair of them he gazed over at the four drawings lined up side by side on the mantelpiece. The second he'd done was the best, he decided. It had that little something extra, that little more depth of character.

He also rose from the table, picked up his plate and hers and took them over to the sink.

'What are you doing?' she queried.

'Helping you clear the table. When the water's ready I'll dry if you wash.'

'Not in my house you won't! That's strictly women's work.'

Her outraged expression amused him. 'I don't mind.'

'But I do. And that's an end of it. Honestly!'

'All right, have it your own way.' He was suddenly terribly aware of her smell, not a put-on scent but personal odour. It was gorgeous and enticing. He wanted it to stay in his nostrils for ever.

The mood between them had changed, she could feel it as well. Her skin had become all alive, and there was an ache between her legs. An ache that desperately wanted attending to.

'Adam?'

'Yes?'

'Kiss me.'

He did, and most willingly. She writhed in his arms as her tongue probed and delved and twined with his.

She was filled with fierce heat and longing. Her nails sank into the back of his jacket as she hugged him tightly to her.

When the kiss was over she broke free, took a deep breath, and walked slowly to the door. There she paused to glance back at him over her shoulder.

'The bedroom's through here,' she husked.

171

In a daze, not quite believing this was happening – though it was what he'd been hoping would happen all along – he followed her into the bedroom. She immediately closed the heavy main curtains. There were also nets, plunging the room into darkness.

He stood where he was, waiting for her to make the next move, which she did by lighting the gas. Pale, somewhat wan, light flooded the bedroom.

'Well?' she queried.

He walked slowly towards her till he was standing directly in front of her. Reaching up he placed his hands on her breasts, something he'd never dared do in the back close.

She gave him a small, crooked smile. And began undoing his tie.

When his shirt was off, lying dropped to the floor, she told him he could do the rest for himself. Moving away she started to strip.

When he was naked he crossed to the bed and pulled the covers back. He slipped inside, taking up a sitting position, his eyes glued to Vera. When she too was naked she turned to face him full frontally on.

He stared at her body in wonder and admiration, thinking how far more beautiful it was compared to those of the women who posed for the life classes at art school. Without exception the latter were middle-aged, ugly, or a combination of both.

Vera's thighs whispered silkily as she came towards him. On reaching the bed she sat beside him.

'Do you like what you see?'

'Oh yes.'

There was that in his voice and expression confirmed what she'd suspected. 'Am I your first woman, Adam?'

He knew it was useless to lie, and nodded.

'I'm pleased about that.' She ran her fingers lightly up and down his arm, which broke out in gooseflesh. 'There's nothing to worry about, just relax and let it all happen naturally.'

It wasn't cold in the room so there was no need for them to be under the bedclothes other than for modesty. Pulling the bedclothes off him she threw them aside.

He touched her left nipple, then her right.

'You can kiss them if you want to,' she said.

He did.

'And the rest of my breasts, all over.'

He did that too.

Smiling, she stroked his hair. She'd known ever since that first night in the front close that they would end up like this, as lovers. She couldn't say how she'd known, but she had.

Taking his hand she placed it over her mound. 'That's right, that's nice,' she crooned.

With her nails she traced patterns on his bare back. She kissed his neck, and ear, then neck again. She dug in her nails, but not enough to break the skin.

He trembled all over when she took him in her hand. Slowly, her hand began to move. 'Do you like that?'

'Yes,' he choked in reply. He was beginning to think he'd died and gone to Heaven. But the best, as he was about to discover, was still to come.

When he was ready for her, and still holding him, Vera rolled over on to her back, gently taking him with her.

'Let me,' she whispered, and guided him in.

'Oh it's been so long,' she sighed after a while. 'So long.'

The sun was cracking down as Sarah and Olivia strolled along the quayside at Port Glasgow. They'd come down with Jock who was bidding at the auction of four ships that were to be sold. He was one of the number of bidders clustered round the auctioneer about a hundred yards away.

'So how's Adam?' Sarah asked. 'I haven't seen him in absolute ages.'

'We're all a bit concerned about his drinking. He's been doing an awful lot of that of late,' Olivia replied.

Sarah's brow creased into a frown. 'Drinking! I never knew Adam was much for that?'

'Neither did we. But most nights now when he comes home he's had a skinful. We think he must have fallen in with bad company from the Art School.' Olivia paused, then added, 'We also believe – though he denies it emphatically – that he's become mixed up with some female.'

'Nothing wrong with that, surely?'

'No, except if he is why doesn't he tell us about her, her name for example, and bring her home to meet the family?'

Sarah had no answer to that.

'The drinking I can understand. But the female? That's the surprising part.'

Sarah noted the man again, the man she'd spotted watching her several times now since Jock had gone off to join the other bidders. He was a well-dressed man, handsome too. Round about Jock's age, she thought, maybe a little older.

'Why the surprising part?' she asked Olivia.

They walked a few steps in silence. Then Olivia said, 'You've never realised, have you?'

'Realised what?' She couldn't think what Ollie was on about.

'That Adam is in love with you. And has been right from the very beginning.'

Sarah was amazed. 'He told you this?'

'No, but I am his sister. I can see the way he's behaving towards you.'

'I don't know what to say.' Sarah shook her head. 'I've never given him any encouragement in that direction, I assure you. I think of him as a friend, and no more than that.'

The man was still staring at her, and now he was smiling. What a cheek! She turned her back on him. If he came over and tried to strike up a conversation she'd call a bobby, of whom there were several somewhere about.

'Whoever this female is that Adam has taken up with,' Olivia said, 'she's got Adam on the rebound.'

'Are you sure there is a female?'

'All the signs are there. Though as I told you Adam denies the fact emphatically.'

'Perhaps he's doing so because . . .' Sarah bit her lip, not certain she should say.

'She's not suitable? Someone the family wouldn't approve of?' Olivia prompted.

Sarah nodded.

'That is a possible explanation.'

'Here's Jock!' Sarah said, pointing to her father who was hurrying in their direction. Behind him the crowd of bidders was breaking up, which meant the auction was over. As Jock got closer Sarah saw that his face was flushed. With success, she presumed. And she was right.

'I did it!' he announced gleefully on reaching them. 'I managed to buy two of the four, the *Talus* and *Loch Tay*, both iron full-rigged vessels ideal for my purposes.'

'Congratulations!' Sarah beamed.

'Congratulations, Mr Hawke!' Olivia echoed, beaming also.

'In one fell swoop I've increased the size of my fleet by fifty per cent. And it's all thanks to you, Sarah, that I'm able to do so. That South African idea of yours is making me money hand over fist.' Beside the *Snowdrop* he also had the *Edward Wake* on that run the *Talus* would now join them, as the South African market for palm oil continued to expand. As he'd originally foreseen other traders, squeezed out of the domestic market by Miller Bros. of Liverpool and McIvor, were also selling down there, but not yet in enough quantity to oversupply the market. Other traders, taking a leaf out of his book, were selling palm oil in Australia and New Zealand whose indigenous product was of extremely low quality.

Sarah was of course delighted that her idea was continuing to be successful. She and Jock still had regular discussions in the library after dinner, and all the while she was learning more about his business in particular, and business in general. Her understanding of accountancy was also coming on by leaps and bounds, but then she'd have been disappointed if it hadn't, considering the amount of effort she was putting into it.

'Can we go aboard your new ships?' Olivia eagerly asked Jock.

'I don't see why not. But first of all I think a little celebration is in order. I thought we might repair to the Railway Hotel and order up some fizz. How does that appeal?'

'Very much,' Sarah responded. She was actually quite peckish; it was a long time since breakfast.

'Hello, Jock. How are you?'

It was the man who'd been staring at Sarah. He now raised his hat to her and Olivia.

Sarah glanced back at her father who wasn't smiling any more. His expression had become grim.

'Hello, Ranald, I noticed you earlier and thought you'd come to bid. But not so, apparently. At least I wasn't aware of you bidding in person.'

'I'm in Port Glasgow to fry other fish,' Ranald replied.

Sarah didn't have to be introduced to know who the man was who'd been staring at her. The name Ranald, and her father's expression, told her.

'And this is your daughter, I believe. I've heard a great deal about her,' McIvor said, smiling at Sarah.

Was that a crack? she wondered. A reference to her life in Netherton?

'Sarah, this is Mr McIvor,' Jock said.

It was surprising that Sarah hadn't met McIvor long before, as Jock had once told her she no doubt would. It was just one of those things, their paths had never crossed up until then.

'I guessed as much,' she replied.

McIvor arched an eyebrow.

'The name Ranald isn't exactly a common one,' she explained. 'Ranald *Cyril* isn't it?' She added that because she knew from Jock that he loathed his second name.

'A small burden I have to bear,' he acknowledged. Nor had he missed the fact she was having a dig at him.

Sarah decided she didn't like McIvor, and that had nothing to do with his being Jock's competitor and rival. It was the man himself. He might be handsome, but underneath there *was* something weasely about him.

'And this is Miss Olivia Tennant,' Jock went on.

When that introduction was over the two men spoke briefly about business, then McIvor excused himself, saying he had a meeting in a few minutes' time.

'Pleased to have met you, Sarah,' he said.

She didn't lie by returning the compliment, instead she nodded. He could make what he would of that.

'Don't be taken in by the polite manner – that one would stick a knife in your back as soon as look at you,' Jock said after McIvor had left them.

'And a rusty knife at that if he had the choice,' Sarah qualified.

Jock laughed. Rusty knife indeed! 'Come on, let's get that fizz,' he said, and crooked out both his arms.

Sarah took his left, Ollie his right, and like that they made for the Railway Hotel.

Adam was in a lather of sweat, his own mingled with Vera's, as he thrust again and again into her willing flesh. Her fingers drummed a tattoo on his upper arms and shoulders. Her head thrashed from side to side.

'Ah!' she cried. 'Ah!'

There was a demon driving Adam on. His lips drew back in a wolfish snarl as Vera writhed and bucked beneath him. The sensation he was experiencing was unbelievable, quite out of this world.

Vera's hands left off their drumming to clutch her breasts, which she squashed against herself. Like him she too was slippery all over, covered in a sheen of sweat.

'Yes! Oh yes!' she choked, inwardly flying to meet the explosion that would lift her soaring.

'Now!' Adam commanded in what was almost a scream, and thrust a last time, as deeply and hard as he could.

A moment? An eternity? It was both. And then it was over. Adam, chest heaving from exertion, collapsed beside Vera. 'That was the best yet,' he smiled.

Vera was aglow inside. Thoroughly satisfied, and satiated. Leaning over she kissed him on a tiny puckered nipple. 'Yes,' she agreed.

Her hair was soaking, she discovered, running a hand through it. Glancing at Adam's she saw his was too.

'I can't get enough of you,' Adam told her.

She felt exactly the same about him. Their lovemaking just got better and better. What a transformation from the shy young man she'd first gone to bed with, she thought, the corners of her mouth crinkling into a wry smile.

'Christ, look at the time!' Adam exclaimed, and leapt out of bed. 'If I don't get my skates on I'll miss my last tram.'

She watched him through half-closed eyelids, her gaze lingering on that which gave her so much pleasure. How innocuous it now looked, and how innocent. And how little compared to when it had been inside her.

Adam was throwing on his clothes, trying desperately to get dressed. It was one hell of a long walk if he missed that tram. He could have taken a hansom cab of course, but that would have been unnecessarily extravagant.

Languidly, Vera rose and shrugged herself into a dressing-gown. Gathering her hair back she tied it with a piece of material. Her neck was running with sweat, as was the rest of her. She'd have a good wash at the sink before returning to bed.

'I must fly!' Adam said, now completely dressed.

'See you tomorrow night?'

'Wild horses couldn't keep me away.'

Going to him, she kissed him on the tip of the nose as had become her custom when privately saying goodbye to him. 'I'll see you then.'

Another glance at the clock tick-tocking on the mantelpiece told him he shouldn't be there. "Bye!" And with that he was out of the bedroom, across the hall and out of the front door, which slammed shut behind him.

Vera folded her arms and hugged herself. Tomorrow night and another dose of the same after work. She could hardly wait.

Douglas Tennant groaned as he held his head in his hands; this headache that had struck earlier was sheer agony. He'd never had such a bad headache before, and prayed he never would again.

'Is there anything I can get you, dear?' Dorrie Tennant, his wife, inquired anxiously.

He'd already taken a pain-relieving powder which wasn't having any effect whatever.

'A nice cup of tea perhaps?'

'No.' He just wished she'd shut up.

'How about some warm milk?'

'No thank you,' he replied through gritted teeth.

'Then I think you should go to bed. When you wake in the morning you'll be right as rain again.'

Why did she have to sound so bloody cheery! 'I wouldn't sleep, I just know it.'

Dorrie tutted in aggravation. Douglas could be so obstinate at times. Of course, bed was the best place for him, why couldn't he see that! And where was Adam? He should have been in before now. What with one thing and another she hardly ever saw him nowadays.

There was the sound of a key in the front door. That was him now, Dorrie thought. Olivia and Primrose had gone through together over an hour since.

Adam came into the room. 'I saw the light was still on in here.' Then he noticed Douglas. 'What's wrong?'

'Headache, terrible headache,' Dorrie explained.

Douglas caught the smell of drink. It came wafting over him, making him feel nauseous. He dry boaked, then dry boaked again.

'You reek of alcohol,' Douglas choked.

'I only had a few,' Adam lied.

Douglas glanced up at his son. 'Don't lie to me. You smell like you've been swimming in the stuff.' He frowned. Alcohol and something else?

The penny dropped with Dorrie and Douglas simultaneously, the something else was sex. Unmistakably so.

'You've been with a woman! You stink of her!' Dorrie accused, horrified.

Adam cursed inwardly. Usually he had a hot water wash at Vera's before coming home, but because he'd been so late he hadn't that night. Trust it to be a night his parents were still up.

'Woman? What woman? You've got it wrong, Mum,' he protested, fixing a smile on to his face.

'She hasn't got it wrong,' Douglas said, lumbering to his feet, his legs partially buckling under him as a reaction to standing. 'You stink of this woman you're seeing.' He spat out the next bit. 'The pair of you have been fornicating.'

Adam had gone white. 'Don't be daft!'

'Don't daft me!' The inside of Douglas's head was spinning and, he wouldn't have believed it possible, the pain was even worse than it had been. 'You've been fornicating with some tart.'

'She's nothing of the sort,' Adam retorted. 'You'll take that back.'

Douglas stuck his face into Adam's. He was going too far, but the pain combined with the shock of discovering that Adam had been sexually with a woman had pushed him over the top. 'Some disease-ridden tart!' And with that his hand flashed to crack against Adam's cheek.

Adam had gone cold with anger to hear Vera called a disease-ridden tart. That anger now erupted at his being slapped. He reacted with a punch that caught Douglas squarely on the jaw.

Douglas went flying backwards to get tangled up in a rug, and fall crashing on to his side. He bit the lining of his mouth as he landed, which caused blood to spurt into his mouth, and from there to rapidly find its way out over his lips, and go running down his chin.

Dorrie stood frozen, eyes on stalks, a hand clutching the centre of her bosom.

The pain was now so brutally intense Douglas thought he must surely faint from it, which would have been some sort of relief. How dare Adam do that to him, how dare he! 'Get out, get out of this house and never come back. Do you hear!' he roared.

Adam couldn't believe he'd struck his father. The idea was inconceivable. But he had. And what's more, the old bastard had deserved it.

'No, Douglas, no,' Dorrie whimpered.

Olivia appeared in the doorway, wakened by the noise.

'It's maybe for the best, Mum,' Adam said, his voice shaking.

'Out, and go now,' Douglas shouted.

Primrose, also wakened by the noise, appeared behind Olivia.

Dorrie was torn between her husband and son. She didn't know what to do, or say. She was totally confused.

Adam marched to the door, past Olivia and Primrose, and made for his bedroom, stopping *en route* at a hall press to take out one of the suitcases it contained. Suitcases that had been used every year when he, Olivia and Primrose had been children for their annual summer fortnight down the Clyde at Helensburgh. Always Helensburgh, never anywhere else, because Douglas liked it there.

In his bedroom Adam threw the suitcase on to his bed, opened it, and then began to cram it with clothes he took from his tallboy and wardrobe.

It was for the best, he told himself. It was.

'Adam, please don't leave. Please!' a tear-stained Primrose pleaded, having come running into his room. Of the two sisters she was the closer to Adam.

He didn't reply.

'But where will you go?'

Where would he go? The answer was obvious.

'Please?' She clutched at his sleeve.

'I'm sorry, Primrose, but I can't remain here after what's been said.'

'But I don't want you to go!'

'Don't make this worse than it has to be. I'm going. He's told me to, I want to, and that's that.'

'But . . .' She trailed off, unable to think of any further objections.

'Now let me get on with this,' he said, removing her hand from his sleeve.

He didn't know what he'd packed as he closed the suitcase again, everything that had gone in had been just a blur. There was lots left behind, but he couldn't help that. He hefted the suitcase and went out into the hall where he found an ashen Olivia standing. He could faintly hear his mother sobbing.

'Don't go, at least stay till morning. Things will look differently then, to you and father.'

He kissed Ollie on the forehead, tried to smile but couldn't, walked on past her and out of the house. He glanced at his pocket watch. Incredibly it was only six minutes since he'd arrived home. He knew that as he'd looked at his watch coming up the stairs.

The suitcase was heavy, and there were no trams or omnibuses, which stopped before the trams. It was going to have to be a hansom despite the cost.

He was lucky, he found one almost right away.

'Who is it?' Vera demanded in response to his knock.

'Adam.'

There was the rattle of a chain being unhooked, then the door was flung open to reveal an astonished Vera. Astonishment that deepened when she saw his suitcase.

'I've been thrown out of the house,' he explained. 'Can I come and live with you?'

The astonishment disappeared to be replaced by an expression of sheer delight. She wasn't going to have to wait till tomorrow night after all.

'Come away in,' she replied, taking him by the arm.

'This is it, Miss Hawke. Three storeys up, left-hand door,' Sheach said to Sarah who was sitting in her carriage, Olivia facing her.

Olivia eyed the close with distaste; it was repugnant to her to think her brother was living here. What a come-down.

Neither the close nor street bothered Sarah, who'd been used to what the people she now mingled with would consider unsavoury surroundings. Netherton hadn't exactly been the Garden of Eden.

Olivia, Primrose and Mrs Tennant were worried sick about Adam and how he was getting on. It was bad enough when he'd left home, but then he'd packed in his job with Jock, without giving proper notice, which had angered Jock, and gone off to do who knows what.

Olivia had approached Sarah, who was also worried about him, and they'd contacted Toshie at the art school who'd assured them Adam was still attending evening classes.

But where was he staying? And was he all right? Was he eating properly? All these and many more questions wanted answering.

They'd considered accosting Adam in the street as he went into the art school, but decided that was unsatisfactory. He could simply refuse to talk to them after all, leaving them none the wiser.

They'd pondered about that, then Sarah had hit on a plan. Sheach had waited outside the Art School the previous night, and followed Adam.

181

Adam had gone to a pub, which he'd left after closing time with a woman. The pair of them had come to this tenement where they'd gone upstairs. Sheach had been able to work out which house they'd gone into by its light coming on.

He'd then stayed for quite some time in the street till eventually the light had gone off again, but neither Adam nor the woman had reappeared back downstairs. A quick check had revealed that the rear light was also off, which meant either Adam and the woman were sitting in the dark, or had gone to bed. It seemed safe to assume the latter was the case.

'Right, let's go on up then,' Sarah said to Olivia.

Olivia was suddenly filled with indecision, and otherwise mixed emotions. 'I'm not so sure I want to now,' she replied slowly, retreating backwards into her seat. 'Perhaps it would be better if you went up alone? You might get more out of him that way.'

'Either we go up together, or not at all. And that's final.' Actually Sarah was so curious about the woman that Adam had become involved with she was quite prepared to confront him on her own, but she much preferred Olivia to accompany her.

Olivia believed what Sarah said, and caved in. 'All right, after you.'

Sheach helped first Sarah out of the carriage, then Olivia. 'Do you wish me to come with you, Miss Hawke?' he queried.

'I don't think that's necessary.'

'It is a fairly rough area, Miss.'

She couldn't deny that. 'Then it's best you stay here and keep an eye on the carriage. I don't want us all to go upstairs only to come down again and find we've only got four wheels left.'

Sheach grinned. She had a good point. 'If you do need my help, Miss, just shout and I'll hear you.' Well, he thought, you never knew who you might run into on stairs like these.

When Sarah and Olivia arrived at the door on the left hand side three storeys up they found it to be painted brown, and very badly scarred and chipped. The nameplate bore the legend *Bryce*.

Sarah tugged the brass bell-pull, and they listened to it clang within.

Olivia wrinkled her nose in disgust. There was a toilet smell pervading the close that was most unsavoury. She dreaded to think what the communal toilets themselves were like. Disgusting, no doubt.

Adam opened the door, his face falling in surprise to see who it was.

'Well, aren't you going to ask us in?' Sarah smiled.

He was carrying a filthy rag which he now used to wipe his hands. His clothes were blotched here and there with paint, and there was a smudge of buttercup yellow on his cheek.

'How on earth did you find me?' he replied.

Sarah tapped her nose. 'Ask us in and all will be revealed.'

He laughed to hear that, and instructed them to follow him through.

He'd been painting in the kitchen and the almost complete picture was propped up on a homemade easel. There was a stack of finished canvases in a corner, and others, varying in size, hanging on the walls.

Olivia gaped at one of the latter; it was of a naked female lying sprawled across a bed. The female positively oozed sex and sensuality.

Adam saw what his sister was goggling at. 'That's Vera and this is her house,' he said softly.

Olivia's mouth opened, and closed again. Then repeated the procedure. Just like a goldfish in a bowl.

Sarah felt a pang of jealousy inside her. There was no reason whatever why she should be jealous, but she was. She had to admit she'd come hoping to see the woman, this Vera, that Adam had taken up with. What she hadn't expected to see was *all* of her.

'She's very pretty,' Sarah said. 'I take it she's not here?'

'She's at work.'

'And what does she do?'

'Barmaid at a pub called Milne's Vaults. That's where I work too now, as a cellarman. Mornings only though, which gives me the afternoons free to draw and paint, and the evenings for my classes.'

Olivia found her voice. 'You earn enough there to keep yourself?'

'The funny thing is I only work mornings as I said but my take-home pay is considerably more than when I was with Mr Hawke. But then that was a job with prospects and a future and a cellarman has neither. Once a cellarman that's it.'

Sarah found her gaze drawn back to the naked Vera. What a pair of bosoms! She had nothing to be ashamed of herself in that department, but Vera quite outdid her.

Adam couldn't help teasing Sarah. 'You once told me to watch out for the nude models, remember? Well, I found them not nearly as terrifying as I thought I would. In fact I thoroughly enjoy painting the naked female body.'

Sarah couldn't help but think what else he must thoroughly enjoy with that particular female body, which caused her ears to go red and burn. She'd never envisaged Adam in that light prior to this, he'd always seemed something of a boy before. But he was clearly a boy no more, Vera Bryce had seen to that.

'So how *did* you find me here?' Adam asked a second time.

Sarah explained about Sheach following him the previous night, then Olivia explained the reason for their visit.

'I'm fine, couldn't be better. Tell Mum and Primrose they have nothing to worry about.'

It was obvious to Olivia that Adam was physically well, though shabbily dressed compared to what she'd been used to. He had a definite air of scruffiness about him now that hadn't been there before. And he badly needed a haircut.

'You're happy then?' she queried.

'As a pig in . . .' He stopped himself from saying what he'd been going to. Some of Vera's coarseness had rubbed off on him, he realised.

'Very much so,' he replied instead.

But was he? he asked himself. He'd certainly thought he was until a few moments ago when Sarah had reappeared in his life. Damnation! And after he'd successfully managed to get her out of his mind, too.

He thought of Sarah next door in the bed he slept in with Vera. In his mind he imagined *her* naked, the pair of them doing some of the things that he and Vera did. The mental vision brought a lump to his throat, and made his heart beat faster.

'And how are Mum and Primrose?' he asked.

'In the pink, though missing you and worried about you as I've just explained,' Olivia replied. She hesitated, then added, 'So too is father, though to be honest with you he's never said that he's worried or in the least way concerned about you, at least not in my presence. But reading between the lines, I think that if you were to ask him to take you back into the house he would agree.'

Adam shook his head.

'He had an absolute blinder of a headache that night. And then to find out that you and this Vera had been . . . Well you know he *is* a church elder.'

Adam glanced sideways at Sarah. He found this embarrassing with her there. 'I won't be going back, Ollie, not ever. It's best for everyone concerned to accept that.'

'You'll be staying on here then?' Sarah queried.

'Yes.'

'And continuing with your evening classes?'

'Oh yes, I wouldn't give those up. Not for all the tea in China.'

'And you can manage, the pair of you can manage, financially?'

'The rent here is very reasonable, and as I told you I'm now earning considerably more than I was. I'm sorry I left your father so abruptly, Sarah, but when the cellarman job came up I had to jump at it.'

'I'll explain that to Jock then. You never did.'

He looked sheepish. 'My leaving was messy. I'm sorry.'

Sarah crossed to the almost-completed picture standing on the easel. It was of a group of shawled wifeys nattering outside a closemouth. They were happy, one of them laughing uproariously, but underneath that the pain and suffering they'd all endured in their lives was clearly evident, movingly so.

'It's excellent, very, very good indeed. You continue to improve,' she acknowledged.

'Thank you.' He twisted the filthy rag he was still holding round a thumb. There was a question he felt compelled to ask, and knew he would have to do so. 'Does the way things have turned out, me leaving your father's employ like I did, make you regret paying my art school fees?'

When Sarah had originally paid Adam's fees, because she'd had the capital there and then, and to get it out of the way, and furthermore because she'd been given a fair-sized reduction for doing so, she'd paid for three years in advance.

She thought about that before replying. 'When Olivia and I encouraged you to go to the School of Art we, all three of us, were opening a door for you beyond which none of us could know what would lie. I must confess things haven't turned out as I expected, but that is hardly relevant. Your own well-being, and the fact you continue to advance artistically, are both counts which I am more than well satisfied on.'

His heart, still beating faster than usual, swelled within him to hear that.

'Now I think we'd better go, Ollie, and let Adam get on with his picture.'

'Yes,' Olivia agreed. All the questions she'd wanted answering had been.

'Won't you stay for a cup of tea?' It didn't bother him one way or the other if his sister did or not, but he desperately wanted Sarah to do so. Any excuse to prolong her visit.

Sarah glanced at Olivia. 'Ollie?'

'No, you're right Sarah. We should get on.' For a great many reasons she was ill at ease there. She didn't wish to linger.

Sarah glanced sideways again at the picture of Vera. Adam saw the glance, and couldn't help himself asking, 'And how's Jardine?'

Sarah frowned, and brought her attention back to him. 'Who?'

'Jardine. You met him that night of the summer ball. I thought, imagined, the two of you would end up going out together?'

Sarah recalled Jardine now, and the amusing incident of Adam telling her that Jardine was married with two children. 'He did write to me but I'd already decided he wasn't my sort at all. Far too arrogant and self-conceited by half.'

Adam thought of the mental agony he'd gone through speculating about that relationship, a relationship it now transpired had never existed. 'Jardine is very arrogant and self-conceited,' he mumbled in reply.

An awkward silence fell between them, finally broken by Olivia saying, 'Shall we then, Sarah?'

Feeling wretched and miserable as sin that Sarah was leaving, Adam saw them out on to the landing. He kissed Olivia goodbye, but didn't kiss Sarah. Nor did he shake her hand. Instead he muttered that it was kind of her to have worried about him, but she mustn't any more.

As soon as they were walking down the stairs he shut the front door, and leant his back against it.

He was sick inside, sick with the knowledge that he was still in love with Sarah, and that what had been between him and Vera would never be the same again.

When he returned to his easel to paint he found he couldn't. All he could think about was Sarah.

Sarah rubbed a hand across her forehead. What was wrong with her! Earlier on she'd been restless and jumpy, now she was the complete opposite, lethargic in the extreme.

She tried again to concentrate on the book she was in the middle of, *The World of Will and Idea*, but her attention kept wandering. She wasn't all that keen on Schopenhauer anyway, she decided. She much preferred Hegel.

'Come in!' she called out, when there was a tap on the library door.

It was Mrs McGuffie carrying a silver tray. 'I've brought you coffee and a nice slice of cake,' Mrs McGuffie announced.

Sarah laid her book by the German philosopher aside, and massaged her temples. Coffee was the very dab, her mouth had gone awfully dry.

Mrs McGuffie placed the tray on a table, then poured coffee from the pot into the solitary cup. 'It's Madeira cake – you like that, don't you?'

'Yes, I do.' A cigarette, she thought. That was what she needed despite her dry mouth. She rose and went over to the mantelpiece where she'd left them earlier.

'Are you feeling all right, Sarah?' Mrs McGuffie queried. 'You certainly don't look it.'

'I'm not at my best, I must admit,' Sarah smiled back. She lit a cigarette, and drew the smoke deep down into her lungs. 'That's better.'

Mrs McGuffie wasn't at all convinced. 'Are you sure?'

'I think I might have a dose of the flu coming on.'

'In which case you should go straight to bed and stay there,' the housekeeper counselled.

Sarah didn't want that, she loathed being in bed during the daytime. There was something terribly slothful about it. 'I'll see how I go,' she prevaricated.

'Well just ring if you want anything.'

'I'll do that.'

Mrs McGuffie was halfway down the corridor when she heard a loud thump coming from the library. Whirling, she raced back the way she'd just come.

Jock closed his office door, and turned the key in the lock. Going over to the safe he opened it and took out a metal box that was padlocked shut.

He put the box on his desk blotter, then stared at the box for almost a full minute before opening the small padlock. Inside was a photograph of a woman, his wife Myrtle, Sarah's mother.

Sitting beside his desk he propped the photograph up against the box, and gazed at it. As he continued to gaze his eyes began to glisten.

The photograph had been taken after Sarah had left Netherton. He'd hired a photographer who'd gone to Netherton with the story that he, the photographer, was there to take photographs for posterity of a typical Scottish mining community.

Literally hundreds of photographs had been taken until eventually the photographer had been able to take the one he was being paid most handsomely to get, that of Myrtle.

Jock was still lost in the past, reliving episodes of when he and Myrtle had been together, when there was an urgent knock on his office door.

'Mr Hawke! Mr Hawke, sir!'

He dimly heard the knock, but was so lost in the past it was as though he was actually part of it, and it was the voice which belonged to another time and place.

'Mr Hawke, sir!'

Jock frowned, and sucked in a deep breath, the past slipping away as he returned to the present.

'Mr Hawke, sir, it's important I speak to you!'

He recognised the voice now, it belonged to Moffat, the Chief Clerk.

'Coming!' he called back, replacing the photograph of Myrtle in the metal box as he did, and snapping the padlock shut again. A few swift paces and the box was once more in the safe, and the safe closed.

He paused for a moment to compose himself, then made for the door which he unlocked and swung open.

Moffat wasn't alone. Sheach the driver was with him.

'Your daughter has collapsed at home, and the doctor sent for. Your housekeeper apparently thinks it best you return to Stiellsmuir right away,' Moffatt said in a rush of words.

'Collapsed?'

'Fainted dead away in the library, sir,' Sheach added.

Jock was galvanised into action. Hurrying to the stand he snatched up his hat and coat. 'Let's go Sheach!' he commanded, striding past the two men. Sheach fell into step behind him.

Jock's own carriage and driver were available, but it would take time for the horses to be harnessed, which was why he elected to go with Sheach.

When they reached Sarah's waiting carriage Jock said, 'Drive as fast as you can, man,' and clambered aboard.

Sheach took Jock at his word, and drove like a fury out of hell.

Mrs McGuffie was waiting for Jock outside Sarah's bedroom. 'Doctor Lambie is with her now,' the housekeeper said. Doctor Lambie was the 'family' doctor with a reputation for being one of the finest in Glasgow. Sarah couldn't be in better hands.

'What happened exactly?'

Mrs McGuffie was still explaining when the bedroom door opened and Doctor Lambie came out.

'How is she?' Jock demanded.

'Brace yourself, Jock, for it's bad news I'm afraid. There's been an outbreak of it recently, a small epidemic. One of the prices we pay for being an international port.'

Jock knew immediately what the doctor was referring to – he'd read about it in the newspapers.

'Aye,' Doctor Lambie said, nodding. 'Smallpox.'

Chapter 5

Somebody began to sob. Jock looked round and there was Elinor, Sarah's maid, who'd come up without his noticing.

'She'll have to be taken to a fever hospital,' Doctor Lambie went on. 'If you let me have the services of one of your people I'll arrange matters.'

Jock might be stunned, but his brain was still functioning. He didn't like the sound of that at all. Fever hospitals were notorious; the majority of those who went in never came out again.

'Wait a minute, does she have to go into hospital? Can't she be looked after here, in her own room and bed?'

'She can, but it's going to be very expensive if she is.'

'Bugger the expense!' Jock exclaimed vehemently. 'I want the best there is for her. The best specialists, nurses, medications, whatever, I don't care what it costs.'

'Right then, leave it all to me. The first thing I'll do is hire four nurses to tend her round the clock, and we'll go from there.'

'The best, mind,' Jock growled.

'I understand.'

'Now can I go in and see her?'

Doctor Lambie shook his head. 'No, after you've been vaccinated perhaps. But not yet.' He knew from long years of being Jock's personal physician that Jock hadn't been vaccinated.

Jock was about to argue, then changed his mind. 'Is she awake?'

'She's in a deep sleep which she should be in for some while. She'll be distressed when she wakes, but we'll be ready for that. Now which one of your staff can I have to help me?'

Mrs McGuffie stepped forward. 'If you'll tell me what you want done, Doctor, I'll see that it is.'

'Good.'

Doctor Lambie and Mrs McGuffie went into a conflab, then the pair of them went off, to disappear down the corridor.

Jock turned to Elinor who was still sobbing. 'Go and get me a bottle of whisky, girl, and a glass.'

'Yes sir,' she mumbled.

He remembered then how highly Sarah thought of Elinor, how Sarah was forever singing her praises.

'And girl –'

'Yes sir?' Her eyes were red, her face blotchy.

'Have a gill yourself before you bring the bottle up.'

She smiled at that, then hurried off on her errand.

'The ants! The ants! There are millions of them crawling all over me!' Sarah shrieked, her entire body twisting and writhing. Her hands were hooked into claws which she would have attacked the imagined ants with if they hadn't been tied down, as were her legs and body, restraining her from doing so.

The imagined ants were small red angry eruptions called macules that covered her face, forearms, the hands themselves, and below the knees. There were also some on her trunk and the upper portion of her limbs, though on these places the rash was scanty.

Soon the macules would turn into papules, flat, raised areas, which after several days would become vesicles, raised areas containing a clear fluid, rather like little water blisters. Eventually the vesicles would become pustules, the latter lasting roughly a week before drying up to form dark scabs.

Jock, sitting on a wooden chair by the door, staring at Sarah – he was strictly forbidden to go any closer – knew this from his many conversations with Doctor Lambie and Mr McKendrick, the latter Scotland's leading authority on infectious fevers.

Jock also knew from these many conversations that all lesions in smallpox develop approximately at the same time and not in separate crops, with the result that all reach each stage simultaneously.

The nurse currently in attendance was Nurse Reilly, a big raw-boned redheaded woman from County Wexford. She was gowned and masked as she hovered over Sarah, as was Jock himself. The room stank of disinfectant – it was washed down with the stuff twice daily, mid-morning and late evening.

'Aaaaahhhhh!' Sarah shrieked.

Every sound she made was like a knife twisting in Jock's belly. How much longer before this delirium broke! How much longer? Providing it did break, that was – many sufferers died without coming out of it.

Jock thrust that thought from his mind. She would survive. *She would!*

Without being aware of what he was doing he reached up and

rubbed his upper right arm where his vaccination was itching like billyo. The entire household had been vaccinated within hours of Doctor Lambie's diagnosis.

'The ants! The ants!' Sarah raved again, her body jerking and twisting, seemingly in all directions at once.

'I'll be back later,' Jock said to Nurse Reilly, and left the room. Outside in the corridor there was a basket into which he dropped his gown and mask. Later they would be burned. McKendrick had said they could be boiled and reused, but where money was no object the best thing of all was to burn each set after being worn. And so burned they were.

Jock leant against a wall, and closed his eyes. He was dead beat, utterly exhausted. But he wouldn't allow himself more than a short catnap or two until Sarah was out of her delirium.

He knew then what he wanted to do next, and where he would do it. In the privacy and intimacy of his own bedroom.

He was entering his bedroom when Mrs McGuffie, who'd been attending to kitchen business, caught sight of him. He looked quite ghastly, she thought.

She attended to one more pressing matter first, then went to his bedroom where she found the door slightly ajar. She pushed it further open, intending to enter, then checked it when she saw that Jock was on his knees by the side of his bed, hands clasped in front of him, praying. Silently she withdrew, closing the door to as it had been before.

Anything that is mine, God, Jock was praying. My life, money, property, *anything*. Just spare Sarah. Please, I beg of you. Anything, just spare Sarah . . .

Mrs McGuffie allowed a few minutes to tick by, then looked into the bedroom again. This time Jock was on his feet pouring himself a hefty dram. Going inside she closed the door behind her.

'Oh Maud!' he whispered.

'I know, Jock. I know.'

Taking his drink from him she placed it on the dressing-table beside the bottle, then gathered him into her arms.

'Oh Maud!' he whispered again.

'I want to see a mirror,' Sarah stated adamantly. She was at the late pustule stage, they on the verge of transforming into scabs. 'I look hideous, I know I do.'

'No mirror, Miss Hawke,' McKendrick replied. Then, to Jock

who was standing by the wooden chair, 'If she's starting to worry about her appearance we know she's doing well, and on the road to recovery.' That was a long road yet, but he didn't say so. But what he had said was true.

Sarah felt terribly weak, completely drained of energy. And the thick gloves she was forced to wear when awake were a damned annoyance. These were to stop her picking, which was a constant overwhelming temptation. When she was asleep they tied her hands again, though now only those.

Nurse Marra waited near by, ready to bathe Sarah's eyes once McKendrick and Doctor Lambie had gone. There were a number of pustules on Sarah's eyelids, clusters of them on the skin directly underneath the eyes. These had to be continuously bathed and attended to in order that the eyes themselves weren't damaged.

McKendrick came to sit on the edge of Sarah's bed. He'd been waiting to have this conversation with her, and judged the time to be now ripe. 'You're very lucky, you know,' he said.

Her chest heaved in a bitter laugh. 'Lucky! How can you say that when I'll end up with a face pitted from top to bottom! I've seen folk who've had smallpox and survived; not a pretty sight. In fact a downright ugly one.'

'Number one, you're alive. There's everything to be thankful for, for that alone.'

Which was true, she thought. Alive, but facially scarred for the remainder of her life. Or she would be once the disease had finished with her. But there she was wrong.

'Number two, and this is where you have been lucky. The classical form of smallpox is called Variola Major, the most severe types of which are confluent and haemorrhagic.'

'And which do I have, confluent or haemorrhagic?'

'Neither. You don't even have Variola Major. What you have is Variola Minor.'

'And that's lucky, Mr McKendrick?'

He smiled at her – he had a lovely smile. 'It is, because Variola Minor doesn't scar nearly so badly as Variola Major. You *will* be left with some scar tissue mind you, but nothing like you would have been left with had you had the Major form of the disease.'

It was such a relief to hear that, unbelievably so. She felt as if an enormous weight had been lifted off her shoulders. 'When you say not nearly so badly, how little do you mean?'

He shrugged. 'That depends, it varies from case to case. At nineteen you're young still, which is very much in your favour. And you had a healthy body when the disease struck, which is another.'

'I certainly don't feel very healthy now,' she replied, and laughed again, a laugh that turned into a racking cough.

'You must take it easy, relax as fully as you're able. That too will be to your benefit, for we also have your heart to be concerned about. The heart can be easily weakened during an attack of smallpox, and that we don't want, do we?'

'No,' she agreed.

'Total bed-rest and the excellent ministrations of Nurse Marra and her colleagues are what's required for quite some time to come I'm afraid.'

Total bed-rest, she thought, and mentally groaned. Torture for someone who loathed lying abed during the day.

'Snap!' Sarah said quickly, and gathered the playing cards to her. It was such a silly game, but one she enjoyed. And it didn't take too much mental effort, in fact it took none at all, which was an attraction. When she played whist and rummy she soon got fagged out.

Elinor eyed the small pile of playing cards left to her. 'You're going to win again, I just know it,' she complained, but only in fun.

'Game's not over yet. Anything can still happen.'

There was a tap on the library door. 'Come in!' Sarah called out.

It was Roderick the footman with a calling card which he presented to Sarah. Her eyebrows shot up when she saw it belonged to the Honourable Ian Monteith; she hadn't seen him since the night he proposed to her. It was as though he'd completely vanished off the face of the earth. Well at least as far as she was concerned.

'Shall I show him in, Miss?' Roderick inquired.

'Yes, of course.'

'I'll leave you,' Elinor said, gathering up the playing cards and putting them back in their box. 'Is there anything you want before I go?'

Sarah shook her head.

Elinor left the library, and shortly afterwards Roderick ushered in Ian who was carrying an enormous bunch of spring flowers. It was April 1893, five months since Sarah had come down with smallpox.

'I only got back to Glasgow last week, and heard about your illness yesterday,' he said in a rush of words.

He'd put on a little weight, she noted. Something she could do with herself. She'd never regained that which she'd lost.

She smiled at him. 'It's good to see you again, Ian.' And she meant that; it was. But then she'd always enjoyed his company.

He came closer. 'You're fully recovered, I believe?'

'Yes, but still not quite my old self again. It takes a long time to get properly over smallpox.'

Again he moved closer, trying not to make it obvious, and failing completely, that he was trying to get a good look at her face.

'I was lucky,' she told him, and went on to explain about Variola Minor, and how it didn't scar nearly as much as Variola Major, the more virulent and more common variety of smallpox.

She'd been left with a band of scar tissue under each eye, and a patch roughly the size of a half crown on her left cheek. Other than that her face and neck had escaped unscathed. She considered herself to have got off very lightly indeed.

'I was worried sick when I heard,' he confessed. 'But now that I've seen you . . .' He shook his head. 'There's no difference really.'

She'd forgotten what a beautiful speaking voice he had, the sort you could listen to all day long. And occasionally it had that hint of a caress in it which still made her go prickly all over.

'Would you like a cup of tea, or whisky perhaps?' she offered.

'No, thank you.'

'Then sit and talk to me. I enjoy receiving guests. My strength isn't yet such that I get out and about a great deal.'

He sat opposite her, laying the flowers on the table between them.

'They're gorgeous, thank you,' she smiled, and he smiled back. 'You never got in touch with me again after that night at your house.'

He glanced down. 'No.'

'Because I refused you?'

'I should have thought that was obvious.'

She decided to tease him. 'So have you found yourself a meal ticket yet?'

Anger flashed across his face, replaced by amusement. 'There is a young lady in the offing.'

'Rich, I take it?'

'Oh, filthy!'

Sarah laughed. 'Is she pretty?'

'Passably so.'

'I see.'

'It is a pity about her hump, though.' He slid that smoothly in, his expression never altering.

'Her hump!' Sarah exclaimed, sitting bolt upright.

'On one of her shoulders. Makes her look a bit like a female Richard the Third.'

His eyes twinkled, giving the game away. He was having her on, Sarah realised. Doing a Chinese prince to her. 'How unfortunate for the poor girl,' Sarah replied, pretending to sympathise.

'If it was only the hump I wouldn't be too bothered. It's the other thing that really puts me off, I'm afraid.'

Sarah went along with it. 'And what's that?'

'Her ginger moustache.'

Sarah guffawed. This was tremendous fun, and the best laugh she'd had since her illness.

'Of course, you might say that a ginger moustache goes with a name like Charlie, short for Charlotte.'

'Stop it!' Sarah exclaimed, slapping her thighs. 'You're being totally outrageous.'

'Well I'm glad I've cheered you up.'

And he had, cheered her up immensely. She felt the better for it. 'Is there really a young lady in the offing?'

'Yes, and her name is Charlotte. But she doesn't have either a hump or a moustache.'

'And she is filthy rich?'

'Disgustingly so. Her family own half of Suffolk.'

Sarah wasn't sure if she should ask this or not. Then decided she would. 'Do you love her?'

'I love you. I told you that.'

So convincing, she thought. Just as he'd been before. She almost believed him. 'And yet you're thinking of marrying this Charlotte?'

'I didn't say that. What I said was there was a young lady in the offing.'

'Well are you going to marry her? She'd solve your problems.'

'She certainly dotes on me, thinks I'm the bee's knees.'

'She's one bird you've succeeded in charming down out the tree?'

'Tweet tweet!'

Sarah laughed again.

'You haven't asked me why I've been away from Glasgow.'

The scent of the spring flowers, strong and fragrant, had filled the room. 'All right, why have you been?'

'I got myself a job.'

She leant back in her chair, thoroughly enjoying the scent wafting all around and over her. 'I'm impressed. What kind of job?'

'A kind I can do extremely well, it transpires. I've joined the diplomatic corps, and all this time have been living in London while being trained. Charlotte is the daughter of the man who's been training me.'

'I see. And what now brings you back to Glasgow?'

'I'm on leave prior to being posted abroad. I'm off to join our embassy in France next month.'

'And what about Charlotte?'

'By remarkable coincidence her father is to be our new ambassador there.'

'Remarkable coincidence,' Sarah agreed drily.

'We shall be seeing each other every day.'

'How cosy for the pair of you.'

'Very.'

Now why was she feeling niggled? She certainly had no right to be. And yet she was. Niggled and . . . a teensy bit jealous? He would marry this Charlotte in the end, everything pointed that way. Half of Suffolk indeed! That was a lot more than Jock Hawke's daughter would have brought him. Yes, he was going to land very neatly on his feet. She could see it coming a mile off.

'I know it's rude to ask about money, but what's the salary like in the diplomatic corps?'

He pulled a face. 'Terrible. Far below what I'd imagined.'

If she needed a clincher that was it, he *definitely* would marry his Charlotte.

He went on. 'The salary does become very good when you reach ambassadorial level. But of course it takes some while to get that far.'

'But not quite so long when you have influence in high places, such as a father-in-law who's already an ambassador?'

He didn't reply to that.

'So it's all working out well for you,' she said.

'It's not what I wanted.'

'I asked you once. No more charades, remember?'

'Oh yes, I remember,' he replied softly.

'Now how's your friend the actor who's also mad keen on cricket?' she inquired, changing the subject.

'C. Aubrey Smith? Why he's fine. In fact I had a letter from him only the other week . . .'

Ian stayed two hours, time that just flashed by for the pair of them.

When he finally left it was with the promise that he'd return soon.

'Take a deep breath,' instructed Mr McKendrick, his stethoscope placed against Sarah's chest. 'And another.'

He gave her a thorough sounding, then had a look at her eyes, and after that the back of her throat.

'You can get yourself done up again,' he said when he was finished. And while Sarah got her various bits and pieces tied, laced and hooked – it was Elinor's day off – he washed his hands, using the pretty patterned jug and bowl placed at his convenience.

When Sarah was once more presentable, McKendrick opened the door and told Jock, who'd been waiting outside, that he could come in.

'What's the verdict then?' Jock asked anxiously.

'I can't find anything physically wrong. And yet she should have fully recovered from her illness long before now.'

'I'm so weak there are some mornings I can hardly find the energy to get myself out of bed,' Sarah said.

McKendrick stared grimly at her while he racked his brains for a suggestion.

'And she still isn't putting on weight,' Jock said.

'I just never have an appetite any more. A bit of a pick and that's it.'

McKendrick packed his things away in his black bag. 'You have had an extended period of convalescence, but that's been entirely at your home here. Perhaps what you need is a complete change of air and surroundings to stimulate your general well-being.'

'That's a thought,' Jock mused, rubbing his chin.

'You mean down the Clyde?' Sarah queried.

'I was thinking more of abroad. Switzerland maybe, or Italy?'

She liked the sound of Italy.

'Then again a sea trip could be the very thing. There's nothing like sea air to revitalise you.'

'A sea trip is easily organised,' Jock said. 'She could take one of the big passenger ships from here. There again, she could leave from Liverpool, Southampton or the Pool of London, depending on her destination.'

'A sea trip or cruise does sound fun,' Sarah said. 'I've always fancied a trip to sea. Except . . .' She trailed off, and bit her lip.

'Except what?' Jock probed.

'There would be all those other passengers aboard, which would mean socialising to an extent, as I could hardly stay in my cabin all the time, and that wouldn't suit me at all. Frankly, I just wouldn't be up to it. Mentally or physically.'

'How about a cargo ship where there would be no other passengers, and therefore no socialising? Surely that could be organised?' McKendrick proposed.

'If a cargo ship is all that's required, Sarah could go on one of my own vessels,' Jock said. 'There's one docking at the end of the week, the *Good Intent*. She's doing a round trip to the West Indies after that.'

Sarah closed her eyes as a ripple of excitement ran through her. She hadn't manipulated this at all, she reminded herself. She hadn't. But of Jock's six ships it would have to be the *Good Intent* and Captain Mathew Wilson. Somehow, there was an inevitability about it.

'A round trip to the West Indies would be excellent,' McKendrick enthused. 'How do you feel about that, Sarah?'

'I think I'd enjoy it,' she replied, managing to keep her voice steady.

'Right then, that's agreed. The West Indies it is for you, girl,' Jock stated.

Sarah let out a long, low sigh.

It was drizzling as Ferguson brought Jock's carriage into Queen's Dock, North Basin, where the *Good Intent* was tied up, and still in the process of loading cargo bound principally for Kingston, Jamaica, with a small amount destined for San Juan in Puerto Rico.

Sarah glanced through the carriage window to see that Captain Wilson was standing on the deck waiting for them. Jock had said they'd arrive at 3 pm and dead on 3 pm it was. Jock was notorious for being punctual, as Wilson knew.

'Terrible weather for July, cold as well as wet,' Jock said. 'But you'll soon be out of it, glorying in the sunshine.'

'I can't tell you how much I'm looking forward to that.'

'And as you're aware, you'll be in good hands with Wilson. A first-class skipper, totally trustworthy.'

In Wilson's hands, she thought, and smiled inwardly. How lovely!

The carriage came to a halt, and Ferguson helped them out. Jock first, then Sarah. Wilson came down the for'ard gangplank to greet them.

'Everything ready and in order for Miss Hawke?' Jock demanded in a voice steely with authority.

'Yes sir. She has my own cabin which her maid has sorted out with all the paraphernalia that came aboard earlier.' Elinor had arrived shortly after breakfast with Sarah's luggage plus many other items that would make Sarah's sojourn aboard the *Good Intent* more comfortable. Included amongst these, at Jock's insistence, were luxury wines and foods of the sort that would have been available to her had she gone on a big passenger ship. He was ensuring she'd want for nothing.

'Hmmm!' Jock growled, nodding his approval. He was feeling very emotional, hating the idea of losing Sarah for a while. He would have loved to have gone with her, but because of the business and what was generally happening at the time it was quite impractical for him to do so.

Wilson turned to Sarah. 'I'm very sorry to hear about your illness, Miss Hawke. I hope and pray our voyage does you the world of good.'

He was truly sincere about that, Sarah could read it in his eyes. It was marvellous to see him again, it being ages since they'd last spoken and been together, a night before her illness when he'd called briefly at Stiellsmuir to discuss something with Jock.

'Thank you,' she replied.

'Then shall we get aboard before you get sodden?' Wilson said.

At a sign from Wilson a burly sailor came rushing down the gangplank to assist Sarah. She wished he'd done the assisting himself.

She hardly recognised Wilson's cabin, compared to how she remembered it. Cushions, quilts, bits of furniture, all manner of things that she was familiar with at Stiellsmuir were there.

'It's just like a home from home,' she breathed.

Jock beamed with pleasure to hear that.

'Will you take a dram before you leave us, sir?' Wilson asked Jock. Jock nodded.

'And you, Miss Hawke?'

'Not for me, thank you, Captain Wilson. But I will have a glass of sherry if one's available?'

He gave a thin smile, knowing this was a reference to the last occasion she'd been aboard when she'd had a dig at him about the sherry he'd offered her then.

While the drinks were being poured by Wilson, Elinor helped Sarah out of her hat and coat, then hung them on a steel rail that was in the cabin for that purpose.

When Wilson went to hand Sarah her sherry it shocked him to see how thin she'd become. That hadn't been noticeable when she'd had her coat on.

'To a successful trip!' Jock toasted when the three of them had their glasses. Nor was he talking about the financial aspect of it either. That didn't matter a damn to him. Sarah's health was all that counted.

After the drink Jock said he'd better get on and leave Sarah to settle in. He told her not to bother coming up on deck with him; he'd say his goodbyes there and then.

There was a glint of wetness about his eyes as he kissed her on the cheek. 'I'll be waiting here on the quayside for you when you get back lass,' he promised, thinking how empty his life, and Stiellsmuir were going to be without her.

Then Jock was off, stomping off and up the companionway that led to the deck.

'Excuse me,' Wilson muttered to Sarah, and hurried after him.

Sarah sat on the bed while Elinor shut the cabin door. She felt exhausted, but elated at the same time. Her insides were churning with a medley of emotions.

Lying back she closed her eyes. This was where *he* normally slept she told herself. She was on *his* bed.

Her thoughts drifted off as she began to daydream, and in that daydream to fantasise about Captain Mathew Wilson.

Adam Tennant stood on the brow of the hill watching the *Good Intent* slowly make its way downriver. He'd learned of Sarah's trip from Olivia, also the name of the ship she was going on, the ship's berth place and time of departure.

There was a lump in his throat as he watched the barque hoist another sail. He'd never gone to see Sarah when she'd started receiving visitors again after her illness. On a dozen occasions he'd resolved to travel out to Stiellsmuir, and once had actually started, only to turn back again, but never had.

'Oh Sarah!' he whispered.

The drizzle had become a downpour that was fairly stotting off the ground, but that didn't bother him any except that it meant his view was not as clear as it might have been.

He watched the *Good Intent* until at long last it turned a bend in the river and was gone from sight.

With a heart heavy as stone, and the sharp wind that had sprung up whistling in his ears, he retraced his footsteps the way he'd come.

Back to Vera.

'I must say this is a tremendous treat. What I eat normally aboard ship is nowhere near as good as this,' Wilson said.

Sarah smiled, and didn't reply. It was their first night at sea, and she had invited Wilson to her cabin to dine with her.

Wilson had a sip of wine, eyeing her over the rim of his glass as he did. He was struggling to make conversation but no matter what he said she was either not replying or else being monosyllabic in reply.

Sarah was well aware of his discomfiture, and thoroughly enjoying it. He was mentally squirming, just as she'd planned.

'And this wine is excellent. The best France is capable of producing, and that's saying something,' he went on.

His mention of France made her think of the Honourable Ian, and wonder how he was getting on. On with the job, and his Charlie.

'More wine, Miss Hawke?'

She shook her head, then wiped the corners of her mouth with her napkin. When she'd done that she carefully moved her knife and fork together, signalling she was finished with that course.

When Wilson saw that Sarah was finished he too moved his knife and fork together.

'How's Miss Bessie Wallace from Boston, Massachusetts?' Sarah asked suddenly.

'She married several months ago. I was invited to the wedding but couldn't manage as I was at sea.'

Sarah raised an eyebrow.

'She married a lawyer. One from Philadelphia.' He laughed, thinking that a fine joke. Not even the glimmer of a smile cracked Sarah's face.

'*Philadelphia*,' he repeated, thinking she hadn't got it first time round.

Her expression remained blank.

'Ye...s.s,' he said, and took a deep breath.

She remained silent, forcing him to speak again. It amused her to note that a faint sheen of sweat had appeared on his brow.

'They're to live in Philadelphia where he already has a house,' Wilson went on.

There was another hiatus. 'I'm sure they'll be very happy together,' Wilson said.

'Why?'

He frowned. 'Why what?'

'Why should you think that?'

'I eh . . .' He shifted uncomfortably in his chair. 'I just presume they'll be.'

'Oh!'

What was wrong with this woman! They'd got on so well together the first time they'd met, but nothing but disaster since. The voyage was going to be very difficult indeed if she kept this up.

'Pity for you, though,' Sarah said.

'How so?'

'I got the impression you had designs there yourself?'

Wilson refilled his own glass. 'Bessie and I were – and still are – good friends, nothing more. I never had any "designs", as you put it, on her.'

A warm glow of pleasure that had nothing to do with the alcohol she'd drunk warmed her insides to hear that. But was it true? 'That wasn't what came over the night of our party at Stiellsmuir.'

'Well it's a fact, I assure you.'

'I must have been wrong then,' she conceded. 'And yes, I will have some more wine, thank you.'

He topped up her glass, and had just done so when there was a rap on the door.

'Come in!' Sarah called out.

'Enter!' he called out simultaneously.

Sarah couldn't help but smile at that, and so too did he. 'Sorry,' he apologised. 'Force of habit.'

The door opened to reveal a sailor.

'Yes Geikie, what is it?' Wilson queried.

'Could you come up on deck, sir. Mr Jolly would like a word.' Mr Jolly was the third mate, and officer of the watch.

'Right. Excuse me, Miss Hawke, I'll be as quick as I can.' And with that Wilson rose and strode from the cabin.

She'd wrongfoot him again, Sarah decided. She was feeling tired and, anyway, it had been a hectic day.

Elinor, who had another of the officers' cabins, entered. She'd eaten earlier.

'Is there anything I can do for you, Miss Hawke?' she asked, having seen Wilson's departure.

'Close the door and start getting me ready for bed. When Captain Wilson returns inform him that I've retired.'

'Yes, Miss.'

The nightdress Sarah put on was amber-coloured silk, the touch of which against her skin she found sensual in the extreme. She smoothed it down over her hips, smiling wickedly as she remembered Jock's comment that she'd be in good hands with Captain Wilson.

She got into bed and lay there, waiting for Wilson to come back. She nodded to Elinor when there was a knock on the door.

Elinor slipped out the cabin, and Sarah listened to her maid's muted voice as Elinor explained the position to Wilson. Then Elinor came back to the cabin.

'He says he understands perfectly,' Elinor reported.

Oh no he didn't. At least, not yet, Sarah told herself, rubbing her thighs very gently one against the other.

After Elinor had cleared up she finally fell asleep listening to the creaking of the wooden hull, and with the sharp tang of the sea in her nostrils.

She slept like a baby.

Mr Jolly, the third officer, was telling a story, and telling it badly. He, Mr Runciman the first officer, Sarah and Elinor were mid-deck, the day after the *Good Intent* had embarked for the West Indies.

What a bore, Sarah thought, then caught sight of Wilson watching her from astern where he was standing beside the wheelman. She hadn't noticed him there until now.

Jolly finished his story, and laughed heartily at it even though — thanks to his telling of it — it had been about as unfunny as could be.

Sarah laughed also, but only for Wilson's benefit. She wanted him to think she was thoroughly enjoying herself with his two officers.

Elinor laughed too, but only out of politeness. She couldn't understand what Sarah found so hilarious.

'That was most amusing,' Sarah said to Jolly, who smirked with self-congratulation at her compliment, and laughed again.

Wilson spoke to the wheelman, then left his position there to make towards Sarah and company. It was clear he intended joining them.

Slowly, deliberately, Sarah turned her back on him, somehow, in her female way, indicating by her body that his presence was neither wanted nor required.

Wilson came to a halt, his expression a mixture of puzzlement and annoyance.

Sarah smiled to herself when she saw him walk past her and the others on the opposite side of the ship.

'Elinor!' Sarah croaked. 'Elinor!' Her voice was barely above a whisper, all she could manage. She'd been calling for what seemed hours now, and still no reply or sign of Elinor. Where was the bloody girl!

The inside of her head was whirling, and she was covered from top to toe in a cold, clammy sweat.

She retched, but this time couldn't keep down the sick that now burst into her mouth. She managed to turn to the side so that the evil mess spewed away from her.

The ship heaved upwards, hung still for a brief moment, then plunged downwards again. Up and down, backwards and forwards, side to side in a screwing motion.

Outside the waves were huge that dashed against the ship. The water was green topped by white, the sky dark and thunderous. Aloft, members of the crew were dancing on the footropes as they struck the fore and mizzen topsails.

Captain Wilson, dressed in oilskins, watched this operation until it was completed. When it had been the crew aloft, like so many circus acrobats, shimmied down the shrouds.

'A bit fresh this morning,' Purcell the second mate commented drily to Wilson, shouting to make himself heard above the roaring elements.

Wilson nodded.

'I wonder how our passengers are taking it?'

Wilson started. He'd completely forgotten about Sarah and Elinor.

'They'll be feeling none too clever, I shouldn't doubt,' Purcell went on.

Wilson gave a low laugh. 'I should imagine so. Neither has been to sea before, far less experienced a force ten.' Force ten meant a whole gale was blowing with wind velocity between fifty-five and sixty-three miles per hour.

He'd better go below and see how they were, Wilson thought. Miss Hawke was the owner's daughter after all.

'Oh!' Sarah groaned. This was even worse than the smallpox. If she'd died there and then she'd have welcomed her passing.

Her feet jerked upwards as the front of the ship reared to a seemingly impossible angle, then she had to grab for the handhold on the side of the bed as she was nearly tossed out of it.

'Oh!' she groaned again.

The stink of sick hung heavily in the air, and she knew she must look a right ratbag, but neither bothered her one whit. All she wanted was relief from this agony, this hell on earth.

There was a knock on the door. 'Come in!' she croaked, thinking it was Elinor at last. But she was wrong, it was Wilson.

He crossed to her bedside to stare down at her, his face creasing with concern.

'I thought you were Elinor,' Sarah croaked.

'I called in on her on the way here. She is also in a bad state, though she hasn't vomited.'

How stupid of her! Sarah thought. She should have realised Elinor was also seasick. It just proved how bad she herself was that that hadn't dawned on her.

'I'll be back,' Wilson said suddenly, and left the cabin abruptly.

'Oh!' Sarah groaned yet again as the ship juddered, then fell away, leaving her stomach behind. The cabin door, which Wilson had left open, banged, then banged again.

It wasn't long before he returned, carrying a cup plus clean sheets and blankets under the other arm.

'Get this down you,' he commanded, lifting her by the shoulders, and putting the cup to her mouth.

The liquid in the cup was black and smelt absolutely vile. Sarah balked, thinking what it must taste like.

'Drink it!' he urged. 'I promise it will do you the world of good.'

It tasted even worse than she'd imagined. For a horrible few seconds she thought she was going to throw up a second time, but then that passed.

'I've told Runciman, who's off duty, to attend to your maid, so you don't have to worry about her,' Wilson said, laying the cup aside.

He went on, 'I'm going to strip and change this bed, then I'll give your face a wash.' With that he ripped off the bed's top covers, took them to the cabin door and threw them outside.

Coming back to the bed he worked the bottom sheet out from under her, and that followed the others out the door.

She wasn't at all embarrassed at his seeing her in her nightdress; the way she was feeling she wouldn't have cared if she'd been stark naked. She just didn't care about anything any more.

He was gentleness itself as, by half lifting her with one hand and using the other to spread the clean sheet, he managed to arrange the sheet over the bed. He tucked that in before starting on the top sheet. The fresh blankets followed.

He left her once more, this time returning with a bucket which he placed beside the bed directly underneath her head. 'If you need to vomit again use that. All right?'

'Yes,' she croaked.

He left her yet again, but soon returned with a steaming bowl of hot water and a large sponge, the latter his own property. Using these he proceeded to wash her face and neck, which he then dried with one of her fluffy towels.

'I don't think this weather will last too long. Hopefully it will have blown itself out by tomorrow,' he said, folding away the towel.

He got no reply to that. When he looked at Sarah again he saw that she was sleeping, which made him smile. The concoction he'd given her had a powerful sedative in it.

'Come in!' Sarah called out in answer to the knock on her cabin door. It was Wilson, as she'd guessed it would be.

'So how do you feel now?' he asked, pleased to see that she was sitting up. She was wearing a frilly cream bed jacket that was shot through with bands of champagne-coloured satin.

It was the evening of the same day. The weather outside was still foul, though nowhere as violent as it had been.

'Human again. Thank you very much. I don't know what that was you gave me but it's done the trick.'

Wilson nodded. 'It usually does. It's an old seafarer's recipe that was passed on to me by my father.'

She indicated the side of the bed – the box part of it below the covers and mattress, and the floor. 'I've noticed all this was cleaned up while I was asleep. You?'

'Not personally. I had one of the crew do that, while I kept an eye on him of course.'

She remembered then that he'd seen her in her nightdress, and a tinge of pink crept over her face. 'I'd happily have died this morning, that's how awful it was.'

'There's something particularly distressing about seasickness. Everyone who's suffered from it says so.'

'Have you?'

'Oh yes, when I first came to sea as a lad. But that's a long while ago now.'

'How's Elinor?' she inquired anxiously, for she was very fond of her maid, thinking of Elinor more as a friend than a servant.

'A great deal better, I'm told. Would you like me to send her to you?'

Sarah shook her head. 'Let her rest. She can come to me in the morning if she's up to it.'

'I'll see she's informed.'

The ship suddenly tilted sharply to port and Wilson had to grab hold of a fitting to stop himself from falling over. 'Shit!' he exclaimed.

Sarah laughed to hear that.

Now it was Wilson who coloured. 'Sorry, I shouldn't have sworn in the presence of a lady. It's just that I was caught completely unawares.'

'Don't be concerned about it, Captain, I've heard far worse in my time.'

He wondered how that could be. For of course he knew nothing about Netherton and Sarah's life prior to her going to stay with Jock at Stiellsmuir.

'Miss Hawke, may I speak plainly?'

'Please do.'

'I was surprised you elected to take your trip on my ship as you don't seem very well disposed towards me.'

Honesty? Why not! 'After it was decided I should take a sea trip yours was the first of my father's ships into Glasgow. It's as simple as that,' she replied.

Well that was clear enough, Wilson thought. 'I see.'

Instinct told her that now was the time to relent, to soften towards him. To change, in an expression he would have understood perfectly, tack.

'I'm well enough disposed towards you, Captain,' she smiled. 'And from now on, as we're going to be together for some while, why don't you call me Sarah?'

His expression was one of astonishment. 'I eh . . . Yes, I'd like that . . . Sarah.'

'And you're Mathew aren't you?'

'Yes.'

'Well then, in private I'll call you Mathew, but Captain in front of the others so as not to undermine your authority in any way. Is that suitable?'

He swallowed hard. He just never knew where he was with this woman.

'Quite.'

Sarah laughed to herself after he'd gone. He was more confused than ever, which wasn't what she'd been aiming for at all.

Removing her bed jacket she snuggled back down into bed. Her stomach still felt odd, but thankfully the nausea and sensation of disorientation had gone. She could have got up, but decided the best place for her was right where she was.

Next morning when she woke the sea was calm as a village pond, and the sun was shining.

'So tell me about yourself, Mathew I'd love to know,' Sarah said. 'You mentioned yesterday evening that you got the recipe of that drink you gave me from your father, and that it is an old seafarer's one. Does that mean he's a sailor as well?'

Mathew Wilson poked a piece of pork round his plate. At Sarah's request he was dining with her in her cabin.

'*Was* a sailor, a captain like myself. His ship the *Inverlyon* was lost through collision with the German barque *Khorasan* in mid-Atlantic. He died in the collision which was entirely the Germans' fault.'

'Oh I am sorry. That must have been awful for you. Was it long ago?'

'No, in eighty-nine, four years back.'

'And what about your mother, is she still alive?'

'Yes, living in Greenock where our family have stayed for generations. The Wilson men have always been sailors.' He barked out a laugh. 'In fact we go so far back at sea I'm sure our remote forebears must have been paddling round that part of the Clyde in coracles.'

What a change in Sarah, he thought. She was warm, pleasant and chatty, just as she'd been that first time they'd met. He was thoroughly enjoying himself.

'Do you have brothers and sisters?' Sarah probed further. She wanted to know everything about Mathew Wilson.

'Two brothers, one older, the other younger. And three sisters. The girls are all married, to Greenock men naturally, and Craig, that's my older brother, is also. He has two bairns of his own.'

'And lots of aunts and uncles and other relations, I presume, from what you've said?'

He nodded. 'We're a veritable clan in and around Greenock.'

He had marvellous hands – quite unsailorlike. The fingers were long and slim, and sensitive-looking, his wrists narrow. She would have loved to have reached out and taken one of them in her own. 'So do you still live in Greenock yourself?' she asked, a slight husk in her voice.

'I wouldn't say I actually live there any more, though I would describe it as my base, and no doubt it's where I'll retire to when the time comes. The *Good Intent* is my home, and whatever ships come after her.'

'And what if you married?'

'Would you mind if I smoked, Sarah?'

'Not in the least. I'll join you.'

She hadn't known until then that he did smoke. He produced a briar and ancient leather tobacco pouch, and proceeded to fill one from the other. When he was ready he held out a struck Lucifer match for Sarah's cigarette, then lit his pipe. A cloud of blue smoke immediately formed round him.

'The question of marriage has never come into it.'

'But if it did?' she persisted.

He shrugged. 'I suppose I'd get a place ashore as my brother Craig did.'

She had a sudden alarming thought. 'You're not a misogynist, are you?'

His lips twitched, then curled into a smile. 'I may be many things, Sarah, but that is not one of them.'

At which point they were interrupted by Borland the steward who was serving their meal. They stayed silent, Mathew puffing contentedly on his pipe, Sarah taking the occasional draw on her cigarette, while Borland cleared away and placed cheese, biscuits and a decanter of port in front of them.

Borland was the sole steward aboard and attended all the officers. His duties also included helping cook in the galley.

When Borland was gone, and they were once more alone, Mathew said, 'As I've told you about me, how about you now telling me about yourself? How is it, for instance, that a well-brought-up young lady has heard the sort of swearing you told me you have?'

Her green eyes twinkled mischievously. 'Who said I was a well-brought-up young lady?'

'Aren't you?'

'Not in the way you mean.'

'But you're Mr Hawke's daughter?'

'That's true, only I never lived with him until the day before I first met you. Up until then I was used to wearing clogs on my feet, and bathing in a zinc tub in front of the kitchen range.'

Mathew stared at her in amazement. 'Are you pulling my leg?'

'Not a bit of it.'

She then went on to tell him all about Netherton. Well, *nearly* all. She didn't mention Gordy.

'This is a lovely fresh egg I'm boiling for you, Bob. You'll be sure to enjoy it,' Myrtle said, looking over at Bob who was lying propped up in bed.

His vacuous gaze stared back at her. Even more vacuous than usual, she thought, if that was possible.

'And I'll make you some toasty soldiers to go with it. A wee bit fun, eh?'

She cut a slice of bread, slid it on to the toasting fork, which she then held in front of the bars of the range where a fine fire was blazing.

'Do you mind how Sarah used to love soldiers when she was toaty? And what a hullabaloo she'd kick up if I dared serve her a boiled egg without them, which did happen the odd time if I'd run out of both bread and money towards the end of the week.'

Myrtle chuckled at the memory. Then her face lengthened. 'I wonder how Sarah's doing?' she mused. Something she often wondered. There wasn't a week went by but she posed that question to the never replying Bob.

With a start she realised her toast was smoking, and quickly changed it round on the fork.

When the toast was made and neatly cut into buttered soldiers, she placed them on a plate, and then the egg in an eggcup alongside them.

'Right then, here we are,' she declared, sitting beside Bob, who was looking awful white. A lot paler than he normally did. Maybe he had a cold coming on.

'Tom Crayk is coming over this evening for a bit of a crack. You'll enjoy that too,' she said, slicing the top off the egg. None of this tapping and peeling for her, she was a slicer.

She dipped a soldier into the yolk, or dook as they called it in Netherton, and raised it to his lips, lips, she now noticed, that were strangely blue.

'Bob?'

His mouth remained steadfastly shut.

'Come on, Bob.'

She tapped him on the side of the jaw, and his mouth fell wide open. And in that instant all the pieces, the more vacuous than usual gaze, the white complexion, the blue lips, the not eating, clicked into place.

'Bob!' she exclaimed, dropping the soldier. 'Bob!'

She grabbed hold of his shoulders, which made him slowly topple sideways, almost as if in slow motion.

He was dead, stone dead. Her Bob was dead!

Something snapped inside Myrtle. She screamed, and continued screaming.

Jumping to her feet she rushed for the door, threw it open, and clamping her hands over her ears went running off down the street past several startled neighbours.

Still screaming she ran and ran. Retired Mr Hamilton tried to stop her but she brushed by him, almost knocking the old soul to the ground.

Kerr Street, Florence Street, Gadshill Wynd, Muckle Row, she ran and ran. Seeing nothing, hearing nothing. One thought alone hammering in her brain. Bob, her beloved Bob, the man she loved and cherished, was dead.

When she regained her senses it took a moment or two for her to realise where she was. She was on top of High Cliff that overlooked Netherton from the east. Below her was a sheer drop of a hundred feet and more.

Closing her eyes, she let the breeze that was blowing play against her face. Oh Bob! she wailed inside her head. I can't lose you! I can't! How could she go on with him gone? How could she face the empty days, the endless nights? Even as he'd been after his stroke he'd still been there. During the day she could talk to him even if he didn't answer back, during the night reach out and touch him.

Her anguish and despair melted like a handful of snow held in front of a cherry-red fire. A profound calmness settled on her, for she knew what she was going to do, what she had to do.

'I'm coming, Bob. I'm coming. Wait for me,' she said in a whisper.

Opening her eyes again, she stared out over Netherton for the last time.

Smiling, she walked to the cliff's edge where, without hesitation of any kind, she stepped out into empty space.

'Would you care to try?' Mathew asked Sarah, having just demonstrated to her how the ship's wheel worked.

Dickson, the wheelman on duty, was standing further aft gazing politely out to sea. He thought the captain showing the bonny lady how to steer a right lark.

Sarah had been hoping Mathew would offer to let her have a go at the wheel, and would have asked if he hadn't. 'Please,' she smiled.

It was a gorgeous day with the fat yellow sun beating down out of a cornflower-blue sky. According to what Mathew had told her earlier they were almost at the Tropic of Cancer in an area of the North Western Atlantic Basin known as Nares Deep.

The spokes of the wheel were smooth in her hands. The feel of them there made her think of something which caused her to smile.

She looked up at the sails billowing in the wind. A line of sailors, tiny at that distance, were making a readjustment to what she now knew, thanks to Mathew's tutoring, to be the main topgallant.

The wheel started to drag to starboard, which she tried to correct, but found she couldn't because she just wasn't strong enough. The wheel dragged further and further, twisting away from her.

'Hold her steady,' Mathew laughed, coming behind her and overlaying her hands with his own. In one fluid movement he brought the *Good Intent* back on course.

The touch of his flesh on hers turned her insides to jelly. Glancing round she found her face only inches from his.

Their eyes met, and locked, as they stared at each other, and into each other. And each saw the same thing. The same emotion, the same desire.

'I'll show you how to use a sextant tomorrow,' Mathew said in a voice that was tight as a coiled spring.

'That'll be nice. I'll look forward to it.'

Mathew called Dickson to come and take the wheel again.

'Yon Mr McKendrick certainly knew what he was about when he suggested this voyage to you,' Elinor said to Sarah. 'The change in you since we left Glasgow is unbelievable. You're your old self again and no mistake.'

It was true, Sarah thought. She was her old self again, completely recovered from the aftereffects of her smallpox attack. Her appetite was back; she'd regained all the weight she'd lost; and she was fair bursting with energy.

But Sarah knew it wasn't just the voyage she had to thank for all this, though of course that was an important contributory factor, but who she was sharing the voyage with, Captain Wilson.

'And you're so happy, it's grand to see that,' Elinor continued.

She *was* happy, gloriously so!

And very much in love.

'Bugger!' Mathew Wilson swore with the realisation that he'd made an elementary mistake in his chart calculations. And he'd made it because his mind wasn't properly on the job. He'd been thinking more about Sarah than what he was doing.

But then he'd been thinking more and more about Sarah as their voyage progressed. At times it seemed that she was never out of his thoughts. Awake and asleep, for he dreamt about her nearly every night.

He'd never been this way about a woman before, he told himself. Never. He was amazed and a little bewildered about what was happening to him. He was also—if he was being honest with himself—just that tiny bit scared. For once in his life he didn't feel in total control of the situation.

He felt wretched when he wasn't with her, downright bloody miserable. He longed for when they were together. Her company, her conversation, her humour.

Damn and blast this chart work! he thought. Normally he thoroughly enjoyed doing it, but not that day.

Up on deck Sarah laughed, which made his face brighten. Then a male voice spoke, that of Purcell the second mate.

Sarah laughed again, and so too did Purcell.

Mathew's expression was now a glower. Purcell was with Sarah, his Sarah, and he resented that. He wanted her to be with him.

'Geikie!' he bellowed.

The cabin door flew open. Mathew was using Runciman's cabin for the duration of the voyage, while Runciman and the other officers had also moved down in strict accordance with rank. Poor Jolly, last in line and with no cabin for him to move into, was having to make do with what was normally a stores cupboard.

'Yes sir?' Geikie queried.

'Ask Mr Purcell to come to me right away.'

'Yes sir.'

Mathew threw down his pencil. Purcell could do the chart work, while he would take Purcell's place on deck. With Sarah.

The glower vanished and he began to hum a jaunty shanty about lime juice and vinegar.

There's nothing in a Limey ship contrary to the Act.
So what's the use of worrying, when you have had your whack,
of lime juice and vinegar, according to the Act . . .

He'd sing the entire shanty to Sarah when he joined her on deck he decided. She'd like that.

'Have you ever tasted mango?' Mathew asked Sarah.

She shook her head.

'Then we'll have two of these.'

The street market was a riot of colour and dinning with noise. It was close to the Port Royal waterfront where the *Good Intent* had docked late the night before. After instructing his officers about the unloading Mathew had taken Sarah ashore, insisting that he would show her the sights.

Mathew told the street trader that they'd have two of his mangoes, and personally selected plump juicy ones he knew would melt in her mouth.

When he'd paid for the mangoes he handed them to the carriage driver who was accompanying them. He'd hired the carriage and driver till sunset when he would have to be back aboard the *Good Intent*.

The driver was carrying a wicker basket which he popped the mangoes into. There they joined bananas, huge misshapen tomatoes and various other fruit and vegetables that Mathew had purchased.

'How about fried goat, would you like to try that?'

Sarah wrinkled her nose. 'Sounds absolutely disgusting.'

'It isn't, I promise you.' Then, with a click of his fingers, 'I know, fish. You can't come to Jamaica and not eat fish.'

That sounded more like it; she adored fish. 'What I don't understand is where we're going to eat all this?'

He gave her a teasing smile. 'In paradise.'

She laughed. What was he havering about? 'I beg your pardon?'

'I said, in paradise. We're going to picnic in paradise.'

She was mystified. What or where was paradise?

'Wait and see,' he replied when she asked him. Then he was dragging her away, across to a fishseller whom he'd spotted.

Their last purchase was a flagon of rough red wine which came in a leather-covered bottle that Sarah thought would make a wonderful souvenir.

When they reached their carriage, which the driver had paid an urchin to mind while they wandered through the teeming market, Mathew assisted Sarah to a seat, then gave the driver whispered orders.

'What was that all about?' she queried as the open carriage, and a very old and rickety one it was too, lurched into motion.

Mathew didn't reply, just smiled enigmatically.

216

After a short while they left Port Royal and Kingston on a dusty track — it certainly couldn't have been called a road — that wound along parallel to the seashore.

'The sea round here is the colour of your eyes,' Mathew said. And it was: the exact same green colour. 'Enjoying yourself?'

'You know I am.'

'So am I. Very much so.'

They turned off the track on to scrubland which quickly plunged them into a cathedral of trees. Birds cried while a million insects moved and rustled.

The air was heavy with humidity, while under the trees the light was dappled and somehow sinister in places. Somewhere close by a largish animal went scampering off, but Sarah saw nothing.

'It's a little spooky here,' she said to Mathew.

'Don't worry, we'll soon be out of this.'

That happened a few minutes later when they burst into a lush valley where a group of laughing chocolate-coloured children were excitedly at play.

The children shouted and waved, and Sarah waved back. The children were barefoot and dressed in rags.

'Plantation workers' children,' Mathew explained. 'There's a large sugar plantation near to here.'

They passed a slow-moving river along whose banks exotic plants and flowers were growing, a river it transpired they didn't have to cross for it bore away again to their right.

'The Blue Mountains,' Mathew said, pointing.

They didn't look very blue to Sarah, but she presumed they must do at certain times of the day or year for them to be so named.

Eventually their carriage plunged into more trees, these so dense that the horse had to slow to a walk, and abruptly out of them on to the shore of a tiny cove.

Sarah gasped with pleasure. It was absolutely beautiful, quite breathtaking.

'I promised you paradise, and this is it. Paradise Cove,' Mathew said.

The sand was honey golden, the water that lapped it so enticing it gave Sarah the almost overwhelming desire to throw off every stitch she had on and plunge in.

The cove was screened by a ring of trees that halted where the sand started, the same trees they'd just come through. On the land

217

on both sides of the cove's open mouth coral gleamed and twinkled in the sunlight.

'According to legend, Captain Morgan used to sometimes anchor here, for despite being a tiny cove the water's deep. It's said that this was his favourite place on the entire island.'

With the help of the driver Sarah stepped down on to the sand, and Mathew followed her.

Mathew looked round, selected a site by a fallen tree that had crashed on to the narrow strip of beach, and told the driver to take their basket over there.

Mathew then arranged a time for the driver to return for them, after which the driver clambered back on to his carriage and drove off, soon to be swallowed up by the dense ring of trees.

Sarah was glad she'd worn her lightest dress; she'd have been sweltering in anything else.

'Why don't you take off your shoes and stockings?' Mathew suggested.

She thought that a good, if somewhat daring, idea. But who was to see or know apart from him? No one. 'All right,' she agreed, and sat on the opposite side of the tree to him while she lifted her skirt to undo her suspenders.

Mathew wasn't watching anyway, he'd gone in search of some driftwood which he found without any bother at all. After that he went into the trees to gather small bits and pieces that he would need to get the fire started.

Sarah ran down to the water's edge, pulled her skirt up a little, then waded out till the water was just above her ankles. The water was warm, in total contrast to that cold stuff to be found in the Clyde, she thought.

Still holding her skirt, she threw back her arms and raised her face to the sun. She was going to have quite a tan when she returned home, which pleased her. She didn't give a damn that it was considered unfashionable amongst ladies to have such, and couldn't wait to show it off to Olivia.

'Mind the sharks don't get you!' Mathew called out.

'Aahh!' she exclaimed, and hastily splashed back to the beach.

Mathew was laughing at her.

She'd been had, she realised. 'There aren't any sharks, are there?' she chided.

'You'd soon know if there were, I assure you,' he said, and

laughed again. He'd thought that great sport to give her a fright.

'Have you ever seen a shark?' she asked.

'Oh aye, lots of them.'

'Up close?'

He bared his teeth. 'That close.'

She shuddered. 'I read about them in a book. They terrify me.'

'You're not the only one. Sharks, crocodiles and snakes, all three give yours truly the heebie jeebies.'

'Me too.'

'That's something we've got in common then,' he said.

They stared at one another, her insides dissolving once again into jelly.

'Will you gut the fish or shall I?' he asked.

'I'll do it. Have you got a knife?'

The black-handled knife he tossed to her had many blades, including a corkscrew. She went to work on the fish they'd bought at the market while he lit the fire.

'We can eat some of the other things till the fire settles a bit,' he said, for having quickly caught it was now blazing away.

He showed her how to clean her dirty blade in the sand, and then used it to slice the delightful huge misshapen tomatoes.

'Have you been here many times before?' she asked him, probing.

'Quite a few.'

'With women?'

'Always.'

Her face dropped a fraction.

'Never before with a woman, actually,' he confessed. 'You're the first.'

Her face lit up again.

He glanced out over the cove, and to the sea beyond which could be glimpsed through the cove's mouth. 'You know I like you,' he said casually, but with a wealth of meaning behind it.

'Yes. And I like you.' She felt as if a hurdle had been overcome. That a declaration, of sorts, had been made.

Sarah began her meal with the tomatoes which, despite their appearance, were delicious. 'We should have brought salt and pepper,' she said.

'Sorry, I never thought.'

'That's all right.' She smiled at him, and he smiled back.

'How about some wine?' he proposed. 'And as we don't have

219

glasses either you'll have to drink it from the bottle, pirate fashion.'

She laughed. 'Sounds fun.'

The wine was very rough, and strong. It went straight to her head, making her feel marvellously woozy.

They chatted, ate and drank for a while, then he set about cooking the fish. He constructed, by notching and tying with a length of green vine that he'd found when gathering the firewood, two wooden crosspieces. Next he speared a brace of fish on to a thin strip of wood, sharpened at one end, which he slung between the crosspieces.

'These won't take long,' he said.

Sarah leant back against the fallen tree, and closed her eyes. She knew this was a very special day, and one she was going to remember for the rest of her life.

She heard him move, come close.

'Sarah?'

She opened her eyes again to find him beside her.

'Sarah.' He reached up to touch her shoulder. Then suddenly, his mouth was on hers, his arms round her holding her tightly to him.

The kiss went on and on, neither of them wishing to break that first magic moment of intimacy.

'Oh!' she sighed when he finally pulled his mouth away. 'I've wanted you to do that since our first meeting aboard the *Good Intent.*'

His eyebrows lifted in surprise. 'You have? I thought there was that period when you didn't like me. Why, at your party at Stiellsmuir you couldn't even remember my name correctly.'

She traced the line of his jaw with her finger. Should she tell him she'd arranged the date of the party specifically so he could be there? No, she decided, she wouldn't. That would remain her secret, at least for now.

'Men can be so completely non-understanding,' she murmured in reply. 'Now kiss me again.'

When everything had been eaten, and the wine drunk, they lay contentedly in each other's arms, occasionally talking in soft voices, occasionally kissing.

And that was how the carriage driver found them when he returned.

'You're very quiet tonight,' Mathew said to Sarah. It was her last night aboard the *Good Intent*, the last time they'd dine together in her cabin.

'And you're nervous, which is unlike you.'

'Yes,' he agreed. He knew he was.

He pushed his plate away; he had no appetite whatever. 'I can't imagine life without you now,' he said in a voice so low she had to strain to hear.

'Nor I without you.'

'I eh . . .'

Come on! she thought. Say it!

He snatched at the whisky bottle and poured himself a large gill, half of which he swallowed in a single gulp.

Say it! she shouted at him in her mind. If he didn't soon she bloody well would.

'It could be considered impertinent of me to ask you this, me being nothing more than a ship's captain and you the daughter of Mr Hawke. But I do love you and . . . want to marry you.'

There, at last he'd said it. Sarah opened her mouth to reply, but before she could do so there was a tap on the door and Borland breezed in.

'Finished, Miss?' Borland queried.

Sarah smiled, and nodded. The steward's timing was impeccable. Impeccably bad. She and Mathew waited silently – and he very impatiently – until Borland had once more left the cabin.

What a wretched speech, Mathew was thinking over and over. He'd meant it to be loquacious, and romantically delivered. Instead of which it had come out as though he'd been a bumbling boy standing up in front of the class.

'*Well*?' he demanded, far more forcefully than he'd intended, the moment the cabin door had clicked shut.

'I accept.'

He rocked back in his chair. 'You do?'

'Oh yes. I love you too, as I thought was obvious by now.'

All his nervousness and uncertainty vanished, replaced by elation and glee. He came to his feet, and to her side, she rising also to slip into his embrace.

'You do appreciate that a sailor spends an awful lot of time at sea?' he said.

'I do.'

'And that won't bother you?'

'Of course it will. But I'll just have to live with it as all sailors' wives do. And anyway, there's no reason, my father being your employer, that I can't travel with you on the ship from time to time, is there?'

He hadn't thought of that. 'No.'

'And I insist our honeymoon is aboard here, which I have no doubt Jock will agree to. Because I'll see he does.'

A niggle of remaining worry twisted in Mathew. 'And it won't come between us that I'm not rich?'

She knew his love to be true, there was no question at all in her mind about that. His love for her was as true as her love for him. 'Not in the least,' she assured him.

He kissed her, a passionate kiss that had her squirming.

'Let's get married as soon as possible,' he suggested.

'Yes, let's not wait. Just as soon as it can be arranged.'

'I can't wait either for . . .' He broke off, slightly embarrassed. 'You know?'

She did know, only too well. She wanted him physically just as fiercely and urgently as he wanted her.

This time she kissed him, their tongues stabbing and twining in each other's mouths.

'I'll call the other officers in to announce our engagement,' Mathew said when the kiss was over.

'No, I wish Jock to be the first that we tell. He'd appreciate that.'

'Then the first he'll be.' Mathew hesitated, then asked, 'Do you think he'll approve?'

'I'm certain of it. He holds you in very high esteem.'

Mathew ran his hands down her back, and on to the swell of her hips. 'I still can't believe this. I was certain you'd turn me down.'

She nibbled under his chin, which caused him to tremble all over. 'Nice?'

'Lovely.'

She pulled his head to her, and flicked a tongue in his ear. His reply to that was to do the same to her.

Her hand made butterfly movements across his chest, then dropped to just above his belt where she made rubbing, massaging movements.

'Someone might come in,' he said, swallowing.

Knowing Borland, the damned steward would, Sarah thought, removing her hand.

'I'd better get up on deck anyway. It's time for the changeover of the watch,' Mathew said.

'Goodnight then.'

'Goodnight.'

He kissed her again, a touching of the lips, then turned for the door.

'Mathew?'

He paused, and looked at her over his shoulder. 'Yes?'

'As we're going to get married just as soon as it can be arranged, why not start the honeymoon tonight?'

He stared at her, hard. Then his face softened into a smile. 'What a good idea. It'll have to be after midnight though, and I'll only be able to stay for a few hours as I wouldn't want anyone to find out. We've your reputation to consider.'

'I'll be waiting,' she said.

'Mrs Mathew Wilson,' Sarah spoke aloud when he was gone. It was music to her ears.

She was still reading, and fighting off sleep, when the door silently opened and Mathew just as silently entered the cabin, closing the door silently again behind him.

She laid her book aside to gaze at him. He was dressed in a white open-necked shirt, his uniform trousers and had only stockings on his feet.

'Hello,' he said.

She was wearing a scarlet nightdress by Paquin that had a plunging neckline and mandarin sleeves. It was made of China silk that was the finest money could buy.

'Hello,' she replied.

The room was filled with warm yellow light from the oil lamp dangling and slightly swaying in the centre of the cabin. She'd turned it up full so that she could read. He now went to it and turned it down.

'Better like that,' he said.

She agreed the low light was far more intimate.

'Would you care for a drink?' he queried.

'Would you?'

He nodded.

He was nervous again, she thought correctly. But then that was understandable. She was herself a little. 'Then I'll have a whisky and soda.'

When the drinks were poured he came to the bed and sat on its edge. 'What'll we toast to?' he asked, giving her a glass.

'Us?'

'Why not. To us!'

'To us!' she echoed, and drank.

Reaching out, he put a hand inside her nightdress to reach for her breast. He caressed it several times, then brought it out of her nightdress where it gleamed palely in his grasp.

'Why don't you take your clothes off and get in here with me?' she suggested.

He placed his glass beside her book then, getting up again, started to strip.

His body was wiry with no excess flesh on it, his buttocks small and hard. A thick rope of pubic hair ran from the tangle round his genitals up to his deeply indented belly button.

When he was naked he stood before her. 'And you?'

Smiling, she pulled the covers back, then whipped her nightdress off over her head to throw it aside. Now they were both naked.

His eyes feasted on her for a few seconds before he climbed in beside her.

'This bed isn't exactly made for two,' she said.

'No.'

'But we'll manage.'

'Yes.'

He'd suddenly gone monosyllabic, reminding her of Douglas Tennant, Adam's father.

He buried his face in the valley of her breasts, moving it slowly from left to right and back again. While he was doing this her hands were continuously moving, touching, probing, feeling.

She gasped when he nipped a nipple, which he then worried with his teeth. She gasped again when he repeated the performance with her other one.

Kissing, sucking, biting, his face slid down her body. Parting her willing legs he delved his tongue into her.

She came immediately, lifting her hips as she did. His tongue continued to flick, bringing her to orgasm once more, this a deeper orgasm than the previous one.

'Come into me, I want you into me,' she husked.

He twisted away from her, and nearly fell out the bed in the process. She wasn't a virgin, he thought. He hadn't known whether she would be or not. It didn't matter that she wasn't.

He pulled himself up, then her head downwards on to himself.

He grinned with pleasure as her head began to move.

Grasping her full breasts he squeezed them. Then alternately squeezed and teased her jutting nipples with his pinkies.

There was a raging furnace between her legs, a furnace she now desperately wanted attending to. She pulled him out, and rolled on to her back.

'Please?' she pleaded.

He plunged into her, and from there they became like two wild animals bucking and tearing at one another till at last, with a strangled cry, he came.

This was heaven on earth, she thought, as he jetted into her. And with that she orgasmed again, the most convulsive one yet, one that made her writhe, grinding herself against him.

'I love you Mathew,' she whispered when the sensations had subsided within her.

'And I love you. More than anyone or anything else,' he whispered in reply.

She didn't know how she was going to bring it about, but somehow she was going to get him to give up the sea and stay ashore. To stay ashore, and be happy doing so.

'There he is, there's Mr Hawke!' Sarah exclaimed excitedly to Elinor, pointing to a distant figure in a 'lum' hat. Jock had promised he'd be there waiting on the quayside when she returned, and he was a man who kept his promises.

She couldn't wait to tell Jock about her and Mathew, and for the two of them to begin making preparations for the wedding. She glanced across to where Mathew was in conversation with Mr Jolly, and a warm glow of satisfaction filled her at the memory of the night before. When he'd finally left her she'd been satiated from their lovemaking, and had slept a wonderfully blissful sleep as a result.

'And there's Sheach,' said Elinor. 'I recognise the carriage.'

Sarah now saw that Sheach was standing a short distance away from Jock, and in front of the carriage. And there too were Royal and Regal, her lovely horses. She was extremely fond of those horses, and knew they'd be just as pleased to see her again as she was to see them.

Mathew came striding over. 'About twenty minutes till the gangplanks go down. I've ordered a couple of hands to start bringing your luggage and other belongings up on deck.'

His eyes were sparkling as he gazed into Sarah's. He too was remembering the previous night.

'And we'll do it over a drink in the cabin,' Sarah said, for that was what had been agreed between them. Jock would undoubtedly ask to inspect the documentation, and during the usual dram she and Mathew would break the news to him. If by any chance he didn't ask to inspect the documentation they would invite him down to the cabin, and then do so.

'Aye,' Mathew replied, nodding.

Something was going on, Elinor surmised. But she had no idea what. Sarah hadn't informed her of Mathew's proposal, and her acceptance of it. As Sarah had told Mathew, she wanted Jock to be the first to know.

The *Good Intent* moved slowly towards the quayside where she would be warped alongside. On the quayside itself gangs of dockies lounged about awaiting the ship's tying up.

'That's not Mr Hawke,' Elinor said a little later.

Frowning, Sarah gazed again at the man in the 'lum' hat. She'd assumed because of the hat and Jock's promising to be there that that was him. But now they were closer she could see that Elinor was right. 'Lum' hat was smaller than her father, and slimmer. So where was Jock?

The ship was about a hundred yards offshore when, with a shock, Sarah recognised 'lum' hat. It was Ranald Cyril McIvor, and there was no sign of Jock whatever. A sense of foreboding gripped her.

Finally the *Good Intent* was tied alongside, and the gangplanks secured in place. McIvor came strutting up the aft gangplank making straight for where Mathew was standing beside Sarah and Elinor.

On reaching them McIvor raised his hat to Sarah, then swung on Mathew. 'This ship now belongs to me, Captain Wilson. Take me to your cabin, where I wish to discuss the new situation with you.'

Sarah was thunderstruck, as was Mathew. This was totally unexpected.

'Yes, of course, sir,' Mathew replied after a stunned pause, completely thrown by this turn of events.

'Good day to you, Miss Hawke. I hope you enjoyed your trip. Now lead on Captain.'

A dazed Mathew strode away, McIvor following hard on his heels.

'My God, what's happened!' Sarah choked to Elinor.

'Sheach will know.'

She should have thought of that, Sarah berated herself. But since McIvor had dropped his bombshell her mind had been numb.

Sheach was at the bottom of the aft gangplank directing the sailors who'd brought Sarah's luggage and other belongings, including Elinor's things, in the loading of them on to the carriage, having brought the carriage close in to the *Good Intent* after the ship had docked.

'What's happened, Sheach?' Sarah demanded the moment she was by his side.

'The master's been taken ill, Miss, and that's all I can tell you. My instructions from Mrs McGuffie are to get you back to Stiellsmuir as soon as possible,' he answered.

'Ill? What's wrong with him?'

Sheach shook his head. 'I don't know, Miss, and that's gospel.'

Sarah turned to face the ship, and bit her lip. She didn't want to go off without speaking to Mathew, but didn't see how she could do in the circumstances. Then she spotted Mr Purcell the second officer.

'Mr Purcell!' she called out, and gesticulated that she wanted a word.

Purcell shouted some orders, then came down the gangplank. She gave him a message for Mathew, stressing that it was private and not to be passed on to Mathew in anyone else's hearing. Purcell replied that he understood.

'Thank you for a wonderful voyage, Mr Purcell. And will you please convey my thanks to Mr Runciman and Mr Jolly. I had intended thanking them myself but events have transpired otherwise.'

Purcell answered that he would be delighted to do that for her, then excused himself and returned on board.

Sarah had one last look at the *Good Intent*, thinking of Mathew and that the ship now belonged to that weasel McIvor.

'Let's go,' she said, and climbed into the carriage on to which her luggage and other belongings had now been fully loaded.

She was grim-faced, and silent, all the way home to Stiellsmuir.

PART 3

The Witching Time of Night

Tis now the very witching time of night,
When churchyards yawn, and hell itself breathes
  out
Contagion to this world. . .

Hamlet by WILLIAM SHAKESPEARE.

Chapter 6

The change in Mrs McGuffie rocked Sarah when she saw her. The housekeeper's eyes had sunk in on themselves, as had her cheeks. Her facial skin had become taut, with an unhealthy yellowish tinge to it. The hair that previously had been pepper and salt was now almost entirely white with only a few streaks of dark remaining.

The two women stared at each other for a few seconds. Then came together, and hugged.

'How ill is he?' Sarah asked.

Mrs McGuffie held Sarah at arms' length, and took a deep breath. 'I'm afraid you're going to have to brace yourself for a shock, Sarah. A number of shocks in fact. Would you like a drink first?'

'No, a cigarette though. You?'

'Please.'

Sarah offered her silver case, a wee treat to herself the year before. And the pair of them lit up.

'Sarah,' Mrs McGuffie said slowly, 'I'm sorry to have to tell you that your mother's dead.'

Sarah stared blankly at the housekeeper. It was her father who was ill. 'I beg your pardon?'

'Your step-father died and your mother was so distraught she . . . killed herself.'

Sarah staggered where she stood. This was a nightmare.

'Killed herself? How?'

'When you lived in Netherton you must have been familiar with a place called High Cliff?'

Sarah nodded.

Mrs McGuffie had already decided she had to be blunt about this. There was no other way. 'Your mother just stepped off the top. We know that for fact because it was witnessed. She just walked towards the edge and . . . off.'

Sarah made a funny animal sound at the back of her throat, and ground a fist into her mouth. Her mother dead! Bob dead! 'Did she . . . did she die right away?'

'Thankfully yes. The same person who saw what occurred, a Mrs McLelland, reached her moments after she landed. That's how we know she was killed on impact.'

Mrs McLelland, her with the terrible teeth and window boxes. 'Mrs McLelland was a neighbour, I mind her fine.'

'Your mother and step-father were buried side by side in Netherwood Cemetery.'

Sarah took a deep draw on her cigarette, and tasted nothing. 'When?'

'Not that long after you left for the West Indies. We had no way of contacting you.'

'And Bob, what did he die of?'

'He just passed on. His stroke finally did for him.'

Her mother and Bob dead! Sarah still couldn't believe it. Bob, yes. That had always been on the cards since they'd brought him home on the flat cart. But for her mother to be gone! And suicide too.

In her mind's eye Sarah pictured High Cliff as it had been the last time she was there. She remembered the sheer, terrifying drop to the ground below, and saw her mother go over the edge to fall . . . fall . . . fall . . . until finally . . .

'I believe I'll have that drink after all,' she whispered.

'I'll get it for you.'

Mrs McGuffie poured herself one as well. 'There's more,' she said, handing a large dram to Sarah.

'Oh!' Sarah exclaimed. She'd temporarily forgotten about Jock.

Mrs McGuffie gulped some of the contents of her glass. 'Your father . . .' A choke rose to block her throat. She swallowed, and started again. 'Your father took your mother's death very badly.'

Sarah was suddenly icy cold all over. 'I imagine he would have done.'

'Very, very badly, Sarah. In fact it . . .' She drained her glass, then turned anguished, despairing eyes brimming with tears on to Sarah.

'Doctor Lambie says it's called schizophrenia, and it's what Jock has been suffering from all these years. The doctor said that by imagining ghosts, tapping on walls, and all the other strange things that Jock did when he was in one of his "moods" – or "funny turns" as I called them – he was displaying classic symptoms.'

She paused, then went on, her voice trembling with emotion. 'I'm sorry to have to tell you that your mother's death has severely worsened his condition, and that Doctor Lambie says that it's entirely possible that he'll stay as he is now for the rest of his life.'

Mrs McGuffie, quite overcome, tottered to the nearest chair and sank into it. Her face was streaming with tears. 'Oh Jock, oh my poor mannie,' she whispered to herself.

Sarah was stunned. First her mother and Bob, now this. She felt as if she was breaking into a thousand pieces, each of which, one by one, was blowing away in the wind.

'You're telling me he's snapped. That he's . . . he's . . .' She forced herself to articulate the word. 'Mad?'

Mrs McGuffie slowly nodded.

'Sweet Jesus!' Sarah whispered.

'You'll want to see him. He's in his room. He rarely leaves it nowadays. Usually only to go to the toilet.'

'He's not dangerous then?'

Mrs McGuffie produced a crumpled handkerchief which she dabbed her face with. 'Not in the least. He never was when having one of his "turns".'

'And now the "turn" is a permanent thing?'

'It would break your heart, Sarah. It's broken mine.'

Sarah had a sip of her whisky, which she hadn't touched up until now. Then she had another.

'Doctor Lambie suggested we have him committed, but I wouldn't have that. I'll look after him as long as I can.'

Sarah placed her glass on an occasional table. 'I'll go to him now.'

Mrs McGuffie sniffed back tears. 'And Sarah, that's not all of it. There's more.'

'More!' God in Heaven! A veritable Greek tragedy was rapidly unfolding. 'What more?'

'See your father and I'll explain when you come down again. I'll order tea for the pair of us.'

What else could possibly have happened, Sarah wondered as she left the room. Then she remembered that the *Good Intent* had been sold to McIvor. It had something to do with that.

Outside Jock's bedroom she paused and listened to him talking, but couldn't make out what he was saying. She knocked, and when she got no reply knocked again. When she still didn't get a reply she opened the door and went in.

Even though it was broad daylight outside the curtains were drawn, and candles lit. Jock was sitting by the fire, staring into it and talking animatedly to himself.

'I think we should go fishing tomorrow Rence, you know how we both enjoy that . . .'

233

Rence, the man he'd stayed in the caravan with as a boy, Sarah thought. The man who'd burned alive trying to save his galah.

'And when we've cooked and eaten our catch we might have a long walk over Mossie Moor; we haven't been out that way in ages. What's that?'

Jock cocked an ear. 'I'm with you. I understand,' he answered to the imaginary voice only he could hear.

'Hello, Jock,' Sarah said softly.

'Yes, rainbow trout *are* delicious. Particularly with almonds . . .'

She went to him, and touched his arm. 'Jock, it's me – Sarah. Your daughter.'

'I've never tasted pike. I would have thought it was a very strong flavour . . .'

She squatted beside him, and looked up into his eyes. 'Jock,' she said insistently. 'It's me, Sarah.'

'A lot better than garbage soup . . .' Jock threw back his head and laughed.

She shook his arm. 'Jock! Jock!'

He suddenly swung on her, his eyes blazing. 'She's dead, you know. Myrtle's dead.'

'I know.'

'You aren't the blue lady.'

'I'm your daughter, Sarah.'

'Why aren't you the blue lady? She promised she'd come today. She promised.'

'Don't you recognise me?'

He screwed up his face, and peered into hers. 'Never seen you before. Are you a new servant?'

'I'm your daughter.'

'She's dead you know. Killed herself.'

'Yes.'

'Myrtle, who left me years ago for Sunter. I could never understand that.'

'She loved him.'

'*I* loved her.' He twisted away. 'Look! Can you see them? Over there!' He pointed to the far corner of the room. 'Aren't they beautiful.'

'Aren't what beautiful?'

'The butterflies of course. There are dozens of them, all fluttering and weaving.' He laughed again. 'Watch out for Mr Murphy! He

234

eats butterflies. He'll gobble you all up!'

Jock turned his attention back to the fire. 'Tell me another tale about when you were a sailor, Rence. You're a born storyteller. You have me hanging on every word.'

Jock's features became set with concentration as he listened to the imaginary voice of his long-dead friend.

After a while Sarah got up, kissed her father on the forehead, and left the room.

When Sarah returned to the library she found Mrs McGuffie composed once again.

'I had some sandwiches prepared as well in case you were hungry,' Mrs McGuffie said, indicating a plate of them beside the tea things.

Sarah shook her head. 'I couldn't eat anything.'

'But you'll have a cup of tea?'

'Yes, please.' Sarah went to the window and looked out. The September garden was resplendent with late summer flowers and flowering shrubs, but it was Jock in the room upstairs she was seeing.

'He didn't know me,' she said to Mrs McGuffie when the housekeeper handed her her tea. 'Does he ever recognise the person with him?'

'He has me several times, but even then the situation is never normal.'

'And there's nothing can be done?'

'I did what Jock did with you when you had smallpox. I instructed Doctor Lambie to get the best specialist there was. So he did. A man from London called Professor Kloehn, a Prussian.'

'And?'

'The professor examined Jock at length, then went back to London to write his report. That went to Doctor Lambie who then conveyed its contents to me. Jock is now totally schizophrenic and, as I told you earlier, it is entirely possible that he'll stay as he is for the rest of his life.

'As for something being done, there are certain treatments. None have had any real positive results, and all of them cause a great deal of pain and general distress to the patient. Professor Kloehn, Doctor Lambie and I were all agreed against these so-called treatments. But of course Jock is your father; if you want to try them it's your right to do so.'

'They don't only sound useless, they sound downright sadistic.

235

So I'm in agreement too, no treatment,' Sarah replied emphatically.

Mrs McGuffie had been sure Sarah would say that. Nonetheless it was a relief to have it verified. 'Of course, Jock *might* get better with the passage of time, with no interference other than letting nature take its course, but the professor, via Doctor Lambie, didn't want to raise any false hopes in that direction.'

'I understand the position now,' Sarah said. She had the beginning of a headache, but there was little wonder at that, considering all she'd been through since getting up that morning. A morning during which she was supposed to have announced her forthcoming marriage to Mathew, but which had turned out quite differently, lurching from one disaster to another.

'You mentioned there was more to come,' Sarah said to Mrs McGuffie. 'To do with selling the *Good Intent*, I take it?'

Mrs McGuffie nodded. 'I don't understand the ins and outs of it, but the firm is in dire financial straits. Hemphill the accountant has been here several times trying to get Jock to sign some paper or other, but hasn't succeeded in getting him to do so.'

Hemphill had been employed by Jock to do the day-to-day accountancy donkey work, thereby giving Jock far more time to spend on the actual running of the firm.

Sarah was baffled. 'How can the firm be in dire financial straits? It was making money hand over fist when I left for the West Indies.'

'It's something to do with Jock's Canadian investment. Though exactly what I couldn't say. But I do know that Hemphill is like a cat on a hot tin roof about the whole business.'

Sarah glanced at the mantelpiece clock, surprised to see it was still so early. 'I think the best thing would be for me to go and have a chat with Hemphill.'

'I think so too Sarah.'

'Right then.' She ran a hand across her brow. Drat this headache. It was getting worse by the second.

'Have Sheach harness the horses again, will you, Maud. I'll join him in ten minutes.'

She'd stop *en route* at a chemist's shop and get something for her headache, she thought.

When Mrs McGuffie left the room she poured herself another cup of tea. She'd had reservations about overseas capital investment right from the start. But what had gone so terribly wrong with

Jock's Canadian investment that it had plunged the firm into dire financial straits, to use Maud's expression, and necessitated the selling of the *Good Intent*?

She'd soon find out.

'If you care to wait here, I'll get Mr Moffat to attend to you,' Holmes, one of the clerks, said.

Sarah was impatient to speak to Hemphill, but decided it best she have a word with the Chief Clerk first. She didn't want to upset him in any way by appearing to go over his head.

Moffat appeared a few minutes later. 'Good-day to you, Miss Hawke and let me say how profoundly sad we all are that Mr Hawke has been taken ill.'

'Thank you, Mr Moffat.' She came straight to the point. 'Mr Hemphill the accountant has been out to Stiellsmuir on several occasions with some papers that need signing. I would like to discuss the matter with him.'

Moffat's eyebrows crawled up his forehead. 'You, Miss Hawke? Why should you want to do that?'

'Perhaps I can help.'

'With all due respect, Miss Hawke, I hardly think so. These aren't things that a young lady should concern herself with.'

She was rapidly becoming irritated. 'Young lady or not, I *am* concerned, Mr Moffat, and want to see Mr Hemphill.'

He was frowning now. 'I fail to understand how you can help, Miss Hawke.'

Irritation gave way to anger. Anger that might not have come on so quickly if she hadn't had a headache. 'I don't give a damn whether you understand or not, Mr Moffat. I wish to discuss the matter of these papers with Mr Hemphill, and shall. Please conduct me to his office.'

Moffat had gone pale. It was unheard of for him to be spoken to like this. 'I . . .' he started to protest.

Sarah brushed past the Chief Clerk, thinking sod him! She had a rough idea where Hemphill's office was, and marched in that direction. She left a spluttering Moffat staring after her.

A word with another of the clerks and she found Hemphill's office with no bother.

'Come in!' he called out when she knocked.

'Miss Hawke!' he exclaimed in surprise, rising from behind his desk.

'I wish to know what's gone awry with my father's Canadian investment,' she declared, and sat facing him without being asked to do so.

Her tone of command and authority further surprised Hemphill. He sat again, and made a pyramid with his hands. 'First of all, about Mr Hawke ...' He shook his head. 'I really am most dreadfully sorry. Mr Hawke was a man I much admired.'

He was sincere about that, it was no false or fawning statement. She nodded. 'Thank you, Mr Hemphill.'

'The Canadian investment,' he said, and took a deep breath. 'What do you know of it?'

'My father and I often discussed business affairs, but in this instance, possibly because he thought I disapproved of it, we never discussed the investment in any detail. I know the investment was Canadian, speculative, and concerned with oil. That's the sum total of my knowledge on the subject, so please go on from there.'

'Before I do, would you care for coffee?' Hemphill inquired.

She shook her head. She'd have a cigarette instead, she decided, reaching into her handbag for her case.

'A syndicate of Scottish businessmen was formed, Miss Hawke, of which your father was one. A syndicate numbering twenty in all, each contributing an equal share of capital, each to have an equal return on that capital.

'Part of the contract between the twenty was, the venture seeming such a surefire one, that should any member withdraw there would be no new member brought in to replace him. There would therefore then be nineteen or eighteen or whatever equal shares instead of the original twenty.'

So far clear enough, Sarah thought, lighting up. Her headache was beginning to fade, thanks to the draught she'd had at the chemist's shop.

'As you correctly stated, Miss Hawke, the investment was to do with oil, or to be more specific the drilling for such. That brings us to to Mr Earl Raisin, one-time hero and now arch villain of the piece.

'Raisin is a well-experienced and well-qualified engineer who had bought a section of land in Manitoba under which, thanks to the myriad tests he's conducted, he's convinced there is a lake of oil. Crude, as he calls it.

'Now, as I'm sure you're well aware, not that many years ago you couldn't give oil away, but with the advent of the internal combustion engine, and its offspring the motor car, oil is becoming more and more in demand with an enormously lucrative future ahead of it according to many people's belief, twenty of whom formed the syndicate which backed Mr Raisin.'

Sarah recalled Jock mentioning a number of times that he believed oil was going to be a very big commodity in the near future.

Hemphill continued. 'Trouble arose when Raisin didn't strike oil as quickly as he'd thought he would, which meant continued drilling, and the continued eating up of capital. Eventually the point was reached where six of the original twenty were forced to drop out, their venture capital exhausted, leaving fourteen.'

Sarah had a horrible suspicion she was beginning to see something of what was coming. 'Go on,' she urged.

'Raisin, it began to emerge, is a fanatic who's convinced beyond all doubt there is oil underneath the section of land he's purchased. He's continued to drill and drill, at huge expense, and continues to do so, despite the fact that just after Mr Hawke took ill another ten members of the syndicate pulled out, *en masse*, after three the month previously, calling it a day and cutting off what was rapidly becoming an enormous capital drain for them.'

'Six, three and ten, that's nineteen,' Sarah said.

Hemphill nodded. 'The twentieth is Mr Hawke, who is the sole member of the syndicate left and now paying for the entire shebang himself.'

'And the papers you want signed are to get him out as well?'

'Correct, Miss Hawke. There is no doubt that is what Mr Hawke would do were he in his right mind, but when I've gone to see him about signing he just won't do so.'

'And it's because of all that that you've had to sell the *Good Intent*?'

'Not only the *Good Intent* but others as well. I've been able to hang on to the *Snowdrop*, but unless this resolves itself satisfactorily soon then that will have to go also to help finance Mr Raisin's drilling. Of course, you do appreciate it isn't just Mr Raisin himself, but him plus a large crew, plus machinery, plus running costs.'

Five of Jock's ships gone; that was a blow, Sarah thought. 'And if Jock doesn't sign the papers?'

'Bankruptcy within a very short period, and I mean short. He would lose everything, including Stiellsmuir.'

Christ! What a mess. 'But how were you able to sell the ships without my father's signature?'

'We were fortunate there. My own signature was sufficient to sell them on behalf of the company.'

'So why can't you sign the Raisin papers?'

Hemphill pulled a face. 'Because that isn't actual company business, but Mr Hawke's personal investment.'

Lose Stiellsmuir! It was inconceivable. And yet it would happen, according to Hemphill, if those papers weren't signed. And soon. 'What about the firm itself, how is that doing without my father here?'

'Not too well, I'm afraid, Miss Hawke. Mr Moffat has taken charge, and is doing his pedestrian best. But without the powerhouse that was Mr Hawke the firm is losing business left, right and centre. Mainly to McIvor, McIvor and Devereaux who bought all of the ships we've so far put up for sale.'

'McIvor knows about my father's illness, then?'

'He's aware that Mr Hawke is ill, but not the nature of the illness. Nor does anyone in the firm, with the exception of myself. I found out when I went to Stiellsmuir but considered it prudent to withhold that information, not even divulging it to Mr Moffat, who believes Mr Hawke will return in the near future.'

'You did the right thing, Mr Hemphill,' Sarah replied. 'I appreciate that. As I only returned from my voyage to the West Indies this morning all that has happened is still somewhat bewildering. I can assure you I will get everything sorted out, but for now the important thing is to get those papers signed.'

Hemphill opened a desk drawer, and extricated a thin sheaf of papers tied together with a blue ribbon. 'Signed and witnessed, Miss Hawke,' he said, handing them over. 'And as soon as possible, please. Time is of the essence where this is concerned.'

'I fully understand.' She rose, and Hemphill hastily did likewise. 'I'll be back to you just as quickly as I can. And in the meantime continue to keep stumm about Mr Hawke's true condition.'

Hemphill gave her a small bow.

'I presume that Moffat and the others in the firm know that, as five of our ships have been sold, the firm is in a crisis?'

'Yes, but not the details or extent of the crisis. I've so far managed to keep that from them.'

She nodded her approval. 'Good, continue to do so.'

He walked her to his office door where he said goodbye.

'I'm most impressed by your handling of all this, Mr Hemphill. I won't forget it,' Sarah said.

She sounds just like her old man, Hemphill thought to himself after she'd gone.

He hoped to God she got Hawke to sign those bloody papers. If she didn't he'd be looking for a new position. And he liked the one he had.

Jock was sitting dozing in front of his bedroom fire. He snorted, then snorted again.

'Jock?' Sarah tapped him on the shoulder. 'Jock, can you wake up? I need you to do something.'

His eyes flew open so suddenly they startled her. 'What is it? What do you want?' he demanded harshly.

'I've got some papers that urgently require your signature. See here they are. And pen and ink.' The papers were on a tray she'd brought up, as were the pen and pot of ink.

He looked suspiciously at the tray which she'd laid beside his chair. 'What papers?'

'Papers to extract you from your Canadian investment. If you don't sign them we stand to lose everything, including Stiellsmuir.'

He grunted.

'How are you feeling, Father?'

His eyes slithered round the room. 'Have you seen Mr Murphy?'

'No Jock. I haven't seen Rence's galah.'

'Intelligent bird that. Very intelligent. Got more brains than some people I know.'

'I'm sure,' she said, lifting the tray and placing it on his lap. 'Why don't you tell me all about Mr Murphy after you've signed these papers.'

She took the top off the pot of ink, dipped the pen in, shook it, and handed it to Jock. 'If you could sign right here where Mr Hemphill the accountant has put the pencilled cross.'

'Why?'

'I just explained Jock. If you don't sign these papers we stand to lose everything, including Stiellsmuir.'

He grunted again.

'So if you'll sign,' she urged.

'You're Sarah aren't you?'

Her heart lifted that he'd recognised her. 'Yes.'

'Your mother's dead, killed herself. Walked off a cliff, smash, strawberry jam.'

Sarah winced at that.

'Was in love with Sunter, you see. He died, so she committed suicide.' Tears welled in his eyes. 'Committed suicide, the silly bitch.'

'Sign, Jock,' she urged.

He brought the pen up in front of him. Suddenly, forcefully, he threw it from him. 'No, it's all a conspiracy. They're out to get me.'

She went after the pen, retrieving it. 'Who's out to get you?'

'They are.'

'And who are *they*?'

Jock tapped the side of his nose, and winked knowingly.

Luckily he hadn't bent the pen's nib for she hadn't brought a spare nib with her. She dipped the pen again in the ink.

'Come on, let's get this done,' she said in a schoolmarmish tone.

'No! They won't catch me out. I'm too fly for them.'

'Who Jock? Who are you talking about?'

He didn't reply to that. Instead he lifted the tray from his lap and placed it back on the floor. Standing, he started to unbutton his shirt.

'Jock, what are you doing?'

He didn't reply to that either. Ripping off his shirt he tossed it aside. He then began unbuckling the belt he was wearing rather than his usual braces.

When his trousers joined his shirt Sarah decided it was time to leave.

'Captain Wilson,' Roderick the footman announced.

It was just past nine o'clock that evening and Sarah had been waiting, hoping that Mathew would manage to come to Stiellsmuir as she'd asked him to in the message she'd sent him via Mr Purcell.

During that evening she'd confided to Mrs McGuffie all about her romance with Mathew, and that it was their intention to marry. Mrs McGuffie had been delighted for her, delight tempered by the present circumstances.

'Mathew!' Sarah exclaimed, and flew into his arms where he hugged her tight.

'I can't stay long. We sail on the morning tide and I still have a thousand things yet to do.'

So soon! She'd hoped, prayed, they might have a few days together.

'What's going on, Sarah. Why has Mr Hawke sold the *Good Intent*?'

'Excuse me, you two will want to be alone,' Mrs McGuffie said, gathering up her knitting which she too, like Sarah, found a soothing pastime.

'By the way, congratulations, Captain! Miss Hawke has told me of your plans.'

'Why, thank you, Mrs McGuffie.'

'As I told her, I wish you both every happiness in the world. Every happiness.' She turned now to Sarah. 'I know it's still fairly early but I'll away to bed now. I'll speak to the servants before I go, though, so you won't be disturbed.'

'Thank you, Maud,' Sarah smiled.

'And I'll look in on himself just to make sure he's all right. I might even linger with him for a wee while as he likes that.'

'Is your father ill?' Mathew inquired after Mrs McGuffie had left them.

'It's a story and a half, Mathew. Sit down and I'll get you a gill, then tell it to you.'

He listened amazed and dumbfounded as she related her harrowing tale.

'My God!' he whispered when she was finally finished.

'So I'm afraid it means that we'll have to postpone the wedding for a while. I can't get married right now the way things are.'

'No, of course not,' he agreed.

'You won't mention what's really wrong with my father to anyone will you? I don't want that getting out and about. At least not yet.'

'You have my word, Sarah,' he promised.

She shook her head. 'Today has just been unbelievable! And to think that only last night you and I . . . That seems like a million years ago. So much has happened since then.'

He crossed to the settee where she was, and sat beside her. 'My poor Sarah,' he murmured, and gathered her to him.

She snuggled against his chest, enjoying the heat and feeling of security his body offered. 'I do love you, Mathew,' she said.

'And I love you.'

'Kiss me then.'

243

He did. Not a passionate kiss, but one of great tenderness and affection.

'Just what the doctor ordered,' she smiled, when the kiss was over.

'Would you like a repeat?'

'Hmmm!'

This time he stroked her breast through the bodice of her dress.

'We could go upstairs if you want. But I'd rather stay here just as we are,' she murmured.

He continued stroking, which made her sigh. 'How long will you be away for this trip?'

'It's only a short one – Lisbon and back.'

'Good.'

'I'll contact you again, just as soon as I can, when I return.'

'Hopefully things might be clearer by then.' Reaching up, she touched his cheek. 'Oh Mathew!'

They kissed again.

After which he told her a joke, which made her laugh. And that made her feel a lot lot better.

Holding the tray in her right hand, Sarah used her left to close Jock's bedroom door behind her. She'd been trying to get him to sign the papers Hemphill had given her but to no avail. Jock had refused point blank, going on about a 'conspiracy' and the mysterious 'they' who were out to get him.

She glanced round as Pansy the parlour maid came hurrying down the corridor towards her.

'It's Mr Hemphill from Carlton Place to see you, Miss,' Pansy said on reaching Sarah.

'Where have you put him?'

'In the drawing-room, Miss.'

Sarah handed Pansy the tray on which were the papers to be signed, plus pen and ink. 'Take these to the library for me, Pansy.'

'Yes, Miss.'

She found Hemphill pacing up and down, his face lined with concern.

'Have you got those papers signed?' he asked the moment she entered the room.

'I'm afraid not. My father's being most resistant to them.'

'Blast!' Hemphill exclaimed. 'There's been a development which has brought me straight out here in the hope those papers had been signed.'

A development? She didn't like the sound of that at all.

244

Hemphill went on. 'Our friend Earl Raisin has pulled a flanker that has really set the cat among the pigeons. Realising that Mr Hawke is the only member of the syndicate left, and that Mr Hawke must also be going to desert his cause, he hired two full extra crews a fortnight ago and now has all three crews drilling like mad on three different sites within the section of land he owns. I can only presume his idea is that with this further increased effort on his part he's bound to succeed in striking oil before we pull the financial rug out from underneath him.'

'Two full extra crews!' Sarah exclaimed angrily.

'The new figures have just arrived in today by first post. They've leapt by almost two hundred and fifty per cent.'

'As much as that?'

'It's involved and complicated. I can explain it to you if you like.'

Sarah shook her head.

'We *must* get those papers signed, *now*.'

It came to her then how she could do that. It was her only solution, she decided.

'The papers will be signed today. I promise you,' she assured the accountant.

'You're certain of that?'

'Absolutely.'

He stared at her hard. 'Do you wish me to wait?'

'No, go back to Carlton Place. I'll send them to you directly they're signed.'

She saw him to the front door, and from there went to the library. Could she manage it? She was going to have to.

It was some hours later that Sarah sent for Mrs McGuffie. When the housekeeper entered the library she found Sarah sitting at the bureau. In a few terse sentences Sarah told her the news that Hemphill had brought earlier.

'So you see, these papers had to be signed now,' Sarah said.

Sarah's use of the past tense wasn't lost on Mrs McGuffie. 'Had to be? You mean you got Jock to do it?'

'Not quite,' Sarah replied slowly. 'But the papers are signed, and it's Jock's signature that's on them.'

The penny dropped. 'You mean . . .?'

Sarah nodded. 'I'm afraid that desperate situations call for desperate measures.'

Mrs McGuffie came to stand beside Sarah. Picking up the papers, she went through them one by one.

'I know Jock's signature well and I couldn't tell the difference,' she pronounced at last.

'There's no other solution, Maud. At least none I can think of.'

'And now you'd like me to witness these.'

'Will you?'

'I'd do anything that would help Jock or be to his benefit.' Her face cracked into a sudden smile. 'Know something?'

'What?'

'It's precisely the sort of thing Jock himself would have done.'

It pleased Sarah tremendously to hear that.

Sarah opened Jock's bedroom door and peered inside. He was sleeping again in front of the fire. He slept a great deal now, Mrs McGuffie had told her.

She went in, and silently closed the door behind her. Just as silently she crossed to the other chair by the fire, and sat in it. Jock snorted, snorted again, and for a moment she thought he was going to wake up. But he didn't. His breathing resumed being regular, and deep.

Her mind went back to the first time she'd met her father, a thunder and lightning night when he'd turned up at their house in Netherton, and that offer he'd made which Myrtle had finally accepted for her to come and live with him at Stiellsmuir.

Now Myrtle was dead, and her step-da Bob. And Jock was mad, raving bonkers. Her mother had gone over the edge of a cliff, and by doing so had driven her father over the edge of sanity.

She hadn't cried since her arrival home from the West Indies, but now she broke down and let it all come. Hot scalding tears coursed the length of her cheeks while, clutching herself under her bosoms, she gently rocked back and forth.

She didn't blubber, or make any noise, though. She didn't want to wake Jock, she wanted him to sleep on in peace.

Luckily she had a handkerchief with her. After a few minutes' agonised weeping she groped for it, and used it to wipe the wet from her face.

What if they lost everything including Stiellsmuir? What would she do then?

One step at a time, she counselled herself. One step at a time.

There was nothing she could do until she knew their exact financial position. And that wouldn't be forthcoming for at least two weeks yet, possibly even three. In the meantime all she could do was hope and pray.

She wiped her nose, feeling a great deal better for her cry. She'd needed that.

For with her weeping had come a new resolve. An iron resolve that made her feel strong again. And yes, a strange word perhaps, but brave also.

'Don't you worry, Jock,' she whispered. 'If the firm and house can be saved I'll save them. I swear to God I will. Just leave everything to me.'

She sat with her father for over half an hour while he slept on. When she left him she'd decided what she wanted to do next, and would do the following day.

She'd go to the grave.

Royal and Regal clip-clopped into Netherton, and almost instantly, bringing a choke to her throat, Sarah caught sight of the big wheel at Dundonald's pit. Slowly spinning, it was bringing the last shift workers to the surface.

She'd go and visit Gordy, of course. The prospect of seeing him again excited her, and scared her too. It was three years and three months since they'd said goodbye. Not that long really, yet it seemed a lifetime ago. An eternity.

How small the houses were, far smaller than she remembered. And how dirty the streets, they too smaller and narrower than she recalled them to be.

Her carriage passed a group of children playing peever. The lassies were wearing clogs just like the ones she'd worn when living here, the lads all barefoot, one with his bare backside literally hanging out of his trousers.

She'd adored peever when wee, and had played it for hours on end. Another great favourite had been skipping ropes. Skipping by yourself, or cawing the rope with a partner while a third person, or a number of others taking it in turn, jumped.

She'd given Sheach explicit instructions before they'd left Stiellsmuir on how to get to the graveyard, where he now took her. She picked up the wreath she'd brought when he opened the carriage door for her.

She didn't have to inquire where the grave would be. As the Sunters hadn't already had a family plot they would be buried in the new part of the cemetery. And that was where she found them.

Myrtle and Bob had been laid side by side as Mrs McGuffie had said they'd been. The granite stone with their names and particulars on it, Myrtle erroneously described as 'Beloved Wife Of', was placed at the top of the double plot, in the middle.

Sarah stared down at the freshly turned earth. She couldn't really believe that her mother and Bob were down there. Myrtle who'd always been so full of life and energy, her step-da who before his stroke had been just the same, and yet it was so. Both were dead, and laid here to rest.

Had her relatives come to the funeral? she wondered. Her Auntie Jessica, Myrtle's sister, and Jessica's husband Dandy? And what about her granda, also from Shotts?

She walked carefully round the side of the grave, and placed her wreath against the stone. And who had paid for that? Not Jock, so who? She would ask Mrs McGuffie when she returned home. Then she walked back the way she'd come to take up her previous position.

After a while she glanced away from the grave, to gaze about her. It was a lovely cemetery, extremely well taken care of. The folk in Netherton might not have much money, but they certainly knew how to look after their dead.

She smiled to herself at a memory. The cemetery was a favourite with courting couples, though never as popular as Bluebell Wood. It was particularly convenient for this part of Netherton from where it was a bit of a hike to Bluebell Wood.

The one place she didn't want to go anywhere near was High Cliff. That would have been too much. She gave Sheach fresh directions, so that they carefully skirted that entire area.

Her heart was in her mouth when the carriage turned into her old street. Still unpaved, still with an open drain running down its middle. How mean it all now seemed to her, and squalid. She rapped for Sheach to stop when they arrived outside what had been the Sunters' door.

There were curtains she didn't recognise at the window, and inside a figure moved. The house had been let again, and quickly too.

A face she'd never seen before came to the window and stared out at her. The woman was mid twenties she guessed, and bonny. A nice woman, she decided. It was good the house she had so many fond memories of had gone to someone nice.

She could chap the door, explain who she was and ask to go in. A look round for old times sake. She nearly did, then decided not to. She shouted to Sheach, and when he jumped down and came to the carriage door she gave him new directions.

She passed Mrs Geddes, and Mrs Buick a little further on. Both women stared into the carriage, and at her. But neither appeared to recognise her.

When they reached the McCallum house she rapped again, and Sheach whoaed! the horses to a stop.

'Mind your feet, Miss Hawke, these streets are filthy,' he warned her as he helped her down.

The streets were even more than filthy, they stank. The whole place did. She supposed that growing up with it she'd just never noticed it. She did now though. It was an unwashed human, excretory smell and quite disgusting.

The McCallum front step was freshly whiteclayed and she smiled to herself to mind how often she'd done that task. In fact that was what she was doing the day they brought Bob back on the flat cart, that day her life changed for ever.

She knocked at the door, and waited. Some people strolled by on the other side of the street, staring curiously at her and her carriage as they passed. The gingerhaired lassie was one of the Robertson girls; she didn't know the others.

A boy opened the door to stare at her in astonishment.

'Hello Stewart, is Gordy home?' she smiled. Stewart was the fractionally elder of the twins.

'I'm Stephen, and yes he is. Who shall I say wants him?'

She'd always had trouble distinguishing between the twins. Her and everybody else in Netherton, including Gordy sometimes. But not Mrs McCallum; she'd never been known to get it wrong.

'Sarah Hawke.'

Stephen's eyes opened wide. 'I didn't recognise you. You look so different. So . . . I'll get Gordy.' With that he fled back into the house. 'Gordy! Gordy! You're never going to guess who's here to see you! Sarah Hawke! Her you used to go out with.'

It started to smir. She was wondering if it was going to get any

249

worse when Gordy appeared at the door. When he saw her his mouth dropped open.

'Hello,' she smiled.

'It really is you. I thought the little bugger was taking the piss. He's forever doing it.'

The blue streaks of ingrained coaldust that all colliers carried on their bodies lined his neck, the backs of his hands, and the lower parts of his arms exposed by his having half rolled up his sleeves. He, too, was smaller than she remembered.

'I wasn't in the country when my mother died and the funeral took place. I came today to lay a wreath,' she explained.

'Not in the country? England were you?'

'The West Indies.'

'Oh!' He nodded significantly. That was where bananas came from. Bananas and coconuts. He'd eaten a banana on several occasions, but never a coconut. 'You eh . . .' His eyes swept over her. 'You're quite the lady now, Sarah. Quite the lady.'

'They're only clothes Gordy, I'm still the same underneath.' Even as she said that she knew it wasn't true. She was a far cry from the lassie in clogs who'd left Netherton three years and three months previously.

He gave a self-conscious cough and ran a hand through his hair. 'Here, I'm not minding my manners keeping you standing on the step. Will you come through?'

'I don't want to disturb you all.'

'Och, don't be daft, come on in.'

The stink was worse inside the house than out. And Gordy smelt. She almost wrinkled her nose as she brushed by him. My God, she must have smelt the same way when she went to Stiellsmuir! How awful. No wonder a bath had been the first thing she'd been offered, a bath with sweet-scented crystals dissolved in it.

She found Mrs McCallum standing in front of the range, wiping her hands on her pinny. Stephen and Stewart were to one side of her. Or was it Stewart and Stephen?

Mrs McCallum took one look at Sarah and dipped in a small curtsey. That shocked Sarah, making her feel embarrassed. It was the last thing she'd expected.

'How are you, Mrs McCallum? It's nice to see you again.'

'I'm well, Sarah. And let me say how sad we all were at what happened. A terrible thing entirely.'

'Yes.'

'Sarah was abroad at the time, the West Indies where bananas and coconuts come from. That's why she wasn't at the funeral,' Gordy explained.

'The West Indies eh! Very grand. Very grand indeed!'

She'd always liked Mrs McCallum but now the bloody woman was irritating her. She had no need to be so obsequious.

There was a mirror over the mantlepiece which Sarah now caught sight of herself in. In her frills and finery, what a contrast she was to them. No wonder Mrs McCallum had dipped to her, it was the natural reaction of a working-class woman when suddenly finding herself in the presence of – as Gordy had so rightly called her – the lady she'd become.

'I've just been to the cemetery and felt I couldn't be in Netherton without paying Gordy a visit,' Sarah smiled.

Gordy shifted uncomfortably.

'Would you care for a cup of tea? The sort you can stand a teaspoon in?' Mrs McCallum offered.

How revolting, Sarah thought. Then chided herself for not only being ungracious but also for being a snob. There was a time she'd have thought such tea mother's milk, sheer ambrosia. Now she preferred delicate China.

'I musn't keep you, you were just about to sit down to your meal,' she replied. For indeed the table was set and there was a black pot of stew bubbling on the range.

'No, no, it'll keep,' Mrs McCallum answered instantly.

Sarah took a deep breath. She'd been so looking forward to this, and now wasn't enjoying it one little bit. 'So how are you then, Gordy? You're certainly looking fit enough.'

'I'm fine thanks.' He hesitated, then said quickly, 'And engaged to be married.'

'Are you! Who's the lucky girl?'

'Do you remember Betty Redhead? We're getting wed next spring.'

'I remember Betty well,' Sarah replied. Gordy marrying Betty, that made sense. Betty had always fancied Gordy something rotten.

It surprised Sarah that her reaction to Gordy's forthcoming nuptials was one of relief rather than anything else. There was certainly no feeling of jealousy on her part. Not one jot, even though Gordy had once been the sun and moon to her.

'I take it the twins are now working?' she said.

'Oh aye, we've been "down by" well over a year now,' one of them replied.

If the twins had been that bit older how different things might have been, Sarah thought. If they'd been working when Bob had his stroke she'd have married Gordy, and never gone to Stiellsmuir.

'How about yourself?' Gordy asked.

'I too am engaged, to a ship's captain. We plan to marry fairly soon.'

'Congratulations!' Gordy smiled thinly.

'A ship's captain. My, my!' Mrs McCallum said, impressed to the point of awe.

'His name is Mathew Wilson and his ship is the *Good Intent*. It was his ship I sailed to the West Indies on.' Sarah paused, then further explained. 'The doctor ordered me to have a sea voyage to help me regain my strength after I'd been down with smallpox.'

'I saw marks on your face but didn't want to pass comment,' Gordy nodded.

'I got off lightly, don't you think?'

'Hardly noticeable at all,' Gordy agreed.

The conversation died. They all looked at one another, each desperately trying to think of what to say next.

'Are you sure you won't have that cup of tea?' Mrs McCallum pressed.

'No, and I've stayed long enough. I only called in for a minute.'

'I'm glad you did, Sarah. It's been a treat seeing you again,' Gordy said.

She didn't believe that. Her presence made him uncomfortable, as in truth the reverse did to her. She didn't fit in these surroundings any more. They were alien to her, and she to them.

'I'll let you get on with your meal then,' she said.

'And I'll see you to the front door,' Gordy volunteered.

Sarah said her farewells to his family, then let him lead the way. Outside the smir had stopped.

'You've done well for yourself, Sarah. I'm pleased,' Gordy said at the door.

She should kiss him on the cheek, she thought. But couldn't bring herself to do so. She extended a hand instead.

'All the very best for the wedding. I hope you and Betty have long life and every happiness,' she said.

'The same for you and your captain. Lang may your lum reek,' he replied, shaking with her.

He stood in the doorway, head slightly bowed, hands deep in pockets, watching as Sheach helped her into the carriage. The new Sarah didn't only make him feel ill at ease, she made him feel downright nervous into the bargain. There had been a part of him that had held back from Betty, a part that belonged to Sarah. But not now. From here on in Betty would have all of him.

'Straight home,' Sarah said to Sheach, who closed the carriage door and then climbed on to the driver's seat.

'Goodbye!' Sarah cried out with a smile, waving to Gordy.

'Tara and good luck!'

As the carriage moved off she sank back into her seat, and closed her eyes. What a disappointment that had been, what a let-down. She didn't mean the grave, that had been all right. But Netherton and Gordy!

She doubted she'd ever return again, she told herself as the carriage left Netherton. Doubted it very much indeed.

The first thing she'd do on getting home was have a bath and hairwash, she promised herself.

The list Sarah was compiling was a long one, all the assets and valuables that Jock owned, and which could be realised, cashed in and sold if need be.

On the assets side there was a small portfolio of shares and holdings, plus a personal bank account containing nearly ten thousand pounds.

The valuables consisted of furniture, ornaments, some very good Georgian silver and, the *pièce de résistance* as far as she was concerned, a diamond the size of a shilling coin.

She had no idea where the diamond had come from, and neither did Mrs McGuffie – she'd asked the housekeeper. She'd found it, and other items, in Jock's strongbox, the key to which had been on his keychain.

Sarah glanced up when there was a tap on the library door. 'Come in!'

It was Hamish the footman. 'Captain Wilson is here to see you, Miss. Shall I show him in?'

'Yes of course!' Sarah exclaimed in delight. This was marvellous, she hadn't expected Mathew back till the end of the week.

She stood, smoothed down the front of her dress which had become slightly rumpled with her sitting, then patted her hair into place. She was beaming radiantly when he came into the room.

They both waited until Hamish had closed the library door before flying into each other's arms. She smothered him in kisses, and he did the same to her.

'How I've missed you,' he whispered, and nibbled her ear.

'And how I've missed you.' She ran an eager hand over his chest, then down a buttock and thigh. 'You're back sooner than I expected,' she husked.

'We made tremendous time both ways. We seemed to be flying rather than sailing.'

She couldn't help herself. Her hand flicked between his legs. 'Hello there,' she whispered.

'Hello to you too.'

She took a deep breath, and broke away. She was filled with exhilaration, profound happiness and . . . love. 'How about a drink?'

'I thought you'd never ask.'

She gave a throaty laugh, and crossed to the decanter.

'How's Mr Hawke?' he queried as she poured.

'The same. But there has been a development regarding the Canadian business.'

He listened tight-lipped as she related what had happened. 'That's bad,' he said when she was finished, and had a swallow of the whisky she'd handed him.

She gestured towards the bureau. 'I'm just making out a list of my father's personal assets and valuables in case the worst comes to the worst and I have to utilise them. I have a valuer coming in tomorrow to give me prices on the furniture, etc.'

Mathew shook his head. 'Do you think the worst will come to the worst?'

'It could well be on the cards according to our Mr Hemphill. But at least I'll know one way or the other before too long. It's the waiting that's the horrible part, like waiting to be told whether or not you're to be executed.'

He had another swallow of his drink. She looked tired, he thought, but still gorgeous with it. 'We're in port for seventy-two hours this time round,' he said.

Her face lit up. 'That's marvellous. Do you have to be back aboard tonight?'

'No, I'm not really needed aboard again till morning.'

'You'll stay the night?'

His lips curled into a smile. 'I was hoping you'd suggest that. I've already informed Runciman where I can be found should I be needed in an emergency.'

'I'll have a spare room made up then.' She laughed at his sudden stricken expression. 'For appearances' sake. You'll be with me, don't worry.'

They sat by the fire and talked until it was time to go to bed. Half an hour after he'd been shown into the room allocated him Mathew left it to go to Sarah's.

She was already in bed waiting for him when her door opened and he slipped inside.

'Lock it, just to be on the safe side,' she smiled.

He did just that, then came to stand beside her. The bedroom was lovely and warm thanks to the fire that Nettie had lit earlier.

They stared longingly into each other's eyes, she wanting him every bit as much as he wanted her.

'Come to bed, my darling,' she whispered.

He hesitated. 'Just one thing, Sarah, as we're not now getting married right away what happens should you get pregnant?'

'We'll cross that bridge if we come to it. But I doubt very much we will. There are ways and means to prevent such accidents as any good herbalist can tell you.' Her tone became urgent. 'Now come to bed.'

He removed his dressing-gown to reveal he was wearing pyjamas underneath.

'You can take those off too,' she said.

When he was naked she threw back the bedclothes. She had on a short flimsy top that fell away round the sides of her full breasts to stop just below her ribcage. Encircling her waist was a thin gold chain that she'd bought in Sauchiehall Street the previous year. It was her own idea to wear it round the waist rather than the neck for where it was intended.

The sight of Sarah like that produced an instant reaction in Mathew, which made her smile.

He lay alongside her, his hot flesh burning her thigh as they kissed. They were still kissing when he opened her thighs to tease her with a finger.

Her tummy muscles were jumping, and she could feel her juices start to flow. Grasping a buttock she squeezed it hard, then did the same to his other one.

He tongued a nipple that was as hard as he himself now was.

'I love you,' he breathed in her ear.

'And I love you.'

He came into a sitting position between her legs from where he slowly and sensuously, stroked her flanks. 'I just want to look at you for a minute,' he said, continuing to stroke.

She groaned when he eventually slid into her, grabbing at his back to force him in as far as was possible.

Lifting her legs she brought them to a position across the top of his buttocks. As he moved she rocked beneath him.

The sensations she was experiencing built and built as he plunged in and out until finally, with a cry of agonised gratification, she orgasmed. And then only seconds later did so again, and yet again.

When it was all over they were both covered in sticky sweat and grinning at each other like a couple of Cheshire cats.

'Thank you', he said.

'Thank you.'

She smoked a cigarette, he his briar for a while. Talking, touching, enjoying the pleasure of one another's company. Till finally passion gripped them both a second time.

He turned her on to her front, raised her hips till they were exactly where he wanted them, and penetrated her from the rear.

Sarah whimpered from the sheer ecstasy of what followed.

'I know it's hardly the thing for me to say in my position, but the French really are a bunch of detestable little creeps,' the Honourable Ian Monteith said to Charlotte Bingwall as he danced with her. The occasion was a party being thrown at the British Embassy in Paris to open British Cultural Week in that city.

'Sssh!' Charlotte hissed back. 'Somebody might hear you.'

He'd drunk too much, but it had been such a dreary evening. 'Puffed up egotistical backstabbers the lot of them, with delusions of grandeur about themselves and their, it has to be admitted, rather beautiful country.'

Charlotte didn't particularly care for the French either, but would never have dreamt of saying so in public. My God, if her father heard Ian speaking like this, or it was reported to him, he'd have a fit.

'You know the trouble with France?' Ian said, lifting an eyebrow.

'What?'

'It's full of Frenchie frog-eaters, nearly all of whom have disgustingly bad breath. And I'll tell you something else; behind all the smiles, nods and overtures of *bonhomie* and affection I doubt there's not one of the little creeps likes us British. And why? Because they're jealous of us. Jealous of our Empire and the success of our language. Particularly the latter.'

'Will you stop it Ian, please? For me?'

Dreary, dreary, it was a terrible evening. A monumental bore. As they danced he fell into a sullen silence.

Sarah Hawke. Why was it that no matter how hard he tried he could never get her out of his mind? The woman haunted him. Day and night she was never far away.

He was being stupid, he told himself. Charlie was just as beautiful as Sarah. Bubbling, vital, with a perfect figure and smashing personality. Why, the two of them got on like a house on fire!

And her family was rich, with half of Suffolk to call their own. Marry Charlie and his future, financial and careerwise, was secure. And yet . . . and yet . . .

Sarah Hawke.

'A penny for them?' Charlotte prompted.

He roused himself from his reverie. 'What?'

'A penny for them?'

'I was just wondering how soon before you and I could escape?'

'We can't, you know that.'

She was right of course, damnably they would both have to stay to the death. It was expected of her, and his duty to do so.

'I think it's all going awfully well, don't you?' Charlotte said.

He grunted non-committally.

'Daddy will be pleased.'

The music ended and they both clapped their appreciation. After which they mingled, having both been instructed to mingle as much as possible, to talk, enthuse about and promote British Cultural Week and British culture in general.

Dreary, Ian thought to himself again. Dreary, dreary, dreary.

He fell into a conversation about the Jacobean playwrights Beaumont and Fletcher and their famous collaboration *The*

Knight of the Burning Pestle, but in his mind he was back in Glasgow, with Sarah Hawke.

She arrived at Carlton Place at five to eleven in the morning, five minutes early for her meeting with Hemphill. Once inside she was confronted by Moffat who, from his expression and overall demeanour, had clearly been lying in ambush for her.

'Miss Hawke, I'd like a word if you please?'

'Yes?'

He indicated a nearby door. 'Could you step in here, please? More private you understand.'

Sanctimonious, she thought. That was how the dry as a stick Moffat came across, as being sanctimonious.

The room he ushered her into was small and dark. 'I believe you're seeing Mr Hemphill at eleven o'clock about matters concerning the firm? I know this because I instructed him to attend on me at that time, only to be informed by him that he was meeting with you.'

'That's correct.'

Moffat pursed his lips. 'And how is Mr Hawke? Any improvement?'

'None,' she replied flatly.

'Does he appreciate that you are . . . are . . . how shall I put it? Involving yourself with the firm?'

She didn't reply to that.

'Miss Hawke, I really must protest. I have no idea what it is you will be discussing with Mr Hemphill but it is most irregular that I have not been consulted first.' He squared back his thin shoulders, and jutted out his jaw. 'I am in charge here after all.'

'Self-appointed in charge,' she countered.

He blinked his beady eyes at her. 'Well of course. I am Chief Clerk, who else would be in charge during Mr Hawke's regrettable absence?'

He was right, she thought. Up to a point. 'I think it best you sit in on my meeting with Mr Hemphill. It's time you became aware of the full facts.'

'Full facts?' he repeated, frowning. 'What full facts?'

'Shall we go?' she said, and left the room, making in the direction of Hemphill's office. A few seconds later a bewildered Moffat went hurrying after her.

Hemphill was waiting for her with various ledgers and account books spread before him on his desk. He looked surprised to see Moffat. Sarah explained that the Chief Clerk would be joining them, then asked bluntly, 'How do we stand?'

Hemphill shook his head. 'It's very bad indeed. I'm not at all sure that the firm can survive.'

Moffat's eyes popped out on stalks when he heard that. 'What are you talking about, Hemphill?' he demanded.

It was Sarah who answered. 'The first thing you should know, Mr Moffat, is that we have deliberately kept quiet about how ill my father really is. It seems likely that he will never work again.'

Moffat's sallow skin became mottled. 'You're exaggerating, surely?'

'I'm afraid not.'

'But . . . but . . . but I had no idea!'

'As I said, we deliberately kept it quiet. And for the time being continue to wish to do so. What you have just been told is in strictest confidence.'

'What exactly is wrong with Mr Hawke?' the Chief Clerk asked.

Sarah's eyes flicked to Hemphill, then back to Moffat. Should she confide to Moffat about Jock's schizophrenia or not? She decided not to.

'There is a name for it which I can never remember,' she lied. 'But it has rendered him unfit to carry on as head of the firm.' That was evasive enough she thought. She glanced again at Hemphill, and saw that he'd got the message.

'And Mr Hawke won't be coming back?' The idea of that seemed unbelievable.

'Most unlikely,' Sarah replied.

Then he remembered the other thing. 'And what's this about the firm not surviving?'

Sarah went on to relate the sorry tale of Jock's Canadian investment, right up to the point where Earl Raisin had hired two full extra crews the previous month.

Moffat sat stunned when she finished.

'We're now completely out of that mess?' Sarah said to Hemphill. 'Fully financially extricated.'

'And you have the final figures?'

'They're all here,' he said, indicating the ledgers and account books in front of him.

'I'll take these home with me. I'll want to go through them myself.'

'Would you like me to come and explain their contents to you?' Hemphill volunteered.

'Thank you, but that's unnecessary. I can read and understand them for myself.'

That impressed Hemphill.

'And in your opinion, things don't look good?'

'Pretty dreadful. Mr Hawke has lost an absolute fortune. My own opinion is, on the facts and figures available to me, that the firm of J. Hawke & Daughter will have to close.'

'Close,' Moffat repeated in a whisper, and swallowed hard.

'Could you bring all this down to the carriage for me?' Sarah said to Hemphill, gesturing at the ledgers and books on his desk. 'I'll take them straight home and begin studying them right away.' To both of them she said, 'And gentlemen, for now I want the fact that the firm might be going under kept among ourselves. If the news of closure has to be broken to the staff I shall do it personally.'

Moffat rose, his hands twisting and twining. All he could think of was that at his age he'd never get another job, far less another position as Chief Clerk. It was the scrapheap for him.

Hemphill began collecting up the ledgers and account books.

Outside, at the carriage, Sarah said quietly to Hemphill, 'I didn't tell Moffat what's wrong with Jock, nor do I intend to tell him or anyone else unless I have to.'

'I understand, Miss Hawke. You can rely on me – mum's the word.'

She believed him. 'Thank you, Mr Hemphill.'

She was anxiously biting a thumbnail as Sheach drove off.

'Come in!' Sarah wearily called out when there was a tap on the library door. The library had long since become her favourite room in the entire house. She spent a great deal of her time here, loving its ambience, and the many books it contained.

It was Mrs McGuffie with a tray. 'I thought you might fancy a cup of tea,' the housekeeper said.

'I couldn't think of anything I'd like more.'

She'd have a break for the tea and a cigarette, Sarah decided, laying down her pencil beside the sheets of paper covered in notes and computations she'd been working on. She felt totally drained, and physically sore, as if she'd been engaged in heavy manual labour.

'What's the verdict, then?' Mrs McGuffie asked, handing Sarah her tea.

'I'm not finished yet, but I believe I can save Stiellsmuir, and the firm.'

Relief washed over Mrs McGuffie's face. 'Oh that's grand!'

Sarah gave a small laugh. 'If only that damned diamond had been worth what I'd got all excited thinking it might be worth.' The diamond she was of course referring to was the one she'd found in Jock's strongbox, and which had raised such high hopes in her. As it had transpired the diamond was so badly internally flawed as to be almost valueless. God knows where Jock had got it from, or why he'd kept it in his strongbox. It was a trinket, nothing more.

She gratefully sipped her tea, which hit the spot.

Mrs McGuffie pulled a chair over, close to where Sarah was at the bureau, and sat there with her tea.

'How's Jock?' Sarah asked.

'Talking to somebody called Mr Love.'

Sarah nodded. 'That was the undertaker who employed Jock after Jock's friend Rence died.'

'Well, whoever, your father is having a good old chinwag with him.'

Sarah had another sip of tea. 'I said I believe I can save Stiellsmuir, but it's going to have to mean a savage cutback on staff. I want you to draw up a list for me of the absolute minimum staff that we can run the house with. And I mean *minimum*.'

'On top of being housekeeper I can also cook, so we can make a start there,' Mrs McGuffie replied.

'Let me have the list as soon as you can. We'll have to keep one of the drivers, and I've decided on Ferguson because he's older and been here longer. Sheach will have to go, and my own carriage and horses sold.'

Sarah took a deep breath. 'I'm also selling Carlton Place.'

'No!' Mrs McGuffie exclaimed.

'It'll fetch a handsome price. And anyway, it will be far too large for the firm after it's suffered its cutbacks. Two thirds of the present personnel will have to be shed.'

'As many as that?'

'McIvor and others have been poaching orders off us left, right

261

and centre. McIvor and Co. have been playing merry hell with the business with Jock away, and Moffat in charge. Moffat may be a competent enough Chief Clerk, but he's a dead loss at actually running the firm.'

'So who is going to run it from here on?'

'I am,' Sarah stated matter of factly.

'I see,' Mrs McGuffie said, and took a deep breath. 'Well, I have every faith in you, and I know Jock would too. He'd approve of you doing this.' She paused, then added slowly, 'Just as long as you appreciate what you're taking on.'

'You mean me being a woman?'

'In Glasgow anyway, women bosses aren't exactly thick on the ground. In fact I don't think I've ever heard of one.'

Sarah smiled. 'There's no rule I know of says that a woman can't sit in the boss's chair, and in this instance necessity dictates precisely that.'

'Good luck to you, then!' Mrs McGuffie replied, raising her cup in a toast.

Sarah raised her cup also, and they both drank.

'You'll be selling the *Snowdrop*, I take it?' Mrs McGuffie said.

'That's the last thing I intend doing,' Sarah replied quickly. 'It was a mistake on Hemphill's part to sell the other five, though I quite understand why he did so. No, I need the *Snowdrop* for the palm oil run to Cape Town. That's by far and away our biggest profit-maker, and the base from which I propose to rebuild the firm.'

Mrs McGuffie was puzzled. 'But why then did Mr Hemphill sell the other five ships if that was such a bad idea?'

'He's a good man, and excellent accountant. But the latter is all he is, a book-keeper. He has no vision outwith his speciality. In other words he had a debit, so he sold the ships to balance the figures. All neat and tidy as far as he was concerned, but wrong from the firm's point of view. At least one of those ships should have been kept, two if at all possible. Their profit-making ability far outweighed their capital value. Do you understand that?'

'I think so.'

'That Cape Town run is the springboard for our eventual recovery, if a recovery there's going to be. You wait and see if it isn't.'

It was almost as if Jock himself was speaking, Mrs McGuffie

marvelled. Sarah even used similar inflections to her father, and certainly Sarah's tone carried the same total conviction that Jock's did when he was discussing business.

'When is your young man coming again?' Mrs McGuffie queried. She thought very highly of Captain Mathew Wilson, very highly indeed. In her opinion he and Sarah made an admirable couple.

'He should be docking within the next couple of days. Perhaps even as early as tomorrow morning's tide if the winds have been exceptionally favourable.'

'You'll want the same spare room at the ready then?' Mrs McGuffie said, the hint of a smile tugging at the corners of her mouth.

'Yes,' Sarah replied, knowing fine well that the housekeeper was aware that she and Mathew were sleeping together. And that Mrs McGuffie approved.

The two women stared at one another, and many things were said between them, none of which were spoken aloud.

Mrs McGuffie finished her tea. 'I'll go and make a start on that list now. I'll leave the tray and things for the moment, and send someone along for them later. There's another cup in the pot if you want it.'

For a short while after Mrs McGuffie left her Sarah sat enjoying her second cup, and thinking of Mathew. Dreaming of when they'd be married, and the life they'd have together.

It was with the utmost difficulty that she forced herself to concentrate again on what she'd been doing before being interrupted.

Moffat was appalled. 'Sack two thirds of our people!' he gasped.

'There's no other way if we're to save the firm, Mr Moffat, I assure you. And even that doesn't guarantee success,' Sarah replied.

'But who . . . which ones . . .?'

'That's your job. But I do wish Hemphill to be amongst those who stay. I don't want him to go.'

Moffat licked his lips. 'And my own position, Miss Hawke?'

'Of course you remain, Mr Moffat. It never crossed my mind otherwise.' He was a competent Chief Clerk after all, and as such useful to her.

Moffat gave her a small bow. 'Thank you.'

'The other piece of bad news is I'm putting these premises on the

263

market. I don't know yet where we'll be moving to, but it'll be a far smaller place than this.'

'Sell Carlton Place, Miss Hawke! Mr Hawke would never do that.'

'My father is a realist, Mr Moffat. He would do whatever was necessary to save his firm.'

'I really think I should speak to him . . .'

'I've already explained to you. That is impossible.'

'But to sell Carlton Place . . .'

'Mr Moffat!' Sarah's voice was tough as steel. 'I thought I'd made it clear to you. I am now running this firm. You will do as I say, and how I say.'

Moffat swallowed hard.

'If you have something positive and constructive to contribute, then do so by all means. I value your advice and experience. But it is I and I alone who will make final decisions, *without* reference to my father who is far too ill to be of any help. Now I hope I don't have to repeat that again, otherwise . . .' She trailed off, and ever so fractionally raised an eyebrow.

Otherwise he would be one of those to go, Moffat said to himself with a sinking heart.

Sarah rose. 'How soon can you have that list ready for me?' she asked.

'Tomorrow?'

'That's fine. I shall see them each at ten-minute intervals and explain the situation myself. I feel that's the least I can do.'

Moffat nodded his approval of that.

'You may go then, Mr Moffat.'

Outside Mr Hawke's office, that was now Sarah's, Moffat leant against a wall, and shut his eyes.

Taking orders from a chit of a lassie! What was the world coming to?

What was the world coming to indeed?

Sarah ran a hand wearily across her face. She was exhausted, completely dead-beat. She wished now she hadn't arranged to meet Olivia after she was finished at the office, but she'd seen so little of her friend since returning from the West Indies she'd felt she really had to make the effort.

She glanced down again at the order form she'd been perusing and the words and figures swam before her eyes. Eyes that felt like gritty lead balls.

'Miss Hawke?'

It was Smith the clerk standing framed in her office doorway. She presumed correctly that he'd knocked and she hadn't heard. 'Yes, Smith?'

'Mr McIvor of McIvor, McIvor and Devereaux is here asking to speak to you.'

Well, well! she mused. What had brought Ranald Cyril to Carlton Place? There was only one way to find out. 'Send him in,' she replied.

As the acting head of *J. Hawke & Daughter* it would have been polite of Sarah to rise and greet McIvor. 'This is unexpected,' she said as he entered the office, remaining sitting.

McIvor inclined his head. 'A pleasure to see you again, Miss Hawke. I hope you will believe me when I tell you I was genuinely distressed to hear about your father's illness.'

I'll just bet you were! she thought, keeping her face impassive. She waved him to a chair, and waited till he was seated before asking, 'And what can I do for you, Mr McIvor? For I take it you haven't come here merely to commiserate with me about Jock being ill?'

'Straight to the point, eh!' McIvor said, and laughed.

Sarah lit a cigarette, but didn't ask McIvor if he'd care for one. There was also a box of Jock's best Havanas inside the roll-top desk she was sitting at, but she didn't proffer one of those either.

He went on. 'Rumour has it that Jock is so ill he will never get in harness again. Is that correct?'

It was bound to have got out sooner or later, Sarah thought. 'You've taken to listening to gossip and idle chatter now, have you?' she replied.

'It *is* correct then,' McIvor said, and sighed.

'I didn't say that.'

'You didn't deny it either. That's the first thing you would have done if it wasn't true. Therefore it is.'

It made Sarah cross she hadn't handled that better. She felt temporarily outsmarted by the weasel.

McIvor produced a leather case of cigars, took one out, clipped its end and lit up.

'That being so I would like to buy Jock out,' he declared.

His statement threw Sarah; she hadn't been expecting such a proposal. 'Why?' she demanded.

'Although Jock and I were fierce business competitors, I also admired him greatly.' He paused to puff on his cigar, his exhalation sending a cloud of blue smoke swirling in front of him.

Sarah resisted the temptation to urge him to continue, knowing that was what he wanted her to do. It was a psychological move to give him superiority over her. It was a trick Jock had often employed, and which Jock had explained to her.

She drew on her cigarette, and continued to wait. She had the satisfaction of seeing a flash of irritation cross McIvor's eyes with the realisation she wasn't to be drawn.

'Greatly admired him,' McIvor tried again.

She deliberately looked away, and out of the window. It was that time of the evening when the starlings, of which literally millions seemed to inhabit central Glasgow, were making their mass flight, which they did twice a day, morning and evening, without fail. Even from Carlton Place, across the river from the centre, she could still see a huge swarm of them, and hear their raucous cries. In the centre of town itself the din would be almost deafening.

McIvor went on. 'As I think Jock admires me.'

Sarah allowed a hint of amusement to play across her face, which was still there when she glanced back at McIvor. That was a fib. He knew it was, but more importantly so did she. His mistake had given her the position of superiority.

McIvor coughed, then cleared his throat. 'I, of course, know of the acute financial difficulty the firm is in after Jock's disastrous Canadian venture, and how business has dramatically fallen away since his illness. In the circumstances it seems to me that Jock will be only too happy to sell out.'

Sarah allowed a few seconds to tick by before replying. 'What sort of figure did you have in mind?'

'I'd like to have a view of your books, of course. But my offer would be a very fair one, I promise you that. It is not my intention to try and take advantage of a fallen opponent, but rather to help him and myself at the same time. For I wouldn't be so silly as to try and deny that it is to my advantage to take over *J. Hawke & Daughter* and for it to cease to be a rival.'

It certainly was a temptation, Sarah thought. The easy way out. And by golly she would make McIvor pay through the nose for the

266

firm. Just how much she began to speculate upon, and wonder if it would be enough to make her, Jock and Maud comfortable for the rest of their lives at Stiellsmuir.

Then McIvor made his second, and by far biggest, mistake. 'You must appreciate that the firm can only go from bad to worse as it is,' he said.

Sarah frowned. 'How so?'

'Well eh . . . that's obvious.'

'Not to me, Mr McIvor.'

He laughed. 'It can only go from bad to worse because, and I mean no disrespect whatever, such an inexperienced person is running it.'

Sarah went cold inside. The cheek of the man. The bloody cheek! 'You mean because a *female* is running it?'

'It's a novel concept I must admit, but hardly a practical or viable one.' He waved a hand at her. 'Don't get me wrong. As I admire Jock so do I admire you for doing your best in trying to keep the firm's head above water, but it just won't work in the long term, will it? You must see that and agree?'

She must have been mad to have been tempted, even for an instant, she thought. She could only put her weakness down to the fact she was so damn tired.

'If you think we'll go under anyway, why do you want to buy us out?' she asked.

'For the firm's goodwill, past and present, which can count for a great deal. It also saves me the time, effort and aggravation of chipping away at you from without. This way everything is neat, tidy and to the mutual benefit of all parties concerned,' he lied smoothly. His real reason for wanting to buy Jock out was the personal satisfaction of doing so. That, and paying Jock back for what Jock had done to him and his father all those years ago by stealing business from McIvor, McIvor and Devereaux and setting up on his own.

'Well, I'm sorry to disappoint you, but we're not interested in any buy-out,' Sarah stated coldly.

'Don't be hasty, Miss Hawke. And shouldn't you really talk this over with Jock?'

'I don't have to talk it over with Jock, Mr McIvor. I know what his answer would be, the same as mine. No.'

McIvor scowled at her. 'Maybe I should speak to him direct.'

'Jock is in no condition to receive visitors, far less discuss business with one. And please don't get the idea you could go out to Stiellsmuir while I'm at the office here. The staff have strict instructions from me to turn everyone away at the door.'

'You have the authority to make these decisions, then?' McIvor probed.

'Oh yes, Mr McIvor, I have the authority. My status has been made quite legal and above board, I assure you.' That was something she'd taken care of through Jock's solicitors.

McIvor could see he was getting nowhere, and decided to try another tack. Taking out his pocket watch he glanced at it. 'I have a suggestion, Miss Hawke. Would you do me the honour of dining with me? It would be far more enjoyable to discuss this matter further over a good meal and bottle of wine.' He flashed her a wide, and what he considered to be disarming, smile. 'What do you say to that eh?'

She'd had enough of Ranald Cyril. 'I already have an engagement Mr McIvor. But even if I didn't I wouldn't accept your invitation. To put it bluntly, there's that about you makes my skin crawl.'

His smile vanished, and he blushed.

'Good evening, Mr McIvor,' she said with finality, and stubbed out what remained of her cigarette.

She didn't extend him the courtesy of walking him to her office door, instead she addressed herself again to the order form she'd been perusing when disturbed by his arrival.

'Condescending creep!' she muttered to herself after the door had snicked shut behind him.

Sarah and Mathew lay satiated in each other's arms. Her ear was against his chest, and she could hear his heart thudding within. A heart that belonged to her.

'It just gets better and better,' she said.

'Aye.' He certainly wouldn't have disagreed with that.

Reaching down she curled her fingers in the thick rope of pubic hair that ran from the tangle round his genitals up to his belly button. Very gently she tugged.

'Ouch!' he said, pretending that was sore.

'Kiss me or I'll pull these out by the roots.'

'You wouldn't!'

'I would.'

'Sadist.'

She gave a soft laugh. How gloriously happy she was. She lifted up her face as his came down to her. Their mouths met, and then their tongues. Slipping her hand further down she cupped his testicles, something she adored doing.

'Be careful,' he whispered when the kiss was over.

'Aren't I always?'

He frowned suddenly. 'I wish I didn't have to go away again so soon.' He was scheduled to sail for South America that afternoon.

'So do I.' She kissed one of his nipples, then the other. 'So do I!' she sighed.

He lightly caressed the swell of her buttock. How soft it was, like satin. But then her skin was the same all over. He never tired of touching and stroking it.

'I didn't suggest this before because you were on short-haul runs, but now that McIvor has you going to South America, and you say its's going to be a regular thing, why don't you come and work for me? You can be captain of the *Snowdrop* in place of MacQuarrie.'

He twisted round to look at her. 'Nigeria, Cape Town and back?'

'That's it.'

'Hmmm!' he mused.

'All you have to do is say, and the *Snowdrop*'s yours.'

'And what about MacQuarrie?'

'I'll give him an excellent reference,' she replied. 'He'll get another ship, no bother.'

Mathew thought about the *Snowdrop*, not a vessel he particularly liked. He'd been aboard her several times and had never been taken with her.

'Don't be offended, but I prefer to stay with the *Good Intent*. That ship and I fit one another the way you and I do.'

She smiled to hear that, understanding exactly what he meant.

It was a decision Mathew Wilson was to regret for the rest of his life.

Chapter 7

It was a freezing cold February night with large snowflakes flying as Ronald Moffat stepped out into Tradeston Street. There he paused to pull his coat collar high round his neck, before glancing back up at the rather dilapidated building from which he'd just emerged.

What a comedown, he thought bitterly. The new premises weren't a patch on the old; there was just no comparison. It had broken his heart to leave Carlton Place, particularly to come somewhere like this. Why, it was the next best thing to a slum!

It was almost 7 pm, but *she* was still working. He'd left her beavering at her desk. She was certainly a grafter same as her father, he had to give her that. He stared at her window from which a pale light glimmered.

'Mr Moffat?'

He turned to find that a carriage had drawn up at the pavement edge.

'Mr Moffat, may I have a word with you?'

The voice was vaguely familiar, but he couldn't make out the face because of the dark and snow.

'It might well be to your advantage, Mr Moffat.'

And then the penny dropped. He knew whose voice that was. He crossed to the waiting carriage.

'Is that you, Mr McIvor?'

'It is indeed, Mr Moffat. Please come inside.' And with that the carriage door swung open.

Now what did McIvor want with him? He hesitated for a brief second, glanced about him and saw that he was unobserved, then climbed into the carriage. McIvor pulled the door shut behind him.

'I've given my driver your home address, Mr Moffat. May I take you there and we can talk on the way?'

When Moffat didn't reply a now thinly smiling McIvor rapped the carriage roof, and the carriage moved off again. There was a wooden box, edged in metal, on the seat beside McIvor, which he opened to extract a bottle and two crystal glasses. He poured them each a hefty tot.

'Uisge beatha, the water of life, was invented for weather such as this,' McIvor said, handing Moffat one of the glasses.

270

'Slainthe!' McIvor toasted.

Moffat raised his glass to match the toast, then drank. It was good whisky, quality stuff. Way beyond his pocket.

'How do you like it?'

'Excellent,' Moffat enthused.

'Blairburnie Malt, a wee Perthshire distillery I bought several years ago. I'll have a case sent round to you.'

Moffat blinked. A whole case of whisky! He'd never had such an extravagance. He'd be able to bum about that to the neighbours right enough.

'Why, thank you.'

'Don't mention it.'

McIvor had a sip from his own glass. So far so good. 'How are you enjoying working for a lassie, then?' he asked genially.

Moffat dropped his gaze. 'It's . . . all right. A bit different, but all right.'

'You don't sound too enthusiastic, Mr Moffat?'

Moffat didn't reply.

'I can well understand your feelings. A man of your age and experience taking orders from a lassie. Must be galling in the extreme.'

Moffat had another swallow of his drink.

'I have to confess your Miss Hawke has surprised me. Since the turn of the year she's started to regain some of the ground that *J. Hawke & Daughter* had lost.' What he didn't say was that most of the ground had been lost during Moffat's stewardship.

'She's a hard worker. I was just thinking that before you called out to me.'

'A hard worker and a shrewd one despite her tender years. I hear she runs the firm with a rod of iron, just like Jock did.'

Moffat grinned sheepishly. 'I won't deny it, there were a few of us got a shock in that department. There are times when it's just like dealing with Mr Hawke himself.'

'Aye, that's what I heard.' McIvor extended the bottle. 'Here, let me top you up.'

The carriage clip-clopped on for a short way in silence, then McIvor said, 'I know it's an impertinent question, Mr Moffat, but I have my reasons for asking. How much does Miss Hawke pay you?'

Moffat named his yearly salary.

'Reasonable for a Chief Clerk. About the going rate, I should say.'

Moffat was no fool. Picked up by McIvor himself in the man's own carriage, escorted home, the promise of a case of whisky. Some sort of proposition was going to be made. Nor was he averse to that being so.

'How would you like to work for me on the side, Mr Moffat? For which service I will pay you the same salary again.'

Moffat's throat went dry. The same salary again! Why, that would put him and Mrs Moffat in clover. By his standards he'd be rich! 'And what precisely will I have to do to earn this money?' he queried, having already guessed the answer.

'I want you to help me put *J. Hawke & Daughter* out of business,' McIvor replied simply.

It was a real snowstorm outside the carriage now, Moffat noted. The trams he normally used to get home had a bad habit of stopping in conditions like this, and with the trams stopped he'd have had to be lucky in the extreme to find an empty hansom. Thank goodness McIvor had come along; McIvor had probably saved him a long walk in appalling conditions. An omen? It could be interpreted as such.

'Mr Hawke has always been a fair employer to me. I couldn't stick the knife in his back,' Moffat said quietly.

'Forget Jock Hawke. He's out of the firm and never returning to it. You know that for fact,' McIvor argued.

'Miss Hawke's exact words were, "it seems likely he will never work again".'

'Semantics, Moffat, nothing more. If Jock has handed over the responsibility for his firm to his daughter then he's finished, and well you know it. Good God, man, the old Jock would have walked a mile over broken glass before allowing the reins to slip from his fingers. No, no, he's through, down the plughole.'

McIvor paused, then asked, 'By the by, do you know what *is* wrong with Jock? That's something I haven't been able to find out.'

Moffat shook his head. 'When Miss Hawke told me about his illness she said she couldn't mind the name of it. Why, is it important?'

McIvor thought about that. 'No, I don't suppose so. The fact that Jock is *hors de combat* is all that matters, all that counts.' He topped up Moffat's glass again, then his own.

He went on. 'I approve and applaud your loyalty to Jock, Mr Moffat. But he's in the past now, history. Why should you be loyal to his daughter, a lassie not even twenty-one years old yet? I truly can't see why you should feel the need to be loyal there.' Sarah was due to celebrate her twenty-first birthday the following month, March 1894.

'You have a point,' Moffat conceded. He knew this was wrong, that McIvor's was a false argument. That it was his duty to be loyal to Sarah as he'd been to her father. If only she'd been a lad it might not have been so bad. But for a female, not even, as McIvor rightly pointed out, the age of majority yet, to be giving him orders, telling him what to do. Oh but that was a bitter pill to have to swallow!

McIvor played his ace. 'And when *J. Hawke & Daughter* does throw in the towel, or should anything go amiss in the meantime, I guarantee you a job with me at the double salary level until retirement.'

Moffat swallowed hard. *Guaranteed job at the double salary level!* This was a golden opportunity he'd be mad to turn down. He couldn't possibly lose out.

'What do you want me to do?' he asked.

McIvor had a sip of his whisky, enjoying the feeling of having ensnared Moffat. For with Moffat on the payroll the destruction of *J. Hawke & Daughter* was a certainty.

'I want full details of each and every transaction they engage in, tenders, etc. – the lot. Can you do that for me?'

Moffat nodded. He had complete access to everything of that nature within the company. Had to have as Chief Clerk.

'Equal emphasis on both sides, export and import, but I'm particularly interested in their import business. Up until now that's been the hardest for me to find out about.'

'How do you wish this information, on a daily or weekly basis?' Moffat enquired.

'Every Tuesday and Thursday evening should be sufficient. What we'll do is arrange a rendezvous. Somewhere convenient but where there will be no one to recognise either of us.'

'So you don't only want a written report but a verbal précis as well,' Moffat said.

'Correct.'

'I understand.'

'Tomorrow is Thursday. Shall we have our first rendezvous tomorrow night then?'

'Fine by me.'

McIvor held out his hand, and the two men shook on it. McIvor had already spoken to his driver about just such a meeting place, the name of which he now gave to Moffat. Then they agreed a time.

Adam Tennant sat in a booth at Milne's Vaults nursing a glass of

Revolver. He was supposed to be at class but, most unusual for him, had decided to give it a miss that night.

He'd been painting at home that afternoon when suddenly he'd become scunnered by the whole thing, and decided to take the rest of the day off to get over it.

He stared morosely at Vera serving behind the bar. The pair of them weren't getting on at all well. They seemed to do nothing but fight and generally lay into one another of late. In fact, not only of late but for some while now. They were becoming like a right married couple.

The bed side of things had degenerated too. Most nights now the pair of them just turned over and went to sleep. And when they did get down to it, it was a case of going through the actions.

His reverie was rudely interrupted when a well-remembered face came into the pub. Old man Moffat himself! The Chief Clerk of *J. Hawke & Daughter*. Now there was a turn up for the book. It took a stretch of the imagination to envisage Moffat going into a pub at all, but one like Milne's Vaults, a nefarious dive some would call it, really took the biscuit.

As Adam watched, Moffat ordered two drinks which he paid for, picked the drinks up and took them over to an empty booth across the room from where Adam was sitting.

Two drinks and an empty booth? That meant Moffat was meeting someone.

Adam smiled to himself. Was it a woman? If it was it wasn't Mrs Moffat, not in Milne's Vaults. A prossie maybe? There were a few who frequented the place.

Could that be it? Had Moffat arranged to meet a prossie? Adam found that rich if it was.

Still smiling Adam settled back in his booth, his face in shadow. He couldn't wait to see what turned up. Blonde? Brunette? A ginger? A wee birdie about the same age as the grand-daughters he knew Moffat had?

Dirty old bugger! he thought. Who would have believed Moffat had it in him? Certainly not Adam Tennant.

A few minutes later the person the second drink was intended for arrived, and Adam's jaw dropped in recognition. Not a prossie at all, but McIvor!

McIvor slid in beside Moffat, and their two heads came close in quiet conversation.

What the hell was going on? Adam asked himself. Why should the

Chief Clerk of *J. Hawke & Daughter* be meeting clandestinely, and what else could you call it, with the head of a rival firm? Something stank here, stank to high heaven.

And then, as he continued to observe, Adam saw Moffat take a folded paper, or it could be papers, from an inside jacket pocket and place it on the table between himself and McIvor. Using a finger as a pointer McIvor appeared to be explaining what was on the paper.

Papers, plural, Adam was now able to verify. Two sheets at least, possibly more.

Adam sank further into his booth to ponder this mystery. Just before Christmas he'd bumped into Jacky Telfer who'd been at *J. Hawke & Daughter* when he had, and who'd told him about Mr Hawke's illness, Sarah's taking over, and two-thirds of the staff being let go. It had come up in the conversation that Moffat was staying, while Jacky was one of the unfortunates being given the heave-ho.

Could it be that Moffat had moved firms since then? Could he now be working for McIvor? But if Moffat was, why on earth were they meeting here?

That didn't wash. So, presuming Moffat was still Chief Clerk at *J. Hawke & Daughter*, the question remained, what was he doing clandestinely meeting with the head of a rival firm?

Moffat left the booth, returned to the bar and ordered another round of drinks. When Moffat glanced about, Adam retreated even deeper into the shadow.

Moffat, carrying a couple of large gills, went back to his booth, and the conversation between him and McIvor resumed.

Adam decided that Sarah should know about this. If there was any humphery mumphery going on, tipping her the wink was a small repayment on his part for what she'd done for him by paying his art school fees.

He stayed well in the shadow till McIvor and Moffat had left, McIvor going first, followed shortly afterwards by Moffat.

If Adam needed any convincing that they were up to no good the manner of their departure clinched it.

Sarah gazed in total and abject despair at the letter she was holding. Yet another tender turned down, the umpteenth in a row. There had been no new business for six weeks now, not a sausage. And as for existing contracts, the ratio was now down to about only one in three being renewed.

She threw the letter on to her desk, and lit a cigarette with trembling hands. What an unholy mess she was making of it all! She'd thought in her arrogance that she could run the firm as well as Jock. What a sick notion that was turning out to be. Thank God for *Snowdrop* and the palm oil run. If it wasn't for that lifeline they'd be in an even worse situation than they now were, which was saying something.

Things had looked so promising at the beginning of the new year, too! The corner had been turned, everything had started to look rosy once more, and then ... Like snakes and ladders they'd hit a snake and down, down down they'd gone. And were still falling, with no sign of a halt.

She had another puff of her cigarette. If only Jock had been able to help her, to advise. She'd gone to his room the previous week and tried to talk to him about what was happening. But she'd got no response. When he finally had spoken it was about his days in Maryhill when he'd lived there with her mother, before Myrtle had gone off with Bob.

She was going to have to let another clerk go, she decided. At this rate, for others had gone since the original butchering, there would soon only be her, Moffat and Hemphill left.

'Jesus!' she swore aloud.

She was stubbing out her cigarette when there was a rap on the door. 'Come in!' she cried out.

It was Smith. 'This came for you in the second post,' he said, handing her a blue envelope.

Personal, the envelope stated in the left hand corner, and underlined three times. She didn't recognise the handwriting.

'Dear Sarah ...' the letter began. She turned the page over to see who it was from, and was pleasantly surprised to discover it was Adam Tennant's signature.

Her smile slowly disappeared as she read. When she had finished the letter she started again at the beginning, and read it through a second time.

She was furious in the extreme, and very, very let down. How could Moffat!

Taking a deep breath she counselled herself to wait a little before confronting her Chief Clerk. She wanted to be fully in control when she did, not ablaze with emotion as she now was.

It was half an hour later that Moffat was summoned to Sarah's office.

'Yes, Miss Hawke?'

'Thirty pieces of silver,' she stated coldly.

Moffat regarded her with astonishment. 'I beg your pardon?'

'Wasn't that what the Romans paid Judas to betray his master, thirty pieces of silver?'

All expression left Moffat's face, which now became a mask out of which his beady eyes glittered. 'I don't know what you're talking about Miss Hawke.'

'No?'

She waited, but he didn't reply to her jibe. Eventually she went on, 'I blamed myself for the firm doing so badly, believing it was all my fault.' She paused, then added very softly, almost in a whisper, 'But it wasn't, was it, Moffat?'

'I'm still not with you, Miss Hawke.'

'Oh I think you are, Mr Moffat. You've been acting as a spy, a traitor, giving away all our business details and secrets.'

He pretended outrage. 'Really, Miss Hawke! That is just too fantastic.'

'Is it? It makes sense to me. It explains all sorts of things that were inexplicable before.'

Moffat drew himself up to his full height, continuing to try and bluff this out. 'I don't know where you've got this ridiculous idea, Miss Hawke, but I really must protest. It's unworthy of you.'

'Ranald Cyril McIvor of McIvor, McIvor and Devereaux,' she said.

'I know of Mr McIvor of course.'

'Not only know of, you know him personally, Mr Moffat.'

'We eh . . . Yes, I recall now that we have met. Though quite some time ago.'

That was it, what she'd been angling for. A straight lie. It confirmed everything.

'Not "quite some time ago" Mr Moffat, but last Tuesday night to be precise. In a pub called Milne's Vaults. And please don't try to deny that, you were seen.'

'By whom!'

Should she name Adam or shouldn't she? Why drag his name into this when it was unnecessary. 'By someone who knows you very well Mr Moffat. You personally bought two rounds of drinks, you and McIvor sat in a booth, and you showed him papers you'd brought along with you.'

Moffat's sallow skin had gone even paler. His lips were thinned, his nose flared, his beady eyes glittering venomously.

'Why, Mr Moffat? Why have you been playing Judas? I really would like to know.'

There was no point in trying to bluff any further. The game was well and truly up. 'It wasn't just for the thirty pieces of silver as you put it, though I will confess the money did influence me considerably. But also because I am now guaranteed a job until retirement, which was something you could most certainly not do.'

He glared at Sarah. 'Another reason, and perhaps the primary one, is have you ever stopped to consider how humiliating it is for me to have to jump when a lassie cracks the whip? A man my age being told what to by a female, and a minor at that!'

'Well you won't have to jump anymore, Mr Moffat,' she snapped in reply, 'because you're fired. Collect your personal belongings and be out of the building within fifteen minutes.'

Turning, he walked stiff-legged from her office, closing the door behind him.

With the closing of the door it was as if a taut wire inside Sarah had snapped. She slumped in her chair. Damn McIvor, and damn Moffat. Damn the pair of them to burn in everlasting hellfire!

How profoundly betrayed she felt. For Moffat to have done that, to have been working against the firm while all this time she'd been working so hard for it!

She hadn't liked the weasel before, now she positively loathed him for putting Moffat up to what he had done. She loathed McIvor, and despised Moffat.

She had to be strong she told herself. Now the cancer had been cut from the firm it truly had a chance from here on in. If she'd worked hard before she'd work harder still. She'd save the firm if it was the last thing she ever did. *As God and all his angels were her judge she would!*

Laying her arms on the desk in front of her, and her head on her arms, she began to weep.

'Please inform Mr McIvor that Mr Moffat is here to see him,' Moffat said to the clerk who appeared when he rang the bell in reception.

'Do you have an appointment, sir?'

'No. But I can assure you Mr McIvor will want to speak with me.'

'I'll tell Mr McIvor that you're here then, sir. Would you please take a seat in the meantime?'

Moffat sat, and gazed about him. The building was an even more handsome one than that in Carlton Place, and superbly appointed, from what he'd so far glimpsed. He would enjoy working here all right. He thanked his lucky stars he would never again have to present himself at that dreadful tenement in Tradeston Street.

The clerk was back almost immediately, which was gratifying. 'Could you please follow me, Mr Moffat.'

They went along several corridors which had carpet underfoot – now there was a luxury! – until finally arriving at a glass-panelled door. The clerk knocked the door, then said to Moffat, 'Go straight in, sir, Mr McIvor is expecting you.'

There was a great deal of window glass in the office, which made it very light and airy, and gave a general feeling of spaciousness. McIvor was standing by a window looking out. He turned the moment Moffat entered the room.

McIvor waited until the door was closed again before exclaiming, 'Mr Moffat, I thought we'd agreed you'd never come here!'

'There's no need for cloak and dagger any more, Mr McIvor.' And with that Moffat launched into the tale of what had happened. McIvor listened in brooding silence.

'Hmmm!' he said when Moffat was finished. Then, 'Damn!' Going to his desk he threw himself into the button-back leather chair behind it.

'Any idea who it was saw us in that bloody pub? I was certain we'd be safe there!'

Moffat shook his head.

'Not that it matters. We were seen, and that's that.' Taking out a cigar he clipped and lit it.

'So when do I start with you, Mr McIvor?' Moffat asked.

McIvor went very still as he studied Moffat through the smoke now surrounding him.

'Monday first is as good a day as any I suppose,' Moffat added, smiling.

'What are you talking about?' McIvor queried, voice completely flat.

Moffat blinked. 'Our deal, our agreement. Your guarantee.'

'What guarantee?'

Panic suddenly flared in Moffat. Was this a joke? If so he

considered it to be in very poor taste. The panic was evident in his voice when he now spoke. 'You guaranteed me a job at double salary level when *J. Hawke & Daughter* threw in the towel or if anything went amiss in the meantime. Well, it most certainly has gone amiss. I've been found out helping you and sacked as a result.'

McIvor felt almost sorry for Moffat, but only almost. 'This guarantee you claim I gave you, have you any written proof of it? A letter, or contract perhaps?'

Moffat could feel his legs begin to go weak. 'You know I haven't, Mr McIvor. Your guarantee was verbal.'

'And as such non-binding, Mr Moffat. It's your word against mine.' His expression became one of false puzzlement. 'Guarantee? I never made you any guarantee, Mr Moffat. I did pay you some cash for information received, but that's as far as it went.'

This was no joke, it was horrible, horrible reality. McIvor was welching on him. 'Oh, you bastard!' he breathed.

'Good-day to you Mr Moffat. If you don't mind I'd like to get on. I have a great deal to do.' And with that McIvor opened a folder in front of him, and pretended to begin studying its contents.

'You can find your own way out, I'm sure,' he said without looking up, when Moffat still hadn't moved.

Moffat didn't remember leaving McIvor's office, or the building either. Next thing he knew, he was several streets away hanging on to some palings.

How was he going to face the wife? How was he going to face Mrs Moffat with the news?

Spying a pub across the way, he lurched over to it and went inside.

'Adam!' Sarah called out, raising her hand to catch his attention.

He'd come out of a classroom with a group of others, all of them talking excitedly and animatedly. On hearing her voice he glanced across to where she was standing, and acknowledged her presence with a wave. He spoke briefly with one of the group he was with, then left them to go to Sarah.

'I met Toshie downstairs. He told me if I stood here I'd be certain not to miss you when you were finished,' she explained.

It was the first time they'd met since her attack of smallpox, and with relief he saw that what Ollie had told him was true enough; Sarah wasn't badly facially scarred at all.

Realising what he was staring at, Sarah hurriedly explained how lucky she'd been.

It was on the tip of his tongue to apologise for not going to see her after her illness, when she'd started receiving visitors again. But he didn't.

'I was terribly sorry to hear about Mr Hawke,' he said instead.

'Yes, it was a blow.'

'I bumped into Jacky Telfer just before Christmas – He told me about what's been happening with the old firm, including you taking over.'

Adam was extremely thin, she thought. And peaky looking. 'I received your letter, and that's why I'm here. To thank you,' she said.

He took hold of her by the arm. 'Listen, there's a coffee shop in the basement. Would you care for some, and perhaps a sticky bun?'

She laughed. 'Coffee sounds marvellous, but if you don't mind I'll forgo the sticky bun.'

'Come on, then.'

She spotted Toshie with Herbert MacNair, and gestured that she'd found Adam.

'He's really beginning to make a name for himself as an architect and designer,' Adam said of Toshie. 'The school is very fortunate that he continues to teach here.'

'Does that mean we're going to have to call him Mr Mackintosh? Or will it be the full title, Mr Charles Rennie Mackintosh?'

This time it was Adam who laughed. 'I think he'd bash us if we did that. I can't say for his clients and business associates, but I'm certain that for the likes of you and I, his "freends" so to speak, he'll always prefer Toshie.'

In the basement Sarah sat at an ancient, much scarred table while Adam fetched the coffee. She wondered about having a cigarette, and decided she could. This was the School of Art after all: they were all Bohemians here.

'So tell me what happened about Moffat?' Adam asked when he rejoined her.

She related all that had been said, on her part and Moffat's.

'I just knew the pair of them were up to no good. I mean, why else would yon dreich Moffat meet a man like McIvor in a pub such as Milne's Vaults? That was the only logical explanation.'

She placed a hand on his wrist, which caused him to flush

slightly. 'Thank you again, I appreciate what you did.'

'It was little enough, considering.'

'Moffat would have done for the firm eventually if he'd gone on as he had been. And probably sooner than later. We were closer to having to shut up shop than I dared admit even to myself.'

'And now?'

'The firm will survive, and prosper again. I'm utterly determined on that.'

Just sitting here with Sarah made him the happiest he'd been in a long time he realised. Her presence filled him with a warm glow, and gave him a sense of completeness.

'Good luck to you then!' he said, a tightness in his throat as he toasted her with his coffee cup.

She drank as well, enjoying his company. Though not in the same way as he was hers.

'It isn't that long now until your time here is up. Have you decided what happens next?' she asked.

'I'll just keep painting and try to sell. I have sold quite a few since that first commission of Stiellsmuir you know. The public seem to like me.'

'The public show good taste,' she smiled. 'Does that mean you'll continue on with your cellarman's job?'

'While I'm in Glasgow anyway. I thought I might go abroad for a while. To the south of France perhaps, or Spain. Somewhere it's warm and the living's dirt cheap.'

'And paint while you're there?'

'Draw and paint as long as I could afford the materials. Or until I got homesick for Glasgow and came back.'

'It's strictly drawing and painting, then? You wouldn't consider architecture or design like our "freen" Toshie?'

Adam shook his head. 'I have no talent, or interest, in that direction. It's with drawing and painting that my ability and interest lie.'

'Your passions,' she said.

He glanced down into his cup, unable to continue staring her in the eyes after she'd said that.

'Are you still with your ladyfriend, what was her name again?'

'Vera.'

'Are you still with her?'

'Yes,' he mumbled.

'Will she go with you if you go abroad?'

She wouldn't be asked, he thought to himself. He replied instead, 'I doubt it. Vera's one of those Glaswegians who think the world ceases to exist outside the city boundaries, or the Clyde coast anyway. No, if I do go it's almost certain she'll remain behind.'

'I see.' For some inexplicable reason Sarah was pleased to hear that.

'Talking of abroad, how was the West Indies? Ollie mentioned you were off there on a convalescent trip.'

'I had a wonderful time. I was supposed to get married on my immediate return, but was unable to do so because of my father and the other problems I found awaiting me on my arrival back.'

Adam fought to keep his feelings out of his face. This was a revelation to him. Ollie had mentioned nothing of Sarah getting married the last meeting they'd had. He knew then with certainty that his elder sister had kept the news from him, not wanting to hurt him. Somewhere along the line Ollie had guessed his secret, that he was in love with Sarah Hawke.

'Congratulations!' he choked.

Sarah had been wondering if he was still in love with her. His reaction to that left her in no doubt as to the answer. Poor Adam, she thought.

'We'll get married when everything has been sorted out with the firm and it's on it's feet again.'

He drank what remained of his coffee, giving himself time to try and pull himself together. He wasn't just hurt, he was devastated. 'And who is the fortunate chap?' he asked eventually.

'His name is Mathew Wilson, and he's captain of the ship I went out to the West Indies on. We'd met before, the ship being one of my father's. Unfortunately it has had to be sold because of the financial problems we've been having.'

'You love him of course?'

That was an obvious, and could even be construed as an odd, question, but she understood his need to ask it. 'Very much so,' she replied softly.

'And he you?'

'So he says.'

'Then all I can do is wish you every happiness.'

'Thank you Adam, I appreciate that coming from someone I consider a dear and true friend.'

He'd been enjoying Sarah's company, now he wanted away from her. He needed to crawl into a corner somewhere and lick his wounds.

It was stupid really that he felt this way about her impending marriage. There had never been any chance for him. And yet, if he was honest, there had always been that hope at the back of his mind that somehow, against all the odds, a miracle might occur.

Now he knew for certain there was to be no miracle and that she would shortly be lost to him forever. If this Captain Mathew Wilson had been there with them he'd cheerfully have strangled the sod.

The thought of another man, this Wilson, doing with Sarah what he and Vera did together brought him out in a cold sweat. Then in his mind he pictured Sarah and Wilson, not in a sexual context, but happy together, sharing things, caring for one another. And that was far, far worse than the sex business. Deep down that was what he really wanted of Sarah, what he would have given an arm and a leg for.

'Is your carriage waiting outside?' he asked.

'Yes.'

'Then I'll see you to it, shall I?' He somehow forced a smile on to his face.

They left the coffee shop in silence, nor did they speak again till they reached Sarah's carriage, where she thanked him yet again for his letter.

He hesitated, unsure how to conclude their meeting, and not wishing to appear oafish about it. She solved his problem by kissing him on the cheek before climbing, helped by Ferguson, into her carriage.

When the carriage was gone he very gently and carefully reached up and touched the spot she'd kissed.

Suddenly his face twisted into murderous fury, and he swore vehemently.

A passer-by looked at him in astonishment, so he swore again.

Exorcism, he thought. A Catholic word, but that's what he needed.

Exorcism.

He was in a fever of painting when Vera returned home from the pub. His glowing eyes were riveted to the canvas where he was creating what seemed to him a part of his very soul.

Vera chucked her purse and shawl on to a chair. 'I'm buggered,' she announced. 'It was one hell of a busy night. I was fair run off my feet, so I was.'

His reply was a grunt.

'I thought you might have stopped off for a Revolver after Art School?'

He grunted again without taking his eyes off the canvas.

Vera sauntered over to see what he was painting. His subject was a female with auburny hair. 'Who's she?'

He was having trouble with the line of Sarah's neck. He wasn't getting it just right. It was the first time he'd painted Sarah since that portrait he'd presented to her three years previously.

'I said, who is she?'

'Chum of my sister Olivia's,' he replied quietly, applying more paint with his palette knife. He sometimes used brushes, sometimes a palette knife. It all depended upon how he felt. Usually it was the brushes when he was in a calm mood, the knife when he was tempestuous inside. The results of both methods were quite different.

'She's pretty,' Vera acknowledged.

Adam grunted again.

Vera gave up, knowing from long experience that there was no talking with Adam when he was engrossed in his work as he now was. She'd make herself a cup of tea, and then go off to bed, she thought. Adam would join her when he was ready, then again he might not. He was quite capable of painting right through the night.

Hours passed, and Adam continued to work feverishly, wishing he had better light to see by, but that was always a complaint of his when he painted during the hours of darkness. He would have to make do with the gas and candles he'd lit.

And then, suddenly, it was over. The painting was complete. All that remained was his signature, which he quickly dashed off.

When he'd done that he stood there, drained, staring at the face he'd had coffee with earlier. And the lips which had announced her forthcoming marriage to Captain Mathew Wilson.

'Fuck you, Wilson!' Adam whispered savagely.

It was a stupid childish thing to do. He knew that, but he did it nonetheless. From top right-hand corner, to bottom left-hand corner, he drew his palette knife across the picture. Then, using the tip and edges of the knife, he jabbed again and again at Sarah's features till he'd horribly disfigured them.

The knife dropped from his now nerveless fingers to the linoleum where it caused a small spatter of paint amongst the many spatters already there.

The same fingers curled into a fist, a fist formed harder and harder till the knuckles showed white through the bloodless flesh.

There was a little whisky in the house, he remembered. Going to the press he located the bottle and poured its contents straight down his throat.

That made his head momentarily swim, and caused him to cough. 'Jesus,' he croaked, and thumped himself on the chest. That whisky was so rough it might have been sheep-dip.

Sarah, going to be married. He felt as though he'd had a death sentence passed on him.

He was drunk he realised. Not from the whisky, but from emotion. A whole medley of swirling, pulsating, negative emotions.

He made another fist and smashed it into his other hand. He smashed the fist again and again. Then he wiped away some of the wet that had crept into his eyes.

He turned out the gas, and blew out the candles with the exception of one. Holding that he went through to the bedroom where he found, as he'd known he would, Vera fast asleep.

She was lying on her front, her face to him, an exposed left breast that had escaped through a tear in her nightdress hanging down the side of the bed.

He stood looking at her for a few seconds, and as he did his breathing became shorter and shorter as passion took hold of him.

Laying his candle on her bedside table – actually a wooden box with a tatty velvet covering over it – he grasped hold of the covers and slowly drew them down till her entire length was revealed.

Vera stirred, muttered crossly, then reaching behind her scratched her backside. But didn't waken.

He removed his clothes, tossing them carelessly aside, not caring where or how they fell. When he was naked he reached down and flipped Vera over onto her back, opened her legs which he now squatted between, and felt her.

Her eyes flew open. 'What are you doing?' she demanded.

She was nowhere near ready, but he didn't care. He thrust himself into her, causing her to cry out in pain.

'Wait! Wait!' she pleaded. But he had no intention of doing that. Grasping hold of her breasts he squeezed them hard as he pounded into her.

'You're hurting me, Adam! For fuck's sake you're hurting me!'

That was precisely what he wanted to do. He squeezed even harder while his continued pounding gradually moved her up the bed till at last her head was jammed against the headboard.

'Bastard! Bastard!' she spat, slapping and punching him on the face and shoulders. One of her nails ripped open his cheek, drawing blood. Blood that began dripping down on to her.

Letting go of her breasts he pulled himself up slightly, and grabbed hold of her waist. He squeezed that just as hard as he'd done her breasts.

The blood from his torn cheek was dripping more fulsomely and faster now. He smiled thinly to see a small river of it run into the top tangle of her pubic hair.

Vera had never known Adam like this before. Brutality was new to him. Come morning she was going to be black and blue from head to toe.

'Turn over!' he commanded, pulling out.

'Like hell I will!' she replied, thinking she'd slide out of bed. She'd hardly begun to move when he slapped her, a slap delivered with such ferocity she thought for one star-filled moment that her head was exploding.

'Over I said, bitch!' he repeated, and grabbing hold of her by the arm he forced her back on to her front.

He pulled her hips up a bit, had trouble with her nightdress which he savagely ripped so that it fell away in two halves, and lunged back into her. Hooking an arm round her waist he stuck a forefinger up her anus.

She screamed at the violation. He had never behaved like this before. He moved his forefinger in time with his penis.

When he tired of that, and feeling as if he could go on forever, he removed his forefinger and using that hand began rhythmically to smack her backside.

When the right buttock was blazing he changed position fractionally and started on her left. Each stinging smack had his full force behind it.

He could feel the pressure mounting now, and knew he would soon ejaculate. Faster and faster he went, still smacking as hard as he could.

He made an animal sound at the back of his throat, and an instant later bucked in orgasm. His sperm seemed red hot as it spurted.

When it was all over, and he'd shrivelled out of her, he sank over on to his own side of the bed.

'That was disgusting,' she whimpered.

He didn't reply.

Gingerly she touched her buttocks, moaning as she did so. Her da had often leathered her bum when she was wee, but that had been nothing compared to this. The combination of the smacking and everything else had left her feeling totally degraded and defiled.

'Why, Adam?'

Again he didn't reply, just continued staring at the ceiling.

'Did you actually *enjoy* that?'

'Yes.'

She shuddered. 'You're not going to say you're sorry, then?'

'No.'

She struggled on to her knees to stare down at him. 'What's happened to us, Adam? What's gone wrong?'

You're not Sarah, he thought. It was as simple as that. She wasn't Sarah Hawke.

She winced as a sharp pain shot through her breast at a point where he'd been squeezing.

'You really hurt me tonight. I hope you're proud of that. I hope it makes you feel like a big man.'

He turned his head away from her.

She got out of bed, dropped the remains of her nightdress to the floor, picked up the candle and went through to the kitchen where the first thing she saw was the disfigured portrait of Sarah. That frightened her; he'd never done anything like that before either.

She was very thoughtful as she soaked a flannel in cold water, wrung it out and applied it to her backside. She did this a number of times, which helped cool down her inflamed flesh, then returned to the bedroom intending to quiz Adam about the portrait.

But, exhausted by his painting, emotions, and sexual exertion, he was already fast asleep.

'It's quite a "do", don't you think?' Charlie Dundonald said to Sarah as they danced to the music of a twenty-piece orchestra installed on a rostrum at the head of the ballroom.

It had been Sarah's idea that Charlie – her calling him Mr had long since gone by the board – take her to The Albion Fiftieth Anniversary Ball, being held at the St Andrew's Halls because the club premises were too small for such a large function.

Charlie had called in at Stiellsmuir one evening to inquire after Jock – he was one of the few Sarah had so far confided in as to what was actually wrong with her father – and to find out how she herself was getting on. During their subsequent chattering he'd told her about the forthcoming ball, and she'd had the brainwave that perhaps she could drum up some business at it. (Nothing ventured nothing gained! she'd thought.) She'd explained the brainwave to Charlie and asked if he'd take her which, being a widower for the past ten years, he'd been only too happy to do.

Sarah glanced about her as she and Charlie danced on. The affair was a glittering one with, amongst other things, jewels all colours of the rainbow sparkling everywhere.

Sarah was the only woman present, or if there was another she hadn't spotted her, not wearing jewellery. All hers had been sold on her return from the West Indies, along with her adored sable coat which had gone for its second-hand cash value.

Having guessed that all the women attending the ball would be dressed up to the nines she'd gone for the opposite effect, simplicity in the extreme.

Her dress was matt black, with no pattern or working of any kind on it. The bodice was figure hugging, the sleeves tight down the length of the arm to the wrist. The waist was pinched, and from there the materials fell away in a cascade to the floor.

The overall effect was even better than she'd hoped. Beside her all the rest looked like Christmas trees.

The dance ended, and they applauded. 'There's someone who might be of help to you,' Charlie said.

'Who's that?'

'Fergus Binnie. His family own a very thriving porcelain factory in Barrhead.'

'What sort of porcelain?'

Charlie grinned. 'They specialise in water closets and urinals which they send all over the world.'

'Then introduce me. And don't be upset if I flirt a bit. I expect to be doing a lot of that tonight.'

'Shameless hussy!' he teased.

'Shameless as they come, if it'll get me orders.'

Grasping Sarah by the elbow, Charlie led her in the direction of Fergus Binnie, who had a right battle-axe of a wife and would therefore enjoy meeting a pretty young woman.

It was some time later when another dance had just ended, and Charlie had left Sarah to fetch refreshments for them both, when a voice behind her said, 'Hello, Sarah. How are you?'

A smile cracked her face when she saw who it was had addressed her. 'The Honourable Ian! How are you?'

'Never better. And yourself?'

'Oh, so so!'

He hesitated, then said slowly, 'Pa told me about your father. I was extremely sorry to hear that.'

'Thank you.'

'Confined to bed, I believe?'

'He's very ill,' she prevaricated.

'And you've taken over *J. Hawke & Daughter*? I must admit I was impressed by that.'

'Why? Think it was beyond me?' she smiled.

'Not at all. I just . . . ' He shrugged. 'It's a man's world, after all. Or so they say.'

'And what do you say?'

'That if anyone is underestimating you they're making a mistake.'

'Flatterer! Still charming the birds down out of the trees I see.'

He touched her very lightly on the arm. 'Are you available to be charmed?'

She was about to reply when Charlie came bustling up. 'Why hello, dear boy, how goes it?' Charlie asked of Ian, for of course the two of them knew one another.

'Fine sir. And you?'

'Feeling on top of the world at having the honour of escorting this delectable creature tonight,' he replied, meaning Sarah, whom he now rounded on, handing her one of the two glasses of punch he was carrying. 'My dear you must come right away and talk to Sir Alexander Robbie. I've just been chatting to him at the punch bowl and he says he'd adore to meet you.' Charlie's eyes flicked to Ian, then back to Sarah. 'Alex is in steel in a big way.'

'Then take me to him,' Sarah replied instantly.

Ian wondered at that. Why should Sarah be so keen to meet someone in steel?

'I have to go,' Sarah said to Ian, whose face dropped.

'Maybe I can speak with you later?'

'Maybe. But the possibility is I'm going to be fairly tied up.' Seeing his expression she added. 'Business.'

Now he understood. 'I'll tell you what. How about lunch tomorrow?'

She frowned, uncertain about that. Her usual practice was to eat a few sandwiches Mrs McGuffie made her at her desk.

'I'm only in Glasgow for a couple of days,' he added.

Why not! she thought. One lunchtime off could hardly hurt the firm.

'All right then. What time?'

They made the arrangements, she giving him the firm's new address in Tradeston Street. And then she was off, moving across the floor with Charlie, eager to meet this Sir Alexander Robbie who was big in steel.

'So how do you consider it went?' Charlie Dundonald asked Sarah as his carriage took them to Stiellsmuir where he'd be dropping her before continuing on home.

'This evening could have been very, very useful indeed. I made some excellent face-to-face contacts, and had several promises of business put my way. Promises I will now have to pursue to ensure they are delivered.'

Charlie chuckled. 'Having got the fish on the line, make sure he doesn't escape again, eh?'

'Exactly.'

'Well I'm only glad I was able to be of assistance.'

'I was thinking, there must be other functions we could attend together which I could use for the same purpose?'

'I suppose so, Sarah. Now let me see.' He brooded in silence for a bit. 'There's an important Masonic "do" coming up next month. How would you fancy going to that?'

'Are you a Mason?'

'I am. And before you ask, Jock isn't. I broached the subject with him a number of times, but he was never interested. Foolishly, in my opinion. But there we are.'

'I'd love to go. And don't the Masons have a female counterpart?'

He gave her a shrewd look, guessing what was on her mind. 'You mean the Eastern Star?'

'I'd be interested to hear what you can tell me about that,' she said.

For what remained of their journey Charlie spoke about the Eastern Star, and the Masons.

The restaurant Ian took Sarah to was a fish one in Springfield Court. Once settled at their table they ordered turbot à la cancalaise, and a bottle of Chablis.

'It really is good to see you again,' Ian declared after they'd placed their order.

'And you. How's Paris?'

'Full of French people. How's Glasgow?'

'Full of drunks.'

He laughed at that.

'Not married or engaged yet?' she queried.

'Not yet. You?'

'I'm unofficially engaged. I, or I should say we, hope to be getting married before too long.'

He hadn't expected that. He hadn't expected it at all. It threw him considerably. He could feel his good humour ooze out of him as if he was a pricked balloon.

'You met Mathew briefly at the party we had at Stielismuir in December 1890, the party where I met you for the first time. He was with a gorgeous woman from Boston, Massachusetts.'

It was coming back to Ian. 'Wasn't he a ship's captain or something?'

'That's right. He's the captain of the ship that took me to the West Indies. One of Jock's ships which, unfortunately, we've had to sell.'

'I suppose congratulations are in order,' Ian said as graciously as he could.

'Thank you.' She paused fractionally, then went on, 'And no, he's not rich, Ian. His background is relatively humble. But what I do know is that he proposed to me because of what I am myself, and his feelings towards me. There were no ulterior motives.'

Ian saw the wine waiter approach. He needed a drink. 'Well, that's put me in my place, and no mistake.'

She reached out and placed a hand over his. 'I didn't intend that to sound nasty or snide.'

They both fell silent while the waiter opened the Chablis and poured.

When the waiter was gone Ian raised his glass. 'To Captain and Mrs . . . What was his surname again?'

'Wilson.'

'To Captain and Mrs Wilson. All the best there is.' He sipped his wine, changed his mind and had a good swallow.

'What about your lady?' Sarah inquired. 'I thought the pair of you would have been engaged by now at least?'

Charlotte was mad keen for them to get engaged; it was he who was holding back. But he wasn't going to tell Sarah that, it might have sounded as if he was boasting. 'It's on the cards, merely a matter of timing,' he replied.

She nodded. 'I understand.'

Oh no you don't! he thought. Sarah getting married! He was furious. Furious and . . . Disappointed was too weak a word for what he felt. Devastated too strong.

'Pa mentioned something about your firm having the hiccups recently? Some sort of financial entanglement?'

Starting at the beginning, she told him everything, with the exception of what was really wrong with Jock. Ian listened, his features creasing more and more with concern.

'This McIvor and Moffat sound a real couple of shits,' he said eventually when she'd concluded her tale. It was rare indeed he used strong language in front of a member of the opposite sex, but just then he'd felt compelled to do so.

'I'd say that was a pretty fair description,' she agreed. She couldn't have put it better herself.

'I had no idea, and clearly neither did Pa, that things were so bad with you.'

'We were in grave danger of losing Stiellsmuir during the Canadian crisis but, thank God, I managed to save it. It would have been absolutely awful to lose the house.'

'And that's now secure?'

'Yes, except in the eventuality of the firm going broke owing debts. Then it would have to be sacrificed. It's the one asset, or piece of collateral, we have left.'

'I appreciate why you were so busy trying to drum up business last night. It's only a pity that . . .' He trailed off.

'What Ian?'

'As a female you're ineligible to join the Albion. Your father, as all of them do, used his membership there to great effect.'

'I can well imagine,' she said, agreeing with the latter. 'That's where it *is* a disadvantage being female. I'm excluded, apart from certain social occasions, from that business inner sanctum so to speak.'

Ian toyed with his glass. 'There is a way I can help you,' he said slowly.

'You mean with the Albion?' she replied, frowning.

He gave a short laugh. 'No, not there.'

'Then how?'

'Through the Embassy. Diplomats do have considerable power in the field of trade and commerce, you know. In fact it is one of our primary functions.'

'Are you saying you can secure orders for me?'

He stared deep into her green eyes, and saw hope and excitement there. His mind was already turning, thinking who he could speak to, what strings he could pull.

It shouldn't be too difficult, he decided. Monsieur Gabiroche the cheese manufacturer for one owed him a personal favour. And then there was Tardiveau's wife who'd approached him only last week begging him to bring some pressure to bear on her behalf in a certain sensitive matter; she too could be useful. A trade for a trade. And of course there was Georges Bordenave who was extremely influential with . . .

'Leave it to me, I'll do all I can,' Ian promised.

Sarah beamed at him.

At which juncture their turbot arrived, and delicious it looked too. Garnished with poached oysters that had been drained and debearded, and shelled crayfish, it was coated with Normande sauce to which the oyster liquid had been added.

As the waiter began serving, Ian changed the subject. Nor did he allow their conversation from there on to revert at any point to Mathew Wilson and Sarah's forthcoming marriage; that was the last thing he wanted to talk about.

Later when he said goodbye to Sarah, he told her she wasn't to worry. He wouldn't forget his promise.

Sarah opened the telegram and read its contents. The message was brief and simple. It was from Ian asking if she could come to Paris on the twenty-fourth to meet some people. A day in the French capital would be all that was required of her.

She glanced at her desk calendar. The twenty-fourth was the following Wednesday, eight days from then. Go to Paris! She was thrilled at the prospect.

Rising, she left her office and went to Hemphill's where she explained the situation to him. Could he mind the shop while she was away?

When Hemphill assured her he was quite capable of looking after things during her short absence she immediately drafted a reply to Ian's telegram saying she would be coming.

Paris! She couldn't wait.

With the staff at Stiellsmuir cut right back to the bone, Sarah had decided that all meals were to be taken in the breakfast room, and that the dining-room was to be shut up, as was the fate of many other rooms in the house. The staff now consisted of Ferguson the coachman, Hettie the parlourmaid and Mrs McGuffie. Everyone else, including Sarah's personal maid Elinor, had been let go.

The reason Sarah had insisted on using the breakfast room was because it was far smaller than the dining-room and made life a great deal easier for Mrs McGuffie during their mealtimes. The meals now came up all at once, and were dished out at the table. It wasn't unknown for Sarah to help with the washing-up.

Ferguson and Hettie still ate downstairs. And more often than not, for convenience sake, ate the same meals as those upstairs.

Sarah looked across at Jock who was staring at his liver and onions.

'Aren't you enjoying your tea, Jock?' she asked.

Using his knife he moved a heap of onions first to one side of the plate, then the other.

'Another slice of bread and butter?' Mrs McGuffie asked him.

He glanced up at the housekeeper and frowned.

'Here, let me do it for you,' Mrs McGuffie said, and buttered a slice of pan loaf which she halved and placed on his side plate.

'I'm going to Paris next week, Father,' Sarah said.

His eyes dropped down, and he again moved the same heap of onions about. Then, very slowly and methodically, as if he was a surgeon at the operating table, he began to slice off a thin piece of liver.

'I'm meeting Ian Monteith there. You know, the Honourable Ian Monteith, Viscount Ascog's second son, whom you once warned me to beware of as he could charm the birds down out of the trees. Well, I'm meeting him in connection with business.'

Jock popped the thin sliver of liver into his mouth, and set about trying to cut an even thinner one.

Sarah had an almost overwhelming urge to shake him hard by the shoulders in the hope she might rattle some comprehension back into his head. But of course that was a silly notion, shaking him, no matter how hard, would have accomplished absolutely nothing.

'I know just how you feel. I often feel that way myself,' Mrs McGuffie said to Sarah, correctly reading what was in Sarah's mind.

Sarah gave the housekeeper a weak smile, then launched into an explanation of her impending trip. This for Mrs McGuffie's benefit rather than her father's. While she spoke he appeared totally and utterly uninterested in what she was saying.

'Do you really think your friend will be able to help you with orders?' Mrs McGuffie asked eagerly when Sarah stopped speaking.

'I have high hopes, Maud, I can tell you. I just can't believe that Ian is the sort of person to lead me on a wild goose chase.'

Mrs McGuffie nodded. 'Well, I sincerely hope you're right, and that you return with a briefcase fair bursting with new business.' The briefcase Mrs McGuffie was referring to was an old one of Jock's which Sarah, much to the amusement of Hemphill and others in the firm, had recently begun taking to and from the office.

Sarah gazed warmly at the housekeeper. As time passed the two of them got closer and closer. In many ways their relationship was now almost that of mother and daughter.

'What's that you say? Eh?' Jock suddenly burst out.

Sarah and Mrs McGuffie thought it was them or one of them, he was talking to. But they were wrong.

'Really!' Jock said, addressing the empty space on his right hand side. 'How very interesting!'

Sarah and Mrs McGuffie glanced at each other. Jock was having a conversation, it seemed, with one of his invisible chums.

'Now, tell me, what clothes do you intend taking with you?' Mrs McGuffie queried of Sarah.

Sarah and Mrs McGuffie proceeded to discuss the wardrobe Sarah would pack for France while Jock continued to chat with, as it now transpired to be, he having mentioned her name several times, the blue lady.

296

That night Sarah thought about Mrs McGuffie in bed with her father, for since the cutting back of staff and closing down of rooms Maud had moved in with Jock. There was no sex any more between them—Jock had completely lost interest in that direction. This information Mrs McGuffie had confided to Sarah without Sarah's inquiring or probing into the matter.

Nowadays the only night-time intimacy between Maud and Jock was the occasional cuddle.

And sometimes Jock held her hand while he cried for seemingly no reason at all.

Sarah's heart was pounding, and she was up to high doh, as the boat train pulled into the Gare du Nord. What a lot of yabberers these French folk were. Yabber yabber yabber, it never stopped! And how strange France smelt. Quite unlike anything else she'd ever smelt before.

The train came to a halt in a huge billow and hiss of steam. Doors were immediately thrown open, banging against the side of the train, followed by even more and louder yabbering. How peculiar it was to listen to a language of which you understand not one word. Odd, and a teensy bit frightening.

She prayed he'd be there to meet her as his telegram—they'd exchanged several before she'd finally left Glasgow—had said he'd be. She didn't know what she'd do if he wasn't and she had to find her own way to the hotel where he'd reserved a room in her name. Since arriving in France she'd only found two of the natives who would speak English, she'd suspected that others she'd tried to communicate with had refused to do so.

She needn't have worried. She'd just stepped on to the platform when she caught sight of Ian hurrying towards her, waving as he came. She waved back.

'Sarah, it's marvellous to see you again so soon!' he said on reaching her side, and taking her right hand lifted it to his mouth and kissed it.

He'd brought a porter with him. After consultation with Sarah he now told the man in French to fetch her belongings from the rack above where she'd been sitting, these consisting of a single suitcase and a hat box.

'How was your journey?' he asked.

'Very enjoyable. No problems whatever.'

'Good.' He snapped out a further instruction to their porter, then led Sarah off down the platform.

'I've got transport waiting, and will escort you straight to your hotel. You've got an hour and a half there to get freshened up and changed, after which time I'll call back for you and take you on to the Embassy. I'm holding a champagne buffet there in your honour.'

Sarah gasped. 'A champagne buffet at the Embassy for *me!*'

He laughed, her expression tickling him pink. 'If you're going to do these things you must do them properly. If we at the Embassy view you seriously, then those you have to meet will do so also. Understand?'

'Yes.' And she did, perfectly.

They emerged into bright August sunshine. 'Have you experienced an automobile ride yet?' he asked.

There were a number of these newfangled contraptions in Glasgow, several of which she'd seen go puttering by, but so far she'd never actually set foot on or in one. She shook her head.

'Then today is your baptism.'

The combination of vehicles they stopped beside – the automobile itself in front with an ordinary carriage, whose two front wheels had been removed, joined to its rear – was startling to say the least. The automobile itself gleamed with highly polished brass and leather, while the body in the main consisted of wickerwork. The carriage, with fold-down hood, had a queer suspended look about it, as if the horse which had originally drawn the carriage had bolted away taking the front wheels with it.

'Does it belong to you?' Sarah queried, anxious about what lay immediately ahead of her. She wasn't at all sure she wanted to be driven in such an oddball contraption. (And certainly a lot more oddball than those she'd seen in Glasgow.)

'It's actually the ambassador's, but he allows me to use it whenever he isn't.' Ian patted the automobile's fender which looked for all the world like an elongated brass snake. 'This model is a French built De Dion Bouton steam automobile. I call her De-Di.'

A chauffeur directed the porter where to store Sarah's suitcase and hat box, and while this was happening Ian assisted Sarah into the carriage, and helped her sit down.

'Steam up!' he called out gaily to the chauffeur.

The chauffeur saluted. 'Yes sir! Six hundred psi, sir!'

'Then off we go when you're ready.'

298

Ian went round to the other side of the carriage, and got in to sit beside Sarah. 'Fun eh?'

'I'll tell you that after it's over.'

He laughed at that. 'Hold on to your hat!' he jokingly warned her as the chauffeur, having tipped the porter, climbed into the automobile's driving seat.

Levers were pulled, knobs turned and twisted, and then with a bang and a jolt they were off.

'Have we got far to go?' Sarah asked, thinking this really wasn't so bad after all. And she certainly didn't need to hold on to her hat which was well pinned down.

'We'll be there before you know it,' he smiled in reply.

Her apprehension and anxiety evaporated after only a short distance. Ian was right, this was fun.

They chatted and joked, enjoying each other's company, Ian pointing out the sights along the way, until they arrived in the Rue de la Paix, and Sarah's hotel, the Hotel Eychenne.

When they stopped outside the hotel, a green-liveried commissionaire came forward to assist. Ian rapped out something in French, then helped Sarah out of the carriage on to the pavement.

'Well you survived your first ride in an automobile,' he teased.

'And enjoyed it. Though I didn't think I was going to.'

To the chauffeur Ian said, 'Keep the steam up, I shan't be long.'

Inside the hotel the initial impression was of opulence and sumptuousness. Ian and Sarah crossed to reception where Ian explained who Sarah was, and the key to her room was produced.

Ian and Sarah now went upstairs in a handsome metal and glass lift, getting out at the third floor where her accommodation was.

With a flourish, and a theatrical tara! Ian opened her door and gestured for Sarah to enter. Once over the threshold she came up short. The room was a sitting-room done out in cream and gilt. It simply screamed elegance and good taste (the latter of the continental variety).

Off the room were two doors. 'Where do those lead to?' Sarah asked Ian, pointing at them.

'Why don't you find out?' he smiled in reply.

En route to the first door she stopped at a table covered in goodies. There were a number of cheeses, pâtés, different kinds of biscuits, a large bowl of black caviare set in a larger bowl of ice, and a basket containing a folded napkin which she later discovered to be concealing blinis, small buckwheat pancakes made with yeast. There was also a bottle of champagne in a cooler packed with ice flakes.

'You laid this on?' she queried.

'In case you're peckish before the buffet,' he replied, eyes twinkling.

'And you're paying for it?' she queried bluntly.

'Not me personally, the Embassy. They're paying for all this. There will be no bill for you when you leave.'

She was amazed. 'But why should the Embassy do that for me?'

'Because you have friends in high places.'

'You mean *friend*,' she smiled.

He gave a mock bow, then said, 'But go on, explore. While you do that I'll pop the bubbly.'

The first door she went through led to the bedroom. The bed was enormous; you could have slept an entire family, if not two, in it. And felt even more comfortable, which was saying something, than the one she had at Stiellsmuir.

The bedroom was en suite. In a connecting room there was a toilet, bidet, basin and shower. The bidet and shower were both new to her, though she knew from having read about them – thank God for Jock's comprehensive library – what they both were.

She returned to the sitting-room where Ian handed her a flute of champagne. 'What do you think so far?'

Her reply to that was to impulsively give him a quick kiss on the cheek. 'I'm flabbergasted,' she breathed.

When she walked away from him to the second door off that room there was a look in his eyes that hadn't been there before.

Sarah opened the second door to stand mesmerised at what was revealed within. The bath was sunken, a replica of an ancient Roman one. Made of green marble, she judged it to be roughly eight feet square, and about two and a half feet deep. The taps that fed it were gilt swans with long curving necks and open beaks from which the water spouted.

There were tapestries on the walls depicting nymphs and lecherous satyrs, while one tapestry, the largest and most dominant, was of a full-blown orgy in which absolutely nothing was left to the imagination. Sarah, certainly no prude, blushed to see it.

'I thought that might amuse you,' Ian said, laughter in his voice.

She glanced sideways at him, the pair of them now just inside the doorway. 'You've seen this before, then?'

'Yes, we have booked other guests into this particular suite.'

'Single women?'

He smiled, and didn't reply, sipping his champagne instead.

'I expected a room, not a suite. And I expected to pay for it myself,' she said.

'For you Sarah, *anything*,' he answered. And she knew he meant exactly that.

He went back into the sitting-room, and she followed him. Rounding on her he said. 'Before I leave you I'll give you a quick briefing on those you're going to meet. The other thing is I shall be stressing the fact that you're Scottish, not English.'

She frowned. 'I'm not with that.'

'To put it simply, the French detest the English. Always have, and probably always will. But the Scots, well that's a different kettle of fish, or should I say race, entirely. Don't forget the Auld Alliance. Traditionally the Scots and French have been thick as thieves, concerted in an ever ongoing effort to do down the common enemy, the hated English. That's what I shall be playing on, the Auld Alliance, and the long history of cooperation our two peoples, the Scots and French, have together.'

He was clever, she told herself. She'd never have thought of that. 'Isn't such a line coming from a British diplomat a bit thick?' she teased.

'Ah! Scots first, British second,' he riposted, which made her laugh.

'You really are lovely, Ian. I shall never forget this.'

He wondered if she would kiss him again. When she didn't, he launched into his briefing.

As soon as Ian was gone Sarah unpacked, and while she was doing that ran the bath. She wouldn't be able to soak for long as he hadn't left her all that much time before he'd be back again.

There were going to be other Embassy folk at the buffet to keep the general chat going while she was introduced around. She'd asked if his Charlotte would be one of them, and been told that Charlotte, because of some prior engagement, was unable to attend.

She would meet Charlotte that evening, however, at the Embassy dinner she'd been invited to, where she'd be sitting down with the ambassador and the ambassador's wife, Charlotte's parents. There were to be other guests at the dinner, Ian had informed her, which he would also be attending. She was looking forward to the occasion.

Now completely unpacked Sarah stripped naked. Slipping on a negligee she crossed to the window to stare out over Paris. It was supposed to be the most romantic city in the world – she only wished that Mathew was there with her.

The insides of her thighs prickled at the memory of the last time they'd been to bed and made love together. She wished, how she wished, that he was there to scoop her up and carry her through to that gorgeous bed. And after that the pair of them to get into the Roman bath where, eventually, they might even find the energy to do it once again.

She plastered a blini with caviare which she munched as she went through to the bathroom. There she again regarded the orgy tapestry.

'Decadent,' she muttered through a mouthful of caviare. 'Disgustingly decadent.'

She was smiling as she climbed into the steaming bath.

'Feeling all right?' Ian queried as he took her along an Embassy corridor leading to the room where the champagne buffet was being held.

'A few butterflies. Or flutterbyes, as my step-father used to call them.'

He squeezed her arm. 'Relax, be yourself and you'll be just fine. And remember I'll be right beside you at all times to help with any language problems.' He flashed her a sudden grin. 'They've already been here about twenty minutes. I wanted to give them the chance to get a few bottles of the old champers down themselves before trundling you on.'

'Is that common Embassy practice?'

He gave her a fly wink. 'We're a devious lot, us diplomats. Drink can be a great seducer, and I'm not merely talking about sex either.'

A hum of conversation came from behind the door he stopped at. 'Chin up!' he said. And with that opened the door and ushered her in.

Monsieur Foucarmont was a portly man with upcurling moustaches who was waxing lyrical about the amount of minerals and chemicals he had to import every year to service his factory on the outskirts of Paris. An attentive Sarah hadn't yet caught what the factory actually produced. He'd mentioned it several times but his accent was so strong she hadn't been able to make out the word.

Monsieur Foucarmont's face was flushed for he'd imbibed well of the neverending flow of champagne. Still talking he exchanged an empty glass for a full one from a passing waiter, not bothering to ask Sarah if she wanted another as her glass had hardly been touched.

His eyes glistened rheumily. 'I'm always prepared to deal with someone else in Britain of course, providing the figures are lower.'

'Perhaps you'd allow me to submit a quote, Monsieur Foucarmont? All I ask is that you let me know what you're already paying, and I shall see if I can better that.'

Ian turned from a few feet away to glance at her, ensuring she wasn't in any trouble. He'd left her alone with Foucarmont knowing Foucarmont spoke English, if heavily accented. Her expression told him Sarah didn't want to be moved on just yet, so he brought his attention back to Madame Tardiveau.

'I always ship directly to London, but there is no reason why my champagne shouldn't go to Glasgow and be sold throughout Scotland from there,' Monsieur Lerat said. It was his Reims champagne that was being served at the buffet. (This was a shrewd move on Ian's part, the champagne having been bought by the Embassy for the 'do', and not donated.)

'Which might affect distribution costs and therefore the Scottish domestic price, which could well work in your favour,' Sarah replied . . .

Finally it was all over, and the last of those invited had gone. Sarah felt drained, but exhilarated at the same time. Seeing that the Embassy folk who'd been helping out wanted to go too she thanked them for all their hard work, after which they excused themselves.

Sarah and Ian were now all who remained. 'So what's the verdict?' he demanded.

'Nothing firm, but very worthwhile I should say.'

'Not sorry you came, then?'

'Not at all! I think today could lead to quite a bit of new business for me. In fact I'm sure of it.'

'Good.'

They talked about the buffet all the way back to the hotel where he dropped her having arranged that he'd return at seven-thirty to take her again to the Embassy, and the dinner they would be attending there.

'It went rather well for you earlier, I'm told,' Ambassador Bingwall said to Sarah.

'Yes, thank you. And I must say it's extremely kind of the Embassy to have done for me what it has.'

'Don't mention it, Miss Hawke. It's all part and parcel of what we're here for.'

Ian was present, chatting to a Mrs Austin-Bartey who had a laugh like a horse's neigh. Not all the guests had arrived yet, apparently, nor had Charlotte. Sarah knew she'd recognise Ian's girlfriend when Charlotte put in an appearance.

Mrs Bingwall came over. 'Will you excuse my husband, Miss Hawke. You really must speak to Humphrey before we go in, Rodney dear,' she said, addressing the latter to her husband.

The Ambassador sighed. 'Yes, I suppose I must.'

'He needs his poor mind put to rest. I've assured him there's no need to worry, but he wants to hear it from you personally.'

Intriguing, Sarah thought. And wondered what it was that was worrying Humphrey. (She hadn't been introduced to a Humphrey anybody yet.)

'Speak to you later, Miss Hawke,' Ambassadoe Bingwall said, and gave Sarah a small, courteous bow. He and his wife moved off.

Sarah glanced around her. She was most impressed by what she'd seen of the Embassy so far. It was a beautiful building inside and out. They would be dining in the Wellington Room, which had amused her no end when Ian mentioned it. Imagine naming a room after him in the British Embassy in Paris! She liked, that, she liked it a lot.

'You're the last person I expected to see here,' a male voice said.

She half turned to confront who'd spoken to her. The face was familiar, now where . . . Then it clicked. 'Jardine!' she exclaimed. The same Jardine who'd danced with her at the Art School summer ball, and whom Adam had been jealous of. The Jardine who'd written to her asking her out, and whom she'd written back to declining.

'Thomas, please.'

He was as raffish as ever, she thought. Still with that saturnine, sardonic appearance. She was pleased to see him.

'What brings you to Paris?'

'I left the art school last year, you know.'

She shook her head, she hadn't.

'And . . . after a short while in London decided to take a studio here, which I have done in Montmartre.'

'Sounds exciting.'

'Oh it is!'

Remembering his reputation, she couldn't help but jibe. 'Are you referring to your painting, or women?'

He smiled wickedly. 'Both.'

Well at least he was honest. 'I hear that French women can be very fast?'

He nodded. 'Yes, it's lovely.'

She laughed at that. 'You're incorrigible, Jardine.'

'*Thomas*, please, I told you.'

She noted Ian was watching them, frowning slightly.

'How did you come to get invited here tonight?' she asked.

'My father and the ambassador are old chums. When my father wrote to the ambassador to say that I was in Paris it was only natural that I be invited one evening. And so here I am.'

'I see. And who's your father – would I have heard of him?'

'Sir Ewan Jardine.'

'The industrialist!'

'That's him,' Jardine confirmed.

Sarah had certainly heard of Sir Ewan Jardine. He was reputed to be the richest man in all Scotland. 'What does your father think about you being a painter?'

'Strangely enough, he approves. His attitude is that if that is what I want to do in life then I should go ahead and do it. After all money isn't a problem, nor ever will be. So why not fulfil my artistic yearnings? I consider that to be very civilised, and modern, of him.'

Charlotte entered the room. Had to be her, Sarah would have bet a pound to a penny on the fact. 'You know the Bingwall family then?' she asked Jardine.

'Well yes, though I have to admit it's years since I last met them. His job takes him all over the world, you'll appreciate.'

'Is that the daughter who's just come in?' Sarah queried. 'Just over there talking to the fat chap.'

Jardine had a sip of his whisky and soda while he studied the female in question. 'Could be I suppose. In fact, yes I believe it probably is. It's yonks since I last saw her. I say, she has turned out to be a smasher, eh!'

She was a smasher, Sarah agreed. Lovely figure, with auburn hair a few shades darker than her own. She was also extremely well bred, that stood out a mile.

Ian moved over to Charlotte, which confirmed that it was indeed Charlotte, exchanged a few words with her and the fat chap, then drew Charlotte away to bring her in their direction.

'Sarah I'd like you to meet Charlotte Bingwall. Charlotte, this is Sarah Hawke, a friend of mine from Glasgow.'

The two women shook hands. A greyhound, Sarah thought. A svelte greyhound, and she meant that as a compliment.

'I'm very pleased to meet you. Ian has talked a lot about you during the past few weeks.'

Did Charlotte know that Ian had once proposed to her? A glance into Ian's face gave her the impression that she didn't. That was good.

'And I'm awfully pleased to meet you Charlotte. Ian has talked a great deal about *you* to me. From what he's said he holds you in very high esteem.' Was that all right? From Charlotte's reaction, and Ian's, it seemed it was.

'And how are you Thomas? Mummy and Daddy told me earlier that you'd be putting in an appearance.'

'It's been a long time, Charlotte.' He gave her a thin, ever so slightly, leering, smile. 'You've changed.'

'For the better I hope?'

'Most certainly.'

'You've changed too.'

'For the better?'

'Of course.' There was that in her tone made them all laugh.

'And you two have already introduced yourselves,' Ian said, meaning Sarah and Jardine.

'Not introduced, we already knew one another,' Jardine replied

'Through your father?' Ian probed, for of course he knew who Jardine was, and what Jardine's background was. It was part of his job to do so.

'The Honourable Ian Monteith, Thomas Jardine,' Charlotte said, and the two men shook hands.

'We didn't meet through our fathers, but at the Glasgow Art School summer ball two years ago,' Sarah explained.

Ian's frown returned. 'I didn't know you had any interest in art?' he said slowly.

'There are all sorts of things about me you don't know,' she riposted.

His frown deepened. He wasn't sure he liked the sound of that. What manner of things was she referring to?

'Was it a good ball?' Charlotte asked Jardine.

'I enjoyed it,' he replied.

'Me too,' Sarah said, not waiting to be asked. 'It was all very Bohemian. There was a man there I swear to God was wearing black tights with a padded-out crotch!'

'Never!' Charlotte breathed.

'He was quite obscene. Isn't that right, Thomas?'

'I thought he was rather amusing actually. And for your information . . .' Thomas paused, and dropped his voice, 'They *weren't* padded.'

Sarah gave a little shriek, then clamped a hand over her mouth.

'I know that for a fact,' Jardine added.

Charlotte was loving this – she adored rudery.

'They must have been!' Sarah protested.

Jardine shook his head.

'Then he's deformed.'

Charlotte sniggered.

'How long is a piece of string?' Jardine replied, trying to hold back his own laughter. He'd thought the evening would be crashingly dull – it was turning out to be anything but.

Ian was feeling quite eclipsed by Jardine, a totally new experience for him. The bloody man just radiated charm and personality, and was handsome with it. Too damned handsome by far.

'I really can't believe that's the truth,' Sarah said to Jardine.

'I swear it! Cross my heart and hope to die,' he replied, making the sign of the cross on the left side of his chest.

'How long is a piece of string?' Charlotte repeated, and sniggered again.

'Terribly long in this case. Absolutely en...or...mously long!'

Charlotte buried her face in her hands.

'Oh!' said Sarah, catching her breath. The vision she had in her mind of black tights with the tights off would have made a cat laugh. Or sent a girl screaming in the opposite direction! She burst out laughing, fumbling for her handkerchief as she did.

Ian signalled over a passing waiter. He wanted another drink.

*

Ian glanced across to where Sarah and Jardine were chatting away nineteen to the dozen, the two of them having been sat side by side at the dinner table. There was no doubt that Sarah was thoroughly enjoying herself, thanks to Jardine's company.

'I beg your pardon?' Ian said, and turned to Humphrey Singleton who was on his left, and who had just addressed him.

When the meal was over everyone repaired to the Red Room for coffee and liqueurs. There Sarah and Jardine, Ian and Charlotte came together in a little group.

'Splendid meal,' Jardine said.

'Absolutely,' Sarah agreed, smiling at him.

'How fascinating that you've become a painter. I had no idea,' Charlotte said to Jardine.

The ambassador and Mrs Bingwall came over. 'Splendid to see you again Thomas, glad you could make it tonight.'

'Most kind of you to invite me, sir.'

There then followed a few minutes' conversation between Jardine and the older Bingwalls, after which the Bingwalls moved off, having to circulate.

'I've had a thought,' Jardine smiled. 'Why don't the four of us go on somewhere from here? As this is Sarah's first time in Paris we could show her some of the nightlife?'

'What an excellent suggestion!' Charlotte exclaimed eagerly.

Ian wasn't keen, but did his best to hide the fact. It would have been all right if it had just been him and Sarah doing the town, but with Charlotte – and especially Jardine – along it wouldn't be the same thing at all.

'I'm game if everyone else is,' Charlotte said.

Jardine looked at Ian. 'Ian?'

'Sounds terrific.'

Jardine took out a half hunter, and eyed it. 'The night is still young. How about the *Folies Bergère* for starters?'

'Oh yes please!' Sarah beamed. She'd heard about the *Folies Bergère*, it would be marvellous to actually go and see it.

'Are we all agreed, the *Folies* it is?' Jardine asked.

The *Folies* it was.

'That was wonderful. I enjoyed every single moment of it,' Sarah said as they emerged from the *Folies* into the warm, slightly humid, night. The show had been so gay, colourful, and delightfully naughty. You'd never see anything like it in Glasgow, not in a month of Sundays. The Church of Scotland would have a canary if you tried to stage anything even a tenth as *risqué*.

'Where to now?' Jardine queried.

'Sarah?' Ian asked her quietly.

'Wherever you think. But I am a bit thirsty.'

'Then how about a drink in one of the cafés?'

'The very thing,' Charlotte enthused, slipping an arm through Ian's.

Jardine held out an arm for Sarah to do likewise, which she did. Ian felt green with envy.

The Café Flore was full of characters. Most of these clearly working class with a lifetime's pain, poverty and despair etched into their faces. It was a far cry from the *Folies*. The other side of the coin.

Jardine ordered absinthe for them, declaring what else could they drink in a French café?

Absinthe transpired to be made of aniseed, and slipped down like smokey velvet. They all drank glass after glass as Jardine kept up an almost non-stop line of banter and jokes.

The women laughed and laughed, having an absolutely tip-top time. Ian laughed too, but he could have seen Jardine far enough.

'Up here, follow me,' Jardine said, leading them into a dingy doorway and up an equally dingy flight of stairs. He was taking them to see his studio.

Inside the studio – Ian stumbling over something on the floor as they went in – Jardine told them to hold on a moment while he lit a candle.

When candles and several lamps were lit the interior of the studio was revealed to be a filthy shambles. The bed was unmade; dirty dishes were piled high in an even dirtier sink, while there were pictures, paints and painting accoutrements everywhere. The air was heavily impregnated with the combined smell of paint and turps.

Sarah spied an article of clothing lying on the floor round the other side of the bed that made her smile. It was a pair of women's bloomers. Which made her wonder, if the woman they belonged to had worn them there, what had she been wearing when she left? It was a nice mystery to ponder on.

Jardine produced wine and more absinthe, and insisted they all imbibe further with him.

While he poured, Charlotte was staring at a half-completed painting on his easel. It was a Montmartre street scene, and very good indeed. Judging from that, and other pictures hanging and strewn around, there was no question about Jardine having talent.

Handing round the absinthe they'd all elected for, Jardine launched into a sparkling monologue about his work, and his approach to that work.

While Jardine spoke Ian was standing a little way off from the other three staring at Sarah and Charlotte.

Sarah was to be married to her ship's captain, he thought with bitterness. She was to become Mrs Mathew Wilson.

And Jardine? Jardine was no more than a temporary irritant, spoiling what might have been a few hours he could have arranged to have had alone with Sarah.

'What do you think?' Charlotte asked eventually, turning to smile at Ian. 'What do you think, darling?'

When he went over to join them where they were standing round the easel he reached down and took Charlotte by the hand. Nor did he let that hand go all the rest of the time they were in the studio.

'Ian, it's been simply fantastic, I can't thank you enough. The hotel, the buffet – particularly the buffet – last night, they were all first class. I'm much indebted to you.'

He caught sight of the Gare du Nord – they would be there shortly. In plenty of time for Sarah's boat train. 'You will let me know what happens about those you met at the buffet. Naturally I'll be eager to hear how that worked out.'

'Of course! I'll keep you well posted.'

'Good, and in the meantime if there is anything else I can steer your way rest assured I shall.'

She squeezed his wrist. 'You're a brick, Ian. A true Spartan brick, and friend.'

'Oh! There's one other item,' he said, and paused.

She waited for him to go on.

'You'll recall that I told you that diplomats have considerable power in the field of trade and commerce? Well, that is a two-way effect.'

She frowned. 'I'm not with you?'

'In other words, one can help, but one can also hinder. By the latter I mean the application of pressure against undesirables, those who are not a credit to our country. I have decided to do that to your Mr McIvor. For, in my opinion, anyone who did what he did to you — malign business practice to say the least — deserves to be censured at the highest level.'

As the De Dion Bouton turned into the Gare du Nord's forecourt Ian went on. 'I have circulated a letter to all our residencies, that is, every British embassy and consulate there is, stating that the firm of McIvor, McIvor and Devereaux is not a firm to be either recommended or supported.'

'Every embassy and consulate?'

'*Every* embassy and consulate,' he confirmed.

'And what effect will that have?'

'I doubt if it will force him to call in the receivers, but he'll certainly suffer as a result. Things that had been easy for him before will no longer be so. Certain cooperations and protections will be removed. As for diplomatic goodwill, that will be non-existent.'

Sarah was astounded.

The automobile drew up to a hissing halt, and the chauffeur got quickly out of his seat and round to Sarah's side of the carriage where he opened the door for her.

'Do you approve?' Ian asked.

She bit her lip. 'I wish I could be nice and feminine and say that I didn't. But I do.'

Ian gave a short, barking laugh. 'Thought you would somehow. Your father, from what I know of him, certainly would.'

She allowed the chauffeur to help her down on to the pavement, from where she and Ian proceeded to the train while the chauffeur arranged for a porter to bring on her suitcase and hat box.

Ian waited till the train's departure so that he could wave goodbye. God knew when he would see Sarah again, perhaps never.

When the train was gone he took a deep breath, and squared his shoulders. He would go straight from the station to a jeweller's the embassy had dealt with in the past, and there buy an engagement ring for Charlotte. He'd present it to her after he'd proposed to her that evening.

No! He thought. That was the wrong way of doing it. He'd propose to Charlotte over lunch, then take her to the jeweller's so *she* could choose the ring.

It was best he forget all about Sarah Hawke, he told himself as he returned to De-Di. From here on there would be only one woman in his life, the one he'd be sharing it with.

Charlotte Bingwall.

Chapter 8

Sarah sat back in the leather-covered captain's chair she'd brought from Carlton Place, reached for her cigarettes, and lit up. She'd just gone over the latest figures for *J. Hawke & Daughter*, and was absolutely delighted with the recovery the firm was making.

She picked up the slim sheets of figures she'd just been reading, and ran through them again. Certainly her Paris trip had borne fruit, but the recovery wasn't due to that alone. Business that had been theirs originally and had been lost to them, was now returning to the fold. And a lot of that was coming from McIvor, McIvor and Devereaux, she was pleased to note.

Rising, she went to her office door, opened it and called for Smith. 'Ask Mr Hemphill to come and see me,' she said to Smith, then returned to her chair.

There she went through the figures yet again. She'd expected them to be good but they were far better than she'd dared hope.

When Hemphill knocked she beckoned him in. 'I think we can afford to engage two new clerks. Would you like to see to it?'

Hemphill beamed at her. 'I knew you'd be pleased with the figures.'

'I'm not merely pleased, Mr Hemphill, I'm cock-a-hoop! But . . .' she paused, gesticulating with her cigarette, 'there's still a long way to go till we're fully recovered, back to where we were before that disastrous Canadian invesment.'

'Oh aye, a long way,' Hemphill agreed.

'But we'll get there, won't we?'

'I believe we will, Miss Hawke. As God is my judge, I truly believe we will.'

'Two new clerks, Mr Hemphill, to start as soon as possible.'

'I'll draw up the advertisement right away, Miss Hawke,' and with that Hemphill left her.

Two new clerks, *and* a new member of staff for Stiellsmuir, Sarah thought. Another parlourmaid maybe, but that would be up to Mrs McGuffie. It was going to give her enormous pleasure to instruct Maud to hire whoever she wanted when she got home that evening.

Thinking of Mrs McGuffie made her think of Jock, and that in turn caused her to glance up at the framed photograph standing on top of her roll-top desk. A photograph of Myrtle, her mother.

Reaching up, she took the photograph down, and stared at it. She'd discovered the photograph hidden in a metal box in the safe when she'd taken over the firm.

What a heart-wrench that had been when she'd found it, having had to force the padlock securing the metal box to get inside.

How on earth had Jock acquired the photograph? Which appeared to have been taken after she'd left Netherton? Must have been taken after she'd left, for she'd never heard of a photographer having been in the community while she lived there. And surely Myrtle would have mentioned she'd had a photograph taken, for her mother was smiling into the camera, fully aware of what was going on.

And why had the photograph been kept locked away, a secret? She thought she knew the answer to that.

'Oh Jock!' she whispered, not for the first time when looking at the photograph, a prized possession of hers as it was the only photograph she knew to be in existence of Myrtle.

'Oh Jock!'

After a while, with a sniff, she replaced the now framed photograph – she'd had it framed shortly after finding it – back atop of her desk, and got on with her work.

What Sarah presumed, correctly, to be Tomtain Castle appeared in the near distance, hidden until then because of the lie of the land. She was deep in Kilsyth Hills, *en route* to spend the weekend with Sir Ewan and Lady Jardine at their home and main residence. They also had town houses in Glasgow, Edinburgh and London.

A fortnight previously she'd received a letter from Thomas saying that he'd had a long chinwag with Ian at a recent embassy dinner he'd attended – he attended quite a few now – and during this conversation had learned for the first time about her taking over her father's firm, etc., etc.

He sympathised with the predicament she'd found herself in, and was extremely pleased to hear from Ian that she and her firm were fighting back, and beginning to do well again.

Now the thing was this, Ian had been able to help her, and so perhaps could he. He wasn't promising anything, mind, but he'd taken the liberty of writing to his father explaining the situation, asking Sir Ewan if he could assist her cause. As she was already aware, Sir Ewan was a very successful industrialist and most influential man. Now that his father knew about her and her present circumstances, why didn't she contact him and arrange a meeting? Such a meeting couldn't do her and the firm any harm, only the contrary.

Sarah had been touched by Thomas's trying to help, and jumped at the opportunity. She'd written to Sir Ewan the very same day she'd received Thomas's letter. The reply had been to invite her to Tomtain Castle for that weekend, to arrive some time during the Saturday morning, and leave on Sunday after tea.

Sarah put these thoughts from her mind as Tomtain Castle loomed closer. It was a real castle, built originally during the latter part of the thirteenth century, and added to since. Sir Ewan had had the castle completely restored and modernised when he had bought it twenty years previously. She knew all this, having done her homework on the subject.

Sarah's carriage, with Ferguson driving, rattled over a cattlegrid set between two stone pillars, and on towards the castle. They temporarily lost sight of the castle as they skirted a wood of Douglas firs, and then it came into view again across a vast well-manicured lawn.

Something cried out, one of the strangest sounds Sarah had ever heard. What manner of beast was that? she wondered. Certainly something weird and spooky.

Then she spotted a man in tweeds with a broken shotgun cradled in his arm watching her as the carriage went past the spot where he was standing, partially concealed by a rhododendron bush. Resident, guest, or gamekeeper? Sarah couldn't tell. Whoever he was, he had a surly, taciturn, look about him.

The carriage halted outside the castle's principal doorway where a footman was already waiting to receive her. The footman had a few words with Ferguson before opening her door.

'Mr Valentine the butler will attend you inside, Miss,' the footman said after he'd helped Sarah down.

'Thank you.'

'So if you will just follow me, miss.'

She did, up well-worn stairs and into a rather dark reception hallway that led directly into a high vaulted room.

Valentine had a 'Presbyterian' air about him and, although considerably younger, reminded Sarah of Moffat.

'Welcome to Tomtain Castle, Miss Hawke,' Valentine stated stiffly. 'Her Ladyship has been sent for and will be with you in a moment.'

She smiled at the butler, but didn't reply.

The footman who'd received her appeared with her luggage, the same suitcase and hat box she'd taken to Paris. At a command from Valentine he took them across the room and through a door.

'Miss Hawke, a pleasure to meet you.'

Sarah took an immediate shine to Lady Jardine, knowing instinctively that the pair of them would get on well together.

Margaret Jardine was of average height with a figure that bore evidence to her age and of having had children. Her eyes were deep blue with a lovely twinkle about them, her smile radiant. She somehow contrived to give the impression of being ethereal on the one hand, extremely sensual and sexual on the other. It was a very strange mixture.

'And I'm pleased to meet you, Lady Jardine,' Sarah responded, accepting the hand that was offered to her. The pair of them shook hands.

'We're having luncheon in about an hour, and my husband thought he might speak privately to you after that.'

Sarah nodded.

'You'll meet everyone over luncheon — we have other guests staying. So till then?'

'Till then,' Sarah echoed, and the two women shook hands again, after which Lady Jardine turned and walked away.

'Christine will show you to your room, and look after your needs while you're here,' Valentine said.

Christine, who'd joined them during Sarah's brief tête-à-tête with Lady Jardine, now gave Sarah a small bob. 'If you'll follow me, Miss.'

'Thank you,' Sarah said to Valentine, then gestured to Christine to lead on.

Sarah wondered how large a staff the Jardines had. Dozens, possibly, to look after a place this size. And then there were the grounds; from what she'd seen they were extensive.

Following Christine as requested, Sarah went up stairways and along corridors until she was quite lost. Christine laughed when she mentioned this.

'Don't you worry, Miss. We're used to that here. There will

always be someone on hand to take you wherever you want to go.'

Well that was considerate of the Jardines, Sarah thought.

'Here we are, Miss.' Christine opened a narrow door and ushered Sarah inside.

The room, like the door, was also narow, and very plainly furnished. Sir Ewan might be the richest man in all Scotland but he certainly didn't lash out on his guest accommodation, Sarah thought.

'I'll unpack for you, Miss,' Christine said, going to the single bed on to which Sarah's luggage had been placed.

'The bathroom is facing across the corridor, the toilet next to that on the right,' Christine explained.

Sarah took off her coat and hat, placed them beside her now open suitcase for Christine to put away, then crossed to the window and stared out.

She smiled with pleasure to see a pair of peacocks strutting and preening on a lawn as well manicured as that at the front of the castle, for her room was at the castle rear.

The nearest peacock lifted its head high, and she heard again that strange cry she'd heard earlier. Definitely weird and spooky she thought. It gave her the creeps.

She began to question Christine about the other weekend guests.

'Please sit down, Miss Hawke,' Sir Ewan Jardine said. They were in his private study where they'd just come direct from luncheon.

Sarah now knew where Thomas got his saturnine, sardonic appearance: from his father. And the raffishness, though in Thomas's case that was far more pronounced than with Sir Ewan.

As for Thomas's good looks, those must have been inherited from Lady Jardine's side. Sir Ewan was anything but handsome, though certainly not ugly.

'Would you mind if I smoked?' he asked.

'Not in the least. Do you mind if I do?'

Sir Ewan blinked at that. In his world women didn't do such a thing.

Sarah guessed why he was momentarily nonplussed. 'Of course, if it offends . . .'

'Not at all,' he replied politely. 'Perhaps you'd care for one of my cigarettes. I have them made in London.'

316

The cigarettes he offered were longer than usual, and cork-tipped. They had a different, slightly sweeter, taste than she was used to. 'Very nice,' she murmured.

Sir Ewan remained standing, cigarette in one hand, the other arm folded behind his back.

'Thomas told me something about you in his letter, but the best thing might be for you to give me your own story,' he suggested.

Sarah recounted a potted history of the firm and then went from there. One item she didn't include was the true nature of Jock's illness. In her opinion Sir Ewan didn't need to know about that.

While she talked Sir Ewan walked slowly up and down, listening but not looking at her.

Finally she concluded her tale, took a puff of her cigarette, and waited expectantly for his reaction.

'You were most fortunate with the smallpox. I had a second cousin who died from it,' Sir Ewan said eventually.

'Yes, I was fortunate. Very much so.'

'And you enjoyed the West Indies, you said. That's one part of the globe I've always hankered after seeing.' He gave a small sigh. 'Maybe one day.'

Sarah was frowning now.

'I met your father once, Miss Hawke, and to be truthful I didn't like him at all.'

Sarah swallowed hard, thought about replying, but didn't.

'What my son didn't make clear in his letter, Miss Hawke, is your precise relationship with him. What is that?'

'I suppose you might say we're friends, Sir Ewan. Recent friends.'

'Ah!' His gaze flicked at her, then flicked away again. 'And what exactly do you mean by *friends*?'

She was bewildered; this interview wasn't turning out at all as she'd expected. 'What the word implies.'

He stopped walking with his back to her, waiting.

'Friends, Sir Ewan, nothing more.'

'There is no, how shall I say? Physical relationship?'

She could feel her ears redden, and her throat flush. 'None whatever. I am shortly to be engaged to be married to a ship's captain.'

Sir Ewan resumed walking. 'It's just that . . . well, Thomas has had a great many girlfriends you understand.'

She was now wishing she'd never come to Tomtain Castle. It was rapidly proving to be a ghastly, embarrassing mistake. 'Yes, he is popular, I believe.'

'And how do you know that?'

'We have a common friend at the Glasgow School of Art. It was at the Art School summer ball that I first met Thomas.'

Sir Ewan went over to a high-backed, tapestry-covered chair at the far side of the study, and sat on it. 'What do you think of his painting? Have you seen any of it?'

'Several of us went to his studio the night I was in Paris, and I saw some canvasses then. I thought them very good.'

'I consider his work to be good also, so we're in agreement there.' He paused briefly, then snapped out, 'You said "several of you". Who were they?'

'Myself, Charlotte Bingwall and Ian Monteith—he's Lord Ascog's son and a member of the embassy staff.'

'Remember Charlotte as a baby. Her father and I are old chums you know.'

'Thomas mentioned that.'

'What's the studio like?'

She decided that she wasn't going to be passive any more. If he was going to bite then she'd damn well bite back. 'Disgusting. Filth everywhere. A proper cesspit.'

Sir Ewan gave a thin smile. 'Just as I imagined it would be.'

'Can I say something to you?'

He raised an eyebrow.

'If you don't like my father, I would suggest it's because the pair of you are very similar. And if you don't like me—which you don't seem to—it's no doubt because I'm out the same mould as my father, and therefore as you, too.'

Sir Ewan laughed.

'It's true.'

'I suspect you're right,' he admitted.

'And I would further point out to you that I never asked Thomas to write to you about me, that was entirely his idea.' She didn't so much stub out as grind out her cigarette in the ashtray by her chair.

'I must admit I had wondered about that.'

She regarded Sir Ewan with a diamond-hard gaze that was pure Jock Hawke. 'I can assure you there was no instigation on my part in any way. And I would be pleased if when you next write to, or see, Thomas you verify that.'

'Would you care for a glass of sherry, Miss Hawke?'

Abruptly change the subject, try to wrongfoot her, throw her off balance. An old trick of Jock's that Jock had taught her long since. 'I'd prefer whisky if you have it.'

'So early in the day?'

That was a dig, which she would turn against him. 'You have the sherry Sir Ewan, I'll have the whisky.'

The dominance factor wasn't lost on him. 'We'll both have whisky, Miss Hawke.'

'I thought it was too early for you?'

He ignored her jibe, and opened a cupboard to reveal an array of bottles. He poured them each a large dram. 'Soda or water?'

'Neat.'

He took his neat also.

'Slainthe!' he toasted.

Up yours too! she thought, and tasted her drink. It really was too early for whisky, and she should have had it with either soda or water. But drink it neat she would. She would have drunk neat bleach if it had meant either standing up to, or scoring against, him.

'I really can't take seriously the concept of a woman, a female, running a business,' Sir Ewan said.

'No?'

'I mean, it's ridiculous.'

'Oh? And why's that?'

'A woman's place is in the home.'

'Not out working,' Sarah qualified, then laughed. 'That's precisely what Jock said to me once when I told him I'd like to be employed by the firm in some capacity. His reply was exactly that, "a woman's place is in the home, not out working".'

'There you are then,' Sir Ewan smiled.

'The more I speak to you the more I see I'm right. Two peas in a pod, you and him. When he met you he probably didn't like you either.'

'You must ask him,' Sir Ewan said.

She didn't reply to that. 'What do you think about female domestics then? Or women who slave in factories? They're working.'

'They're also working class,' he answered sharply.

'I see, that's different?'

'Totally.'

'Working-class women can work their fingers to the bone, but the middle-class and aristocratic ladies don't?'

He frowned at her. 'Are you one of those . . . what's the word?' His frown deepened as he cudgelled his mind. 'Emancipated females?'

She leaned forward in her chair. 'I'll tell you what I am, Sir Ewan. I'm a woman who believes that a female brain can be just as good as a male one. In fact, sometimes better.'

He looked shocked, which pleased Sarah. She'd given up hope anyway of his helping her.

She went on. 'Apart from the physical limitations, I don't see why women can't do any job that a man does. It's only tradition, and because we bear the children, that decrees otherwise.'

'You're saying tradition is wrong?'

'I'm saying that males have a puffed-up notion of their own importance and ability.'

He drained his glass. 'You're absurd, Miss Hawke.'

'So too was Jesus Christ, if you only took him at face value.'

Sir Ewan shrank back into his chair. 'That's heresy!'

'Nonsense.'

He quickly rose, and returned to the small bar where he refilled his glass.

Sarah wasn't going to be outdone. Not on your Nellie Duff! She swallowed the whisky that remained in her glass, then held it out. 'I'll have another as well, thank you very much.'

'Neat again?'

'Neat again,' she confirmed.

'I have a proposition to make,' he said handing her her second drink.

That surprised Sarah. 'Which is?'

'It's possible I could use a little company such as yours. Let me have a look at your books, and providing everything is as it should be I'll make you an offer.'

'You mean buy us out?'

He nodded.

She hadn't expected that at all. It had never entered her head to sell the firm, or that Sir Ewan might make a bid for it.

'Well, Miss Hawke?'

She didn't even have to ask herself what Jock's answer would be, she knew just as surely as she knew two and two equalled four.

320

'The firm's not for sale, Sir Ewan. Thank you all the same.'

'If I do make an offer it will be a good one.'

She regarded him coldly. 'What you're really saying is that you doubt my competence in running it.'

'I feel that as you're Thomas's friend I should try and help as he requested I do.'

'Don't patronise me, Sir Ewan! What you're doing is trying to help yourself. Our firm has been turned around and is on the up and up again. I'll get it back to what it was, with or without orders from you. It's only a matter of time, and determination.'

He smiled. 'I can see you're a most determined woman, Miss Hawke.'

'I am.'

He took a deep breath. 'You're turning down my proposal, I presume?'

'Flat.'

'Well I don't think you should be so hasty. Why don't you sleep on it, that's what I always do with important matters, and we'll talk again tomorrow?'

'We can talk again tomorrow if you wish. I won't have changed my mind. The firm of *J. Hawke & Daughter* won't be sold. Not to you or anyone else.'

'Do you ride, Miss Hawke?'

'Why, Sir Ewan, I thought you'd never ask!'

She smiled inwardly at his expression, and sipped her whisky, He sipped his, after which he remained silent.

She remained silent also, the two of them staring at one another.

Finally it was he who was forced to speak first. A tiny victory she thoroughly enjoyed.

They discussed chamber music which it transpired he was extremely knowledgeable about.

Esme Manners finished her song on a high note, then bowed her head. Those listening applauded enthusiastically, for she had a fine voice.

Esme's husband Barton was sitting close to Sarah, with Sir Ewan beside him. Lady Jardine, the Duke and Duchess of Kyle, and Alexandra Buchanan – the Jardines' daughter and Thomas's elder sister – were playing whist at a green-baized table set up for that purpose. Iain Buchanan, Alexandra's husband, and an employee of

321

Sir Ewan's was standing by the canary cage, drink in hand, from which vantage point he'd been listening intently to Esme's singing.

The final person to make up the Jardines' house party was Robert Forbes, a bachelor solicitor friend of the Jardines who'd been accompanying Esme on the piano.

Barton Manners picked up the port decanter and refilled his glass. He'd been drinking heavily before dinner, during dinner, and was now continuing to do so after dinner.

'More port, Sir Ewan?' Barton inquired, waving the decanter at his host.

'Not for me, thank you.'

'How about another for you, Miss Hawke?'

She covered the top of her own glass. 'Perhaps later.'

'Another song, Esme!' Iain Buchanan called out. He adored her singing.

Esme patted the bottom of her throat. 'That's all for now, Iain. But why don't you perform for us?' Iain's party piece was conjuring tricks, which he was rather good at.

'Didn't bring me bits and pieces with me, worse luck. Sorry!' he apologised.

At the card table Lady Jardine gathered up the deck, expertly shuffled it, and began dealing.

'What happened about that strike you had on your hands?' Sir Ewan asked Barton Manners.

'Oh they're back. I knew they couldn't stay out for long. Couldn't afford to.' Barton Manners took a deep swallow of his port. 'Bloody miners!' he swore in a low voice.

That caught Sarah's attention. Up till then she'd found Barton Manners boring in the extreme. 'Do you have something to do with colliers, Mr Manners?' she asked pleasantly.

'I should say so.' He barked out a laugh. 'I own four pits out in Hamilton. Been in the family since my grandfather's day.'

She was trying to recall Hamilton. 'The Shoe Horn is in Hamilton?'

'That's the biggest.'

'And where the accident was. Isn't that right?' Sir Ewan said. Barton Manners nodded. 'Aye.'

'A bad accident?' Sarah probed.

'Bad enough. I lost twenty-three men dead, another dozen injured.'

Sarah took a deep breath—to hear such a thing made her blood run cold with memory. 'Was the strike connected with the accident?' she further queried.

Barton Manners regarded her quizzically. 'Are you interested in this sort of thing, Miss Hawke?'

She smiled at him, awaiting his reply.

He shrugged. 'The strike was a direct result of the accident. The men wanted safety equipment installed in all four mines. Well I ask you, have you any idea what that would have cost!'

'So you refused,' Sarah stated.

'Too tooting I did!'

Sarah closed her eyes, her mind filled with pictures from the past. That terrible afternoon when there had been a gas explosion in Dundonald's Pit and five men had been lost. Another day when a huge fall of stone had done for seven others.

'How long were the men out for?' Sarah asked.

'Three weeks. I knew it wouldn't be much longer than that.'

'I suppose they did, too, and that what they were actually making was a gesture. A gesture to try and drive it home to you how strongly they felt about the situation.'

Barton Manners was now glowering at Sarah, while the atmosphere in the room had gone decidedly chill. Sarah noted that the Duke of Kyle's expression was particularly disapproving.

'You seem to have some sympathy with these people?' Barton Manners said.

Sarah glanced at Sir Ewan, whose face had become impassive. 'I certainly have,' she replied to Manners.

'And why would that be?'

'Because I grew up, and have lived most of my life, in Netherton, where my step-father worked down the pit there. "Down by" as they called it.'

Iain Buchanan was staring at her in astonishment, as were several others.

She said softly, but with a voice filled with steel, 'I know what it's like to have someone brought home on a flat cart. They did that to my step-father, though to be truthful it was a stroke that got him and not the mine.

'And I know damn well what it's like to hear the hooter sound telling us there's been an accident, and the agony of standing at the pit head waiting to find out who the casualties are. Do you still have

323

a husband, brother, or in my case step-father? And if he is alive does he still have all his arms, legs, eyes and what have you?

'And I also know what it's like to go hungry because the money has run out and there's no more food, not even a crust, till Friday pay night. Of course the men couldn't stay on strike for more than three weeks, and even that is stretching it. The reason is a simple one, as well you know. It's difficult enough to make ends meet without putting anything by.'

Barton Manners poured himself more port. His expression was one of contempt for Sarah. 'If your step-father was a miner, how do you come to be here tonight, Miss Hawke?'

'As *my* guest, Barton,' Sir Ewan said in a low, warning voice.

Sarah was upset now, and very angry. She fixed Barton Manners with a glittering gaze. 'Your men were only asking for safety equipment because it can be so dangerous down the pit,' she stated.

'Of course it's dangerous, mining is,' he sneered in reply.

'But you can lessen that danger, that's within your power,' she retaliated.

'What they're asking would cost money, my money.'

'You make the profits.'

'I also provide jobs.'

She swallowed hard. For two beans she'd have scratched Barton Manners's face to shreds – he was having that sort of effect on her.

'It's good that you provide jobs,' she said. 'And I've certainly nothing against making profits, quite the contrary. But can't you slice a little of those profits in order to save lives?'

She was aware that everyone in the room was staring at her now. Those who'd been playing cards made no pretence of still doing so. The impression Sarah got, with the exception of Lady Jardine who was regarding her sympathetically, was that some awful egg odour had suddenly gone off in their midst.

'The trouble with demands from the workforce,' Barton Manners replied, 'is that once you give in, where do you stop? One demand becomes two which in turn becomes three and so on and so forth, until in the end you have no profits left at all!'

'A bit extreme, surely?' Sarah countered.

'I don't believe so, Miss Hawke. I know these people. Be kind to them, expose yourself in any way, and they'll tear you to shreds as surely as any pack of ravening wolves would.'

'Hear hear!' the Duke of Kyle muttered.

Sarah had to wait for a few seconds before she could go on, forcing herself to control her mounting anger. 'Do you have any children, Mr Manners?' she asked eventually.

'Yes, three sons.'

'Grown up?'

He nodded.

'How would you feel if one fine day they were brought home to you on a flat cart, dead because the man they worked for was too greedy to spend a few measly quid on equipment that would have saved their lives?'

'Really!' Esme Manners exclaimed.

She'd gone too far, Sarah thought. But what the hell! In for a penny, in for a pound.

'Your sons, Mr Manners,' she continued ruthlessly, 'just think of them, picture them in your mind. Remember all the trials and tribulations you and your wife went through, as all parents do, bringing them up. How they grew, and learned, were a source of alternating joy and despair to the pair of you. How they finally turned out as they are now. And then . . .' She paused for emphasis. 'And then try and imagine them brought home to you dead on a flat cart because some other father couldn't bear to give up a fraction of his profits. Couldn't bear to give up *money*!' she almost spat that last word out.

Barton Manners's eyes had gone very hot-looking, as though they were cooking on the inside. His colouring, already choleric to begin with, had become a great deal more so. 'I don't think I need lecturing from you, Miss Hawke,' he replied venomously.

It was time for her to be out of there, away to bed. Rising, she smoothed down the front of her dress.

'Goodnight, Sir Ewan, Lady Jardine. I don't apologise for anything I've said, only that it may have disrupted your evening.'

And with that she left the room, every pair of eyes following her as she went.

She came awake with a start to find herself covered in prickles. What on earth had wakened her? And why did she feel as she did, as if she'd been given a fright?

Out on the lawn a peacock cried, and she knew then what had disturbed her. Reaching for the glass of water on her bedside table she drank some of it, and felt the better for that.

Closing her eyes again she tried to go back to sleep, but sleep wouldn't return.

She shouldn't have stayed the night, she told herself, but gone home directly after her interview with Sir Ewan. It was only politeness that had caused her to stay, for she certainly wasn't going to change her mind about selling the firm to him.

She thrust a leg outside the bed because she was too hot, but within seconds the leg was frozen stiff and she had to bring it back in again.

She tossed and turned, wondering what time it was. The peacock cried again. Or perhaps it was the second peacock. (Or were there more?) Whatever, she hated the sound. It sent shivers up her spine.

She thought about Mathew *en route* to South America, which calmed her somewhat. How she wished he was here with her now so that she could snuggle up to him, enjoy the closeness of his body, and the warm, male smell of him.

'Damn!' she muttered, she had pins and needles in her left leg. She stretched the leg first this way, then that, but the pins and needles continued. She stretched her left toes, then waggled them, which did the trick. The pain passed off.

Barton Manners — she disliked that man intensely. How could anyone be so tightfisted when lives were at stake! She wondered if he'd ever actually been down a pit, and doubted it. Few owners knew from first-hand experience what hell it was down there in the dark, narrow twisting tunnels, where face-men could do — and often did — an entire shift crouched up in a three foot high seam, their bodies twisted and contorted as they hacked and dug.

She'd never been 'down by' either, but appreciated what it was like. She'd heard Bob and his pals describe the conditions often enough. A verse from an old miners' lullaby began to drift through her mind.

> 'Your daddy coories doon ma darlin',
> doon in a three-fit seam.
> So you can coorie doon ma darlin',
> coorie doon an' dream . . .'

She was still wide awake when the dawn crept into her bedroom, and with the dawn she decided what she was going to do.

Getting out of bed she washed herself at the jug and basinful of water provided, after which she started dressing. She was halfway through that when she heard a noise outside in the corridor.

Peeping out her door she spied a maid, and called quietly to the lass. The maid came right away.

'Wait a second,' Sarah whispered, then went back into her bedroom to search out her purse.

'I need a message taken to my driver Ferguson. Can you do that for me?' Sarah asked, holding up a two-shilling piece.

The maid eyed the florin, a big tip in her book. 'Aye, missus, what is the message?'

'Tell him I want to leave here just as soon as he can get ready. Understand?'

'Aye, missus, just as soon as he can get ready.'

'Right then.' She gave the maid the pee shilling toosh as her step-da Bob had always called the coin. 'Deliver your message and come back to me. There will be another two shillings in it for you if you take me to the stables just as soon as I'm packed.'

This was her lucky day! the maid, whose name was Irene, thought jubilantly.

'Do you want Christine to pack for you?' Irene asked, knowing Christine wasn't on duty for another half an hour.

'I'll pack myself, don't you worry about that. Now on you go to my driver Ferguson, then straight back here to me.'

When Irene was gone Sarah finished dressing, ran a comb through her hair, then set about packing. She had just completed that when there was a tap on the door announcing Irene's return.

Sarah let out a huge sigh of relief when she was in her carriage and it was under way. Thank God, she was spared the ordeal of breakfast – that would have been sheer murder. What she was doing was extremely bad mannered, but easier all round. She would drop Lady Jardine a note thanking her for her hospitality and explaining why she'd done what she had, though an explanation was hardly necessary.

One of the peacocks cried out again, making her shudder from head to toe.

'There's a Sir Ewan Jardine here to see you,' Smith said to Sarah. Then, in a whisper, '*The* Sir Ewan Jardine.' As if there might have been more than one.

Sarah laid down the pen she'd been using, and patted her hair. Sir Ewan was the last person she'd expected to come calling to Tradeston Street.

'Then you'd better show him in,' she replied.

She stood when Sir Ewan entered her office. 'This is a surprise.'

'Yes, I'm sure it is.'

It wasn't only a surprise, it was embarrassing, she thought. 'Please have a seat.' She half expected him to refuse but, again a surprise, he didn't.

'I take it you got home safely the other morning?' he smiled.

It was now Thursday, four days after she'd done her dawn flit. Sarah realised she was blushing. 'I did write to Lady Jardine.'

'She mentioned you had.'

'I thought it better for all concerned if I wasn't there for breakfast.'

'I appreciate why you left so early, Miss Hawke, but there was no need for you to have done so, certainly not as far as I or Lady Jardine were concerned.'

'It's kind of you to say that,' she replied, giving him a small inclination of her head.

'I mean it. I was most impressed with what you said to Barton, and the way you stood up to him. I wasn't only impressed with the way you stood up to him, but how you stood up to me earlier. It's a long time since anyone other than my wife has done that.'

She sat again behind her desk. 'If you've come about buying the firm I'm sorry to disappoint you but the answer still is, and always will be, no.'

'Ah!' he breathed, and made a pyramid with his hands.

'I'm afraid you've had a wasted journey.'

'I don't think so.'

'I'm serious Sir Ewan, I won't sell,' she said levelly.

'I'd have been disappointed if you had.'

That puzzled her. Then, in a flash of insight, several things clicked into place. 'Was your proposition a test of some sort? Was that it?'

He gave her a thin smile. 'You're very quick, Miss Hawke. I like that.'

'So it was a test?'

'I have no interest in acquiring an import/export concern. It's completely outside my field of reference. What I wanted to establish was your commitment to your firm, your belief in it, which I think I have.'

She digested that. 'Was the charade because I'm a woman?'

'I'd have engaged in the same charade, as you call it, even if you'd been of the male gender.'

'But you are prejudiced against women in business?'

'There are exceptions to every rule,' he countered, 'and my instincts tell me you're one.'

'Your instincts and Lady Jardine?'

Amusement dawned in his eyes. 'Very good, Miss Hawke. I'm rapidly becoming convinced that neither my wife nor I are wrong about you.'

She decided to tease him. 'You're admitting you do take your wife's advice then?'

'Certainly. It's advice I have a great deal of respect for.'

'And what if she wanted to go into business, run her own firm?'

He laughed. 'She has no inclinations in that direction, so the situation will never arise.'

'But if she *did*?'

He patted his pockets. 'Do you have a cigarette? I seem to have come out without mine.'

She went to him, offered him her case, then returned to her chair. They both lit up.

He went on. 'We live in a changing world, Miss Hawke, a new century only five years away. Who's to say what great changes and revolutions lie just over the horizon? For great changes and revolutions there will certainly be.'

'I think you're more open minded than you pretend, Sir Ewan.'

He gestured at her with his cigarette. 'Now it's you who's being patronising, Miss Hawke.'

'You're right. I stand admonished.'

He was thoroughly enjoying this conversation, and Sarah's company. He'd been disconcerted on Sunday morning when told she'd done a disappearing act, as his wife Sybil had been. They'd both taken to Sarah, finding her a breath of fresh air.

Opening the pigskin attaché case he'd brought with him he took out a sheaf of papers, rose from where he was sitting and placed the papers in front of Sarah.

'Those are orders for, and instructions from, my factory in Camlachie, one of half a dozen factories I own on Clydeside. Everything has already been quoted for by Gemmil, MacRae & Lumsden with whom I deal a lot. If you can match the figures quoted then the business is yours.'

A thrill of excitement ran through Sarah. 'I can match them,' she said quickly.

Doubt invaded his mind. Had he made a mistake about Sarah? 'How do you know that without going into them?'

'Simple. Gemmil, MacRae & Lumsden are a first-rate, reputable company. Whatever figures they have quoted will be fair ones, to you and them, and ones I can match. And, being a smaller firm with less overheads, probably even undercut slightly.'

His doubt vanished – he hadn't made a mistake after all. 'You know where my office is – send me round your figures when they're ready.'

'Sir Ewan, is this a singular transaction between us? Or could more follow?'

'Provided I'm happy, more will follow, and continue to follow.' She could have jumped for joy to hear that. 'Thank you, you won't regret this. I promise you.'

'I believe that, Miss Hawke. I sincerely do.' He paused for a brief second, then said, 'Perhaps you'd care to visit us again at Tomtain Castle? Lady Jardine and I would both relish it if you did.'

When he saw Sarah's expression he added, 'And next time there will be no other guests. No types such as Barton Manners to annoy you.'

'That would be marvellous, except . . .' She trailed off.

He frowned. 'Except what?'

'Those peacocks of yours give me the heebie jeebies. That cry of theirs makes my blood run cold.'

His frown vanished, and he laughed. 'I promise you this, when you do come again the peacocks will be moved far enough away so that you won't hear them. What do you say to that?'

She rose and stuck out her hand. 'I'll await your invitation.'

They shook on it. And for Sarah they were shaking on more than the invitation.

Sarah sat astride Mathew, moving slowly up and down as he writhed beneath her.

On this occasion there was no fierce heat in her as there usually was in her lovemaking, but a languorous sensuality that she wanted to go on and on forever.

Placing her hands on her buttocks she continued to move up and down on his maleness, smiling at the pleasure it gave her, and the obvious pleasure it was giving him.

'Oh Sarah! Sarah!' he husked, his fingers hooked like talons, digging into the bed.

She felt him go even more rigid, prelude to his orgasm. And with that let herself go, gave herself over to the tidal wave of sensation she'd been keeping at bay.

'Christ!' he gasped as he ejaculated within her. And as he did he thrust his pelvis up at her, while at the same time she, smiling broadly now, ground herself down on to him.

Closing her eyes, she dropped her head forward so that her hair tumbled down to brush his chest. She remained in that position, extracting every last ounce of gratification there was to be had from the now rapidly receding tidal wave, till finally, sexual sensation ceased, and there was only satiated mind and flesh left.

Opening her eyes again she looked down at his face, to discover he was kissing the ends of her hair.

'I love you,' he whispered.

'And I wouldn't be here like this if I didn't you.'

He laughed at that.

She broke their joining, then flopped beside him. 'Know something darling?'

'What?'

'When you're ashore we seem to spend most of our time together making love.'

'Are you complaining?'

Now it was her turn to laugh. 'Not in the slightest. I was merely remarking, that's all.'

'If I had my way we'd spend all our time together in bed.'

'You'd soon wear yourself and that out,' she replied, touching his glistening penis.

He sighed. 'What a way to go. Shagged to death!'

'Mathew, that's rude!' she exclaimed, flicking his penis with a forefinger.

'Ow that hurt!'

'Serves you right for using a dirty word. I don't like dirty words. And that one in particular demeans an act that's pure and good. Well certainly in our case it is anyway.'

He gently kissed first one nipple, then the other. 'There are times when you sound like a Sunday school teacher,' he teased.

'And what's wrong with that?'

'I just find it funny, that's all. And adorable too.' He brought her

331

to him, and kissed her deeply.

'I can't get enough of you,' he said when the kiss was over.

'Nor I you.'

'He looked over at the blazing bedroom fire, a fire they'd lit before getting into bed. Outside, the early December weather was bitter cold, and due to get colder before Christmas.

'I spoke to your friend McIvor this morning,' he said.

'McIvor's no friend of mine!'

'Aye, well, you know what I mean.' He turned to face her, a small smile playing round his lips. For some reason, right at that moment, she reminded him of puff candy he'd loved as a wean. He'd never been able to get enough of that either. 'You want some good news?'

'I'm always keen for that.'

'Next trip in the *Good Intent* is to have her hull scraped, followed by a total refit. That means I'll have a month at least ashore with you. Maybe even more.'

She squealed with delight. 'Mathew, that's absolutely wonderful!'

'Exactly what I thought.'

It was too good a chance to miss. 'That's when we'll get married then.'

Which was precisely what he'd been hoping she'd say. It was now fifteen months since they'd originally planned to wed on their arrival back from the West Indies.

'You're confident you now have everything sorted out well enough for us to go ahead?' he probed.

'Business is snowballing, particularly so since my trip to Paris and, more importantly, Sir Ewan Jardine deciding to use *J. Hawke & Daughter*. I see no reason whatever that we can't now get married whenever we like.'

'Then at the end of my next trip it is,' he agreed.

'I don't want you to worry about anything, darling. Just leave it all to me. I'll arrange everything. We'll stay at Stiellsmuir, of course. I couldn't move out.'

'Of course not,' he smiled.

'Olivia Tennant will be one of my bridesmaids and. . .'

They fell to discussing details.

Sarah paused in her writing to jiggle the pencil between her teeth — she was making a rough list of guests to be invited to the wedding.

The wedding would be a fairly small affair, the reception held in town. That was how she wanted it, principally because of Jock. It broke her heart that he wouldn't be giving her away, but that was impossible. He wouldn't even be attending.

'I'll tell you who I would have liked to invite,' Sarah said to Olivia Tennant, sitting opposite drinking tea.

'Who?'

'Adam. I would have liked him to be there.'

Olivia set down her cup. 'Even if he was in Glasgow I don't know that he'd come.' The last thing they'd heard of Adam he was travelling and painting in southern Spain, never staying long in one spot, continually on the move.

Sarah knew exactly what Ollie meant by that. 'Maybe not,' she said, and shrugged. 'But I would have liked him to be there.'

She thought of her last meeting with Adam, and how it was he who'd saved her from Moffat and McIvor. She owed him a lot for that.

Another name, a must on Mathew's side, popped into her mind. She hastily added it to the list, and Adam was forgotten.

Mathew Wilson took a swallow of tepid beer and stared out over the harbour at the many ships tied up or riding at anchor, his own *Good Intent* among them. The humidity was awful, the hot season having come early to Maracaibo that year. He'd put on the shirt he was wearing only half an hour previously, just prior to leaving the ship, and already it was sodden.

This was their last day in Maracaibo. They sailed on the morning tide for La Guaira, the port for Caracas, where they would make a brief stopover, after which it was home to Glasgow, and Sarah.

He smiled at the thought of his bride-to-be, and wondered about the preparations for the wedding.

'Mathew Wilson! By all that's holy! How are you?'

He turned to find a vaguely familiar face beaming at him, and then it clicked who the face belonged to. 'Bill McFarlane!' Bill was another Greenock man.

The two of them warmly shook hands, and as Bill sat at his table Mathew called out for another beer.

'It's great to see you again, Mathew,' Bill said. 'How many years is it?'

They both made mental calculations. 'Six, I think,' Mathew ventured.

'I make it seven. Whichever, it's a damned long time.'

'I heard you'd been made captain, Bill. Congratulations!'

'Aye, three years and a bit since. I'm sailing out of Fowey on the *Little Secret*, as trim a schooner as you'll come across in many a long day. Look,' he pointed, 'that's her yonder, tied up behind that black-painted Swedish slättoparre.'

'She looks a right smasher, Bill.'

'Handles like a dream. I tell you, you'll travel far and wide before you'll find a sweeter ship than my *Little Secret*.'

That sounded just like himself talking about the *Good Intent* Mathew thought, smiling inwardly. The *Little Secret* was obviously a good'un.

'It took me a moment to recognise you behind all that fuzz,' Mathew said.

Bill stroked his beard which was a full foot in length. The moustaches above the beard had a reddish tinge to them that the beard itself, basically mouse-brown in colour, didn't. 'Think it suits me, don't you?'

Mathew remembered then that Bill had always been somewhat vain. 'Gives you charisma,' he replied, a word he'd learned from Sarah.

Bill frowned, he didn't know what charisma meant. Nor was he about to show his ignorance of the fact by asking.

The beer Mathew had called for arrived. 'All the best!' Bill toasted, and promptly downed most of it. 'Bring us another couple,' he instructed the waiter who'd just begun to move away from them.

'Get back to Greenock much?' Mathew asked.

'Some, but not nearly as often as I'd like. It's being based in Cornwall that does it. Fowey being a Cornish port.'

Mathew nodded that he understood. Bill was saying that he only got to Greenock when his ship docked in Clydeside.

'And what about you Mathew? I suppose you're there a fair amount, sailing out of Glasgow as you do?'

'Not nearly as much as I used to. When I am in Glasgow I rarely get out of the city itself nowadays.'

'Oh? And why's that?'

Mathew gave him a sheepish grin. 'A woman I have there.'

Bill let out a great roar, and thumped the table. 'A woman is it!'

'We're to be married when I dock at the end of this trip.'

'Married! Now it's my turn with the congratulations!' And with that Bill, a bear of a man, reached over and grabbed Mathew's hand which he proceeded vigorously to pump up and down.

Still pumping, Bill turned in the direction of the bar and bellowed. 'Bring us tequilas to go with the beers! You hear!'

'Si señor!' came back the reply.

'No, not for me!' Mathew protested.

'Just the one, what's the harm? It's a celebration after all,' Bill argued.

It wasn't often he met another captain, and old friend in this instance, whom he could have a drink with, Mathew thought. For he never drank ashore with any of his officers, or any other officer of inferior rank, as that just wasn't done. And Bill was right, it was a celebration.

'Aye, all right,' he agreed.

The beers and tequilas arrived together. Bill snatched up his tequila, indicating for Mathew to do the same. 'What's your lassie's name?' he demanded.

'Sarah.'

'Bonnie name, right enough. Well here's to you and Sarah!' And with that Bill threw the tequila down his throat.

'Another two of these!' Bill shouted to the bar.

'Now wait a minute!' Mathew protested.

'Another one won't do you any harm. And it's good stuff this.'

The tequila was particularly good, Mathew thought, having another swallow of it. Better quality than he was used to being served up and down this coast.

'You don't have to rush back to your ship, do you?' Bill asked.

'Not really.'

'How's your Number One?'

'Excellent. I've never known a better.'

'You're all right there then.'

The two tequilas each became three, which in turn, became four. After that Bill instructed the waiter just to bring the bloody bottle, they'd pour for themselves.

'I'm pissed as a fart. Must get back aboard,' Mathew slurred. They were in a bar somewhere, the latest in a long line of many they'd visited since meeting up with each other hours previously. It had been afternoon then, it was now night.

'Listen,' said Bill, grasping hold of Mathew by the sleeve, 'I have to go somewhere. Will you come with me? Support an old Greenock pal?'

'Go where?'

Bill tapped the side of his nose. 'That's for me to know and you to find out. But will you come? I need you.'

Mathew was undecided. He really should get back to the *Good Intent*. Not that he was worried, everything there would be fine in Runciman's hands. But he should get back nevertheless.

'Here, have another one of these,' Bill said, and slopped more tequila into Mathew's glass.

Mathew stared at the glass, which seemed to shimmer. Pissed as a fart, he repeated to himself. And thoroughly enjoying the experience.

'Bottoms up!' Bill said, and had a gulp from his glass.

Mathew had a sip from his.

'So will you come with me? Support an old Greenock pal?' Bill repeated.

His brain had gone quite numb, Mathew realised. He couldn't think straight any more. In fact he couldn't damn well think at all. He giggled, then giggled again.

'Not far from here,' Bill said, rising, and pulling Mathew to his feet.

Bill settled their account at the bar. Then, arm in arm, the two of them lurched outside.

'I come to Maracaibo often. Did I tell you that?' Bill queried.

Mathew shook his head.

'Regular port of call.'

They turned off the dirt street into a narrow alleyway. From an adjoining house came the sound of a guitar being played, the tune a melancholy one.

'Almost there,' Bill said as they emerged from the alley into another street, the houses on this street being of a better class than the others in the immediate neighbourhood.

Bill stopped suddenly. 'Know the worst thing about being a master?'

Mathew shook his head.

'The loneliness. You can't be one of the lads any more.'

Mathew patted Bill on the chest. 'I know exactly what you mean.'

'The loneliness,' Bill repeated, and belched. 'That's the only thing about being a master I don't like.'

'Me too,' Mathew agreed.

'Come on,' Bill said, resuming walking. Mathew was forced to go with him as their arms were still linked.

They mounted a short flight of steps, and Bill knocked at an ornately carved wooden door. Seconds later a panel set into the door slid back and a brown male face peered out at them.

'Bill McFarlane and friend, Mustard,' Bill stated.

Mustard! Mathew wondered.

The panel slid shut again, and the door opened to reveal a very powerful-looking Venezuelan dressed in suit and tie. 'Come in, Captain McFarlane, you always welcome here,' Mustard said.

'This is Captain Wilson,' Bill said, indicating Mathew whose arm he'd now let go.

'Any friend of Captain McFarlane is welcome here,' Mustard smiled, gesturing they should enter.

It was beginning to dawn on Mathew the sort of place that Bill had taken him to. They went along a sumptuously decorated hallway, into a salon, and as soon as he saw the many females there he knew that he was right.

'This is a brothel!' he hissed at Bill.

'The best in Maracaibo. Or at least, one of the best.'

'What have you brought me here for?'

'Because I want a bit of nookie, that's why.'

A waiter in white jacket and black tie came up to them carrying a tray of drinks. 'Champagne, whisky, or brandy, gentlemen?' the waiter politely inquired.

'Whisky for me,' Bill said, helping himself to a large dram.

Mathew hesitated. He wasn't sure mixing his drinks was at all wise. 'Any tequila?' he asked.

'Certainly sir.'

'Then I'll have a glass of that.'

'I'll bring it to you presently, sir,' the waiter said, and moved away.

Mathew gazed about him. This couldn't be anything other than a brothel. It simply screamed the fact.

The women, and they were all colours, nationalities, varieties and sorts, were, without exception, dressed provocatively, though they were fully dressed, and not in a state of partial undress.

'What do you think?' Bill beamed.

'I'm hardly an expert on these places.'

'But you have been to one before?' Then, when Mathew didn't reply, 'Surely?'

'Captain McFarlane, how delightful to see you again.'

Mathew and Bill turned to face the speaker, an apparently middle-aged Venezuelan woman who had clearly been a beauty in her day. She was still undeniably attractive for her age which Mathew judged to be early forties. Very few people knew that she was actually sixty-three.

'Gisela! How are you!' Bill exclaimed, and taking a heavily bejewelled hand kissed the back of it.

'This is Gisela whose establishment we're in,' Bill explained to Mathew.

Bill completed the introductions, at which point the waiter returned with Mathew's tequila.

'How long are you in Maracaibo for, Captain?' Gisela asked Mathew.

'My ship sails on the morning tide.'

'Ah!' she replied, making an exaggerated facial expression of disappointment. 'We lose you so soon, huh!' She winked salaciously. 'But at least we have you for tonight.'

Mathew cleared his throat. 'I eh . . .'

'My friend is shy,' Bill said, and let out another of his roars of laughter.

Mathew blushed.

One of the many reasons that Gisela was good at what she did was that she knew when to push, and more importantly, when not to. 'There is no obligation or pressure of any kind, Captain Wilson,' she smiled. 'Enjoy the alcohol if that is all you want. It is my pleasure to have you here.'

Mathew relaxed a little on hearing that. 'You're most gracious,' he replied.

'Well I intend to do more than just drink,' Bill said, glancing round. 'There are new faces here, I see.'

'There is always a constant turnover. Our regulars prefer it that way. Have you met Kaarina?'

Bill thought for a moment. 'Don't remember that name,' he answered, shaking his head.

'She's Finnish. I recall you like the blonde, blue-eyed ladies. Isn't that so?'

'My preference is in that direction, yes. Though I do like to ring the changes once in a while.'

338

'I shall send her over to you.' To Mathew Gisela said, 'Perhaps we shall speak again later. In the meantime, enjoy yourself. I shall be upset if you don't.'

Gisela left them, and Bill beckoned to a nearby waiter. He had more whisky, but Mathew declared he would stay with what he had.

'You don't get places like this in Glasgow, do you?' Bill said, and laughed again.

Mathew didn't reply to that. He realised he wasn't quite as drunk as when he'd entered Gisela's, but still far from sober.

'So what about you?' Bill demanded.

'How do you mean?'

Bill gestured about him. 'Going to dip your wick?'

'Not me. I told you, I'm getting married when I return to Glasgow.'

'What's that got to do with it?' Bill replied, genuinely baffled.

'Well, if you don't know I'm not going to try and explain.'

'Ach mannie, it's a long trip here and a long trip home again. A wee bit of fleshly gratification in the middle doesn't do any harm. On the contrary, it probably does a great deal of good.'

'I'm in love with Sarah,' Mathew replied simply.

'Fine! Dandy! I'm all for you being in love with your lassie. There's only one thing wrong with that though.'

'Which is?'

Bill gave him a wicked grin. 'She's in Glasgow and you're here.'

Mathew glanced over to a winding staircase at the far end of the salon. Two couples were going up it, while another couple were coming down. That must lead to the bedrooms, he surmised.

'Captain McFarlane?'

The speaker was blonde and blue-eyed, as Gisela had promised, with a voluptuous – to the point of being slightly over-ripe – figure.

'You must be Kaarina?'

'Full marks, Captain,' the Finn replied in a voice that just oozed sex.

'Bill please.'

'Then Bill it is.'

He had to look no further, Bill was thinking. Kaarina was going to do very nicely. Oh yes! Very nicely indeed.

Mathew was staring at the girl who was with Kaarina, and as different to the northener as could be imagined. Her skin was shiny brown, her eyes the same colour, with a deep-set glow to them that Mathew found fascinating. Her features, combined with thick black hair chopped off at the neck, told that there was a lot of Indian in her. Overall she had a waiflike, vunerable quality. She couldn't have been more than fifteen years of age. Yet was, at the same time, ageless.

'Hello,' the girl said to him.

'Hello,' Mathew replied, smiling.

'My Englis she no ver good. You spik Spanish?'

Mathew shook his head. 'Sorry.'

'Then I jus hav to spik in Englis.'

She was an absolute stunner, Mathew thought. A coffee-coloured work of art. But he musn't get involved when he wasn't going upstairs, he reminded himself. 'I eh . . .'

The girl was ahead of him. 'S'all right. Madame Gisela she explain, you no wan the jig-a-jig. You shy.'

Mathew blushed for the second time that evening.

'Well I bloody well do,' Bill leered, and stroked Kaarina's bottom.

'You wan sit, hav nother drink? I wan drink,' the girl said to Mathew.

'Then we'll have a drink and sit,' Mathew agreed. 'By the way, my name is Mathew.'

'Me Juanita. That no my rel name you unnerstan? You no able to say that.'

He turned to Bill and Kaarina. 'What about you two?'

'We'll leave you for now. Rejoin you after a while,' Bill answered quickly. He couldn't wait to get Kaarina upstairs.

'Right then. We'll be sitting somewhere.'

'Or dancin in otter room,' Juanita added.

Bill hooked an arm around Kaarina's waist and the pair of them headed for the winding stairs. Mathew called over a waiter from whom Juanita accepted a glass of bubbly. Rather than go through the business of having the waiter go off and get him a tequila he decided to have a whisky instead. What the hell! He was getting tired of tequila anyway.

There were open curtained alcoves along the sides of the salon, and Juanita now took him to one of these. There was a large sofa in the unlit alcove. Juanita sat on the sofa, he beside her.

'Now tell me all about yourself Mathu, I wanna hear,' Juanita said.

The one thing Mathew didn't speak about was Sarah, but he spoke of nearly everything else. Juanita listened, nodding from time to time, occasionally interjecting with a question. Somewhere during this, without Mathew noticing at first, she began touching, then lightly caressing, his upper thigh and buttock.

They had another round of drinks, and another after that. Mathew was very drunk again, but still aware of what was going on, and extremely aware of Juanita. If asked to describe his state he would have replied that it was like being borne along on the crest of a wave.

When he finally finished talking about himself Juanita led him out of the alcove and salon, to the room where a small band was quietly playing, and the dancing was taking place.

They danced for a short while, then Juanita led him back to the same alcove where fresh drinks were waiting for them.

She sipped her champagne, her brown glowing eyes studying him over the glass's rim. 'I like you ver much, Mathu,' she whispered.

'And I like you.' Which was certainly no lie.

Placing her glass aside she grasped him by the hand and laid the hand on her breast. 'Nice, Mathu?'

The breast was soft, and oh so tempting! 'Very.'

She slipped the hand down the front of her bodice till his fingers came into contact with her nipple. 'And that?'

He should leave now, he told himself. As God was his judge he certainly hadn't meant things to go this far.

Take your hand out of there, he thought. Take it out. The hand stayed where it was.

'Kiss me,' she breathed.

Her lips met his, and her tongue darted into his mouth. She tasted primeval, and there was something about that which was exciting in the extreme. As her tongue probed and twisted in his mouth he felt himself begin to respond physically.

She was aware of that also, sensing it happen. She took her mouth from his, and smiled. A smile that was full of beguiling innocence, sensuality, and somehow unbridled lust. It was an impossible combination, but there it was.

'Come, enough foolishness. Show me the man you are,' she pleaded.

She raised him to his feet, and he came willingly. Hand in hand they left the alcove and made for the winding stairs.

Wasn't every man entitled to a last fling? he asked himself as they

341

climbed the stairs. Of course he was. That was how he should view this, a last fling before the altar.

Where was the harm after all?

Mathew emerged on to the deck to glance up at the sheets and rigging. His face was drawn, his expression grim.

Silently he strode over to where Purcell and Jolly were standing. 'Who's officer of the watch?' he demanded.

'I am, sir.' Jolly replied.

Mathew gave him a shrivelling look. 'More sail I think, Mr Jolly, don't you?'

'If you say so, Captain.'

Mathew now positively glared at his third officer. 'Do I detect a tone of insolence, Mr Jolly?'

'No sir! I mean sir, there was certainly none intended, sir!'

'Hmmm!' Mathew growled.

This wasn't like the old man at all, Purcell thought. But then Mathew hadn't been the same since Maracaibo.

'You're getting slack, Mr Jolly. S-L-A-C-K, slack. Do you hear me?'

'Yes Captain,' came the tremulous reply.

'Well I won't have slackness aboard my ship, Mr Jolly. Won't have it. So unless you mend your ways, and right quickly too, I'll pay you off in Glasgow. Understand?'

Jolly licked his lips that had suddenly gone dry. It would be disastrous for his career if he was paid off with a bad report, which was what Mathew was implying. 'Yes sir. Perfectly sir. It won't happen again sir.'

Mathew gave another growl, then stalked off towards the wheel, and the aft of the ship.

Jolly spat out orders which the crew on watch, some of whom had overheard the interchange between Mathew and the Third, hastened to obey.

'You know what?' Purcell whispered to Jolly.

'What?'

'I think he's getting cold feet about the wedding. I think the bugger's taken fright.'

'Could be,' Jolly muttered in reply. 'Could be.'

At the stern rail Mathew stood watching the ship's wake. Slowly he began to fill his pipe, his expression even grimmer than it had been before.

*

'Ship's tied up, Captain,' Runciman reported to Mathew who'd been overseeing the operation. There was the rattle and clank of the for'rad and aft gangplanks being fixed into place.

'Start unloading just as soon as you can, Mr Runciman,' Mathew replied. 'In the meantime I'm going ashore for a few hours. Any queries or questions?'

'No, Captain.'

And with that Mathew hurried off along the deck, and down the aft gangplank. He was walking so quickly it was almost a run.

'Mathew!' Sarah exclaimed in delight, having glanced up from her desk to find him standing in the open doorway of her office.

Jumping to her feet she came round the desk, and while she was doing that he entered the office and closed the door behind him.

'No!' he exclaimed, holding her at bay when she attempted to embrace him.

'Mathew?'

'I'll explain in a second.'

Puzzled, and frowning, she retreated a few feet. She noticed now how ghastly he looked. The glands in his neck appeared to be up, and he also seemed to have something of a rash round the same area. 'Have you got the flu?'

He took a deep breath, and sighed. 'No, not the flu.'

'Not mumps!' she laughed, thinking how funny that would be. 'How are you?'

Her laughter died at the intense seriousness of his expression. How oddly he was behaving, quite unlike his normal self. 'Fine, never better. Have you just docked?'

He rubbed his hands together. This was going to be even more difficult than he'd imagined. 'No, two days ago.'

She stared at him blankly. 'I beg your pardon?'

'Two days ago, Sarah. We docked two days ago at Queen's Dock, North Basin.'

'And . . .' She was totally baffled. 'It's taken you this long to come and see me.'

He didn't reply to that.

This was rapidly getting odder and odder. 'Has there been some sort of trouble?'

'I had to go and visit a doctor, Sarah, which I did. Since then I've been trying to screw up the courage to come and tell you what he told me.'

A sudden fear clutched her throat. 'Tell me what?'

He tried to stare her straight in the eye, and couldn't. He dropped his gaze to the floor. 'There isn't going to be a wedding. I can't marry you. I'm sorry.'

She hadn't heard correctly, couldn't have. 'I beg your pardon?'

'There isn't going to be a wedding. I can't marry you,' he repeated.

She went cold inside, cold and numb. 'What is wrong with you, Mathew?' she asked.

'I've got the pox,' he stated bluntly.

She stared at him, incredulous. 'The pox, you mean syphilis?' He nodded.

She couldn't stand any longer, she had to sit down. She tottered back to her chair and sank into it. When she placed her hands on her desk a part of her brain noted they were shaking.

'You're certain about . . .'

'Yes,' he interrupted. 'The doctor said there's no question. The symptoms are unmistakable.' He paused, then added unnecessarily, but wanting to enunciate it all the same, 'As I'm sure you know, there's no cure.'

No cure, the words were an eventual death sentence. And a most horrible death too, from what she'd heard. She had a sudden, alarming, thought. 'Me! what about . . .?' She stopped when he shook his head.

'You've no cause for worry. I caught it this trip in Maracaibo. I just can't believe she was infected. It seems impossible . . . And yet, she was. She could only have caught it shortly before I went with her. I'm sure she didn't know.'

'Who?' Sarah asked, tears spurting into her eyes. 'Sure who didn't know?'

Mathew told her the whole story then, from meeting up with Bill McFarlane to staggering back aboard the *Good Intent* in the early hours of the following morning.

Sarah listened in stony silence, and when he finally finished her whole world lay in ruins around her.

Remembering she had a handkerchief in one of her desk drawers she got it out and dabbed her face with it.

'I'm sorry,' he said again. 'You'll never know how much. One awful mistake and . . .' He bit his lip.

'Please go,' she muttered.

She was right, he thought. What else was there to say? Nothing. Without speaking further he left her.

For ever.

She had iron control over herself as she stepped down, with Ferguson's assistance, from the carriage outside Stiellsmuir. She'd never left work early before, far less abandoned it in the middle of the day. The fact that she'd done the latter had caused a few eyebrows to be raised. Not that she cared, she doubted she cared about anything any more.

She found Mrs McGuffie in the housekeeper's study, busy with some household paperwork that had been piling up.

'There isn't going to be a wedding, Maud,' Sarah announced abruptly.

Mrs McGuffie's reaction to that statement was a combined one of shock and disbelief.

'It's Mathew. He went to a brothel when he was away and caught syphilis.'

The pen Mrs McGuffie had been holding dropped out of her hand.

'Could you please write to all those we've invited explaining that the wedding has been cancelled. And the minister, yes, you'll have to notify him as well.'

'The minister, aye,' Mrs McGuffie jerked out in a low, tight, voice.

'I'm going to go down and sit in the library for a while. Can you see that I'm not disturbed.'

'Of course. I'll instruct the servants to leave you completely alone.'

'Thank you Maud.' She started to turn away.

'Sarah?'

Sarah glanced back at the housekeeper.

Mrs McGuffie just shook her head.

'I understand, Maud. Thank you.'

Feeling ethereal, like some ghost, only partly there, she went down to the library where she poured herself a huge dram and soda.

Having sat, she proceeded to stare into empty space. Remembering, thinking of what might have been.

*

She hadn't moved from the chair in the library, and darkness had long since fallen, when suddenly, quick as a finger click, something snapped within her.

She knew then she didn't want to live without Mathew.

It was sheer luck Jock was at the window he was, the only window in the house from where one of the ornamental turrets could be seen. And it was further luck that it was that particular turret Sarah chose. But then, what is luck, if perhaps not the divine manipulation of things?

A shadowy figure behind the turret window glass caught his attention. Seconds later the window swung open.

He saw a face, pale in the moonlight, and then the figure the face belonged to begin to clamber out of the window.

'Myrtle!' he gasped. It was Myrtle, his wife, about to go over High Cliff.

Whirling, he ran from the room, and as hard and fast as he was able along the corridor that would take him to the stairs leading up to the turret door.

'Myrtle!' he choked. 'Wait, love! Wait! I'm coming! Jock's coming!'

'Myrtle!' he screamed.

Sarah was out the window now, her feet on the outside sill, supporting herself erect by holding on to the top of the outswung window.

She smiled. All she had to do was let go and that would be it. Any pain she'd have to experience would be over in the briefest instant.

She was just about to topple forwards when she heard a shout, someone calling her mother's name. That caused her to hesitate, a hesitation which saved her life.

Jock charged into the turret whose door was wide open, took the turret stairs three at a time, and lunged at the top of them to grab the legs standing on the outside window sill.

Sarah immediately tried to throw herself into space, but failed. Jock had her firm.

She suffered several nasty bangs, lacerations and grazes, which she didn't feel then but did later, and a pane of glass went crashing. Then Jock, exerting all his strength, succeeded in pulling and wrestling her back through the window into the interior of the turret.

'What do you think you're doing!' he yelled angrily, and shook

346

her as a dog will a rat. 'One suicide in the family is quite enough. Do you hear me, my girl! Do you hear!'

'You're hurting me, Jock!'

'I'll hurt you all right. By God and I will!' And with that he slapped her hard.

He manhandled her down the turret stairs to the landing below where he thrust her up against a wall, his chest heaving from exertion, his breathing laboured.

'What a fright you gave me, Sarah. I thought there that I'd lost you, too. What possessed you to attempt such a thing girl? Eh? Answer me that?'

'The wedding's been called off. Mathew can't marry me.'

He regarded her blankly. 'What wedding? Mathew who?'

'Mathew Wilson, captain of the . . .' She trailed off, and her eyes went wide. 'Jock?'

'Aye?'

'You . . . you're making sense.'

He released her, took a deep breath and ran a hand over his face. 'I haven't been well.'

'No, you haven't.'

'Your mother, she . . . ' he swallowed.

'Killed herself,' Sarah finished for him, her own anguish and despair temporarily forgotten. Had a miracle really happened?

'I thought . . . I was standing at a window downstairs when I saw you in the turret and, somehow, thought it was Myrtle at High Cliff. I came running, intending to save her. Only it wasn't Myrtle, it was you.' He gave a great shudder. 'You,' he repeated in a whisper.

'Have they all gone?' she probed. 'The imaginary people you've been talking to? The butterflies and other things you've been seeing?'

Slowly, haltingly he replied. 'Yes, I can remember something of that. Images, voices.'

She knew precisely how to find out if he really was his old self again. Business, the firm. 'We had to sell five of our ships. I now run *J. Hawke & Daughter*.'

'What! Who sold the bloody ships? Why?'

A smile twisted her lips upwards. Jock was back, that was her father speaking.

'And what are you doing running the firm? Lassies don't run firms.' He clutched his head.

'What is it?' she asked anxiously.

'It's all right. A sudden splitting headache. But I am all right, I promise you.'

He closed his eyes. 'It's as if I've been asleep, dreaming,' he said.

'You've been suffering from what's known as schizophrenia. Let's go downstairs and I'll tell you all about it. That, and what's been happening.'

He grasped hold of her shoulders. 'You won't try anything silly again, will you, Sarah?'

Only minutes before she'd wanted to die, thinking she had nothing left to live for. Now, in the space of those few minutes, everything had changed. The outlook was no longer as totally black and desolate as it had been. A new light had appeared, something to live for after all. Her father.

'I won't try anything silly again. I swear.'

He drew her to him, and held her tight. 'I couldn't bear to lose you too, Sarah.'

'You won't, Jock. Not now.'

She felt drained, weak as the proverbial kitten. But strangely, and this amazed her, she also felt happy. Happiness was growing within her with every passing second.

'Before we have our chat, we must break the news to Maud,' she said.

'Only about me though, not a word of what you just tried to do.'

'Right,' she agreed.

He cupped her face in his hands, and kissed her first on one cheek and then the other Sarah offered up a silent prayer that this wasn't merely a temporary recovery on Jock's part, that he was back from the dark recesses of his mind for good.

Hand in hand, as if each was scared to let the other go in case he or she might disappear, they went looking for Mrs McGuffie.

Mrs McGuffie came out with Sarah and Jock to see them into the carriage and wave them goodbye. It was six weeks since Sarah's thwarted suicide bid and Jock's recovery, and so far there had been no relapse on his part, or any signs of one. Not even a hint of the 'moods' he'd suffered from at nights before Myrtle's death, and the pitching of his mind into full-blown schizophrenia.

For the past month Sarah had been taking work and files home in the evening to explain what was currently happening at the firm to Jock, and generally bring him up to date.

He'd been furious to learn of the McIvor/Moffat conspiracy, and delighted to discover just how well Sarah had been doing as head of the firm. Now he was raring to get back to the helm, a helm they had agreed to share as equal partners.

Jock helped Sarah into the carriage, then turned to Mrs McGuffie. He smiled at her, and the housekeeper smiled back. Their relationship had emerged from his illness stronger than it had ever been.

She wanted to reach out and touch him, but couldn't do so because of the presence of Ferguson. 'Good luck,' she said.

He surprised her by doing, in front of Ferguson, what she'd wanted to do. Taking hold of her arm he gave it a gentle squeeze. 'Thank you, Maud.' he replied quietly.

He further surprised her by waving back to her as the carriage clattered off towards town.

'That's it,' Sarah said, gesturing up at the Tradeston Street building which now housed *J. Hawke & Daughter*.

Jock studied the building, his expression one of distaste. 'It's not exactly Carlton Place, is it?'

'Not exactly.'

Jock nodded. 'Well it's serving its purpose, and will do for now.'

His meaning wasn't lost on Sarah. 'Yes, for now,' she agreed.

'Let's away in then,' he said.

Upstairs the entire staff, new and old, of their own volition and not organised by Sarah, were standing in a group awaiting Jock's arrival. As soon as he appeared they all burst into applause. It didn't matter that they all believed, with the exception of Hemphill who of course knew the truth, that Jock had been physically and not mentally ill, this was their gesture to welcome him back.

Jock's expression was one of pride and pleasure as he acknowledged their salute.

Sarah emerged from Jock's office carrying a quotation she'd been discussing with her father. It was a quotation for a new client, recommended by Sir Ewan Jardine, and she had wanted to make sure he agreed her figures. Which he had.

It was August 1895, and they'd moved from Tradeston Street in June. Their new building, which they occupied in full, was in Adelphi Street, a continuation of Carlton Place, and just as smart. Business was booming. Not only had they moved to Adelphi Street, but they had also bought a second ship, the *Port Jackson*, a handsome four-masted iron barque which they had immediately put on the palm oil run. They'd borrowed most of the capital to buy the ship from their bank, and the hope was, if everything went according to plan, that the *Port Jackson* would soon pay for itself.

On entering her office, just along the passageway from Jock's, Sarah came up short on finding she had a visitor. 'Ian!' she smiled.

The Honourable Ian Monteith bowed to her. Then came over and kissed the back of her hand.

'Très galant!' she mumured.

'Merci, belle femme,' he replied, and kissed her hand again. 'It's marvellous to see you, Ian,' she said, disentangling her hand. 'What brings you to Glasgow?'

'A tale and a half. I thought I might tell it to you over lunch.'

'That's an invitation, I take it?'

'How about that fish restaurant I took you to in Springfield Court?'

There was no reason why she shouldn't go. Jock had no plans to lunch out, so he would be here if needed. And how could she turn Ian down after what he'd done for her through the embassy? It would be downright churlish for her to do so.

'What's the time now?' she queried. She'd been so busy she'd completely lost track of the clock.

'Half past twelve. Lunchtime. I have a carriage waiting outside.'

He assisted her into the light linen coat she was wearing that day. Then, when she had pinned her hat into place, they were off. They stopped first to put Jock into the picture, and for Ian to congratulate Jock on his return to work.

'How's Paris?' Sarah asked after they were settled into Ian's carriage and it had moved off.

'Fine.'

'And Charlotte?' Ian and Charlotte had been engaged for a year now, but as far as Sarah knew they hadn't yet set the date.

'In the pink. Never better. I must say it was tremendous to hear about your father. What a relief for you!'

More than you'll ever know, she thought grimly.

On reaching the restaurant they were shown to a good table where they perused the menu, then ordered.

'So why *are* you in Glasgow?' Sarah asked a second time.

'Family complications. My brother James is to marry in the new year.'

350

She frowned. 'I don't understand. Why does that cause family complications?'

'He's marrying Lady Mary Foynes, daughter and only child of the Marquess of Limerick.'

'A love match?'

'Oh most certainly. The pair of them are as in love as any two people can be.'

'That's good then.'

'For them, yes. For my father, no.'

'Why ever not?'

'Because, dear Sarah, the lady in question is a Catholic, and James is in the process of turning so that he can marry her. Lady Mary is the Marquess's only offspring. James will never inherit the title, but his firstborn son – providing he has one – will.'

It was now beginning to make sense to Sarah. 'And Bertie objects to his title eventually going to the same son?'

'Ours is a Protestant family, and Bertie is determined that our title will remain as such. He has no wish for our title to become Catholic, or for it to be swallowed up, and become an appendage of a greater one.'

The wine they ordered arrived, and they fell silent while it was poured.

'James is disclaiming the Ascog peerage, which will then fall to the second in line. Namely, *me*. When my father dies I will become Viscount Ascog, and inherit.'

Sarah clapped her hands in glee. 'I'm so pleased for you, Ian!'

'Who would ever have imagined this would happen, eh? What a turn up for the book. It means I'll be leaving the diplomatic corps, of course.'

'Why do you have to do that?'

'I have to learn to manage the estate, something I know very little about.'

'So you'll be coming back to Glasgow permanently, then?'

'In a few months' time. It will take that long to resign properly and get everything on that side of things sorted out.'

Sarah had a sip of her wine. 'What about you and Charlotte?'

'We'll marry after James and Lady Mary. Charlotte will stay in Paris till then, the two of us visiting the other whenever we can.'

'I hope I shall be invited to the wedding? Yours and Charlotte's that is.'

Ian glanced down at the tablecloth, the corners of his mouth tightening slightly. 'Naturally.'

Sarah then went on to pump Ian about this Lady Mary Foynes. What was she like, how had James met her? etc., etc.

They were getting on towards the end of the main course when Ian said casually, 'Talking of marriage, what about your own? When does that take place?'

Sarah suddenly lost her appetite which had been so excellent up until that moment. She'd come to terms with losing Mathew, but there was still an awful dull ache inside her every time she thought of him.

'I'm not getting married now,' she replied quietly. 'We called it off.'

Ian was astonished. 'You called it off?'

She was damned if she was going to tell Ian the real reason for her and Mathew parting. 'In the end it just didn't work out between us.'

'I'm sorry, Sarah. Truly I am.'

She shrugged, carrying on the pretence. 'Better to find out you're not suited before the marriage rather than after it.'

'Yes, I couldn't agree more.'

'I eh . . . I really don't want to talk about it, if you don't mind, Ian.'

'Of course.'

She laid down her knife and fork, picked up her glass and had a gulp of its contents. That made her feel better, so she had another even larger swallow, forcing herself to feel and appear bright again.

'So how is Thomas Jardine getting on? His parents and I have become great friends, you know. His father has been terribly good to us businesswise.'

'Thomas has been . . .'

Ian told her a story about a night out he, Charlotte and Thomas had had recently that soon had Sarah laughing because of how outrageously funny it was.

That evening Sarah, Jock and Mrs McGuffie had just risen from dinner – although the staff was now again at full complement Mrs McGuffie continued to eat as one of the family – when Henry the footman announced that Sarah had a gentleman caller, the Honourable Ian Monteith.

'Show him through,' Sarah instructed, wondering what it was had brought Ian to Stiellsmuir when she'd already seen him earlier.

When Ian was shown into the library he was clearly in a state of agitation, completely unlike his normally cool, contained self.

'Mr Hawke, Mrs McGuffie,' Ian said, giving them both a rather stiff, formal bow. A totally different bow to the casual easy one he'd given Sarah that lunchtime in her office.

He now turned to Sarah and gave her a nervous smile. 'Hello again, Sarah.'

'Has something happened?' she demanded.

He raised an eyebrow. 'No. What makes you ask that?'

'You seem a bit . . . well out of sorts.'

'Do I?' His expression was one of puzzled innocence.

'Would you care for a dram?' Jock inquired.

'Yes please.'

Sarah waited for an explanation of his visit.

'It's been a beautiful day, hasn't it,' Ian said to Mrs McGuffie.

'Very.'

'I went for a long walk in Kelvingrove Park this afternoon. They have an absolutely gorgeous display of flowers there just now.'

'Really,' Mrs McGuffie replied, nodding her head.

What was he wittering on about? Sarah wondered. This was all becoming most curious.

'Sarah, you?' Jock questioned, waving the whisky decanter at her.

'No thank you.'

'Maud?'

'Me neither.'

'Then it's just you and I,' Jock said to Ian, and poured himself as generous a dram as that he'd poured for Ian.

Sarah noted that Ian's continuing nervous smile was rapidly getting a fixed look about it. What was wrong with the man?

'Slainthe!' Jock toasted, having given Ian his whisky and soda.

'Slainthe!' Ian responded and drank.

'Well then,' Jock said, and cleared his throat. He, Sarah and Mrs McGuffie stared expectantly at Ian whose continuing nervous smile was now so fixed it might have been glued on.

'It's been an excellent summer so far for flowers,' Mrs McGuffie said after a while.

'Vegetables too, I believe,' Jock added.

Ian, smile unwavering, licked his lips.

'Cigar?' Jock offered.

'Not for me,' Ian replied.

Jock took a cigar from the humidor, clipped its end, and lit up. He then regarded Ian through a haze of smoke.

Ian suddenly, in fact so suddenly it gave Mrs McGuffie a bit of a start, downed the rest of his drink. 'Do you think I could possibly speak to Sarah alone?' he requested in a rush of words.

Jock's eyes slid to Sarah, then back again to Ian. 'I don't see why not. Mrs McGuffie and I have some things to attend to elsewhere anyway.'

Mrs McGuffie, taking her cue, now rose from where she'd been sitting, while Sarah couldn't imagine what it was Ian wanted to speak to her about alone.

'Can I have another whisky?' Ian asked as soon as Jock and Mrs McGuffie had left the room.

'Certainly. Help yourself.'

The dram which he poured was an even heftier one than that Jock had given him, which made it very large indeed.

'Now what is it? What's bothering you?' Sarah asked gently.

'I was all right until I got to your front door, then I sort of went to pieces inside. I've never been so bloody nervous in my life!'

'You're certainly that,' she agreed.

'I eh . . . That walk I mentioned in Kelvingrove Park. I took it because I wanted to think. You see, after I left you this afternoon, I realised something.'

He paused, but when Sarah didn't say anything went on. 'Three and a half years ago I asked you to marry me, and you turned me down saying you wouldn't be mine or any other man's mealticket. Remember?'

'Yes.'

'Well I really did mean what I said at the time, that I was in love with you and wanted you for youself and not your money.'

Had she been wrong? Sarah wondered. *Had* he been speaking the truth then?

'I'm still in love with you, Sarah, and now you can't believe I'm after your money because as I explained to you this afternoon I am now to inherit. Will you marry me? Will you be my wife, and the future Viscountess Ascog?'

She went weak all over. She hadn't expected this at all.

'First of all the money was between us, then you met your sea captain. Now neither is a problem.'

'But . . . but . . .' She didn't know what to say, she was completely flabbergasted. 'But what about Charlotte?'

'Charlotte is a good woman, whom I think very highly of. If I married her she would make an excellent wife, there's no doubt about that. But she was always second choice after you. If I break with her she'll soon find someone else. And I wouldn't be at all surprised if that someone wasn't Thomas Jardine – those two might have been made for each other.'

Marry Ian? Eventually become Viscountess Ascog? And it wasn't as if she didn't care for Ian. She did, and always had. But she didn't love him.

As though reading her mind he said, 'I appreciate you don't love me, but given time I'm certain I can rectify that. And I do love you; I love you desperately.'

She didn't know what to think. It was so soon after Mathew. How could she marry Ian still feeling as she did about Mathew!

Laying his glass aside Ian went to Sarah and gathered her hands into his. 'This must have been meant to be, can't you see that? It's all too much of a coincidence for it not to be. Say you'll marry me and you'll make me the happiest man alive.'

Meant to be? He could well be right. And if she was going to marry someone other than Mathew she wouldn't do better than Ian Monteith, whom she could well have married anyway if it hadn't been that she'd believed him to be after her money.

'Agree and you'll never regret it. Not for one instant. I swear that to you on my life.'

Closing her eyes she thought of Mathew. Lost to her for always, she reminded herself. If only . . .

Then warm, urgent, lips were pressing against hers, and the scent of Ian was warm in her nostrils.

Damn Mathew Wilson and his poxridden Venezuelan whore! Damn them both to everlasting hell!

'Well?' Ian demanded when the kiss was over.

There and then she made up her mind. She had to think of the future, not the past. She loved Mathew, but he had forfeited her love. A new opportunity had been offered her, an opportunity she'd be a fool not to grab with both hands.

'Yes.'

Ian blinked at her.

'Yes,' she repeated emphatically.

This time she kissed him. After which the pair of them, bursting with excitement, went to tell Jock and Mrs McGuffie.

'How do you feel?' Hemphill asked Sarah as their carriage drew up outside the church.

'Not as bad as I thought I would. But I'll be glad when it's over nonetheless.'

'Aye, I know what you mean. That's exactly how Mrs Hemphill and I felt on our wedding day. A curious blend of happiness, nervousness, and sheer terror.'

Sarah grinned at that. He'd just summed up her emotions to a T.

Hemphill got out the carriage, then helped Sarah out. Behind them a second carriage had drawn up, this one containing Maud McGuffie and Smith the clerk from the firm. Hemphill was giving Sarah away, Smith doing the same for Maud.

Jock had proposed several weeks after Ian had to Sarah, and it had been her idea they have a double wedding. Initially Jock had been against it, as had Maud, not wanting, as they thought, to spoil her big day. But finally Sarah had convinced the pair of them that rather than spoiling it a double wedding with her father and Maud would actually enhance it. And so, with Ian also keen on the idea, it had been agreed.

Jock would normally have given Sarah away, but as he was unable to do so on account of being one of the bridegrooms, Hemphill had been drafted in for the job.

As for Maud, her father was long dead and she had no other male relatives to fit the bill. It had been Hemphill's suggestion that they ask Smith, an old bachelor, who'd been delighted to oblige.

Up the church steps the four of them went, while high above the church bell rang out.

The vestibule was dark, while further in the ambience was of peace and sanctity.

Sarah and Hemphill took up their positions at the entrance to the left hand aisle, Maud and Smith at the entrance to the right. From where she was Sarah had a clear view right down the church, and could see Ian and Jock standing waiting in front of the altar.

Sarah glanced over at Maud, caught her eye, and smiled. A smile of mutual encouragement.

The organist struck up 'Here Comes the Bride', or 'Brides' as it was in this instance.

'Ready?' Hemphill asked her.

'As I'll ever be.'

Hemphill signed to Smith, as had been their arrangement, and both couples started off down their respective aisles.

Fifteen minutes later Sarah was a Monteith, Maud her stepmother.

PART 4

Over the Water and Far Away

Chapter 9

'Aren't you the most gorgeous baby in the whole wide world,' smiled Sarah, tickling the Honourable Robert Ian John Monteith on his bright pink tum. The Honourable Robert gurgled back as if he'd understood every word despite the fact he was only three months old.

'He is indeed bonny. A right smasher of a boy,' agreed Nanny Tate who also doted on the wee lad, but understandably wasn't quite as extravagant in her praise of him as Sarah.

Sarah smoothed back Robert's already thick straw-coloured hair – which could do with a snip she noted – and gazed into those liquid brown eyes that were identical to his father's. He was the spit of Ian, though far slimmer and more delicate in build, the latter the one obvious physical inheritance from her.

Sarah blew her son a kiss, and he blew bubbles in return, which delighted her.

'How's that water?' she asked.

Nurse Tate tested the newly poured water in the enamelled baby bath which was standing on a table in the middle of the nursery floor. 'Just right,' she pronounced. 'Shall I?'

'No, let me do it this time.' Sarah couldn't get enough of Robert, and in some ways was sorry (which was no reflection whatever on Miss Tate personally) that they'd hired a nanny. But it would have been unthinkable for a couple in their position not to have done.

It was a great sadness to both Ian and Sarah that Bertie had never lived to see his grandchild, but he had finally succumbed to his old liver problem in July of the previous year, 1900.

Sarah removed the shawl Robert was wrapped in – it might be February and bitter out but the nursery was warm as toast thanks to the huge fire blazing in the grate – and then slowly immersed his naked body in the bath till he was in a half sitting, half lying position with the water several inches above his belly button.

Robert kicked his legs, and blew more bubbles. 'Did he drink all his breakfast?' Sarah inquired as she gently lathered him with mild soap.

'A full eight-ounce bottle, after which he had a zizz,' Nanny Tate reported.

'That's my boy,' chuckled Sarah. He was a grand feeder, usually good as gold in that department. It was the same with sleeping and performing his other functions; rarely a hiccup to cause anxiety.

Sarah rinsed Robert off using a cup kept in the nursery for that purpose, then lifted him from the bath to enfold him in a thick Egyptian towel – even nicer and fluffier than the Turkish variety.

Nanny Tate removed the bath, setting it on the floor, then placed a small mattress on the table where the bath had been. Over this she put a fine cotton sheet.

Sarah carefully laid Robert on the sheet, and began drying him, not forgetting the areas between fingers and toes. As she dried she softly sang, a lullaby she'd learned during those far-off days in Netherton.

When Robert was dried to her satisfaction she powdered him, first on the front, then the rear. After which she slipped him into a warm semmit, with a cosy top following that.

Nanny Tate handed her the triangularly folded nappy which Sarah wormed under Robert's bottom, and then secured with pins. She had just completed that when there was a knock on the door.

'Come in!' Sarah called out, thinking it was one of the servants. But she was wrong. It was Ian.

'How's my son and heir this morning?' he beamed. It had become a great habit of his to refer to Robert as his son and heir.

'Never better. Come and have a look.'

It pleased Sarah that Ian was completely at ease with Robert. Not nervous and unsure as many men were with their baby offspring. Indeed, offspring up to the age of reason, and often beyond.

Ian chucked Robert under the chin. 'Hello, young chap. I've brought you a surprise.'

'A surprise?' Sarah echoed. Now wasn't that just like Ian! He was forever producing things for Robert.

'Something special,' Ian said to her, eyes twinkling. 'Only this minute delivered from the town. The men are bringing it up now.'

Sarah couldn't think what on earth it could be. 'Bringing it in here?' she queried.

'Pearson is showing them the way.' Pearson was one of the footmen.

Sarah raised an eyebrow, and looked at Nanny Tate, who shrugged. They both glanced at the nursery door when there was a noise outside.

The door, already partially open, swung further open as two burly men carrying a large cardboard-encased object came through, Pearson fussing behind them telling them to see and mind not to scrape paint or wallpaper.

The object the men were carrying was instantly recognisable by the head sticking out of the top, and the legs from the bottom.

'A rocking horse!' Sarah exclaimed.

'The best in Glasgow, I made sure of that,' Ian replied, indicating to the men where he wanted the horse.

When the horse was in position the men took their leave, and Pearson shut the door behind him and them.

'Wait till you see this,' Ian enthused, hurriedly stripping away string and cardboard.

The rocking horse was truly magnificent. Its mane was long and made of real horsehair, while the saddle was of bright red padded leather. The wood underneath the yellow paint dotted with large black spots was mahogany.

'What do you think?' Ian asked Sarah, obviously pleased as punch with himself.

Nurse Tate was smothering a smile.

'It's . . . eh . . . lovely,' Sarah answered, thinking exactly the same as Nanny Tate.

'I knew you'd like it. As I'm sure Robert does.' He swung his attention on to his three-month-old son. 'Don't you, lad?'

Sarah hefted Robert into the crook of her arm. 'I'm sure he will when he grows up a bit, Ian. It's just that a rocking horse is somewhat too old for him at present, wouldn't you say?'

Nanny Tate had to turn away so that Ian wouldn't see her expression. Daft bugger! she thought, but kindly.

Ian's brow creased. 'I suppose it is.' Then, his brow clearing, 'But not for long. He'll be on that horse before you know it. Damned if he won't!'

Smiling broadly, Sarah took Robert over to the horse and sat him in the saddle. Holding him firmly, and manipulating the horse with her foot, she very gently rocked Robert to and fro.

'He's enjoying it,' Ian declared.

Sarah wouldn't have exactly said that, but he wasn't not enjoying it either. 'A born horseman,' she said, knowing that would please Ian no end. Which it clearly did.

'Takes after his father, eh?'

'No doubt about it.'

It was a tremendous source of pride to Ian that Robert looked like him. As far as he was concerned Sarah had given him a son completely in his own image, a tiny replica of himself.

'Can I?' Ian held out his hands, asking if he could hold the baby. Sarah lifted Robert off the rocking horse, and gave him to Ian who cradled the wee fellow to his bosom.

The two of them together like that made a beautiful picture, Sarah thought, not realising it was an image that was going to stay with her, burned indelibly into her mind and memory, till the end of her days.

She didn't care about Nanny Tate being present, that didn't inhibit her one whit. She kissed Ian on the cheek, then whispered, 'You're lovely, do you know that?'

Nanny Tate glanced away.

'You're not so bad yourself,' he replied in a low voice.

For the space of several seconds magic flowed between them, the magic of two people very much in love, utterly content with each other.

It was Ian who finally broke the spell. 'Tell you what, I have to ride over to Burnie Wood so why don't you come with me?' he grinned. 'It'll be good for the figure.' He was referring to the fact that Sarah was still carrying a spare tyre as a result of her pregnancy. Something she was rather touchy about.

She refused to be drawn, knowing full well he was teasing her. 'You're right, a ride will do me good. When are you leaving?'

'I've a few things to attend to first. An hour say?'

'I'll meet you in the stables.'

He handed Robert back to her. 'See you then.'

When he was gone Nanny Tate gave a small sigh. What a perfect couple Lord and Lady Ascog were. Sometimes it was like watching a real live fairy story.

Together Sarah and Nanny Tate put Robert down for a nap, then Sarah went off to get changed into riding gear.

'Do you think it's going to snow?' Sarah asked Ian as they left the stables. She was on her mare Goldy, while he was on Boy, a young hunter he'd only recently acquired.

Ian glanced up at the leaden sky. It wasn't quite as cold out as it had been, and he knew that was what had made her ask. 'Difficult to say,' he replied. 'It certainly feels as though something's brewing up there.'

Not just brewing, she thought, staring at the low grey ceiling above, but somehow ominously so. She suddenly shuddered, her feeling the one commonly described as 'somebody having just walked over her grave'.

'How do you want to go to Burnie Wood?' she inquired a little further on. For there were a number of routes through the estate that would take them there.

Ian shook his head. 'Doesn't matter to me. Any preference?'

'As the cows are inside let's go across the north pastureland. There's a good view over Meikleour Vale that way.' Meikleour Vale belonged to a neighbouring estate, and was a firm favourite of Sarah's. During the summer months she and Ian occasionally took picnics there.

The cows Sarah had referred to were their herd of forty Ayrshires which they had three full-time employees looking after. The herd was at present installed in the estate's two byres for the winter, and wouldn't be let out again till spring.

Sarah's cheeks were already burning from the sharp wind that was blowing. They would return to the house via the barley and turnip fields, she decided. There would be less wind there thanks to that entire section being well shielded by Coldfall Wood and the smaller Ten Acre Wood.

They had five woods on the estate altogether, all of which were cover for pheasant, partridge and woodcock. The shooting and selling of these game birds, plus the grouse that also bred on other parts of the estate, provided a substantial part of the estate's income.

The estate also boasted a small herd of deer – twelve to be exact – which included two bucks. It was Ian's intention to allow the herd to expand, having introduced it eighteen months previously, to the point where it too would be a source of estate income.

'Why are we going to Burnie Wood?' Sarah queried as they jogged along. The wood was so called because of the shallow burn that traversed it from top to bottom.

'Do you remember that fire we had there when the lightning struck just after Hogmanay?'

She nodded.

'Well, the burnt remains and those trees damaged beyond saving are starting to be cut down and dragged away today. I want to ensure everything is going as it should.'

The lightning Ian was talking about had occurred during a violent storm. Despite the lashing rain fire had not only broken out but persisted for quite some time before finally being extinguished by the downpour. Half an acre of trees had been destroyed and badly damaged, Ian had told her the next day after he'd visited that part of the wood where the fire had taken place.

Ian and Sarah changed direction, veering to the right. From there Sarah could see, below her now as they were on rising ground, the estate's timber yard and sawmill.

Finally they had to leave the north pastureland, going through a gate into a large field containing sheep. Some of these sheep were grazing at fodder racks, racks made from their own timber in the yard below.

Sarah twisted round to have a last look at Meikleour Vale, an idyllic place in the summer, and then that was lost to view.

Soon Burnie Wood came into sight, and a few minutes later that part of it where the fire had occurred. A pair of Clydesdales were plodding towards them, hauling several chained trees in their wake.

The Clydesdales were being led by Bobby Thom, a young man in his late teens who'd been born on the estate, his dad having been born in the same cottage, and bed, forty years previously. Bobby's great-grandfather had been a young man himself when he'd come to work for the then Lord Ascog.

Ian exchanged a few words with Bobby, then he and Sarah continued on their way along what was once more level ground.

On reaching the spot where his men were working Ian dismounted, and Sarah followed suit. All the men stopped what they were doing to touch either their forehead or cap.

'How's it going, Harry?' Ian inquired, Harry Sampson being in charge of the work party.

'Nae sae bad yur Lordship. Should be finished no bother at a' by the night after next.'

That was what Ian had estimated, and had wanted to hear. 'Good,' he acknowledged with a nod of his head.

Sarah gazed about her. A blackened stump about five feet high was all that remained of one tree. Pointed at the top it looked for all the world like some giant toothpick, thought Sarah, staring at it.

Closer inspection on her part revealed that the carbon formed by the fire was about an inch and a half thick.

She walked into the wood till she came to the furthest extent of the fire where the trees, bare and stark, were untouched.

After a short while she returned to the horses where Ian joined her.

'We're only taking out what's above ground for now. We'll excavate the root systems in the spring when I'll also plant some saplings to replace those trees we've lost,' he explained.

That made sense to Sarah. She would have considered it daft to attempt to excavate the root systems while the earth was hard as iron.

'Done everything here you wanted to?' she asked.

'I have.'

'Then let's start back.'

She was about to remount Goldy when he suggested, 'Do you mind if we walk for a bit? I could do with a stretch of the legs.'

'That suits me fine,' she smiled.

They strolled side by side with their respective horses to the outside of them. When they'd left the work party well behind, Ian reached down and took Sarah by the hand. 'When will we have the next one?' he asked.

'Next what?'

'Baby, of course.'

She laughed. 'Give me a chance! Robert is only three months old after all.'

'I think I'd like a girl next time. And from there on in we'll have them turn about. Boy, girl, boy, girl . . .'

Sarah's expression was one of pretended outrage. 'What do you think I am! One of your breeding cows?' she interrupted.

He brought his head close to hers, and whispered, 'Mooooo!'

That earned him a swift slap on the face, but only in fun.

'You know something?' he said, rubbing the spot where she'd made contact.

'What?'

'The nicest thing about having children by you is the getting of them.'

'You're certainly most diligent in that department,' she acknowledged.

'I never hear you complaining,' he countered.

'I'm a dutiful wife.'

He let go of Boy and caught her in his arms. 'Is that all it is, being dutiful?'

'You know it's not,' she replied softly.

He kissed her deeply, a kiss that was not only passionate but also full of love and affection.

'I feel like being diligent again,' he whispered when the kiss was over.

'Well, not here. Your bum would freeze.'

He threw back his head and roared. Sarah could be so delightfully rude at times. He adored that. 'I was thinking more of our double bed back at the house.'

'Bed during the day! What would the servants say?'

He smiled wickedly. 'I pay them. I don't care what they say.'

'Know what?'

'What?'

'Neither do I.'

She cuddled up tightly to him. Hugging him, and being hugged by him in return.

Closing her eyes she thought how good life had turned out for her. Ian, Robert, position and wealth – she couldn't have asked for anything more. Not for one moment had she regretted marrying Ian, not for one single solitary moment.

Disengaging herself she went round to the other side of Goldy and climbed into the saddle. And Ian climbed into his. 'Want to race?' he challenged.

'No fear. Boy would leave Goldy standing, as well you know.'

'I wouldn't say that exactly.'

'Well I would. Poor Goldy and yours truly wouldn't have a chance.'

It was in the second barleyfield they came to that it happened. They were approaching the gate that would let them out of that field into the next when a hare suddenly bolted from almost directly underneath Boy's hooves. The hare had been so well blended in with the hard brown earth that neither of them – or the horses – had seen it.

Boy, a very young and inexperienced horse, reared in fright. Bucking on to his hind legs he stabbed and pawed the air with his front ones.

Ian should never have come off, but he'd been caught completely unawares with his mind on the double bed at home which he and Sarah were heading for.

With an exclamation he went toppling sideways to land with a jarring thump.

Sarah couldn't help but laugh. She'd never known Ian come off a horse before. And for the damn horse to be walking at the time, that was priceless!

Ian was lying on his back staring up at her, an odd, bemused expression on his face. Boy was a dozen feet away, snorting and blowing but clearly calming down again. The hare, through the hedge and into the next field, was only a speck in the distance.

'That's what I call a very hairy experience,' Sarah said, guffawing at her own wit.

Ian continued staring up at her, that same odd, bemused expression on his face.

'Oh come on, there's no need to make a meal of it,' she said when he still hadn't moved half a minute later.

He wants me to get down there with him, then he's going to grab me, she thought. Well, she was fly to that one.

'If you don't get up I'm going to just leave you there,' she warned.

His expression remained the same.

She was becoming irritable now. 'Ian, will you stop mucking about?'

Boy snickered. Coming to Ian he nudged Ian with his nose, also urging Ian to get up.

'This isn't funny any more. It's boring. So will you please come on!'

Boy licked Ian's face, and as he did Ian's head moved slowly round till it was at an impossible angle to his neck.

Sarah, filled with sudden horror, stared at her husband in disbelief. 'Ian?' she croaked. Then, in a tight scream, 'Ian!'

She threw herself from Goldy to kneel beside him. Tentatively she touched the cheek nearest his shoulder, still half expecting him to grab her and shout 'Gotcha!', and pushed his head upwards till it was horizontal to his body.

'Ian?'

His eyes were open, and staring, but different to any way she'd ever seen them before. His eyes might be open but they were closed at the same time. As if shutters inside them had been drawn.

'Oh my God!' she whispered. She didn't have to feel for his pulse, or listen for his heartbeat to know her husband was dead. She just knew.

'Oh my God!' she repeated.

And with that it began to snow.

She wasn't enjoying her cigarette; it tasted like ashes in her mouth. Nor her drink which didn't seem to be having any effect on her although it was her fifth large one.

It was that evening, and she was sitting with Jock and Maud who'd come straight over directly they'd been contacted. Nanny Tate and Samuel the butler had both been pillars of strength, doing what had to be done after the body was brought home by the work party from Burnie Wood.

'I just can't believe . . .' Maud started to say, then changed her mind about going on. She bit her lower lip.

Jock toyed with his whisky and soda, then saw off what remained in his glass. 'A refill?' he asked Sarah, whose glass was almost empty. Her reply was a shake of the head.

'Maud?'

Maud wasn't usually much of a drinker, but she needed bolstering that night. 'Please,' she answered quietly, and held out her glass which Jock took from her.

Sarah ground out what remained of her cigarette in the ashtray balanced on the arm of her chair and, without thinking, immediately lit another. She was dry-eyed, and hard-faced. A face almost completely devoid of colour. After the initial shock it was now slowly sinking in that Ian was dead, that she'd never see him alive ever again, that their life together was finished. That she was a widow.

'If Boy had been galloping, or cantering even, it might have made sense. But he was only walking when that hare . . .' She looked at Jock. 'It's so silly, isn't it. At the time I laughed because it was so silly.'

Jock was worried about Sarah. He'd expected her to go to pieces, but she hadn't. She was fiercely in control of herself. Doctor Lambie had been earlier, but she'd refused the sedative he'd offered her. Lambie had left the sedative telling her she could have it later if she felt she needed it. He'd promised to return in the morning to see how she was doing.

Sarah glanced up at the ceiling. Ian was in their double bed, the double bed they'd been returning to when it had happened. She intended he'd stay there in their bed, in their house, on their estate where he belonged, till it was time for the burial. The undertakers, already contacted by Samuel, were calling in the morning to discuss details.

There was a tap at the door. 'Come in!' Sarah called out.

It was Samuel. 'I was wondering if you and Mr and Mrs Hawke would care for a little supper, your Ladyship?' he inquired in a sombre tone.

'Not for me. How about you, Maud? Jock?'

Maud waited to hear what Jock replied. She wouldn't have minded a bite herself. 'Me neither,' he said. 'You dear?' Maud shook her head, feeling it would have been inappropriate to eat on her own.

Samuel left them, quietly closing the door behind him.

Silence reigned once more.

'If you'd like, we'll stay the night,' Jock volunteered.

'That's not necessary.'

'It would be no trouble, Sarah. We can stay the night, and as long as you wish.'

She gave her father a wan smile. 'You mean miss work?'

He smiled back, knowing that was a teasing jibe. 'I mean precisely that. I'll take as much time off as is needed.'

She came over all warm inside. Good old Jock, how much she loved him. 'Thank you, but your taking time off won't be required. I appreciate the offer though.'

Sarah had left the firm of *J. Hawke & Daughter* soon after she'd realised she was pregnant with Robert. A married woman working was one thing, but a pregnant married one something else altogether. That hadn't seemed right. And so she'd left Jock to run the firm on his own again.

The firm itself had prospered greatly under their dual management, long since surpassing what it had been before Jock had degenerated into full-blown schizophrenia.

On that front there was nothing but good news. Since that night in the tower at Stiellsmuir when Jock had recovered to become himself again, there had been no relapsing on his part. Not even a single nocturnal 'mood'. It was their profound hope – Jock, Maud and Sarah's – that his schizophrenia was now completely in the past. And so it was certainly appearing to be.

'Excuse me,' Maud said, and left the room, needing to go to the toilet.

Jock had been waiting to get Sarah alone, and had intended soon organising this if a suitable opportunity hadn't presented itself. Which it now had.

'Sarah?'

She'd been staring blankly into space; now she brought her attention onto her father.

'I was just thinking about what happened after Captain Wilson. You won't . . .'

'No,' she interjected. 'There won't be a repeat of that, Jock. I promise you.'

He searched her face, and what he saw there convinced him she was telling the truth. He breathed a silent sigh of relief. 'Right then,' he acknowledged, and nodded.

She lit another cigarette. Just for something to do, she thought. Something to hold in her hand. 'I'm only twenty-seven – twenty-eight next month. Ridiculously young to be widowed, don't you think?'

'Yes,' Jock agreed grimly.

She put a hand across her mouth, and returned to staring blankly into space.

Maud arrived back and said she would have another drink when Jock asked her.

Jock produced a cigar, clipped one end then carefully lit it. He stood in front of the fire staring at Sarah, wishing there was some way he could lessen her pain.

After a while Sarah ground out the cigarette she'd only had two puffs from, rose and crossed to the bellpull which she gave a sharp tug. It was Samuel who answered.

'Regarding the rocking horse that arrived earlier today,' she said levelly. 'First thing in the morning have it removed from the nursery and get rid of it.' She paused to reconsider that. 'No, don't get rid of it, take it outside and have one of the men smash it to smithereens. Understand?'

'Yes, your Ladyship.'

'And Samuel, I mean precisely that. I want it smashed to smithereens, not someone spiriting it away for themselves, thinking I'll be none the wiser.'

'I'll personally supervise the smashing, your Ladyship.'

'Good,' she answered, and made a sign of dismissal.

Jock was frowning at her, Maud clearly puzzled. But she didn't explain.

Lighting yet another cigarette she again retreated into a dream, staring blankly off into space.

The funeral service was held in Glasgow Cathedral as befitted a peer of the realm. Sarah was sitting with Jock on one side of her, Ian's brother James over from Ireland on the other. All she could think of was how cold she was. It was freezing in the cathedral, there being no form of heating whatever. At least none she could detect.

You would have imagined they'd have done better than that! she thought. If she'd realised this was going to be the case she'd have worn heavier clothes. She pitied the old folk present, they must be really feeling it.

The congregation rose and began to sing, 'Onward Christian Soldiers . . .'

It was a tremendous turn-out, Sarah reflected. Thomas and Charlotte Jardine had come over from Paris for the ceremony, and were sitting with Sir Ewan and Lady Jardine. (Ian had been right in his prophecy that Thomas and Charlotte would marry.)

Friends of Ian's from his diplomatic corps days were there, as were a host of school, personal and family friends.

Olivia McQueen – as Olivia Tennant now was – had come along with her husband Archibald, the two of them having married the year after Sarah and Ian, as had Primrose, now Mrs Tucker. Her husband, a captain with the 60th Rifles, hadn't been able to accompany Primrose as he was away fighting the Boers.

One section of the congregation was composed entirely of house and estate staff, every one of them being there with the exception of Nanny Tate, who'd remained at home looking after Robert.

Charlie Dundonald was sitting several rows behind Sarah with Maud, and beside them Lady Mary, James's wife.

Hemphill was in the row behind that, as was Smith who'd given Maud away at the wedding.

C. Aubrey Smith, involved in rehearsals for a play that was scheduled to open the following week in London's West End, had tried to make it but had been unfortunately unable to do so. Sarah had a telegram from him back at the house, one of nearly fifty she'd received.

Originally Sarah had considered having the ceremony in the church where they'd been married, but in the end had decided against that, not wanting to confuse in any way the memory of her marriage to Ian with that of his funeral. She wanted them quite distinct, and in different buildings. She didn't know why, only that was how she wanted it.

Besides, when they'd married Ian hadn't yet succeeded to the title. Now that he had, the cathedral was far more appropriate. Jock had agreed with her on that when she'd spoken to him about it.

There was also a large contingent of neighbours present to pay their respects. For Ian had been well liked amongst them, as had Bertie before him.

They finished the hymn, sat down again and began to pray. Our Father, Who art in Heaven, hallowed be Thy name . . .

Jock surreptitiously glanced sideways to Sarah to see that she was smiling. A smile to break the heart.

'Sarah, I have to talk to you. It's important,' James Monteith said to her. Others had been invited back to the house, but now only the immediate family were left. That was Sarah, Jock, Maud, James and Lady Mary. They were in the main drawing-room.

Sarah frowned. 'On you go then.'

James glanced over at the door to the 'snug room'. 'Why don't we go in there?' he suggested, gesturing.

Sarah ran a hand over her forehead. She was incredibly weary, weary beyond belief. Yet she knew if she went to bed she wouldn't sleep. 'You mean just the two of us?'

'We can discuss matters here if you wish. It's entirely up to you.'

Sarah stared at the 'snug room' door, recalling the night she'd been in there with Ian and overheard that loudmouth Carrick Holme talking about her. The same night Ian had first proposed.

Closing her eyes she visualised Ian as he'd been that night, saw the two of them sitting on the 'snug room' settee drinking mulled wine. And remembered her horror and mortification, not to mention blazing anger, to hear Carrick Holme describe her as common as muck, and Myrtle as a trollop.

How magnificent Ian had been, threatening to take Carrick outside and give him the thrashing of his life if he didn't apologise to her, which he had.

She'd adored the 'snug room' that night, but since then, and coming to live in the house, had only been into it on four or five occasions. The odious Carrick and his snooty wife Henrietta – whatever had become of them? – had quite blighted it for her.

'I'd prefer to remain here, if you don't mind. I'm sure there's nothing you have to say to me which can't be said before those present,' Sarah replied.

Jock was pleased to hear that. Sarah was hardly herself. If there were any important decisions to be made regarding her and the child he wanted to be in on them. Sarah had always spoken highly of James, but nonetheless Ian's brother was basically an unknown quantity to him, the pair of them only ever having met before briefly and socially.

'Fine,' James said with a shrug. 'I know it's a distressing time for you, Sarah, but nonetheless life goes on. And there are practical matters to be dealt with. What I'm referring to is the running of the estate – are you up to dealing with that yourself?'

The continued running of the estate was something that hadn't even entered her head. 'To be honest with you, James, Ian handled that entire side of things. Nor did I ever take an interest, first of all because I had my own job with Jock, and then because of the pregnancy and baby. Ian did talk over the occasional problem with me when he wanted my advice, but that's about it.'

James nodded. 'I guessed as much.'

'There's nothing to stop you learning though, is there?' Jock queried. Then, to James, spelling our her ability, 'She's an extremely competent person, James, I can certainly vouch for that.'

'Do you wish to learn estate management? Is that what you want?' James asked her.

Sarah shook her head. 'Right now I really couldn't say. Though I suppose, yes, that's what I will end up doing.'

'It's not that hard actually, but it does take some while to learn the ropes. In the meantime you need an expert to help you, to ensure things don't fall apart as they can so quickly do.'

'That makes sense to me,' Jock chipped in.

'Yes, I suppose you're right,' Sarah said slowly to James. If only she could think straight, but her head felt as if it was stuffed full of soggy cotton wool.

'What I suggest is this,' James went on. 'We have a chap called Tommy Walsh working for us at Foynes whom I'd recommend to anybody, even the new King himself, God bless him! So why don't I send Walsh over to run the estate for you until you've learned enough from him to be able to manage it yourself? I can assure you he's a first-class man.'

Sarah glanced at Jock, who gave her the nod that he approved this idea. 'Sounds ideal,' she answered. 'But are you sure Mr Walsh will want to come?'

'Oh he'll want to come all right. There's a post falling vacant in the not too distant future that is just the carrot to dangle in front of him. I'll make it clear to him that if he scratches our back, and by that I mean Lord Limerick and myself, we'll scratch his in return.'

'That's settled then,' Lady Mary said firmly in the softest of Irish brogues, her voice a musical delight to listen to whenever she spoke.

'I'll write to Lord Limerick later today, explaining the situation to him, and he can speak to Walsh. I'll stay on here keeping an eye on matters for you until Walsh arrives. How's that?'

'Absolutely splendid,' Sarah smiled weakly.

Sarah slid from Goldy's back on to the ground. 'Good girl,' she said, patting Goldy's slightly steaming rump.

She was in Meikleour Vale where winter was rapidly giving way to spring. There were clumps of crocuses near to where she'd stopped and beyond them a scattering of snowdrops. Somewhere close by a bird was twittering cheerfully, as if declaring to the world how pleased it was that the weather was on the turn.

She raised her eyes to the high ground on the estate which she and Ian had passed over that day he'd died. She could see him now, he on Boy, she on Goldy, the pair of them heading for Burnie Wood.

It was strange to remember that she hadn't loved Ian when they were married. But time had changed that. His goodness, his tenderness, his thoughtfulness, his wit, his charm, that gentle way he'd had of touching her, of caring for, and cherishing her, all those combined had brought love bubbling to the surface, until at last she was as much in love with him as he with her.

At that moment something broke inside Sarah, something that had desperately needed breaking. Tears welled in her eyes, the first she'd shed since his death.

'Oh!' she choked, ramming a fist into her mouth, then, 'Oh!' again.

As the tears flowed down her cheeks her face crumpled in on itself.

The dam was now well and truly breached. Her entire body shook with grief, while at the same time she clutched her heaving bosoms.

'Ian . . . Ian . . . Ian . . .' she repeated over and over in a voice that was riven with emotion.

Why had he had to die? It wasn't fair. It just wasn't. Not for him, not for her, not for Robert.

Crushed, that was how she felt. Bereft, and utterly crushed.

She laid a wet cheek against Goldy's neck, and in that position cried and cried. A flood of tears.

Jock stared stony faced at the latest figures to come from Cape Town, his glittering eyes shooting off sparks of cold green fire. The palm oil, and many other things he'd started shipping out there since the war began, were still making a handsome profit, but a profit that was down considerably on what it had been that time the previous year when Burnet had been his agent. Ten months ago Burnet had quit and gone off, God alone knew where, and Furness had taken over the agency. During the last four months the profit margin had gone into decline. And as far as he was concerned, without justifiable reason. In fact without any reason at all.

Jock tossed the sheets of figures aside, picked up his half-smoked Havana and clamped it between his teeth.

He smelt a rat, and a bloody big rat at that. And the rat's name was Theodore Furness. The man was on the fiddle, had to be. There was no other explanation for what was happening.

What mystified him was that Furness had been given the agency on Burnet's recommendation, and Burnet was no fool either in business or character analysis. Was Burnet somehow in on this? No, he couldn't believe that. Not Burnet, his record had been impeccable.

Well, there was only one way to solve this problem. He would inform Maud directly he got home to Stiellsmuir that evening.

'You must try and eat more to regain the weight you've lost,' a worried Maud advised Sarah. It was now July, five months after Ian's tragic death.

Sarah sipped her tea. There were crumpets, griddle scones,

potato scones, teabread and teacakes on plates in front of her, but they were there for Maud's benefit, not hers. Nowadays she never touched anything between meals, and at mealtimes themselves all she ever did was pick. She'd become the despair of Mrs Darling, the cook.

'I will,' she replied listlessly, knowing full well she had no intention of doing so. Food didn't interest her any more. Cigarettes, tea and coffee had become her staple diet.

'Perhaps you should see Doctor Lambie again?' Maud suggested.

'I saw him only last Tuesday. He says there's absolutely nothing physically wrong with me.'

Aye, *physically*, Maud thought. But there was in other ways, that stood out a mile. The loss of Ian had gutted Sarah.

'And how's the wee lad?' Maud asked.

'All right, just the same,' Sarah answered vaguely.

Maud munched a teacake. 'This is delicious,' she smiled, hoping Sarah would take the hint. But Sarah didn't.

There was a tap on the door. 'Come in!' Sarah called out.

It was Nanny Tate with Robert. 'I thought I'd take him out into the garden for a crawl in the grass,' Nanny Tate said.

'When did he start crawling!' Maud exclaimed to Sarah.

Sarah frowned. 'When was it, Nanny?'

'The end of last week, your Ladyship.'

'Oh yes, that's right. I remember now.'

It amazed Maud that Sarah had forgotten the date of such an important event so soon.

'I think he'd enjoy a cuddle from his mum before I take him out,' Nanny Tate said, proffering Robert to Sarah.

To Maud's surprise Sarah pushed Robert away. 'Not now, Nanny, perhaps later.'

For a split second there was a look of anxiety in Nanny Tate's eyes, then it was gone.

Maud saw the look, and knew she was going to have to speak to Nanny Tate privately before she left. 'Well, I'd love to give him a cuddle,' she beamed.

Robert was lovely and warm and soft and smelling of powder, a right little adorable baby. And so like his father! A chip off the old block if ever there was one.

Maud gently bounced him on her knee, which he approved of, cuddled him, then gave him a couple of big smackers before handing him back. It was a great sadness to her that she'd never had children of her own. Now it was too late for that.

'Another cup?' Sarah asked Maud after Nanny Tate and Robert had left them.

'Please.'

Sarah refilled both their cups.

'And when are you coming to Stiellsmuir? We haven't seen you there for ages.'

'I keep meaning to come but . . . I just never seem to get round to it,' Sarah ended lamely.

'Well, there is a lot for you to do here. Overseeing the running of the house, and learning to manage the estate.'

'I actually have very little to do with the house,' Sarah replied. 'Samuel and Mrs Darling more or less do it all by themselves. As for the estate . . .' She shrugged. 'I just can't seem to get interested in it.'

'You must remember that Walsh won't be here with you forever,' Maud said quietly, trying not to make it sound like a rebuke, which it was.

'I know,' Sarah sighed, and lit a cigarette.

Maud and Sarah chatted for about another fifteen minutes, Maud doing most of the talking, then Maud said, 'I really must be on my way. I have an appointment at Madame Baptiste's in an hour.'

'As always, it's been lovely having you here.'

Both women rose.

'Before I leave I must go and say goodbye to Robert,' Maud smiled, ready to put Sarah off should Sarah volunteer to accompany her into the garden. But Sarah didn't.

It was a beautiful day out. Warm, without being too much so. And with the gentlest of breezes blowing.

Nanny Tate had spread a tartan travelling rug on the grass on which she was now seated. Robert, when mobile, was crawling from the rug on to the grass, then back again and so forth.

'No, don't get up!' Maud instructed Nanny Tate who'd begun to come to her feet on realising that Maud was joining her.

Nanny Tate relaxed back into a sitting position, and Maud went down on her knees beside her.

'He's quite young to crawl, isn't he?' Maud queried.

'Youngish. His being able to do so now is what we call being fairly advanced. I would imagine it'll be the same with his walking and eventual reading.'

377

'You're saying he's clever?'

'No, not clever. Advanced. It's not quite the same thing.'

Maud reached over and scooped Robert into her arms. 'I've come to say tatti-byes, young man. I have to be off.'

He grinned cheekily at her.

'Who's a cheeky monkey then? Is it you?' And having said that she kissed him.

'Nanny?'

'Yes, Mrs Hawke?'

'Is there something wrong between her Ladyship and the baby?'

Nanny Tate dropped her gaze.

'You must know that Mr Hawke and I dearly love both of them. If something is amiss, and I get the definite impression there is, then it's to their advantage that you tell me.'

Nanny Tate twisted her hands together. It was a breach of confidence, she knew, but Mrs Hawke was right, she should say. If anyone could help, Mr and Mrs Hawke could.

'Her Ladyship just doesn't seem to care for Robert any more. It's as pure and simple as that,' she answered haltingly.

'You're not intimating she's cruel to him in any way, are you?'

Nanny Tate shook her head. 'No, no, nothing like that! She'd never hurt the mite, I'd lay my life on that. What she's become is indifferent to him. She never helps with his bath any more, or with dressing or feeding him. I can't even recall the last time she was in the nursery. She doesn't even want to hold him any more. At least once a day I try to get her to do so, but it's rare that she'll actually take him.'

'And this has been the case since his Lordship's death?'

'I first noticed the change in her attitude towards Robert about a week after that. Since then that attitude has got steadily worse, more and more indifferent. Least, that's how it seems to me.'

Maud, her heart swollen with emotion and concern, kissed Robert again, then laid him back on the rug where he immediately made a bee-line for the grass.

'Thank you for telling me this, Nanny. Now that I know what's what perhaps Mr Hawke and I can do something about it.'

'I sincerely hope you can, Mrs Hawke, for I tell you it fair upsets me to have things as they are.'

Maud stood up, and smoothed out the front of her dress which had become somewhat rumpled. 'Goodbye for now then, Nanny, and thank you again.'

Sarah came out to see Maud off in her carriage. Maud stayed as bright and cheerful as she could until a waving Sarah was lost to view. Then her face fell, and from there she brooded deeply all the way to Madame Baptiste's.

'Well?' Jock prompted softly, having just confronted Sarah about her uncaring attitude towards Robert.

She puffed on her cigarette. She was smoking far too many of the wretched things, and had developed a cough as a result. She kept meaning to cut down, but so far hadn't actually made the effort.

'I didn't realise it was so obvious.'

'I'm afraid it is. Maud particularly noticed it when she was here yesterday.' He and Maud had agreed not to mention her conversation with Nanny Tate.

Sarah sighed. 'I do love him, you know. It's just that . . . I can't bear to look at him.'

'But why?'

Her expression became tortured. 'Because every time I do I see Ian staring back at me. Looking at Robert is like having a knife that's already stuck in me being slowly twisted.'

'Ah!' Jock breathed. Now he understood. And it was true, Robert was the image of Ian.

'Those liquid brown eyes, that straw-blond hair, the way he has of . . .' Sarah broke off, and sucked on her cigarette. 'I keep hoping, for Robert's sake as well as my own, that it'll pass. But it doesn't.'

Jock went to the decanter and poured himself a stiff whisky to which he added only a taste of soda. He then said, in a flat, calm, metallic voice, 'I can appreciate what it's like for you losing Ian, the terrible hurt and pain. Pain that can be so deep and profound it can drive you right out of your mind as it did to me when Myrtle killed herself.'

He drank off half his whisky, and having done that made a decision. 'I think a break is what you need. A complete break away from Robert, this house, Glasgow and Scotland even.'

'You mean like I had after the smallpox?'

'Precisely. Only this time instead of the West Indies how about Cape Town?'

Sarah blinked. 'Why there in particular?'

'Because Theodore Furness who took over as our agent from Burnet is on the fiddle, and I need to have that sorted out. I intended going myself, but Maud insisted she accompany me for reasons I don't have to explain to you . . .'

'To be on the safe side,' Sarah cut in. 'Just in case—'

'Exactly,' he nodded. 'But you could go in my stead, which would certainly make things an awful lot easier for me, as it would mean I wouldn't have to abandon the office for a couple of months. That's about how long I calculate the trip will take.'

Cape Town? The idea of visiting there certainly appealed, she couldn't deny it. That entire area had been one of interest to her ever since she'd heard C. Aubrey Smith enthuse about it.

'What about the war that's going on there?' she queried.

'The war's nowhere near Cape Town. The entire Cape is quiet, as I understand it. It's in the Orange Free State, the South African Republic as the Boers call Transvaal, and northern Natal where the fighting is taking place. So you'll be quite safe. I wouldn't suggest you go if you wouldn't be.'

She bit her lip. It was tempting right enough. And yet . . . 'I know you say a complete break from Robert, but despite how I've been towards him since Ian's death I would still feel guilty as hell at leaving him.'

'There would be no reason for you to feel guilty,' Jock said quickly. 'He'd have Nanny Tate to care for him, and I'd insist the two of them came to live at Stiellsmuir until your return. That would give Maud and I a chance to spoil our grandson a wee bit.'

Excitement was fluttering inside her. A sea voyage, Cape Town, a job of work to do. The whole thing sounded just the ticket.

'All right, then,' she agreed. 'I'll go.'

Jock saw off what remained of his drink. 'I'll telegraph the authorities there and warn them to expect you. I'll ask them to give you their full backing regarding Furness. Now, when would you like to sail?'

'The sooner the better, I suppose.'

He nodded his approval. 'I'll have a booking made, and in the meantime if you come to Adelphi Street I'll show you the figures and brief you as much as I'm able.'

'I'll come to Adelphi Street in the morning. How's that?'

'Excellent.'

She stubbed out her cigarette and stood up, her eyes shining. 'I'd better go and discuss with Alice what to pack. I'll have to take her with me, you appreciate.' Alice was her personal maid, a woman in her early thirties who was best of chums with Nanny Tate.

'Of course.'

She went to her father, and kissed him on the cheek. 'Thank you, Jock.'

He pulled her to him, holding her tight for a few seconds. Then released her again.

'I should imagine this time next week you'll be well at sea,' he said.

At 7,000 tons the Union Castle's SS *Scot* – holder of the record for the Cape Town run – was a big ship whose usual steaming speed was between eighteen and twenty knots.

Sarah stood on the upper deck watching the English coastline fade into the evening light. It was five days since Jock had proposed she make the trip, five days of hectic planning, packing and generally getting organised.

She and Alice had taken the train the day before down to London where they'd spent the night at the Savoy in the Strand. After dinner she'd hired a hansom and instructed the driver to show them some of the sights.

Big Ben, the Houses of Parliament, the Abbey, Piccadilly Circus, Trafalgar Square, London Bridge, Fleet Street, St Paul's. They'd stopped and gone into the Abbey, which had been awesome inside. She'd also liked to have gone into St Paul's, but that had been closed to the public. She intended trying again to view the inside of the latter when she returned back through London.

Now the English coast was gone, leaving only the sea and sky to be seen, and the seagulls wheeling and raucously crying overhead.

Sarah closed her eyes. Already she was feeling the better for being away. A new lightness had entered into her, a lightness that had started in London, and seemed to be growing all the time. She prayed it would continue to do so.

Opening her eyes again she took a deep breath of heavily salt-impregnated air that made her nose tingle. That was a tonic in itself.

She smiled up at the now circling gulls, and would have waved to them if it wouldn't have looked totally stupid to the other passengers on deck.

Glasgow seemed a million miles away, the house and estate even further. As for Robert, her feelings about him were ambivalent.

On the one hand if he'd been there she still wouldn't have wanted

381

to look at him, on the other she was missing him, considerably so. Surely a good sign.

How Ian had adored that boy, his son and heir as he had so often called him. It was only eight months since Robert's birth. Who would have thought then that three months later . . .

She stopped herself thinking further along those lines. Ian was gone and nothing in the whole wide world was going to bring him back again. Nothing.

She brought herself out of her reverie. It was time for her to go and get changed for dinner. She'd been invited to sit at the captain's table, one of the advantages of being titled.

Although Robert was now Viscount Ascog, or the Rt Honourable Viscount Ascog to give him his full and formal description, she remained Viscountess Ascog, and would do so until Robert married, when she would become the Rt Honourable the Dowager Viscountess Ascog, or more simply, as she would prefer, Sarah, Lady Ascog. (She didn't fancy at all being called Dowager, it had such a geriatric ring to it.)

Leaving the port rail where she'd been standing, she went below.

Sarah lay in her bunk unable to sleep because of the ship's motion, something she was going to have to get used to again.

She'd thoroughly enjoyed dinner, Captain Broadhurst turning out to be quite a card.

The nicest thing about the meal was that during it she'd actually laughed, another first for her since Ian's death. That had cheered her enormously.

She started to reach for a cigarette, then changed her mind. She would begin cutting down as from now. Right there and then.

What was she smoking? Somewhere in the region of forty a day. Well, she'd ration herself to ten tomorrow. Ten at the maximum, and she'd stick to it. She promised herself.

When she did finally fall asleep it was a better, more refreshing sleep than she'd enjoyed in a long time.

Table Mountain had its tablecloth on, a layer of white cloud, and was just as she'd imagined it would be. Not bigger, or smaller, or more or less impressive, but just as she'd imagined.

The SS *Scot*, which had docked ten minutes previously, was abustle with activity, some of its passengers already disembarking.

'Lady Ascog!' Mr and Mrs Zemanovic, Americans from New York State, came hurrying over. They were two of a number of people Sarah had struck up a friendship with during the voyage.

'As you know we'll be in Cape Town for a couple of weeks and do hope we'll see you again during that time,' Wally Zemanovic said.

'You can count on it. I have your address and will be in touch as soon as I can,' Sarah promised them, not wishing to commit herself to a definite date until she'd got settled in and made at least initial inquiries into the Furness business.

After the Zemanovics, the Lyttleton-Turners appeared to make their final goodbyes, their destination being inland to Citrusdal where Freddy Lyttleton-Turner's brother had a farm.

Whilst they were talking a sleek grey warship passed behind the SS *Scot* heading out of the harbour. This was HMS *Powerful* which had brought in 400 men of the Yorkshire Light Infantry from India, and was now headed back there again.

Alice came on deck to signal to Sarah that they were now repacked and ready to go ashore whenever Sarah wanted.

'Excuse me a moment,' Sarah said to the Lyttleton-Turners, and beckoned Alice over.

'Have the luggage taken on to the quayside, then secure a cab or carriage for us. Come back here and tell me when you've done that.'

'Yes, your Ladyship.' And with that Alice left Sarah and went to do as she'd been instructed.

Sarah was still talking to the Lyttleton-Turners, having been joined by a Major Greenhive with whom she had danced several times, when Captain Broadhurst came towards them. Union Castle would have been furious with him if he'd allowed a Viscountess to leave the ship without a personal farewell from him.

It was about fifteen minutes later, Sarah now chatting to a Miss Smithers, when Alice reappeared to announce that a carriage with their luggage loaded aboard was waiting below.

Sarah and Miss Smithers shook hands and said goodbye, after which Sarah followed Alice down the aft gangplank and on to the thronged quayside.

'This way, your Ladyship,' Alice said, carving a passage through the crowd. Sarah tucked herself closely in behind her.

'Excited?' Sarah smiled as their carriage moved off, knowing this was Alice's first time abroad.

'Yes, your Ladyship. Very much so.'

'I have to confess, I'm excited myself.'

They soon left the dock area to enter the city proper. Although winter here, it was pleasantly mild. Sarah was wearing a light coat which she felt she could actually have done without.

As they rattled along a cobbled Adderley Street, Sarah noted that there were khaki uniforms everywhere, and here and there the flash of a kilt to remind her of Scotland.

At the top of Adderley Street, they turned into Orange Street, having come through the entire town centre. Immediately their destination, the Mount Nelson Hotel, could be seen further along the road.

The hotel building was a splendid one. There was a certain refined elegance about it which immediately appealed to Sarah. She knew she was going to enjoy staying there.

She was expected and a suite of rooms had been reserved for her, Jock having arranged this by telegram. After being shown to her suite Sarah declared to Alice that the first thing she wanted was a good hot soak. There had been bathing facilities on board the SS *Scot*, but they'd left a great deal to be desired.

Bath over, and dressed again, Sarah was about to order some tea when there was a knock on the door, which Alice answered.

'There's a gentleman from Government House downstairs to see you, your Ladyship,' Alice reported back to Sarah. 'He's asking if he can come up.'

She'd been expecting to be contacted by the authorities once she'd arrived; they were certainly being extremely prompt about it.

'Yes, and have them send up a tray of tea and biscuits,' Sarah answered.

Shortly there was another knock on the door, which Alice again answered. She ushered the man through to the sitting-room where Sarah had positioned herself on a couch.

The man gave her a courteous bow. 'Welcome to Cape Town, Lady Ascog. I'm John Buchan, Sir Alfred Milner's Private Secretary. As I'm sure you know, Sir Alfred is High Commissioner for South Africa, and Governor of Cape Colony.'

'I'm pleased to meet you, Mr Buchan,' Sarah replied, extending a hand which Buchan shook.

Buchan was carrying a champagne bottle which he now held up in front of Sarah. 'I took the liberty of bringing you a chilled magnum of our best Cape champagne, Lady Ascog. There are those who swear it's up to French standards, but that of course is a matter of taste.'

Sarah smiled. What a charming gesture. 'I have ordered tea, but what do you say we have that instead?'

Buchan's face cracked into a smile to match hers. 'Excellent! Just what I was hoping you'd propose.'

Alice found some glasses in a cabinet, and with those at the ready, Buchan popped the cork.

Sarah had to admit the champagne was good, though she was hardly connoisseur enough to agree or disagree that it was on a par with the French original.

'Before we go further,' Buchan said, 'Sir Alfred is holding a reception at Government House on Saturday evening. We do hope you'll be able to attend.'

'How kind! I shall be delighted to attend.'

'Perhaps you would allow me to escort you? You would do me great honour if you did.'

Sarah thought that a splendid idea. Going in the company of Mr Buchan would certainly make things a great deal easier for her as the reception would be comprised completely of 'strange faces'.

'I shall look forward to that, Mr Buchan. Very much so.'

He gave her a little nod; that was settled then. It would certainly be no hardship taking Lady Ascog to the reception, none at all. 'May I sit?'

'Please do.'

He chose a chair facing her. 'I have been instructed by Sir Alfred to tell you that, as requested by your father, Mr Hawke, we are prepared to give you every assistance that you may require during your visit here.' He paused, to frown slightly. 'What we don't understand is what kind of assistance you will want.'

They were dancing such prompt attendance because of her title, Sarah suddenly realised. Until the discovery of diamonds and gold Cape Town had been little more than a backwater. Not so now, though it hadn't yet changed to the extent that the arrival of a title wasn't still an event.

'I'm here on business,' Sarah stated.

Buchan tried to hide his surprise. He hadn't expected that.

'Have you heard of a Theodore Furness?'

'Furness,' Buchan repeated, searching his memory. 'No, I don't believe I have. In fact I'm certain I haven't.'

'Well, he's my father's agent in Cape Town, and my father and I suspect he is being less than honest in his dealings with us. I'm here to find out precisely what's what and, if we are correct in our suspicions, to sort matters out.'

'I see,' Buchan said, stroking his chin.

'What I would ask you for the moment is to find out all you can about Furness. And if possible the current whereabouts of Charles Burnet, who was our original agent here but who resigned with the recommendation that Furness succeed him. We personally have no knowledge of Burnet after his resignation, or indeed if he's still in this part of the world at all.'

'Do you know why Burnet resigned?' Buchan probed.

'No explanation was given.'

'Leave this to me then,' Buchan said, 'and I'll do all that I can.'

What a lovely man, Sarah thought, after John Buchan had gone. She liked him a great deal.

'This is it, madam,' the black driver announced, gesturing with his whip at a rundown, dilapidated timber-framed structure.

Sarah glanced around her. The area wasn't at all a nice one – it was quite sinister in fact. She would later learn that it bordered on the Malay Quarter, the present-day Malays descendants of the slaves brought to the Cape from the east in the seventeenth century by the Dutch East India Company.

A shifty-eyed individual peered at them from an adjacent window, then hurriedly ducked out of view. A black appeared round a corner leading an ox pulling a cart loaded with fresh fruit and vegetables.

After Furness had taken over from Burnet the address that *J. Hawke & Daughter* dealt with had changed to this one. Burnet's address had been in Waterkant Street which was not only central, but respectable. This was neither.

'You want me to come in with you?' Alice asked. She didn't fancy this place either. It was the sort of street where you just *knew* you could get your throat cut.

'I think you'd better,' Sarah replied, glad of the company. Not that she was scared to go in by herself – apprehensive, yes, but not scared. If being honest, however, she would have had to admit that she much preferred Alice to accompany her.

The driver helped Sarah down, then Alice. There was no brass plaque on the door, which was hardly surprising, but instead a small painted sign which stated simply, *T. Furness*.

Sarah knocked, at the same time catching another glimpse of the shifty-eyed individual, on this occasion peering at them from a doorway.

The air was pungent with the ripe smell of produce, also heavier than the other parts of the city where she'd so far been. It reminded her of Port Royal.

Sarah rapped again, having to do so because there was no knocker or bellpull. The door itself was extremely old, and badly scarred.

Somewhere near by two voices, one a female's, were suddenly raised loudly in anger. The female shrieked an obscenity, which was followed by a splintering crash.

A white man dressed in filthy clothes walked towards them. When he was about a dozen feet away he took a long thin cigar from his mouth and treated them to a smile full of rotten teeth.

For an awful moment Sarah feared he was going to stop, but he didn't. He muttered something in a guttural language – Afrikaans? – and continued on his way.

Sarah gave a glance to check that their driver, a sturdy chap, was still there and hadn't somehow disappeared. She was glad of his presence. He gave the impression of being able to look after himself – and them, she hoped.

She rapped a third time, harder than before. It was past eleven o'clock on a working morning, surely Furness or a member of his staff were on the premises?

A small furry shape darted across the street, and hard on its heels another. Rats, Sarah thought, filled with revulsion. She loathed rats, they gave her the willies.

A cat scampered after the rats. A big marmalade tom who had killer written all over him.

'Maybe Mr Furness isn't in?' Alice ventured.

Another carriage rattled into the street, the occupant a fat white man wearing a panama hat. He gazed curiously at them as his carriage went by.

'Up there, on the left,' Alice whispered, nudging Sarah.

Sarah slowly lifted her eyes in that direction. A brown-skinned woman clearly of mixed blood – Cape Coloureds, they were known as – was standing on a verandah looking down at them. The woman's hair was long and wild, her legs bare, as were her feet. The

387

kneelength slip she was wearing appeared to be all that she had on.

The woman spat over the verandah railing into the street below, turned and went back inside.

To hell with ladylike knocking, Sarah thought. Forming a fist she banged Furness's door. If he or anyone else was inside they would most certainly hear that. They would have to be stone deaf not to.

'I think we're wasting our time,' Alice said when there was still no answer.

Sarah marched to the next door down the street and knocked that. After a few moments there was a rustling sound within, then the tread of footsteps.

The man who opened the door had a broad nose and exceptionally strong chin. His greying hair was shoulderlength, and greasy. It gave the impression of not having seen soap and water in a long while.

'Jah?'

'We wished to speak to Mr Furness but he doesn't appear to be there this morning. Have you any idea when he or any of his staff will be?'

The man's eyes narrowed slightly. When he spoke it was in the same guttural language that rotten teeth had used.

'I'm sorry I don't speak Afrikaans. Do you speak English?'

The man rattled off a reply, then spat into the street just as the woman on the verandah had done.

Alice exlaimed in disgust as he spat.

He understood her all right, Sarah thought. She could read so in his eyes. But he was refusing to speak English.

She turned round and beckoned the driver. 'Do you speak Afrikaans?' she asked him when he joined them.

The driver glanced nervously at the man, then nodded. She repeated to the driver what she'd asked the man, and requested he put it to the man in Afrikaans.

The driver was still talking when the man took a step backwards and slammed the door in their faces.

'Really!' Alice exclaimed, outraged that Sarah should be shown such behaviour.

'Don't forget their people and ours are at war,' Sarah said softly.

The driver swallowed hard, his slightly bulging eyes showing the fear he was feeling.

'We'd better return to the hotel for now. We can come back later,' Sarah said to Alice.

Alice was relieved to hear they were leaving there, but not at all pleased to know they'd be coming back again. She thought of that with trepidation.

The driver assisted Sarah and Alice into the carriage, after which he literally leapt into his seat. He cracked his whip, then cracked it again, taking them away from there far more quickly than he'd brought them.

'I have to say, Lady Ascog, that you look absolutely stunning,' John Buchan smiled.

'Why thank you, Mr Buchan. You are *très galant.*'

'Call me John, please.'

'Only if you call me Sarah.'

He gave her a little bob of the head. 'Thank you, Sarah.'

Alice came into the room with a light cloak that she draped over Sarah's shoulders. 'Have a lovely evening, your Ladyship.'

'I'm certain I shall. And what will you do?'

'I have a good book to catch up on.'

'Ah! You enjoy reading,' John said.

'Oh yes, sir. There's nothing better than a good book.'

'I couldn't agree more. I dabble a bit myself, you know.'

'Really!' Sarah exclaimed. 'You mean you've actually written a book?'

'A number, actually. I'll tell you all about them on the way to Government House.'

And he did, keeping Sarah enthralled during the entire journey which she ended up wishing was longer than it actually was.

'Vicountess Ascog, Sir Alfred Milner,' John introduced.

Sarah's first impression of the High Commissioner for South Africa and Governor of the Cape Colony was that here was a shy, austere, melancholy person. He had a long, thin face with downcast grey-brown eyes. He made Sarah think of a sad dog.

'Welcome to Cape Town, Viscountess, I hope your stay will be a happy and fruitful one.'

'I'm sure it will, Sir Alfred.'

'And this is Lady Edward Cecil,' Sir Alfred said, gesturing to the woman on his left.

'How nice to meet you,' Lady Edward smiled.

'And for I to meet you,' Sarah smiled in return.

The four of them chatted for a few moments, then Sarah and John moved on as new guests arrived whom Sir Alfred would have to receive.

'Lady Edward is the Prime Minister's daughter-in-law,' John explained quietly to Sarah when they were out of earshot. 'She's married to Major Lord Edward Cecil who was second-in-command to Baden-Powell at the siege of Mafeking.'

'She's a striking woman.'

'Sir Arthur thinks the world of her. His godsend, he calls her.'

A waiter approached them carrying a tray of champagne. Sarah declined for the moment, but John had a glass.

'Cape or French?' Sarah queried in a whisper, eyes twinkling mischievously.

'Cape. Sir Alfred wouldn't dare serve otherwise with some of those present,' John whispered in reply. Then, 'Do you see that stout fellow over there beside the pillar? The one talking to the lady in turquoise.'

Sarah spotted the man. 'Yes, I see him.'

'He owns a great deal of the land, and the vineyards on that land, surrounding Stellenbosch, one of the main centres for the Cape's winemaking industry. He's a very rich and powerful gentleman.'

Who likes his own product, judging by the looks of him, Sarah thought. He had a bright puce complexion and a large-veined reddish nose.

Sarah gazed about her. What passed for Cape society was a mixed bag as far as she could make out. A great many dress uniforms in evidence as a reminder that a bloody war was taking place in the north.

A stocky chap in ill-fitting tails came swaggering over. 'Hello, Buchan, how are you this evening?'

The voice was guttural and abrasive. The accent not at all a pleasant one. An Afrikaner, Sarah thought.

'Viscountess Ascog, may I introduce you to Mynheer Klopper. The Viscountess is newly arrived from Scotland, Mynheer.'

Klopper took Sarah's hand in his own huge, rough one and kissed the back of it. 'Delighted, Viscountess. Delighted.'

'And I'm delighted to meet you, Mynheer Klopper.' She was pleased with herself that she hadn't stumbled over the unfamiliar word Mynheer.

Klopper released Sarah's hand to stare at her in what could only be described as an impertinent fashion. And behind the impertinence something else, a lascivious sizing up of her. As if he was mentally imagining her stripped naked. And more.

Sarah felt her neck colour.

'Mynheer Klopper fought against us, didn't you, Mynheer?' John said levelly.

'Oh, jah! I did indeed, Buchan, as you well know.' Then, to Sarah, 'I was amongst those who surrendered with General Cronje at Paardeberg a year last February to your Field-Marshall "Bobs". On that day I made my peace with the British.' The Field-Marshall 'Bobs' he was referring to was Field-Marshall Lord Roberts, VC, British Commander-in-Chief, and hero of the march to Kandahar.

Sarah nodded, not sure what to reply to that.

Klopper, eyes glinting, went on. 'I was with Cronje at Magersfontein where many of your Scottish countrymen were killed. We were in trenches, they attacked. Let me see if I can recall the regiments now!' And with that Klopper pretended to think back, to recollect.

Sarah glanced at John who'd gone tight round the jaw. Klopper was getting at the pair of them, she realised, for John was also a Scot, having been born in Perth.

'The Seaforths,' Klopper smiled. 'And the Argylls. And then there was the Black Watch, the Gordons, the Highland Light Infantry. Brave men we'd been told, but not brave enough. For as you will remember, Buchan, they broke and ran.'

It was true, Buchan couldn't deny it. Nine hours of terror, boredom, being without water and with a scorching sun blasting down had finally combined to accomplish what up until then withering Mauser fire had failed to do.

'How many were killed again?' Klopper asked, still smiling.

'Nine hundred something, I believe.'

'That's right. Nine hundred and two to be precise. With only two hundred and thirty-six lost on our side. A remarkable victory for the volk, eh?'

'Yes, a remarkable victory,' John agreed. He paused, then added icily, 'Irrelevant, however, for in the end you'll lose the war.'

Klopper's smile changed to a scowl, knowing in his heart of hearts, and despite desperately wishing it otherwise, that what Buchan said was correct. Ultimately the British would win, overwhelming numerical superiority on their part would assure it.

That, and the terrible international loss of face they would have to endure if they didn't.

'Now, if you'll excuse us,' John said, and taking Sarah by the arm led her away.

'What an odious creature. Quite foul,' Sarah declared.

'He is rather. What you have to appreciate though is that the Boers truly hate us. There isn't one of them, male or female, who wouldn't stick a knife in a British back if they thought they could get away with it.'

'That look he was giving me made me want to slap him silly.'

'Yes, I must apologise for that.'

She turned to John. 'There's no reason why you should apologise. It was hardly your fault that he was so . . . well, so lecherously rude.'

'How about that champagne now?'

'Please.'

He beckoned over a waiter, handed Sarah a glass, then swapped his now empty one for a full one.

'Did the Highlanders really break and run?' Sarah asked softly.

'I'm afraid so. Almost unbelievable with their military record, but happen it did. The whole engagement was an awful mistake, of which we've made far too many in this war. But as I told Klopper, we'll win in the end, of that there is no doubt.'

She wondered how old John was. A couple of years younger than herself, she guessed. And she was right, he was twenty-six to her twenty-eight.

'I can see two people who will be absolutely furious if I don't introduce them to you,' John said.

'Oh?'

'Would you mind?'

'Not in the least.'

'Come on then.'

The two men were standing apart talking in low undertones, as if exchanging secrets. They abruptly stopped speaking as soon as they realised that John and Sarah were joining them.

'Viscountess Ascog, may I introduce you to Mr Alfred Beit. Mr. Beit, Viscountess Ascog.'

Beit was short, plump and bald, with large, pale, luminous eyes. 'Great pleasure to meet you, Viscountess,' he said, and shook hands with Sarah. Directly the handshake was over he tugged nervously at his grey moustache.

'And this is Mr Barney Barnato.'

'How are you enjoying Cape Town so far, Lady Ascog?' Barnato inquired in a pronounced cockney accent as he shook hands with her.

'Very much. Though to be truthful I haven't seen a great deal of it yet.'

'If God was to come down to live on earth, he'd live in Cape Town,' Barnato enthused.

'I thought he already did, out at Groote Schuur,' Beit commented drily.

Barnato sniggered at this witticism. 'Have you met C.J. yet?' he inquired of Sarah.

'I'm afraid I'm lost. C.J. who?'

'C.J. who!' Barnato laughed, and slapped his thigh, thinking that priceless.

Sarah looked to John for help.

'Cecil Rhodes,' John explained. 'Groote Schuur is the name of his home. It means Great Barn.'

She turned again to Barnato and Beit. 'No, I'm afraid I haven't.'

'Then we've met you before him. He'll be livid!' Beit said with clear self-satisfaction.

'I thought he would have been here this evening?' Barnato queried of John.

'He was invited of course, but according to the reply we had to his invitation he isn't feeling too well.'

'Nothing terminal I hope,' Barnato smiled.

Sarah thought that an awful thing to say. For although it might have been said as a joke there was obviously a large element of wishful thinking behind it.

'I wonder ...' mused Beit, tugging nervously again at his moustache.

'What, Alfred?' Barnato asked.

'It's unlike him to miss a reception at Government House. Now it may be that he isn't well as he claims, on the other hand, could he be up to something? You know C.J!'

Barnato's good humour vanished. 'What sort of something?'

Beit shrugged. 'With him, who knows?'

Barnato was now twitchy and agitated. 'Perhaps we should drive out to Groote Schuur to wish him a speedy return to health?'

'Exactly what I was thinking,' Beit agreed.

'Right away?'

'Right away,' Beit further agreed.

The two men excused themselves, then hurried off, the pair of them walking so fast they were almost running.

'What was all that about?' Sarah asked.

'Do you know who Rhodes is?'

'I have heard of him, yes.'

'And Beit and Barnato?'

She shook her head.

'All three are what's known here as "gold bugs" and Rand Lords. They own gold mines on Witwatersrand, hence the nicknames. Barnato and Rhodes are also co-directors of De Beers diamond monopoly, which was the foundation of their individual fortunes. Beit also started in Kimberley, as did most of South Africa's other multi-millionaires.'

'They're that rich?' Sarah said.

'Wealth beyond your wildest dreams. And the funny thing is that not one of them doesn't want to get wealthier. It's become like a game between them, each trying to outdo the other.'

'I take it none of them was born to money?'

'Barnato is a good example. He's a Whitechapel Jew who came out here as a travelling salesman touting cigars and braces round the diamond diggings, buying up claims with the money he made from music-hall turns and the winning share of prizefight purses.'

'Fascinating,' Sarah breathed. As a young man Jock would have loved this country, she thought. He would have taken to it like the proverbial duck to water.

'As for Rhodes –'

'Good evening, Mr Buchan.'

Neither John or Sarah had seen or heard the newcomer approach them.

'Superintendent, how are you?' John replied.

'Never better, sir.'

'Viscountess Ascog, may I present Superintendent Wetherspoon of the Cape Town Police.'

The customary pleasantries were exchanged, then John explained to Sarah, dropping his voice, 'You asked me to find out all I could about your friend Furness, a brief I handed over to Superintendent Wetherspoon, who has the reputation of being one of our most able senior officers.'

'I see,' Sarah said, nodding.

'Are you wishing to speak now about Furness?' John asked Wetherspoon.

'On being told by one of the other guests that this was Lady Ascog I thought I might take the opportunity. However, if it's inconvenient we can talk tomorrow.'

John glanced at Sarah.

'It's fine by me,' Sarah said.

John gave Wetherspoon the nod to go ahead.

'Mr Furness was unknown to us until you mentioned him, sir, which means he has no criminal record in the Cape. When we discovered that he came to Kaapstad from Jo'burg I contacted my colleagues there inquiring about him. Thankfully the Zarps' records were captured intact when the city was retaken, which enabled my colleagues to confirm that he's also clean in Jo'burg and the Transvaal.'

'Kaapstad? Zarps?' Sarah queried.

'Sorry, your Ladyship. Kaapstad is Afrikaans for Cape Town – I've just been talking to an Afrikaner – and Zarps is from Zuid Afrika Republik which the Afrikaner Jo'burg police had written on their shoulder flashes.'

'They were hated by the Uitlanders,' John further explained.

Sarah laughed. All these new words were suddenly coming thick and fast. 'Uitlanders?'

'Foreigners,' John smiled. 'It usually means English speakers.'

'Of which there are a great many in Transvaal and Jo'burg in particular, thanks to the mines,' Wetherspoon said.

'You talk of these people in the past tense; does that mean they're no longer in control in Johannesburg?' asked Sarah.

'They escaped from the city when it was retaken, and fought as a unit under General Botha at the battle of Bergendal, where they were annihilated after – it has to be admitted – fighting extremely bravely and well,' John said.

Wetherspoon went on. 'After they'd fled the city during its recapture, English-speaking police officers were drafted in to take over their duties.'

'I understand now,' Sarah said. 'But why were they hated by the Uitlanders?'

'They were brutal and cruel to the English speakers. Very much so,' John replied.

'In fact it was an incident by them when they shot and killed an innocent English working man that sparked off this entire conflagration. They were the match that lit the fire,' Wetherspoon elaborated.

John had a swig of his champagne. 'Leaving the Zarps, what else have you found out about Furness, Superintendent?'

'Not a great deal. He was in business in Jo'burg in a small way, now he's in business here in a bigger one. *J. Hawke & Daughter* are his largest clients, the others tiddlers by comparison.'

'I've called on him several times now at his business premises but there has never been anyone there,' Sarah said to Wetherspoon.

'That's because he's currently in PE, Lady Ascog.' Then, seeing Sarah's expression, 'Sorry, Port Elizabeth. It's in the Eastern Cape.'

'And what's he doing there?' Sarah probed.

'Arranging a consignment of stinkwood to be shipped to Japan.'

'Stinkwood!' Sarah exclaimed.

'A South African wood that's highly prized not only here but in other parts of the world,' Wetherspoon explained.

Sarah was still puzzled. 'I can understand him being away on business, but why are his premises closed? Are you saying he's a one-man band?'

Wetherspoon became embarrassed. 'No, he does have a permanent secretary who usually holds the fort, so to speak. But she . . .' He cleared his throat. 'She and Furness are apparently, eh . . . Well, let me put it this way, she's gone to PE with him.'

Sarah couldn't help but smile at Wetherspoon's embarrassment. Was it because she was a woman? Titled? Or both? 'You mean they're having a relationship together?'

'So I'm led to believe,' he replied, his gaze fixed on the floor.

'Do you know when they'll be back?' John asked.

Wetherspoon looked at him. 'Some time Tuesday, my sources said.'

'Then I'll call on him on Wednesday,' Sarah declared.

'Do you want me to accompany you?' Wetherspoon queried.

Sarah thought about that. 'No, I don't think so. I don't want to alarm him until I've at least had a chance to go through his books, or those sections of his books relating to our firm anyway.'

'You're still convinced he's a crook, then?'

'Has the Cape economy fallen away during the past months, Superintendent?'

Wetherspoon shook his head. 'On the contrary, from what I understand it's hitting new heights.'

'Then my father and I are still convinced he's on the fiddle with us,' Sarah said firmly.

'Now what about Charles Burnet?' John prompted.

'Another seemingly honest businessman who about a year ago apparently developed a taste for the card tables. Then one day he just dropped out of sight and was never seen locally again.'

'Do you think he's left the country?' Sarah asked.

'We're still trying to find that out. I can certainly say that he hasn't left Cape Town by ship, at least not under the name of Charles Burnet. Nor Durban, that has also been confirmed.'

They spoke for a few minutes more, then Wetherspoon took his leave of Sarah and John, returning to Mrs Wetherspoon whom he'd left chatting to friends.

'Burnet's disappearance would seem to be most mysterious,' John said.

'Yes.' She lapsed into a brooding silence, going over in her mind what Superintendent Wetherspoon had told them.

'Would you like to dance?'

'Why not!' she replied, snapping out of her reverie. They got rid of their glasses and then joined those already dancing, a colourful swirl of people, some of whom were more exuberant than accomplished.

Sarah and John were laughing when they eventually came off the floor, intent on having a breather and another glass of bubbly.

'You wait here and I'll hunt down a waiter,' John said, and left her.

Sarah gazed about. She was having a smashing time, thoroughly enjoying herself.

The man was sitting close to a window deep in conversation with a pretty blonde-haired young lady. His face struck a chord; she was sure she knew him.

He was deeply tanned, as were many of the males present, with hair that was swept straight back from his forehead. The lower part of his face was covered by a thick beard and moustache.

And then the penny dropped. 'My God!' she breathed. The man she was staring at was Adam Tennant.

Chapter 10

'Hello, Adam, it's been a long time.'

Adam glanced up at Sarah, and his jaw dropped.

'I was as surprised to see you,' she smiled.

'Sarah Hawke! Of all that's holy!' And having said that he rose to his feet.

'Adam Tennant, I'd like you to meet John Buchan, who's my escort tonight.'

'Pleased to meet you,' John said, and the two men shook hands.

'And this is Gillian Garlicke.'

'Pleased to meet you, Mrs Hawke,' Gillian said, having spotted Sarah's wedding ring.

'Not Mrs Hawke, but Monteith.'

Adam was even more bewildered. 'But I thought . . . Wilson was the name you told me.'

'I never married Mathew Wilson, instead I married a chap called Ian Monteith.'

'But . . .' Adam shook his head. 'So many questions, I don't know where to start.'

'I take it the pair of you are old chums?' Gillian smiled.

'We're both Glaswegians,' Sarah explained. 'Adam used to work for my father before he went to Art School and became a painter. I'm also great friends with his sisters, Olivia and Primrose.'

'How . . . ?' Adam bit his lip.

'They're married now. Primrose to an army captain who's out here fighting.'

Adam nodded, then turned to Gillian. 'I lost touch with my family some years back. It's a long story.'

'You stopped writing to them,' Sarah said quietly, her tone ever so slightly reproving.

'When I was still in Spain,' Adam answered, just as quietly.

John's eyes flicked between Sarah and Adam – he could sense undercurrents here, and guessed that Sarah and Adam wanted to talk alone for a while. If so, he'd endeavour to provide the opportunity.

'Miss Garlicke, would you care to take a turn round the dance floor with me?' John proposed. 'It'll give these two a chance to catch up on each other.'

Gillian didn't see any harm in that. Why not! 'Of course, I'd be delighted to.'

When Gillian had taken his arm John gave a small bow. 'Mr Tennant, Lady Ascog.' He'd been using Sarah's Christian name, as she'd requested, when they were alone together, but preferred, as a matter of form, to use her title when with others.

'What did he just call you?' Adam queried after John and Gillian had left them.

How much older he looked, she thought. There had always been a boyish element about him before, but not now. That was completely gone. The new lines in his face, combined with the tan, moustache and beard made him quite rugged in appearance.

'Lady Ascog.'

A bemused expression came over his face. 'You married a lord, then?'

'A Viscount to be precise.'

'Which makes you a Viscountess.'

'That's right. Viscountess Ascog when being formal, Lady Ascog for other occasions and situations.'

'Well I'll be . . .' he shook his head again.

'Did you ever marry?'

'No.'

She wanted to ask why, but thought that would be rude. And what if it was because of her? Then it would be embarrassing.

'So what are you doing in . . .' They broke off and laughed, both having started simultaneously to ask the same question.

'You first,' she said.

'I'm here as an artist, or illustrator, for the *Illustrated London News,* and have been in South Africa as such for the past two years. Normally I'm far upcountry, but was sent to Cape Town for convalescence a month ago.'

'Convalescence?'

'I caught a bullet in my right shoulder while with Colonel Douglas Haig. On leaving hospital I was packed off down here to rest and recover, and will be rejoining Haig or whomever when the medics consider me fully fit again.'

Revelation upon revelation, Sarah thought. 'And when will that be?'

'Any day now, I should think.' He flexed his right arm for her. 'Good as new, see!'

'We had no idea that you had become an illustrator, or were in this part of the world. Not that we had any notion where you were, mind you, but we never dreamt it was South Africa.'

'And you say that Ollie and Primrose are now married?'

'Both happily. Ollie is a Mrs Archibald McQueen. Her husband works in a bank.'

Adam smiled ruefully. 'My father would certainly approve of that; jobs don't come more respectable. Is he nice?'

'Who, Archibald? Yes, very.'

He heard the reservation in her voice, and also saw it in her face. He immediately guessed why. 'But boring, is that it?'

'I have to admit he's somewhat staid.'

Sounded dreary as hell, Adam thought. 'And what about Primrose's husband?'

'Jack's a different kettle of fish entirely. Full of personality, and funny with it. He's out here with the 60th Rifles.'

'What's his surname?' Adam queried.

'Tucker.'

Adam screwed up his forehead in concentration. 'I was briefly with the 60th some while ago, but don't remember a Captain Tucker. We can't have been introduced.'

'I'm certain you would recall him if you had been. He's not the sort of man you forget.'

Sarah glanced across at the dancers, immediately spying John and Gillian. The music stopped, and the dancers and some spectators applauded. John said something to Gillian, who nodded. They were going to stay up.

Sarah brought her attention back to Adam. 'I still can't believe this. How on earth did you become a newspaper illustrator?'

He sipped his drink, then said, 'From Spain, the last place I wrote home about, I went to the south of France where I lived for a few months, drawing and painting. But I didn't get on with the French as well as I had with the Spanish, and decided to go home when the money started getting thin on the ground. I had intended returning to Glasgow, but got stuck in London.

'I adored London, and sold quite a bit to begin with. Then that dried up and it was hard times again. One evening I was in a pub nursing a half pint and sketching a few of the characters round about when the chap who was sitting next to me struck up a conversation. His name was Fleetwood, and it transpired he was editor of the *Illustrated London News*. To cut a long story short he asked me if I'd be interested in doing some work for him and, needing the cash, I said yes. From there on in the whole thing just snowballed, with me ending up out here doing war illustrations for them.'

'And painting proper?'

He shrugged. 'I occasionally do a canvas, and eventually hope to return to it full time. In the meanwhile illustrating provides a tidy income, and is very satisfying to do.'

Sarah hesitated, then asked, 'Would you mind if I wrote to Ollie and Primrose telling them that we'd bumped into one another, and what you're doing out here?'

He considered that. 'Better still, if you give me their addresses I'll write to them myself. I should never have stopped, but . . . well, I did and let's just leave it at that.'

'You've never forgiven your father, then?'

'I don't think forgive is the proper word. I understand him a lot better than I did then. I don't wish to sound superior, or condescending, but he was merely a little man trying to do what he undoubtedly thought was right.' He paused, then asked, 'Are my parents both well?'

'Last time Ollie mentioned them to me they were. Maybe you should write to them too? For your mother's sake if not your father's.'

'I'll think about it,' he promised. 'But now, enough of me, what about you? Is your husband in Cape Town with you? And why are you here?'

'No, Ian isn't in Cape Town with me,' she replied in a voice that had suddenly gone brittle. 'You see he was killed in a riding accident last February.'

Adam stared at her, his expression one of shock. 'I am sorry. How awful.'

'I was with Ian when it happened. A hare leapt directly in front of his horse, and off he came. He broke his neck on landing.'

She took a deep breath, then another. 'At least there was no pain. I was thankful for that.'

Adam thought grimly of some of the deaths he'd witnessed since coming to South Africa. Men with limbs blown off, screaming in agony as their life's blood drained out of them, men with their bellies ripped open and their guts hanging out; one man in particular whom he'd never forget who'd been accidentally impaled. Horrible deaths from fevers, snakebites, sunstroke and dehydration.

'Yes, he was lucky there,' Adam agreed quietly.

'We have a son, Robert. A grand wee soul who's the spit of his dad.'

'How old is he?'

'Nearly ten months old,' Sarah smiled. 'My father and stepmother, with the help of a nanny, are looking after him while I'm away.'

'Your father married again, then?'

'It was a double ceremony, Jock and Maud, Ian and I. That was . . .' She did a rapid mental calculation. 'Five and a half years ago now.'

'You didn't have long together,' Adam sympathised.

'Not long, but what we had was good. I'd much rather have five good years than twenty bad ones.' She attempted a laugh which didn't come out sounding like a laugh at all.

An acquaintance passing by called to Adam, who waved a hand in acknowledgement.

'And coming to Cape Town?' he queried of Sarah.

'I suppose I could say convalescence, like you. We're having trouble with our agent here and Jock thought the trip would be beneficial to me.' She then went on to explain about Furness and Burnet. She had just come to the finish of that when John and Gillian reappeared.

'I mustn't monopolise you,' Sarah said to Adam, rising.

'I have a suggestion,' Gillian smiled. 'My family and I are having a few friends round tomorrow afternoon for a cookout. Perhaps you, Lady Ascog, and Mr Buchan would like to come?'

'Excuse my ignorance, but what's a cookout?' Sarah asked.

'Steaks, chops and suchlike cooked over an open-air charcoal fire. It's become quite the rage in Cape Town,' John explained.

'Adam will be there, so you two can chat further,' Gillian went on. It would be a definite social coup for her and her family to have Sarah visit them. Besides which, they were naturally friendly people who adored entertaining.

John looked at Sarah. 'I'm free if you are.'

'Done then, we'll come,' Sarah said to Gillian.

Gillian gave John her address, and while he was writing it down in his notebook Sarah told Adam that she'd bring Ollie and Primrose's addresses with her the next day.

The Garlickes' house was set on a cliff overlooking the ocean. Painted a gleaming white, the house was limited to two levels only, but was spread over a great deal of ground, making it a far larger house than it at first appeared.

Behind the house was a patio and garden, the garden ending abruptly at the cliff edge which wasn't sheer, but rather fell away at about a thirty-degree angle. Steps had been cut into the rockface, and handrails installed so that it was possible to go right down to the water.

'It's a beautiful location,' Sarah said to John, knowing the district was called Bantry Bay, John having told her that on their way there.

'That's the Atlantic Ocean,' John replied, pointing directly ahead of them. 'While on the other side of the Cape of Good Hope is the Indian Ocean, the nearest point to which is roughly eight miles east of here. In the summer Cape Towners and other locals bathe in the Atlantic because it's cool, while in the winter they use the Indian because it's warm.'

Sarah laughed. 'Is that true!'

'Yes, it is. Amazing, isn't it? Having different oceans on your doorstep to choose from in accordance with the time of year.'

'Are the two oceans different other than in temperature?' Sarah queried.

'Totally. The Atlantic, as you can see, is either blue or bluey-grey, and basically clear. The Indian on the other hand is green and cloudy, the latter I believe due to it being far saltier than the Atlantic.'

'And this difference in temperature is quite noticeable?'

'Oh quite! Taking a dip in the Indian is like having a tepid, or lukewarm bath; the Atlantic is a cool, bordering on cold, shower.'

Out of the corner of her eye she saw Adam coming over. 'I wonder when the food is going to be served, I'm starved!' she said to John.

'I have to admit, I'm somewhat peckish myself.' He sniffed the air. 'Gorgeous smell, don't you think?'

Sarah had to agree the aroma from the cooking wasn't only gorgeous, it was mouth-watering.

She glanced across to where the cooking was taking place. The fire itself was contained in a brick construction several feet high, with a metal grille laid over the top of this. The meat, watched and attended to by two black men, was being cooked on that.

'Hello again,' Adam smiled, joining them. So far the three of them had only had a few words together earlier when Sarah and John had been introduced around.

403

'I've just been hearing about the difference between the Atlantic and Indian Oceans,' Sarah said.

'I say, look!' exclaimed John, gesturing to a rock a short way out.

The seal that had clambered on to the rock gave what appeared to be a yawn, then settled down as if for a sleep. It closed one eye, but the other remained open, watching.

Sarah turned to Adam to discover he'd produced a sketchpad and was swiftly drawing. His pencil fairly flew over the paper as the seal and its surroundings quickly took shape.

When the sketch was completed he tore it from his pad and presented it to Sarah. 'Something to remember today by,' he smiled.

John peered at the sketch. 'That's excellent!'

'And so fast, too,' Sarah said.

'As an illustrator, particularly of war situations where events can change very rapidly, you have to learn to be fast,' Adam replied sombrely.

Sarah glanced again at the sketch. 'Now what shall I do with this until it's time to leave?'

'I'll take it to our carriage and have the driver look after it,' John suggested.

'Thank you.'

Sarah handed John the sketch, and he strode away, making for the front of the house where the carriages and several motorcars were parked.

'I want to mention again how sorry I am about your husband,' Adam said quietly to Sarah.

'Thank you.'

'And you with an infant son, too.'

She didn't comment about that, guilty about how she'd been towards the bairn since losing Ian.

'Can I ask something?'

She glanced at Adam.

'What happened between you and Wilson? I kept wondering that all last night. You seemed so set on him.' When Sarah didn't reply straight away he added apologetically, 'Sorry. If I'm being too inquisitive then just tell me to shut up.'

She certainly wasn't going to explain about Mathew catching syphilis from a Venezuelan whore – how humiliating and degrading that would be! But she could well understand why Adam wanted to know. After all, he'd been painfully in love with her himself at the time.

404

'There's no mystery. It just didn't work out between us. In the end we decided we weren't suited,' she lied.

'Oh!'

She thought of Mathew who, she'd heard, had been forced through ill health to give up the sea the year before. He'd retired home to Greenock, she'd been told, the breakdown in his health due to an illness he'd caught when abroad. That had made her smile, it being true enough as far as it went. Except the illness was called syphilis and he'd caught it in a tart's bed.

'And again if you don't mind me asking, how did you come to meet Viscount Ascog?'

'That was absolutely ages ago when ...' She broke off, recollecting. 'Wait a minute, you were there!'

'I was?'

'Do you recall the party Jock gave me at Stiellsmuir to celebrate the fact the firm had become *J. Hawke & Daughter*, the same party during which you invited me to your home to meet your sisters? Well, I met Ian for the first time that night.'

'As far back as that! Why that party was ...'

'Eleven years ago,' Sarah interjected. 'It was in the December of the same year I went to stay at Stiellsmuir.'

'Eleven years,' Adam mused. He'd forgotten he'd known Sarah so long. While on the other hand it seemed as if he'd known her forever.

'I remember how much I enjoyed that evening. It was a lovely party.'

'I enjoyed it too. Dancing with you was the highlight of it for me.'

She didn't reply to that.

'How young I was then. How young and dreadfully gauche.'

'Young, perhaps, but I wouldn't say gauche.' The fib was intended as a face-saver for him, for she had thought him that.

'Oh I was, Sarah! Gauche as can be. Wet behind the ears, and green as grass.'

She laughed. 'Now you really are going too far. It's beginning to sound like self-pity.'

She bit her lip. She hadn't meant to say that.

'Self-pity? I wouldn't agree, I've long since grown out of that. No, it's genuinely and objectively how I see myself as I was then.'

She stared into his eyes, and saw there that he didn't love her any more. That he'd long got over her. The spark of love he'd had for her had died, and blown away in the winds of time.

She was pleased about that. But also, she had to admit, somewhat saddened, for herself, not Adam. Selfish as it may be, it's a lovely thing to be loved, even when you can't return that love.

'You were always a good friend to me, Adam. I hope you'll continue to be,' she said softly.

'You can count on it. Just as I know I can count on your friendship.'

On impulse, and not caring who might be watching, she kissed him on the cheek. 'I'm glad I know you, Adam Tennant.'

'And I you, Sarah.'

Even though you've caused me a great deal of pain and suffering, she thought to herself, that being what Adam had left unspoken.

Strength, she thought, she could perceive a great deal of inner strength in Adam now. Before he'd been soft and malleable, as copper was. Now he was tempered steel.

'Food's about to be served,' Amy Garlicke, Gillian's younger sister, announced, joining them. Amy was an exceptionally good-looking girl, about eighteen years old and with a stunning figure. A sun-ripened South African peach.

Amy slipped an arm round Adam's. 'I've instructed the chief cook boy to see that you get the biggest and juiciest T-bone. How about that?' she purred.

Well, Sarah thought, there was one young lady who wasn't slow in coming forward.

Adam flashed Amy a broad smile. 'Sounds marvellous.'

John returned. 'That's the sketch safe,' he said to Sarah.

'Shall we, then?' Amy smiled, and pulled Adam in the direction of the fire where the servants began handing out stacked-high platters.

The older Adam certainly didn't lack for admirers, Sarah thought, with just the teensiest stab of jealousy.

Looking at Amy Garlicke, and Gillian who was only a few years senior, made her feel quite matronly. Which was ridiculous really, but it did nonetheless.

She turned her attention to John who'd started to speak as they followed on behind Adam and Amy.

She mustn't forget to give Adam those addresses before either of them left, she reminded herself. Olivia and Primrose would be thrilled to hear from him.

*

On Wednesday morning, with Alice accompanying her, Sarah again presented herself at Furness's office. This time her knocking was answered by an attractive woman, if slightly coarse in appearance, whom Sarah judged to be in her mid twenties.

'Can I help you?' the woman asked pleasantly.

'My card,' Sarah replied.

The woman glanced at the card Sarah had given her, eyebrows shooting up as she read what was embossed there.

'I'd like to speak to Mr Furness,' Sarah stated.

The woman had become quite flustered. 'Yes, yes, of course, Viscountess. Please come on up.'

The stairs were bare and dirty, the walls screaming out for a fresh coat of paint.

'In here, please,' the woman requested, opening a door.

The sole occupant of the room was sitting behind a desk, a scattering of papers in front of him.

The carpet on the floor was old and threadbare in patches, the curtains hanging on the two windows of the same vintage. About a third of the way along the right-hand wall was a door. The overall impression was seedy in the extreme.

Furness frowned to see Sarah and Alice. 'Yes, Miss Kaufmann?'

Miss Kaufmann crossed to Furness and handed him Sarah's card. 'I thought I'd better bring the Viscountess straight up,' she said.

Furness jumped to his feet. 'Welcome Viscountess, eh . . .' He had another quick look at the card. 'Viscountess Ascog. Please be seated.'

The chair he placed in front of his desk was old, like everything else in the office, and rickety.

'This is my personal maid,' Sarah explained, gesturing to Alice who'd taken up a position by her side.

Furness, once more behind his desk, flashed Alice a smile, then brought his attention back to Sarah. 'Can I offer you something? A sherry? Or a cup of tea, perhaps?'

'No, thank you,' Sarah replied, keeping her voice neutral.

Furness clasped his hands together and smiled broadly at Sarah. 'Now what assistance can I be to you, Viscountess?'

'You call her your Ladyship,' Alice said, conferring on him the status of employee or menial.

'My apologies, your Ladyship,' Furness said instantly. 'You must appreciate that we're not used to dealing all that much with the nobility in Cape Town.'

Sarah winced inwardly. The man was a clod, but a smooth clod. Cheap, that was another word she would have applied to him. The suit he was wearing was appallingly tailored, his rings and other jewellery ostentatious and vulgar.

She wondered about his accent, certainly English, Midlands perhaps. She wasn't all that *au fait* with regional English accents. In fact, Furness was from Salford.

'You're the South African agent for the Glasgow firm of *J. Hawke & Daughter*,' she said.

He nodded. 'That's correct.'

'I'm the daughter.'

Furness's broad smile sort of slipped off his face and for a brief second there was panic in his eyes. 'I beg your pardon?'

'I'm the daughter, Mr Furness. My maiden name was Hawke.'

Furness fumbled in a pocket to produce a packet of cigarettes. 'Do you mind if I smoke?' he asked.

'Not in the least.'

He was about to extract one, then remembered his manners. The smile came back on to his face. 'How about you, your Ladyship?'

'I do, but not now, thank you.'

He lit up, nor did Sarah fail to notice that his hands were trembling ever so slightly. He wasn't even an accomplished crook, she thought, but the third-rate variety. Furness was going to rue the day he'd had the idea to defraud Jock Hawke.

'Well, well,' Furness said. 'And what brings you to South Africa?'

'This and that,' she replied ambiguously.

He gestured about him. 'Please excuse these offices, they're only temporary. A stop-gap until the ones I have my eye on become available.'

'They're not exactly salubrious, are they?'

'No, not exactly.'

He didn't know what salubrious meant, she thought. But he'd got the drift.

'I'm surprised you didn't keep on Mr Burnet's offices in Waterkant Street when you took over our agency from him,' she said.

'Ah! There was a slight problem there.'

She didn't say anything, forcing him to elaborate.

'To do with the other tenants in the building,' Furness went on. 'In the end I decided I'd prefer to be elsewhere.'

Sarah glanced at Miss Kaufmann who looked as though if she'd said boo! to her she'd have jumped a foot in the air.

Sarah couldn't resist it. 'How was your trip to Port Elizabeth?' she asked Furness.

He swallowed hard. 'You know about that?'

'I called here several times last week. I found out then.'

Furness's eyes flicked to Miss Kaufmann, then back again to Sarah.

'The very least I can do in the circumstances is offer you lunch. I know a tip-top . . .'

'Thank you, but I already have a luncheon appointment,' she lied.

He appeared relieved to hear that.

'In the meantime, as I'm here, perhaps I might have a look through your books, or those sections of your books relating to our firm.' That wasn't a request, but a statement of intent.

His eyes narrowed. 'Why should you want to do that, your Ladyship?'

'Routine, nothing more,' she lied.

'I see. I understand.' He puffed on his cigarette, then asked, 'How far back would you like to go?'

'You have Burnet's books as well, then?' She was curious about that.

'Naturally.'

'I think the last year would be fine, thank you very much.' He'd been their agent for eleven months now.

He signalled to Miss Kaufmann. 'Bring the blue ledger through please, Miss Kaufmann.'

'Yes, Mr Furness, right away.'

Miss Kaufmann went to the door in the right-hand wall, opened and went through it.

Sarah glimpsed another office, Miss Kaufmann's presumably, just as seedy as the one she was in.

Furness rose. 'You'd better sit here, your Ladyship. More comfortable for you.' As he spoke he gathered up the papers atop the desk and slipped them into a drawer.

'Are you certain you won't have that sherry or tea? How about coffee?' he pressed.

'No, thank you, Mr Furness.' She sat in the seat he'd just vacated, and moments later Miss Kaufmann returned with a thick blue ledger.

'As you'll soon see *J. Hawke & Daughter* are our main clients,' Furness said as Miss Kaufmann placed the ledger in front of Sarah.

Sarah opened the ledger, and flicked through to the last page of entries. 'I'll also want receipts, invoices, bills of sale, all corroborating documentation,' she stated mildly, expecting him to balk at that. But he surprised her by not doing so.

'Could you fetch those as well, please,' he instructed Miss Kaufmann.

'According to the figures you've been sending us in Glasgow profits have gone into decline during the past months.'

'I think that's because the war is almost over. Demand for many items has been slipping,' he countered.

'I didn't realise the war was almost concluded, Mr Furness?'

'Oh yes. Brother Boer is on his knees. What's left of Brother Boer anyway!' And having said that Furness laughed.

'I would have thought Sir Alfred Milner would have mentioned the fact when we discussed the war the other night,' she riposted with a smile.

'You know Milner!'

'He invited me to a reception at Government House last Saturday,' she elaborated.

Was it her imagination, or was that a sheen of sweat that had appeared on Furness's brow?

'Tell me something before I start, Mr Furness.' She paused for effect, then asked, 'What's become of Mr Burnet? I've been trying to locate him but it appears he's dropped right out of sight. Has he left Cape Town, do you know?'

'I believe he has. Though I couldn't say where.'

'Pity. I did want to have a few words with him. He'd been our agent – and an excellent one too – for quite some while, you know.'

'Yes, I did know.'

'Strange, his disappearing like that. Was he a personal friend?'

'Not exactly. More of an acquaintance.'

'Only that!' She pretended surprise. 'And yet he recommended you to us?'

'He had every confidence in me through several dealings we'd had in the past. He also knew of my reputation.'

'Quite,' she murmured, staring at Furness.

'I bought the agency from him if that's what you're wondering.

410

For a fairly substantial sum actually. I understand there were a number of people interested in acquiring the agency, but he chose me, as he told me himself, because he knew he could trust me to do a good job for you.'

'With Mr Burnet's recommendation backing you we had no doubt about either your ability or integrity,' Sarah said. Which was perfectly true – the doubt and suspicion had come later.

Furness visibly relaxed on hearing that.

Miss Kaufmann returned with the filed documentation, placing it beside the blue ledger.

'It's just a pity about the war, though,' Sarah said, referring to his statement that the war was almost over.

'There are a lot of soldiers wouldn't agree with you!'

'Yes!' she laughed. 'I take your point.'

He relaxed even more, a certain pert cockiness taking over. 'I'll leave you to get on with it then, shall I?' Turning to Miss Kaufmann he went on, 'You remain here in case there's anything further her Ladyship needs or wants.'

'There's no necessity for Miss Kaufmann to stay,' Sarah protested. 'I'm sure I have everything I require.' When she saw his hesitation she added disarmingly. 'It's only a routine, cursory examination of your figures after all. I'm not the city auditor.'

He laughed, and so too did Sarah.

'Come along then, Miss Kaufmann, and I'll treat you to a coffee at Perle's.' To Sarah he said, 'Perle's serve by far the best coffee in Cape Town.'

'I'll remember that,' she nodded.

Miss Kaufmann collected her hat which she pinned on. 'I'm ready then,' she said to Furness. She too had relaxed during the past couple of minutes.

'About an hour?' Furness queried of Sarah.

'Make it an hour and a half, I'm not as clever or quick at figures as I might be,' she lied, disarming him even further.

When Furness and Miss Kaufmann were gone Sarah whispered to Alice to go to one of the windows and check that they had actually left the building.

'They're away,' Alice confirmed as Furness and Miss Kaufmann headed on up the street.

'So what do you make of him, then?' Sarah asked, Alice being in her confidence about the reason behind her trip to Cape Town.

411

'Well, let me put it this way, if I shook his hand I'd count my fingers afterwards.'

Sarah laughed, a genuine laugh this time. That was Furness to a T.

She laid out a small jotting book she'd brought with her, then got down to his figures.

With a sigh Sarah refolded the letter she'd received from Jock, and replaced it in its envelope. It was her first letter from home since her arrival.

According to Jock, Robert was well and appeared to be enjoying his stay at Stiellsmuir, as Jock and Maud were thoroughly enjoying having him there.

Everything at the house and on the estate was running smoothly, Walsh continuing to do an expert job with the latter.

They'd had a lot of unseasonal rain, but the forecast was that September would be warmer than usual. How was she enjoying the Cape Town climate? They were all envying her that.

And what about the Furness business? Jock was dying to hear.

Sarah wiggled the envelope in front of her, then tossed it down beside a huge bowl of fruit that the hotel management provided daily.

A smile of grim satisfaction crossed her face. The most interesting part of Jock's letter was that Ranald Cyril McIvor had decided to retire and had duly put the firm of McIvor, McIvor and Devereaux up for sale.

The letter that Ian had circulated to every British embassy and consulate had cooked McIvor's goose. His trade had fallen right away to become a mere rump of what it had been at its height. The last years had been a desperate struggle for McIvor, and now he'd finally chucked in the towel.

That pleased her; it pleased her enormously. Served him right for what he'd tried to do to her, and Jock, through Moffat.

If only Jock could buy McIvor, McIvor and Devereaux! That would really be sweet revenge. But she doubted McIvor would sell to Jock. Anyone but Jock.

Still, you never knew. She would mention it to Jock in the reply she was about to write him.

Ian and his letter, and the smashing time they'd had in Paris when he'd done so much to help her. The memory brought a lump to her throat.

Ian, how she missed him.

She wiped her nose with her hanky, then went to search out her writing materials.

She would write to Jock, after which she'd pen a note to Superintendent Wetherspoon.

'Everything balanced, there wasn't a single item I could fault him on,' Sarah said.

Wetherspoon nodded, stirring his tea.

'It was the receipts, invoices, bills of sale that amazed me; without exception they tallied with the entries.'

'And yet you still think he's a crook?'

'Oh yes, he's that all right, a cheap smoothie, a clod and a crook. But not quite as stupid as I initially took him to be.'

'Another crumpet, Lady Ascog?' Wetherspoon asked her, extending a plate on which there were several left, the pair of them having already had one each.

'No thank you, Superintendent. I don't like them nearly as much as Scots crumpets.'

'There's a difference?'

'Oh totally! Scots crumpets are rolled thin, brown on one side, yellowish on the other, and served cold. Nothing whatever like these English ones.'

'Well, well!' murmured Wetherspoon, thinking you learn something new every day. Even if it was only the difference between Scots and English crumpets.

'I've discovered more about Furness himself,' he said.

Sarah raised an eyebrow.

'Originally he came out to South Africa to try his luck as a digger on the Rand. He stuck it for a while, without success. Then he gave that up and went into business, where he at least started to make money, if not a great deal.'

'He doesn't look the physical type to me. I can't see him knocking his pan out with spade and shovel.'

'Something else, your Ladyship. He's a bit of a gambler. Track and casino, he loves them both.'

Her memory flashed back to the conversation she'd had with Wetherspoon at Sir Alfred's reception. 'Didn't you tell me that Burnet had developed a taste for the card tables?'

'Exactly what struck me. There could be a connection. If only we could find Burnet.'

'Still no sign of him?'

'Not a whisper. It's as if the earth has just opened and swallowed him up.' Wetherspoon gave a small laugh. 'Mind you, that has literally happened in South Africa before now.'

'What about Burnet's home?' Sarah queried.

'He was unmarried, and lived in a rather nice house out at Bloubergstrand, which he owned—or still owns as the case may be.

'There are still personal effects there which could mean a number of things. It could mean he's gone off intending to return; then again it could also mean he's gone and wants us, or anyone else looking for him, to think he's going to return when in actual fact he has no intention of doing so. There again he could be lying dead somewhere, which isn't as unlikely as it may sound.'

'When you say dead, do you mean murdered?' Sarah queried.

'We have an extremely high incidence of murder in South Africa,' Wetherspoon replied ominously.

'What about him having lost his memory?'

'That too is a possiblity, though becoming more and more unlikely. If that had been the case I'm sure my people would have found him by now.'

'You think he's dead, don't you? You keep referring to him in the past tense.'

Wetherspoon wiped his face with his napkin. 'It's beginning to "feel" that way to me. I don't know why, just instinct.'

'That which makes you a good policeman?' she smiled.

'Amongst other things,' he prevaricated, ever so slightly embarrassed by her forthright compliment.

A woman in a particularly pretty dress walked by. A London or Paris garment, Sarah thought to herself. It had to be one or the other. Probably Paris, and very, very expensive.

'If Burnet has been murdered perhaps the motive was robbery?' she said. 'Furness did mention that he paid Burnet a substantial sum for the agency, though I suppose there's no reason why Burnet should be carrying that around as cash.'

'Interesting,' Wetherspoon mused. 'I've already checked Burnet's bank account which had only fifteen pounds in it. And there hadn't been much more than that in it for some time before his disappearance.'

'So he never banked the money Furness paid him?'

'Apparently not.'

'Then robbery could well be a motive?'

'I can't think why he would want to abscond with his own money, can you?'

Sarah couldn't. She glanced out of the conservatory windows at the Mount Nelson gardens beyond. 'Do you suggest the next move regarding Furness, or do I?'

Wetherspoon smiled, he liked that. 'What do you propose?'

She produced the jotting book she'd had with her in Furness's office, opened it and stared at what she'd noted inside. 'The first item we shipped out to South Africa was palm oil which we brought here from Nigeria, and continue to do so. According to Mr Furness's blue ledger the factory which buys that palm oil is located at a place called Rosebank. I think we should talk to the owner of that factory.'

It was precisely the step that Wetherspoon had next intended taking, though he hadn't narrowed it down to a specific firm, or firms, yet.

'When would you like to go there?' he queried.

'No time like the present. How about directly after we've finished tea?'

She certainly didn't let the grass grow under her feet, he thought. He wished that some of those under his command that he could think of were as enthusiastic and diligent.

'Fine,' he agreed.

She offered him the final English crumpet.

Rosebank was out past Groote Schuur, where Cecil Rhodes lived. The factory that Furness supplied with palm oil was a rambling wooden affair tucked in below a rock escarpment that towered overhead.

On entering the factory, Wetherspoon made himself and Sarah known, and they were ushered into the presence of the factory owner, a Mr Gerrard.

After introductions had been made, Sarah and Wetherspoon sat down, and coffee was sent for.

'How can I help you, Superintendent?' Gerrard, an oldish, crusty-looking individual queried.

'I understand you acquire the palm oil you use in making your soap from a Mr Theodore Furness,' Wetherspoon stated.

Gerrard's brow darkened. 'I do indeed, sir. Him and that roguish company he represents.' He was as yet unaware that Sarah was Jock Hawke's daughter.

'Why roguish, Mr Gerrard?' Wetherspoon asked softly.

'Since Furness became their agent their price has jumped a full thirty-three and a third per cent. That's daylight robbery in anyone's book!'

Wetherspoon glanced at Sarah, who shook her head. 'We haven't increased our price for some while,' Sarah told him.

Wetherspoon explained to Gerrard. 'Lady Ascog is the daughter in *J. Hawke & Daughter*. The idea of bringing palm oil to South Africa from Nigeria was hers in the first place.'

'It was a brilliant idea, and an opportunity I grabbed with both hands,' Gerrard said. 'But what do you mean your price hasn't been increased for some while? I can assure you it has.'

'Furness hasn't received any instruction from us to implement a price increase, or increases, as the case may be. You have my word for that.'

Gerrard's expression became grim. 'Are you telling me that Furness has been lining his own pockets with my money?'

'Not only your money, Mr Gerrard,' she replied in a steely tone, 'but ours as well. Though that I still have to prove.'

Gerrard swore vehemently, then immediately apologised to Sarah for having done so in her company.

'That's all right, Mr Gerrard, I can well understand your feelings.'

A black man – or Bantu, as Sarah was learning to call the local black people – arrived with their coffee.

When the Bantu had left them, and the coffee had been poured, Sarah said, 'I wonder if I might make a request of you, Mr Gerrard?'

'Certainly, Lady Ascog.'

'Can I examine one of your receipts, please?'

That puzzled Gerrard. What did she want a receipt for? 'Of course, I have a pad of them right here.' Having said that he opened a drawer in his desk, took out a thick pad, got up, came round the desk and handed it to Sarah.

One look was enough for her. 'Have you recently changed the design of your receipts?'

Gerrard stared blankly at her. 'No.'

She turned to Wetherspoon. 'This isn't the same design receipt as those filed at Furness's. They are far plainer than these, and white, whereas these are green.'

'How can that be?' Gerrard questioned.

'You're absolutely certain of this?' Wetherspoon queried of Sarah.

'Absolutely. White and green with a totally different design on each.'

'Then the only explanation is,' Wetherspoon said slowly to Gerrard, 'that Furness is having receipts printed in your firm's name.'

'What!' Gerrard exploded.

'And if he's having receipts printed in your firm's name then it's a certainty that he's doing the same with his other major clients.'

Sarah took a deep breath, then went on, speaking to Gerrard. 'Our South African profits have dropped recently, which caused my father to smell a rat, as he couldn't think why they should have done so. I came out here specifically to find out what was going on. I've been through Furness's accounts, and was amazed to discover that everything tallied. Now I know why – his corroborative documentation is phoney.'

'Which means his returns to *J. Hawke & Daughter* are false,' Wetherspoon said to her.

'Exactly.'

'And not content with that he's also been upping my price so that he can make another layer of personal profit that way,' Gerrard said, clenching his hands into fists.

'Fraud and more fraud. But now we have him,' Wetherspoon smiled. He enjoyed working with Lady Ascog, he thought. She had the sort of mind he admired. They would have made a great team.

'This calls for something stronger than coffee,' Gerrard muttered, crossing to a cupboard.

'Brandy, Lady Ascog?' he asked over his shoulder.

'I believe I will, Mr Gerrard.' She was as pleased as punch that they'd nailed Furness. It hadn't been that difficult after all, as she'd feared it might be before arriving in Cape Town.

'Superintendent?'

'I shouldn't while on duty but . . .' He trailed off.

'You will anyway?' Gerrard prompted.

'I will anyway.'

Gerrard poured three liberal measures and handed them round. 'When will you nab him?' he asked Wetherspoon.

'I'll visit a few more of his major clients and pick up examples of their receipts, invoices etc. When I have a variety of those I'll arrest him, and his female friend Miss Kaufmann, for she's certainly in on this.'

'I wonder who does his bookwork?' Sarah mused. 'It was of a high standard, which he doesn't strike me as being capable of.'

'Probably has a book-keeper come in,' Wetherspoon said. The Indians – of whom we have a large contingent in Cape Town – are very good at that.'

Sarah frowned, then queried of Gerrard, 'One thing mystifies me. When Furness raised the price of our palm oil why didn't you just take your business elsewhere? I'm sure some of those others bringing palm oil into South Africa would have been able, and only too happy, to accommodate you.'

'Then Burnet never told you about our contract?'

Sarah shook her head. 'Neither my father nor I have ever heard of any contract involving you. In fact, because we only get a simplified financial statement back in Glasgow, I didn't know the name of your firm, far less its address, until I went through Furness's accounts.'

Gerrard had a gulp of brandy. 'When I initially approached Burnet about buying your palm oil he said he would only sell to me if I agreed to sign a loyalty contract. The deal was that I would be the first to have the Nigerian palm oil here, in return for which I had to remain loyal to Burnet and to *J. Hawke & Daughter*.

'When the quantity you were bringing in dropped off some years ago, Burnet allowed me to purchase from others, but as your quantity increased again so I had to revert back to you.'

Gerrard was referring to the time when Sarah had returned from the West Indies to find that five of their ships had been sold.

Gerrard went on. 'The contract was never a problem until Furness took over, when the price went haywire.'

'So you *had* to pay the increase, no matter what it was, because of the contract,' Sarah said.

'That's it, Lady Ascog. A contract I only signed in the first place because I desperately wanted that palm oil, and because Burnet was such a reputable man.'

'And if you hadn't paid the increase?' Sarah probed.

'Furness threatened to sue me for everything if I broke the contract. Which he could have done, and won the case I've no doubt.'

'What an unsavoury person Mr Furness is turning out to be,' Sarah mused.

'You were certainly right about him being a crook. He's that through and through,' Wetherspoon told her.

'Regarding the price I'm now paying . . .' Gerrard began.

Sarah cut in. 'Leave all that to me, Mr Gerrard. The next

418

consignment of palm oil you buy from us will be at the correct price, I promise you. And furthermore, whatever happens you'll be reimbursed for the extra you've been paying. I know my father would insist on that.'

Gerrard beamed.

When Sarah and Wetherspoon left the factory they had with them, Wetherspoon carrying Sarah's, gifts of soap from a grateful Gerrard. A dozen bars of Cape Orange, ladies' scented, for Sarah; a dozen bars of Cape White, gentlemen's plain, for Wetherspoon.

John Buchan listened intently as Sarah recounted the story to him.

'Good grief!' he muttered.

Sarah continued. 'Apparently what happened was that Burnet lost heavily to Furness in a card game, and didn't have the wherewithal to honour his IOU. Desperate, he offered Furness the one thing of value he had left which was the agency, and Furness accepted. For the agency, and most importantly Burnet's recommendation to my father, Furness tore up the IOU.'

'Wait a minute,' said John, frowning. 'Didn't you say that Burnet had a house in Bloubergstrand? Why didn't he sell that to offset his IOU?'

'I doubt that would have been enough. Anyway, as it transpired, Burnet had lost the house in another card game some time previously. The new owner, a friend of his, had allowed him to stay on there on a rental basis.'

Sarah drew deeply on her cigarette (she was still managing to keep her daily quota down, and was now thinking about giving them up altogether) then said, 'Acquiring the agency was the biggest thing that had ever happened to Furness, and he could have made a good living out of it, as Burnet had done before him. Except that he was too greedy. Why settle for a small slice of the cake, he thought, when with a bit of jiggery-pokery he could have a far bigger one.

'And so he fiddled the accounts with those phoney receipts, etc. of his, but well enough so that an independent auditor called in by us, the principals, would have been entirely fooled. What just never entered his head was, I suppose because of the distance involved, that we would come out and investigate ourselves. And not only check the accounts but take it further than that. Then, of course, the whole charade quickly fell apart.'

'And what about Burnet?'

She shook her head. 'That's still a mystery which Superintendent Wetherspoon is continuing to work on.'

John spotted a chum of his and waved. 'So how can I help you?' he asked Sarah. 'You stated in your note that you had a favour to ask.'

'I need someone to replace Furness as our agent, and wondered if you could suggest a suitable person? In your position I would think you were ideally placed to make a recommendation.'

He nodded. 'Leave it to me, Sarah. I'll instigate inquiries right away.'

'Good. Thank you.'

'I take it you'll want to get this matter resolved as soon as possible?'

'Please, John. I can handle things in the meantime. We have one of our ships docking at the beginning of next week and I shall deal with that. But I would like an agent to be appointed before the cargo after that arrives.'

'Now,' John said, fishing in an inside pocket, 'I have something for you.' He took out a heavily embossed card which he placed in front of Sarah.

'What's this?'

'Lady Edward Cecil is throwing a birthday party for Sir Alfred, and that is your invitation. She was about to send it on from Government House, but when I realised I would be seeing you today I brought it instead.'

Sarah picked up the card and stared at it. There was no reason why she shouldn't go. 'I'd be delighted to accept.'

'Topping! Would you like us to go together as we did to Sir Alfred's reception?'

'Would *you*, John?'

'Oh, yes, rather.'

She couldn't help but smile at his eagerness. The two of them had become close friends in a short time. They genuinely enjoyed being with one another without there being any romantic overtones whatever. John knew about Ian's death the previous February, though she hadn't told him. But then the High Commissioner's Private Secretary should know, as part of his job, the background and details of those important and influential visitors to South Africa.

Sarah went on to relate more about Furness and Miss Kaufmann. The latter now proved to be up to her neck in it, as Wetherspoon had said she was.

*

The Boer Commando comprising two hundred and fifty men was heading for Kiba Drift. Ahead of them lay a long dark line, the lip of the great canyon cut by the Orange River as it comes swirling out of the mountains of Basutoland.

For several days now the Commando had been scouring the brown veld to the north, hunting for a suitable drift. The Orange River was still low due to the spring rains not yet having broken, but every sandy footpath leading down to the river seemed to be blocked by files of white tents belonging to the hated khakis.

'Oom' Jannie glanced gloomily off to his right at the local farmer Commandant Wessels had found to guide them over the river. The farmer, a veteran of the Basuto war, was certain that the bridle path to Kiba Drift, the path to the Native Reserve at Herschel, was still open. He prayed that the farmer was right.

'Oom' Jannie thought of the country they had come through during the past couple of weeks. Dams everywhere full of rotting animals that rendered the water undrinkable. Veld covered with slaughtered herds of sheep, goats, cattle and horses. Death, destruction and horror everywhere. And everywhere, like an encirling human tidal wave, the British.

He thought of ammunition, and his mouth twisted downwards. The Commando desperately needed bullets for their Mausers. And food for their bellies; the burghers were starving. How long was it since they had last tasted hot coffee? He couldn't remember, it had been so long.

And tobacco. There wasn't one among the Commando who wouldn't have sold his soul for tobacco. Coffee and tobacco, there's nothing the Boer likes better, or feels the deprivation of more, than those two commodities.

The wind sighed, while overhead the low clouds scudded. At least they weren't short of horses, having almost two apiece, and pack animals. If only forage wasn't so scarce, but what else could they expect at that time of year?

Ammunition, medical supplies and food: they had to have those soon or they would be finished. They might just as well wait for the pursuing khakis and fight it out to the end, make a last-ditch stand of it.

Or surrender, there was always that alternative which so many of the burghers had recently taken.

Resolve filled him. He would never surrender. That way wasn't for him. They would never put him in one of their concentration camps as they called them – hell on earth they were known to be. No, he would fight and continue fighting till either he was dead, or the volk were triumphant.

Somewhere behind a horse snickered, followed instantly by a low word of reprimand from its owner.

With all metal parts of their gear and equipment bound and wrapped against making a noise, the Commando melted silently into the night.

'And then would you believe,' said Major Long to Sarah and others in their company, 'six of the blighters popped up and started blasting away.'

'No!' Sarah exclaimed.

'I swear it as God is my judge. As soon as they started blasting, the beggar with the white flag dropped out of sight. Four men I lost because of that. Four fine men.'

'It's not the first time that's been reported,' John Buchan said.

'Nor the last either I suppose,' commented Colonel Clery drily.

'So what did you do then?' Sarah asked Long.

'Charged them, of course, and captured them. And my goodness what a change of face then! As soon as we had them it was down on their knees squealing for mercy. Well, I gave them mercy all right.'

'You shot them?'

John was looking uncomfortable, which Long saw. And suddenly remembered who John was.

'We were attacked again shortly afterwards and they were all killed in that mêlée,' Long said.

Sarah stared into his face, and didn't believe a word of it. But how provoked Long and his men must have been. To renegue on a white flag was despicable.

'Excuse me, Lady Ascog, could I speak to you?'

She turned to find Adam by her side. She'd noted him earlier but hadn't had an opportunity to talk to him yet. 'Why yes, of course.'

'I'd like you to meet someone who's just this minute given me some rather upsetting news,' he said quietly.

Sarah excused herself, gave John a small, personal smile, then went with Adam in the direction of the main door leading from the ballroom.

'What's this all about?' she queried.

'I'll let Doyle explain.'

They left the ballroom, crossed a black and white marble-floored hall and plunged into a corridor. Some yards down the corridor Adam opened a door into a study where a solitary man was revealed sitting on a leather chesterfield drinking whisky. He rose as Sarah entered the room.

'Viscountess Ascog, I'd like to introduce you to Doctor Conan Doyle. Doctor Doyle, Viscountess Ascog.'

'Pleased to meet you, Doctor.'

'And I you, Lady Ascog.'

'I know Doyle from up-country where he's been working in various field hospitals,' Adam said to Sarah.

'I see.'

Doyle ran a hand through his hair. 'I've been sent back to Cape Town for a while before being reassigned. The powers that be seemed to believe that I needed a break.'

'Did you tend Adam's wound?' Sarah asked.

'No, I'm afraid not. That was a surgeon called Devitt, I believe.'

'An excellent surgeon too,' Adam said. Then, directly to Sarah, 'Would you care for a drink?'

'Not for now, thank you.'

'Let's all sit then, shall we,' Adam suggested. Sarah sat on a matching leather armchair to the chesterfield while Adam sat beside Doyle.

'You said some rather upsetting news?' Sarah prompted.

Adam glanced at Doyle, then back at Sarah. 'Conan and I got fed up with the scrum out there and decided to come in here to catch up on one another. But . . . Well you tell her, Conan.'

'My last hospital was a typhoid one which unfortunately has a large number of cases from the 60th Rifles, which has had a recent outbreak of the fever . . .'

Sarah saw it coming. Mention of the 60th Rifles gave the game away. 'Jack!' she exclaimed, cutting in.

'I'm afraid so,' Doyle confirmed.

'How bad is he?'

'All typhoid is bad, Lady Ascog, particularly under war conditions. We do our best, of course.'

'Conan just happened to mention the 60th and I asked him, being naturally curious, if he'd ever come across a Captain Tucker, and that was that.'

'You must go to him immediately,' Sarah said to Adam.

'I've never even met the man!'

'Nonetheless, he is your brother-in-law. What would Primrose think if she found out you'd known about Jack and hadn't done all you could to help?'

Adam became shamefaced at this admonishment.

'Where exactly is this hospital where Jack's a patient?' Sarah asked Doyle.

'Just outside Estcourt in Natal.'

'And you say conditions there are bad?'

'Pretty appalling, actually.'

'What could we do that would help Jack?'

'The food is basic and not all that nourishing. And they're pretty short-staffed. If something as simple as daily laundry could be arranged that would be a tremendous boost for any of the patients there.'

'It sounds fairly grim,' Sarah said.

Doyle shrugged. 'There are a lot of people in high places, one or two of them here tonight, who have a lot to answer for. I could tell you stories that I guarantee would make your hair stand on end. Myself and most of the other medical staff do the best we can, while others . . .' He shrugged again. 'Others worry more about paperwork and their careers than patients.'

Sarah swung on Adam. 'No buts about it, whether you've met your brother-in-law or not you must go.'

'Yes, I suppose so,' he agreed reluctantly.

'How about your own wound. Have you been discharged yet?'

Adam shook his head. 'It's taking a little longer than I thought.'

'So you've no work commitment that stops you going to this . . . What was it called again, Doctor?'

'Estcourt.'

'None,' Adam admitted. He knew he was being churlish about this but he genuinely didn't fancy charging off to become involved with a sick brother-in-law whom he'd never met, and whose existence – up until Sarah's arrival in Cape Town – he hadn't even been aware of.

'If you'll draw up a list of the things I should take, and arrange in Estcourt, I'll leave just as soon as possible,' Adam said to Doyle, who nodded his approval.

Sarah was pleased also; that was more like it. 'Would you like me to go with you?' she asked Adam, who immediately brightened.

'Would you?'

'I'm sure a familiar face from home would be bound to cheer Jack up.'

'Could be the best medicine of all,' Doyle said.

There wasn't anything to detain her now in Cape Town, Sarah thought, the business of appointing a new agent having been just concluded. John had come up with a splendid chap called Simon Dawkins, a local man, Cape born and bred. She'd intended booking her passage home within the next few days, but now that would have to wait. She felt a clear responsibility after all. Primrose might not be as close a friend as Ollie, but was a friend all the same.

Sarah and Adam, with Doctor Doyle advising, fell to discussing the details of their trip to Estcourt.

Sarah had never seen an armoured train engine before, and found the sight of the one now before her quite astonishing. Its slate-coloured funnel and boiler were encased in half-inch steel plates, like the funnel of a dreadnought.

Behind the engine was an armoured truck packed with troops, behind that two tarpaulin-covered trucks containing the supplies. Behind the second of these was an ordinary passenger carriage and behind that a final armoured truck, this one boasting, besides troops, a mounted seven-pounder ship's gun.

'This lot would cause them to stop and stare in Glasgow,' Sarah said to John, which made him laugh.

'It would indeed,' he agreed.

John supervised Sarah's luggage being taken aboard the carriage, which belonged to the officers amongst whom she was to be an honoured guest for the trip, and had just completed this when Adam appeared with his things.

The large canvas bag dangling at Adam's hip was secured to him by means of a leather shoulder strap. When Sarah asked him what the bag was for, he told her it contained paper, pens, pencils and other illustrating materials. When they got to the hospital outside Estcourt he intended making drawings of what he saw there.

'Ten minutes till departure,' John said. It was he who had arranged that they go by this supply train which was not only travelling direct to Pietermaritzburg, the nearest large town to Estcourt, but would be doing so far more quickly than any of the scheduled trains.

Adam waited on the platform with Sarah and John while his belongings were loaded into the carriage, and as they were standing talking the figure of Superintendent Wetherspoon came hurrying into view.

'Thank goodness, I thought I was going to miss you,' he puffed to Sarah on joining them.

Aliced poked her head out of an open carriage window. 'Everything is ready in here for you when you are, your Ladyship,' she announced.

'Thank you, Alice. I'll be there in a moment.' Having said that, Sarah turned her attention back to Wetherspoon.

'Well, Burnet isn't dead after all,' the Superintendent declared proudly. 'We've finally found out what's become of him.'

Sarah clapped her hands. This was marvellous. 'Which is?'

'He joined the South African Light Horse the day after Furness officially took over as your agent. The reason it's taken us so long to discover the fact was because he signed on under the name of Herbert Burnet, rather than the Charles Burnet we've been looking for.'

That Burnet had signed up surprised Sarah. She'd always imagined him to be older, somehow. In his late fifties, or sixties. Certainly beyond active fighting. It seemed she was wrong.

'Where did the Herbert come from?' John inquired.

'Apparently that's his real name, the one on his birth certificate. It seems he always hated it though and adopted Charles way back when.'

'And you're certain it *is* the same man?' Sarah queried.

'No doubt about it, your Ladyship. That Herbert Burnet and Charles Burnet are one and the same has been confirmed to me personally by the actual Lieutenant who recruited him into the Light Horse, and who's been an acquaintance of his for years.'

'That's that, then. Well done, Superintendent,' Sarah said. At long last the mystery of the disappearing ex-agent was solved and all ends were neatly tied.

'Thank you, your Ladyship.'

His news delivered, Wetherspoon now wished Sarah and Adam all the best for their trip, then took his leave of them.

After that John saw them into the carriage where a pair of facing three-seater seats had been set aside for their use.

The carriage was an open one without any compartments or sectionalisation of any kind. A number of seats had been removed with various supplies and kit stacked in these spaces.

The officers present were delighted to have a female accompany them on what would otherwise have been a dull and dreary journey, and quickly introduced themselves.

'Thank you for everything, John. I'll see you when I return to Cape Town,' Sarah said to Buchan as the warning whistle proclaiming imminent departure blew.

'If you have any trouble at the hospital, you can always contact me at Government House and I'll do whatever I can for you.'

He was a real sweetie, she thought.

Half a minute later, with a jolt and several clanks, they moved off. Sarah waved to John till he was lost to sight, then joined Adam who was already seated.

'A gin and tonic, your Ladyship?' an army servant inquired.

'Yes, that would be very nice.'

'And you, sir?'

'I'll have one as well,' Adam smiled.

Alice came bustling up to sit beside Sarah. 'The "facilities" are down the far end, your Ladyship,' she whispered, making sure Adam couldn't hear.

'What are they like?' Sarah whispered back.

Alice screwed up her nose.

Sarah could just imagine. Still, she was sure she'd endured worse in her lifetime.

'You'll never guess what I managed to lay my hands on just before we left,' Sarah said to Adam.

'What?'

'A genuine Fortnum and Mason hamper crammed chock-full of scrumptious goodies. Jack will think that a proper treat.'

Adam settled back into his seat, looking forward to a good old chat with Sarah, when they were suddenly approached by a Major Newbigging inquiring if either of them would care to join in a game of whist.

'Why I'd love a game of whist!' Sarah exclaimed, surprising Adam, and irritating him.

'Not for me, thanks,' he said to Newbigging.

'If you'd like to come this way, Lady Ascog, we have a folding table set up further along the carriage.'

With Sarah gone Adam was left with Alice for company, she knitting and staring blandly at him. When his g & t arrived he took a deep swallow of it, and immediately felt the better for that.

Then he thought of Gillian Garlicke and the farewell she'd given him the night before. You had to give it to these South African women, they weren't just hot, as the saying went, they fair sizzled!

Alice leant forward. 'Are you all right, Mr Tennant? You have a very odd expression on your face.'

He smiled mysteriously at her. 'I'm fine, Alice. I was just remembering something.'

'Oh!'

And with that he closed his eyes and went on remembering. When Sarah laughed a few moments later it irritated him not in the slightest.

Sarah woke to find she had a tacky mouth.

'A good nap, your Ladyship?' Alice inquired.

'Excellent, thank you.'

'How about a nice cup of tea?'

'That would be lovely, Alice.'

'Just leave it to me.' Laying her knitting aside, Alice rose and bustled off down the carriage to where the spirit-fuelled kettle was.

Sarah yawned, then stretched. She would haved adored a bath, but of course that was impossible. What a long train journey; it was beginning to seem interminable. When Alice returned she would ask the maid to wet a flannel and bring that to her so that she could wipe down her face and neck.

She glanced over at Adam who had his sketch pad out and open, his features screwed up in concentration as his pencil flew.

'What are you doing?' she asked.

Adam stopped, grinned impishly at her, and put a finger across his lips. He then used the same finger to point to the other side of the carriage.

Captain Driscoll was a fat man with balding ginger hair and large upsweeping ginger moustaches. He was sitting fast asleep, hands clasped in his ample lap, his mouth puckering every time he noisily breathed out.

Sarah couldn't help but giggle. If ever there was a frog in human shape, Captain Driscoll was it.

'Can I see?' she asked Adam quietly.

He motioned her over.

As soon as she saw what he'd already drawn, croak! croak! she thought. She giggled again.

*

As the train went into the blind bend, Driver Hartley increased speed knowing that he would need that speed to climb the steep gradient that lay immediately beyond the bend.

He flicked a sideways glance at his fireman, Jakey Harris, shovelling coal into the boiler, flames licking out of the aperture. Then he brought his attention back to the track.

An instant later, halfway round the bend, his face froze in disbelief when he saw the obstruction – a huge boulder – sitting squarely on the tracks. Behind this boulder were a number of smaller ones.

'Jesus!' he breathed, his hand snaking to the brake lever. Even as he applied it he knew it to be futile. There was nothing like the room needed for the train to stop in time.

As the brakes took hold a great screeching, rending noise shredded the air, while a million glittering sparks showered and cascaded from the now locked wheels.

Sarah was thrown forward in the seat as the brakes were applied, and Adam's pencil – which he'd been holding loosely as was his wont when drawing – went flying from his hand.

'What the hell's going on!' an irate male voice bellowed.

Captain Driscoll bounced out of his seat to land with a thump on the floor.

Major Newbigging, sitting in the toilet with his trousers and underwear round his ankles, grabbed for them and hastily tried to pull them back up again. In doing so he lost his balance, fell backwards and was knocked cold by the plumbing.

Sarah grabbed for Adam as the train continued to slither. Then there was the most god-almighty crash, followed by a bang. At which point the train, Driver Hartley and Fireman Harris already dead, proceeded to both jack-knife and corkscrew, trucks and carriage going in all directions at once.

Sarah never managed to get hold of Adam. She didn't know how it happened, but somehow she was in mid-air with the carriage revolving around her.

It was the end, she thought. She was going to die. Robert! she shrieked silently inside her head. I love you, son. I love you!

Then there was another bang, louder than the first. And after that, nothing.

Chapter 11

Sarah regained consciousness to discover Adam bending over her, his face grey and full of concern. The inside of her head was whirling, and she felt slightly nauseous.

'Are you all right?' he asked anxiously, having to raise his voice to be heard above the noise, noise that Sarah was now becoming aware of.

Shots were being fired, lots of them. Orders were being shouted. Men were cursing. And somewhere, close by, someone was keening in agony.

'What happened?' she husked.

'Boer attack. They seem to have totally wrecked the train.'

Zip! A bullet scythed the air above them. Then zip! zip! Two more did the same in rapid succession.

Confusion, she thought. That was her impression of what was going on all around. Confusion, filled with fear. The sort of fear that brings a cold sweat to the skin and makes you stink.

'Have you broken anything?' Adam demanded.

She gingerly moved her legs, then arms, then hips. 'Doesn't feel as if I have.'

'Good.'

'Where's Alice?'

He'd forgotten about the maid. 'Don't know. She was down the other end when it happened.'

Crack! That was a revolver firing, quite a different sound to the others. It was young Lieutenant Crudgington kneeling about a dozen feet away, firing through a window.

'Got one of the bast –' He turned to shout jubilantly, but never finished the sentence when a bullet drilled his ear, blood, pieces of bone and pink gore spattering out the other side.

Sarah stared in horror as he slowly toppled sideways. He'd been one of the whist players.

'Oh my good God!' she whispered.

The acrid smell of cordite was now heavy in the air. And other smells, without exception all unpleasant, that Sarah couldn't put a name to.

Ting! A Boer bullet glanced off metal, followed by chunk! as it bit into wood.

'I'm surprised we landed upright. The carriage went arse over tip a number of times,' Adam said.

She remembered that. She in mid-air, the carriage revolving around her. 'Did we hit something?' she asked, for now she came to think of it, it seemed that's what must have happened.

'A boulder, or boulders apparently. I heard a tommy call that out to a couple of his mates.'

'Your Ladyship! Your Ladyship!' Alice came wriggling towards them, her face bright with blood.

Ting! Ting! Ting! That was a ricochet that hummed round the interior of the carriage. Everyone ducked or fell flat until it had stopped.

'I got stuck, trapped down there,' Alice said, on reaching Sarah and Adam. 'A box of supplies fell across my legs and I couldn't move. One of the officers has just released me.'

'Your face!' Sarah said.

'Only a cut, nothing to worry about. Though it is making me bleed like a stuck pig.'

'Wait a minute,' Sarah said. Pulling up her skirt she tore off a piece of petticoat. She used this to wipe and dab the worst of the blood away. Then tore off another piece of petticoat with which she bound the wound, the bandage encircling Alice's forehead and the back of her head.

'I wish I could see what's going on,' Adam muttered.

Alice coughed. The cordite fumes, getting stronger with every passing second, were hurting her chest.

'Come on lads!' someone shouted. That was instantly followed by a fusillade of shots from further off. Bodies crashed to the ground.

A horse whinnied shrilly, and a command was given in Afrikaans. *'Skiet, kerels, skiet hulle!'*

Another fusillade rang out.

Someone, a tommy, screamed in terrible agony. A scream that was never finished, but ceased abruptly halfway through. The scream stopping the way it did was even worse than the scream itself.

Glass crashed, and a metal object rattled over the carriage floor. 'Bomb!' an officer shouted.

Adam didn't think about what he did next, but did it instinctively. He threw himself across Sarah, pressing them both as flat against the floor as he was able.

The bomb exploded with a roaring, rushing sound that filled the carriage with bright orange light and flying metal fragments.

Captain Driscoll, the same 'frog' that Sarah and Adam had been so amused by only minutes before, died instantly as a flying fragment pierced the nape of his neck to travel upwards and lodge in his brain.

Adam was bearing down so hard on Sarah that she couldn't breathe. 'Ah . . . Ah . . .' she gasped, trying to speak his name but unable to do so.

Adam opened his eyes to discover dust and debris swirling everywhere. Some of this caught in his throat causing him to choke. Still choking he rolled off Sarah.

Alice came into a semi-sitting position and shook her head. Her ears were clanging as though bells were being rung inside them. She noted absently that the side of her dress had been sliced open by a flying fragment. But there was no further damage to her person.

Sarah sucked in a deep breath, and another.

Zip! Ping! More bullets.

Over his choking fit, Adam was feeling himself. He too had escaped damage of any sort. They'd been lucky, thanks to their position in the carriage in relation to where the bomb had exploded.

The carriage door had gone, blown away. Sarah looked through the now gaping space to glimpse an incline beyond. Something dark moved, a flitting motion, then moved again. One of the Boers, she presumed.

Khaki uniforms flashed by the hole. Then one, in the process of running by, was suddenly propelled sideways. His arms whirled backwards, ending up in a position that wedged his upper torso in the open doorway, while his lower torso dangled outside. He'd been shot straight through the centre of the forehead.

'What are we to do?' Sarah whispered to Adam.

'Nothing. What can we do? Go out there and we're meat for certain.'

She blanched to hear that, and again thought of Robert. Closing her eyes she silently began to pray, asking God if she was to die that day could He please make sure that Robert grew up knowing that his mother had truly loved him. Which she did. At least the wee chap would have Jock and Maud to look after him. He couldn't have better substitute parents than them.

Opening her eyes again she reached across and placed her hand over Adam's. 'Thank you for that.'

'For what?'

'Throwing yourself over me. Protecting me with your own body as you did.'

The hint of a flush crept into Adam's neck.

Impulsively she kissed him lightly on the cheek. Outside the sounds of fighting were, if anything, even more intense than they'd been.

Adam spotted his canvas bag containing his illustrating materials, and crawled over to retrieve it. Whatever happened he didn't want to lose that.

Sarah lit a cigarette. If ever she needed one it was then. As she smoked she savoured the taste of the tobacco, wondering if this was going to be her last ever cigarette.

It was odd, she thought. Faced with, and surrounded by, death she'd never felt more alive. Her blood was racing while her skin was as sensitive as surely skin could be.

And she was sexually aroused. The ache between her legs a terrible need for hard male flesh.

'Do you think we're winning?' Alice asked Adam.

He shrugged. 'I've no more idea than you, Alice.'

Again there was the crack of an officer's revolver, then it cracked a second time.

Sarah glanced down the carriage thinking she would see other figures. But she didn't. At least none that were alive. What officers had survived the bomb appeared to have vacated the carriage, though how they'd got out she didn't know. It certainly hadn't been through the blown-open doorway. She would have seen that.

A fusillade of shots, the largest yet, rang out. Then another and another. Boer fusillades, as all the fusillades had been. She was able to distinguish the rifles now. Those belonging to the Boers had a distinctive high-pitched whine, the British a lower, more solid, sound.

Alice started to cry. 'I'm sorry. I'm sorry,' she apologised to Sarah, shoulders shaking as she dashed away the tears using the back of her hand.

'That's all right,' Sarah replied softly, taking Alice into her embrace and holding the maid tight. She would never have imagined that Alice would fall apart like this. She'd always thought Alice to be made of sterner stuff than that.

Another fusillade banged out, followed by . . . silence. Sarah glanced at Adam; what did that mean?

The silence continued, stretching on and eerily on. Then a voice called out in Afrikaans, and the same person laughed.

A sudden solitary shot sang out, but that was the last of the engagement.

A medley of male Afrikaner voices were now talking loudly and excitedly, laughing and joking with one another.

Sarah's lips thinned, her expression becoming grim. There could be no doubt who had won.

The dead tommy in the doorway disappeared as he was jerked out.

'If there's anyone left alive in there you have ten seconds to get out before I throw in another bomb,' a heavily accented voice called into the carriage. 'One . . . two . . . three . . .'

'We're coming!' Adam yelled, jumping to his feet. Quickly he helped Sarah and Alice to theirs.

'We're civilians and unarmed,' he said loudly as they approached the doorway.

On arriving at the doorway Sarah found herself looking into the eyes of half a dozen rifles pointed directly at them.

'We're unarmed,' Adam repeated.

Sarah's first impression of these Boers was that she was staring at a collection of tramps or scarecrows. Their clothes were in absolute tatters.

'Jump down!' one of the Boers commanded, waggling his rifle.

Adam leapt to the ground where he stumbled, having nearly fallen over the corpse of the soldier who'd been lying in the doorway.

'Alice next,' Sarah instructed him. When Alice was on the ground she followed.

Sarah had never seen anything like it, nor did she ever want to again. Dead, dying and badly wounded were everywhere. Khaki uniforms lay higgledy-piggledy, most with red stains on them.

Faint groaning and moaning, which they hadn't heard inside the carriage, came from some of the wounded.

'Very pretty,' a Boer said, leering at Sarah. He was thin as a stick with a long, matted, unkempt beard. His facial skin was burnt the colour of mahogany.

Reaching out, the same man put a hand on Sarah's breast.

Adam made to go for the man, but before he could several pairs of strong arms grabbed him, forcing him to remain where he was.

434

'Officer's wife, eh?' the Boer with the hand on Sarah's breast said, and squeezed it.

'Leave her Ladyship along, you filthy brute!' Alice exclaimed vehemently, incensed by what was happening to Sarah.

'A Ladyship, eh?' the Boer touching Sarah said, but didn't take his hand away.

'Viscountess Ascog,' Sarah declared quietly, and with dignity.

'Viscountess,' the Boer repeated, and guffawed.

Sarah attempted to remove the hand from her breast, but the Boer wouldn't let go. Instead his fingers tightened, catching her nipple.

Fear of rape, and multiple rape, blossomed in Sarah. The latter too horrible to contemplate. Death was preferable. What she did next was a terrible gamble, but in the event a gamble that came off.

Her own hand flashed to smack hard against the side of the Boer's face, the ferocity and force with which the blow was delivered causing him to cry out in surprise and pain, and send him reeling backwards.

'And I'm not an officer's wife. I'm not anyone's wife,' Sarah said, speaking as quietly as she had done before.

For a moment or two it was touch and go, anything might have happened. Adam found himself holding his breath. Then the Boer Sarah had hit laughed, uttered something in Afrikaans, and his companions also laughed.

'Would you like to try and slap one of us?' a Boer who had no shirt under his ragged coat, and who was wearing well-patched rawhide sandals on his feet, asked Adam.

Adam shook his head.

'Just as well, Mynheer.'

'What's in his bag, heh? Food?' Another of the Boers snatched at the bag dangling at Adam's hip which he had slung on before leaving the carriage.

'No food. Only the tools of my trade,' Adam said as the Boer peered into the bag.

'Paper? Pencils? What sort of tools are those?'

'I'm an illustrator for the *Illustrated London News*,' Adam explained.

'A newspaperman, heh?'

Alarm bells jangled in Adam's brain. A newspaperman, as the Boer put it, might not be a good thing to be. 'I don't write the words, I only draw pictures of what I see. I'm an artist, not a journalist.'

A middle-aged Boer appeared at a run round the side of the carriage, spoke hurriedly to the Boer Sarah had slapped, who let out an oath, then the pair of them ran back the way the first had come.

'It seems Hennie's brother has been killed,' the Boer who'd been talking to Adam said slowly, and spat.

Adam didn't care for the way those Boers surrounding them were looking at him, so he dropped his gaze to the ground. And kept it there.

Boers were swarming over the trucks containing the supplies. One of them now let out a joyous halloo! and held a cardboard carton triumphantly aloft.

'Come!' the Boer with no shirt on under his coat said to Sarah, Adam and Alice, and gestured with his rifle in the direction in which he wanted them to walk.

Alice gagged and clutched at Sarah when they passed a dead tommy whose bloody face was a nightmare. Flies were buzzing round the face, and feasting on it. One awful eye socket was full of huge ants.

The armoured truck containing the mounted seven-pounder ship's gun was smashed to smithereens, the gun's barrel bent by impact. Sarah had wondered about the gun and why they hadn't heard its boom during the attack. Now she knew why.

The engine itself had concertinaed at the very front before being thrown upwards and over on to its back. Fire that had come from its boiler was raging round it.

A tall, slightly built man with yellow hair was standing surrounded by others who appeared deferential towards him. As soon as Sarah saw this man she knew him to be the Boers' leader. He had the unmistakable aura of command about him.

Besides the yellow hair the man had a pointed yellow beard clipped in the French style, and was wearing grey riding breeches. Overall he was far better dressed than his men, though he was still scruffy in the extreme.

As Sarah, Adam and Alice reached this group the leader shaded his eyes to stare into the distance. Sarah followed his gaze to see a blinking light. The light continued to blink out its message for a few seconds more, then stopped. Heliograph, Sarah thought correctly.

A member of the small group attending the leader rattled off a sentence, which the leader replied to.

'Jah "Oom" Jannie,' the man said almost reverentially.

When Adam heard that his eyebrows leapt up his forehead. 'You're Smuts!' he exclaimed to the leader addressed as 'Oom' Jannie.

Slowly, Smuts turned his gaze on to Adam, a gaze that had a frightening intensity about it. The grey-blue eyes were strained and hard.

'I am General Smuts,' the leader acknowledged.

He was far younger than he'd initially appeared, Sarah thought. Why he might even be younger than herself! Young for a general.

'And you are?' Smuts queried.

'Adam Tennant, an illustrator for the *Illustrated London News*. And this is Viscountess Ascog. We were both passengers on the train.'

The grey-blue eyes came to rest on Sarah, making her go cold inside. She knew she couldn't lie to those eyes without them realising it, not that she had any intention of trying to do so.

'Viscountess,' Smuts said, and gave a small inclination of the head.

'General.'

'And this is . .?' Smuts gestured at Alice, who bobbed to him.

'My personal maidservant,' Sarah explained.

'I see.'

' "Oom" Jannie!' one of the Boer group exclaimed, pointing towards a far-off hill.

It was another message by heliograph, this one coming from a totally different position to the previous one.

'Ah! Good!' Smuts muttered when the message was over. He said something in a whisper to the man closest to him, who then strode away.

'Civilian passengers on a military train, most unusual. Your husband must be high-ranking,' he declared, the latter addressed to Sarah.

'I've already explained, I'm not an officer's wife. Nor am I anyone's wife.'

'Yet you're wearing a wedding ring?' Smuts said almost lazily.

Sarah had forgotten about that. She lifted her ring to look at it, and nodded. 'I was married. My husband, Viscount Ascog, was killed last February in a riding accident. He had nothing whatever to do with the army, or this war.'

437

'So why were you aboard the train?'

'Adam is an old friend of mine from Glasgow where I come from and live. While in Cape Town on business our paths crossed again. And then, only two days ago, he learned that his brother-in-law is ill with typhoid, and we decided – I also know Jack – that we would both go to see him in hospital, and there do all that we could for him.'

'And this brother-in-law Jack, is he in the military?'

'Yes. He's a captain with the 60th Rifles.'

Smuts stroked his beard. 'The 60th Rifles, heh!'

'You've heard of them, then?'

'Oh yes, Lady Ascog,' Smuts smiled softly, a smile with a chilling quality about it.

'You still haven't explained how you came to be aboard a military train,' Smuts continued to probe.

Sarah sensed a trap here, but didn't see how she could sidestep it. 'A Mr Buchan arranged it for us. He's an acquaintance of mine, and Private Secretary to Sir Alfred Milner. We were trying to get to Jack as quickly as possible.'

The Boer with no shirt said something to Smuts.

'Be quiet, Deneys. I shall decide what happens to them.'

Deneys spoke again to Smuts, who now turned to regard him coldly. A rapid exchange in Afrikaans followed, after which Smuts brought his attention back to Sarah.

'Deneys wants to kill the three of you here and now. What do you say to that?'

'I would have thought there had been enough killing for one day,' she replied quietly.

Smuts nodded his approval. It was a good answer. 'You are also an acquaintance of Sir Alfred's, I take it?'

'Yes, we've met several times. Do you know him?'

Anger crowded the grey-blue eyes. That and contempt. 'I know Sir Alfred. We have met on a number of occasions.'

'And you don't like him?'

'All this!' Smuts waved a hand about him. 'Could have been avoided if Sir Alfred had wished it so. The man is an empire builder.'

Several riders each trailing a string of pack animals went past, the lead rider calling out to Smuts who answered with a smile and wave.

'What are you going to do with us?' Sarah asked the Boer general.

'I'm not sure yet,' he answered softly. 'I shall have to think on it. In the meantime, remain here. And you, Louis, stand guard on them.'

Louis, it transpired, was one of the Boers who'd taken them prisoner at the carriage.

Smuts broke back into Afrikaans, and moved away. The original group surrounding him went with him, while the other Boers, including Deneys who'd wanted to shoot them, dispersed.

'He's young for a general,' Sarah said to Adam.

'Don't let his age fool you – he's one of the most able of the Boer high command. There are those who argue that only De Wet himself is more capable.'

Sarah looked at Louis, taking him in properly for the first time. He was so thin she could plainly see his ribs sticking through his shirt. In other circumstances he seemed as if he might be a pleasant enough lad.

'I'm scared, your Ladyship,' Alice whispered.

'That's nothing to be ashamed of. I am too, I can assure you.'

'And me,' Adam chipped in. He didn't think the Boers would kill either Sarah or Alice, not with Smuts in charge. But they could well kill him. He might be a civilian, but he was an enemy male.

To take his mind off what might shortly happen to him, and to give his hands something to do, he decided he might as well draw.

He explained what he wished to do to Louis who, reluctantly and suspiciously, agreed that he could. The Boer watched him closely, Mauser aimed straight at his belly, as he took out a sketchpad and pencil. Quickly, he began to draw the scene of carnage that lay all around.

'I haven't spotted any British prisoners,' Sarah said to Adam after a while. 'Badly wounded, yes, but no walking wounded or unharmed men.'

Adam paused in his drawing. Now that she mentioned it, neither had he.

'What about walking wounded and unharmed British prisoners?' Sarah asked Louis, whose reply was a shrug.

'There must be some, surely?' Sarah said.

She remembered then that she had her cigarette case with her. Producing it, she extracted a cigarette, and lit it. As she blew smoke away she became aware of Louis' expression.

'Would you like one?' she offered, extending her case.

He stared fixedly at the case for a few moments, appeared to be trying to be resolute, then caved in. '*Jah!*' he replied, and slid a cigarette from the case.

His first draw was down to the very bottom of his lungs where he held the smoke, savouring it. Finally, after what seemed an age, he exhaled slowly, the smoke trickling from between slightly parted lips.

'Gasping, eh?' Sarah smiled.

He looked blank.

'You needed that?'

'Oh *jah*!' he agreed softly. 'Oh *jah*!'

Sarah glanced over at the supply trucks which had now been completely unloaded, their contents stacked on the ground where they were being reloaded into panniers on the pack animals.

The Boers were in high spirits, with a great deal of laughing, back slapping, handshaking and general skylarking going on. But none of this was affecting the work in progress which was moving along very efficiently.

Out of the corner of her eye Sarah glimpsed another heliograph message, this again coming from a totally different direction to the other two.

It was about ten minutes later that a Boer figure appeared heading straight for them. This one was different to the others in not having a beard or moustache.

When the figure got closer Sarah realised with a shock why that was so. It wasn't a man, but a woman.

The woman was dressed identically to the other Boers, which is to say trousers, upper garments and a hat. (Only a handful of them weren't wearing hats.) She also carried a Mauser with a near-empty bandolier slung over her right shoulder. She walked like a man with long purposeful strides, and her body posture and movements were mannish too. Yet, despite all this, she remained very feminine.

'Isie!' Louis smiled, obviously pleased to see her.

Isie had a brief conversation with Louis in Afrikaans, then rounded on Sarah. 'You come with me.'

'Why? Where to?'

' "Oom" Jannie's orders. You come.'

'Right then,' Sarah said.

Alice made to go with Sarah, but was immediately stopped. 'Not you, only her.'

'Alice is my maidservant,' Sarah explained.

'Not matter. Only you come.'

'You stay here with Mr Tennant,' Sarah said.

Alice bit her lip. The last thing she wanted was to be separated from Sarah.

They returned to the carriage Sarah, Adam and Alice had been travelling in, and Isie instructed her to go inside. When Sarah did, Isie followed her.

'You have luggage here?' Isie inquired.

'I do.'

'Then change clothes. Clothes to ride horse on.'

Isie's English wasn't all that comprehensive, Sarah realised. Still it was good enough for the Afrikaans woman to make herself understood.

Sarah located her cases and opened them. She wasn't absolutely certain about what Alice had packed, a lot of her things having been left behind at Mount Nelson. It was as she'd thought.

'I have nothing here suitable for riding,' she said to Isie, who gave a dark, irritated scowl.

'Look for yourself. Neither myself nor my maid anticipated that I'd have need for riding clothes.'

Isie considered that. Then the solution came to her. 'Man with you, he have luggage here?'

'Yes, he has.'

'Put on his clothes. Trousers, shirt, jacket.'

'Adam's clothes!' Sarah exclaimed.

'Do so now,' Isie commanded.

There was nothing for it, Sarah thought, but to obey. She located one of Adam's two cases, tried to open it and found it locked. Isie solved that problem with a wicked-looking knife with which she quickly snapped the locks.

Sarah chose a pair of herringbone trousers, a crisp cotton shirt, pullover and socks. She started to strip, and was halfway through that when to her amazement she saw that Isie was stripping also.

'What are you doing!' Sarah exclaimed. She'd heard about 'strange' women.

'New clothes for me, replace those I'm wearing,' Isie explained.

So that was it, the Afrikaans female was taking this opportunity to replace her rags.

Isie exclaimed with delight when, on rummaging through Adam's

441

case, she discovered several heavy vests. She hugged them to her as though they were gold.

In Adam's other case Sarah found a Norfolk jacket that was too big for her, like the trousers which she'd had to roll up at their bottoms, but would have to do.

The only other jacket belonged to a set of tails. Isie considered wearing this, but then decided against doing so. Crossing to where Lieutenant Crudgington lay in a huddled heap she pulled his uniform jacket from his body, and shrugged herself into that.

When Isie saw the way Sarah was looking at her she said, 'Well, he won't be needing it any more, will he? And still damned cold at night.'

'What about walking wounded, and those British soldiers who gave themselves up? I haven't seen any of those,' Sarah replied quietly.

'No one give themselves up.' She paused, then added slyly, 'Khakis very brave men.'

'You mean you never gave anyone a chance to surrender?' Sarah said.

'*You* here, heh?' And with that Isie laughed.

'But I'm not a soldier.'

'You still here though.'

The two women stared hard at one another. 'If I'm to go off with you, as I presume that's what all this means, can I take along a few bits and pieces?' Sarah asked in what she judged to be a reasonable tone of voice.

'You got perfume?'

That surprised Sarah. 'Several bottles. Why?'

'You keep one, you give me one. That fair as you British say?'

Sarah would just never have imagined Isie using perfume. The two together seemed quite incongruous somehow.

Sarah gave Isie the cheaper bottle of perfume, then swiftly made up a small bag for herself. Toilet articles with some warm undergarments. What Isie had said about cold nights hadn't been lost on her.

Outside the carriage again Isie led Sarah back to where Adam and Alice were, Sarah quickly explaining to Adam why she was now dressed in his clothes. Shortly after that they were rejoined by General Smuts and several of his entourage.

'As you will have no doubt guessed, you will be coming with the Commando, Lady Ascog,' Smuts said.

'May I ask why?'

'The pleasure of your company?' he smiled.

'I hardly think so.'

'Then let's just say I believe it might be to our future advantage to have you with us.'

'A bargaining counter should you need one,' Adam said.

'Precisely, Mr Tennant. Most astute of you.'

'Or hostage,' Sarah added softly.

Those grey-blue eyes fastened on to Sarah's green ones. The intensity and power in the former made most people glance away, but not Sarah. Smuts liked that.

'Let me put it this way, you are an ace up my sleeve should I need an ace.'

Sarah nodded; she understood. 'I think this is the first time I've regretted having a title,' she said drily, her voice tinged with irony.

Smuts laughed. 'Very good, Lady Ascog! I just know you and I are going to get along.'

Alice stepped forward a pace. 'If her Ladyship is going with you then so too am I.'

'No, you will remain here with the British wounded, of which I am informed there are eighteen . . .'

Only eighteen out of all those soldiers who'd started the train journey, Sarah thought. My God!

Smuts held up a hand to silence Alice who was about to protest. 'You will tend to those soldiers as best you are able until help arrives, which will be no later than nightfall, I assure you. When the train fails to be accounted for at its next spotting stage the British will have a mounted column on the move within the hour.'

'But I know nothing about nursing,' Alice said.

'I'm sure you will cope.'

'But I don't want to be separated from her Ladyship!' Alice persisted.

'It's better, and safer, you remain here,' Sarah said firmly.

'If that's what you want, my Lady.'

'It is.'

Alice bowed her head in acquiescence. Her heart was hammering. She was so totally confused and scared. She'd never been so scared before. These Boers with their beards and guns terrified the living daylights out of her. She would have given anything to have been back home safe in Glasgow.

'And what about me? What's to happen to me?' Adam queried of Smuts.

'You stay here with the maid.'

Relief surged in Adam; he was to live after all. Then he thought of Sarah, alone with the Boers. 'If Lady Ascog is to go with you then I would like to also,' he forced himself to say.

'No, Adam!' Sarah exclaimed.

'I feel a responsibility towards you. It was because of me you were on the train after all.'

'You're being silly!' she admonished.

He coloured. 'Silly or not, it's what I feel I should do. *Want* to do!'

'He's to stay here with Alice,' Sarah said to Smuts.

'The General makes the decisions, not you,' Adam told her hotly.

Smuts was amused by this interchange – it reminded him of some of those he'd had with his own dear wife, whom he missed dreadfully.

'What sort of ace up the sleeve would you be? None,' Sarah said to Adam.

And with that a new thought came into Smuts' mind. Perhaps the illustrator could be useful after all. He'd just come from Kaapstad where he would have been mixing with all manner of important people, military and otherwise. Who knew what intelligence the man possessed? Intelligence he might be coaxed into divulging without being aware he was doing so.

'You can ride with us if you wish. To keep your friend company,' Smuts said mildly to Adam.

'Thank you, General.'

Sarah shot Adam a look that quite plainly said, fool! She considered him to be endangering himself unnecessarily.

Bang! The report was loud, and immediately caught everyone's attention.

The seven-pounder may have had a bent barrel, but the Boers had ensured it was never fixed. The bang was them blowing the gun up.

The Boers had now loaded their pack animals with the maximum these animals could carry. Those supplies that were left were being taken over to the fire raging round the engine and there burnt.

Sarah noticed that the Boers were now carrying two rifles apiece, their own Mausers plus either a captured British Lee-Enfield or Lee-Metford. She deduced correctly that the ammunition for the

British rifles didn't fit the German Mausers, hence the reason the Boers were taking along the British weapons until such time as they could replenish their own ammunition.

Everything was now happening in a great flurry, Boers hurrying hither and thither, a sense of imminent departure in the air.

Louis, who'd been despatched by Smuts, returned leading a pair of horses. The reins of one he handed to Sarah, of the other to Adam.

Alice burst into tears, her face flooding with them.

'There, there,' Sarah consoled, gathering Alice into an embrace. 'If the General says that a column will be here before nightfall then I'm sure that's the case.'

'But what about wild beasts!' Alice wailed. 'What if some of those appear?'

Smuts, who'd overheard this, said, 'Don't worry, there are no wild beasts in this part of the Cape. There never have been many hereabouts, and those there were have all been slaughtered since the war started.'

Adam glanced round in surprise when he heard Smuts declare they were still in Cape Colony. There shouldn't be any armed Boers in the Colony, which was supposedly firmly under British control and domination. So why were Smuts and his Commando here? A raiding party of some sort?

'Oh, my Lady!' Alice husked, wiping her face and nose.

'Pull youself together, Alice. You're going to be all right. There are no wild beasts, and help will be on hand before nightfall. All you have to do is tend to those poor soldiers, giving them what comfort and solace you can.'

Alice took a deep breath, which helped steady her. 'Yes, Lady Ascog. Please excuse me for breaking down. It's just all so . . .' She trailed off.

'I understand.' And with that Sarah gave Alice another hug.

'We go south,' Smuts said quite distinctly to one of his entourage, who was in fact Commandant Wessels.

'South,' Wessels repeated.

'South,' Smuts confirmed. An exchange in Afrikaans followed, during which Smuts issued an instruction to Louis.

Louis came over to Alice. 'I'll take you to where the soldiers are now.'

Off in the distance a heliograph, the same one that Smuts had been watching when Sarah and company first joined him, winked furiously.

'My Lady,' Alice muttered, and curtsied.

Louis led Alice away, the maid having to hurry to keep up with him, for he was walking fairly quickly.

All around the train Boers were mounting horses and forming themselves into groups.

'Hi! hi! hi!' someone shouted, followed by what was obviously a warning.

The explosion was very loud, and made the ground tremble. Sarah looked to Adam for an explanation.

'Must have been the shells for the seven-pounder,' he guessed correctly.

They later found out that to begin with the Boers had thought to take the shells with them, then at the last minute had changed their minds.

An old Boer, a gnarled oak of a man, made his way from the rear of the train trailing a short string of horses behind him. These he delivered to General Smuts and entourage.

'On-saddle!' Smuts called out.

Sarah and Adam mounted, tucking themselves in behind the General and his party as they trotted across to where the rest of the Commando was now fully assembled ready to ride.

Sarah glanced round to discover that the Boer called Deneys was right behind her, Isie and Louis flanking him.

She saw someone waving to her, and there was Alice beside a line of figures stretched out on the ground. These were the eighteen wounded. She waved back.

With Smuts in the lead the Commando rode between one of the supply trucks and what remained of the truck that had been carrying the seven-pounder. They veered right, along the incline there, to where four wooden crosses were suddenly revealed, planted in the ground.

As they neared the crosses, Smuts swept off his hat, as did every other hat-wearer. These were the four Commando members who'd been killed during the engagement, and who'd been buried and read over, without Sarah or Adam being aware of it, since the end of the engagement. Smuts had personally conducted the brief service while Sarah was changing her clothes.

Past the graves they went, and then started up the steep gradient that lay immediately beyond.

*

Sarah sat beside Adam watching in amazement at the manner in which the Boers were eating. She'd never seen anything like it. Why, they were going at the food like a pack of crazed animals.

Smuts strolled out of the night, and as he walked by members of the Commando called out to him and he replied to every one in turn.

When he reached Sarah and Adam he smiled at them. 'May I join you?'

Sarah indicated the ground. 'Please do.'

Smuts sat, and sipped from the tin cup of coffee he was carrying. 'You've had enough to eat?'

'Thank you,' Sarah said.

'And drink?'

Sarah nodded.

Smuts sipped more coffee, wondered if he should have another pipe and decided he would, but not just yet. 'You British have an expression, hunger is a good sauce, heh?'

'That's right,' Sarah answered.

He gestured at the Boers surrounding them. 'As you can see the expression is a true one.'

'May I ask something?' Adam queried.

'You may *ask*,' Smuts replied ambiguously.

'How long since they've all eaten?"

Smuts turned away so that neither Sarah nor Adam could see his pained expression. He had another sip of coffee before turning to face them again. He held out his tin cup and moved it slightly from side to side. 'I was just talking to Commandant Wessels – we were trying to recall the last time we had a cup of coffee. We knew it had been a long time, but it surprised us to work out just how long.' He smiled, a smile that was a combination of amusement and bitterness.

'How long?' Sarah prompted.

'A year.'

'No!'

'Yes, Lady Ascog, a full year,' Smuts said, nodding.

Sarah thought about that. 'And food?' she asked softly.

'We've foraged as best we could. But it has been many, many months since the Commando last had a meal that could even begin to compare with the one they're enjoying tonight.'

That was why there were all so thin, skin and bones, Sarah thought. They'd been on a starvation regime. 'What about your own people, those on the farms, haven't they been able to help you?'

'You clearly don't know too much about this war, Lady Ascog. Our people, the volk, have little enough for themselves; your Kitchener sees to that. He burns them out, kills their cattle and sheep, destroys their crops whenever and wherever he can. He wages total war, not just war against those in arms against the British, but also the housewife and child left behind by those who have gone on Commando.'

Adam took out a sketch pad and pencil from his canvas bag. 'Do you mind?' he asked Smuts.

'Me?'

'Please.'

'Go ahead. Why not, heh?'

'Why do they call you "Oom" Jannie? What does it mean?' Sarah queried.

He sipped more of his coffee. What pleasure, what great satisfaction there could be in the contents of a tin cup. 'Jannie is my Christian name. Or I should say Jan is, Jannie of course is the familiar diminutive.'

'And "Oom"?'

'What you might call a term of endearment. Literally translated it means uncle.'

'They see you as an uncle?'

'And the connotations that implies.'

'You mean respected, and loved?'

'Certainly that is what is implied when they refer to President Kruger, whom they call "Oom" Paul. There isn't an Afrikaner, a member of the volk, who doesn't love, respect and honour him. He is our leader and light.'

'I've heard you once thought that of Rhodes?' Adam said quietly, his pencil flying.

The grey-blue eyes fastened themselves on to Adam. 'I once thought highly of Rhodes, that is true. I believed he shared my then ideal of South African unity under the British flag. I envisioned a "great Temple of Peace and Unity" in which both white races would assemble, "joyfully" accepting their differences, until, at last, they finally coalesced into a single great white nation spanning South Africa from the Zambezi to the Cape. And Rhodes was the man, I fondly imagined, who would help build the foundations of the temple.'

Sarah was entranced. Something mystical had seemed to envelop Smuts as he spoke. 'So how did you come to lose faith in Rhodes?'

Smuts' expression changed to one of sadness. 'I found him to be what his enemies had always claimed he was, a plotter and a traitor. This man we had followed, who was to lead us to victory, had not only deserted us, he had betrayed us. That was when I gave up my dreams of a united South Africa under the British flag, and went north to the South African Republic, the Transvaal, where I transferred my allegiance to Paul Kruger.'

Smuts finished his coffee which no longer tasted as good as it had. It had turned bitter on him.

'I haven't met Rhodes,' Sarah said.

'Take my advice, and don't. And certainly never become his friend. For if you did he'd only betray you as he's betrayed every friend he's ever had. He's undeniably a genius, but as a person hideously flawed.'

Sarah produced her cigarette case, offered Smuts one which he refused, and lit up.

He threw away the dregs of his coffee, and decided he'd now have that other pipe. He silently praised God for the tobacco that had been found in large quantity amongst the British supplies.

'You speak excellent English,' Sarah said.

'I come from the Cape, thanks to which I was brought up speaking both languages. My first language, for the purpose of writing, is English.'

'Really!' she exclaimed.

'Really,' he laughed. 'It may interest you to know that my favourite poets are all English. Shelley, Shakespeare and a whole list of others. I'm also fond of Walt Whitman who, of course, isn't English, but American.'

Adam tore the top sheet of paper from his pad and was about to put it in his canvas bag amongst the hardbacked file of others he intended keeping when Smuts said, 'May I?'

Adam handed over the sketch.

'You're very talented, Mr Tennant.'

'Thank you, General.'

Smuts stared at the sketch for a while, his eyes slightly narrowed, his mind clearly elsewhere. 'Can I have this?' he requested after a while. 'I'm sure my wife would appreciate it – if I can get it to her, that is.'

'Certainly you can have it,' Adam replied. 'As long as you don't object to me making other drawings of you.'

Smuts placed the sketch aside, then pulled out a briar which he proceeded to fill.

'Have you ever been to Britain?' Sarah asked, fascinated by this most charismatic of men.

'Oh yes. I went to Cambridge where I took a double first in law. I was there at the same time as two other chaps who're making something of a name for themselves, Bertrand Russell and G.E. Moore.'

'You sound as though you enjoyed your spell there.'

'Very much so, Lady Ascog. It was a golden era for me.'

Adam began sketching again, this time a group of Boers about twenty feet away. They had now stopped wolfing and guzzling their food, and had settled back to drink coffee and smoke. Their faces were reflected in the firelight, one of a number of fires the Commando had lit on which to cook.

'I thought we were supposed to be going south?' Adam queried lightly.

'And how do you know that we aren't?' Smuts replied, eyes suddenly twinkling.

'I may be a civilian, but I've been out here long enough now to know which way is which. We started off going south, but that changed after the rock area we crossed over late afternoon. By my reckoning, we're now travelling due east.'

Smuts nodded. 'Very good, Mr Tennant.'

Adam stopped sketching to glance at Smuts. 'You deliberately mentioned going south in front of Alice so that she would tell the mounted column and thereby mislead them, and those the column would pass the information on to?'

'Confusion is part of the game, Mr Tennant. Hopefully, that ploy gave us an extra hour or so.'

'I guessed it must be something like that.' Smiling at this artifice, Adam resumed sketching.

Smuts smoked a while in silence, listening to the night sounds. Somewhere in the darkness someone was singing, an old Dutch lovesong. He couldn't make out to whom the voice belonged.

He brought his attention back to Sarah, and smiled at her. 'So tell me about Cape Town? What did you think of it?'

'Very beautiful.'

'There are those who swear it is one of the most beautiful cities in the world. I, for one, certainly wouldn't disagree with them.'

450

'I'll tell you this, it knocks spots off Glasgow where we come from. Isn't that so, Adam?'

'Its weather certainly knocks spots off Glasgow's. Even the most ardent and fanatical Glaswegian couldn't deny that.'

The three of them laughed. 'I've heard about Glasgow weather. Brrr!' Smuts joked.

'It turns out a hardy breed, mind. Hardy, and kind. They don't come hardier or kinder than Glasgow folk,' Sarah said proudly.

'I have always been fond of Scots people. Of whom there are many in Cape Town at the present. You both must have met a lot of them when you were there?' And with that he turned the conversation back to the route along which he intended it would go.

From then on in Smuts used his considerable skill as a lawyer to probe, oh so gently and deviously, for information that might be of use to him and the volk.

When he finally excused himself from Sarah and Adam's company he'd gleaned several very useful nuggets of intelligence from the unsuspecting pair, particularly from Adam.

Sarah was miserable, completely sodden through. The spring rains had begun at last, and having started hadn't stopped. The deluge had been incessant for the past two days, only occasionally varying in intensity.

Sarah sat huddled under her blanket, Adam beside her huddled under his. Neither of them had slept a wink the previous night, thanks to the rain and bitter night cold. If she managed to sleep that night Sarah knew it would only be because exhaustion had overwhelmed her.

Sarah glanced over to where Deneys Reitz was sitting talking quietly to Isie. Every so often he slapped the ground with an officer's sword he now carried, a trophy from the train engagement. Sarah had no idea who the sword had originally belonged to, she hadn't noticed any officer carrying a sword during the journey.

'If this bloody rain doesn't stop soon, we'll all die of drowning,' Adam grumbled. He was clutching his canvas bag tight to his middle, protecting it as best he was able from the wet.

Sarah ran a hand over her face. She didn't need a mirror to know she had dark, puffy bags under her eyes. She felt she would have sold her soul for a hot bath followed by a clean, warm bed.

Adam pulled out his pocket watch and looked at it. 'Smuts has been gone for over six hours,' he said.

Only six hours! Sarah thought. It seemed longer. Smuts, taking three of the Commando with him, had left the others that morning, going on ahead to reconnoitre personally. He should have been back long before now.

Sarah had to go to the lavatory, and couldn't put it off any longer. Telling Adam where she was going, she rose and went over to Isie, explaining to the Afrikaner woman that she needed her, and why. Sarah was forbidden to go to the lavatory by herself, as was Adam, in case she tried to escape and therefore always had to take another female with her from the five amongst the Commando.

With Isie walking beside Sarah they splashed off to a stand of trees where Sarah did what she had to, Isie hovering a few feet away.

Sarah hated the business of being accompanied when she did this; it was so humiliating. But Smuts had been adamant; someone had to go with her.

When she was finished Sarah readjusted her clothes. 'The General is overdue,' she said to Isie.

Isie grunted, concern showing in her eyes. She, like the rest of the Commando, was becoming more and more worried. Soon Commandant Wessels would send out a party to try and locate the General and those with him. She knew that Wessels was angry with Smuts for taking what he, Wessels, saw as an unnecessary personal risk. But that was the General for you, never asking anyone else to do what he himself wasn't prepared to. And one of the many reasons why he was held in such high regard and esteem.

Lightning crackled overhead, and then crackled again. There had been a steady light wind blowing. Now it began to gust and eddy.

Sarah and Isie started back to where Adam and Deneys were, when a sudden commotion caught their attention.

' "Oom" Jannie! "Oom" Jannie!'

Isie smiled in relief. The General had returned safe and sound, all was well.

But Smuts had returned alone, having lost his three companions to khaki bullets. One of the dead was Hennie Meyer, the same Hennie whose brother had been killed during the train engagement. The Hennie Sarah had slapped.

It was much later, and many hard-ridden miles away, before Sarah and Adam got the story of what had happened. Louis told them when he brought them a cold supper.

452

Disaster had struck at a place called Mordenaar's Poort (Murderer's Gorge) when Smuts and company had suddenly run into a tommy patrol. A rapid exchange of fire had ensued during which Hennie and the two others had been shot dead. It was only by a miracle, and reduced visibility on account of the weather, that Smuts himself had avoided either death or capture. This he had done by escaping down a ditch. Having become separated from his horse in the mêlée he'd had to walk all the way back to where the Commando was anxiously waiting for him.

'Where's the General now?' Sarah asked after Louis had finished his tale, pleased that Smuts had survived, even if he was Britain's enemy.

'With Commandant Wessels and Deneys Reitz. The three of them are having a meeting.'

'About what?'

Louis shrugged. 'I've no idea. And even if I did I wouldn't let on as it's bound to be Commando business.'

Sarah chewed on some of the precooked meat that had been given her. Cold and gristly, it tasted quite foul. 'I didn't know that Deneys was part of the Commando hierarchy. Is he?'

'Oh *jah*! Deneys is leader of the Rijk section, the Dandy Fifth!' Seeing Sarah's expression, Louis burst out laughing. 'You appreciate the joke, *jah*? His section, to which I belong, comprises the youngest members, and is also the worst dressed in the entire Commando. It is because we are so badly dressed that we call ourselves the Dandies!'

'Very droll,' Sarah replied.

'It was Deneys's idea. He has a big sense of humour. He is the son of President Kruger's State Secretary, you know.'

'No, I didn't.'

'Oh, *jah*!'

What she did know about Deneys Reitz was that he was the one who had wanted to shoot her, Adam and Alice. She was very fearful of that young man.

'I go now,' Louis said, and abruptly left Sarah and Adam.

'I wonder what the meeting is about?' Sarah mused.

Smuts was morose. He'd come within a whisker of dying that day, and three fine men had. He still felt sick inside, blaming himself for not having spotted that damn patrol before they blundered into one another. But these things happened, and the rain had been particularly heavy at that point, absolutely sheeting down.

With a sigh he came out of his reverie to stare at Wessels and Deneys squatting before him. He had already guessed why they had requested to speak with him.

He stuck his pipe in his mouth upside down, lit and smoked it that way so that the still teeming rain wouldn't put it out.

'I think the time has come for you to confide in us what the Commando's mission in the Cape is,' Wessels said softly.

Smuts sucked on his pipe – Wessels was right, the time was ripe for him to share the knowledge of what their mission was.

'If you had been killed today . . .' Deneys said, and trailed off.

Smuts snapped two fingers. 'It was as close as that. The bullet that Lucas de Villiers took in the throat missed me by a fraction. A very small fraction. If I hadn't been leaning slightly to the right in my saddle I wouldn't be here now.'

Wessels thought of the de Villiers family. Walter, the father, was a good friend of his. He'd been there to drink the baby's health when Lucas was born.

'Why do you think we have come into the Cape, Deneys? You must have speculated.'

'Of course, "Oom" Jannie. And, whatever the reason, it must be important when all previous incursions from the republics have, without exception, failed with great loss of life.'

Smuts watched Deneys keenly. The young man had an excellent head on his shoulders. If he survived the war, and the volk won, he would go far. His intelligence and connections would ensure that.

Deneys went on. 'It is my conclusion, General, that the Commando has been ordered into the central districts of the Cape to test the difficulties of launching a large-scale invasion later on, an invasion to relieve the increasing pressure against our main armies in the north.'

Smuts nodded, and continued to suck his pipe.

'I'm right, then?'

Smuts transferred his attention to Wessels. 'And what do you conjecture our purpose to be, Commandant?'

Wessels knew he was being teased. He was a man of action, not of theory or policy. He was a natural second-in-command. He decided to do a bit of teasing himself. 'I believe we are in the Cape, Jan, because you have been feeling homesick.'

Smuts laughed, enjoying the joke.

'So why are we here?' Deneys prompted.

'First, let me say that previous missions into the Cape, all from the Free State, failed for the same reason; they were uncoordinated, there was no joint strategy between them, let alone with the Transvaal. That is why we were beaten back across the Orange River.'

Smuts puffed further on his pipe, marshalling and ordering his thoughts. 'We are here,' he said eventually, 'to create a third front. To carry the war into the enemy's country, into the Cape which we recognise as being politically British, but morally the Afrikaner heartland, where, outside the towns, the volk are still the overwhelming majority.'

Deneys was filled with leaping elation to hear these words. Establish a third front! Sweet music to his ears. Eagerly he waited for Smuts to continue.

'As you are both aware things are going badly for us in the republics where our bases are being destroyed, where our men are surrendering at the rate of hundreds a month, and where the number of recruits has fallen away dramatically. Kitchener with his sweep and scour strategy is winning, the new blockhouses that he is building to criss-cross the country slowly and inexorably strangling us. And so we must do something to alter the balance back into our favour. That something is this mission, and establishment of a third front.'

'How?' Wessels asked simply.

'We are to join forces with Assistant Commandant-General Kritzinger to help him reorganise the surviving Free State bands holed up in the mountains of the Eastern Cape. After that we will cut our way through to the Western Cape to prepare the ground for a large-scale invasion of Transvaalers led by De la Rey.'

Smuts took a deep breath, then said levelly. 'At best this will set the whole Cape alight, raise the fire storm of a great Afrikaner rising that will represent the last positive hope the volk have of winning this war by force of arms.'

'Aaahh!' Deneys breathed, eyes gleaming with fervour and fanaticism.

'So that is our mission,' Wessels said quietly.

'That is it,' Smuts confirmed.

Wessels levelled a thick, stubby finger at Smuts. 'If you fall I cannot replace you in all this, none of us can. Therefore you must never risk yourself again unnecessarily the way you did today. Never!'

'Never, "Oom" Jannie,' Denys agreed.

'You are too precious to us,' Wessels stated.

'But if I fall you must try,' Smuts ordered Wessels. Then to Deneys, 'And you must support the Commandant to the fullest of your ability.'

'You mustn't fall. You cannot,' Deneys replied.

'Our *last* hope by force of arms?' Wessels queried of Smuts.

'Our last hope.'

'You're sure of that?'

'Oh yes. I have no doubt whatever. If we fail in our mission it is the British who will triumph. And all that will be left to us, the volk, will be to salvage what we can through the terms of capitulation and surrender.'

Silence settled between them, each lost in his own thoughts.

'You know what?' Smuts said at last.

'What?' Wessels asked.

'I could use a drink, some of that Scotch whisky we found on the train.'

Deneys laughed. 'A brilliant idea, "Oom" Jannie. And I shall join you if I may. I'll go and get a bottle of it.'

Smuts waited till Deneys had gone, then said to Wessels, 'Kitchener is bringing in another twenty-five thousand crack troops from India. Cavalry, mounted infantry and infantry.'

'How do you know this?'

'Our friend the illustrator spoke, during a conversation I had with him the other night, of a colleague of his with the *Westminster Gazette* who is accompanying them. Apparently they are already at sea.'

'Twenty-five thousand crack troops,' Wessels echoed, and shook his head. 'That is the big difference between our two nations. The British have bottomless manpower resources to call upon, whereas we are strictly limited. Each man we have killed is one less, one who cannot be replaced.'

'Which is why our mission must succeed,' Smuts said. '*Must*. It is *now* or never.'

Sarah and Adam considered themselves lucky. They had managed to get themselves under a five-foot overhang of rock which would keep the worst of the rain off them during the night.

Closing her eyes, Sarah said her prayers, asking God to bless and look after Jock, Maud and Robert.

She pictured Robert in her mind, which made her smile. More

456

and more she was missing her wee son. What she wouldn't have given to be able to take him in her arms for a few seconds and cuddle him. Cuddle and kiss him.

How far away Glasgow seemed now. Years away in time. As for Ian and his accident, somehow in the past few days she'd come more to terms with that than she had in the last seven months.

Adam coughed. 'Christ! You wouldn't believe it could rain so hard for so long. Not a minute's let-up since it started.' He coughed again.

'Are you all right?'

'Apart from the fact I'm lying in several inches of stinking mud, am soaked through to the skin and freezing cold, I'm absolutely fine. No complaints whatever!'

Sarah gave a low laugh. 'It is pretty awful, isn't it?' Eyes open again she reached up to readjust the position of the saddle she was using as a pillow.

'That's putting it mildly. The only consolation as far as I'm concerned is that Louis gave me a square of oilskin to wrap my canvas bag in so that I can stop worrying about my paper and drawings getting destroyed.'

Close by, outside the overhang, somebody was snoring softly, the snoring contrasting oddly to the constant thut! thut! thut! of drumming rain.

'I wonder where Alice is and what she's doing now?' Sarah mused.

'Wherever she is, and whatever she's doing, she's safe.'

'You could have been safe too, Adam.'

'I said, I feel a responsibility towards you. It was because of me that you were on that train. It was me who put you in jeopardy.'

He pulled his blanket more tightly about him, trying to block out the draught that was blowing up his legs.

'Well, I still think you were silly to do what you did,' Sarah said.

He snorted. 'Silly or not, I did what I believed to be right. And what's more, if I had the decision to make over I'd do the same thing again.'

She allowed a few seconds to tick by, then said gently, 'It was very kind and sweet of you, Adam. I want you to know that I appreciate it.'

He didn't reply.

'Adam? I said thank you.'

'I know Sarah. Now try and get some sleep.'

She closed her eyes again, smiling to herself when she felt the exhaustion well within her. She had to somehow relax, forget about the cold and wet and let the exhaustion claim her. If she had another night without a wink of sleep God alone knew what she'd be like in the morning. A total mindless wreck.

'Sarah?'

'Yes, Adam?'

'Who would ever have thought when you and I met all those years ago in your father's office that one day we would end up like this?'

A chill ran through her that had nothing to do with the cold. 'Not *end up*, I hope,' she whispered in reply.

'I didn't mean it that way. I meant . . .' He bit his lip.

'Adam?'

'Yes, Sarah?'

'Put your hand out to me.'

He wriggled his hand free of the blanket, and stretched it in her direction. Their groping hands found one another, and clasped. She squeezed tight, and so did he.

'Goodnight,' she said.

'Goodnight.'

Releasing his hand she wrapped herself in her blanket again, as did Adam.

The hand-clasping had done them both good, made them both feel better. Given them both fresh heart.

A few minutes later they were both fast asleep.

The horse, one of a group in front of Sarah and Adam, squealed as it stumbled badly, throwing its rider. The horse then sank to its knees, and from there crashed on to its side, its erstwhile rider having to quickly scramble out of the way to avoid being squashed under the animal.

Sarah and Adam reined in, as did the others round about. The fallen horse, its eyes rolling wildly, panted heavily where it lay.

It was the sixth horse that day to go down, victim of the relentless weather, forced riding and lack of forage. Unfortunately there had been no grain or other animal fodder amongst the supplies on the train.

Christiaan Bingle, the horse's owner and rider, swore vehemently as he came to his feet and caught hold of the animal's reins. He continued swearing as he tugged and pulled, trying to get the horse upright again. But the animal steadfastly refused his efforts. It was through, and knew it.

'Come on, you don't have to watch,' Adam said to Sarah and urged his own mount on, and hers, with a quick slap on the haunch.

Sarah and Adam were a little further on, their heads bowed against the driving rain, when a solitary, muffled shot rang out. Bingle had put his horse out of its misery.

Half an hour later yet another horse dropped stone dead in its tracks.

Isie's Lee-Metford was pointed at a spot equidistant between Sarah and Adam as they lay, having been instructed to do so, on the side of the *kop*, as the Afrikaners called a hill. They had been warned, one peep out of either of them and they would both be instantly killed.

Smuts, Wessels, Deneys Reitz and several others were at the brow of the *kop* silently watching the British mounted column traversing the veld below.

A column of five hundred, Smuts calculated. Double the size of the Commando. And unless he was mistaken, that was the distinctive figure of Major-General French at its head, as clever a soldier and as formidable an opponent as you could find.

Smuts glanced at Wessels who was grim-faced. 'French,' he whispered.

Wessel's face became even grimmer. He too knew of French.

As the mounted column vanished into the distance Smuts turned to Wessels and said, 'It's my guess that they're doing a loop which will take them eastwards and then south. We'll alter direction so that we slip out behind them, on the outside of their loop.'

Wessels nodded his agreement.

'We must find food for the horses soon or we'll all be walking before long,' Deneys said.

Smuts was more worried about the horses than he cared to admit. Despite the weather conditions the men could soldier on thanks to the supplies they'd taken from the British train. But the horses? They were another matter entirely.

'Let's go,' Smuts said, rising and leading the way back down the *kop* to where the dismounted Commando waited for them.

Sarah spied the scout coming in hell for leather. 'Look!' she said to Adam, pointing.

The scout galloped up to Smuts, reining in beside the General. Less than a minute later the scout fell back into the main body of the Commando.

'We're changing direction again,' Adam commented as Smuts swung the Commando about thirty degrees to the right.

'More British troops must have been sighted,' Sarah said.

'It seems to me that the whole area is alive with our boys,' Adam replied.

'And closing in, I feel.'

Adam looked at her, remembering that Smuts had brought her along as a bargaining counter or hostage, an ace up Smuts' sleeve. If he needed to, how would Smuts put that ace into effect? What would the mechanics of the situation be? One thing Adam did know, it made him feel sick to think that any harm might come to Sarah. He would do anything he could – anything – to protect her.

Another scout broke ranks and galloped off, replacing the scout who'd just rejoined the Commando.

Sarah drew the blanket that was draped over her head and shoulders further over her head.

The rain continued, relentless as ever.

'What mountains are those over there?' Sarah asked the Boer riding beside her. A man unknown to her.

The Boer stared uncomprehendingly back.

'Kowie doesn't speak a word of English, only the Taal,' the next Boer down the line explained to her, leaning forward in his saddle to do so. Taal meaning the Afrikaans language. There were fifteen riders in that line, with Sarah and Adam in the middle.

Sarah shivered. The wind that was blowing had turned icy. She wouldn't have been at all surprised if it had started to snow. And in spring, too!

'They're lovely-looking mountains,' Sarah said. And they were. Tall and imposing, illuminated by a halo of white light.

'They are the Stormberg Mountains,' the Boer who had spoken declared. He was about to elaborate on that when there was a volley of long-range gunfire.

The Boer next to Sarah, the one who couldn't speak English, toppled from his horse, shot through the chest.

'*De Britische!*' someone snarled.

A second volley was loosed at the Commando, and more Boers fell dead and wounded.

Smuts shouted an order and the Commando broke into a gallop, away from the direction of the gunfire. Some of the Commando remained behind, friends of the fallen, to gather up the wounded. A

460

number of them fell when a third volley was fired.

Sarah hugged the neck of her horse, presenting as small a profile as possible to the unseen marksmen. Dressed as she was, with the blanket round her, there was no distinguishing her from the Boers.

About two miles further on, Smuts reined in, the rest of the Commando following suit, dropping from the pace of a full-blown gallop to a walk.

'We should have charged the British!' Deneys said furiously, he having been riding beside Smuts and Wessels at the time of the first volley.

'Do you know how many there were, Deneys?' Smuts retorted.

'Two dozen guns, no more.'

Smuts gave a thin smile. 'If two dozen guns open up on a Commando our size then either those firing the guns are suicidal madmen, or else they are up to something.'

Deneys regarded his leader, staring hard. 'You mean a trap? Trying to lure us into engaging them?'

'I tell you this, Deneys. On one hand the British can be incredibly stupid, do incredibly stupid things. On the other, they are just naturally devious and guileful. I have no idea why two dozen guns opened fire on us but I certainly had no intention of taking the Commando to them to find out. I much prefer, whenever possible, to fight on my terms, not theirs.'

Deneys nodded. It was a salutary lesson. 'I understand, "Oom" Jannie.'

'Good. Now find out how many men we lost, how many are wounded and how badly so, and report back to me.'

This time the volley was withering, the number of guns far greater than before. Louis died, shot through the eye.

Two other members of the Dandy Fifth were hit, one fatally, the other only superficially.

Again the Commando broke into a gallop, away from the guns firing at them.

Horses went down that hadn't been hit, unable to go any further because of their condition.

A pack animal fell, the string behind it careering into it to topple over like ninepins. These, and the supplies they were carrying, were lost to the Commando.

The bullets, being fired individually now, might have been angry bees or flies. Bzz! Bzz! Bzz!

She could die at any second, Sarah thought. What would it be like? Would there be pain, would she suffer? Or would it be a matter of being here one moment, absolutely nothing the next? Would she . . . Bzz! That had been close. She glanced quickly at Adam to make sure he was all right, relieved to see he was. The skin of his face was taut, his eyes bulging. She wondered what she looked like? A drowned rat probably.

Bzz! Bzz! She had to come through this, she told herself. Had to for Robert's sake. The only trouble was, the whole situation was completely and utterly outside her control.

The Commando continued at a gallop, heading for the Stormberg Mountains.

Sarah sat slumped on her horse. Was this nightmare never going to end? For nightmare it had truly become.

The wind was cold and sharp as a surgeon's knife, cutting and slicing into her. While the rain — was it really a Second Deluge? — just continued to pour and pour and pour.

The ground underfoot was a mire, the horses' hooves making obscene sucking noises every time they were lifted.

A solitary shot rang out. Bzz! She didn't even bother looking up and around to see if anyone had been hit. Instead she conserved her energy, concentrating on staying in the saddle and not toppling off, which she could easily have done, being so utterly tired and exhausted. She knew if she did fall off the Boers would put her back on again, and tie her there.

'Sarah?'

Wearily she glanced sideways at Adam.

'Chin up!'

What a support Adam was being, a veritable Samson. 'Chin up, yourself!' she grinned weakly back.

Bzz! Bzz!

She and Adam had talked in whispers the previous night. The British were herding the Commando, they'd decided. Herding them the way a shepherd and his dogs herd sheep. And didn't sheep always end up in a pen?

Had Smuts also realised this? they'd wondered. They didn't know, they hadn't spoken to Smuts for the past several days. When not riding he was always in conference with his staff.

'You know what I would love right now?' Adam said.

'What?'

462

'I used to drink a beer called Younger's Revolver Brand export.'
He changed his accent to broadest Glasgow. 'I could just murder
one of those so I could.'

Sarah laughed. 'Did you use to drink that in . . . what was the
name of that pub you worked in for a while?'

'Milne's Vaults. And yes, I did.'

Somebody swore. Heads turned. Voices muttered.

Sarah and Adam both swung in the direction everyone was
staring. What she saw made Sarah's stomach contract.

A great arc of mounted British troops, tiny in the distance but
clearly discernible, were slowly advancing towards them. Several
thousand strong at least, Sarah judged.

'Holy Christ!' Adam whispered.

At the head of the Commando a thoroughly dismayed Smuts was
surveying the advancing arc of khaki. So many of them! *So many!*

'What do we do, General?' Wessels asked through clenched teeth.

Smuts only wished he knew the answer to that. 'Get me the
woman,' he instructed an aide. He didn't have to specify which
woman, the aide knew. Wheeling about, the aide began weaving his
way back through the ranks.

On reaching Sarah, the aide wheeled round again. 'Follow me,' he
told her.

Adam attempted to go with Sarah, but was restrained by Isie who
was riding on his right.

'There was . . .' She couldn't think of the English. 'You stay
here,' she said instead.

'But . . .' Adam trailed off when he saw the expression on Isie's
face. Any argument on his part would be futile.

'Time to play your ace?' Sarah said to Smuts on joining him.

'Perhaps.'

Sarah wasn't at all certain that the British would make any
allowances for her safety, particularly if that meant Smuts, even
temporarily, wriggling out of their grasp. From what Adam had said
Smuts was a prize the British were most eager to pluck. It depended
very much on what line Sir Alfred Milner and Kitchener had taken on
her capture, the latter bound to have been informed of that event. And
Kitchener was not only a hard bastard, but ruthless in the extreme. No,
she wasn't at all certain that they'd make any allowances.

And if they didn't? Well the Commando could surrender, but she
doubted that, knowing Smuts. So it would be a fight, and during

that fight one of the Boers, Deneys Reitz for example, might just do for her out of sheer spite.

Smuts waited for Swart, the last scout to report in, to confirm what he already knew. The Commando was surrounded, trapped on the summit of the Stormberg. Every pass out was blocked by khakis.

It was twilight now, the British would close in with the coming of dawn. That was when he would try and barter the Viscountess. The British were notoriously sentimental about, and protective of, their aristocracy. It might just work.

There was Swart now, and from the dejected way Swart held himself it was clear the news was as he'd expected. He swore, then swore again.

Damn French! Damn the rain! Damn his luck for not being with him when he needed it most.

'What now?' Wessels asked after Swart had made his report.

'I tell you this, Commandant, whatever happens they will never put me in one of their concentration camps. I swear that.'

'Me neither, "Oom" Jannie. We are of like mind on this.'

Smuts reached out and took Wessels by the hand. The pair of them shook hands. If needs be they would die side by side, just as they'd fought.

But Smuts was wrong about one thing. His luck hadn't deserted him. Quite the contrary.

Smuts was about to give the order to off-saddle, thinking their present spot was as good as any to spend the night, when ahead in the quickly gathering dusk he spied the outline of a low building. A farmhouse by the looks of it.

They would continue on to there he decided. Even if it was uninhabited they would be able, providing it still had a roof that is, which it appeared to, to cook a meal inside, and the Commando could have its first hot meal since the one directly after the taking of the train. That would uplift them, put them in better spirits for whatever lay ahead on the morrow.

The farmhouse did have its roof, nor was it uninhabited. As they neared it the front door flew open and a man on crutches hobbled out to greet them.

Closer to the man Smuts saw that he wasn't only a cripple, but also a hunchback.

The man stared from face to face, his own beaming with delight. 'Welcome! Welcome to my poor farm!' he exclaimed.

Smuts gave the order to off-saddle, and swung down from his horse. The man was of the volk, a friend.

What on earth was going on? Adam wondered. Why was Smuts roaring with laughter and slapping his thigh! And what a weird-looking chap had come out of the house. Talk about Quasimodo!

Minutes later night proper had fallen, and shortly after that Adam was rejoined by Sarah, escorted by the same aide who'd taken her to Smuts. The aide spoke in Afrikaans to Isie, who replied in the same language.

'What's to do?' Adam asked Sarah.

'I've no idea. But whatever the hunchback told Smuts has made the General very happy indeed.'

'I could hear and see that.' Adam turned to Isie. 'Do you know what's happening?'

'Hot food soon,' Isie replied.

'Is that all?'

Isie didn't reply to that. Instead she smiled mysteriously.

'Something more than hot food is up, that's for sure,' Sarah said to Adam, who nodded his agreement.

Close to where they were two of the pack animals were unloaded, their panniers taken into the farmhouse.

Sarah sniffed. 'I can smell smoke.'

Adam glanced at the farmhouse chimney, and could just make out several grey wisps drifting skywards. 'Fire's on, food shouldn't be too long.' He was absolutely ravenous.

'Can we go into the house?' Sarah asked Isie.

'No,' came the hard, flat refusal.

'Why not?'

' "Oom" Jannie send you here. If he had wanted you there he would have said so.'

'God, it's bitter!' Sarah complained, stamping her feet. After that she patted her horse's neck, telling the mare what a good girl she was. The bugger's just about done in, she thought. But then all the horses were on their last legs, or close as dammit to it.

The meal when it came was piping hot beans and bacon, and delicious. Sarah smiled to herself, remembering the sight of the Boers wolfing down their food after the taking of the train. Now she was wolfing just like the rest of them. Blowing on each spoonful to cool it a bit before gobbling it down.

465

The hot food immediately made her feel better. It brought back some of her strength, while her tiredness receded a little.

'There's bound to be a bed in there,' Sarah said, staring at the farmhouse. The thought was tantalising.

Sarah suddenly realised that the command hadn't been given to unsaddle the horses. That was strange. She asked Isie why this was so.

'You see,' Isie replied.

'Do you mean we're not stopping here?' Adam queried.

'You see,' Isie repeated. And would be drawn no further on the subject.

A little later the Boers began checking the metal parts of their gear and equipment, ensuring that they were securely bound and wrapped against making a noise. When Isie had gone over hers she checked Adam's horse, then Sarah's.

'We must be going on,' Adam whispered to Sarah.

'Or maybe they intend trying to double back and sneak through the British line?'

Adam shook his head. 'That would be madness on their part. The British would be on the lookout for just such a move, and would cut them to pieces.'

'But if it's simply a case of resuming going forward why the precautions they've just taken?'

Adam had no answer to that.

'This time –' Sarah started to say, then stopped. She'd been about to say that this time next day they might both be dead.

She suddenly felt very vulnerable and scared, and alone. No, not alone. Adam was here. 'Adam, would you do something for me? A favour?'

'If I can.'

'Take me in your arms and hold me close.'

He didn't care about Isie or any of the other Boers round about. He gathered Sarah into his embrace, and held her there.

He could feel her heart hammering, as his own now was. He surprised himself then by doing something he'd wanted to do since that long ago morning when he'd first met her in Jock Hawke's office.

Taking her gently by the chin he tilted her face up to his, and kissed her.

For the briefest of seconds she resisted, then her resistance melted.

'I meant no disrespect to your husband by doing that,' he murmured when the kiss was over.

'I know. And Adam. Thank you.'

'Romance heh?' Isie said to them, then made what was obviously a coarse crack to one of the nearby Boers.

'Isie?' Adam smiled. And when he had her attention. 'We have an expression in Glasgow. Away and bile yer heid hen.'

Isie looked blank. 'I no understand?'

'It's double Dutch to her,' Sarah quipped to Adam, which caused them both to burst out laughing.

Isie didn't get that either.

'Utter a single sound and it's your last, I promise you,' Deneys said, brandishing a long, well-honed knife in front of Adam's face. 'I'll cut your throat, then hers.' He turned to Sarah. 'Same for you. Just one sound and that's it for the pair of you. Understand?'

'Yes,' Sarah breathed, while Adam nodded.

'Good.'

The Commando was assembled, ready to move out. The instruction was that they were to lead their horses, total silence being essential. The worst of the wounded were left behind, having been already moved into the farmhouse.

Smuts was at his usual place at the head of the Commando, Wessels to one side of him, Mynheer Treurnicht the crippled hunchback at the other. Mynheer Treurnicht was to be their guide.

For the first time since the rain had started Smuts was glad of it. It would have just been like the damn thing if the rain had stopped when its continuance would be to their advantage.

Once under way, the Commando flitted through the night, the only sound being the sucking noises the horses made when they lifted their hooves, but there was nothing could be done about that.

If Treurnicht was right and there was a route off the Stormberg that would allow them to escape the British noose, it would be a miracle, Smuts thought. And one in the eye for Major-General bloody French. But most importantly, it would mean the Commando would still be intact to carry on with its mission.

Smuts offered up a silent prayer to the Almighty, pleading on behalf of the volk that this would be the case.

Sarah stiffened when she heard voices, and immediately Deneys's knife was against her throat. The voices became clearer, Cockneys by their accents. British soldiers bivouacked for the night.

At the head of the Commando, Treurnicht was thinking that

another ten minutes would bring them to the escarpment. He was moving swiftly on the crutches that he'd been using for years, ever since the illness that had shrivelled his left leg and twisted his upper torso, turning him into a hunchback. So adept was he with his crutches that he could hobble on them for miles without it bothering him in the slightest.

The Commando was a little further on when someone called out, another cockney accent. This was followed by the champing of bits.

Treurnicht immediately signed to Smuts that the Commando was to halt. And this was accomplished without a word being spoken.

Sarah stood in the darkness, Deneys and his knife beside her on her right, Adam a couple of feet away on her left. The same voice called out again, but further away this time. Another voice replied from further away still.

Treurnicht signed for the Commando to resume its progress, which it did.

When they eventually arrived at the edge of the escarpment, Treurnicht stopped, and gave a whispered warning. A warning that was quickly passed back through the ranks.

Smuts stared into the plunging blackness before him, the reality of what faced the Commando now coming home to him. 'How far down is it?' he asked Treurnicht softly.

'All the way down the south face of the Stormberg.'

Wessels swore in a whisper.

If only they could see, Smuts thought.

'Men maybe, but horses too?' Wessels said to Treurnicht.

'It can be done, and has been. I warned you it would be difficult.'

'Have you ever been down it?' Smuts queried.

Treurnicht gave a low laugh, and waggled a crutch in front of Smuts. 'Not I personally, but my two brothers have on several occasions. Of course it was daytime when they did it, but you can't afford that luxury. If you are still here when the light breaks, or on the escarpment itself, the British will spy you and that will be that.'

Sarah gazed in horror down the little she could make out of the escarpment drop. Surely some terrible mistake had been made. They weren't going to be expected to go down there!

God in heaven! Adam thought. He glanced at Deneys and was gratified to see the young Boer looked thoroughly shaken.

'There is thick grass on the escarpment, that's what makes its descent possible,' Treurnicht explained.

Thick grass! Smuts thought wryly. Any other place but this and his starving horses could have had a fine feed.

'Good luck, General,' Treurnicht said, holding out a hand.

Smuts shook hands with Treurnicht, Treurnicht with Wessels after that.

Smuts then passed the order along. They were going to descend the escarpment as quietly as they could. Good luck to everyone.

'I wouldn't mind a swallow or two of gin before attempting this,' Wessels whispered to Smuts, who smiled. Truth was, he wouldn't have minded a swallow or two of gin either.

'Well then,' said Smuts, and took a deep breath. 'Here we go.' And with that he stepped out on to the escarpment, dragging his very unwilling horse with him.

Wessels went after Smuts, the entire Commando after him. A woman called Ester was the first to fall, landing with a jarring thump to go bouncing and rolling before she managed to regain her feet.

Sarah's horse broke away from her early on; she just couldn'* keep hold of the animal. It slid and slithered off ahead of her.

Sarah grabbed Adam's hand, linking up with him. That made matters slightly better for the two of them, each giving the other support, and each acting as a counterbalance to his partner.

Someone went skidding past Sarah, whoever it was stretched flat out on his back. Then she glimpsed a pack animal comically sitting on its rump as it descended.

Sarah and Adam were running now. The terrifying thing was they were running into pitch blackness.

Something went crack! A bone, Sarah thought. Somebody close by had snapped a bone.

A number of horses were squealing, others snorting and neighing. Not one human voice was heard, however, the Boers were maintaining their silence.

At the top of the escarpment, Mynheer Treurnicht was smiling. At long last he had been able to help the volk in their war against the detested British. He, the hunchback cripple, had saved the great General Smuts and Smuts' Commando from either certain capture or death. It also paid the British back a little for killing his brothers, Henning and Francis, the year before at the Battle of Diamond Hill.

Hand in hand Sarah and Adam, he still maintaining the hold on his horse, glissaded down the escarpment while all around them Boers and animals did the same.

And then suddenly, abruptly, it was all over, and they were at the bottom of the escarpment having got down safely.

Amazingly not one member of the Commando was killed, nor were any of the animals. Scrapes, scratches and cuts there were aplenty. Plus several broken bones. But not one life lost.

Smuts' miracle had come to pass. The Commando had escaped the British noose. Their mission was still viable.

A bemused Smuts gave the Commando a few minutes in which to catch its collective breath, then led them in a short prayer of thanks for their deliverance.

After which the command was given to mount, and ride.

Chapter 12

Sarah came awake with the realisation that something was different, something had changed. Without opening her eyes she tried to think what that something was. And then the answer dawned on her. It had stopped raining.

Her eyes snapped open to gaze up into a clear morning sky, a sky completely devoid of cloud.

Raising herself into a sitting position she threw her sodden blanket from her and stretched. Not only had the rain stopped but it was actually warmish. How glorious!

'Adam! Wake up!'

'Wh . . . what is it?' He too sat up. Then the penny dropped for him also.

'I don't believe it!' he breathed. 'I was beginning to think it was going to rain forever.'

Taking out his pocket watch he glanced at it. 'Ten o'clock!' They'd been allowed to sleep late. But then they'd alternately ridden and walked the entire previous day and half the night before that away from the Stormberg Mountains.

Getting to his feet he groaned and clutched his right shoulder.

'What is it?' Sarah queried.

'Where I was wounded. Coming down that escarpment hasn't exactly done it a power of good.'

She had totally forgotten about his wound: he had not mentioned it once since their capture. 'Let me have a look and I'll see if I can do anything.'

He took off his jacket and laid it to one side, then stripped, above the waist, down to his vest.

There was a bandage on his shoulder which Sarah now carefully removed. The wound when revealed was a pucker of scar tissue slightly red round the edges.

'Well, it hasn't been opened up again,' Sarah said. 'Perhaps all that activity jarred and wrenched it somewhat.'

Adam gingerly touched the pucker. Now that he came to analyse it the pain did seem muscular. 'Could be you're right.'

'Is this angry circle round it new?'

'No, in fact it's less angry now than when we left Cape Town.'

'I'm hardly a doctor but it would seem to me that the jarring and wrenching is what you're feeling as opposed to any further damage to the wound itself.'

She then rebandaged his shoulder, securing the tailpiece with the brace of brass safety pins that had originally held it in place.

When she finished he was smiling softly. Reaching up, he placed his fingertips very lightly, the suggestion of a caress in the action, on her cheek. 'Thank you.'

For the space of a few seconds it was as if a spell had been woven between them, a spell that popped when they heard a loud halloo! Sarah immediately glanced in the direction of the halloo, as did Adam.

The scout slid from his horse to talk very animatedly to the waiting Smuts and Wessels. When the scout's report was completed Smuts called to Deneys Reitz and held a brief conversation with him.

When that conversation was over, Deneys gathered together the Dandy Fifth, who then rode off in the direction the scout had come from.

It was then Sarah realised the area where they'd camped was covered in luscious spring grass. All the tethered horses were grazing very contentedly, and already looking better for the first proper nourishment they'd had in ages.

Shortly after this some of the Boers began collecting wood from a nearby clump of trees, and soon had two sizeable fires blazing. Before long the mouth-watering aroma of coffee was wafting on the air.

'It looks like Smuts is coming over,' Adam said to Sarah, the General making straight in their direction.

'So how are you both, heh?' Smuts inquired politely on reaching them.

'Feeling better now that the rain has finally stopped,' Sarah replied.

'I'm sure I can say we're all feeling better for that,' Smuts smiled. 'And you, Mr Tennant?'

'Wondering what happens next.'

Smuts produced a cigar, bit off its end and spat the end away. Then, carefully, and with obvious great enjoyment, he lit the cigar. 'I'll tell you. For today, nothing. My scouts report there are no British within a wide circle of here, so we will have a day of rest to hopefully recuperate from our recent exertions, get ourselves and clothes dried, and have a feast.'

'A feast!' Sarah exclaimed.

'That last scout who came in told me he spotted a herd of waterbuck a few miles away, so I've despatched Deneys Reitz and his section to bring back as many as they can. If you haven't had waterbuck before they make excellent eating.'

'Right now just about anything would make excellent eating as far as I'm concerned,' Sarah retorted.

Smuts laughed. 'Hunger is a good sauce, heh! Remember I said that?'

'Oh, I remember all right.'

'You also said that all the wild beasts in this part of the Cape had been slaughtered since the war started, and I presumed that included game?' Adam queried of Smuts.

'I did mean that. But we have come quite a distance since the train, you know. Nonetheless, we are fortunate to have found waterbuck. I can only presume there haven't been any British in strength hereabouts, for as I told you before it is part of their policy to slaughter every animal they come across. It is one of their many methods of trying to break the spirit of the volk – which they will never do, I assure you.'

Adam looked over at the two fires where a number of the Commando were already stripping and beginning to dry their clothes. 'Would you mind if Lady Ascog and I have our own little fire here?' Adam asked Smuts.

'I don't see why not. If that's what you want.'

'Please.'

'Do you wish to cook your own meat?'

Adam glanced at Sarah, then back to Smuts. 'Yes, if you've no objection.'

'None whatever.' And having said that Smuts strode away.

Adam turned to a puzzled Sarah. 'If you want to get your clothes dried properly you're going to have to take them off. I thought it would be more private, and less embarrassing, for you if we had our own fire.'

'How very thoughtful of you. Thank you.'

'I'll get wood then. You do have matches don't you?'

'I have indeed.'

He tapped her gently on the arm. 'Shan't be long.'

She stared after him, the hint of a smile playing round her lips, and a warmth in her that had nothing to do with the change of weather.

Sarah decided it would be best to dry their blankets first so they could wrap themselves snugly in these while doing their clothes. The blankets were steaming nicely by the fire Adam had made when Deneys and the Dandy Fifth returned with the waterbuck they'd killed, twenty carcases in all.

When the animals had been skinned Adam was given a piece of hindquarter which he skewered and proceeded to roast on the spit he'd constructed from sticks.

Sarah ran a hand through her hair. How greasy and awful it felt — rats' tails. And itchy. She gave her scalp a vigorous scratch, but that only made the itch even worse.

'Where did the water for the coffee come from?' she asked Adam.

'There's a small stream, the Boers call it a *spruit*, beyond the trees. It came from there.'

Amongst the toilet articles she'd brought from the train was a bar of the Cape Orange soap that Mr Gerrard had given her. She explained to Adam where she was going, and what she was going to do, then went off in search of Isie. For, like the lavatory, she presumed she wouldn't be allowed to disappear off without being accompanied.

She found Isie not far away lying chatting to a Boer she'd never noticed before. A handsome chap, she judged, underneath all that dirt, matted hair and chest-length beard. Isie's sweetheart?

When Isie heard what Sarah intended, her eyes opened wide. '*Jah*, I come with you,' she hastily agreed.

The stream when they reached it was about three feet across and filled with fast-moving water. Rainwater, Isie said. *Spruits* were usually dry except in the rainy season.

Sarah took off her jacket and threw it down, then considered removing her shirt, but decided against that. Kneeling by the stream she plunged her head fully into it, gasped on pulling it out again, then began to get as good a lather as she was able with cold water.

She lathered and rinsed her head twice, after which she squeezed her hair as dry as possible.

'Me?' Isie requested, pointing at the soap.

Sarah had guessed this was why the Boer woman had so readily agreed to accompany her. 'Help yourself.'

There was nothing shy or modest about Isie. In a trice she was naked to the waist, revealing small, firm breasts that had tiny pink nipples, and kneeling on the bank of the stream. After a quick immersion she began to vigorously lather her hair.

'Good,' Sarah said when Isie was done.

Isie sighed. *'Oh jah, gut!'*

Laughing together the two women returned to the main camp area.

Sarah had only been back with Adam a few minutes when Isie reappeared carrying several items which she gave to Sarah. 'Yours,' Isie declared, and promptly left them again.

The items were a pot of strawberry jam, a pottery container of Stilton cheese, a packet of savoury biscuits and a half-pound of salted butter that had been partially used.

Sarah stared at these things in bewilderment for a few seconds, then it clicked. 'From the Fortnum and Mason hamper I intended taking to Jack,' she explained to Adam.

Adam opened the pot of jam, scooped out a fingerful and stuck the finger into his mouth.

'Scrumptious!' he declared.

'Strawberry jam, Stilton, savoury biscuits, butter and waterbuck. What a mixture!' Sarah said.

'But delicious, I'm sure.'

'Oh, I'm *sure*!'

'Here.' He wiped his finger, stuck it back in the jam, then offered the resulting fingerful to Sarah.

She took his finger fully into her mouth and slowly sucked it clean.

'More?' Adam asked, his voice suddenly husky.

She nodded.

He scooped out another dollop, and again her mouth closed over his finger. This time she used her tongue, licking even more slowly than she'd sucked.

'I wonder what's become of poor Jack?' she said after that was over.

Adam was about to answer that he just hoped they lived to find out, then changed his mind. 'I hope he's all right. That he's managing to hang on.'

Sarah hoped so too. 'How long will that meat be?'

'A while yet.'

She felt the blankets which had stopped steaming and was surprised to find that they were dry, if not exactly bone dry. 'I think I'll start drying my wet togs, then,' she said.

'And I'll go and get some more wood.'

He was being tactful again, she thought when he was gone, leaving her alone to get out of her clothes.

She swathed herself in her blanket, and undressed completely under that.

When she was at the *spruit* she should have taken the opportunity to wash her underclothes also, she now realised. She had been wearing three complete sets of underwear: the set she'd been wearing when captured, plus the other two sets she'd taken from her luggage.

Adam returned with his arms heaped high with wood, saying that the Boers had produced a couple of hatchets and there wouldn't be much left of the clump of trees by the time they'd finished.

Then he noticed Sarah's cross expression, and asked her the reason for it. She explained about her underwear.

'That's not a problem. You watch the meat and I'll go and wash them for you now.'

She looked shocked. 'You can't do that!'

'Why not?'

'They're female things.'

'So?'

'Well . . . it just wouldn't be nice.'

He gave her a level stare. 'Do you think any of what we've been through so far has been nice?'

'I know, but . . . underclothes are personal.'

'It wouldn't bother me. Not when I know the person and . . .' He paused, then added softly, 'Like her.'

They stared at one another. 'What about your own underclothes? Surely you'll want to wash those also?'

'And my hair. I'll do all that while I'm there.'

'Here's the soap,' she said, handing it to him. Was it her imagination or did she feel a tingle when their fingers touched?

He gathered up her underwear, then went off to find someone to go with him.

Sarah closed her eyes. It was odd considering the circumstances, but she was filled with happiness. Happiness, well-being and a sort of zinging elation.

Singing quietly to herself she turned the meat on the makeshift spit. It smelt absolutely wonderful.

Sarah was trimming Adam's beard and moustache, using the pair of small nail scissors that came from her toilet articles, when there was a sudden commotion. Glancing round she saw two mounted Boers, each trailing a string of blacks whom they were in the process of bringing into camp. The blacks, tied and roped as if pack animals, were trotting along behind the Boers' horses.

'They're all women,' Adam noticed.

They were all women, Sarah confirmed mentally. Eleven in all.

A large group of Boers was gathering round the now stationary women, laughing, joking and making what were clearly ribald remarks.

Then General Smuts was there, talking to the two mounted men who'd brought in these new captives.

Smuts and Wessels pushed their way out of the throng, while behind them the women simply vanished from view. One of the women screamed, a high shrill sound that ceased abruptly.

Sarah swallowed hard. 'What do you think's happening?' she queried softly.

'I don't know.'

'They're not killing them, are they?' Then she remembered her own fear when captured. 'Oh no! Surely not?'

Adam was bleak faced as he stared at the solid wall of Boer backs. The Boers began yelling and jeering, some of them waving their hats in the air.

Two of the wall detached themselves, and began strolling away. One was Isie, the other Ester.

'Isie?' Sarah called out.

Isie and Ester, the pair of them grinning hugely, came over. '*Jah*?' Isie asked.

'What are those men doing?'

Ester sniggered. Isie clenched a hand into a fist, and made a pumping motion.

'You mean the women are being raped?' Sarah said, voice tight and brittle.

Ester spat on to the grass, then rubbed the spot with her foot. 'Their men working for British. Our men decide have little fun.'

'Fun!' Sarah exclaimed. 'You call that fun?'

'Our men think it is.' Ester said something short and sharp to Isie in Afrikaans, and the two of them strode off.

Sarah looked again at the wall of men, the wall part of a circle that had formed. She blanched to imagine what was happening within that circle.

'Don't interfere. There's nothing we can do,' Adam warned her.

'I can't believe that Smuts sanctioned what's going on. I just can't.'

'He must have.'

'No,' she said, shaking her head.

'He must have,' Adam repeated. 'You saw him talking with them.'

A ragged cheer went up from the circle of Boers, and several hats were flung high into the air.

Sarah tossed the scissors to one side, and rose to her feet.

'For God's sake don't try and stop that lot!' Adam said in alarm.

'I'm going to speak to Smuts,' Sarah declared, jaw firm with determination, and marched across to where the General was in conversation with Wessels and several others.

'General?'

He gave her a polite nod of the head. 'Lady Ascog.'

'I can't believe that you gave permission for what's happening over there.'

He frowned. 'Why shouldn't I have given permission?'

'Those women are being raped, violated by your men. It's disgusting, disgraceful. And totally inhuman.'

'My men have been on Commando for a long while, Lady Ascog. A little sexual release, for those who wish to indulge, will do them the world of good.'

She was astonished to hear him say that. 'But it's *rape*! You can't tell me the women have agreed to what's being done to them.'

Smuts produced his pipe and started to fill it. He shot Wessels an amused glance. 'I don't understand your concern, Lady Ascog.'

'Those women, as you well know, are being raped,' she repeated.

'Why should this upset you? They're not white women, only Kaffirs.'

'Black or white, they're still women.'

'No, Lady Ascog,' he said emphatically, his tone as if he was addressing a child. Explaining to the child a fundamental fact of life. 'They're Kaffirs. Little better than beasts.'

She was appalled. 'You really mean that?'

'Most certainly.'

In that instant Sarah realised the sheer callousness of the volk, a callousness that was breathtakingly coupled with their sublimely arrogant – and total – belief in their own white supremacy.

478

'Those Kaffirs, as you call them, have feelings, just as you do,' she stated quietly.

'A dog has feelings, Lady Ascog, yet it remains a dog.'

She had the almost overwhelming urge to slap him, but wisely stopped herself from doing so.

Wessels muttered something in Afrikaans, which Smuts laughed at.

'How can you call yourselves Christians, and yet believe as you do?' she queried. One of the things she'd learned about the Boers was how extremely religious they were.

Smuts shrugged. 'I fail to see how that has anything to do with the subject in question.'

'Christianity teaches us to love our neighbours . . .'

'And I do!' Smuts exclaimed.

'Those black women are neighbours.'

He shook his head in despair. 'You don't seem able to understand, Lady Ascog. Those black women are Kaffirs. They have their place in the order of things, just as we have ours. But the places, the stations, are quite different. Besides . . .' His face lit up in an impish grin. 'Isn't that precisely what my men are doing?'

He'd lost her. 'What?'

'Loving their neighbours.'

Wessels let out a great hoot of laughter, and slapped his thigh. The others present also joined in the laughter.

'Oh "Oom" Jannie! "Oom" Jannie!' Wessels said, wiping away tears of mirth.

Another cheer went up from the circle of men.

Sarah could see it was useless arguing further. Smuts and the Arikaner ideology would not be moved.

Feeling sick inside she turned about, and walked back to Adam.

Sarah woke to find herself chittering. It was that night and since falling asleep the temperature had plummeted.

At least she had dry clothes on, and her blanket was dry. That was something. But it was still freezing, the coldest night of all since her capture.

She looked at Adam a few feet away. He was curled up foetus-style, his back to her.

'Adam?'

He grunted.

'Adam, are you awake?'

He rolled over to face her. 'I am now. What is it?'

'I was just thinking . . . Oh!' she exclaimed as a blast of icy wind stabbed through her.

Scuttling sideways like a crab she closed the gap between them, while he stared at her in astonishment.

'It seems downright daft for us not to share our blankets, and body temperatures,' she explained. 'If we cuddle up, that should make us both warmer.'

The thought had crossed his mind before now, but he hadn't dared suggest it.

'Good idea,' he replied.

'You don't object, then?'

'Not in the least.'

'Right.' And with that she threw her own blanket off her, grabbed his which was wound round him, tugged it free, then wrapped it round the pair of them, her blanket being wrapped over that.

Still chittering she snuggled up close to him. 'Turn back the way you were.'

He did as she'd instructed, and instantly she had an arm round his chest, and was pressing her body hard against his.

'That's better,' she muttered after a while, her chittering having stopped.

How often he'd dreamt of this when younger, he thought. To be sleeping with Sarah Hawke, her cuddling up tight against him.

'Yes, it is,' he agreed.

When they eventually fell asleep again they were both smiling.

The Commando, with Sarah and Adam approximately in the centre of it, moved forward at a steady pace which ate up the miles.

The British were pressing them again, and weren't all that far away. On top of a kop about a mile distant a heliograph winked out a message to Smuts. With the weather staying clear, and a pale yellow sun in the sky, the heliographs – reduced to two as one had been smashed to pieces coming down the Stormberg – were once more in action.

Sarah ran a hand over her face. The veld seemed endless. Something that went on and on and forever on. No beginning, no end, just constantly unfolding landscape.

Time too had altered. Out here a minute was like an hour, an hour a day, a week a year. Was it really still September 1901? It seemed that at least a decade had passed since her capture.

She glanced at Adam riding beside, but fractionally in front of her. She was having disturbing thoughts about him of late, seeing him in an entirely different light to that she had done previously.

How kind he was, and caring. God knew what this journey would have been like if he hadn't volunteered to accompany her. An even worse nightmare than it was.

Reaching out, but without him being aware of it, she gently touched him.

Smuts was angry, angry with himself. What he hadn't told Wessels, Deneys Reitz or anyone else was that as the Commando progressed towards the Eastern Cape he had expected a great many of the local volk in the districts they passed through to join the Commando, swelling the number of the Commando to far, far more than it had been originally when it had slipped across the Orange River. That this would happen had been an integral part of his argument to the High Command at Cypherfontein the previous December when he had first advocated his raid, and the eventual linking up with Kritzinger and De la Rey.

The Cape volk, under hated British domination, would rise and flood to his side, he had assured President Kruger and the others at Cypherfontein: De Wet, Hertzog, Kritzinger, De la Rey, Louis Botha to name but an illustrious few.

And how many of the volk had actually joined the Commando since it had come into the Cape? Two. *Two!* When he'd hoped for anything between five hundred and a thousand plus.

Glancing up at the sky he cursed under his breath. Those were rain clouds if ever there were. Huge ones, dark and glowering. He'd never known a Cape spring like it for rain.

Twenty minutes later the first spots spattered the ground.

Sarah acted instantly and instinctively.

The Commando had stopped for a few hours' rest, the rain that had been bucketing down all that day and the day before having thankfully ceased about an hour previously.

Sarah had been to the lavatory with Ester accompanying her – she hadn't been able to find Isie – and was now returning to her horse. She had left Ester on the periphery of the Commando talking to a friend.

Suddenly the horses round about squealed in fright, several of them rearing on to their hind legs. Deneys Reitz, who'd been about to place his saddle on the ground, was knocked by his horse's rump, it being one of those who'd reared, and sent sprawling.

The shape was moving so quickly it appeared to be flying over the ground, and was headed straight for Deneys.

Before undoing his saddle, Deneys had stuck the sword he now carried, his trophy from the train, into the ground.

There was no time to give warning, or even for thought. Sarah took a few swift steps forward, snatched up the sword by its handle, and swung the blade with an overhand motion. More by luck than good judgement her aim was perfect: she sliced the snake in half.

Swearing, Deneys grabbed at the Lee-Enfield thonged to his saddle, pulled it free and twisted round, thinking he was being attacked from the rear. Which was true, only he'd got the wrong attacker.

His finger was tightening on the trigger when Swart, who'd seen what had happened, cried out for him to stop.

'It was going straight for you,' Sarah mumbled.

'What was?'

Using the tip of the sword she pointed at the dead snake which Deneys now noticed for the first time.

Deneys stared at the snake, a black mamba. One bite from that and he would have died horribly, raving and in excruciating pain. The thought made the inside of his mouth go dry.

Sarah's hand was trembling as she stuck the sword back in the ground. All around her Boers were staring at her, some nodding, others smiling.

She'd resumed walking and was about twenty feet further on from where the incident had taken place, when a vicelike grip grasped her arm.

'Lady Ascog?'

It was Deneys, the strangest expression on his face.

She looked at him, but didn't reply.

'Thank you.'

'You're welcome.'

'Lucky for me the General didn't take my advice and have you shot, heh?' he joked.

'Yes, lucky for you,' she agreed softly, and removed his hand from her arm.

She continued on her way back to her horse, and Adam.

*

'Listen!' Wessels said, low and urgently.

The sound was faint, but unmistakable. A train. A few seconds later both men knew it was coming towards them rather than away.

Smuts and Wessels had been aware there was a railway line not far ahead. The maps they carried told them so. And earlier scouts had confirmed it.

'If we hurry we might be able to derail it,' Wessels suggested.

Smuts shook his head. 'In this darkness we won't be able to tell until the last minute whether it's a military train or an ordinary scheduled one. I can't take the chance that it's the latter. I will not attack—far less kill—civilians in Cape Colony.' He turned in his saddle and looked at Wessels. 'That would be a tactical mistake.'

Wessels nodded that he understood.

The Commando reached the railway line with the lights of the train fast approaching. Smuts issued the order that they would halt and wait this side of the tracks until the train had passed, then they'd cross over and on their way.

Clickety-clack! Clickety-clack! Sarah's heart was in her mouth as she listened to the train thunder towards them. And then, whoosh! The engine was by, the long line of carriages following.

Carriage after carriage, until at last the dining car came into view.

Sarah stared wistfully at the sight of British officers and civilians smoking, drinking and tucking into plates of food. 'Oh!' she sighed. If ever she'd envied anyone it was those she was now seeing. She would have given anything to have been suddenly transported amongst them. Her *and* Adam transported amongst them, she corrected herself. Her and Adam.

When the train was past the Commando allowed it to travel several hundred yards further on before silently crossing the tracks and continuing on their way.

Sarah watched the train till at last its lights were lost to view. When they finally were gone she couldn't hold back the small sob that escaped her lips.

At the head of the Commando, Smuts would have been livid if he'd known that Major-General French and many of the Major-General's staff had been aboard that train. A train he could probably have taken if it hadn't been that he didn't want to attack or kill civilians in Cape Colony.

Major-General French and staff who were in hot pursuit of Smuts and his Commando.

Sarah sat slumped in her saddle, head bent into the driving rain. High above it was thunder and lightning, one following the other, over and over again.

She felt herself slipping slowly to the right, but just didn't seem to have the energy to stop herself.

She was about to fall when Adam wrapped an arm round her, stopping her from doing so.

'Can't . . . can't go on,' she whispered.

'You have to!'

'No. Just want to sleep. Close my eyes and sleep.'

'Pull yourself upright again, Sarah. I can't hold you like this for long.'

'Can't . . . No strength.'

Dropping the reins he'd been holding in his free hand he swung round and attempted to push her back upright. Because he was as weak as she it was like trying to push a ton weight.

'Pull!' he commanded. 'Pull, Sarah!'

She whimpered.

'Pull!'

She found herself thinking of the dining car again – the memory of it had been haunting her. In her mind she was sitting at one of the tables with a heaped plate of –

'Pull, dammit!'

'Eh?'

They were both going to fall off, he thought. This was it. The Boers were too far gone to stop and remount them. They would either be trampled to death by those behind, or perish alone on the veld.

No, this wasn't it! he told himself, a wave of rage erupting within him. He'd be buggered if it was.

His rage lent him the strength he hadn't had, and with a final mighty shove Sarah was back upright on her saddle.

'Now stay there. You've got to stay there,' he urged fiercely.

She slowly shook her head. 'Finished, Adam. Nothing left. Done for.'

Leaning over he hit her a stinging blow on the cheek. 'Don't talk like that, woman! Don't be so bloody selfish!'

'How, selfish?'

'Think of Robert, your son. He's already lost his father. You give in now and he becomes an orphan. Is that what you want? Your child to become an orphan?'

'Of course not.'

'Then stick with it. Think of Robert and going back to him.'

'Yes,' she mumbled. Robert and going back to him, her wee son. The image of Ian. She couldn't let him down, she couldn't.

'Remember what you told Smuts,' Adam went on. 'We're Glasgow folk and they don't come any hardier. Prove now that you were right, that it was no empty boast.'

'Did I say that?' she replied, smiling lazily.

'You did. I was there. You told the General to his face that there is no hardier breed than Glaswegians. So anything this lot can put up with we can as well. Can't we, Sarah?'

'Yes.'

'Good.'

'Won't give in. Will stick with it. For Robert's sake.'

'For Robert's sake, Sarah.'

She took a deep breath, then another.

The loudest clap of thunder yet, like some mighty cannon being fired, boomed out.

It was about midnight when the rain turned to sleet. The Commando floundered along through inches deep mud – that was what the ground had been turned into. Those who were reduced to walking, whose horses were dead, held on to their comrades' stirrups to help keep them going.

Every so often, with sickening regularity, there would be a splash and thud as yet another horse went down. Few of those that went down got up again.

This was hell on earth right enough, Adam thought as his horse put one weary foot in front of the other. In his mind's eye he pictured the Commando. Some day, if he lived through all this, he would paint – not draw – but paint this night.

He glanced at Sarah sitting slumped with head bent. If her horse was one of those to go he would give her his. Insist she took it.

Smuts peered into the murk. The scouts were all in, any out in the weather this had become stood an excellent chance of getting separated from the Commando and lost.

The British following them would have stopped and bivouacked. They'd be warm and snug in tents, he thought bitterly. Despair rose up in him, terrible black despair. Everything was going wrong, nothing was happening as it should, as he'd envisioned it would.

Damn these spring rains! Damn them! For the umpteenth time he told himself he'd never known a Cape spring like it for rain.

How could he have foreseen these abnormal rains? How could he possibly!

But that was no consolation.

'House!' croaked Hermann Malan, pointing ahead. He was in the front line of the Commando riding alongside Smuts and Wessels.

Smuts passed a hand over his eyes. Was it a house? It certainly looked as if something was there.

'House,' Wessels confirmed a moment later.

The word spread like wildfire back through the Commando. They were coming up to a house.

At the front of the Commando rifles were unslung, and bolts clicked. You could never be too careful.

Smuts halted the Commando and instructed Malan to ride forward and investigate. He told van Rinsberg and Pelzer to go with Malan.

A few minutes later Malan was back reporting to Smuts. 'A farmhouse, "Oom" Jannie, and this one *is* deserted, though some furniture and other bits and pieces have been left behind.'

'Roof?'

'Still on, and in good repair. The house is an exceptionally big one: the entire Commando should be able to squeeze inside.'

That cheered Smuts — precisely what the doctor ordered. He barked out an order, and the Commando moved forward towards the farmhouse.

Not only did the farmhouse still have its roof intact — it was khaki policy to burn roofs whenever and wherever possible, this to deny shelter to just such as the Commando — so too were its windows.

'Build a fire with whatever you can find,' Smuts instructed, the moment he was through the door.

The men took him at his word. A long kitchen table was smashed to pieces, as were the chairs that had been surrounding it.

The Boers scoured the house, but didn't find a morsel of food.

That was a bitter disappointment as the supplies they'd taken when they'd captured Sarah and Adam were now all gone.

Food wasn't found, but a small cache of oil was. That and two lamps. Some of the oil was used to start the fire, then the lamps were lit.

Sarah and Adam claimed a corner of the main room as their own. There they huddled, slapping themselves with their hands, trying to restore some warmth.

Soon the fire was roaring, and another started in the adjoining kitchen where the table and chairs had come from.

The temperature in the house quickly rose, which began to revive everyone.

'How do you feel now?' Adam asked Sarah.

'Better than I did, and that's for certain.' Taking him by the hand she squeezed it. 'Thank you for what you did earlier.'

He smiled weakly. 'I can't lose you now. We've come too far together for that to happen.'

'Lady Ascog?'

It was Deneys Reitz who had spoken. He was standing over them, a hat in one hand, what appeared to be a blanket in the other.

'I'm sure you can use these. They belonged to one of the Dandy Fifth who won't be needing them any more.'

Sarah stared up at Deneys. 'Dead?'

'A few miles back. He was wounded before the Stormberg, and although not all that bad to begin with the wound finally killed him.'

'I'm sorry,' Sarah said quietly.

'He was a good man. We will miss him.' And with that Deneys gave Sarah the hat and blanket.

'Now it's my turn to thank you.'

He nodded, and she could see he felt he was repaying part of his debt to her. Then he moved away from her and Adam.

When she opened the blanket she discovered it wasn't just that, but a poncho. A headhole had been cut in the centre of the blanket and reinforced with leather and stitching. This was going to come in very useful, as was the hat.

They heard a smashing sound, bang! bang! bang! and on inquiring what was going on, were informed that members of the Commando were using hatchets to take up parts of the wooden floors. All fuel available to them would be used to keep the fires burning for the duration of the night.

Adam managed to dry their blankets, jackets and trousers in front of the nearest fire, after which they decided they'd try and sleep.

'No, you wear the poncho yourself and we'll share the other two blankets,' Adam protested when Sarah made to wrap them both in the poncho prior to winding the two blankets round that.

'Don't be silly. Share and share alike, Adam. What's mine is yours and yours mine. All right?'

He thought of a rude answer to that, and laughed softly. 'If you insist.'

'I most certainly do. That's settled then.'

She snuggled tightly into his back, an arm over his chest. She listened to his breathing, slow and regular. And matched her own to it.

She tried not to think that if it hadn't been for him she too would be dead back there on the veld.

It was in the second barley field they came to that it happened. They were approaching the gate that would let them out of that field into the next when a hare suddenly bolted from almost directly underneath Boy's front hooves. The hare had been so well blended in with the hard brown earth that neither of them, or the horses, had seen it.

Boy reared in fright. Bucking on to his hind legs he stabbed and pawed at the air with his front ones.

With an exclamation Ian went toppling sideways to land with a jarring thump.

Sarah couldn't help but laugh. She'd never known Ian come off a horse before. And for the damn horse to be walking at the time, that was priceless!

Ian was on his back staring up at her, an odd, bemused expression on his face. Boy was a dozen feet away, snorting and blowing but clearly calming down again. The hare, through the hedge and into the next field, was only a speck in the distance.

'That's what I call a very "hairy" experience.' And having said that she guffawed at her own wit.

Ian continued staring up at her, that same odd, bemused expression on his face.

'Oh come on, there's no need to make a meal of it,' she admonished when he still hadn't moved half a minute later.

He wants me to get down there with him then he's going to grab me, she thought. Well she was fly to that one.

488

'If you don't get up I'm going to just leave you there,' she warned.

His expression remained the same.

She was becoming irritable now. 'Ian, will you stop mucking about?'

Boy snickered. He nudged Ian with his nose, also urging Ian to get up.

'This isn't funny any more. It's boring. So will you please come on!'

Boy licked Ian's face, and as he did Ian's head moved slowly round till it was at an impossible angle to his neck.

Sarah, filled with sudden horror, stared at her husband in disbelief. 'Ian?' she croaked.

And with that Ian's features somehow rearranged themselves till it wasn't Ian she was staring at any more, but Adam. Adam, dead as mutton.

'Ah!!'

'It's all right, it's all right!' Adam said. 'You were only having a bad dream.'

Sarah's chest was heaving, and there was sweat on her brow. She was in a sitting position, having dragged Adam into one also when she'd abruptly sat up.

'My God!' she whispered.

Adam pushed her hair first behind one ear, then the other. With his sleeve he mopped up the perspiration on her forehead.

'I dreamt about Ian,' she whispered. 'That last day when . . .'She took a deep breath. 'Ian and you.'

'Me?' Adam queried in surprise.

In a quiet voice she recounted her dream to him, including the part where Ian's face had turned into his.

Silence fell between them when she was finally finished.

'Adam?'

'Yes?'

'Hold me close, Adam. Hold me as close as you can.' And having requested that she began to noiselessly cry, the tears running down her grimy cheeks.

'Oh, Sarah!' he whispered, drawing her to him as tightly as was possible. 'Oh Sarah!'

'I'm so frightened, Adam.'

'I know. I am too.'

He very gently pulled her back on to the floor. And there they lay side by side, he with an arm round her shoulders.

She then did a strange thing. Taking his free hand she placed it over the breast closest to him, deriving enormous comfort from that intimacy.

After a while she fell asleep again, and this time didn't dream.

Adam lay beside Sarah watching the flickering reflections from the fire dancing on the ceiling, a ceiling partially illuminated by the soft yellow glow from one of the oil-lamps.

The discordant sound of snoring filled the room, while from the kitchen came the muted hum of voices in quiet conversation.

Sarah's scent was strong in Adam's nostrils, a scent that made him feel totally at peace with himself, and the world at large. He would have been content to lie there, with her beside him, forever.

He still loved her. He knew that beyond question now. He'd thought he'd fallen out of love with her years ago, and maybe he even had. But if he had he was back in love with her again. More likely, being unrequited, his love had become dormant till their chance meeting again, and the events which had reactivated it.

He loved her the way he had when young, so much that it hurt. A physical ache that seemed to squeeze and squeeze and continue squeezing.

He moved the hand that was on her breast, lightly caressing her. There had been other breasts, and other women, but they meant nothing now. Nothing at all.

Turning his head he kissed her on the cheek. If it came to the bit – and that was entirely possible in their present circumstances – he'd lay down his life for her, and willingly.

Bang! Bang! Bang! In another part of the house some of the Boers had resumed hatcheting up wood for the fires.

Eventually, Adam too drifted back to sleep.

Smuts, Wessels, Deneys and many others stood outside the farmhouse staring aghast at the bodies of the horses and pack animals who'd died during the night. Somebody began to count, the terrible final number they arrived at being fifty-seven.

'And the fourteen men who're unaccounted for,' Deneys added grimly. Nobody mentioned the word 'deserters', preferring to believe that the missing men had all expired on the veld without their deaths being noticed. In the conditions that had prevailed the night before it had been possible after all.

Smuts turned away so that no one could see the look on his face, the look of a man an inch away from defeat. It was impossible to live off this country, he told himself. The khakis had taken the food, the forage, any horses that might have been had. Everything. It was as simple as that. And that was why the Cape volk hadn't risen in their thousands as he'd said they would when at Cypherfontein.

Meanwhile, out there the khaki noose was drawing tight again. Tighter and tighter. And this time he couldn't expect another miracle as happened on the Stormberg to spirit them out of the final pull of that noose.

'What now?' Deneys asked. The question Commandant Wessels wanted to ask, but was afraid to.

Smuts didn't reply.

The Commando came to a long gorge that led to the Elands River valley. Their horses were so weak that those still mounted had to dismount and drag the animals after them. At least the sun was out, shining on their backs.

Sarah patted her horse. The poor beast looked as knackered as she felt, which was saying something. 'Come on beauty, come on,' she urged, pulling on its reins. It gamely followed her into the gorge.

Further on the gorge widened, and it was here that a farmer suddenly appeared out of the brush, shouting excitedly in Afrikaans.

The entire Commando halted, waiting while the farmer talked with Smuts and Wessels.

Sarah unscrewed the top from her water bottle, and had several swigs of the river water it contained. She then passed the bottle over to Adam.

'What do you think that's all about?' she asked quietly.

'Your guess is as good as mine.'

Sarah screwed the top back on her bottle while continuing to watch the farmer who was now gesticulating fiercely.

'Two hundred khakis with mountain guns and Maxims. Laagered on the pass at the end of the gorge,' the farmer said to Smuts.

'*Mounted* troops?'

'*Jah!*'

Smuts glanced at Wessels. Was this the answer to his prayers? It could well be.

491

'Do we attack?' Wessels queried.

'Horses and supplies, no doubt. Do we have a choice?'

Wessel's weatherbeaten face cracked into a grin. 'None at all.'

'So attack it is.'

The Dandy Fifth trotted down the valley, forded a stream, and were brushing through a mimosa wood when, surprising both parties, they met British troops cantering towards them. The distance separating Boers and British was less than ten yards.

The Dandy Fifth fired almost as one man.

Sarah and Adam had been warned that a fight was about to take place. They were amongst the main body of the Commando when the volley of gunfire crackled in the air. The gunfire coming from the Dandy Fifth and their opponents.

'Shit,' Adam said to himself.

Sarah overheard him. Those were her sentiments exactly.

The morning had turned foggy, which was to the Boers' advantage. Mausers, Lee-Enfields, Lee-Metfords at the ready, the main body of the Commando moved silently forward.

The 17th Lancers (the 'death and glory boys', with a skull-and-crossbones blazoned on their uniforms) were relative amateurs. They were no match whatever for the Commando whose battle skills had been honed and polished by two years' grind in the Transvaal.

'Irregulars,' Captain Sandeman said to Lord Vivian, pointing at the khaki-clad horsemen who had appeared out of the trees.

He was wrong. The men were the Dandy Fifth wearing khaki uniforms taken from the dead after the train engagement, and from the troopers they'd killed in the mimosa wood.

Deneys Reitz raised an arm, waved to Sandeman, gesturing that Sandeman and the 17th should follow him. He and the rest of the Dandy Fifth then wheeled about and rode back into the trees.

'Must be part of Colonel Gorringe's column,' Sandeman said.

'Must be,' Lord Vivian agreed.

Captain Sandeman glanced behind him. Each and every face he saw was keen and eager to come to grips with the enemy.

'Forward!' he commanded, and kicked his horse into action.

The Battle of Elands River was brief, bloody and a massacre. The first the 17th knew that they'd walked into a trap was when a hail of Boer bullets from the hidden Commando scythed through their ranks, that initial volley causing terrible carnage amongst them.

Deneys Reitz laughed as he shot a lancer through the throat, the lancer throwing his hands high into the air before toppling from his horse. The next lancer he killed he shot through the chin.

Sarah lay on the ground, her hands covering her ears. She and Adam were with the horses, about fifty yards to the rear of where the main dismounted body of the Commando were hidden. Adam was beside her wishing he could witness the events now taking place so that he could later sketch them. He would have joined the Commando if possible, but had been ordered to remain where he was. Knowing the Boers, that was an order he didn't care to disobey.

Many of the 17th, of those still alive that is, were on the ground trying to return fire. Lieutenant Sheridan, Winston Churchill's cousin, rose to his feet with the intention of leading a charge. Before he could shout the command he was dead, shot through the brain.

Isie fired, a bad shot which hit her target on the heel. The man leapt into the air, and was still in the air when Jack Borrius, the Commando's field cornet, drilled him through the heart.

Lancer Perkins was crying over the corpse of Bobby Alford. 'The bastards . . . the fucking bastards,' he choked. He and Bobby had been best friends ever since they'd joined the 17th, which they'd done on the same day. Now Bobby was dead, and not only that but killed by a dum-dum. Bobby's entire head had been blown apart when the dum-dum exploded inside it.

A lancer lay screaming in agony, blood spouting out of his chest. A few feet away another lancer was staring mesmerised at the blood fountaining out of both thighs, he having been shot in each.

Close by was Lancer Winterton, rolling around in the dirt, alternately clawing at and beating it with his fists. Both his testicles had been shot away.

493

Lancer Perkins, bent on revenging Bobby Alford, had somehow managed to work round the Commando's flank without being either wounded or killed. He was carrying Bobby's rifle, having lost his own.

He melted into a patch of fog, most of the fog having dispersed by now, which gave him good cover. When he emerged from the fog he found himself only yards away from the tethered Boers' horses and the three Boers guarding them.

In fact there was only one Boer guarding the horses – Francis Koornhof. Francis was cursing his luck at being delegated guard duty and thereby missing the action, and wondering exactly how events were progressing. With his mind distracted he was not even aware of Lancer Perkins's presence, or of Lancer Perkins raising his rifle to take aim.

Lancer Perkins grunted with satisfaction as Koornhof slid to the ground. If he'd had access to dum-dums he would have used one to kill Koornhof.

Lancer Perkins swiftly reloaded, and swung his rifle towards the next figure, the nearest of the two lying on the ground. That figure was Sarah.

Adam was of course unarmed, as was Sarah. He stared in horror at the rifle pointed at Sarah, and watched Lancer Perkins begin to squeeze the trigger.

Sarah was convinced she was a dead person. Her mind totally froze over and stopped. She held her breath, thinking it was to be her last.

Adam wasn't in the least concerned about himself. Sarah was all that mattered. He had to try and save her, somehow, anyhow.

'No!!' he shrieked, leaping to his feet and throwing himself towards Lancer Perkins, getting himself between Sarah and the rifle.

Adam's shriek, and throwing himself at Lancer Perkins, made Lancer Perkins involuntarily recoil. As he did he completed squeezing the rifle's trigger, and the rifle went off.

Zip!

Adam actually heard the bullet zip by his ear. Lancer Perkins had amazingly missed. Before Lancer Perkins could reload, Adam literally fell on him, grabbing the rifle and trying to wrestle it from Perkins's grasp. The two men tumbled to the ground.

Sarah screwed a fist into her mouth. She couldn't believe she was still alive.

Adam was a madman. Releasing his right hand from the rifle he punched Perkins hard on the face. Then punched Perkins again and again, one of his punches breaking the lancer's nose.

Lancer Perkins heaved, and got himself on top of Adam. Then Adam heaved, and it was he who was on top.

Lancer Perkins tried to hit Adam with the butt of the rifle, attempting to smash it into Adam's face, but failed to do so.

It never dawned on Adam to speak in English, to try and tell Lancer Perkins that he wasn't a Boer, but a British prisoner. Anyway, in the mental state Perkins was in it's doubtful if anything Adam would have said would have penetrated, including the fact Adam was speaking in English rather than Afrikaans.

Adam and Lancer Perkins continued struggling, and then Adam spotted the rock behind Lancer Perkins's head. With every ounce of force he could muster Adam smashed Perkins's head down on to that rock.

Blood spattered as the back of Lancer Perkins's head was stove in. Lancer Perkins's lips twisted into a fearful grimace, while his eyes snapped wide open as though in surprise. His entire body jerked all over. Then jerked a second time.

With a sigh, Lancer Perkins died.

Adam snatched the rifle from the dead man and chucked it aside. Sitting astride the corpse he sucked in deep breath after deep breath. He noted almost absentmindedly that his hands were trembling violently.

Rising from the corpse Adam slowly returned to Sarah. 'He was going to kill you,' Adam said simply.

'Yes.'

'Well he won't . . . can't now.'

'No.'

Adam closed his eyes. 'Christ!' he swore softly.

The Boers were jubilant with their victory, and the spoils of that victory. One hundred and thirty horses had been taken, all prime animals, fresh and well fed. There were also a number of wagons filled with supplies. Supplies that were mainly food, but also included ammunition, clothing, saddlery, boots and a case of gin. (The latter the Boers' favourite tipple.)

Deneys Reitz was delighted with the Arab polo pony he'd claimed as his own, a pony which had belonged to Lieutenant Sheridan.

495

He'd never seen such a fine mount before, far less owned one of that quality.

'Look at me, heh!' he cried out to Bingle, turning the pony round in a tight circle. 'Look at me, heh!'

'You look like a prince, man,' Bingle called back.

Deneys laughed to hear that.

Besides the mounts several dozen pack animals had been captured. Smuts now ordered these to be loaded with supplies, the supplies remaining to be burnt along with the wagons. He also ordered a field gun, too immobile to be of any use to the Commando, to be blown up.

The wagons were blazing like torches when Deneys Reitz paid a personal visit to see the lancers he had killed, check his personal bag so to speak. There were eight of them, all lying close to one another.

He gazed down at the bodies, all young men roughly his own age. He didn't hate the British, he told himself. But he was certainly proud of his day's work. Yes indeed, proud! A fight was a fight after all.

An hour later the Commando, filled with new heart, broke out of the Bamboo Mountains into the open plain. Leaving behind the prisoners and the 17th's African retinue to shift for themselves.

Colonel Douglas Haig was the newly appointed C.O. of the 17th Lancers, directly responsible – under the overall direction of General French – for that section of the cordon. Besides the 17th, French had given him three packs – that is three columns totalling roughly two thousand men.

Now C Squadron of the 17th had been annihilated, among the wounded survivors (thank God!) Lord Vivian, whose sister he planned to marry.

It was 5.55 pm. He had been informed at 4.30 pm of what had occurred, and had galloped the fourteen miles from where he'd been to here in an hour and a quarter, splashing down the waterlogged track.

He was appalled at what he'd found. Four of the six officers dead, the men themselves decimated. And to top it all dum-dums had been used. The latter unforgivable.

'Brutes,' he muttered to himself. 'Brutes.'

Since crossing the Orange River, Smuts and his Commando had been pursued hard by British troops. Well, that pursuit would be nothing to what he'd now engage in. The supply of fresh horses would be so organised that his columns would march day and night if necessary.

Smuts and his Commando would pay for this. And account personally to him.

He swore that on his life and future career.

'Would you like more coffee?' Sarah asked.

Adam shook his head.

The Commando had off-saddled shortly after night had fallen, and because of the surrounding terrain it had been decided that fires could be safely lit. Within a short while of that being done everyone had been guzzling on captured food, washing it down with captured coffee.

Now that he'd eaten his fill Adam had fallen into a gloomy, introspective silence.

'There was nothing else you could do,' Sarah said quietly, guessing correctly what was bothering Adam. 'Another second or two and he would have killed me, and then you after that.'

Adam laid his tin cup aside and wrung his hands together. 'I know that, but it doesn't make it any easier.' He looked Sarah straight in the eye. 'I killed a British soldier, one of ours. A lad on our side.'

She went to him and squatted beside him. 'You had no option Adam. It was either him or us.'

'That's what I keep telling myself.'

Reaching up she touched his cheek. 'It was a very brave thing you did.'

'I . . .' He trailed off.

'Yes?' she prompted.

'It was you. I had to try and save you. I couldn't bear the thought of you being killed.'

Tears sprang into her eyes. 'Oh Adam!' she whispered.

He placed a hand on her neck, and drew her face to his.

She offered her lips willingly.

Sarah was sitting on a fallen tree, numb with exhaustion. The Commando had stopped for half an hour to give the horses a breather, then they would ride again.

If it had been bad before the fight with the 17th Lancers, it had been a lot worse since. The British pursuit had become relentless, forever driving them on, never giving time to stop and have a proper rest. The horses taken from the 17th had begun to look very much the worse for wear. Another couple of days and they too would start to drop in their tracks as the original horses had done, and were still doing.

'I hallucinated this afternoon,' Adam said matter-of-factly. He screwed up his face. 'Or was it this morning? Whatever, I hallucinated.'

'Oh?'

'I was back at Art School with Toshie and Herbert McNair.'

Sarah shuddered. She didn't like the sound of that at all. It reminded her all too much of Jock when Jock had been out of his mind with schizophrenia.

'It's the tiredness that's doing it,' Adam added.

'I find myself sleeping in the saddle sometimes. I'm just surprised I don't fall off, but so far I haven't. I suppose I've done so much riding since all this began it's as if a horse and I have become as one.'

Smuts loomed out of the darkness. 'Good evening. How are you both tonight?'

'Buggered,' Adam answered truthfully, which made Smuts laugh.

'How about some gin? There was a case of it amongst those supplies we took from the khakis.'

'Have you any tonic to go with it?' Sarah joked.

Smuts laughed again. 'I'm afraid not Lady Ascog. Just best London gin.'

Sarah rinsed out her cup and Adam's, after which Smuts gave them both hefty measures from the bottle he produced from a pocket.

'During one of our chats didn't you mention that you'd been with Colonel Douglas Haig before you were wounded?' Smuts asked Adam casually.

'That's right.'

'What's he like?'

Adam had a sip of his gin, which was like liquid fire going down, but good nonetheless. 'Why do you ask?'

Smuts decided to be honest. 'He's the one currently on our tail. And has been since Elands River.'

Adam was curious. 'How do you know that?'

Smuts tapped his nose. 'I have my ways and means.'

'The bush telegraph. Word of mouth. Boer farmers and other of the volk telling your scouts?' Sarah ventured.

Smuts smiled at Sarah, and gave her a small nod acknowledging this was so. He turned his attention again to Adam. 'Haig?'

Adam had another sip of his gin, thinking back to Haig whom he'd thought highly of and respected enormously as a person and military commander.

'There are those who say he's far more clever than French, while others describe him simply as a man of destiny.'

That amused Smuts. 'A man of destiny, heh?'

'So many people consider him to be.'

Smuts's finger stabbed at Adam. 'Napoleon Bonaparte was considered a man of destiny, but in the end he was beaten.'

'Yes, General,' Adam replied. Then, added cuttingly, 'By the British. In the end they all lose to us.'

Smuts' amused expression turned to a scowl. 'The Americans beat you, heh? George Washington and his minutemen.'

'The Americans at the time were predominantly British stock, Washington himself a prime example. The British didn't lose to a foreign power, but to our colonial cousins. Because of the blood tie that was one war the British had no stomach for, and why they lost it.'

Depression, like a dark cloud, settled on Smuts. He scowled at Adam.

'This is good gin,' Sarah commented after a while, half smiling.

'Dutch gin is better,' Smuts instantly replied, almost belligerently.

Sarah knew the wise thing to do would be to keep her mouth shut, but for some reason – national and personal pride? – she just wasn't in the mood to do the wise thing. 'Certainly different, but hardly better.'

Smuts regarded her with a steady, unblinking gaze. 'I say *better*.'

'You're entitled to your opinion, General, but that doesn't make it right.'

His depression deepened. He felt he'd been having one of those bad dreams where you find yourself falling down an endless tunnel. And had then wakened to find it was actually true, he *was* falling down an endless tunnel. He swung his gaze back to Adam. 'Man of destiny, heh?'

'So many people consider Haig to be,' Adam repeated.

Smuts sighed, then had a swig of gin from the bottle. Without another word he recorked the bottle, returned it to his pocket and strode away.

Adam suddenly shook all over, and found himself covered in clammy gooseflesh.

'Are you all right?' Sarah asked anxiously.

'I'm fine. It's just that . . .' He stopped himself from completing the sentence.

'Just what?'

'Nothing.'

What he'd been going to say was that the sensation he'd suddenly experienced was that known as 'someone walking over your grave'.

A silly expression, of course. Quite silly.

'Look, "Oom" Jannie,' said Wessels, pointing back the way they'd just come.

The smoke curling skywards could originate from only one source. The farmhouse they'd passed less than an hour previously.

'Haig,' Smuts muttered to himself. Haig must have burnt the farmhouse roof as a matter of policy, but also, and he was certain of this, as a knife-twist to remind him how close the British were. Close, and closing.

Shortly after that they came to another farm where they were greeted as conquering heroes. Smuts could hardly look the farmer or the farmer's wife in the eye.

Later, another finger of smoke punctuated the sky behind them.

'Let the pack animals go. Release them,' Smuts said wearily to Wessels.

'Our supplies?'

'We have to make better time and they're holding us back. Haig and his men are only half an hour behind now. If we don't make better time they'll be on us some time tomorrow.'

'How long do you think before we link with Assistant Commandant-General Kritzinger?' Wessels asked.

Smuts shook his head. 'Three days, maybe four. We could have been with him now if we hadn't tried so hard to shake off Haig.' The Commando had attempted all manner of tricks, to no avail.

Haig had stuck to their trail as if they'd been deliberately leaving clear signs for him to follow.

'I'll order the pack animals to be turned loose,' Wessels said. He didn't even bother to ask about stopping to burn the supplies the animals were carrying, he knew there wasn't time for that.

'My name is Tottie Malherbe and I've been looking everywhere for you, General,' the man said, falling his horse in alongside Smuts'. A forward-ranging scout had found the man and brought him in.

'Who are you from?' Smuts demanded.

'Assistant Commandant-General Kritzinger.'

'Is he that close?' Smuts queried eagerly.

'No, General, I'm sorry to say he is not. He has taken his army and retreated back into the Free State.'

Wessels swore to hear that. Deneys Reitz dropped his head in profound disappointment.

It was over, Smuts thought. The mission was finished. 'Why did Kritzinger do that?' he asked slowly.

'A new British army from India was entrained up to the border. Cavalry, mounted infantry and infantry. They knew the whereabouts of the Assistant Commandant-General and were advancing rapidly upon him when he decided, the odds being so against him, that the only thing he could do in the circumstances was retreat.'

Smuts' mind had already flown back to that first proper conversation he'd had with Adam Tennant. 'An army consisting of twenty-five thousand men, Tottie?'

Malherbe looked surprised. 'The estimate was round that figure. But how did you know that, General?'

Smuts tapped his nose. 'As the British say, a little bird told me.'

Wessels couldn't contain his question any longer. 'What about De la Rey?' he asked anxiously.

Malherbe glanced back at Smuts. 'The Assistant Commandant-General has instructed me to inform you that General De la Rey and his Transvaalers will not now be crossing into Cape Colony. General De la Rey now apparently feels that would be a mistake on his part when we wouldn't have the Assistant Commandant-General to back him up.'

'I fully agree with Koos,' Smuts said. Koos being De la Rey's Christian name.

Smuts swung on Wessels. 'Haig?'

'No more than fifteen minutes behind us now. He and his columns will have us before dark.'

There was a thud as one of the horses went down.

'Now I try and play the one card I have left up my sleeve. Viscountess Ascog,' Smuts said.

'You think Haig will let us go in exchange for their lives?' Wessels queried.

'No. From what I now know about Haig he would never agree to such a thing. But he might, just might, exchange their lives for a little time.'

'Get the time and I can lead you to fresh horses,' Malherbe said.

'What!' Smuts exclaimed, new hope blossoming within him.

'I hadn't got to that yet,' Malherbe went on. 'The Assistant Commandant-General was aware of the situation you're in, and appreciated what his retreat could mean to you and your Commando. He therefore ordered a cache of horses to be hidden, which I am to lead you to.'

'How far away?' Smuts demanded, voice suddenly hoarse.

'Further than nightfall, General,' Malherbe answered heavily.

Deneys had been listening, and thinking. 'May I make a suggestion "Oom" Jannie?'

'Certainly Deneys.'

'In attempting to exchange the Viscountess and illustrator for time do you intend stopping and allowing the British to catch up with us?'

Smuts frowned. 'I can see no other way to conduct such a transaction, can you?'

'I think so.' Deneys plucked a pistol from his belt, removed all the bullets bar two, which he left in the chamber. He then handed the pistol to Smuts.

Smuts regarded the pistol, then looked back at Deneys. 'I don't understand.'

'The British pride themselves on their sense of fair play. Let us leave the woman and the illustrator behind with that pistol and a simple message for Haig.'

Smuts was intrigued. 'And the message is?'

'*Two hours*. Just that, no more.'

Smuts's forehead creased as he thought about that, trying to puzzle it out. Then he realised the subtlety of what Deneys was proposing. 'Two hours for two lives, the bullets the two we might have used to kill Lady Ascog and Tennant?'

Deneys nodded. 'And Haig, being a British officer and gentleman, with all that implies, will feel obliged to honour the request because, with our prisoners already delivered safely into his hands, it just wouldn't be cricket for him not to.'

Smuts couldn't help but laugh. He liked it, he liked it very much indeed. And it might just work.

Sarah and Adam, she holding the pistol, watched the Commando disappear into the distance. The end of their captivity, when it had finally arrived, had done so with bewildering speed.

'Well,' said Adam. 'That's that then.'

She turned to smile at him. 'So it seems.'

'About fifteen minutes before our lads get here.'

'That's what the General said.' She was filled with elation, yet feeling sick at the same time.

'We made it. We came out of this alive,' Adam said. 'There were occasions when I honestly didn't think we would.'

'Me neither.'

An awkwardness fell between them. 'You'll be back home in Glasgow with your son before you know it,' Adam said.

'Yes. And what about you?'

'I'm going to stay on here till the war's finished, Sarah. I feel I owe that to my paper. And, strangely, myself.'

'I understand that,' she replied.

'But when the war is over I shall return to Glasgow and take up painting again. That's where I want to be, and what I want to be doing.'

Her heart seemed to leap inside her to hear that. She looked at him and their eyes locked. And during that gaze an understanding arose between them.

'I'll come and see you as soon as I get back. The very next day,' he said quietly.

'I'll be waiting,' she replied, just as quietly.

That was settled then. Each knew precisely what was what. The future was decided for both of them.

Then three things happened simultaneously. It began to rain. A rainbow arced on the horizon. And the first dark specks that were British mounted troops appeared.

The rainbow was still shining brightly when she delivered the pistol and message that went with it.

STARK
BEN ELTON

Stark have more money than God and the social
conscience of a dog on a croquet lawn. What's more,
they know the Earth is dying.

Deep in Western Australia where the Aboriginals used
to milk the trees, a planet-sized plot takes shape. Some
green freaks pick up the scent. A Pommie poseur, a
brain-fried Vietnam Vet, Aboriginals who lost their land
. . . not much against a conspiracy that controls society.
But EcoAction isn't in society; it just lives in the same
place, along with the cockroaches.

If you're facing the richest and most disgusting
conspiracy in history, you have to do more than stick up
two fingers and say "peace".

0 7474 40390 2   GENERAL FICTION   £00.00

Nancy Thayer
MORNING

'THERE HE WAS, THE PERFECT HUSBAND, AND HERE SHE SAT, NOT PREGNANT, THE IMPERFECT WIFE. THE FLAWED WIFE. THE INFERIOR WIFE. THE RAPIDLY-MENTALLY-DETERIORATING WIFE.

SHE WANTED TO BREAK ALL THE DISHES OVER HIS PERFECT, UNDERSTANDING, LOVING HEAD.'

But it wasn't Steve's fault. It was nobody's fault that she couldn't have the child she so desperately wanted. So Sara channelled her energies into her work as an editor. And then she read a manuscript that led her to a creative life of a different kind; the autobiographical novel of a beautiful, terrifying recluse with a mysterious past . . . and a painful obsession.

Also by Nancy Thayer in Sphere Books:
NELL
STEPPING
THREE WOMEN
BODIES AND SOULS

0 7474 0104 7   GENERAL FICTION   £3.50